the Island

and

the Return

Victoria

Hislop

The Island first published in Great Britain in 2005 by
HEADLINE REVIEW
An imprint of HEADLINE PUBLISHING GROUP

The Return first published in Great Britain in 2008 by
HEADLINE REVIEW
An imprint of HEADLINE PUBLISHING GROUP

First published in this omnibus edition in 2014 by
HEADLINE REVIEW
An imprint of HEADLINE PUBLISHING GROUP

1

Cataloguing in Publication Data is available from the British Library

ISBN 978 1 47222 039 4

Typeset in Bembo by Palimpsest Book Production Limited, Falkirk, Stirlingshire
Printed and bound in Great Britain by Clays Ltd, St Ives plc

HEADLINE PUBLISHING GROUP
An Hachette UK Company
338 Euston Road
London NW1 3BH

www.headline.co.uk
www.hachette.co.uk

Victoria Hislop read English at Oxford, and worked in publishing, PR and as a journalist before becoming a novelist. She is married with two children. Her first novel, *The Island*, held the Number One slot in the *Sunday Times* paperback chart for eight consecutive weeks and has sold over two million copies worldwide. Victoria acted as script consultant on a 26-part TV adaptation in Greece, which achieved record ratings for Greek television. Victoria was Newcomer of the Year at the Galaxy British Book Awards 2007, and her second novel, *The Return,* was also a Number One bestseller. Her third novel, *The Thread*, was a hardback and paperback bestseller, and was also widely acclaimed. Victoria's books have been translated into more than 25 languages.

Visit www.victoriahislop.com

Praise for *The Thread*

'Hislop's fast-paced narrative and utterly convincing sense of place make her novel a rare treat' *Guardian*

'Pleasingly complex . . . Hislop has done well to tell a story as diverse and tempestuous as Thessaloniki's with such lightness of touch' *Spectator*

Praise for *the Return*

'Aims to open the eyes and tug the heartstrings . . . Hislop deserves a medal for opening a breach into the holiday beach bag' *Independent*

'Like a literary Nigella, she whips up a cracking historical romance mixed with a dash of family secrets and a splash of female self-discovery' *Time Out*

Praise for *the Island*

'Passionately engaged with its subject . . . the author has meticulously researched her fascinating background and medical facts' *The Sunday Times*

'A beautiful tale of enduring love and unthinking prejudice' *Observer*

By Victoria Hislop

The Island
The Return
The Thread

The Last Dance and Other Stories

the Island

For my mother, Mary

With special thanks to:

Professor Richard Groves, Academic Dermatology, Imperial College
Professor Diana Lockwood, London School of Hygiene and Tropical Medicine

The island of Spinalonga, off the north coast of Crete, was Greece's main leper colony from 1903 until 1957.

Plaka, 1953

A cold wind whipped through the narrow streets of Plaka and the chill of the autumnal air encircled the woman, paralysing her body and mind with a numbness that almost blocked her senses but could do nothing to alleviate her grief. As she stumbled the last few metres to the jetty she leaned heavily on her father, her gait that of an old crone for whom every step brought a stab of pain. But her pain was not physical. Her body was as strong as any young woman who had spent her life breathing the pure Cretan air, and her skin was as youthful and her eyes as intensely brown and bright as those of any girl on this island.

The little boat, unstable with its cargo of oddly shaped bundles lashed together with string, bobbed and lurched on the sea. The elderly man lowered himself in slowly, and with one hand trying to hold the craft steady reached out with the other to help his daughter. Once she was safely on board he wrapped her protectively in a blanket to shield her from the elements. The only visible indication then that she was not simply another piece of cargo were the long strands of dark hair that flew and danced freely in the wind. He carefully released his vessel from its mooring – there was nothing more to be said or done – and their journey began. This was not the start of a short trip to deliver supplies. It was the beginning of a one-way journey to start a new life. Life on a leper colony. Life on Spinalonga.

Part 1

Chapter One

Plaka, 2001

UNFURLED FROM ITS mooring, the rope flew through the air and sprayed the woman's bare arms with droplets of seawater. They soon dried, and as the sun beat down on her from a cloudless sky she noticed that her skin sparkled with intricate patterns of salty crystals, like a tattoo in diamonds. Alexis was the only passenger in the small, battered boat, and as it chugged away from the quay in the direction of the lonely, unpeopled island ahead of them she shuddered, as she thought of all the men and women who had travelled there before her.

Spinalonga. She played with the word, rolling it around her tongue like an olive stone. The island lay directly ahead, and as the boat approached the great Venetian fortification which fronted the sea, she felt both the pull of its past and an overpowering sense of what it still meant in the present. This, she speculated, might be a place where history was still warm, not stone cold, where the inhabitants were real not mythical. How different that would make it from the ancient palaces and sites she had spent the past few weeks, months – even years – visiting.

Alexis could have spent another day clambering over the ruins of Knossos, conjuring up in her mind from those chunky fragments how life had been lived there over four thousand years before. Of late, however, she had begun to feel that this was a past so remote as to be almost beyond the reach of her imagination, and certainly beyond her caring. Though she had a degree in archaeology and a job in a museum, she felt her interest in the subject waning by the day. Her father was an academic with a passion for his subject, and in a childlike way she had simply grown up to believe she would follow in his dusty footsteps. To someone like Marcus Fielding there was no ancient civilisation too far in the past to arouse his interest, but for Alexis, now twenty-five, the bullock she had passed on the road earlier that day had considerably more reality and relevance to her life than the Minotaur at the centre of the legendary Cretan labyrinth ever could.

The direction her career was taking was not, currently, the burning issue in her life. More pressing was her dilemma over Ed. All the while they soaked up the steady warmth of the late summer rays on their Greek island holiday, a line was slowly being drawn under the era of a once promising love affair. Theirs was a relationship that had blossomed in the rarefied microcosm of a university, but in the outside world it had withered and, three years on, was like a sickly cutting that had failed to survive being transplanted from greenhouse to border.

Ed was handsome. This was a matter of fact rather than opinion. But it was his good looks that sometimes annoyed her as much as anything and she was certain that they added to his air of arrogance and his sometimes enviable self-belief.

They had gone together, in an 'opposites attract' sort of way, Alexis with her pale skin and dark hair and eyes and Ed with his blond, blue-eyed, almost Aryan looks. Sometimes, however, she felt her own wilder nature being bleached out by Ed's need for discipline and order and she knew this was not what she wanted; even the small measure of spontaneity she craved seemed anathema to him.

Many of his other good qualities, most of them regarded as assets by the world at large, had begun to madden her. An unshakeable confidence for a start. It was the inevitable result of his rock-solid certainty about what lay ahead and had always lain ahead from the moment of his birth. Ed was promised a lifetime job in a law firm and the years would unfold for him in a preordained pattern of career progression and homes in predictable locations. Alexis's only certainty was their growing incompatibility. As the holiday progressed, she had spent more and more time mulling over the future and did not picture Ed in it at all. Even domestically they did not match. The toothpaste was being squeezed from the wrong end. But it was she who was the culprit, not Ed. His reaction to her sloppiness was symptomatic of his approach to life in general, and she found his demands for things to be shipshape unpleasantly controlling. She tried to appreciate his need for tidiness but resented the unspoken criticism of the slightly chaotic way in which she lived her life, often recalling that it was in her father's dark, messy study that she felt at home, and that her parents' bedroom, her mother's choice of pale walls and tidy surfaces, made her shiver.

Everything had always gone Ed's way. He was one of life's golden boys: effortlessly top of the class and unchallenged victor ludorum year after year. The perfect head boy. It would hurt to see his bubble burst. He had been brought up to believe that the world was his oyster, but Alexis had begun to see that she could not be enclosed within it. Could she really give up her independence to go and live with him, however obvious it might seem that she should? A slightly tatty rented flat in Crouch End versus a smart apartment in Kensington – was she insane to reject the latter? In spite of Ed's expectations that she would be moving in with him in the autumn, these were questions she had to ask herself: What was the point of living with him if their intention wasn't to marry? And was he the man she would want as father of her children, in any case? Such uncertainties had circled in her mind for weeks, even months now, and sooner or later she would have to be bold enough to do something about them. Ed did so much of the talking, the organising and the managing on this holiday he seemed scarcely to notice that her silences were getting longer by the day.

How different this trip was from the island-hopping holidays she had taken round the Greek islands in her student days when she and her friends were all free spirits and nothing but whim dictated the routine of their long, sun-drenched days; decisions on which bar to visit, what beach to bake on and how long to stay on any island had been made with the toss of a twenty-drachma coin. It was hard to believe that life had ever been so carefree. This trip was so full of conflict, argument and self-questioning; it was a struggle that had begun long before she had found herself on Cretan soil.

How can I be twenty-five and so *hopelessly* uncertain of the future? she had asked herself as she packed her bag for the trip. Here I am, in a flat I don't own, about to take a holiday from a job I don't like with a man I hardly care about. What's wrong with me?

By the time her mother, Sofia, was Alexis's age, she had already been married for several years and had two children. What were the circumstances that had made her so mature at so young an age? How could she have been so settled when Alexis still felt such a child? If she knew more about how her mother had approached life, perhaps it would help her to make her own decisions.

Sofia had always been extremely guarded about her background, though, and over the years her secrecy had become a barrier between herself and her daughter. It seemed ironic to Alexis that the study and understanding of the past was so encouraged in her family and yet she was prevented from holding up a magnifying glass to her own history; this sense that Sofia was hiding something from her children cast a shadow of mistrust. Sofia Fielding appeared not just to have buried her roots but to have trodden down hard on the earth above them.

Alexis had only one clue to her mother's past: a faded wedding picture which had stood on Sofia's bedside table for as long as Alexis could remember, the ornate silver frame worn thin with polishing. In early childhood when Alexis used her parents' big lumpy bed as a trampoline, the image of the smiling but rather stiffly posed couple in the picture had floated up and down in front of her. Sometimes she asked her mother questions about the beautiful lady in lace and the chiselled platinum-haired man. What were their names? Why did he have grey hair? Where were they now? Sofia had given the briefest of answers: that they were her Aunt Maria and Uncle Nikolaos, that they had lived in Crete and that they were now both dead. This information had satisfied Alexis then – but now she needed to know more. It was the status of this picture – the only framed photograph in the entire house apart from those of herself and her younger brother, Nick – that intrigued her as much as anything. This couple had clearly been significant in her mother's childhood and yet Sofia always seemed so reluctant to talk about them. It was more than reluctance, in fact; it was stubborn refusal. As Alexis grew into adolescence she had learned to respect her mother's desire for privacy – it was as keen as her own teenage instinct to lock herself away and avoid communication. But she had grown beyond all that now.

On the night before she was to leave for her holiday, she had gone to her parents' home, a Victorian terraced house in a quiet Battersea street. It had always been a family tradition to eat out at the local Greek taverna before either Alexis or Nick left for a new university term or a trip abroad, but this time Alexis had another motive for the visit. She wanted her mother's advice on what to do about Ed and, just as importantly, she planned to ask her a few questions about her past. Arriving a good hour early, Alexis had resolved to try and get her mother to lift the shutters. Even a little light would do.

She let herself into the house, dropped her heavy rucksack on to the tiled floor and tossed her key into the tarnished brass tray on the hall shelf. It landed with a loud clatter. Alexis knew there was nothing her mother hated more than being taken by surprise.

'Hi, Mum!' she called into the silent space of the hallway.

Guessing that her mother would be upstairs, she took the steps two at a time, and as she entered her parents' room she marvelled as usual at its extreme orderliness. A modest collection of beads was strung across the corner of the mirror and three bottles of perfume stood neatly lined up on Sofia's dressing table. Otherwise the room was entirely devoid of clutter. There were no clues to her mother's personality or past, not a picture on the wall, not a book by the bedside. Just the one framed photograph next to the bed. Even though she shared it with Marcus, this room was Sofia's space, and her need for tidiness dominated here. Every member of the family had his or her own place and each was entirely idiosyncratic.

If the sparse minimalism of the master bedroom made it Sofia's, Marcus's space was his study, where books were piled in columns on the floor. Sometimes these heavyweight towers would topple and the tomes would scatter across the room; the only way across to his desk then was to use the leather-bound volumes as stepping stones. Marcus enjoyed working in this ruined temple of books; it reminded him of being in the midst of an archaeological dig, where every stone had been carefully labelled even if they all looked to the untrained eye like so many bits of abandoned rubble. It was always warm in this room, and even when she was a child Alexis had often sneaked in to read a book, curling up on the soft leather chair that continually oozed stuffing but was somehow still the cosiest and most embracing seat in the house.

In spite of the fact that they had left home long ago, the children's rooms remained untouched. Alexis's was still painted in the rather oppressive purple that she had chosen when she was a sulky fifteen year old. The bedspread, rug and wardrobe were in a matching shade of mauve, the colour of migraines and tantrums – even Alexis thought so now, though at the time she had insisted on having it. One day her parents might get round to repainting it, but in a house where interior design and soft furnishings took low priority it might be another decade before this happened. The colour of the walls in Nick's room had long since ceased to be relevant – not a square inch could be seen between the posters of Arsenal players, heavy metal bands and improbably busty blondes. The drawing room was a space shared by Alexis and Nick, who during two decades must have spent a million and one hours silently watching television in the semi-darkness. But the kitchen was for everyone. The round 1970s pine table – the first piece of furniture that Sofia and Marcus had ever bought together – was the focal point, the place where everyone came together, talked, played games, ate and, in spite of the heated debates and disagreements that often raged around it, became a family.

'Hello,' said Sofia, greeting her daughter's reflection in the mirror. She was simultaneously combing her short blonde-streaked hair and rummaging in a small jewellery box. 'I'm nearly ready,' she added, fastening some coral earrings that matched her blouse.

Though Alexis would never have known it, a knot tightened in Sofia's stomach as she prepared for this family ritual. The moment reminded her of all those nights before her daughter's university terms began when she feigned jollity but felt anguished that Alexis would soon be gone. Sofia's ability to hide her emotions seemed to strengthen in proportion to the feelings she was suppressing. She looked at her daughter's mirrored image and at her own face next to it, and a shock wave passed through her. It was not the teenager's face that she always held in her mind's eye but the face of an adult, whose questioning eyes now engaged with her own.

'Hello, Mum,' Alexis said quietly. 'When's Dad back?'

'Quite soon, I hope. He knows you've got to be up early tomorrow so he promised not to be late.'

Alexis picked up the familiar photograph and took a deep breath. Even in her mid-twenties she still found herself having to summon up courage to force her way into the no-go region of her mother's past, as though she was ducking under the striped tape that cordoned off the scene of a crime. She needed to know what her mother thought. Sofia had married before she was twenty, so was she, Alexis, foolish to throw away the opportunity of spending the rest of her life with someone like Ed? Or might her mother think, as she did herself, that if these thoughts were even present in her head then he was, indeed, not the right person? Inwardly, she rehearsed her questions. How had her mother known with such certainty and at such an early age that the man she was to marry was 'the one'? How could she have known that she would be happy for the next fifty, sixty, perhaps even seventy years? Or had she not thought of it that way? Just at the moment when all these questions were to spill out, she demurred, suddenly fearful of rejection. There was, however, one question she *had* to ask.

'Could I . . .' asked Alexis, 'could I go and see where you grew up?' Apart from a Christian name that acknowledged her Greek blood, the only outward sign Alexis had of her maternal origins were her dark brown eyes, and that night she used them to full effect, locking her mother in her gaze. 'We're going to Crete at the end of our trip and it would be such a waste to travel all that way and miss the chance.'

Sofia was a woman who found it hard to smile, to show her feelings, to embrace. Reticence was her natural state and her immediate response was to search for an excuse. Something stopped her, however. It was Marcus's often-repeated words to her that Alexis would always be their child, but not forever *a* child that came back to her. Even if she struggled against the notion, she knew it was true, and seeing in front of her this independent young woman finally confirmed it. Instead of clamming up as she usually did when the subject of the past even hovered over a conversation, Sofia responded with unexpected warmth, recognising for the first time that her daughter's curiosity to know more about her roots was not only natural; it was possibly even a right.

'Yes . . .' she said hesitantly. 'I suppose you could.'

Alexis tried to hide her amazement, hardly daring to breathe in case her mother changed her mind.

Then, more certainly, Sofia said: 'Yes, it would be a good opportunity. I'll write a note for you to take to Fotini Davaras. She knew my family. She must be quite elderly now but she's lived in the village where I was born for her whole life and married the owner of the local taverna – so you might even get a good meal.'

Alexis shone with excitement. 'Thanks, Mum . . . Where exactly is the village?' she added. 'In relation to Hania?'

'It's about two hours' east of Iraklion,' Sofia said. 'So from Hania it might take you four or five hours – it's quite a distance for a day. Dad will be home any minute, but when we get back from dinner I'll write that letter for Fotini and show you exactly where Plaka is on a map.'

The careless bang of the front door announced Marcus's return from the university library. His worn leather briefcase stood, bulging, in the middle of the hallway, stray scraps of paper protruding through gaps in every seam. A bespectacled bear of a man with thick silvery hair who probably weighed as much as his wife and daughter combined, he greeted Alexis with a huge smile as she ran down from her mother's room and took off from the final stair, flying into his arms in just the way she had done since she was three years old.

'Dad!' said Alexis simply, and even that was superfluous.

'My beautiful girl,' he said, enveloping her in the sort of warm and comfortable embrace that only fathers of such generous proportions can offer.

They left for the restaurant soon after, a five-minute walk from the house. Nestling in the row of glossy wine bars, over-priced patisseries and trendy fusion restaurants, Taverna Loukakis was the constant. It had opened not long after the Fieldings had bought their house and in the meantime had seen a hundred other shops and eating places come and go. The owner, Gregorio, greeted the trio as the old friends they were, and so ritualistic were their visits that he knew even before they sat down what they would order. As ever, they listened politely to the day's specials, and then Gregorio pointed to each of them in turn and recited: '*Meze* of the day, moussaka, stifado, kalamari, a bottle of retsina and a large sparkling water.' They nodded and all of them laughed as he turned away in mock disgust at their rejection of his chef's more innovative dishes.

Alexis (moussaka) did most of the talking. She described her projected trip with Ed, and her father (kalamari) occasionally interjected with suggestions on archaeological sites they might visit.

'But Dad,' Alexis groaned despairingly, 'you *know* Ed's not really interested in looking at ruins!'

'I know, I know,' he replied patiently. 'But only a philistine would go to Crete without visiting Knossos. It would be like going to Paris and not bothering with the Louvre. Even Ed should realise that.'

They all knew perfectly well that Ed was more than capable of bypassing anything if there was a whiff of high culture about it, and as usual there was a subtle hint of disdain in Marcus's voice when Ed came into the conversation. It was not that he disliked him, or even really disapproved of him. Ed was exactly the sort that a father was meant to hope for as a son-in-law, but Marcus could not help his feelings of disappointment whenever he pictured this well-connected boy becoming his daughter's future. Sofia, on the other hand, adored Ed. He was the embodiment of all that she aspired to for her daughter: respectability, certainty and a family tree that lent him the confidence of someone linked (albeit extremely tenuously) with English aristocracy.

It was a light-hearted evening. The three of them had not been together for several months and Alexis had much to catch up on, not least all the tales of Nick's love life. In Manchester doing postgraduate work, Alexis's brother was in no hurry to grow up and his family were constantly amazed at the complexity of his relationships.

Alexis and her father then began to exchange anecdotes

about their work and Sofia found her mind wandering back to when they had first come to this restaurant and Gregorio had stacked up a pile of cushions so that Alexis could reach the table. By the time Nick was born, the taverna had invested in a highchair and soon the children had learned to love the strong tastes of taramasalata and tzatziki that the waiters brought out for them on tiny plates. For more than twenty years almost every landmark of their lives had been celebrated there, with the same tape of popular Greek tunes playing on a loop in the background. The realisation that Alexis was no longer a child struck Sofia more strongly than ever and she began to think of Plaka and the letter she was soon to write. For many years she had corresponded quite regularly with Fotini and over a quarter of a century earlier had described the arrival of her first child; within a few weeks, a small, perfectly embroidered dress had arrived in which Sofia had dressed the baby for her christening, in the absence of a traditional robe. The two women had stopped writing a while back, but Sofia was certain that Fotini's husband would have let her know if anything had happened to his wife. Sofia wondered what Plaka would be like now, and tried to block out an image of the little village overrun with noisy pubs selling English beer; she very much hoped Alexis would find it just as it was when she had left.

As the evening progressed Alexis felt a growing excitement that at last she was to delve further into her family history. In spite of the tensions she knew would have to be faced on her holiday, at least the visit to her mother's birthplace was something she could look forward to. Alexis and Sofia exchanged smiles and Marcus found himself wondering whether his days of playing mediator and truce-maker between his wife and daughter were drawing to a close. He was warmed by the thought and basked in the company of the two women he loved most in the world.

They finished their meal, politely drank the complimentary raki to the halfway mark and left for home. Alexis would sleep in her old room tonight, and she looked forward to those few hours in her childhood bed before she had to get up and take the underground to Heathrow in the morning. She felt strangely contented in spite of the fact that she had singularly failed to ask her mother's advice. It seemed much more important at this very moment that she was going, with her mother's full co-operation, to visit Sofia's birthplace. All her pressing anxieties over the more distant future were, for a moment, put aside.

When they returned from the restaurant, Alexis made her mother some coffee and Sofia sat at the kitchen table composing the letter to Fotini, rejecting three drafts before finally sealing an envelope and passing it across the table to her daughter. The whole process was conducted in silence, absorbing Sofia completely. Alexis had sensed that if she spoke the spell might be broken and her mother might have a change of heart after all.

For two and a half weeks now, Sofia's letter had sat in the safe inner pocket of Alexis's bag, as precious as her passport. Indeed, it was a passport in its own right, since it would be her way of gaining access to her mother's past. It had travelled with her from Athens and onwards on the fume-filled, sometimes storm-tossed ferries to Paros, Santorini and now

Crete. They had arrived on the island a few days earlier and found a room to rent on the seafront in Hania – an easy task at this stage of the season when most holidaymakers had already departed.

These were the last days of their vacation, and having reluctantly visited Knossos and the archaeological museum at Iraklion, Ed was keen to spend the few days before their long boat journey back to Piraeus on the beach. Alexis, however, had other plans.

'I'm going to visit an old friend of my mother's tomorrow,' she announced as they sat in a harbourside taverna waiting to give their order. 'She lives the other side of Iraklion, so I'll be gone most of the day.'

It was the first time she had mentioned her pilgrimage to Ed and she braced herself for his reaction.

'That's terrific!' he snapped, adding resentfully: 'Presumably you're taking the car?'

'Yes, I will if that's okay. It's a good hundred and fifty miles and it'll take me days if I have to go on local buses.'

'Well I suppose I don't really have a choice, do I? And I certainly don't want to come with you.'

Ed's angry eyes flashed at her like sapphires as his suntanned face disappeared behind his menu. He would sulk for the rest of the evening but Alexis could take that given that she had rather sprung this on him. What was harder to cope with, even though it was equally typical of him, was his total lack of interest in her plan. He did not even ask the name of the person she was going to visit.

Not long after the sun had risen over the hills the following morning, she crept out of bed and left their hotel.

Something very unexpected had struck her when she looked Plaka up in her guidebook. Something her mother had not mentioned. There was an island opposite the village just off the coast, and although the entry for it was minimal, missable even, it had captured her imagination:

> *SPINALONGA: Dominated by a massive Venetian fortress, this island was seized by the Turks in the eighteenth century. The majority of Turks left Crete when it was declared autonomous in 1898 but the inhabitants refused to give up their homes and their lucrative smuggling trade on Spinalonga. They only left in 1903 when the island was turned into a leper colony. In 1941, Crete was invaded by the Germans and occupied until 1945, but the presence of lepers meant Spinalonga was left alone. Abandoned in 1957.*

It appeared that the *raison d'être* of Plaka itself had been to act as a supply centre for the leper colony, and it intrigued Alexis that her mother had made no mention of this at all. As she sat at the wheel of the hired Cinquecento, she hoped she might have time to visit Spinalonga. She spread the map of Crete out on the empty passenger seat and noticed, for the first time, that the island was shaped like a languid animal asleep on its back.

The journey took her eastwards past Iraklion, and along the smooth, straight coastal road that passed through the insanely overdeveloped modern strips of Hersonisos and Malia. Occasionally she would spot a brown signpost indicating some ancient ruin nestling incongruously among the sprawling hotels. Alexis ignored all these signs. Today her destination was a settlement that had thrived not in the twentieth century BC but in the twentieth century AD and beyond.

Passing mile upon mile of olive groves and, in places where the ground became flatter on the coastal plains, huge plantations of reddening tomatoes and ripening grapes, she eventually turned off the main road and began the final stage of her journey towards Plaka. From here, the road narrowed and she was forced to drive in a more leisurely way, avoiding small piles of rocks which had spilled down from the mountains into the middle of the road and, from time to time, a goat ambling across in front of her, its devilishly close-set eyes glaring at her as she passed. After a while the road began to climb, and after one particularly sharp hairpin bend she drew in to the side, her tyres crackling on the gravelly surface. Way below her, in the blindingly blue waters of the Gulf of Mirabello, she could see the great arc of an almost circular natural harbour, and just where the arms of it seemed to join in embrace there was a piece of land that looked like a small, rounded hillock. From a distance it appeared to be connected to the mainland, but from her map Alexis knew this was the island of Spinalonga and that to reach it there was a strip of water to be crossed. Dwarfed by the landscape around it, the island stood proud of the water, the remains of the Venetian fortress clearly visible at one end, and behind it, fainter but still distinct, a series of lines mapped out; these were its streets. So there it was: the empty island. It had been continuously inhabited for thousands of years and then, less than fifty years ago, for some reason abandoned.

She took the last few miles of her journey down to Plaka slowly, the windows of her cheap rented car wound down to let in the warm breeze and the fragrant smell of thyme. It was two o'clock in the afternoon when she finally rattled to a halt in the silent village square. Her hands were glistening with sweat from gripping the hard plastic steering wheel and she noticed that her left arm had been scorched by the early afternoon sun. It was a ghostly time to arrive in a Greek village. Dogs played dead in the shade and a few cats prowled for scraps. There were no other signs of life, simply some vague indications that people had been there not long before – an abandoned moped leaning against a tree, half a packet of cigarettes on a bench and a backgammon set lying open next to it. Cicadas kept up their relentless chorus that would only be silenced at dusk when the fierce heat finally cooled. The village probably looked exactly as it had done in the 1970s when her mother had left. There had been few reasons for it to change.

Alexis had already decided that she would try to visit Spinalonga before she tracked down Fotini Davaras. She was enjoying this sense of complete freedom and independence, and once she had found the old woman it might then seem rude to go off on a boat trip. It was clear to Alexis that she would be pushed to get back to Hania that night, but just for now she would enjoy her afternoon and would deal with the logistics of ringing Ed and finding somewhere to stay later on.

Deciding to take the guidebook at its word ('Try the bar in the small fishing village of Plaka where, for a few thousand drachma, there is usually a fisherman willing to take you across'), she made her way purposefully across the square and pushed aside the sticky rainbow of plastic strips that hung in the doorway of the village bar. These grubby ribbons were an attempt to keep the flies out and the coolness in, but all they actually did was gather dust and keep the place in a permanent state of semi-darkness. Staring into the gloom, Alexis could just about make out the shape of a woman seated at a table, and as she groped her way towards her, the shadowy figure got up and moved behind the bar. By now Alexis's throat was desiccated with dust.

'*Nero, parakalo*,' she said, hesitantly.

The woman shuffled past a series of giant glass vats of olives and several half-empty bottles of clear, thick ouzo and reached into the fridge for some chilled mineral water. She poured carefully into a tall, straight-edged glass, adding a thick wedge of rough-skinned lemon before passing it to Alexis. She then dried her hands, wet with condensation from the icy bottle, on a huge floral apron that just about reached around her generous waist, and spoke. 'English?' she asked.

Alexis nodded. It was a half-truth after all. It took her just one word to communicate her next wish. 'Spinalonga?' she said.

The woman turned on her heel and vanished through a little doorway behind the bar. Alexis could hear the muffled yells of 'Gerasimo! Gerasimo!' and, soon after, the sound of footsteps on a wooden staircase. An elderly man, bleary-eyed from his disturbed siesta, appeared. The woman gabbled away at him, and the only word that meant anything to Alexis was 'drachma', which was repeated several times. It was quite clear that, in no uncertain terms, he was being told that there was good money to be earned here. The man stood there blinking, taking in this torrent of instructions but saying nothing.

The woman turned to Alexis and, grabbing her order pad from the bar, scribbled down some figures and a diagram. Even if Alexis had spoken fluent Greek it could not have been clearer. With the help of plenty of pointing and circular movements in the air and marks on the paper, she deduced that her return trip to Spinalonga, with a two-hour stop on the island, would cost 20,000 drachma, around £35. It wasn't going to be a cheap day out, but she was in no position to negotiate – and besides, she was more committed than ever to visiting the island. She nodded and smiled at the boatman, who nodded gravely back at her. It was at that moment that it dawned on Alexis that there was more to the ferryman's silence than she had at first realised. He could not have spoken even if he had wished. Gerasimo was dumb.

It was a short walk to the quayside where Gerasimo's battered old boat was moored. They walked in silence past the sleeping dogs and the shuttered buildings. Nothing stirred. The only sounds were the soft padding of their own rubber-soled feet and the cicadas. Even the sea was flat and soundless.

So here she was being ferried on this 500-metre journey by a man who occasionally smiled, but no more. He was as leather-faced as any Cretan fisherman who had spent decades on storm-tossed seas, battling the elements by night and mending his nets in the baking sunshine by day. He was probably somewhere beyond sixty years old, but if wrinkles were like the rings of an oak tree and could be used to measure age, a rough calculation would leave him little short of eighty. His features betrayed nothing. No pain, no misery, but no particular joy either. They were simply the quiet features of resigned old age and a reflection of all that he had lived through in the previous century. Though tourists had been Crete's most recent invaders, following the Venetians, the Turks and, in the old man's lifetime, the Germans, few of them had bothered to learn any Greek. Alexis now castigated herself for not getting her mother to teach her some useful vocabulary – presumably Sofia could still speak fluently even if her daughter had never heard her utter a word. All Alexis could now offer the boatman was a polite '*efharisto*' – 'thank you' – as he helped her on board, at which he touched the brim of his battered straw hat in reply.

Now approaching Spinalonga, Alexis gathered up her camera and the plastic two-litre bottle of water that the woman in the café had pressed upon her, indicating that she must drink plenty. As the boat bumped against the jetty, old Gerasimo offered her a hand and she stepped across the wooden seat on to the uneven surface of the deserted quay. She noticed then that the engine was still running. The old man was not, it appeared, intending to stay. They managed to communicate to each other that he would return in two hours, and she watched as he slowly turned the boat and set off back in the direction of Plaka.

Alexis was now stranded on Spinalonga and felt a wave of fear sweep over her. Supposing Gerasimo forgot her? How long would it take before Ed came in search? Could she swim the distance back to the mainland? She had never been so entirely alone, had rarely been more than a few metres from the next human being and, except in her sleep, never out of touch with other people for more than an hour or so. Her dependency suddenly felt like a millstone and she resolved to pull herself together. She would embrace this period of solitude – her few hours of isolation were a mere pinprick of time compared with the life sentence of loneliness that past inhabitants of Spinalonga must have faced.

The massive stone walls of the Venetian fortification loomed above her. How was she to get past this apparently impregnable obstacle? It was then that she noticed, in the rounded section of the wall, a small entrance that was just about head height. It was a tiny, dark opening in the pale expanse of stonework, and as she approached she saw that it was the way into a long tunnel which curved away to block the view of what lay at its far end. With the sea behind her and the walls in front, there was only one way to go – forward into the dark, claustrophobic passageway. It went on for some metres, and when she emerged from the semi-darkness once again into the dazzling early afternoon light she saw that the scale of the place had changed completely. She stopped, transfixed.

She was at the lower end of a long street lined on both sides with small two-storey houses. At one time this might have looked like any village in Crete, but these buildings had been reduced to a state of semi-dereliction. Window frames hung at strange angles on broken hinges, and shutters twitched and creaked in the slight sea breeze. She walked hesitantly down the dusty street, taking in everything she saw: a church on her right with a solid carved door, a building which, judging by its large ground-floor window frames, had evidently been a shop, and a slightly grander detached building with a wooden balcony, arched doorway and the remains of a walled garden. A profound, eerie silence hung over it all.

In the downstairs rooms of the houses clumps of bright

wild flowers grew in abundance, and on the upper storeys wallflowers peeped out from between cracks in the plaster. Many of the house numbers were still visible, the fading figures – 11, 18, 29 – focusing Alexis's imagination on the fact that behind each of these front doors real lives had been lived. She continued to stroll, spellbound. It was like sleep-walking. This was not a dream and yet there was something entirely unreal about it all.

She passed what must have been a café, a larger hall and a building with rows of concrete basins, which she deduced must have been a laundry. Next to them were the remains of an ugly three-storey block with functional cast-iron balcony railings. The scale of the building was in strange contrast with the houses, and it was odd to think that someone must have put this building up only seventy years ago and thought it the height of modernity. Now its huge windows gaped open to the sea breeze and electric wires hung down from the ceilings like clumps of coagulated spaghetti. It was almost the saddest building of all.

Beyond the town she came to an overgrown path that led away to a spot beyond all signs of civilisation. It was a natural promontory with a sheer drop into the sea hundreds of feet below. Here she allowed herself to imagine the misery of the lepers and to wonder whether in desperation they might ever have come to this place to contemplate ending it all. She stared out towards the curved horizon. Until now she had been so absorbed by her surroundings, so entirely immersed in the dense atmosphere of the place, that all thoughts of her own situation had been suspended. She was the only person on this entire island and it made her face a fact: solitude did not have to mean loneliness. You could be lonely in a crowd. The thought gave her strength for what she might have to do when she returned: begin the next stage of her life alone.

Retracing her steps into the silent town, Alexis rested for a while on a stone doorstep, gulping back some of the water she had carried with her. Nothing stirred except for the occasional lizard scuttling through the dry leaves that now carpeted the floors of these decaying homes. Through a gap in the derelict house in front of her she caught a glimpse of the sea, and beyond it the mainland. Each day the lepers must have looked across at Plaka and been able to see every building, every boat – perhaps even people going about their daily business. She could only begin to imagine how much its proximity must have tantalised them.

What stories could the walls of this town tell? They must have seen great suffering. It went without saying that being a leper, stuck out here on this rock, must have been as bad a card as life could deal. Alexis was, however, well practised in making deductions from archaeological fragments, and she could tell from what remained of this place that life here had held a more complex range of emotions for the inhabitants than simply misery and despair. If their existence had been entirely abject, why would there have been cafés? Why was there a building that could only have been a town hall? She sensed melancholy, but she also saw signs of normality. It was these that had taken her by surprise. This tiny island had been a community, not just a place to come and die – that much was clear from the remains of the infrastructure.

Time had passed quickly. When Alexis glanced at her watch

she saw that it was already five o'clock. The sun had seemed so high still and its heat so intense that she had lost all track of time. She leapt up, her heart pounding. Though she had enjoyed the silence and the peace here, she did not relish the idea of Gerasimo leaving without her. She hurried back through the long dark tunnel and out on to the quay the other side. The old fisherman was sitting in his boat waiting for her, and immediately she appeared, he twisted the key to start the motor. Clearly he had no intention of staying around longer than necessary.

The journey back to Plaka was over within minutes. With a sense of relief she spotted the bar where her journey had begun and saw the comfortingly familiar hire car parked just opposite. By now the village had come to life. Outside doorways women sat talking, and under the trees in the open space by the bar a group of men were huddled over a game of cards, a pall of smoke from their strong cigarettes hanging in the air. She and Gerasimo walked back to the bar in their now accustomed silence and were greeted by the woman, who Alexis deduced was Gerasimo's wife. Alexis counted out a handful of scruffy notes and handed them to her. 'Do you want drink?' asked the woman in her rough English. Alexis realised that it was not only a drink she needed, but also food. She had eaten nothing all day and the combination of heat and the sea journey had left her feeling shaky.

Recalling that her mother's friend ran a local taverna, she hastily rummaged inside her backpack for the crumpled envelope containing Sofia's letter. She showed the address to the woman, who registered immediate recognition. Taking Alexis by the arm, she led her out into the street and along the seafront. About fifty metres down the road, and extending on a small pier out into the sea, was a taverna. Like an oasis, its painted blue chairs and checked indigo and white tablecloths seemed to summon Alexis, and the moment she was greeted by its owner, the restaurant's eponymous Stephanos, she knew she would be happy to sit there and watch the sun go down.

Stephanos had one thing in common with every other taverna owner Alexis had met: a thick, well-clipped moustache. Unlike the majority of them, however, he did not look as though he ate as much as he served. It was much too early for local people to eat, so Alexis sat alone, at a table right on the edge by the sea.

'Is Fotini Davaras here today?' Alexis asked tentatively. 'My mother knew her when she was growing up here and I have a letter for her.'

Stephanos, who spoke a great deal more English than the couple at the bar, warmly replied that his wife was indeed there and would come out to see her as soon as she had finished preparing today's dishes. He suggested meanwhile that he bring her a selection of local specialities so that she didn't have to bother with a menu. With a glass of chilled retsina in her hand and some coarse bread on the table in front of her to sate her immediate hunger, Alexis felt a wave of contentment pass over her. She had derived great pleasure from her day of solitude and relished this moment of freedom and independence. She looked across at Spinalonga. Freedom was not something any of the lepers would ever have enjoyed, she thought, but had they gained something else instead?

Stephanos returned with a series of small white plates stacked up his arm, each one charged with a tiny portion of something tasty and freshly prepared from his kitchen – prawns, stuffed zucchini flowers, tzatziki and miniature cheese pies. Alexis wondered if she had ever felt such hunger or been presented with such delicious-looking food.

As he approached her table Stephanos had noticed her gazing out towards the island. He was intrigued by this lone Englishwoman who had, as Andriana, Gerasimo's wife, explained, spent the afternoon alone on Spinalonga. In high summer several boatloads of tourists a day were ferried across – but most of them only stayed for half an hour at most and then were driven back by coach to one of the big resorts further down the coast. The majority only came out of ghoulish curiosity, and judging by the snatches of conversation he sometimes overheard if they ever bothered to stop in Plaka for a meal, they were usually disappointed. It seemed that they expected to see more than a few derelict houses and a boarded-up church. What did they want? he was always tempted to ask. Bodies? Abandoned crutches? Their insensitivity never failed to arouse his irritation. But this woman was not like them.

'What did you think of the island?' he asked.

'It surprised me,' she replied. 'I expected it to be terribly melancholy – and it was – but there was much more to it than that. It was obvious that the people who lived there did more than just sit around feeling sorry for themselves. At least that's how it seemed to me.'

This was not at all the usual reaction from visitors to Spinalonga, but the young woman had obviously spent more time there than most. Alexis was happy to make conversation, and since Stephanos was always keen to practise his English he was not going to discourage her.

'I don't really know why I think that – but am I right?' she asked.

'May I sit down?' asked Stephanos, not waiting for an answer before scraping a chair across the floor and perching on it. He felt instinctively that this woman was open to the magic of Spinalonga. 'My wife had a friend who used to live there,' he said. 'She is one of the few people round here who still has any connections at all with the island. Everyone else went as far away as possible once the cure had been found. Apart from old Gerasimo, of course.'

'Gerasimo . . . was a leper?' asked Alexis, slightly aghast. It would certainly explain his haste to get away from the island once he had dropped her off there. Her curiosity was fully aroused now. 'And your wife, did she ever visit the island?'

'Many, many times,' replied Stephanos. 'She knows more about it than anyone else around here.'

By now, other customers were arriving, and Stephanos got up from the wicker-seated chair to show them to their tables and present them with menus. The sun had now fallen below the horizon and the sky had turned a deep pink. Swallows dived and swooped, catching insects on the rapidly cooling air. What seemed like an age went by. Alexis had eaten everything that Stephanos had put in front of her but she was still hungry.

Just as she was wondering whether to go into the kitchen to choose what to have next, as was perfectly acceptable for customers in Crete, her main course arrived.

'This is today's catch,' said the waitress, setting down an oval platter. 'It is *barbouni*. I think that is red mullet in English. I hope I have cooked it as you like it – just grilled with fresh herbs and a little olive oil.'

Alexis was astonished. Not just by the perfectly presented dish. Not even by the woman's soft, almost accentless English. What took her by surprise was her beauty. She had always wondered what kind of face could possibly have launched a thousand ships. It must have been one like this.

'Thank you,' she said finally. 'That looks wonderful.'

The vision seemed about to turn away, but then she paused. 'My husband said you were asking for me.'

Alexis looked up in surprise. Her mother had told her that Fotini was in her early seventies, but this woman was slim, scarcely lined, and her hair, piled high on her head, was still the colour of ripe chestnuts. She was not the old woman Alexis had been expecting to meet.

'You're not . . . Fotini Davaras?' she said uncertainly, getting to her feet.

'I am she,' the woman asserted gently.

'I have a letter for you,' Alexis said, recovering. 'From my mother, Sofia Fielding.'

Fotini Davaras's face lit up. 'You're Sofia's daughter! My goodness, how wonderful!' she said. 'How is she? How is she?'

Fotini accepted with huge enthusiasm the letter which Alexis held out to her, hugging it to her chest as though Sofia herself were there in person. 'I am so happy. I haven't heard from her since her aunt died a few years ago. Until then she used to write to me every month, then she just stopped. I was very worried when some of my last letters went unanswered.'

All of this was news to Alexis. She had been unaware that her mother used to send letters to Crete so regularly – and certainly had no idea that she had ever received any. How odd during all those years that Alexis herself had never once seen a letter bearing a Greek postmark – she felt sure she would have remembered it, since she had always been an early riser, and invariably the one to sweep up any letters from the doormat. It seemed that her mother had gone to great lengths to conceal this correspondence.

By now Fotini was holding Alexis by the shoulders and scrutinising her face with her almond-shaped eyes.

'Let me see – yes, yes, you do look a bit like her. You look even more like poor Anna.'

Anna? On all those occasions when she had tried to extract information from her mother about the sepia-toned aunt and uncle who had brought her up, Alexis had never heard this name.

'Your mother's mother,' Fotini added quickly, immediately spotting the quizzical look on the girl's face. Something like a shudder went down Alexis's spine. Standing in the dusky half-light, with the now ink-black sea behind her, she was all but knocked backwards by the scale of her mother's secretiveness, and the realisation that she was talking to someone who might hold some of the answers.

'Come on, sit down, sit down. You must eat the *barbouni*,' said Fotini. By now Alexis had almost lost her appetite, but she felt it polite to co-operate and the two women sat down.

In spite of the fact that she wanted to ask all the questions – she was bursting with them – Alexis allowed herself to be interviewed by Fotini, whose enquiries were all more searching than they appeared. How was her mother? Was she happy? What was her father like? What had brought her to Crete?

Fotini was as warm as the night, and Alexis found herself

answering her questions very openly. This woman was old enough to be her grandmother, and yet was so unlike how she would expect a grandmother to be. Fotini Davaras was the antithesis of the bent old lady in black that she had imagined when her mother had handed her the letter. Her interest in Alexis seemed totally genuine. It was a long time – if it had ever happened at all – since Alexis had talked to someone like this. Her university tutor had occasionally listened to her as though what she said really mattered, but in her heart she knew that was only because she was paid to do so. It wasn't long before Alexis was confiding in Fotini.

'My mother has always been terribly secretive about her early life,' she said. 'All I really know is that she was born near here and brought up by her uncle and aunt – and that she left altogether when she was eighteen and never came back.'

'Is that *really* all you know?' Fotini asked. 'Hasn't she told you any more than that?'

'No, nothing at all. That's partly why I'm here. I want to know more. I want to know what made her turn her back on the past like that.'

'But why now?' enquired Fotini.

'Oh, lots of reasons,' said Alexis, looking down at her plate. 'But mostly it's to do with my boyfriend. I've realised lately how lucky my mother was to find my father – I'd always assumed that their relationship was typical.'

'I'm glad they're happy. It was a bit of a whirlwind at the time, but we were all very hopeful because they seemed so blissfully content.'

'It's odd, though. I know so little about my mother. She never talks about her childhood, never talks about living here—'

'Doesn't she?' interjected Fotini.

'What I feel,' said Alexis, 'is that to find out more about my mother might help me. She was fortunate to meet someone she could care so much about, but how did she *know* he would be the right person for ever? I've been with Ed for more than five years, and I'm not sure whether we should be together or not.'

This statement was very uncharacteristic of the normally pragmatic Alexis, and she was aware that it might sound rather nebulous, almost fanciful, to someone she had known for less than two hours. Besides, she had strayed off the agenda; how could she expect this Greek woman, kindly as she was, to be interested in her?

Stephanos approached at this moment to clear the dishes, and within minutes he was back with cups of coffee and two generous balloons of molasses-coloured brandy. Other customers had come and gone during the evening and, once again, the table Alexis occupied was the only one in use.

Warmed by the hot coffee and even more so by the fiery Metaxa, Alexis asked Fotini how long she had known her mother.

'Practically from the day she was born,' the older woman replied. But she stopped there, feeling a great weight of responsibility. Who was she, Fotini Davaras, to tell this girl things about her family's past that her own mother had clearly wanted to conceal from her? It was only at that moment that Fotini remembered the letter she had tucked into her apron.

She pulled it out and, picking up a knife from the next table, quickly slit it open.

Dear Fotini,

Please forgive me for being out of touch for so long. I know I don't need to explain the reasons to you, but believe me when I tell you that I think of you often. This is my daughter, Alexis. Will you treat her as kindly as you always treated me – I hardly need to ask it, do I?

Alexis is very curious about her history – it's understandable, but I have found it almost impossible to tell her anything. Isn't it odd how the passage of time can make it harder than ever to bring things out into the open?

I know she will ask you plenty of questions – she is a natural historian. Will you answer them? Your eyes and ears witnessed the whole story – I think you will be able to give her a truer account than I ever could.

Paint a picture of it all for her, Fotini. She will be eternally grateful. Who knows – she may even return to England and be able to tell me things I never knew. Will you show her where I was born – I know she will be interested in that – and take her to Agios Nikolaos?

This comes with much love to you and Stephanos – and please send warm best wishes to your sons too.

Thank you, Fotini.

Yours ever,
Sofia

When she had finished reading the letter, Fotini folded it carefully and returned it to its envelope. She looked across at Alexis, who had been studying her every expression with curiosity as she scanned the crumpled sheet of paper.

'Your mother has asked me to tell you all about your family,' said Fotini, 'but it's not really a bed-time story. We close the taverna on Sunday and Monday and I have all the time in the world at this end of the season. Why don't you stay with us for a couple of days? I would be delighted if you would.' Fotini's eyes glittered in the darkness. They looked watery – with tears or excitement, Alexis couldn't tell.

She knew instinctively that this might be the best investment of time she could ever make, and there was no doubt that her mother's story could help her more in the long term than yet another museum visit. Why examine the cool relics of past civilisations when she could be breathing life into her own history? There was nothing to stop her staying. Just a brief text message telling Ed that she was going to be here for a day or so would be all it would take. Even though she knew it was an act of almost callous disregard for him, she felt this opportunity justified a little selfishness. She was essentially free to do what she pleased. It was a moment of stillness. The dark, flat sea almost seemed to hold its breath, and in the clear sky above, the brightest constellation of all, Orion, who had been killed and placed in the sky by the gods, seemed to wait for her decision.

This might be the one chance Alexis was offered in her lifetime to grab at the fragments of her own history before they were dissipated in the breeze. She knew there was only one response to the invitation. 'Thank you,' she said quietly, suddenly overwhelmed with tiredness. 'I'd love to stay.'

Chapter Two

ALEXIS SLEPT DEEPLY that night. When she and Fotini finally went to bed, it was after one o'clock in the morning, and the cumulative effect of the long drive to Plaka, the afternoon on Spinalonga and the heady mix of meze and Metaxa drew her into a deep and dreamless sleep.

It was nearly ten when luminous sunshine came streaming through the gap between the thick hessian curtains and threw a beam across Alexis's pillow. As it woke her, she instinctively slid further under the sheets to hide her face. In the past fortnight she had slept in several unfamiliar rooms, and each time she surfaced there was a moment of confusion as she adjusted to her surroundings and dragged herself into the here and now. Most of the mattresses in the cheap pensions where she and Ed had stayed had either sagged in the middle or had metal springs protruding through the ticking. It had never been hard to get up from those beds in the morning. But this bed was altogether different. In fact the whole room was different. The round table with a lace cloth, the stool with its faded woven seat, the group of framed watercolours on the wall, the candlestick thickly coated with organ pipes of wax, the fragrant lavender which hung in a bunch on the back of the door, and the walls painted in a soft blue to match the bed linen: all of these things made it homelier than home.

When she drew back the curtains she was greeted by the dazzling vista of a sparkling sea and the island of Spinalonga, which, in the shimmering haze of heat, seemed further away, more remote than it had yesterday.

When she had set off from Hania early the previous day, she had had no intention of staying in Plaka. She had imagined a brief meeting with the elderly woman from her mother's childhood and a short tour of the village before rejoining Ed. For that reason she had brought nothing more than a map and her camera – and had certainly not anticipated needing spare clothes or a toothbrush. Fotini, however, had been quick to come to her rescue, lending her everything she needed – one of Stephanos's shirts to sleep in, and a clean if rather threadbare towel. This morning, at the end of her bed, she found a floral shirt – not at all her style, but after the heat and dust of the previous day she was glad for the change of clothing. It was a gesture of such maternal kindness that she could hardly ignore it – even if the pale pinks and blues of the blouse looked rather incongruous with her khaki shorts, what did it really matter? Alexis splashed her face with cold water at the tiny sink in the corner and then scrutinised her tanned face in the mirror. She was as excited as a child who was about to be read the crucial chapter of a story. Today Fotini was going to be her Scheherazade.

Dressed in the unfamiliar feel of crisp, ironed cotton, she wandered down the dark back stairway and found herself in the restaurant kitchen, drawn there by the powerful aroma of strong, freshly brewed coffee. Fotini sat at a huge, gnarled table in the middle of the room. Though thoroughly scrubbed, it still seemed to bear the stains from every piece of meat that had been pulverised there and every herb that had been crushed on its surface. It must have also witnessed a thousand moments of frayed temper which had simmered and boiled over in the intense heat of the kitchen. Fotini rose to greet her.

'*Kalimera*, Alexis!' she said warmly.

She was wearing a blouse similar to the one she had lent Alexis, though Fotini's was in shades of ochre that matched the full skirt that billowed out from her slender waist and nearly reached her ankles. The first impression of her beauty that had struck Alexis so forcibly the night before in the kindly dusk light had not been wrong. The Cretan woman's statuesque physique and large eyes reminded her of the images on the great Minoan fresco at Knossos, those vivid portraits which had survived several thousand years of time's ravages and yet had a remarkable simplicity that made them seem so contemporary.

'Did you sleep well?' asked Fotini.

Alexis stifled a yawn, nodded and then smiled at Fotini, who was now busily loading a tray with a coffee pot, some generously proportioned cups and saucers and a loaf that she had just removed from the oven.

'I'm sorry – it's reheated. That's the only bad thing about Sundays here – the baker doesn't get out of bed. So it's dry crusts or fresh air,' Fotini said laughingly.

'I'd be more than happy with fresh air, as long as it was washed down with fresh coffee,' responded Alexis, following Fotini out through a set of the ubiquitous plastic strips and on to the terrace, where all last night's tables had been stripped of their paper cloths and now looked strangely bare with their red Formica tops.

The two women sat overlooking the sea which lapped the rocks below. Fotini poured and the dense black liquid gushed in a dark stream into the white china. After the endless disappointing cups of Nescafé, served as though the tasteless dissolving granules of instant coffee were a delicacy, Alexis felt no cup of coffee had ever tasted as powerful and delicious as this. It seemed that nobody had the heart to tell the Greeks that Nescafé was no longer a novelty – it was this old-fashioned thick and treacly fluid that everyone, including her, craved. The September sunshine had a clear brilliance and a kindly warmth that, after the intensity of the August heat, made it one of the most welcome months in Crete. The furnace-strong temperatures of midsummer had dropped and the hot, angry winds had gone too. The two women sat opposite each other beneath the shade of the awning and Fotini put her dark, lined hand on Alexis's.

'I'm so pleased you have come,' she said. 'You can't imagine how pleased. I was very hurt when your mother stopped writing – I understood perfectly, but it broke such an important link with the past.'

'I had no idea she used to write to you,' said Alexis, feeling as though she should apologise on her mother's behalf.

'The very beginning of her life was difficult,' continued Fotini, 'but we all tried, we really did, to make her happy and to do our best for her.'

Looking at Alexis's slightly puzzled expression, Fotini realised that she had to slow her pace. She poured them both another cup of coffee, giving herself a moment to think about where to start. It seemed she would have to go back even further than she had originally imagined would be necessary.

'I could say, "I'll begin at the beginning", but there is no real beginning here,' she said. 'Your mother's story is your grandmother's story, and it is also your great-grandmother's story. It's your great-aunt's story too. Their lives were intertwined, and that's what we really mean when we talk about fate in Greece. Our so-called fate is largely ordained by our ancestors, not by the stars. When we talk about ancient history here we always refer to destiny – but we don't really mean the uncontrollable. Of course events seem to take place out of the blue that change the course of our lives, but what really determines what happens to us are the actions of those around us now and those who came before us.'

Alexis began to feel slightly edgy. The impregnable safe of her mother's past, which had been so resolutely locked for her entire life, was now to be opened. All the secrets would come spilling out, and she found herself questioning whether she really wanted that. She stared out across the sea at the pale outline of Spinalonga and remembered her solitary afternoon there, already with nostalgia. Pandora regretted opening her box. Would it be the same for her?

Fotini spotted the direction of her gaze.

'Your great-grandmother lived on that island,' she said. 'She was a leper.' She didn't expect her words to sound quite so blunt, quite so heartless, and she saw straightaway that they had made Alexis wince.

'A *leper*?' Alexis asked in a voice that was almost choked with shock. She was repelled by this thought even though she knew her reaction was probably irrational, and found it difficult to hide her feelings. She had learned that the old boatman had been a leper and had seen for herself that he was not visibly disfigured. Nevertheless, she was horrified to hear that her own flesh and blood had been leprous. That was entirely different, and she felt strangely disgusted.

For Fotini, who had grown up in the shadow of the colony, leprosy had always been a fact of life. She had seen more lepers arrive in Plaka to cross over the water to Spinalonga than she could count. She had also seen the varied states of the victims of the disease: some cripplingly disfigured, others apparently untouched. Untouchable had, in fact, been the last thing they seemed. But she understood Alexis's reaction. It was the natural response for someone whose knowledge of leprosy came from Old Testament stories and the image of a bell-swinging sufferer crying, 'Unclean! Unclean!'

'Let me explain more,' she offered. 'I know what you imagine leprosy to be like, but it's important that you know the truth of it, otherwise you will never understand the real Spinalonga, the Spinalonga that was home to so many good people.'

Alexis continued to gaze at the little island across the shimmering water. Her visit there yesterday had seemed so full of conflicting images: the remains of elegant Italianate villas, gardens and even shops, and overshadowing them all the spectre of a disease which she had seen portrayed in epic films as a living death. She took another gulp of the thick coffee.

'I know it's not fatal in every case,' she said, almost defensively, 'but it is always horribly disfiguring, isn't it?'

'Not to the extent that you might think,' replied Fotini. 'It's not a rampantly fast-spreading disease like the plague. It sometimes takes ages to develop – those images you have seen of people who are so terribly maimed are of those who have suffered for years, maybe decades. There are two strains of leprosy, one much slower to develop than the other. Both are curable now. Your great-grandmother was unfortunate, though. She had the faster-developing of the two types and neither time nor history was on her side.'

Alexis was feeling ashamed of her initial reaction, humbled by her ignorance, but the revelation that a member of her family had been a leper had been a bolt out of the bluest of skies.

'Your great-grandmother may have been the one with the disease, but your great-grandfather, Giorgis, bore deep scars too. Even before his wife was exiled to Spinalonga, he used to make deliveries to the island with his fishing boat, and he continued to do so when she went there. It meant that he watched on an almost daily basis as she was gradually destroyed by the disease. When Eleni first went to Spinalonga hygiene was poor, and though it improved a great deal during the time she was there, some irreparable damage was done in her early years. I shall spare you the details. Giorgis spared Maria and Anna from them. But you do know how it happens, don't you? Leprosy can affect nerve endings, and the result of this is that you can't feel it if you burn or cut yourself. That's why people with leprosy are so vulnerable to inflicting permanent damage on themselves, and the consequences of that can be disastrous.'

Fotini paused. She was concerned not to offend this young

woman's sensibilities, but was also very aware that there were elements of the story that were nothing less than shocking. It was simply a case of treading carefully.

'I don't want your image of your mother's family to be dominated by disease. It wasn't like that,' she added hastily. 'Look. I've got some photographs of them here.'

On the big wooden tray propped against the coffee pot there was a tatty manila envelope. Fotini opened it and the contents spilled out on to the table. Some of the photographs were no bigger than train tickets, others were postcard size. Some were shiny, with white borders, others were matt, but all were monochrome, many faded almost to invisibility. Most had been taken in a studio in the days before the spontaneous snapshot was possible, and the stiffness of the subjects made them seem as distant and remote as King Minos.

The first photo Alexis focused on was one she recognised. It was the picture that her mother had next to her bed of the lady in lace and the platinum-haired man. She picked it up.

'That's your great-aunt Maria and great-uncle Nikolaos,' said Fotini, with a detectable hint of pride. 'And this one,' she said, pulling out a battered picture from the bottom of the pile, 'was the last picture taken of your great-grandparents and their two girls all together.'

She passed it to Alexis. The man was about the same height as the woman, but broad-shouldered. He had dark, wavy hair, a clipped moustache, a strong nose, and eyes that smiled even though the expression he maintained for this photograph was serious and posed. His hands seemed big in comparison with his body. The woman next to him was slim, long-necked and strikingly beautiful; her hair was wound into plaits which were coiled up on top of her head, and her smile was broad and spontaneous. Seated in front of them were two girls in cotton dresses. One had strong, thick hair worn loose about her shoulders and her eyes were slanted almost like a cat's. She had mischief in her eyes and plump lips that did not smile. The other had neatly plaited hair, more delicate features and a nose that wrinkled as she smiled at the camera. She could almost be described as skinny and, of the two girls, was much more like the mother, with her hands held softly in her lap in a demure pose while her sister had her arms folded and glared, as if in defiance, at the person taking the photograph.

'That's Maria,' said Fotini, pointing at the child who smiled. 'And that's Anna, your grandmother,' she said, indicating the other. 'And those are their parents, Eleni and Giorgis.'

She spread the pictures out on the table, and occasionally the breeze lifted them gently from its surface and seemed to bring them to life. Alexis saw pictures of the two sisters when they were babes in arms, then as schoolgirls, and then as young women, by that stage just with their father. There was also a picture of Anna arm in arm with a man in full traditional Cretan dress. It was a wedding picture.

'So that must be my grandfather,' said Alexis. 'Anna looks really beautiful there,' she added admiringly. 'Really happy.'

'Mmm . . . the radiance of young love,' said Fotini. There was a hint of sarcasm in her voice that took Alexis by surprise, and she was about to quiz her further when another picture surfaced which seized her interest.

'That looks like my mother!' she exclaimed. The little girl

in the photograph had a distinctive aquiline nose and a sweet but rather shy smile.

'It *is* your mother. She must have been about five then.'

Like any collection of family photographs, it was a random selection that told only fragments of a story. The real tale would be revealed by the pictures that were missing or never even taken at all, not the ones that had been so carefully framed or packed away neatly in an envelope. Alexis was aware of that, but at least she had now been given a glimpse of these family members that her mother had kept so secret for so long.

'It all began here in Plaka,' said Fotini. 'Just behind us, over there. That's where the Petrakis family lived.'

She pointed to a small house on the corner, a pebble's throw from where they sat sipping their coffee. It was a tatty, whitewashed building, as shabby as every other home in the ramshackle village, but charming nevertheless. Its plastered walls were flaking and the shutters, repainted time and time again since Alexis's great-grandparents had lived there, were a shade of bright aqua that had peeled and cracked in the heat. A balcony, perched above the doorway, sagged under the weight of several huge urns from which flame-red geraniums cascaded downwards, as though making their escape through the carved wooden railings. It was typical of almost every home on every Greek island and could have been built at any time in the past few hundred years. Plaka, like any village lucky enough to have been spared the ravages of mass tourism, was timeless.

'That's where your grandmother and her sister grew up. Maria was my best friend; she was just over a year younger than Anna. Their father, Giorgis, was a fisherman, like most of the local men, and Eleni, his wife, was a teacher. In fact she was really much more than a teacher – she more or less ran the local elementary school. It was just down the road in Elounda, the town you must have come through to reach us here. She loved children – not just her own daughters, but *all* the children who were in her classes. I think Anna found that difficult. She was a possessive child and hated sharing anything, especially her mother's affection. But Eleni was generous in every way and had enough time for all her children, whether they were her own flesh and blood or simply her pupils.

'I used to pretend that I was another of Giorgis and Eleni's daughters. I was always at their house; I had two brothers so you can imagine how my own home differed from theirs. My mother, Savina, didn't seem to mind. She and Eleni had been friends since childhood and had shared everything from an early age, so I don't think she worried about losing me. In fact, I believe she always harboured a fantasy that either Maria or Anna would end up marrying one of my brothers.

'When I was little I probably spent more time at the Petrakis place than I did at my own, but the tables turned later on and Anna and Maria more or less lived with us.

'Our playground at that time, and for our whole childhood, was the beach. It was ever-changing and we never tired of it. We would swim each day from late May to early October and would have restless nights from the unbearable grittiness of the sand that had hidden in between our toes and then worked its way out on to our sheets. In the evenings we fished for our own picarel, tiny fish, and in the morning we'd go and see what the fishermen had brought in. The winters bring higher tides and there was usually something washed up for us to inspect: jellyfish, eels, octopus, and a few times the sight of a turtle lying motionless on the shore. Whatever the season, we would go back to Anna and Maria's as it was getting dark and the fragrant smell of warm pastry often greeted us when we arrived – Eleni would make us fresh cheese pies and I'd usually be nibbling on one as I trudged up the hill to my own house when it was time for bed—'

'It does sound an idyllic way to grow up,' interrupted Alexis, beguiled by Fotini's descriptions of this perfect and almost fairy-tale childhood. What she really wanted to find out, though, was how it all came to an end. 'How did Eleni catch leprosy?' she asked abruptly. 'Were lepers allowed off the island?'

'No, of course they weren't. That was why the island was feared so much. Back at the beginning of the century, the government had declared that all lepers in Crete should be confined on Spinalonga. The moment that doctors were certain of the diagnosis, people had to leave their families for good and go there. It was known as "The Place of the Living Dead" and there was no better description.

'In those days people did everything they could to conceal symptoms, mostly because the consequences of being diagnosed were so horrific. It was hardly surprising that Eleni was vulnerable to leprosy. She never gave a second thought to the risk of catching infections from her pupils – she couldn't teach them without having them sitting close, and if a child fell in the dusty schoolyard she would be the first to scoop them up. And it turned out that one of her pupils did have leprosy.' Fotini paused.

'So you think the parents knew their child was infected?' asked Alexis incredulously.

'Almost certainly,' replied Fotini. 'They knew they would never see the child again if anyone found out. There was only one responsible action Eleni could take once she knew she was infected – and she took it. She gave instructions that every child in the school should be checked so that the sufferer could be identified, and, sure enough, there was a nine-year-old boy, called Dimitri, whose wretched parents had to endure the horror of having their son taken away from them. But the alternative was a great deal worse. Think of the contact that children have with each other when they play! They're not like adults, who keep their distance. They scuffle and wrestle and fall in heaps on top of each other. We know now that the disease is generally only spread through persistent close contact, but what people were afraid of in those days was that the school in Elounda would become a leper colony in its own right if they didn't pull out the infected child as soon as they possibly could.'

'That must have been a very difficult thing for Eleni to do – particularly if she had that kind of relationship with her pupils,' said Alexis thoughtfully.

'Yes, it was awful. Awful for everyone concerned,' replied Fotini.

Alexis's lips had dried and she hardly trusted herself to speak in case no sound came. To help the moment pass, she moved her empty cup towards Fotini, who filled it once more and pushed it back across the table. As she carefully stirred sugar into the dark swirling liquid, Alexis felt herself being pulled into Eleni's vortex of grief and suffering.

What had it felt like? To sail away from your home and be effectively imprisoned within sight of your family, everything that was precious to you stripped away? She thought not only of the woman who had been her great-grandmother, but also of the boy, both of them innocent of any crime and yet condemned.

Fotini reached out and put her hand on Alexis's. Perhaps she had been in too much of a hurry to tell the story, without really knowing this young woman well enough. It was no fairytale, however, and she could not simply choose which chapters to tell and which ones to omit. If she trod too carefully now, the real story might never be told. She watched the clouds pass across Alexis's face. Unlike the pale wisps that hung in the blue sky that morning, these were sombre and brooding. Until now, Fotini suspected, the only darkness in Alexis's life had been the vague shadow of her mother's hidden past. It had been nothing more than a question mark, nothing that had kept her awake at night. She had not seen disease, let alone death. Now she had to learn about them both.

'Let's go for a walk, Alexis.' Fotini stood up. 'We'll get Gerasimo to take us out to the island later – everything will make more sense when we're over there.'

A walk was exactly what Alexis needed. These fragments of her mother's history and a surfeit of caffeine had made her head spin, and as they descended the wooden steps on to the shingly beach below, Alexis gulped in the salty air.

'Why has my mother never told me any of this?' she asked.

'She had her reasons, I'm sure,' said Fotini, knowing that there was so much more left to tell. 'And perhaps when you get back to England she'll explain why she was so secretive.'

They strolled the length of the beach and began to ascend the stony path lined with teasels and lavender that led away from the village. The breeze was stronger here and Fotini's walk slowed. Though she was fit for a woman in her seventies, she didn't always have her old stamina, and her pace became more careful and more faltering as the path began to steepen.

Occasionally she stopped, once or twice pointing out places on Spinalonga that came into view. Eventually they came to a huge rock worn smooth by wind, rain and its long use as a bench. They sat down and looked out to sea, the wind rustling the scrubby bushes of wild thyme that grew in profusion around them. It was here that Fotini began to relate Sofia's story.

Over the next few days Fotini told Alexis everything she knew of her family's history, leaving no pebble unturned – from the small shingle of childhood minutiae to the larger boulders of Crete's own history. In the time they had together, the two women strolled along the coastal paths, sat for hours over the dinner table and made journeys to local towns and villages in Alexis's hired car, with Fotini laying the pieces of the Petrakis jigsaw before them. These were days during which Alexis felt herself grow older and wiser, and Fotini, in retelling so much of her past, felt herself young again. The half-century that separated the two women disappeared to vanishing point, and as they strolled arm in arm, they might even have been mistaken for sisters.

Part 2

Chapter Three

1939

EARLY MAY BRINGS Crete its most perfect and heaven-sent days. On one such day, when the trees were heavy with blossom and the very last of the mountain snows had melted into crystal streams, Eleni left the mainland for Spinalonga. In cruel contrast to this blackest of events, the sky was brilliant, a cloudless blue. A crowd had gathered to watch, to weep, to wave a final goodbye. Even if the school had not officially closed for the day out of respect for the departing teacher, the classrooms would have echoed with emptiness. Pupils and teachers alike had deserted. No one would have missed the chance to wave goodbye to their beloved 'Kyria Petrakis'.

Eleni Petrakis was loved in Plaka and the surrounding villages. She had a magnetism that attracted children and adults alike to her and was admired and respected by them all. The reason was simple. For Eleni, teaching was a vocation, and her enthusiasm touched the children like a torch. 'If they love it they will learn it' was her mantra. These were not her own words, but the saying of the teacher with fire in his belly who had been her own doorway into learning twenty years before.

The night before she left her home for ever, Eleni had filled a vase with spring flowers. She put this in the centre of the table and the small spray of pale blooms magically transformed the room. She understood the potency of the simple act, the power of detail. She knew, for example, that recollection of a child's birthday or favourite colour could be the key to winning the heart and then the mind. Children absorbed information in her classroom largely because they wanted to please her, not because they were forced to learn, and the process was helped by the way she displayed facts and figures, each one written on a card and suspended from the ceiling so it seemed as though a flock of exotic birds hovered permanently overhead.

But it was not just a favourite teacher who would be making her way over the water to Spinalonga that day. They were saying goodbye to a friend as well: nine-year-old Dimitri, whose parents had gone to such lengths for a year or more to conceal the signs of his leprosy. Each month there had been some new attempt to hide his blemishes – his knee-length shorts were replaced by long trousers, open sandals by heavy boots, and in the summer he was banned from swimming in the sea with his friends lest the patches on his back should be noticed. 'Say you're afraid of the waves!' pleaded his mother, which was of course ridiculous. These children had all grown up to enjoy the exhilarating power of the sea and actually looked forward to those days when the Meltemi wind turned the glassy Mediterranean into a wild ocean. Only a sissy was afraid of the breakers. The child had lived with the fear of discovery for many months, always knowing in his heart that this was a temporary state and that sooner or later he would be found out.

Anyone unacquainted with the extraordinary circumstances of this summer morning might well have assumed that the crowd had gathered for a funeral. They were nearly one hundred in number, mostly women and children, and there was a sad stillness about them. They stood in the village square, one great body, silent, waiting, breathing in unison. Close by, in an adjacent side street, Eleni Petrakis opened her front door. She was confronted by the unusual sight of this great mass of people in the normally empty space and her instinct was to retreat inside. This was not an option. Giorgis was waiting for her by the jetty, his boat already loaded up with some of her possessions. She needed few, since Giorgis could bring more to her during the following weeks, and she had no desire to remove anything but bare essentials from the family home. Anna and Maria remained behind the closed door. The last few minutes with them had been the most agonising of Eleni's life. She felt the strongest desire to hold them, to crush them in her embrace, to feel their hot tears on her skin, to still their shaking bodies. But she could do none of these things. Not without risk. Their faces were contorted with grief and their eyes swollen with crying. There was nothing left to say. Almost nothing left to feel. Their mother was leaving. She would not be coming back early that evening weighed down with books, sallow with exhaustion, but beaming with pleasure to be at home with them. There would be no return.

The girls had behaved precisely as Eleni would have anticipated. Anna, the elder, had always been volatile, and there was never any doubt about what she was feeling. Maria, on the other hand, was a quieter, more patient child who was slower to lose her temper. True to form, Anna had been more openly distressed than her sister in the days leading up to her mother's departure, and her inability to control her emotions had never been more on display than on this day. She had begged her mother not to go, beseeched her to stay, ranted, raved and torn her hair. By contrast, Maria had wept, silently at first and then with huge racking sobs that could be heard out in the street. The final stage for both of them, however, was the same: they both became subdued, exhausted, spent.

Eleni was determined to contain the volcanic eruption of grief that threatened to overwhelm her. She could vent it in full once she was away from Plaka, but the only hope any of them had at this moment was that her self-possession would remain intact. If she caved in, they were all done for. The girls were to stay in the house. They would be spared the vision of their mother's receding figure, a sight that might burn itself for ever on to their memory.

This was the hardest moment of Eleni's life and now the least private. She was watched by rows of sad eyes. She knew they were there to wish her farewell but never before had she yearned so much to be alone. Every face in the crowd was familiar to her, each was one she loved. 'Goodbye,' she said softly. 'Goodbye.' She kept her distance from them. Her old instincts to embrace had died a sudden death ten days ago, that fateful morning when she had noticed the strange patches on the back of her leg. They were unmistakable, especially when she compared them with a picture on the leaflet that had been circulated to warn people of the symptoms. She hardly needed to see a specialist to understand the awful truth. She knew, even before she visited the doctor, that she had somehow contracted that most dreaded of diseases. The words from Leviticus, read out with more frequency than strictly necessary by the local priest, had resounded inside her head:

> *As the leprosy appeareth in the skin of the flesh, he is a leprous man, he is unclean and the priest shall pronounce him utterly unclean. And the leper in whom the plague is, his clothes shall be rent and his head bared and he shall put a covering upon his upper lip and shall cry 'Unclean, Unclean.'*

Many people still believed that the Old Testament's brutal instructions for the treatment of lepers should be followed. This passage had been heard in church for hundreds of years, and the image of the leper as a man, woman or even child to be cast out of society was deeply ingrained.

As she approached through the crowd Giorgis could just make out the top of Eleni's head, and he knew the moment he had been dreading was upon him. He had been to Spinalonga a thousand times, for years supplementing his meagre fisherman's income by making regular deliveries to the leper colony, but he had never imagined making a journey such as this. The boat was ready and he stood watching her as she approached, his arms wrapped tightly across his chest, his head bowed. He thought that if he stood like this, his body tense, rigid, he could subdue his raging emotions and prevent them from spilling out as huge involuntary cries of anguish. His built-in ability to hide his feelings was bolstered by his wife's exemplary self-control. Inside, though, he was stricken with grief. I must do this, he told himself, as though it is just another ordinary boat journey. To the thousand crossings he had already made would be added this one and a thousand more.

As Eleni approached the jetty, the crowd remained silent. One child cried, but was hushed by its mother. One false emotional move and these grieving people would lose their composure. The control, the formality would be gone and the dignity of this farewell would be no more. Though the few hundred metres had seemed an impossible distance, Eleni's walk to the jetty was nearly over, and she turned round to look at the throng for the last time. Her house was out of sight now, but she knew the shutters would remain closed and that her daughters would be weeping in the darkness.

Suddenly there were cries to be heard. They were the loud, heartbreaking sobs of a grown woman, and her display of grief was as unchecked as Eleni's was controlled. For a moment Eleni halted. These sounds seemed to echo her own emotional state. They were the precise outward expression of everything she felt inside, but she knew she was not their author. The crowd stirred, taking their eyes off Eleni and looking back towards the far corner of the square where a mule had been tethered to a tree and, close by, a man and a woman stood. Though he had all but disappeared within the woman's embrace, there was also a boy. The top of his head barely reached her chest and she was bent over him, her arms wrapped around his body as though she would never let go. 'My boy!' she cried despairingly. 'My boy, my darling boy!' Her husband was at their side. 'Katerina,' he coaxed. 'Dimitri must go. We have no choice. The boat is waiting.' Gently he prised the mother's arms away from the child. She spoke her son's name one final time, softly, indistinctly: 'Dimitri . . .' but the boy did not look up. His gaze was fixed on the dusty ground. 'Come, Dimitri,' his father said firmly. And the boy followed.

He kept his eyes focused on his father's worn leather boots. All he had to do was plant his own feet in the prints they made in the dust. It was mechanical – a game they had played so many times, when his father would take giant strides and Dimitri would jump and leap until his legs could stretch no more and he would fall over, helpless with laughter. This time, however, his father's pace was slow and faltering. Dimitri had no trouble keeping up. His father had relieved the sad-faced mule of its burden and now balanced the small crate of the boy's possessions on his shoulder, the very same shoulder on which his son had been carried so many times. It seemed a long way, past the crowd, to the water's edge.

The final goodbye between father and son was a brief, almost manly one. Eleni, aware of this awkwardness, greeted Dimitri, her focus now solely on the boy whose life, from this moment on, would be her greatest responsibility. 'Come,' she said, encouragingly. 'Let's go and see our new home.' And she took the child's hand and helped him on to the boat as though they were going on an adventure and the boxes packed around them contained supplies for a picnic.

The crowd watched the departure, maintaining its silence. There was no protocol for this moment. Should they wave? Should they shout goodbye? Skin paled, stomachs contracted, hearts felt heavy. Some had ambivalent feelings about the boy, blaming him for Eleni's situation and for the unease they now had about their own children's health. At the very moment of their departure, though, the mothers and fathers felt only pity for the two unfortunates who were leaving their families behind for ever. Giorgis pushed the boat away from the jetty and soon his oars were engaged in the usual battle with the current. It was as though the sea did not want them to go. For a short while the crowd watched, but as the figures became less distinct they began to disperse.

The last to turn away and leave the square were a woman of about Eleni's own age and a girl. The woman was Savina Angelopoulos, who had grown up with Eleni, and the girl was her daughter Fotini, who, in the way of small village life, was the best friend of Eleni's youngest daughter, Maria. Savina wore a head scarf, which hid her thick hair but accentuated her huge kind eyes; childbearing had not been kind to her body and she was now stocky, with heavy legs. By contrast, Fotini was as slim as an olive sapling but she had inherited her mother's beautiful eyes. When the little boat had all but disappeared, the two of them turned and walked swiftly across the square. Their destination was the house with the faded green door, the house from which Eleni had emerged some time earlier. The shutters were closed, but the front door was unlocked and mother and daughter stepped inside. Soon Savina would hold the girls and provide the embrace that their own mother, in her wisdom, had been unable to give.

As the boat neared the island, Eleni held Dimitri's hand ever more tightly. She was glad that this poor boy would have someone to care for him and at this moment did not give a second thought to the irony of this position. She would teach him and nurture him as though he was her own son, and do her best to ensure that his schooling was not cut short by this terrible turn of events. She was now close enough to see that there were a few people standing just outside the fortress wall and realised they must be waiting for her. Why else would they be there? It was unlikely that they were on the point of leaving the island themselves.

Giorgis guided the boat expertly towards the jetty and soon he was helping his wife and Dimitri on to dry land. Almost subconsciously, he found himself avoiding contact with the boy's bare skin, taking his elbow not his hand as he helped him out of the boat. He then concentrated fiercely on tying the boat fast so that he could unload the boxes safely, distracting himself from the thought of leaving the island without his wife. The small wooden crate that was the boy's and the larger one that belonged to Eleni soon sat on the quayside.

Now that they were on Spinalonga, it seemed to both Eleni and Dimitri that they had crossed a wide ocean and that their old lives were already a million miles away.

Before Eleni had thought to look around once more, Giorgis had gone. They had agreed the night before that there would be no goodbyes between them, and they had both been true to their resolve. Giorgis had already set off on the return journey and was a hundred metres away, his hat pulled down low so that the boat's dark strips of wood were all that lay in his field of vision.

Chapter Four

THE CLUSTER OF people Eleni had noticed earlier now moved towards them. Dimitri remained silent, staring down at his feet, while Eleni held out her hand to the man who came forward to greet them. It was a gesture that demonstrated an acceptance that this was her new home. She found herself reaching out to take a hand that was as bent as a shepherd's crook, a hand so badly deformed now by leprosy that the elderly man could not grasp Eleni's outstretched hand. But his smile said enough, and Eleni responded with a polite '*Kalimera*.' Dimitri stood back, silent. He would remain in this state of shock for several more days.

It was a custom on Spinalonga for new members of the colony to be received with some degree of formality, and Eleni and Dimitri were welcomed just as if they had finally reached a far-off, long-dreamed-of destination. The reality was that for some lepers this was truly the case. The island could provide a welcome refuge from a life of vagrancy; many of the lepers had spent months or even years living outside society, sleeping in shacks and surviving off pilfered scraps. For these victims of the disease, Spinalonga was a relief, respite from the abject misery they had endured as outcasts.

The man who greeted them was Petros Kontomaris, the island leader. He had been voted in, along with a group of elders, by the three hundred or so inhabitants in the annual election; Spinalonga was a model of democracy and the regularity of the elections was intended to ensure that dissatisfaction never festered. It was Kontomaris's duty to welcome all newcomers, and only he and a handful of other appointed individuals were permitted to come and go through the great gateway.

Eleni and Dimitri followed Petros Kontomaris through the tunnel, their hands locked together. Eleni probably knew more about Spinalonga than most people on the mainland because of Giorgis's first-hand knowledge. Even so, the scene that greeted her was a surprise. In the narrow street ahead of them was a throng of people. It looked just like market day in Plaka. People went to and fro with baskets full of produce, a priest emerged from a church doorway and two elderly women made their way slowly up the street, riding side-saddle on their weary-looking donkeys. Some turned to stare at the new arrivals and several nodded their heads in a gesture of greeting. Eleni looked around her, anxious not to be rude but unable to contain her curiosity. What had always been rumoured was true. Most of the lepers looked as she did: ostensibly unblemished.

One woman, however, whose head was obscured by a shawl, stopped to let them pass. Eleni glimpsed a face deformed by lumps the size of walnuts and shuddered. Never had she seen anything more hideous, and she prayed that Dimitri had not noticed the woman.

The group of three continued to walk up the street,

followed by another elderly man who led two donkeys bearing the weight of their possessions. Petros Kontomaris chatted to Eleni. 'We have a house for you,' he explained. 'It became vacant last week.'

In Spinalonga, vacancies were only created by death. People continued to arrive regardless of whether there was space, and this meant that the island was overcrowded. Since it was the government's policy to encourage lepers to live on Spinalonga, it was entirely in its own interests to minimise unrest on the island, so from time to time it would provide funds for new housing or small grants to restore the old. The previous year, just when existing buildings were reaching the limit of their capacity, an ugly but functional block had been completed and a housing crisis averted. Once again, every islander had some privacy. The man who made the final decision on where newcomers should live was Kontomaris. He regarded Eleni and Dimitri as a special case; they were to be treated as mother and son, and for that reason he had decided that they should not be housed in the new block, but should take over the newly vacant house in the high street. Dimitri at least might be there for many years to come.

'Kyria Petrakis,' he said. 'This is to be your home.'

At the end of the central street where the shops ended, standing back from the road, stood a single house. It struck Eleni that it bore more than a little resemblance to her own home. Then she told herself she must stop thinking in this way – this old stone house in front of her *was* now her home. Kontomaris unlocked the door and held it open for her. The interior was dark, even on this luminously bright day, and her heart sank. For the hundredth time that day, the limits of her bravery were tested. This was undoubtedly the best there was and it was imperative that she pretend to be pleased. Her best acting skills, the ability to perform that contributed so much to her remarkable teaching style, were in heavy demand.

'I'll leave you to settle in,' Kontomaris said. 'My wife will be over to see you later and she will show you round the colony.'

'Your wife?' exclaimed Eleni with more surprise in her voice than she had quite intended. But he was used to such a reaction.

'Yes, my wife. We met and married here. It's not unusual, you know.'

'No, no, I'm sure it isn't,' said Eleni, abashed, realising that she had much to learn. Kontomaris gave the slightest of bows and left. Eleni and Dimitri were now alone, and they both stood looking about them in the daytime darkness. Apart from a threadbare rug, all that furnished the room was a wooden chest, a small table and two spindly wooden chairs. Tears pricked Eleni's eyes. Her life was reduced to this. Two souls in a sombre room and a pair of fragile chairs that looked as though they might crumble with a hand's touch, let alone the full weight of a human body. What difference between she and Dimitri and those frail pieces of furniture? Once again, there was an imperative for false cheer.

'Come on, Dimitri, shall we go and look upstairs?'

They crossed the unlit room and climbed the stairs. At the top were two doors. Eleni opened the left-hand one and went in, throwing open the shutters. The light poured in. The windows looked over the street and from here the sparkle of the sea could be seen in the distance. A metal bed and yet another decrepit chair was all that this bare cell contained. Eleni left Dimitri standing there and went into the other bedroom, which was smaller and somehow greyer. She returned to the first, where Dimitri still stood.

'This one will be your room,' she announced.

'My room?' he asked incredulously. 'Just for me?' He had always shared a room with his two brothers and two sisters. For the first time his small face showed some expression. Quite unexpectedly he found that one thing at least had improved in his life.

As they descended the stairs a cockroach scuttled across the room and disappeared behind the wooden chest which stood in the corner. Eleni would hunt it out later, but for now she would light the three oil lamps which would help to brighten this gloomy dwelling. Opening her box of possessions – which contained mostly books and other materials that she would need for teaching Dimitri – she found paper and pencil and began to make a list: three lengths of cotton for curtains, two pictures, some cushions, five blankets, a large saucepan and a few pieces of her best china. She knew her family would enjoy the idea that they were all eating from the same flower-sprigged plates. Another important item she requested was seeds. Although the house was dismal, Eleni was greatly cheered by the little courtyard in front of it and had already begun to plan what she would grow. Giorgis would be back in a few days, so within a week or two she would have this place looking as she wanted it. This would be the first of many lists for Giorgis, and Eleni knew that he would fulfil her requirements to the very last letter.

Dimitri sat and watched Eleni as she drew up her inventory of essentials. He was slightly in awe of this woman who only yesterday had been his teacher and now was to care for him not just between the hours of eight in the morning and two in the afternoon but for all the others as well. She was to be his mother, his *meetera*. But he would never call her by any name other than 'Kyria Petrakis'. He wondered what his real mother was doing now. She would probably be stirring the big cooking pot, preparing the evening meal. In Dimitri's eyes that was how she seemed to spend most of her time, while he and his brothers and sisters played outside in the street. He wondered if he would ever see them again and wished with all his heart that he was there now, messing about in the dust. If he missed them this much after only a few hours, how much more would he miss them each day, each week, each month? he wondered. His throat tightened until it hurt so much the tears flowed down his face. Then Kyria Petrakis was by his side, holding him close and whispering: 'There, there, Dimitri. Everything will be all right . . . Everything will be all right.' If only he believed her.

That afternoon they unpacked their boxes. Surrounding themselves with a few familiar objects should have lifted their mood, but each time a new possession emerged it came with all the associations of their past lives and did not help them forget. Every new trinket, book or toy reminded them more intensely than the last of what they had left behind.

One of Eleni's treasures was a small clock, a gift from her parents on her wedding day. She placed it in the centre of the mantelpiece and a gentle tick-tock now filled the long silences. It struck on the hour, and at precisely three o'clock, before the chimes had quite died away, there was a gentle knock on the door.

Eleni opened the door wide to admit her visitor, a small, round-faced woman with flecks of silver in her hair.

'*Kalispera,*' said Eleni. 'Kyrios Kontomaris told me to expect your visit. Please come in.'

'This must be Dimitri,' said the woman immediately, walking over to the boy, who remained seated, his head resting in his hands. 'Come,' she said, holding out her hand to him. 'I am going to show you round. My name is Elpida Kontomaris, but please call me Elpida.'

There was a note of forced jollity in her voice and the kind of enthusiasm you would summon up if you were taking a terrified child to have a tooth pulled. They emerged from the gloom of the house into the late afternoon light and turned right.

'The most important thing is the water supply,' she began, her matter-of-fact tone betraying that she had taken new arrivals on a tour of the island many times before. Whenever a woman arrived, her husband would dispatch Elpida to welcome her. This was the first time that she had given her talk with a child present, so she knew she would have to modify some of the information she usually imparted. She would certainly have to control the vitriol that rose up inside her when she was describing the island's facilities.

'This,' she said brightly, pointing to a huge cistern at the foot of the hill, 'is where we collect our water. It's a sociable place and we all spend plenty of time here chatting and catching up with each other's news.'

In truth, the fact that they had to trudge several hundred metres downhill to fetch water and then all the way back with it angered her beyond words. She could cope, but there were others more crippled than her who could barely lift an empty vessel let alone one that brimmed with water. Before she lived on Spinalonga she had rarely lifted more than a glassful of water, but now carrying bucketfuls was part of life's daily grind. It had taken her several years to get used to this. Things had perhaps changed more drastically for Elpida than for many. Coming from a wealthy family in Hania, she had been a stranger to manual work until she arrived in Spinalonga ten years earlier; the hardest assignment she had ever undertaken prior to that was to embroider a bedspread.

As usual, Elpida put on a brave front for her introduction to the island and presented only the positive aspects of it all. She showed Eleni Petrakis the few shops as though they were the finest in Iraklion, pointed out where the bi-weekly market was held and where they did their laundry. She also took her to the pharmacy, which for many was the most important building of all. She told her the times when the baker's oven was lit and where the *kafenion* was situated, tucked away down a little side street. The priest would call on her later, but meanwhile she indicated where he lived and took them to the church. She enthused to the boy about the puppet shows which were put on for the children once a week in the town hall and finally she pointed out the schoolhouse, which stood empty today, but on three mornings each week contained the island's small population of children.

She told Dimitri about other children of his own age and attempted to prise a smile out of him by describing the fun and games they had together, but no matter how hard she tried, his face remained impassive.

What she refrained from speaking of today, especially in

front of the boy, was the restlessness that was brewing on Spinalonga. Though many of the lepers were initially grateful for the sanctuary that the island provided, they became disenchanted after a while and believed themselves abandoned, feeling their needs were met only minimally. Elpida could see that Eleni would soon become aware of the bitterness that consumed many of the lepers. It hung in the very air.

As the wife of the island leader she was in a difficult position. Petros Kontomaris had been elected by the people of Spinalonga, but his most important task was to act as mediator and go-between with the government. He was a reasonable man and knew where the boundaries lay with the authorities on Crete, but Elpida saw him battling continually against a vociferous and sometimes radical minority in the leper colony who felt that they were being badly treated and who agitated constantly for improvements to the island's facilities. Some felt that they were mere squatters in the Turkish rubble even though Kontomaris had done everything he could in the years he had been in charge. He had negotiated a monthly allowance of twenty-five drachma for every inhabitant, a grant to build the new block of flats, a decent pharmacy and clinic and regular visits from a doctor from the mainland. He had also constructed a plan which allocated land to each person on Spinalonga who wished to cultivate their own fruit and vegetables either to eat themselves or to sell at the weekly market. In short, he had done everything he humanly could, but the population of Spinalonga always wanted more and Elpida was not sure that her husband had the energy to fulfil their expectations. She worried about him constantly. He was in his late fifties, like her, but his health was failing. Leprosy was beginning to win the battle for his body.

Elpida had seen huge changes since she had arrived, and most of these had been achieved through her husband's endeavours. Still the rumbles of dissatisfaction grew by the day. The water situation was the main focus of unrest, particularly in the summer. The Venetian water system, constructed hundreds of years earlier, collected rainwater in tunnelled watersheds and stored it in underground tanks to prevent evaporation. It was ingeniously simple, but the tunnels were now beginning to crumble. Additionally, fresh water was brought over from the mainland every week, but there was never enough to keep more than two hundred people well washed and watered. It was a daily struggle, even with the help of mules, especially for the elderly and crippled. In the winter it was electricity they needed. A generator had been installed a couple of years earlier and everyone had anticipated the pleasure of warmth and light in the dark, chilly days from November to February. This was not to be. The generator packed up after only three weeks and had never worked again; requests for new parts were ignored and the machinery stood abandoned, almost entirely covered now with a tangle of weeds.

Water and electricity were not luxuries but necessities, and they were all aware that the inadequacy of the water supply in particular could shorten their lives. Elpida knew that, although the government had to keep their lives tolerable, its commitment to making them better was perfunctory. The inhabitants of Spinalonga seethed with anger and she shared their fury. Why, in a country where huge mountains reared up into the sky, their snowy peaks clearly visible on a wintry day, were they rationed? They wanted a reliable fresh water supply. They wanted it soon. There had been, as far as there could be amongst men and women, some of whom were crippled, violent arguments about what to do. Elpida remembered the time when one group had threatened to storm the mainland and another suggested the taking of hostages. In the end they had realised what a pathetic straggling crew they would make, with no boats, no weapons and, above all, very little strength.

All they could do was try and make their voices heard. And that was where Petros's powers of argument and diplomacy became the most valuable weapon they had. Elpida had to maintain some distance between herself and the rest of the community but her ear was continually bent, mostly by the women, who regarded her as a conduit to her husband. She was tired of it all and secretly pressurised Petros not to stand in the next elections. Had he not given enough?

As she led Eleni and Dimitri around the little streets of the island, Elpida kept all these thoughts to herself. She saw Dimitri clutch the edge of Eleni's billowing skirt as they walked, as if for comfort, and sighed to herself. What sort of future did the boy have in this place? She almost hoped it would not be a long one.

Eleni found the gentle tug at her skirt reassuring. It reminded her that she was not alone and had someone to care for. Only yesterday she had had a husband and daughters, and the day before a hundred eager faces at school had looked up into hers. All of them had needed her and she had thrived on that. This new reality was hard to grasp. For a moment she wondered if she had already died and this woman was a chimera showing her round Hades, telling where the dead souls could wash their shrouds and buy their insubstantial rations. Her mind, however, told her it was all real. It had not been Charon but her own husband who had brought her to hell and left her here to die. She came to a halt and Dimitri stopped too. Her head dropped to her chest and she could feel huge tears well up in her eyes. For the first time she lost control. Her throat contracted as if to deny her another breath and she took one desperate gasp to drag air into her lungs. Elpida, until now so matter-of-fact, so businesslike, turned to face her and grasped her by the arms. Dimitri looked up at both women. He had seen his own mother cry for the first time that day. Now it was the turn of his teacher. The tears coursed freely down her cheeks.

'Don't be afraid to cry,' said Elpida gently. 'The boy will see plenty of tears here. Believe me, they're shed freely on Spinalonga.'

Eleni buried her head in Elpida's shoulder. Two passers-by stopped and stared. Not at the sight of a woman weeping, but simply because they were curious about the newcomers. Dimitri looked away, doubly embarrassed by Eleni's weeping and the strangers' stares. He wished the ground beneath him would part just like in the earthquakes he had learned about in school, and then swallow him up. He knew that Crete was regularly shaken, but why not today?

Elpida could see what Dimitri was feeling. Eleni's sobbing had begun to affect her too: she sympathised terribly but she wanted her to stop. By good fortune they had come to a halt outside her own house, and she led Eleni firmly inside. For a moment she felt self-conscious about the size of her home, which she knew contrasted starkly with the place Eleni and Dimitri had just moved into. The Kontomaris house, the official residence of the island leader, was one of the buildings from the island's period of occupation by the Venetians, with a balcony that could almost be described as grand and a porticoed front door.

They had lived here for the past six years, and so sure was Elpida of her husband's majority in the yearly elections that she had never even imagined what it would be like to live anywhere else. Now, of course, it was she who was discouraging him from staying on in his position, and this was what they would give up if Petros chose not to stand. 'But who is there to take over?' he would ask. It was true. The only others who were rumoured to be putting themselves up had few supporters. One of them was the chief among the agitators, Theodoros Makridakis, and though many of his causes were sound, it would be disastrous for the island if he was given any power. His lack of diplomacy would mean that any progress that had already been made with the government would be undone and it was quite likely that privileges could be subtly withdrawn rather than added to. The only other candidate for the role was Spyros Kazakis, a kind but weak individual whose only real interest in the position was to secure himself the house everyone on Spinalonga secretly coveted.

The interior provided an extraordinary contrast with almost every other home on the island. Floor-to-ceiling windows allowed light to flood in on three sides, and an ornate crystal lamp hung down into the middle of the room on a long dusty chain, the small, irregular shapes of coloured crystal projecting a kaleidoscopic pattern on to the pastel walls.

The furniture was worn but comfortable, and Elpida gestured to Eleni to take a seat. Dimitri wandered about the room, examining the framed photos and staring into a glass-fronted cabinet that housed precious pieces of Kontomaris memorabilia: an etched silver jug, a row of lace bobbins, some pieces of precious china, more framed pictures and, most intriguingly of all, row upon row of tiny soldiers. He stood gazing into the cabinet for some minutes, not looking beyond the glass at these objects but mesmerised by his own reflection. His face seemed as strange to him as the room where he stood and he met his own gaze with some disquiet, as though he did not recognise the dark eyes that stared back at him. This was a boy whose entire universe had encompassed the towns of Agios Nikolaos, Elounda and a few hamlets in between where cousins, aunts and uncles lived and he felt he had been transported into another galaxy. His face was mirrored in the highly polished pane and behind him he could see Kyria Kontomaris, her arms wrapped around Kyria Petrakis, comforting her as she wept. He watched for some moments and then refocused his eyes so that they could once more study the soldiers so neatly arranged in their regiments.

When he turned around to face the women, Kyria Petrakis had regained her composure and reached out both hands towards him. 'Dimitri,' she said, 'I am sorry.' Her crying had shocked as well as embarrassed him and the thought suddenly occurred to him that she might be missing her children as much as he was missing his mother. He tried to imagine what his mother would be feeling if she had been sent to Spinalonga instead of him. He took Kyria Petrakis's hands and squeezed them hard. 'Don't be sorry,' he said.

Elpida disappeared into her kitchen to make coffee for Eleni and, using sugared water with a twist of lemon, some lemonade for Dimitri. When she returned she found her visitors sitting, talking quietly. The boy's eyes lit up when he saw his drink and he had soon drained it to the bottom. As for Eleni, whether it was the sweetness of the coffee or the kindness, she could not tell, but she felt herself enveloped in Elpida's warm concern. It had always been her role to dispense such sympathy and she found it harder to receive than to give. She would be challenged by this reversal.

The afternoon light was beginning to fade. For a few minutes they sat absorbed in their own thoughts, the silence broken only by the careful clink of their cups. Dimitri nursed a second glass of lemonade. Never had he been in a house like this one, where the light shone in rainbow patterns and the chairs were softer than anything he had ever slept on. It was so unlike his own home, where every bench became a sleeping place at night and every rug doubled up as a blanket. He had thought that was how everyone lived. But not here.

When they had all finished their drinks, Elpida spoke.

'Shall we continue our walk?' she asked, rising out of her seat. 'There's someone waiting to meet you.'

Eleni and Dimitri followed her from the house. Dimitri was reluctant to leave. He had liked it there and hoped he might go back one day and sip lemonade, and perhaps pluck up courage to ask Kyria Kontomaris to open the cabinet so that he could take a closer look at the soldiers, maybe even pick them up.

Further up the street was a building several hundred years

newer than the leader's residence. With its crisp, straight lines, it lacked the classical aesthetics of the home they had just left. This functional structure was the hospital and was their next stop.

Eleni and Dimitri's arrival had coincided with one of the days on which the doctor came from the mainland. This innovation and the building of the hospital had been the result of Petros Kontomaris's campaign to improve medical treatment for the lepers. The first hurdle had been to persuade the government to fund such a project and the second to convince them that a careful doctor could treat and help them without danger of infection to himself. Finally they relented on all counts, and every Monday, Wednesday and Friday a doctor would arrive from Agios Nikolaos. The doctor who had put himself forward for what many of his colleagues thought was a dangerous and foolhardy assignment was Christos Lapakis. He was a jovial, red-faced fellow in his early thirties, well liked by the staff in the dermatovenereology department at the hospital and loved by his patients on Spinalonga. His great girth was evidence of his hedonism, in itself a reflection of his belief that the here and now was all you had so you might as well enjoy it. It disappointed his respectable family in Agios Nikolaos that he was still a bachelor, and he knew himself that he was not helping his marriage prospects by working in a leper colony. This did not bother him unduly, however. He was fulfilled in this work and enjoyed the difference, albeit limited, that he could make to these poor people's lives. In his own opinion, there was no afterlife, no second chance.

Dr Lapakis spent his time on Spinalonga treating wounds

and advising his patients on all the extra precautions they could take and how exercise could help them. With new arrivals he would always do a thorough examination. The introduction of the Doctor's Days, as they became known throughout the community, had done a huge amount to lift morale on the island and had already improved the health of many of the sufferers. His emphasis on cleanliness, sanitation and physiotherapy gave them a reason to get up in the morning and a feeling that they were not simply rising from their beds in order to continue their gradual degeneration. Dr Lapakis had been shocked when he arrived on Spinalonga at the conditions many of the lepers lived in. He knew it was essential for good health that they keep their wounds clean, but when he had first arrived, he had discovered something akin to apathy among many of them. Their sense of abandonment was catastrophic and the psychological damage inflicted by being on the island was actually greater than the physical harm caused by the disease. Many could simply no longer be bothered with life. Why should they? Life had ceased to bother with them.

Christos Lapakis treated both their minds and their bodies. He told them that there always had to be hope and that they should never give up. He was authoritative but often blunt: 'You will die if you don't wash your wounds,' he would say. He was pragmatic and told them the truth dispassionately, but also with enough feeling to show that he cared, and he was practical too, telling them precisely how they needed to care for themselves. 'This is how you wash your wounds,' he would say, 'and this is how you exercise your hands and legs if you don't want to lose your fingers and toes.' As he told them these things, he demonstrated the movements. He made them all realise more than ever the vital importance of clean water. Water was life. And for them the difference between life and death. Lapakis was a great supporter of Kontomaris and gave him all the backing he could in lobbying for the fresh water supply that could transform the island and the prognosis of many who lived there.

'Here's the hospital,' said Elpida. 'Dr Lapakis is expecting you. He has just finished seeing his regular patients.'

They found themselves in a space as cool and white as a sepulchre and sat on the bench that ran down one side of the room. They were not seated for long. The doctor soon came out to greet them, and in turn, the woman and the boy were examined. They showed him their patches and he studied them carefully, examining their naked skin for himself and looking for signs of development in their condition that they might not even have noticed themselves. The pale-faced Dimitri had a few large, dry patches on his back and legs, indicating that at this stage he had the less damaging, tuberculoid strain of the disease. The smaller, shinier lesions on Eleni Petrakis's legs and feet worried Dr Lapakis much more. Without any doubt she had the more virulent, lepromatous form and there was a distinct possibility that she might have had it for some time before these signs had appeared.

The boy's prognosis is not too bad, Lapakis mused. But that poor woman, she's not long for this island. His face, however, did not betray the merest hint of what he had discovered.

Chapter Five

WHEN ELENI LEFT for Spinalonga, Anna was twelve and Maria ten. Giorgis was faced with managing the job of home-making single-handedly and, more importantly, the task of bringing up the girls without their mother. Of the two, Anna had always been the more difficult. She had been obstreperous to the point of uncontrollability even before she could walk, and from the day her younger sister was born it seemed she was furious with life. It was no surprise to Giorgis that once Eleni was no longer there Anna rebelled furiously against domesticity, refusing to take on the maternal mantle just because she was the elder of the two girls. She made this painfully clear to her father and to her sister.

Maria had an altogether gentler nature. Two people with her sister's temper could not have lived under the same roof, and Maria fell into the role of peacekeeper even if she often had to fight an instinct to react against Anna's aggression. Unlike Anna, Maria did not find domestic work belittling. She was naturally practical and sometimes enjoyed helping her father clean and cook, a tendency for which Giorgis silently thanked God. Like most men of his generation he could no more darn a sock than fly to the moon.

To the world at large, Giorgis seemed a man of few words. Even those endless lonely hours at sea had not made him yearn for conversation when he was on dry land. He loved the sound of silence, and when he passed the evening at the *kafenion* table – a requirement of manhood rather an optional social activity – he remained quiet, listening to the people around him just as though he was out at sea listening to the lap of the waves against the hull of his boat.

Though his family knew his warm heart and his affectionate embrace, casual acquaintances found his uncommunicative behaviour almost antisocial at times. Those who knew him better saw it as a reflection of a quiet stoicism, a quality that stood him in good stead now that his circumstances had changed so drastically.

Life for Giorgis had rarely been anything but tough. He was a fisherman like his father and grandfather before him, and like them he had become hardened to long stretches spent at sea. These would usually be whiled away in tedious hours of chilly inactivity, but sometimes the long, dark nights would be spent battling against the wild waves, and at times like those there was a distinct danger that the sea might have its way and consume him once and for all. It was a life spent crouched low in the hull of a wooden caique, but a Cretan fisherman never questioned his lot. For him it was fate, not choice.

For several years before Eleni had been exiled there, Giorgis had supplemented his income by making deliveries to Spinalonga. Nowadays he had a boat with a motor and would go there once a week with crates of essential items, dropping them off on the jetty for collection by the lepers.

For the first few days after Eleni left, Giorgis dared not leave his daughters for a moment. Their distress seemed to intensify the longer their mother was away, but he knew that sooner or later they would have to find a new way of living. Although kind neighbours came with food, Giorgis still had the responsibility of getting the girls to eat. One evening, when he faced the task of cooking a meal himself, his woeful inadequacy at the stove almost brought a smile to Maria's lips. Anna, though, could only mock her father's efforts.

'I'm not eating this!' she cried, throwing her fork down into her plate of mutton stew. 'A starving *animal* wouldn't eat it!' With that she burst into tears for the tenth time that day and flounced from the room. It was the third night that she had eaten nothing but bread.

'Starvation will soon crack her stubbornness,' her father said lightly to Maria, who patiently chewed a piece of the overcooked meat. The two of them sat at opposite ends of the table. Conversation did not flow and the silence was punctuated by the occasional chink of their forks on china and the sound of Anna's anguished sobs.

The day eventually came when they had to return to school. This worked like a spell. As soon as their minds had something other than their mother to focus on, their grief began to abate. This was also the day when Giorgis could point the prow of his boat once more in the direction of Spinalonga. With a curious mix of dread and excitement he made his way across the narrow strip of water. Eleni would not know he was coming, and a message would have to be sent to alert her to his arrival. But news travelled fast on Spinalonga, and before he had even tied his boat to the mooring post, Eleni had appeared round the corner of the huge wall and stood in its shadow.

What could they say? How could they react? They did not touch though they desperately wanted to. Instead they just spoke each other's names. They were words they had uttered a thousand times before, but today their syllables sounded like noises with no meaning. At that moment Giorgis wished he had not come. He had mourned his wife this last week, and yet here she was, just as she always had been, as vivid and lovely as ever, which only added to the unbearable ache of their impending separation. Soon he would have to leave the island again and take his boat back to Plaka. Each time he visited there would be this painful parting. His was a gloomy soul and for a fleeting moment he wished them both dead.

Eleni's first week on the island had been full of activity and had passed more quickly than it had done for Giorgis, but when she heard that his boat had been spotted on its way from Plaka, her emotions were thrown into a state of turmoil. Since her arrival she had had plenty of distractions, almost enough to keep her mind away from the sea change which had taken place, but now that Giorgis was standing there before her, his deep green eyes gazing into hers, there was only one focus for her thoughts: how much she loved this strong, broad-shouldered man and how much it hurt her to the very core of her being to be separated from him.

They asked almost formally about each other's health, and Eleni enquired after the girls. How could he respond, except with an answer that only just brushed the surface of the truth? Sooner or later they would get used to it all, he knew that, and then he would be able to tell her honestly how they were. The only truth today was in Eleni's answer to Giorgis's question.

'What's it like in there?' He nodded in the direction of the great stone wall.

'It is not as dreadful as you imagine, and things are going to get better,' she replied, with such conviction and determination that Giorgis found his fears for her instantly suppressed.

'Dimitri and I have a house all to ourselves,' she told him, 'and it's not unlike our home in Plaka. It's more primitive but we're making the best of it. We have our own courtyard and by next spring we should have a herb garden, if you can bring me some seeds. There are roses already in bloom on our doorstep and soon there'll be hollyhocks out too. It's not bad really.'

Giorgis was relieved to hear such words. Eleni now produced a folded sheet of paper from her pocket and gave it to him.

'Is it for the girls?' enquired Giorgis.

'No, it's not,' she said apologetically. 'I thought it might be too early for that, but I'll have a letter for them next time you come. This is a list of things we need for the house.'

Giorgis noted the use of 'we' and a pang of envy hit him. Once, 'we' had included Anna, Maria and himself, he reflected. Then a bitter thought of which he was almost instantly ashamed came into his head: now 'we' meant the hated child who had taken Eleni away from them. The 'we' of his family no longer existed. It had been split asunder and redefined, its rock solidity replaced by such fragility he hardly dared contemplate it. Giorgis was finding it hard to believe that God had not deserted them all. One moment he had been the head of a household; the next he was just a man with two daughters. The two states were as far apart as different planets.

It was time for Giorgis to go. The girls would be back from school soon and he wanted to be there for their return.

'I shall be across again soon,' he promised. 'And I'll bring everything you've asked for.'

'Let's agree on something,' said Eleni. 'Shall we *not* say goodbye? There's no real sense in the word.'

'You're right,' responded Giorgis. 'We'll have no goodbyes.'

They smiled and simultaneously turned away from each other, Eleni towards the shadowy entrance in the high Venetian wall and Giorgis to his boat. Neither looked back.

On his next visit, Eleni had written a letter for Giorgis to take back for the girls, but the moment her father held out the envelope, Anna's impatience got the better of her and, as she tried to snatch it out of his hands, it was ripped in two.

'But that letter's for both of us!' protested Maria. 'I want to read it too!'

By now Anna was at the front door.

'I don't care. I'm the oldest and I get to look at it first!' and with that she turned on her heels and ran off down the street, leaving Maria weeping tears of frustration and anger.

A few hundred yards from their home was a little alleyway that ran between two houses, and this was where Anna, crouched in the shadows and, holding the two halves together, read her mother's first letter:

Dear Anna and Maria,

I wonder how you both are? I hope you are being good and kind and working hard at school. Your father tells me that his first attempts at cooking were not very successful but I am sure he will get better at it and that soon he will know the difference between a cucumber and a courgette! I hope it won't be long before you are helping him in the kitchen too, but meanwhile be patient with him while he is learning.

Let me tell you about Spinalonga. I am living in a small, tumbledown house in the main street with one room downstairs and two bedrooms upstairs, rather like at home. It is quite dark but I am planning to whitewash the walls, and once I have put my pictures up and displayed my pieces of china I think it will look quite pretty. Dimitri likes having his own room – he has always had to share so it is quite a novelty for him.

I have a new friend. Her name is Elpida and she is the wife of the man who is in charge of the government of Spinalonga. They are both very kind people and we have had a few meals at their home, which is the biggest and the grandest on the whole island. It has chandeliers and every table and every chair has some kind of lace draped across it. Anna especially would love it.

I have already planted some geranium cuttings in the courtyard and roses are beginning to bloom on our doorstep, just like at home. I will write and tell you lots more in my next letter. Meanwhile, be good, I think of you every day.

With love and kisses,
Your loving Mother xxxxx

P.S. I hope the bees are working hard – don't forget to collect the honey.

Anna read the letter over and over again before walking slowly home. She knew she would be in trouble. From that day on, Eleni wrote separate letters to the two girls.

Giorgis visited the island much more regularly now than before and his meetings with Eleni were his oxygen. He lived for those moments when she would appear through the archway in the wall. Sometimes they would sit on the stone mooring posts; at other times they would remain standing in the shade of the pines that grew, as if for the purpose, out of the dry earth. Giorgis would tell her how the girls were, what they had been doing, and would confide in her about Anna's behaviour.

'Sometimes it's as though she has the devil in her,' said Giorgis one day as they sat talking. 'She doesn't seem to get any easier with time.'

'Well, it's just as well that Maria isn't the same,' replied Eleni.

'That's probably why Anna is so disobedient half the time, because Maria doesn't seem to have a wicked bone in her body,' reflected Giorgis. 'And I thought tantrums were meant to be something children grew out of.'

'I'm sorry to leave you with such a burden, Giorgis, I really am,' sighed Eleni, knowing that she would give anything to be facing the daily battle of wills involved in bringing Anna up instead of being stuck here on this island.

* * *

Giorgis was not even forty when Eleni left, but he was already stooped with anxiety, and over the next few months he was to age beyond recognition. His hair turned from olive black to the silvery grey of the eucalyptus, and people seemed always to refer to him as 'Poor Giorgis'. It became his name.

Savina Angelopoulos did as much as she was able, whilst managing her own home too. On still, moonless nights, knowing that there could be a rich catch, Giorgis would want to fish, and it became a regular event for Maria and Fotini to sleep, top to tail, in the latter's narrow bed, with Anna on the floor next to them, two thick blankets for her mattress. Maria and Anna also found they were eating more meals at the Angelopoulos home than their own, and it was as if Fotini's own family had suddenly grown and she had the sisters she had always wanted. On those nights there would be eight at the table: Fotini and her two brothers, Antonis and Angelos, her parents, and Giorgis, Anna and Maria. Some days, if she had the time, Savina would try to teach Anna and Maria how to keep their house tidy, how to beat a carpet and how to make up a bed, but quite often she would end up doing it all for them. They were just children, and Anna for one had no interest in anything domestic. Why should she learn to patch a sheet, gut a fish or bake a loaf? She was determined that she would never need such skills and from an early age had a powerful urge to escape and get away from what she regarded as pointless domestic drudgery.

The girls' lives could not have been more altered if a tornado had snatched them and dropped them on Santorini. They acted out their days with a fixed routine, for only with a rigid, unthinking pattern of activity could they rise in the morning.

Anna battled against it all, constantly complaining and questioning why things were as they were; Maria simply accepted. She knew that complaining achieved nothing at all and probably just made things worse. Her sister had no such wisdom. Anna always wanted to fight the status quo.

'Why do *I* have to go and get the bread every morning?' she complained one day.

'You don't,' her father replied patiently. 'Maria gets it every other day.'

'Well why can't she get it *every* day? I'm the oldest and I don't see why I have to get bread for her.'

'If everyone questioned why they should do things for each other, the world would stop turning, Anna. Now go and get the bread. Right this minute!'

Giorgis's fist came down with a bang on the table. He was weary of Anna turning every small domestic task she was asked to perform into an argument and now even she knew that she had pushed her father to the edge.

On Spinalonga, meanwhile, Eleni tried to grow accustomed to what would be regarded as unacceptable on the mainland but on the colony passed for normality; she failed, however, and found herself wanting to change whatever she could. Just as Giorgis did not protect Eleni from his worries, she in turn shared her concerns about her life and her future on Spinalonga.

The first really disagreeable encounter she experienced on the island was with Kristina Kroustalakis, the woman who ran the school.

'I don't expect her to like me,' she commented to Giorgis, 'but she's acting like an animal that's been driven into a tight corner.'

'Why does she do that?' asked Giorgis, already knowing the answer.

'She's a useless teacher, who doesn't care a drachma for the children – and she knows that's what I think of her,' answered Eleni.

Giorgis sighed. Eleni had never been reticent about her views.

Almost as soon as they had arrived, Eleni had seen that the school had little to offer Dimitri. After his first day, he returned silent and sullen, and when she enquired what he had done in class his reply was 'Nothing.'

'What do you mean, nothing? You must have done something.'

'The teacher was writing all the letters and numbers on the board and I was sent to the back of the class for saying that I already knew them. After that the oldest children were allowed to do some really easy sums and when I shouted out one of the answers I was sent out of the room for the rest of the day.'

After this, Eleni started to teach Dimitri herself, and his friends then began to come to her for lessons. Soon children who had barely been able to distinguish their letters and numbers could read fluently and do their sums and within a few months her small house was filled with children on five long mornings a week. They ranged in age from six to sixteen and, with one exception, a boy who had been born on the island, they had all been sent to the island from Crete when they had shown the symptoms of leprosy. The majority of them had received some basic education before they arrived, but most of them, even the older ones, had made little progress in all the time they had spent in a classroom with Kristina Kroustalakis. She treated them like fools, so fools they remained.

The tension between Kristina Kroustalakis and Eleni began to build up. It was evident to almost everyone that Eleni should take over the school and that the valuable teacher's stipend should be hers. Kristina Kroustalakis fought her own corner, refusing to concede or even consider the possibility of sharing her role, but Eleni was tenacious. She drove the situation to a conclusion, not for her own gain but for the good of the island's seventeen children, who deserved so much more than they would ever get from the lackadaisical Kroustalakis. Pedagogy was an investment in the future, and Kristina Kroustalakis saw little point in expending much energy on those who might not be around for long.

Finally, one day, Eleni was invited to put her case before the elders. She brought with her examples of the work the children had been doing both before and after she arrived on the island. 'But this simply shows natural progress,' protested one elder, known to be a close friend of Kyria Kroustalakis. To most of them there, however, the evidence was plain. Eleni's zeal and commitment to her task showed results. Her driving force was the belief that education was not a means to some nebulous end but had intrinsic value, and made the children better people. The strong possibility that several of them might not live to see their twenty-first birthdays was of no relevance to Eleni.

There were a few dissenting voices, but the majority of elders were in favour of the controversial decision to remove the established teacher from her position and install Eleni instead. For ever after there would be people on the island who regarded Eleni as a usurper, but she was profoundly unbothered by such an attitude. The children were what mattered.

The school provided Dimitri with almost everything he needed: a structure to his day, stimulation for his mind, and companionship, in the form of a new friend, Nikos, who was the only child to have been born on the island but not taken to the mainland for adoption. The reason for this was that he had developed signs of the disease as a baby. If he had been healthy he would have been taken away from his parents, who, although they were overwhelmed with guilt that the child shared their affliction, were also overjoyed to be able to keep him.

Every moment of Dimitri's life was filled, successfully keeping him from dwelling on how things used to be. In some ways this life was an improvement. The small, dark-eyed boy now endured less hardship, less anxiety and fewer worries than had burdened him as the oldest of five children in a peasant family. Each afternoon, however, when he left the school building to return to the semi-darkness of his new home, he would become aware of the undercurrents of adult disquiet. He would hear snatches of conversation as he passed the *kafenion* or whispered discussions between people as they talked in the street.

Sometimes there were new rumours mixed in with the old. There was the endlessly recycled discussion over whether they would be getting a new generator and the perennial debate over the water supply. In the past few months there had been whispers about a grant for new accommodation and an increased 'pension' for every member of the colony. Dimitri listened to a great deal of adult talk and observed that grown-ups endlessly chewed over the same matter, like dogs with old bones long since stripped of their flesh. The smallest events, as well as the larger ones such as illness and death, were anticipated and mulled over. One day, though, something took place for which there had been no build-up and little forewarning but which was to have a huge impact on the life of the island.

One night a few months after Dimitri and Eleni had arrived they were eating supper when they were disturbed by an insistent banging on the door. It was Elpida, and the elderly woman was out of breath and flushed with excitement.

'Eleni, please come,' she panted. 'There are boatloads of them – *boatloads* – and they need our help. Come!'

Eleni knew Elpida well enough by now to realise that if she said help was called for, no questions needed to be asked. Dimitri's curiosity was aroused. He dropped his cutlery and followed the women as they hastened down the twilit street, listening as Kyria Kontomaris blurted out the story, her words tumbling out one after the other.

'They're from Athens,' she gasped. 'Giorgis has already brought over two boatloads and he's about to arrive with the third. They're mostly men but I noticed a few women as well. They look like prisoners, sick prisoners.'

By now they had reached the entrance to the long tunnel which led to the quay, and Eleni turned to Dimitri.

'You'll have to stay here,' she said firmly. 'Please go back to the house and finish your supper.'

Even from the end of the tunnel Dimitri could hear the

muffled echo of male voices, and he was more curious than ever about what was causing such commotion. The two women hurried on and were soon out of sight. Dimitri aimlessly kicked a stone about at the tunnel entrance and then, looking furtively behind him, darted into the dark passageway, making sure he kept close to the sides. As he turned the corner he could see quite clearly what the fuss was all about.

New inhabitants usually arrived one by one and after a quiet welcome from Petros Kontomaris slipped as discreetly into the community as they could. Initially, the best anyone hoped for on Spinalonga was anonymity, and most people remained silent as they were welcomed. On the quayside tonight, however, there was no such calm. As they tumbled off Giorgis's small boat, many of the new arrivals lost their balance before landing heavily on the stony ground. They shouted, writhed and howled, some of them clearly in pain, and from his shadowy position, Dimitri could see why they had fallen. The newcomers seemed not to have arms, at least not arms that hung freely by their sides, and when he looked closer, he realised that they were all wearing strange jackets that trapped their arms behind their backs.

Dimitri watched as Eleni and Elpida bent down, one by one undid the straps that kept these people tied up like packages, and released them from their hessian prisons. Lying in heaps on the dusty ground these creatures seemed less than human. One of them then staggered to the water's edge, leant towards the sea and vomited copiously. Another did the same – and then a third.

Dimitri watched both fascinated and fearful, as still as the rocky wall which screened him. As the newcomers unfurled themselves and slowly stood upright they regained a little dignity. Even from a hundred metres, he could feel the anger and aggression that emanated from them. Gathering round one particular man who appeared to be attempting to calm them, several talked at once, their voices raised.

Dimitri counted. There were eighteen of them here, and Giorgis was turning his boat around again to return to Plaka. One more boatload was still to arrive.

Close to the quayside in Plaka, a crowd had gathered in the square to study this curious group. A few days before, Giorgis had taken a letter from Athens across to Petros Kontomaris warning him of the lepers' imminent arrival. Between them they had agreed to keep their own counsel. The prospect of nearly two dozen new patients arriving simultaneously on Spinalonga would send the islanders into a state of panic. All Kontomaris had been told was that these lepers had created trouble at the hospital in Athens – and as a consequence had been dispatched to Spinalonga. They had been shipped like cattle from Piraeus to Iraklion on two days of rough seas. Stricken with sunstroke and sea sickness, they were then transferred to a smaller vessel bound for Plaka. From there Giorgis was to bring them, six at a time, on the final stretch of their journey. It was plain for anyone to see that this bedraggled mob of abused and uncared-for humanity would not survive such treatment for long.

The village children in Plaka, unafraid to stare, had gathered to watch. Fotini, Anna and Maria were among them, and Anna questioned her father as he took a short break before taking the final load across the water.

'Why are they here? What have they done? Why couldn't they stay in Athens?' she demanded. Giorgis had no real answers to her persistent questions. But he did tell her one thing. While he was transporting his first batch of passengers to the island, he had listened intently to their conversation and, in spite of their anger and disenchantment, the voices he heard were those of educated and articulate men.

'I have no answers for you, Anna,' he told her. 'But Spinalonga will make room for them, that's what matters.'

'What about our mother?' she persisted. 'Her life will be worse than ever.'

'I think you might be wrong,' said Giorgis, drawing on the deep well of patience that he held in reserve for his elder daughter. 'These newcomers could be the best thing that ever happened to that island.'

'How can that *possibly* be?' Anna cried, dancing up and down in disbelief. 'What do you mean? They look like *animals*!' She was right about that. They did indeed resemble animals and, bundled into crates like cattle, had been treated like little more than that.

Giorgis turned his back on his daughter and returned to his boat. There were just five passengers this time. When they reached Spinalonga, the other new arrivals were wandering about. It was the first time in thirty-six hours that they had stood upright. The four women among them remained in a quiet huddle. Petros Kontomaris was walking from one person to another asking for names, ages, occupations, and number of years since diagnosis.

All the while he did this task, his mind was spinning. Every additional minute that he could detain them here with this bureaucracy gave him more time for some kind of inspiration about where, in heaven's name, these people were going to be housed. Each second of procrastination delayed the moment when they would be led through the tunnel to find that they did not have homes and that, potentially, they were even worse off than they had been in the Athenian hospital. Each short interview took a few minutes, and by the time he had finished, one thing was very clear to him. In the past, when he had taken details of new arrivals, the majority had been fishermen, smallholders or shopkeepers. This time, he had a list of trained professionals: lawyer, teacher, doctor, master stonemason, editor, engineer . . . the catalogue went on. This was an entirely different category of folk from those who made up the bulk of the population on Spinalonga, and for a moment, Kontomaris felt slightly fearful of this band of Athenian citizens who had arrived in the guise of beggars.

It was time now to take them into their new world. Kontomaris led the group through the tunnel. Word had got around that newcomers had arrived and people came out of their houses to stare. In the square, the Athenians drew to a halt behind the leader, who now turned to face them, waiting until he had their attention before he spoke.

'As a temporary measure, apart from the women, who will be housed in a vacant room at the top of the hill, you will be accommodated in the town hall.'

A crowd had now gathered around them and there was a murmur of unrest as they too listened to the announcement. Kontomaris, however, was prepared for hostility to the plan and continued.

'Let me assure you that this is only a temporary measure.

Your arrival swells our population by nearly ten per cent and we now expect the government to provide money for new housing, as they have long promised.'

The reason for the antagonism to the town hall being used as a dormitory was that it was where the social life of Spinalonga, such as it was, took place. It represented, as much as anything could, the social and political normality of life on Spinalonga, and to commandeer it was to strip the islanders of a key resource. But where else was there? There was one empty room in 'the block', the soulless new apartment building, and this was where the Athenian women would be housed. Kontomaris would ask Elpida to take them there while he got the men settled into their makeshift quarters. His heart sank when he thought about his wife's task; the only difference between the new block and a prison was that the doors there were bolted from the inside rather than from the outside. But for the men it had to be the town hall.

That night, Spinalonga became home to the twenty-three Athenian newcomers. Soon, many of those who had come to gawp realised that more constructive action was needed and made offers of food, drink and bedding. Any donation from their meagre stores meant significant sacrifice, but all, bar very few, managed some gesture.

The first few days were tense. Everyone waited to see what impact these new arrivals would have, but for forty-eight hours most of them were hardly seen, many lying impassively on their improvised bedding. Dr Lapakis visited them and noted that they were all suffering not just from leprosy but also from the rigours of a journey without adequate food or water and without shade from the relentless sun. It would take each one of them several weeks to recover from the months, perhaps years, of mistreatment they had endured even before they had embarked on their journey from Athens. Lapakis had heard that there was no discernible difference between conditions in the leprosy hospital and those in the gaol just a few hundred metres away on the edge of the city. The story went that the lepers were fed on scraps from the prison and that their clothes were cast-offs stripped from corpses in the city's main hospital. He soon learned that this was not just a myth.

All the patients had been treated barbarically, and this group who had arrived in Crete had been the driving force behind a rebellion. Mostly professional, educated people, they had led a hunger strike, drafted letters which were smuggled out to friends and politicians and stirred up dissent throughout the hospital. Rather than agreeing to any change, however, the governor of the hospital decided to evict them; or, as he preferred to term it, 'transfer them to more suitable accommodation'. Their expulsion to Spinalonga marked an end for them, and a new beginning for the island.

The women were visited each day by Elpida and were soon recovered enough to have their tour of the island and to take coffee at the Kontomaris house, and even to begin planning how they would make use of the small plot of ground which had been cleared for them to grow vegetables. They recognised very quickly that this life was an improvement on the old. At least it *was* a life. Conditions at the Athenian hospital had been horrific. The fires of hell could not have been more stifling than the suffocating summer heat in their mean, claustrophobic rooms. Add to that the rats that scratched about on the floors during the night, and they had felt no worthier than vermin.

Spinalonga, by contrast, was paradise. It offered unimagined freedom, with fresh air, birdsong and a street to amble down; here they could rediscover their humanity. During the long days of their journey from Athens, some had considered taking their own lives, assuming that they were being sent to an even worse place than the vile Hades where they had been struggling to survive. On Spinalonga, from their window on the second floor, the women could see the sun rise, and during their first days on the island they were entranced by the sight of the slow-breaking dawn.

Just as Eleni had done, they turned the space they were given into a home. Embroidered cotton cloths hung across the windows at night and woven rugs spread across their beds transformed the room and made it look like any simple Cretan dwelling.

For the men, it was a different story. They languished on their beds for several days, many of them still weakened by the hunger strike they had staged in Athens. Kontomaris organised for food to be brought to the hall and left in the vestibule, but when the dishes were collected on the first day the islanders saw that their offerings had scarcely been touched. The great metal cooking pot was still full to the brim with lamb stew; the only indication that there was any life in the building was that of the five loaves brought to the town hall, only three remained.

On the second day all the bread was eaten, and on the third, a pan of rabbit casserole was scraped clean. Each day such signs of increased appetite signified the revival of these pitiful creatures. On the fourth day, Nikos Papadimitriou emerged, blinking, into the dazzling sunlight. Forty-five years old and a lawyer, Papadimitriou had once been at the centre of Athenian life. Now he was the leader and spokesman for a group of lepers, playing this role with just as much energy as he had put into his legal career. Nikos was a natural trouble-maker, and if he had not gone into law, he might have chosen crime instead. His attempts to oppose the Athenian authorities by organising the revolt in the hospital had not been entirely successful, but he was more determined than ever to win better conditions for his fellow lepers now that they were on Spinalonga.

Though sharp-tongued, Papadimitriou had great charm and could always gather supporters. His great ally and friend was Mihalis Kouris, an engineer who had, like Papadimitriou, been in the Athenian hospital for nearly five years. That day, Kontomaris took them around Spinalonga. Unlike the majority of newcomers shown the island for the first time, a constant stream of questions flowed from these two men: 'So where is the water source?' 'How long have you been waiting for the generator?' 'How often does the doctor visit?' 'What is the mortality rate?' 'What are the current building plans?'

Kontomaris answered their questions as well as he could, but could tell by their every grunt and sigh that they were rarely satisfied with the answers. The island leader knew perfectly well that Spinalonga was underresourced. He had worked tirelessly for six years to improve things and in many areas he had succeeded, though never to the degree that everyone wanted. It was a thankless task, and as he strolled out beyond the town towards the cemetery, he wondered why he had bothered at all. This was where they would all end up, however hard he strived to make things better. All three of them would eventually lie beneath a stone slab in one of these subterranean concrete bunkers until their bones were moved to one side to make way for the next corpse. The futility of it all and the distant sound of Papadimitriou's insistent questioning made him want to sit down and weep. He decided at that very moment that he would tell the Athenians the bald facts. If they were more interested in reality than in simply being made to feel welcome, then so be it.

'I'll tell you,' he said, stopping in his tracks and turning round to face them both, 'everything you want to know. But if I do that, the burden becomes yours too. Do you understand?'

They nodded in assent, and Kontomaris began to give them the details of the island's shortcomings. He described every hoop he had jumped through in order to make any changes and told them about all the issues currently under negotiation. Then the three of them went back to the leader's house and, with Papadimitriou and Kouris's fresh perspective on the island's facilities, drew up a new plan. This included works in progress, projects to be started and finished within the coming year and an outline of what would be undertaken in the forthcoming five-year period. Such prospects in themselves would create the sense of moving forward that these people needed so much.

From that day, Papadimitriou and Kouris became Kontomaris's great supporters. No longer did they feel like condemned men, but as though they had been given a new start. Life had not held so much potential for a very long time. Within weeks, the proposals, which included specifications for building and reconstruction, were ready to be submitted to the government. Papadimitriou knew how to lean on the politicians, and his law firm in Athens, a family practice of some influence, became involved. 'Everyone on this island is a citizen of Greece,' he insisted. 'They have rights and I'm damned if I won't fight for them.' To the amazement of everyone – apart from Papadimitrou himself – within a month the government had agreed to provide the sum of money they had asked for.

The other Athenians, once they had risen from their torpor, threw themselves into new building projects. No longer were they abandoned invalids but members of a community where everyone had to pull their weight. It was now late September, and though temperatures were more moderate, the issue of water was still pressing – the addition of twenty-three new inhabitants had placed more demand than ever on the supply from the mainland and the crumbling water tunnels. Something had to be done, and Mihalis Kouris was the man to do it.

Once repairs were complete, everyone looked to the heavens for rain, and one night in early November their prayers were answered. In a spectacular display of sound and light, the skies opened, noisily emptying their contents on to the island, the mainland and the sea all around. Pebble-sized hailstones bounced down, breaking windows and sending goats scampering for safety on the hillsides, as flashes of lightning bathed the landscape in an apocalyptic luminescence. Next morning the islanders woke to find their watersheds brimful of cool, clear water. Having resolved the most pressing issue of all, the Athenians then turned their attention to creating homes for themselves. There was a derelict area between the main street and the sea; it was where the Turks had built their first houses. The dwellings, mere shells, were constructed right up against the fortress walls and would have been among the most sheltered of all enclaves. With the sort of industry and efficiency rarely seen on Crete, the old houses were restored and raised up out of the rubble, with good-as-new masonry and skilfully planed carpentry. Well before the first snowfall crowned Mount Dhikti they were ready to be occupied and the town hall was once again available for everyone. Not that the initial resentment against the Athenian lepers had lasted for long. It had only been a matter of weeks before the population of Spinalonga had recognised the potential of the new islanders and realised that what they might give would far exceed what they could ever take.

Then, as winter approached, the campaign for the generator began again in earnest. Heat and light would become the most valuable commodities as the winds began to find their way through chinks in every door and window, whipping through the draughty homes in the fading mid-afternoon light. Now that the government had discovered that Spinalonga had a more strident voice, one that could not be disregarded, it was not long before a letter came promising everything that was required. Many of the islanders were cynical. 'I wouldn't put money on them keeping their word,' some would say. 'Until I can turn on a lamp in my own house, I won't trust them to deliver,' agreed others. The general view among people who had been on Spinalonga for more than a few years was that the government's promise was worth no more than the flimsy paper it was written on.

Just ten days before all the parts arrived, labelled and complete, the anticipation of the generator was the main topic of Eleni's identical letters to Anna and Maria:

The generator is going to make so much difference to our lives. There was one here once before so some of the electric fittings are already in place and two of the men from Athens are expert in how to make it all work (thank goodness). Every house is promised at least one light and a small heater and those are due to arrive at the same time as the rest of the equipment.

Anna read her letter in the dying light of a winter's afternoon. A low fire burned in the grate but she could see her breath on the cold air. A candle cast a flickering light across the page and she idly poked a corner of the sheet into its flame. Slowly the fire crept across, melting the paper until she held nothing but a fingertip-sized piece which she then dropped into the wax. Why did her mother have to write so often? Did she really think that they all wanted to hear of her warm, contented and now well-lit life with that boy? Her father made them reply to every letter, and Anna struggled over every word. She was not happy and she was not going to pretend.

Maria read her letter and showed it to her father.

'It's good news, isn't it?' Giorgis commented. 'And it's all thanks to those Athenians. Who would have thought that a ragbag like that could make such a difference?'

By the beginning of winter, before the sharpness of the December winds arrived, the island had warmth and, after darkness fell, those who wished could now read by the dimmest of dim electric lights.

When Advent began, Giorgis and Eleni needed to decide how to deal with Christmas. It was to be their first one apart for fifteen years. The festival did not have the importance of Easter, but it was a time for ritual and feasting within the family and Eleni's absence would be a gaping void.

For a few days before and after Christmas Giorgis did not cross the choppy waters to visit Eleni. Not just because the vicious wind would bite into his hands and face until they were raw, but because his daughters needed him to stay. Similarly, Eleni's attentions had to be on Dimitri and they played out in parallel the age-old traditions. As they always had, the girls sang tuneful *kalanda* from house to house and were rewarded with sweets and dried fruit, and after early morning mass on Christmas Day they feasted with the Angelopoulos family on pork and delicious *kourambiethes*, sweet nutty biscuits baked by Savina. Things were not so very different on Spinalonga. The children sang in the square, helped bake the ornate seasonal loaves known as *christopsomo*, Christ's bread, and ate as never before. For Dimitri it was the first time he had enjoyed such plentiful quantities of rich food and witnessed such hedonism.

Throughout the twelve days of Christmas, Giorgis and Eleni sprinkled a little holy water in each room of their respective houses to deter the *kallikantzari*, seasonal goblins that were said to play havoc in the home, and on 1 January, St Basil's Day, Giorgis visited Eleni once again, bringing her presents from the children and from Savina. The ending of the old year and the beginning of the new was a watershed, a milestone that had been safely passed, taking the Petrakis family into a different era. Although Anna and Maria still missed their mother, they now knew that they could survive without her.

Chapter Six

1940

AFTER ITS BEST winter in years came Spinalonga's most glorious spring. It was not just the carpets of wild flowers that spread across the slopes of the island's north side and peeped out of every crack in the rocks that made it so, but also the sense of new life that had been breathed into the community.

Spinalonga's main street, only a few months earlier a series of dilapidated buildings, was now a smart row of shops with shutters and doors freshly painted in deep blues and greens. They were now places where shopkeepers displayed their wares with pride and islanders shopped not just out of necessity but for pleasure too. For the first time, the island had its own economy. People were productive: they bartered, bought and sold, sometimes at a profit, sometimes at a loss.

The *kafenion* was flourishing too and a new taverna opened which specialised in *kakavia*, fish soup, freshly made each day. One of the busiest places in the main street was the barber. Stelios Vandis had been the top hair stylist in Rethimnon, Crete's second city, but had abandoned his trade when he had been exiled to Spinalonga. When Papadimitriou learned that they had such a man in their midst, he insisted Vandis resume his work. The Athenian men were all peacocks. They had the swaggering vanity of the city type and in their former days had all enjoyed the ritual of the fortnightly trim to both hair and moustache, the condition and shape of which almost defined their manliness. Life took a turn for the better now that they had found someone who could make them handsome again. It was not individual style that they aspired to but identically luxurious and well-coiffed hair.

'Stelios,' Papadimitriou would say, 'give me your best Venizelos.' Venizelos, the Cretan lawyer who had become prime minister of Greece, was thought to have had the most handsome moustache in the Christian world, and it was appropriate, the menfolk joked, that Papadimitriou should emulate him, since he clearly aspired to a position of leadership on the island.

As Kontomaris's strength began to fail, the leader relied more and more on Papadimitriou, and the popularity of the Athenian grew among the islanders. The men respected him for what he had achieved in such a short time; the women were grateful too; and soon he enjoyed a sort of hero-worship, no doubt enhanced by his silver-screen looks. Like most of the Athenians he had always lived in the city, and one result of this was that he did not have the bent and grizzled appearance of the average Cretan male who had spent the best part of his life in the open air, scraping a living off the land or out of the sea. Until the past few months of manual labour, his skin had seen little sunlight and even less wind.

Although the Athenian had ambitions, he was not a ruthless man, and he would not stand for election unless Kontomaris was ready to retire.

'Papadimitriou, I'm more than ready to give up this position,' the older man said one night in early March over a game of backgammon. 'I've told you that a thousand times. The job needs fresh blood – and look at what you have done for the island already! My supporters will back you, there's no question of it. Believe me, I'm just too weary now.'

Papadimitriou was unsurprised at this last comment. During the six months since his arrival he had seen Kontomaris's condition deteriorate. The two men had been close for some time and he had known that the elderly leader was grooming him as his successor.

'I'll take it on if you really are ready to let go,' he said quietly, 'but I think you should give it a few more days' thought.'

'I've given it *months* of thought already,' replied Petros grumpily. 'I know I can't go on.'

The two men played on in a silence only broken by the clack of the counters.

'There's one other thing I want you to know,' said Papadimitriou when the game finished and it was time for him to go. 'If I do win the election, I shall not want to live in your house.'

'But it isn't my house,' retorted Kontomaris. 'It's the leader's house. It goes with the position and always has done.'

Papadimitriou drew on his cigarette and paused a moment as he exhaled. He decided to let the matter rest. The issue might be hypothetical in any case since the election was not entirely a fait accompli. It would be contested by two others, one of whom had been on the island for some six or seven years and had a large following; the election of Theodoros Makridakis seemed, to Papadimitriou at least, a distinct possibility. A large contingent of the population responded to Makridakis's negativity, and although they loved to lap up the benefits of all Papadimitriou's hard work and the dramatic changes of the past six months, they also felt that their interests could be better served by someone who was driven by anger. It was easy to believe that the fire that propelled Makridakis might help him achieve things that reason and diplomacy could not.

The annual elections in late March were the mostly hotly contested in the history of the island, and this time the results actually mattered. Spinalonga was somewhere worth governing and leadership was no longer a poisoned chalice. Three men stood: Papadimitriou, Spyros Kazakis and Theodoros Makridakis. On the day of the election every man and woman placed a vote, and even the lepers who were confined in the hospital with little chance of ever emerging again from their sickbeds were taken a ballot paper which was duly returned to the town hall in a sealed envelope.

Spyros Kazakis won a mere handful of votes and Makridakis, to Papadimitriou's relief and surprise, gained fewer than one hundred. This left the lion's share and the clear majority to the Athenian. The population had voted with their hearts, but also with wisdom. Makridakis's posturing was all very well, but achievement counted for more, and for this Papadimitriou knew at last that he was recognised. It was a pivotal moment in the civilising of the island.

'Fellow inhabitants of Spinalonga,' he said. 'My wishes for this island are your wishes too.' He was speaking to the crowd gathered in the small square outside the town hall on the night following the election. The count had just been double-checked and the results announced.

'We have already made Spinalonga a more civilised place, and in some ways it is now an even better place to live than the towns and villages that serve us.' He waved his hand in the direction of Plaka. 'We have electricity when Plaka does not. We have diligent medical staff and the most dedicated of teachers. On the mainland, many people are living at subsistence level, starving when we are not. Last week, some of them rowed out to us from Elounda. Rumours of our new prosperity had reached them and they came to ask *us* for food. Is that not a turnaround?' A murmur of assent rippled through the throng. 'No longer are we the outcasts with begging bowls crying, "Unclean! Unclean!"' he continued. 'Now others come to us to seek alms.'

He paused for a moment, enough time for someone to shout out from the crowd: 'Three cheers for Papadimitriou!' When the cheers died down, he added one final note to his message.

'There is one thing that binds us together. The disease of leprosy. When we have our disagreements, let us not forget there is no escape from one another. While we have life, let us make it as good as we can – this must be our common purpose.' He raised his hand in the air, pointing his finger upwards into the sky, a sign of celebration and victory. 'To Spinalonga!' he shouted.

The crowd of two hundred mirrored the gesture, and with

a cry that was heard across the water in Plaka they cried out in unison: 'To Spinalonga!'

Theodoros Makridakis, unnoticed by anyone, sloped away into the shadows. He had long yearned to be the leader and his disappointment was as bitter as an unripe olive.

The next afternoon, Elpida Kontomaris began to pack her possessions. Within a day or two she and Petros would need to move out of this house and into Papadimitriou's current accommodation. She had expected this moment for a long time but it did not lessen the feeling of dread that weighed her down so that she could scarcely summon the energy to move one foot in front of the other. She went about packing in a desultory fashion, her heavy body unwilling to do the task and her misshapen feet more painful than ever before. As she stood contemplating the prospect of tidying away the precious contents of the glass-fronted cabinet – the rows of soldiers, the tiny pieces of porcelain and the engraved silver that had been in her family for many generations – she asked herself where these valuables would go when she and Petros were no more. The two of them were the end of the line.

A gentle tap on the door interrupted her thoughts. That must be Eleni, she thought. Though busy with school and the task of motherhood, Eleni had promised to come by that afternoon to help her, and she was always true to her word. When Elpida opened the door, however, expecting to see her slim, fine-featured friend, a large, darkly dressed male figure filled the frame instead. It was Papadimitriou.

'*Kalispera*, Kyria Kontomaris. May I come in?' he asked gently, conscious of her surprise.

'Yes . . . please do,' she answered, moving away from the door to let him in.

'I have only one thing to say,' he told her as they stood facing each other, surrounded by the half-filled crates of books, china and photographs. 'There is no need for you to move out of here. I have no intention of taking this house away from you. There is no need. Petros has given so much of his life to being leader of this island that I have decided to endow him with it – call it his pension, if you like.'

'But it's where the leader has always lived. It's yours now, and besides, Petros wouldn't hear of it.'

'I have no interest in what has happened in the past,' replied Papadimitriou. 'I want you to stay here, and in any case I want to live in the house I'm restoring. Please,' he insisted. 'It will suit all of us better this way.'

Elpida's eyes glistened with tears. 'It's so kind of you,' she said, extending both her hands towards him. 'So very kind. I can see that you mean it, but I don't know how we are going to persuade Petros.'

'He has no choice,' said Papadimitriou with determination. 'I'm in charge now. What I want you to do is unpack all your things from these boxes and put them back exactly where they were. I'll come back later to make sure you've done that.'

Elpida could see that this was no idle gesture. The man meant what he said and was used to getting what he wanted. This was why he had been elected leader, and as she repositioned the lead soldiers in their ranks she tried to analyse what it was that made Papadimitriou so hard to disagree with. It was not merely his physical stature. That on its own might simply have made him a bully. He had other, more subtle techniques. Sometimes he moved people round to his point of view simply through the modulations of his voice. On other occasions he would achieve the same end by overpowering them with the force of his logic. His lawyer's skills were as sharp as ever, even on Spinalonga.

Before Papadimitriou went on his way, Elpida asked him to eat with them when he returned that evening. Her great talent was in the kitchen. She cooked as no one else on Spinalonga, and only a fool would ever turn down such an invitation. As soon as he had gone she went about preparing the meal, fashioning her favourite *kefethes*, meat balls in egg-lemon sauce, and measuring out the ingredients for *revani*, a sweet cake made with semolina and syrup.

When Kontomaris came home that evening, his duties as leader finally completed, there was a lightness in his step. As he entered his home, the fragrant smells of baking wafted over him and an apron-clad Elpida came towards him, her arms outstretched in welcome. They embraced, his head resting on her shoulder.

'It's all over,' he murmured. 'At long last it's over.'

As he glanced up, he noticed that the room looked just as it always had. There was no sign of the half-filled crates that had been standing about the room when he had left that morning.

'Why haven't you packed?' There was more than a note of irritation in his voice. He was weary and he so much wanted the next few days to be over. Wishing they were already transported to their new house, the fact that nothing seemed even vaguely ready to go upset him greatly and made him feel more exhausted than ever.

'I packed and then I unpacked,' Elpida replied mysteriously. 'We're staying here.'

Precisely on cue, there was a firm knock at the door. Papadimitriou had arrived.

'Kyria Kontomaris invited me to eat with you,' he said simply.

Once they were all seated and a generous glass of ouzo had been poured for each of them, Kontomaris regained his composure.

'I think there's been some kind of conspiracy,' he said. 'I should be angry, but I know you both well enough to realise I've no choice in this matter.'

His smile belied his stern tone and the formality of his words. He was secretly delighted at Papadimitriou's generosity, not least because he knew how much it meant to his wife. The three of them toasted each other in ratification of the deal that had been struck, and the issue of the leader's house was never mentioned between them again. There were a few rumbles of dissent among the council members and fervent discussions about what would happen if a future leader wished to reclaim the splendid house, but a compromise was eventually reached: tenancy of the house would be reassessed every five years.

After the election, work continued apace with the renovation of the island. Papadimitriou's efforts had not merely been an electioneering ploy. Repairing and rebuilding went on until everyone had a decent place to live, their own oven, usually in the courtyard in front of their home, and, even more importantly for their sense of pride, a private outdoor latrine.

Now that water was being collected efficiently there was

plenty for everyone, and an extensive communal laundry was built with a long row of smooth concrete sinks. It was little less than a luxury for the women, who would linger over their washing, making the area a vibrant social focus.

The social aspect of their lives was also enhanced, however, in less workaday situations. For Panos Sklavounis, an Athenian who had once been an actor, the working day began when everyone else's had ended. Not long after the election, he took Papadimitriou to one side. Sklavounis's approach was aggressive, which was typical of the man's manner. He liked confrontation and as an actor back in Athens had been used to hustling.

'Boredom is growing like a fungus here,' he said. 'What people need is entertainment. Lots of them can't look forward to next year, but they might as well have something to look forward to next week.'

'I see your point and I agree entirely,' responded Papadimitriou. 'But what do you propose?'

'Entertainment. Large-scale entertainment,' replied Sklavounis rather grandly.

'Which means what?' asked Papadimitriou.

'Movies,' said Sklavounis.

Six months earlier, such a proposal would have seemed ambitious beyond words and as laughable as telling the lepers they could swim across to Elounda to visit the cinema. Now, however, it was not beyond the realms of possibility.

'Well, we have a generator,' said Papadimitriou, 'which is a good start, but it's not all that's required, is it?'

Keeping the islanders happy and occupied in the evening might indeed help rule out much of the discontent that still lingered. While people sat in rows in the dark, thought Papadimitriou, they could not be drinking to excess or hatching plots in the *kafenion*.

'What else do you need?' he asked.

Sklavounis was quick to reply. He had already worked out how many people could fit into the town hall and where he could get a projector, a screen and the film reels. He had also, very importantly, done the figures. The missing element, until he had committee approval, was money, but given that so many of the lepers were now earning some kind of income, an entry fee could be charged to the new cinema and the cost of the entire enterprise might eventually cover itself.

Within a few weeks of his initial request, posters appeared around the town:

Saturday 13 April
7.00 p.m.
Town Hall
The Apaches of Athens
Tickets 2 drachma

By six o'clock that evening, over one hundred people were queuing outside the town hall. At least another eighty had arrived by the time the doors opened at six-thirty, and the same enthusiasm greeted the film the following Saturday.

Eleni bubbled with excitement when she wrote to her daughters about the new entertainment:

We are all so enjoying the films – they're the highlight of the week. Things don't always go to plan, though. Last Saturday the reels did not arrive from Agios Nikolaos. There was such disappointment when people realised that the film was cancelled that there was nearly a riot, and for several days people went about long-faced, as though the harvest had failed! Anyway, everyone cheered up as the week progressed, and we were all so relieved when your father was spotted carrying the reels ashore.

Within weeks, however, Giorgis began to bring more than the latest feature film from Athens. He also had a newsreel, which brought the audience sharply up to date with the sinister events that were taking place in the outside world. Though copies of Crete's weekly newspaper made their way to the island and radios occasionally crackled with the latest news bulletin, no one had had any idea of the scale of the growing havoc being wreaked across Europe by Nazi Germany. At this stage these outrages seemed remote and the inhabitants of Spinalonga had other more immediate things to concern them. With the elections behind them, Easter was approaching.

In previous years, the observance of this, the greatest of Christian festivals, had been subdued. The festivities taking place in Plaka made plenty of noise, and although a reduced version of the same dramatic rituals was always held in Spinalonga's little church of St Pantaleimon, there was a sense that it was not the same as the full-scale celebrations taking place across the water.

This year it was to be different. Papadimitriou would make sure of that. The commemoration of Christ's resurrection in Spinalonga was to be no less extravagant in expression than anything held on Crete or in mainland Greece itself.

Lent had been strictly observed. Most people had gone without meat and fish for forty days, and in the final week, wine and olive oil had been consigned to the darkest recesses. By Thursday of Passion Week the wooden cross in the church that was big enough to accommodate perhaps one hundred souls (so long as they were as tight-packed as grains in an ear of wheat) was laden with lemon blossom and a long line formed down the street to mourn Christ and kiss his feet. The throng of worshippers both inside and outside the church stood hushed. This was a melancholy moment, and all the more so when they looked on the icon of St Pantaleimon, who was, as the more cynical of the lepers described him, the supposed patron saint of healing. Many had lost faith in him some time earlier, but his life story had made him the perfect choice for such a church. A young doctor in Roman times, Pantaleimon followed his mother's lead and became a Christian, an act which would almost certainly result in persecution. His success in healing the sick aroused suspicions and he was arrested, stretched out on a wheel and finally boiled alive.

However cynical the islanders might be about the healing powers of the saint, they all joined in Christ's great funeral procession the next day. A coffin was decorated in the morning, and in the late afternoon the floral *epitaphoi* was carried through the streets. It was a solemn procession.

'We have plenty of practice at this, don't we?' Elpida commented sardonically to Eleni as they walked slowly along the street, the two-hundred-strong snake of people winding its way through the little town and up on to the path that led round to the north side of the island.

'We do,' she agreed, 'but this is different. This man comes alive again—'

'Which is more than we'll ever do,' interjected Theodoros Makridakis, who happened to be walking behind them and who was always ready with a negative comment. Resurrection of the body seemed an unlikely concept, but the strong believers among them knew that this was what was promised: a new, unblemished, resurrected body. It was the whole point of the story and the meaning of the ritual. The believers clung to that.

Saturday was a quiet day. Men, women and children were meant to be in mourning. Everyone was busy, however. Eleni organised the children into a working party to paint eggs and then decorate them with tiny leaf stencils. Meanwhile other women baked the traditional cakes. By contrast with such gentle activities, the men all helped in the slaughter and preparation of the lambs which had been shipped over a few weeks before. Once all such chores were done, people again visited the church to decorate it with sprigs of rosemary, laurel leaves and myrtle branches, and by early evening a bittersweet smell emanated from the building and the air was heavy with anticipation and incense.

Eleni stood in the doorway of the crowded church. The people were silent, subdued and expectant, straining to hear the initial whispers of the Kyrie Eleison. It began so softly it might have been the breeze stirring the leaves but then grew into something almost tangible, filling the building and exploding into the world outside. The candles which had burned inside the church were now extinguished and under a starless, moonless sky, the world was plunged into darkness.

For a few moments Eleni could sense nothing but the heavy scent of molten tallow that pervaded the air.

At midnight, when the bell from the church in Plaka could be heard tolling resonantly across the still water, the priest lit a single candle.

'Come and receive the light,' he commanded. Papa Kazakos spoke the sacred words with reverence, but also with directness, and the islanders were in no doubt that this was a command to approach him. One by one those closest reached out with tapers, and from these the light was shared around until both inside and outside the church there was a flickering forest of flames. In less than a minute darkness had turned to light.

Papa Kazakos, a warm-natured, heavily bearded man with a love for good living – making some justifiably sceptical about whether he had observed any kind of abstinence during Lent – now began to read the Gospel. It was a familiar passage and many of the older islanders moved their lips in perfect synchronicity.

'*Christos anesti!*' he proclaimed at the end of the passage. Christ is risen.

'*Christos anesti! Christos anesti!*' the crowd shouted back in unison.

The great triumphant cry carried on in the street for some time as people wished each other many happy years – '*Chronia polla!*' – responding with enthusiasm: '*E pisis*' – 'Same to you'.

Then it was time to carry the lighted candles carefully home.

'Come, Dimitri,' Eleni encouraged the boy. 'Let's see if we can get this home without it going out.'

If they could reach their house with the candle still lit, it would bring good luck for a whole year, and on this still April night it was perfectly feasible to do so. Within a few minutes every home on the island had a candle glowing in its window.

The final stage of the ritual was the lighting of the bonfire, the symbolic burning of the traitor Judas Iscariot. All day people had brought their spare kindling, and bushes had been stripped of dry branches. Now the priest lit the pyre and there was more rejoicing as it crackled and then finally went up with a roar while rockets soared into the sky all around. The real celebrations had begun. In every far-flung village, town and city, from Plaka to Athens, there would be great merrymaking, and this year it would be as noisy on Spinalonga as anywhere across the land. Sure enough, over in Plaka, they could hear the lively blasts of the bouzouki as the dancing on the island began.

Many of the lepers had not danced for years, but unless they were so crippled that they could not walk, they were encouraged to get up and join the circle as it slowly rotated. Out of their dust-filled trunks had come pieces of traditional costume, so that among them there were several men in fringed turbans, long boots and knickerbockers, and many of the women had donned their embroidered waistcoats and bright headscarves for the night.

Some of the dances were stately, but when they were not, the fit and active would take their turn, spinning and whirling as though it was the last time they would ever dance. After the dances came the songs, the *mantinades*. Some were sweet, some melancholy; some were ballads telling long stories that lulled the old folk and children almost to a slumber.

By the time day broke, most people had found their way to bed, but some had passed out across rows of chairs in the taverna, full not just of raki but of the sweetest lamb they had ever feasted on. Not since the Turks had occupied the island had Spinalonga seen such high spirits and hedonism. It was in God's name that they were celebrating. Christ was risen and in certain ways there had been some kind of rising from the dead for them too, a resurrection of their spirits.

What was left of April became a period of intense activity. Several more lepers had arrived from Athens in March, adding to the half-dozen who had come from various parts of Crete during the winter months. This meant more restoration work was needed, and everyone was aware that once the temperatures had soared there would be many tasks that would be abandoned until the autumn. The Turkish quarter was finally finished and the repairs to the Venetian water tanks were completed. Front doors and shutters had another coat of paint and the tiles on the church roof were all fastened into place.

As Spinalonga rose from its own ashes, Eleni began to decline. She watched the continuing restoration process and could not help comparing it to her own gradual deterioration. For months she had pretended to herself that the disease had met resistance in her body and that there was no development, but then she began to notice changes, almost by the day. The smooth lumps on her feet had multiplied, and for many weeks now she had walked without feeling in them.

'Isn't there anything the doctor can do to help?' Giorgis asked quietly.

'No,' she said. 'I think we have to face that.'

'How is Dimitri?' he asked, trying to change the subject.

'He's fine. He's being very helpful now that I'm finding it harder to walk, and in the last few months he's grown a lot and can carry all the groceries for me. I can't help thinking that he is happier here than he was before, though I don't doubt that he misses his parents.'

'Does he ever mention them?'

'He hasn't said a word about them for weeks and weeks. Do you know something? He hasn't received one letter from them all the time that he's been here. Poor child.'

By the end of May, life had settled into its usual summer pattern of long siestas and sultry nights. Flies buzzed around and a haze of heat settled over the island from midday till dusk. Scarcely anything moved during these hours of simmering heat. There was a sense of permanence here now and, though it was unspoken, the majority of people felt that life was worth living. As Eleni hobbled slowly to school on a typical morning, she relished the strong smell of coffee mingling with the sweet scent of mimosa in the street; the sight of a man walking down the hill, his donkey laden with oranges; the sound of ivory backgammon counters click-clacking as they were pushed about the baize and the rattle of the dice punctuating a buzz of conversation in the *kafenion*. Just as they did in any Cretan village, elderly women sat in doorways facing the street and nodded a greeting as she passed. These women never looked directly at each other when they spoke in case they should miss any comings and goings.

There was plenty happening on Spinalonga. Occasionally

there was even a marriage. Such major events, the burgeoning social life on the island and other significant information which the population needed to know soon created the need for a newspaper. Yiannis Solomonidis, formerly a journalist in Athens, took charge and, once he had got hold of a press, printed fifty copies of a weekly newssheet, *The Spinalonga Star.* These were passed around and devoured with interest by everyone on the island. To start with the newspaper contained the parochial affairs of the island, the title of that week's film, the opening times of the pharmacy, items lost, found and for sale, and, of course, marriages and deaths. As time went on it began to include a digest of events on the mainland, opinion pieces and even cartoons.

One day in November there was a significant event that went unreported by the newspaper. Not a sentence, not a word recorded the visit of a mysterious dark-haired man whose smart appearance would have made him blend into a crowd in Iraklion. In Plaka however, he was noticed by several people because it was rare for someone to be seen in the village wearing a suit, unless of course there was a wedding or a funeral, and there was neither that day.

Chapter Seven

Dr Lapakis had informed Giorgis that he was expecting a visitor who would need to be brought across to Spinalonga and returned to Plaka a few hours later. His name was Nikolaos Kyritsis. In his early thirties, with thick, black hair, he was slight by comparison with most Cretans and a well-cut suit accentuated his slender build. His skin was taut across his prominent cheek bones. Some considered him distinguished-looking, while others thought he appeared undernourished, and neither view was wrong.

Kyritsis looked incongruous on the Plaka quayside. He had no baggage, no boxes and no tearful family as did most of the people Giorgis took across, just the slimmest of leather portfolios which he held to his chest. The only other people who went to Spinalonga were Lapakis and the very occasional government representative making a quick visit to assess financial requests. This man was the first real visitor Giorgis had ever taken there, and he overcame his usual reticence with strangers and spoke to him.

'What's your business on the island?'

'I'm a doctor,' the man replied.

'But there's already a doctor there,' said Giorgis. 'I took him this morning.'

'Yes, I know. It's Dr Lapakis I'm going to visit. He is a friend and colleague of mine from many years back.'

'You aren't a leper, are you?' asked Giorgis.

'No,' answered the stranger, his face almost creasing into a smile. 'And one day none of the people on the island will be either.'

This was a bold statement and Giorgis's heart quickened at the thought. Snippets of news – or was it just rumour? – occasionally filtered through that so-and-so's uncle or friend had heard something about a development in the cure for leprosy. There had been talk of injections of gold, arsenic and snake venom, for example, but there was a hint of madness about such treatments, and even if they were affordable, would they really work? Only the Athenians, people gossiped, could possibly entertain thoughts of paying for such quack remedies. For a moment, Giorgis day-dreamed as he loosened the boat from its moorings and prepared to take this new doctor across. Eleni's condition had been getting visibly worse in the past few months and he had begun to lose hope that a cure would ever be found to bring her home, but for the first time since he had taken her to Spinalonga, eighteen months earlier, his heart lifted. Just a little.

Papadimitriou was waiting on the quayside to greet the doctor, and Giorgis watched as they both disappeared out of sight through the tunnel, the dapper figure with his slim leather case and the powerful figure of the island's leader towering over him.

An icy blast of wind blew across the water, fighting against

Giorgis's boat, but in spite of this, he found himself humming. He would not be perturbed by the elements today.

As the two men walked up the main street together, Papadimitriou grilled Kyritsis. He had enough information at his fingertips to know what questions to ask.

'Where are they with the latest research? When are they going to start testing it out? How long will it take to reach us here? How closely involved are you?' It was a cross-examination that Kyritsis had not expected, but then he had not anticipated meeting someone like Papadimitriou.

'It's early days,' he said cautiously. 'I'm part of a widespread research programme being funded by the Pasteur Foundation, but it's not just the cure we're hunting for. There are new guidelines on treatment and prevention that were set down at the Cairo Conference a couple of years ago, and that's my main interest in coming here. I want to make sure that we are doing all we can – I don't want the cure, if and when it's found, to be too late for everyone here.'

Papadimitriou, a consummate actor, concealed his mild disappointment that the longed-for cure was still out of reach by laughing it off: 'That's too bad. I'd promised my family I'd be back in Athens by Christmas, so I was relying on you for a magic potion.'

Kyritsis was a realist. He knew it could be some years until these people received successful treatment and he would not raise their hopes. Leprosy was a disease almost as old as the hills themselves and was not going to vanish overnight.

As the men walked together to the hospital, Kyritsis took in the sights and sounds around him with some incredulity.

It looked like any normal village, albeit less run-down than many in that part of Crete. Except for the occasional inhabitant he spotted with an enlarged earlobe or perhaps a crippled foot – signs which might not have been noticed by most – the people living there could have been ordinary folk going about their business. At this time of year there were few faces in full view. Men wore their caps pulled down and their collars turned up and women had their woollen shawls furled tightly around their heads and shoulders, protecting themselves from the elements, the wind which grew wilder by the day and the rain which fell in torrents and turned streets into streams.

The two men passed the glass-fronted shops with their brightly painted shutters, and the baker, removing a batch of sandy-coloured loaves from his oven, caught Kyritsis's eye and nodded. Kyritsis touched the brim of his hat in reply. Just before the church, they turned off the central street. High above them was the hospital. Particularly from below, it was an imposing sight, a building far grander than any other on the island.

Lapakis was at the front entrance to greet Kyritsis, and the two men embraced in a spontaneous display of genuine affection. For a few moments greetings and questions overlapped each other in a helter-skelter of enthusiasm. 'How are you? How long have you been here? What's happening in Athens? Tell me your news!' Eventually, their mutual delight at seeing each other gave way to practicalities. Time was running away. Lapakis took Kyritsis on a swift guided tour of the hospital, showing him the outpatients' clinic and treatment rooms and finally the ward.

'We have so few resources at present. More people should

be coming in for a few days, but we simply have to treat the majority and send them back home,' said Lapakis wearily.

In the ward, ten beds were packed in with no more than half a metre between each. All of them were occupied, some by men and some by women, though it was hard to tell which was which, since the shutters were closed and only a few faint streaks of light filtered through. Most of these patients were at the end of the line. Kyritsis, who had spent some time in the leprosy hospital in Athens, was unshocked. The conditions, the overcrowding and the smell there had been a hundred times worse. Here, at least, there was some attention to hygiene, which could mean the difference between life and death for someone with infected ulcers.

'All of these patients are in a reactive state,' said Lapakis quietly, leaning against the doorframe. This was the phase of leprosy where the symptoms of the disease intensified, sometimes for days or even weeks. During their time in this state patients were in terrible pain, with a raging fever and sores that were more agonising than ever. Lepra reaction could leave them sicker than before, but sometimes it indicated that the body was struggling to eliminate the disease and when their suffering subsided they might find themselves healed.

As the two men stood looking into the room, most of the patients were quiet. One moaned intermittently and another, whom Kyritsis thought was a woman but could not be sure, groaned. Lapakis and Kyritsis withdrew from the doorway. It seemed intrusive to stand there.

'Come to my office,' said Lapakis. 'We'll talk there.'

He led Kyritsis down a dark corridor to the very last door on the left. Unlike the ward, this was a room with a view.

Huge windows which reached from waist height almost to the lofty ceiling looked out towards Plaka and the mountains that rose up behind it. Pinned up on the wall was a large architectural drawing of the hospital as it was now and, in red, the outline of an additional building.

Lapakis saw that the drawing had caught Kyritsis's eye.

'These are my plans,' he said. 'We need another ward and several more treatment rooms. The men and women ought to be separated – if they can't have their lives, the very least we can give them is their dignity.'

Kyritsis strolled over to look at the scheme. He knew how low a priority the government gave to health, particularly of those they regarded as terminally ill, and he could not help but let his cynicism show.

'That's going to cost some money,' he said.

'I know, I know,' replied Lapakis wearily, 'but now that our patients are coming from mainland Greece as well as Crete, the government is obliged to come up with some funding. And when you meet a few more of the lepers we have here, you'll see they're not the sort to take no for an answer. But what brought you back to Crete? I was so glad to get your letter, but you didn't really say why you were coming here.'

The two men began to speak with the easy intimacy of those who had spent their student years together. They had both been at medical school in Athens, and although six years had passed since they had last met, they were able to pick up their friendship as if they had never been apart.

'It's quite simple, really,' said Kyritsis. 'I'd grown tired of Athens, and when I saw a post advertised at the hospital in Iraklion in the Department of Dermatovenereology I applied.

I knew I'd be able to continue my research, especially with the large number of lepers you now have here. Spinalonga is altogether a perfect place for a case study. Would you be happy for me to make occasional visits – and, more importantly, do you think the patients would tolerate it?'

'I certainly have no objection, and I am sure they wouldn't either.'

'At some point, there might even be some new treatments to try out – though I'm not promising anything dramatic. To be honest, the results of the latest remedies have been singularly unimpressive. But we can't stand still, can we?'

Lapakis sat at his desk. He had listened intently and his heart had lifted with every word that Kyritsis had spoken. For five long years he had been the only doctor prepared to visit Spinalonga, and during that time he had treated a relentless stream of the sick and the dying. Every night when he undressed for bed he checked his ample body for signs of the disease. He knew this was ridiculous and that the bacteria could be living in his system for months or even years before he was aware of their presence, but his deep anxieties were one of the reasons he only came across to Spinalonga on three days a week. He had to give himself a fighting chance. His role here was a calling that he had felt obliged to follow, but he feared the possibility of his remaining free of leprosy was no greater than the prospect of a long life for a man who regularly played Russian roulette.

Lapakis did have some help now. It was at precisely the moment when he could no longer cope with the slow wave of the sick who hobbled up the hill each day, some to stay for weeks and others just to have their bandages and dressings replaced, that Athina Manakis arrived. She had been a doctor in Athens before discovering that she had leprosy and admitting herself to the leprosarium there before being sent to Spinalonga with the rest of the Athenian rebels. Here she had a new role. Lapakis could not believe his luck: here was someone not only willing to live in at the hospital but who also had an encyclopaedic knowledge of general practice; just because they were leprous it did not stop the inhabitants of Spinalonga from suffering from a whole gamut of other complaints, such as mumps, measles and simple earache, and these ailments were often left unattended. Athina Manakis's twenty-five years' experience and her willingness to work every hour except those when she slept made her invaluable, and Lapakis did not at all mind the fact that she treated him as though he was a younger brother who needed knocking into shape. If he had believed in God, he would have thanked Him heartily.

Now, out of the blue – or, more accurately, out of the grey of this November day when sea and sky competed with each other for drabness – Nikolaos Kyritsis had arrived, asking if he could make regular visits. Lapakis could have wept with relief. His had been a lonely and thankless job and now his isolation had come to an end. When he left the hospital at the end of each day, washing himself down with a sulphurous solution in the great Venetian arsenal that now served as the disinfection room, there would no longer be a nagging sense of inadequacy. There was Athina, and now there would sometimes be Kyritsis.

'Please,' he said. 'Come as often as you wish. I can't tell you how delighted I would be. Tell me what you'd be doing exactly.'

'Well,' said Kyritsis, taking off his jacket and hanging it carefully over the back of the chair, 'there are people in the field of leprosy research who are sure that we are getting closer to a cure. I'm still attached to the Pasteur Institute in Athens and our director-general is very keen on pushing things forward as fast as we can. Imagine what it would mean, not just to the hundreds of people here but to thousands around the world – millions even in India and South America. The impact of a cure would be enormous. In my cautious opinion we're still a long way off, but every piece of evidence, every case study, helps build a picture of how we can prevent the disease spreading.'

'I'd like to think you're wrong about it being a long way off,' responded Lapakis. 'I'm under such pressure these days to use quack remedies. These people are so vulnerable and they'll grasp at any straw, particularly if they have the resources to pay. So what's your plan here exactly?'

'What I need are a few dozen cases that I can monitor very minutely over the next few months, even years, if it works out that way. I've been rather stuck in Iraklion on the diagnosis side and after that I lose my patients because they all come here! Nothing could be a better outcome for them from what I've seen, but I need to do some follow-ups.'

Lapakis was smiling. This was an arrangement that would suit them both equally. Along one wall of his office, reaching from floor to ceiling, were rows of filing cabinets. Some contained the medical records of every living inhabitant of Spinalonga. Others were where the records were transferred when they died. Until Lapakis had volunteered to work on the island, no papers had been kept. There had scarcely been any treatment worth noting and the only progress had been towards gradual degeneration. All that remained to remember the lepers by during the first few decades of the colony's existence was a large black ledger listing name, date of arrival and date of death. Their lives were reduced to a single entry in a macabre visitors' book and their bones now lay jumbled and indistinguishable under the stone slabs of the communal graves on the far side of the island.

'I've got records of everyone who has been here since I came in 1934,' said Lapakis. 'I make detailed notes on their state when they arrive, and record every change as it happens. They're in age order – it seemed as logical a way as any. Why don't you go through them and pull out the ones you'd like to see, and when you next visit I can make appointments for them to come and meet you.'

Lapakis tugged open the heavy top drawer of the cabinet nearest to him. It overflowed with papers, and with a sweep of his arm he gave Kyritsis an open invitation to browse.

'I'll leave you to it,' he said. 'I'd better get back to the ward. Some of the patients will be in need of attention.'

An hour and a half later, when Lapakis returned to his office, there was a stack of files on the floor; the name on the front of the top one was 'Eleni Petrakis'.

'You met her husband this morning,' commented Lapakis. 'He's the boatman.'

They made a note of all the chosen patients, had a brief discussion about each and then Kyritsis glanced at the clock on the wall. It was time to go. Before he entered the disinfectant room to spray himself – though he knew this measure to try and limit the spreading of bacteria was futile – the two men shook hands firmly. Lapakis then led him back down the hill to the tunnel entrance, and Kyritsis continued alone to the quayside, where Giorgis was waiting, ready to take him on the first stage of his long journey back to Iraklion.

Few words were exchanged on the return journey to the mainland. It seemed that they had run out of things to say on the way over. When they reached Plaka, however, Kyritsis asked Giorgis whether he could be there on the same day the following week to take him across to Spinalonga. For some reason he could not quite fathom, Giorgis felt pleased. Not just because of the fare. He was simply glad to know that the new doctor, as he thought of him, would be back.

Through the bitter cold of December, the arctic temperatures of January and February and the howling gales of March, Nikolaos Kyritsis continued to visit every Wednesday. Neither he nor Giorgis was a man for small talk, but they did strike up short conversations as they crossed the water to the leper colony.

'Kyrie Petrakis, how are you today?' Kyritsis would ask.

'I'm well, God willing,' Giorgis would reply with caution.

'And how is your wife?' the doctor would ask, a question that made Giorgis feel like a man with an ordinary married life. Neither of them dwelt on the irony that the person asking the question knew the answer better than anyone.

Giorgis looked forward to Kyritsis's visits, and so did twelve-year-old Maria, as they brought a hint of optimism and the possibility that she might see her father smile. Nothing was said, it was just something she could sense. In the late afternoon she would go to the quayside and wait for them to return. Wrapping her woollen coat tightly around her, she would sit and watch the little boat making its way back across the water in the greyness of dusk, catching the rope from her father and tying it expertly to the post to secure it for the night.

By April, the winds had lost their bite and there was a subtle change in the air. The earth was warming up. Purple spring anemones and pale pink orchids had broken through, and migrating birds flew over Crete making their way back from Africa after winter. Everyone welcomed the change of season and the keenly anticipated warmth that would now arrive, but there were also less positive changes in the air.

War had raged in Europe for some time, but that very month Greece itself was overrun. The people of Crete were now living under the sword of Damocles; the colony's newspaper, *The Spinalonga Star*, carried regular bulletins on the situation, and the newsreels that came with the weekly film stirred the population into a state of anxiety. What they feared most then happened: the Germans turned their sights on Crete.

Chapter Eight

'MARIA, MARIA!' SCREAMED Anna from the street below her sister's window. 'They're here! The Germans are here!' There was panic in her voice, and as Maria galloped two steps at a time down the stairs, she fully expected to hear the sound of steel-tipped boots marching down the central street of Plaka.

'Where?' Maria demanded breathlessly, colliding with her sister in the street. 'Where are they? I can't see them.'

'They're not right here, you idiot,' retorted Anna. 'Not yet anyway, but they are here on Crete and they could be coming this way.'

Anyone who knew Anna well would have spotted a hint of excitement in her voice. Her view was that anything that broke the monotony of an existence governed by the predictable pattern of the seasons and the prospect of living the rest of her life in this same village was to be welcomed.

Anna had run all the way from Fotini's house, where a group of them had been gathered around a crackling radio. They had just about made out the news that German paratroopers had landed in the west of Crete. Now the girls both raced to the village square where, at times like this, everyone would gather.

It was late afternoon but the bar was overflowing with men and, unusually, women, all clamouring to listen to the radio, though of course drowning much of it out with their din.

The broadcast information was stark and limited. 'At around six o'clock this morning a number of paratroopers landed on Cretan soil near the airfield of Maleme. They are all believed to be dead.'

It seemed after all that Anna was wrong. The Germans had not really arrived at all. As usual, thought Maria, her sister had overreacted.

There was tension in the air, however. Athens had fallen four weeks earlier and the German flag had fluttered over the Acropolis since then. This had been disturbing enough, but to Maria, who had never been there, Athens seemed a long way off. Why should events there bother the people of Plaka? Besides, thousands of Allied troops had just arrived on Crete from the mainland, so surely that would make them safe? When Maria listened to the adults around her arguing and debating and throwing in their opinions on the war, her sense of security was reinforced by what they said.

'They haven't got a chance!' scoffed Vangelis Lidaki, the bar owner. 'The mainland's one thing, but not Crete. Not in a million years! Look at our landscape! They couldn't *begin* to get across our mountains with their tanks!'

'We didn't exactly manage to keep the Turks out,' retorted Pavlos Angelopoulos pessimistically.

'Or the Venetians,' piped up a voice in the crowd.

'Well, if this lot come anywhere near here, they'll get more than they bargained for,' growled another, punching a fist into his open palm.

This was not an empty threat, and all those in the room knew it. Even if Crete had been invaded in the past, the inhabitants had always put up the fiercest resistance. The history of their island was a long catalogue of fighting, reprisals and nationalism, and there wasn't a single house to be found that was not equipped with a bandolier, rifle or pistol. The rhythm of life might have appeared gentle, but behind the façade there often simmered feuds between families or villages, and among males over the age of fourteen there were few untrained in the use of a lethal weapon.

Savina Angelopoulos, who stood in the doorway with Fotini and the two Petrakis girls, well knew why the threat was real this time. The speed of flight was the simple reason. The German planes that had dropped the paratroopers could cover the distance from their base in Athens to this island in not much more time than it took the children to walk to school in Elounda. But she kept quiet. Even the presence of the tens of thousands of Allied troops evacuated from the mainland to Crete made her feel more vulnerable than safe. She did not have the confidence of the menfolk. They wanted to believe that the killing of a few hundred Germans who had landed by parachute was the end of the story. Savina felt instinctively that it was not.

Within a week, the true picture was clearer. Each day everyone congregated at the bar, spilling out into the square on those late May evenings which were the first of the year when the warmth of the day did not disappear with the sun. A hundred or so miles as they were from the centre of the action, the people of Plaka were relying on rumours and fragments of information, and every day more pieces of the story would drift over from the west like thistle seeds carried on the air. It seemed that although many of the men who had dropped from the sky had died, some of them had miraculously survived and fled into hiding, from where they were now managing to take up strategic positions. The early stories had told only of spilt German blood and of men speared by bamboo canes, strangled by their own parachutes in the olive trees or dashed on to rocks, but now the truth emerged that a worrying number of them had survived, the airfield had been used to land thousands more and the tide was turning in the Germans' favour. Within a week of the first landing, Germany claimed Crete as its own.

That night, everyone gathered in the bar once again. Maria and Fotini were outside, playing tick-tack-toe by scratching the dusty ground with sharp sticks, but their ears pricked up when they heard the sound of raised voices.

'Why weren't we ready?' demanded Antonis Angelopoulos, banging his glass down on the metal table. 'It was obvious they'd come by air.' Antonis had enough passion for both himself and his brother, and at the best of times it took little to arouse it. Beneath dark lashes, his hooded green eyes flashed with anger. The boys were unalike in every way. Angelos was soft-edged in both body and mind, while Antonis was sharp, thin-faced and eager to attack.

'No it wasn't,' said Angelos, with a dismissive wave of his pudgy hand. 'That's the last thing anyone expected.'

Not for the first time Pavlos wondered why his sons could never agree on anything. He drew on his cigarette and delivered his own verdict.

'I'm with Angelos,' he said. 'No one imagined an air attack.

It's a suicidal way to invade this place – dropping out of the sky to be shot as you land!'

Pavlos was right. For many of them it had been little more than suicide, but the Germans thought nothing of sacrificing a few thousand men in order to achieve their aim, and before the Allies had organised themselves to react, the key airport of Maleme, near Hania, was in their hands.

For the first few days, Plaka went about its business as usual. No one knew what it would actually mean for them having Germans now resident on Cretan soil. For several days they were in a state of shock that it had been allowed to happen at all. News filtered through that the picture was bleaker than they had ever imagined. Within a week the 40,000 combined Greek and Allied troops on Crete had been routed and thousands of Allies had to be evacuated with huge numbers of casualties and loss of life. Debate at the bar intensified and there were further mutterings about how the village should prepare to defend itself for when the Germans came east. The desire to take up arms began to spread like a religious fervour. The villagers were not afraid of bloodshed. Many of them looked forward to picking up a weapon.

It became reality for the people of Plaka when the first German troops marched into Agios Nikolaos and a small unit was dispatched from there to Elounda. The Petrakis girls were walking home from school when Anna stopped and tugged her sister's sleeve.

'Look, Maria!' she urged. 'Look! Coming down the street!'

Maria's heart missed a beat. This time Anna was right. The Germans really were here. Two soldiers were walking purposefully towards them. What did occupying troops do once they invaded? She assumed they went about killing everyone. Why else come? Her legs turned to jelly.

'What shall we do?' she whispered.

'Keep walking,' hissed Anna.

'Shouldn't we run back the other way?' Maria asked pleadingly.

'Don't be stupid. Just keep going. I want to see what they look like close up.' She grabbed her sister's arm and propelled her along.

The soldiers were inscrutable, their blue gazes fixed straight ahead of them. They were dressed in heavy grey woollen jackets, and their steel-capped boots clicked rhythmically on the cobbled street. As they passed they appeared not to see the girls. It was as if they did not exist.

'They didn't even look at us!' cried Anna, as soon as they were out of earshot. Now nearly fifteen years old, she was affronted if anyone of the opposite sex failed to notice her.

Only days later Plaka was given its own small battalion of German soldiers. At the far end of the village one family had a rude early morning awakening.

'Open up!' shouted the soldiers, banging on the door with their rifle butts.

Despite not having a word of common language, the family understood the command, and those that followed. They were to vacate their home by midday or face the consequences. From that day, the presence Anna had excitedly predicted was in their midst, and the atmosphere in the village darkened.

Day to day, there was little substantial news of what was going on elsewhere on Crete, but there was plenty of rumour, including talk that some small groups of Allies were moving eastwards towards Sitia. One night, as dusk fell, four heavily disguised British soldiers came down from the hills where they had been sleeping in an abandoned shepherd's hut and strolled insouciantly into the village. They would not have received a warmer welcome had they appeared in their own villages in the Home Counties. It was not just the hunger for first-hand news that drew people to them; it was also the innate desire of the villagers to be hospitable and to treat every stranger as though he might have been sent from God. The men made excellent guests. They ate and drank everything that was offered, but only after one member of the group, who had a good grasp of Greek, had given a first-hand account of the previous week's events on the north-west coast.

'The last thing we expected was for them to come by air – and certainly not in those numbers,' he said. 'Everyone thought they would come by sea. Lots died immediately but plenty of them landed safely and then regrouped.' The young Englishman hesitated. Almost against his better judgement, he added: 'There were a few, however, who were helped to die.'

He made it sound almost humane, but when he went on to explain, many of the villagers paled.

'Some of the wounded Germans were hacked to pieces,' he said, staring into his beer. 'By local villagers.'

One of the other soldiers then took a folded sheet of paper from his breast pocket and, carefully flattening it out, spread it on the table in front of him. Below the original printed German someone had scribbled translations in both Greek and English.

'I think you all ought to see this. The head of the German

air corps, General Student, issued these orders a couple of days ago.'

The villagers crowded round the table to read what was written on the paper.

There is evidence that Cretan civilians have been responsible for the mutilation and murder of our wounded soldiers. Reprisals and punishment must be carried out without delay or restraint.

I hereby authorise any units which have been victims of these atrocities to carry out the following:

1. *Shooting*
2. *Total destruction of villages*
3. *Extermination of the entire male population in any village harbouring perpetrators of the above crimes*

Military tribunals will not be required to pass judgement on those who have assassinated our troops.

'Extermination of the entire male population'. The words leapt off the paper. The villagers were as still as dead men, the only sound was their breathing; but how much longer would they be free to breathe at all?

The Englishman broke the silence. 'The Germans have never before encountered the kind of resistance they are meeting in Crete. It has taken them completely by surprise. And it's not just from men but from women and children too – and even priests. They expected a full and uncompromising surrender, from you as well as the Allies. But it's only fair to warn you that they have already dealt brutally with several villages over in the west. They've razed them to the ground – even the churches and the schools—'

He was unable to continue. Uproar broke out in the room.

'Shall we resist them?' roared Pavlos Angelopoulos over the hubbub.

'Yes,' shouted the forty or so men in reply.

'To the death!' roared Angelopoulos.

'To the death!' echoed the crowd.

Even though the Germans rarely ventured out after dark, men took turns to keep watch at the door of the bar. They talked long into the small hours of the morning, until the air was thick with smoke and silvery forests of empty raki bottles sat on the tables. Knowing it would be a fatal error to be spotted in daylight, the soldiers rose to go just before dawn. From now on they were in hiding. Tens of thousands of Allied troops had been evacuated to Alexandria a few days earlier and those left had to avoid capture by the Germans if they were to perform their vital intelligence operations. This group was on its way to Sitia, where the Italians had already landed and taken control.

In the Englishmen's view, the farewells and embraces were long and affectionate for such a short acquaintance, but the Cretans thought nothing of putting on such an effusive emotional display. While the men had been drinking, some of the wives had come to the bar with parcels of provisions almost too heavy for the soldiers to lift. They would have enough to last them a fortnight and were fulsome in their gratitude. '*Efharisto, efharisto,*' repeated one of them over and over again, using the only word of the Greek language he knew.

'It's nothing,' the villagers said. 'You are helping us. It is we who should be saying thank you.'

While they were all still in the bar, Antonis Angelopolous, the older of Fotini's brothers, had slipped away, crept into the house and gathered a few possessions: a sharp knife, a woollen blanket, a spare shirt and his gun, a small pistol which his father had given him at the age of eighteen. At the last minute he grabbed the wooden pipe which lived on a shelf along with his father's more precious and ornate lyre. This was his *thiaboli*, a wooden flute, which he had played since he was a child, and since he did not know when he would be home again, he could not leave it behind.

Just as he was fastening the buckle of his leather bag, Savina appeared in the doorway. For everyone in Plaka sleep had been elusive in the past few days. They were all on alert, restless with worry, occasionally roused from their beds by bright flashes in the sky that told of enemy bombs blasting their towns and cities. How could they sleep when they half expected their own homes to be rocked by the impact of shell fire or even to hear the strident voices of the German soldiers who now lived at the end of the street? Savina had been sleeping only lightly and was easily woken by the sound of footsteps on the hard earth floor and the scrape of the pistol on the rough wall as it was lifted from its hook. Above all, Antonis had not wanted to be seen by his mother. Savina might try to stop him.

'What are you doing?' she asked.

'I'm going to help them. I'm going to guide those soldiers – they won't last a day in the mountains without someone who knows the terrain.' Antonis launched into a passionate defence of his actions, like a man who expected fierce opposition. To his surprise, however, he realised his mother was nodding in agreement. Her instinct to protect him was as strong as ever, but she knew that this was how it had to be.

'You're right,' she said, adding in a rather matter-of-fact fashion: 'It's our duty to support them however we can.'

Savina held her son for a fleeting moment and then he was gone, anxious not to miss the four strangers who might already be making their way out of the village.

'Keep safe,' his mother murmured to his shadow, though he was already out of earshot. 'Promise me you'll keep safe.'

Antonis ran back to the bar. By now the soldiers were in the square and the last farewells had been said. He raced up to them.

'I'm going to be your guide,' he informed them. 'You'll need to know where the caves, crevasses and gorges are because on your own you could die out there. And I can teach you how to survive – where to find bird's eggs, edible berries and water where you wouldn't expect it.'

There was a murmur of appreciation from the soldiers and the Greek-speaker stepped forward. 'It's treacherous out there. We have already discovered that to our cost, on many occasions. We are very grateful to you.'

Pavlos stood back. Like his wife, he felt sick with fear at what his firstborn was committing himself to, but he also felt admiration. He had brought his two boys up to understand how the land worked and he knew Antonis had the knowledge to help these men sustain themselves, like goats on apparently barren land. He knew what would poison them and what would nourish them; he even knew which type of scrub made the best tobacco. Proud of Antonis's courage and touched by his almost naïve enthusiasm, Pavlos embraced his son, then, before the five men were out of sight, he turned away and began walking home, knowing that Savina would be waiting for him.

Giorgis related all of this to Eleni when he visited the following day.

'Poor Savina!' she exclaimed hoarsely. 'She'll be worried sick.'

'Someone has to do it – and that young man was ready for an adventure,' replied Giorgis flippantly, trying to make light of Antonis's departure.

'But how long will he be away?'

'Nobody knows. That's like asking how long this war is going to last.'

They looked out across the strait to Plaka. A few figures moved about on the waterfront, going about their daily business. From this distance everything looked normal. No one would have known that Crete was an island occupied by an enemy force.

'Have the Germans been causing any trouble?' asked Eleni.

'You would hardly know they were there,' answered Giorgis. 'They patrol up and down in the day but at night they're nowhere to be seen. Yet it's as though we're being watched all the time.'

The last thing Giorgis wanted to do was make Eleni aware of the sense of menace that now pervaded the atmosphere. He changed the subject.

'But how are you feeling, Eleni?'

His wife's health was beginning to fail. The lesions on her face had spread and her voice had become gravelly.

'My throat is a bit sore,' she admitted, 'but I'm sure it's just a cold. Tell me about the girls.'

Giorgis could tell that she wanted to change the subject. He knew not to dwell on the subject of her health.

'Anna seems a bit happier at the moment. She's working hard at school but she's not much better round the house. In fact she's probably lazier than ever. She can just about clear away her own plate but she wouldn't dream of picking up Maria's. I've almost given up nagging her—'

'You shouldn't let her get away with it, you know,' interjected Eleni. 'She's just going to get into worse and worse habits. And it puts so much more pressure on Maria.'

'I know it does. And Maria seems so quiet at the moment. I think she's even more anxious about the occupation than Anna.'

'She's had enough upheaval in her life already, poor child,' said Eleni. At moments like these she felt overwhelmed with guilt that her daughters were growing up without her.

'It's so strange,' she said. 'We're almost completely unaffected by the war here. I feel more isolated than ever. I can't even share the danger you're in.' Her quiet voice shook and she fought against the possibility of breaking down in front of her husband. It would not help. Not in any way at all.

'We're not in danger, Eleni.'

His words were a lie, of course. Antonis was not the only one of the local boys to have joined the resistance, and tales of the Germans' infamously vicious behaviour at the slightest whiff of espionage made the people of Plaka shiver with fear. But somehow life appeared to go on as normal. There were daily tasks and those that the seasons dictated. When the late summer came, the grapes had to be trodden; when the autumn arrived it was time for the olives to be harvested; and all year round there were goats to be milked, cheese to be churned and weaving to be done. The sun rose, the moon saturated the night sky with its silver light and the stars blazed, indifferent to the events happening below them.

Always, however, there was tension in the air and the expectation of violence. The Cretan resistance became more organised, and several more men from the village disappeared to play their role in the unfolding events of the war. This added to the sense of anticipation that sooner or later life might change dramatically. Villages just like theirs, where men had become *andarte*, members of the resistance, were being marked out by the Germans and targeted for the most brutal reprisals.

One day early in 1942 a group of children, including Anna and Maria, were taking the long walk home from school along the water's edge.

'Look!' shouted Maria. 'Look – it's snowing!'

Snow had ceased to fall some weeks ago and it would only be a matter of time before there was a thaw on the mountaintops. So what was this flurry of white around them?

Maria was the first to realise the truth. It was not snow that was falling from the sky. It was paper. Moments earlier a small aircraft had buzzed overhead, but they had barely looked up, so common was it for German planes to fly low along this part of the coast. It had dropped a blizzard of leaflets, and Anna grabbed one as it floated down towards her.

'Look at this,' she said. 'It's from the Germans.' They clustered round to read the leaflet.

A WARNING
TO
THE PEOPLE OF CRETE

IF YOUR COMMUNITY GIVES SHELTER OR SUPPLIES TO ALLIED SOLDIERS OR MEMBERS OF THE RESISTANCE MOVEMENT, YOU WILL BE PUNISHED SEVERELY. IF YOU ARE FOUND GUILTY, RETRIBUTION WILL BE HARSH AND SWIFT FOR YOUR ENTIRE VILLAGE.

The paper continued to drift down, creating a carpet of white that swirled around their feet before being lifted into the sea and merging into the foamy surf. The children stood quietly.

'We must take some of these back to our parents,' suggested one, gathering a handful before they blew away. 'We need to warn them.' They trudged on, their pockets full of propaganda and their hearts pounding with fear.

Other villages had been similarly targeted with this warning, but the effect was not the one the Germans had hoped for.

'You're crazy,' said Anna, as her father read the leaflet and shrugged his shoulders. 'How can you dismiss it like that? These *andarte* are putting all our lives at risk. Just for the sake of their own little adventures!'

Maria cowered in the corner of the room. She could sense

an impending explosion. Giorgis took a deep breath. He was struggling to control his temper, resisting the urge to tear his daughter to shreds in his anger.

'Do you really think they are doing it for themselves? Freezing to death in caves and living off grass like *animals*! How dare you?'

Anna shrank. She loved to provoke these scenes but had rarely seen her father vent such fury.

'You haven't heard their stories,' he continued. 'You haven't seen them when they stagger into the bar at dead of night, almost dying of hunger, the soles of their shoes worn down as thin as onion skin and their bones almost piercing their cheeks! They're doing it for you, Anna, and me and Maria.'

'And for our mother,' said Maria quietly from the corner.

Everything Giorgis said was true. In the winter, when the mountains were capped with snow and the wind moaned round the twisted ilexes, the men of the resistance nearly froze to death; cowering in the network of caves high above the villages in the mountains, where the only drink was the moisture from the dripping stalactites, some reached the limits of their endurance. In the summer, when the weather was the very opposite, they experienced the full blaze of the island's heat and a thirst which was unquenchable when the streams lay dry.

Such leaflets only reinforced the Cretan determination to resist. There was no question of surrender and they would carry the risks that went with it. With increasing regularity, the Germans appeared in Plaka, searching houses for signs of the resistance, such as radio equipment, and interrogating Vangelis Lidaki since, as the owner of the bar, he was generally the only male in the village during daylight hours. Other working men were in the hills or on the sea. The Germans did not come at night and this was a certainty that the Cretans came to value; the foreigners were too fearful to go anywhere after dusk, suspicious of the island's rocky and difficult terrain and aware of their vulnerability to attack in the dark.

One night in September, Giorgis and Pavlos were at their usual corner table in the bar when three strangers walked in. The two elderly men looked up briefly but soon resumed their conversation and the rhythmic clicking of their worry beads. Before the occupation and the development of the resistance it had been rare to see any outsiders in the village, but now it was commonplace. One of the strangers walked over to them.

'Father,' he said quietly.

Pavlos looked up, open-mouthed with amazement. It was Antonis, almost unrecognisable from the boyish youth who had joined up so idealistically the previous year. His clothes hung off him and his belt was wrapped twice around his waist to keep his trousers in place.

Pavlos's face was still damp with tears when Savina, Fotini and Angelos arrived. Lidaki's son had been hastily dispatched to bring them to the bar, and it was just as a reunion should be between people who loved each other and who had not, until then, been separated for even a day in their lives. There was not just pleasure, there was pain too when they saw Antonis, who looked starved, drawn and not just one year but a whole decade older than when they had last seen him.

Antonis was accompanied by two Englishmen. There was nothing, however, in their appearance to betray their true nationality. Swarthy-skinned and with extravagant moustaches that they had trained to curl in the local style, they now had enough grasp of Greek to be able to converse with their hosts, and they told tales of encountering enemy soldiers and, in the guise of shepherds, fooling them into believing that they were Cretan. They had travelled across the island several times in the past year, and one of their tasks was to observe Italian troop movements. The Italian headquarters was in Neapoli, the largest town in their own region of Lasithi, and the troops there seemed to do little but eat, drink and be merry, particularly with the local prostitutes. Other troops, however, were stationed around the west of the island, and their manoeuvres were more arduous to monitor.

With their shrunken stomachs now bloated with lamb stew and their heads whirling with *tsikoudia*, the three men told stories long into the night.

'Your son is an excellent cook now,' one of the Englishmen told Savina. 'Nobody can make acorn bread like his.'

'Or snail and thyme stew!' joked the other.

'No wonder you're all so thin,' answered Savina. 'Antonis hadn't cooked much more than a potato before all this began.'

'Antonis, tell them about the time we fooled the krauts into thinking we were brothers,' said one, and so the evening continued, with their moments of fear and anxiety turned into humorous anecdotes for everyone's entertainment. Then the lyres were brought out from behind the bar and the singing began. *Mantinades* were sung and the Englishmen struggled to learn the lines which told of love and death, struggle and freedom, their hearts and voices now blending almost completely with those of their Cretan hosts who owed them so much.

Antonis spent one night with his family, and the two

Englishmen were garrisoned with other families willing to take the risk. It was the first time any of them had slept on anything but hard ground in nearly a year. Since they had to leave before dawn, the luxury of their straw-filled mattresses was a short-lived one, and as soon as they had pulled on their long boots and put their fringed black turbans back on their heads, they walked out of the village. Not even a local would have questioned whether these were true natives of Crete. There was nothing to give them away. Nothing, that is, except someone who might succumb to a bribe.

Levels of starvation in Crete were, by now, reaching such high levels that it was not unheard of for local people to accept what was known as the 'Deutsche drachma' for a tip-off about the whereabouts of resistance fighters. Famine and hunger could corrupt even honest people, and such betrayals led to some of the worst atrocities of the war, with mass executions and the destruction of whole villages. The old and sick were incinerated in their beds and men forced to hand over their weapons before being shot in cold blood. The dangers of betrayal were real and meant that Antonis and all like him made only rare and brief visits to their families, knowing that their presence might endanger those they loved the most.

Throughout the war, the only place that really remained immune from the Germans was Spinalonga, where the lepers were protected from the worst disease of all: the occupation. Leprosy might have disrupted families and friends but the Germans made an even more effective job of destroying everything they touched.

As a result of the occupation, Nikolaos Kyritsis's visits to Plaka immediately ceased, since unnecessary travel to and from

Iraklion was regarded with suspicion by the occupying troops. Loath as he was to do it, Kyritsis abandoned his research for the time being; the needs of the wounded and dying all around him in Iraklion could not be ignored. The repercussions of this insane invasion meant that anyone with any medical expertise found himself working round the clock to help the ill and the mutilated, applying dressings, fixing splints and treating the symptoms of dysentery, tuberculosis and malaria, which were rife in the field hospitals. When he returned from the hospital at night, Kyritsis was so exhausted he rarely thought of the lepers who, for such a tantalisingly brief time, had been the focus of his efforts.

The absence of Dr Kyritsis was perhaps the worst side-effect of the war on the inhabitants of Spinalonga. In the months during which he had been making his weekly visits they had nurtured hopes for the future. Now, once again, the present was their only certainty.

Giorgis's routine of coming and going from the island was more fixed than ever. He was soon aware that the Athenians had no difficulty in affording the same luxuries as they had done before the war, in spite of the soaring prices they had to pay.

'Look,' he said to his friends on the quayside one evening as they sat repairing their nets, 'I'd be a fool to ask too many questions. They have the money to pay me, so what right do I have to question their being able to afford to buy on the black market?'

'But there are people round here who are down to their last handful of flour,' protested one of the other fishermen.

Jealousy of the Athenians' wealth dominated conversation in the bar.

'Why should they eat better than we do?' demanded Pavlos. 'And how come they can afford chocolate and good tobacco?'

'They have money, that's why,' said Giorgis. 'Even if they don't have their freedom.'

'Freedom!' scoffed Lidaki. 'You call this freedom? Our country taken over by the bloody Germans, our young men brutalised and the old people burnt to death in their beds? *They're* the ones who are free!' he said, stabbing his finger in the direction of Spinalonga.

Giorgis knew it was pointless arguing with them and said nothing more. Even the friends who had known her well now occasionally forgot that Eleni was on the island. Sometimes he would get a muttered apology for their lack of tact. Only he and Dr Lapakis knew the reality, and even then Giorgis was conscious that he only knew the half of it. He saw little more than the gateway and the lofty walls but he heard plenty of stories from Eleni.

On his last visit, there had been a further change in her condition. First it had been the unsightly lumps that had spread to her chest and back and, most horrifyingly, to her face. Now her voice was becoming less and less audible, and though Giorgis thought this could sometimes be attributed to emotion, he knew it was not the entire cause. She said her throat felt constricted and promised she would go and see Dr Lapakis to get something for it. Meanwhile she tried to remain cheerful with Giorgis so that he did not take his downcast face back home to the girls.

He knew the disease was taking her over and that she, like the majority of the lepers on the island, whether they were impoverished or sitting on a fortune, was losing hope.

These men with whom Giorgis mended nets and sat in the bar whiling away the time playing backgammon and cards were the same people he had grown up with. Their bigoted, narrow views would have been his too if he had not been set apart by his connection with Spinalonga. This one element in his life had given him an understanding they would never have. He would keep his temper and excuse their ignorance, for that was all it was.

Giorgis continued to take his packages and parcels to the island. What did he care if the contents were procured under the counter? Would everyone not have bought the best if only they had the resources of the Athenians? He himself yearned to be able to buy the luxuries for his daughters that only some of the inhabitants of Spinalonga could now afford. For his own part, he very consciously took the best of his catch – once Anna and Maria had eaten their fill – to the leper colony. Why should they not have his biggest bream or bass? These people were sick and cast out of society, but they were not criminals. That was something the people of Plaka conveniently forgot.

The Germans feared Spinalonga with its hundreds of lepers living just across the water and allowed deliveries to continue, since the last thing they wanted was for any of them to leave the island to search out their own supplies on the mainland. One of them did, however, take his chance to escape. It was in the late summer of 1943, and the Italian armistice had led to a heavier German presence in the province of Lasithi.

Late one afternoon, Fotini, Anna, Maria and a group of five or six others were playing as usual on the beach. They were accustomed now to the presence of German soldiers among them, and the fact that there was one patrolling close by on the beach did not attract their interest.

'Let's skim stones,' shouted one of the boys.

'Yes, first to twenty!' replied another.

There was no shortage of smooth, flat pebbles on the beach, and soon their stones were flying across the water, bouncing lightly across the still surface, as they all tried to reach the ambitious target.

Suddenly one of the boys was shouting at them all: 'Stop! Stop! There's someone out there!'

He was right. There was a figure swimming out from the island. The German soldier could see it too and was watching, his arms folded in contempt. The children jumped up and down, screaming at the swimmer to turn back, anticipating the awful outcome.

'What's he doing?' cried Maria. 'Doesn't he know he's going to get killed?'

The leper's progress was slow but relentless. He was either unaware of the soldier's presence or just prepared to take the risk – however suicidal it was – because he could no longer bear life on the colony. The children continued to shout at the tops of their voices, but at the moment when the German raised his gun to fire they were all silenced by fear. He waited until the man had swum to within fifty metres of the beach and then shot him. It was a cold-blooded execution. Simply target practice. At that stage of the war the air was thick with stories of bloodshed and execution but the children had witnessed none of it themselves. In that moment they saw the difference between stories and reality. A single shot ricocheted across the water, the noise amplified by the echo from the mountains behind, and a crimson blanket spread itself slowly across the still sea.

Anna, the oldest among them, screamed abuse at the soldier. 'You bastard! You German bastard!'

A few of the younger children wept with fear and shock. These were the tears of lost innocence. By now dozens of people had rushed from their homes and saw them huddled together, sobbing and crying. Rumours had reached Plaka only that week that the enemy had adopted a new tactic: whenever they suspected the possibility of a guerrilla attack, the Germans would take all the young girls from a village and use them as hostages. Knowing that the safety of their children was far from guaranteed, the villagers' first thought was that some atrocity had been committed against one of them by the lone soldier who stood facing them a few metres down the beach. They were ready, although unarmed, to tear him to shreds. But with the utmost sang-froid he turned to face the sea and gestured defiantly towards the island. The body had long since disappeared but the patch of crimson still floated, clinging to the surface like an oil slick.

Anna, always the ringleader, broke from the wailing group and shouted to the group of anxious adults: 'A leper!'

They understood immediately and turned away from the German soldier. Their attitude had changed now. Some of them were less than bothered by the death of a leper. There were still plenty left. In the short time it took for the parents to reassure themselves that their children were unharmed, the soldier had vanished. So too had the victim and all traces of him. Everyone could forget all about him.

Giorgis, however, would not find it so easy. His feelings about the inhabitants of Spinalonga were anything but neutral. That night, when he took his battered old caique across the water, Eleni told him that the leper whose cold-blooded execution they had all witnessed was a young man called Nikos. It transpired that he had been making regular forays from the island when it was pitch dark to visit his wife and child. Rumour had it that it had been his son's third birthday on the day he died and he wished for once to see him before nightfall.

The children on the shore at Plaka had not been Nikos's only audience. A crowd had also gathered to watch him on Spinalonga. There were no rules or regulations to protect people from such folly and few felt the restraining hand of husband, wife or lover when they were spurred to some spontaneous act of insanity as this. Nikos had been like a starving man and his hunger dominated his every thought and waking moment. He craved the company of his wife, but even more the sight of his son, his own flesh and blood, the image of his unscarred, unblemished boyhood, a mirror of himself as a child. He had paid for his desire with his life.

Nikos was mourned on the little island that night. Prayers were said in the church and a wake was held for him even though there was no body to bury. Death was never ignored on Spinalonga. It was handled with as much dignity there as it would be anywhere else on Crete.

After this incident, Fotini, Anna and Maria and all the other children playing with them that day lived under a cloud of anxiety. In a single moment on this stretch of warm pebbles where they had enjoyed so much carefree childhood happiness, everything had changed.

Chapter Nine

ALTHOUGH THE LEPER executed just metres off their shore had meant little to most of them personally, the hatred the people of Plaka felt for the Germans intensified after this incident. It had brought the reality of war to the very threshold of their homes and made them realise that their village was now as vulnerable as anywhere in this worldwide conflict. Reactions varied. For many people, God was the only source of true peace, and the churches were sometimes full to overflowing with people bent in prayer. A few of the old people, Fotini's grandmother, for instance, spent so much time in the company of the priest that they permanently carried the sweet perfume of incense with them. 'Grandma smells like candle wax!' Fotini would cry, dancing around the old lady, who smiled indulgently at her only granddaughter. Even if He did not appear to be doing much to help them win it, her faith told her that God was on their side in this war, and when stories of the destruction and desecration of churches reached her, it only intensified her belief.

The *panegyria*, saints' days, were still celebrated. Icons would be taken from their safe places and carried in procession by the priests, the town band following them with an almost unholy cacophony of brass and drums. Lavish feasting and the sound of fireworks may have been missing, but when the relics had been safely returned to the church, people still danced wildly and sang their haunting songs with even more passion than in times of peace. Fury and frustration at the continuing occupation would be washed away with the best wines, but as dawn broke and sobriety returned, everything was as it had been before. It was then that those whose faith was less than rock solid began to question why God had not answered their prayers.

The Germans were no doubt bemused by these displays of the sacred and the curiously profane but knew better than to ban them. They did, however, do what they could to interfere, demanding to question the priest just as he was about to begin a service or to search houses as the dancing got into full swing.

On Spinalonga, candles were lit daily for those suffering on the mainland. The islanders were well aware that the Cretans were living in fear of German cruelty, and prayed for a swift end to the occupation.

Dr Lapakis, who believed in the power of medicine rather than divine intervention, began to grow disillusioned. He knew that research and testing had been more or less abandoned. He had sent letters to Kyritsis in Iraklion, but since they had gone unanswered for many months, he came to the conclusion that his colleague must be dealing with more pressing issues and resigned himself to a long wait before he saw him again. Lapakis increased the number of visits he made to Spinalonga from three to six days a week. Some of the lepers needed constant attention, and Athina Manakis could not cope alone. One such patient was Eleni.

Giorgis would never forget the day he came to the island and saw, instead of the slender silhouette of his wife, the squatter figure of Elpida, her friend. His heartbeat had quickened. What had happened to Eleni? It was the first time she had not been there to greet him. Elpida spoke first.

'Don't worry, Giorgis,' she said, trying to inject reassurance into her voice. 'Eleni is fine.'

'Where is she then?' There was an unmistakable note of panic in his tone.

'She has to spend a few days in the hospital. Dr Lapakis is keeping her under observation for a while until her throat improves.'

'And *will* it improve?' he asked.

'I hope so,' said Elpida. 'I'm sure the doctors are doing everything they can.'

Her statement was noncommittal. Elpida knew no more about the chances of Eleni's survival than Giorgis himself.

Giorgis left the packages he was delivering and quickly returned to Plaka. It was a Saturday, and Maria noticed that her father was back much earlier than usual.

'That was a short visit,' she said. 'How is Mother? Did you bring a letter?'

'I'm afraid there's no letter,' he replied. 'She hasn't had time to write this week.'

This much was entirely true, but he left the house quickly before Maria could ask any more questions.

'I'll be back by four,' he said. 'I need to go and mend my nets.'

Maria could tell something was wrong, and the feeling lingered with her all day.

For the next four months Eleni lay in the hospital, too ill to struggle through the tunnel to meet Giorgis. Each day when he brought Lapakis to Spinalonga he looked in vain, expecting her to be waiting under the pine trees for him. Every evening Lapakis would report to him, at first with a diluted version of the truth.

'Her body is still fighting the disease,' he would say, or 'I think her temperature has gone down slightly today.'

But the doctor soon realised that he was building false hopes, and that the more these were reinforced the harder it would be when the final days came, as he knew, in the pit of his stomach, they would. It was not as though he was lying when he said that Eleni's body was fighting. It was engaged in a raging battle, with every tissue fighting the bacteria that struggled to dominate. Lepra fever had two possible outcomes: deterioration or improvement. The lesions on Eleni's legs, back, neck and face had now multiplied, and she lay racked with pain, finding no comfort whichever way she turned. Her body was a mass of ulcers which Lapakis did everything he could to treat, holding on to the basic principle that if they were kept clean and disinfected he might be able to minimise the virulently multiplying bacteria.

It was during this phase that Elpida took Dimitri to see Eleni. He was now living at the Kontomaris house, an arrangement they had all hoped would be temporary but that was now looking as though it might be permanent.

'Hello, Dimitri,' Eleni said weakly. Then, turning her head towards Elpida, she managed just two more words: 'Thank you.'

Her voice was very quiet but Elpida knew what her words had acknowledged: that the thirteen-year-old boy was now in her capable hands. This at least might give her some peace of mind.

Eleni had been moved into a small room where she could be alone, away from the stares of the other patients and neither disturbed by them nor a disturbance to them in the dead of night, when the agony worsened and her sheets became saturated with fever and her groans continuous. Athina Manakis tended to her in those dark hours, spooning watery soup between her lips and sponging down her fiery brow. The quantities of soup were ever-diminishing, however, and one night she ceased to be able to swallow at all. Not even water could slip down her throat.

It was when Lapakis found his patient gasping for breath the next morning and incapable of replying to any of his usual questions that he realised Eleni had entered a new and perhaps final stage.

'Kyria Petrakis, I need to look at your throat,' he said gently. With the new sores around her lips, he knew that even getting her to open her mouth wide enough to look inside would be uncomfortable. The examination only confirmed his fears. He glanced up at Dr Manakis, who was standing on the other side of the bed.

'We'll be back in one moment,' he said, taking Eleni's hand as he spoke.

The two doctors left the room, closing the door quietly behind them. Dr Lapakis spoke quietly and hurriedly.

'There are at least half a dozen lesions in her throat and the epiglottis is inflamed. I can't even see the back of the pharynx for swelling. We need to keep her comfortable – I don't think she has long.'

He returned to the room, sat down beside Eleni and took her hand. Her breathlessness seemed to have worsened in the moments they had been away. It was the point he had reached before with so many patients, when he knew that there was nothing more he could do for them, except keep them company for the last hours. The hospital's elevated position gave it the best views of anywhere in Spinalonga, and as he sat by Eleni's bedside, listening to her increasingly laboured breathing, he gazed through the huge window which looked out across the water to Plaka. He thought of Giorgis, who would be setting off towards Spinalonga later that day to race with the white horses across the sea.

Eleni's breathing now came in short gasps, and her eyes were wide open, brimming with tears and full of fear. He could see there would be no peace at the end of this life and gripped her hands in both of his as if to try and reassure her. It may have been for two, maybe even three hours that he sat like this before the end finally came. Eleni's last breath was a futile struggle for another which failed to arrive.

The best any doctor could tell a bereaved family was that their loved one had died peacefully. It was an untruth Lapakis had told before and would willingly tell again. He hurried out of the hospital. He wanted to be waiting at the quayside when Giorgis arrived.

Some way off shore, the boat lurched up and down in the high, early spring waves. Giorgis was puzzled that Dr Lapakis was already waiting. It was unusual for his passenger to be there first, but there was also something in his manner that made Giorgis nervous.

'Can we stay here a moment?' Lapakis asked him, conscious that he must break the news here and now and give Giorgis time to compose himself before they were back in Plaka and he had to confront his daughters. He held out his hand to Giorgis to help him off the boat, then folded his arms and stared at the ground, nervously moving a stone about with the tip of his right shoe.

Giorgis knew even before the doctor spoke that his hopes were about to be destroyed.

They sat down on the low stone wall that had been built around the pine trees and both men looked out across the sea.

'She's dead,' Giorgis said quietly. It was not just the lines of distress left on Lapakis's face by a gruelling day that had given the news away. A man can simply feel it in the air when his wife is no longer there.

'I am so, so sorry,' said the doctor. 'There was nothing we could do in the end. She died peacefully.'

He had his arm around Giorgis's shoulder, and the older man, head in hands, now shed such heavy and copious tears that they splashed his dirty shoes and darkened the dust around his feet. They sat like this for more than an hour, and it was nearly seven o'clock, the sky almost dark and the air now crisp and cold, when the tears no longer coursed down his face. He was as dry as a wrung cloth and had reached the moment of grieving when exhaustion and a strange sense of relief descend as those first intense tidal waves of grief pass.

'The girls will be wondering where I am,' he said. 'We must get back.'

As they bumped up and down across the water in near darkness towards the lights of Plaka, Giorgis confessed to Lapakis that he had kept the seriousness of Eleni's condition from his daughters.

'You were right to do that,' Lapakis said comfortingly. 'Only a month ago I still believed she could win the fight. It's never wrong to have hope.'

It was much later than usual when Giorgis arrived home, and the girls had been growing anxious about him. The moment he walked in the door they knew something was terribly wrong.

'It's our mother, isn't it?' demanded Anna. 'Something has happened to her!'

Giorgis's face crumpled. He gripped the back of a chair, his features contorted. Maria stepped forward and put her arms round him.

'Sit down, Father,' she said. 'Tell us what's happened . . . please.'

Giorgis sat at the table trying to compose himself. A few minutes elapsed before he could speak.

'Your mother . . . is dead.' He almost choked on the words.

'Dead!' shrieked Anna. 'But we didn't know she was going to *die*!'

Anna had never accepted that her mother's illness could have only one real, inevitable conclusion. Giorgis's decision to keep the news of her deterioration from them meant that this came as a huge shock to them both. It was as though their mother had died twice and the distress they had felt nearly five years before had to be experienced all over again. Older, but little wiser than she had been as a twelve-year-old, Anna's first reaction was one of anger that their father had not given them any warning and that this cataclysmic event had come out of the blue.

For half a decade, the photograph of Giorgis and Eleni which hung on the wall by the fireplace had provided the image of their mother which Anna and Maria carried around in their heads. Their only memories of her were general ones, of maternal kindness and the aura of happy routine. They had long since forgotten the reality of Eleni and had only this idealised picture of her in traditional dress, a long, richly draped skirt, a narrow apron and a splendid *saltamarka*, an embroidered blouse with sleeves slit to the elbows. With her smiling face and long dark hair, braided and wound round her head, she was the archetype of Cretan beauty, captured for ever in the moment when the camera's shutters had snapped. The finality of their mother's death was hard to grasp. They had always cherished the hope that she would return, and as talk of a cure had increased, their hopes had risen. And now this.

Anna's sobs from the upstairs room were audible down the street and as far as the village square. Maria's tears did not come so easily. She looked at her father and saw a man physically diminished by grief. Eleni's death not only represented an end to his hopes and expectations, but the end of a friendship. His life had been turned upside down when she was exiled, but now it was changed beyond repair.

'She died peacefully,' he told Maria that night, as the two of them ate supper. A place had been laid for Anna but she could not be coaxed down the stairs, let alone to eat.

Nothing had prepared any of them for the impact of Eleni's

death. Their three-cornered family unit was only meant to be temporary, wasn't it? For forty days an oil lamp burned in the front room as a mark of respect and the doors and windows of their home remained closed. Eleni had been buried on Spinalonga under one of the concrete slabs that formed the communal graveyard, but she was remembered in Plaka by the lighting of a single candle in the church of Agia Marina on the edge of the village, where the sea was so close it lapped against the church steps.

After a few months, Maria, and even Anna, moved beyond the stages of mourning. For a time, their own personal tragedy had eclipsed wider world events, but when they emerged from their cocoon of grief, all continued to go on around them just as it had before.

In April, the daring kidnap of General Kreipe, commander of the Sebastopol Division in Crete, added to the state of tension across the island. With the help of members of the resistance, Kreipe had been ambushed by Allied troops disguised as Germans and, in spite of a massive manhunt, was smuggled from his headquarters outside Iraklion over the mountains to the south coast of Crete. From here he was shipped off to Egypt, the Allies' most valuable prisoner of war. There were fears that the reprisals for this audacious abduction might be more barbaric than ever. The Germans made it clear, however, that the terror they were still perpetrating would have happened in any case. One of the worst waves of all took place in May. Vangelis Lidaki had been returning from Neapoli when he saw the awful burnt-out villages.

'They've destroyed them,' he ranted. 'They've burned them to the ground.'

The men in the bar listened in disbelief to his descriptions of the smoke still rising from the ashes of the flame-engulfed villages south of the Lasithi mountains, and their hearts went cold.

A few days after this event, a copy of a newssheet published by the Germans found its way to Plaka via Antonis, who had visited briefly to reassure his parents that he was still alive. The tone of it was as threatening as ever:

The villages of Margarikari, Lokhria, Kamares and Saktouria and the nearby parts of the Nome of Iraklion have been razed to the ground and their inhabitants have been dealt with.

These villages had offered protection to Communist bands and we find the entire population guilty of failing to report these treasonable practices.

Bandits have roamed freely in the Saktouria region with the full support of the local populace and have been given shelter by them. At Margarikari, the traitor Petrakgeorgis openly celebrated Easter with the inhabitants.

Listen carefully to us, Cretans. Recognise who your real enemies are and protect yourselves from those who cause retribution to be brought down on you. We have always warned you of the dangers of collaboration with the British. We are losing patience now. The German sword will destroy everyone who associates with the bandits and the British.

The sheet was passed around, read and reread until the paper was worn thin with handling. It did not dampen the villagers' resolve.

'It just shows they're getting desperate,' said Lidaki.

'Yes, but we're getting desperate too,' answered his wife. 'How much longer can we stand it? If we stopped helping the *andarte*, we could sleep easy in our beds.'

Conversation continued long into the night. To surrender and co-operate went against everything that was instinctive to most Cretans. They should resist, they should fight. Besides, they liked fighting. From a minor argument to a decade-old blood feud between families, the men thrived on conflict. Many of the women, by contrast, prayed hard for peace and thought their prayers had been answered as they read between the lines and detected sinking morale among their occupiers.

The printing and distribution of such threats might well be an act of desperation, but, whatever the motivation behind them, it was a fact that villages had been razed to the ground. Every home in them had been reduced to a smoking ruin and the landscape around was now scarred with the eerie silhouettes of blackened, twisted trees. Anna insisted to her father that they should tell the Germans everything they knew.

'Why should we risk Plaka being destroyed?' she demanded.

'Some of it's just propaganda,' interjected Maria.

'But not all of it!' retorted Anna.

The propaganda war was not only being waged by the Germans, however. The British were orchestrating their own campaign and finding it an effective weapon. They produced newssheets that gave the impression that the enemy's position was weakening, spread rumours of a British landing and exaggerated the success of resistance activities. '*Kapitulation*' was the theme, and the Germans would wake to the sight of huge letter Ks daubed liberally on their sentry boxes, barrack walls and vehicles. Even in villages such as Plaka, mothers waited nervously for their sons to return after trips to perpetrate acts of graffiti vandalism; the boys, of course, were thrilled to be contributing something to the effort, never imagining for a minute that they were putting themselves in any danger.

Such attempts to undermine the Germans may have been small in themselves but they helped to change the bigger picture. The tide was turning throughout Europe, and cracks had appeared in the Nazis' firm hold on the continent. In Crete, morale was now so low that German troops were starting to withdraw; some, even, to desert.

It was Maria who noticed that the small garrison in Plaka had cleared out. At six o'clock sharp there was always a show of force, a supposedly intimidating march through the main street and back again with the occasional interrogation of someone en route.

'Something's strange,' she said to Fotini. 'Something's different.'

It did not take long to work it out. It was now ten past six and the familiar sound of steel-capped boots had not been heard.

'You're right,' replied Fotini. 'It's quiet.'

The tension that hung in the air seemed to have lifted.

'Let's go for a walk,' suggested Maria.

The two girls, rather than ambling on to the beach as they usually did, kept to the main street until it ran out. Right at this point was the house where the German garrison had their headquarters. The front door and the shutters were wide open.

'Come on,' said Fotini. 'I'm going to look inside.'

She stood on tiptoes and peered through the front window. She could see a table, bare but for an ashtray piled high with cigarette butts, and four chairs, two of them tipped carelessly on to the floor.

'It looks like they've gone,' she said excitedly. 'I'm going inside.'

'Are you *sure* there's no one in there?' asked Maria.

'Pretty positive,' whispered Fotini as she stepped across the threshold.

Except for a few stray bits of rubbish and a yellowing German newspaper discarded on the floor, the house was empty. The two girls ran home and reported the news to Pavlos, who went immediately to the bar. Within an hour word had swept round the village, and that evening the square was filled with people celebrating the release of their own small corner of the island.

Only days later, on 11 October 1944, Iraklion was liberated. Remarkably, given all the bloodshed of the previous few years, the German troops were calmly escorted out of the city gate without any loss of life; the violence was saved for anyone who was perceived to have collaborated. German troops did, however, continue to occupy parts of western Crete, and it was some months before that situation changed.

One morning in early summer the following year, Lidaki had the radio blaring in the bar. He was washing glasses from the night before in his customary slapdash manner, sluicing them in a bowl of grey water before wiping them with a cloth that had already been used to mop a few puddles on the floor. He was mildly irritated when the music was suddenly interrupted for a news announcement, but his ears pricked up when he caught the solemnity of the tone.

'Today, the eighth of May 1945, the Germans have officially surrendered. Within a few days all enemy troops will have withdrawn from the Hania area and Crete will once again be free.'

The music resumed and Lidaki wondered if the announcement had just been a trick of his own mind. He stuck his head out of the door of the bar and saw Giorgis hastening towards him.

'Have you heard?' he asked.

'I have!' replied Lidaki.

It was true then. The tyranny was over. Though the people of Crete had always believed that they would drive the enemy from their island, when the moment came their joy was unrestrained. A celebration to end all celebrations would have to be held.

Part 3

Chapter Ten

1945

IT WAS AS though they had been breathing in a poisonous gas and now once again there was oxygen in the atmosphere. Members of the resistance were arriving back in their villages, often after travelling hundreds of miles to reach them, and fresh bottles of raki were uncorked to toast every return. Within a fortnight of the end of occupation it was the feast of Agios Konstandinos, and the celebration of this saint's day was the excuse everyone needed to throw all caution to the wind. A cloud had lifted and madness descended in its place. Fatted goats and well-fed sheep rotated on spits the length and breadth of Crete, and fireworks crackled in the sky across the island, reminding some people of the explosions which had ripped through their cities and illuminated the skies in the early days of the war. No one dwelt on this comparison, however; they wanted to look forward now, not back.

For the feast of Agios Konstandinos, the girls of Plaka donned their finery. They had been to church, but their minds were on things other than the sacred nature of the event. These adolescent girls had few restrictions placed on them because they were still perceived as children and innocence was presumed in all they said and did. It was only later, when their womanliness was already developed, that their parents woke up to their sexuality and began to keep a close eye on them, sometimes rather too late. By then, of course, many of these girls had stolen kisses from village boys and engaged in secret trysts in the olive groves or fields on the way home from school.

Whilst neither Maria nor Fotini had ever been kissed, Anna had become a well-practised flirt. She was never happier than when she was in the company of boys and could toss her mane of hair and flash her engaging smile knowing that her audience would not look away. She was like a cat on heat.

'Tonight's going to be special,' announced Anna. 'I can feel it in the air.'

'Why's that then?' asked Fotini.

'Most of the boys are back, that's why,' she answered.

There were several dozen young men in the village, mere boys when they had left to fight with the *andarte* at the beginning of the occupation. Some of them had now chosen to join the Communists and had gone to take part in the struggle against right-wing forces that was brewing on mainland Greece, bringing new hardship and bloodshed.

Fotini's brother Antonis was one of those who had returned to Plaka. Sympathetic as he was to the ideals of the left and the new campaign on the mainland, after four years away he had been more than ready to come home. It was Crete that he had been fighting for, and here he wanted to stay. During his time away Antonis had grown wiry and strong and was unrecognisable from the emaciated figure who had staggered back after those first few months in the resistance to see his family. Now he had not only a moustache, but a beard too, which added at least five years to his twenty-three. He had lived on a diet of mountain greens, snails and whatever wild animals he could ensnare, and endured extremes of heat and cold that had given him a sense of indestructibility.

It was the romantic figure of Antonis that Anna had set her heart on that night. She was not alone in that ambition, but she was confident of winning at least a kiss from him. He was lean and slim-hipped, and when the dancing began, Anna was determined to make him notice her. If he failed to, he would be the only man in the village who had. Everyone was aware of Anna, not only because she was half a head taller than most of the other girls, but because her hair was longer, wavier and glossier than all the rest, and even when plaited it reached down to her hips. The whites of her huge oval eyes were as bright as the dazzling cotton shirts which the girls all wore, and her pearly teeth gleamed as she laughed and chattered with her friends, supremely conscious of her beauty under the watchful gaze of the groups of young men who stood about the square, anticipating the moment when music would mark the real launch of the festivities. Anna was almost luminous in the dusk of this great feast day. The other girls were in her shadow.

Tables and chairs had been set out on three sides of the square, and on the fourth a long trestle table took the weight of a dozen dishes piled high with cheese pies and spicy sausages, sweet pastries and pyramids of waxy-skinned oranges and ripe apricots. The smell of roasting lamb wafted over the square and brought with it the mouth-watering anticipation of pleasure. There was a strict order of events. Eating and drinking would come later, but before that there would be dancing.

At first the boys and men all stood talking together and the girls stood apart, giggling excitedly. The separation was not to last. The band struck up and the swirling and stamping of feet began. Men and women rose from their seats and girls and boys broke away from their huddles. Soon the dusty space was filled. Anna knew as the inner female circle rotated that sooner or later she would find herself opposite Antonis and that for a few moments they would dance together before moving on. How can I make him see me as someone more than his little sister's friend? she asked herself.

She did not have to try. Antonis stood in front of her. The slow *pentozali* dance gave her a few moments to study the pair of fathomless eyes that looked out through the black tassled fringe of his traditional headdress. The *sariki* was the warrior's hat that many young men now wore to show that they had graduated into manhood, not just through the passage of time but because they had the blood of another man on their hands. In Antonis's case, it was not merely one but several enemy soldiers. He prayed that he would never again hear the distinctive cry of surprise as his blade penetrated the soft flesh between the shoulder blades, and the strangulated gasp that followed. It never felt like victory, but it did give him the right to associate himself with the fearless warriors of Crete's past, the *pallikaria*, in their breeches and long boots.

Anna flashed her broad smile at this boy who had become a man, but he did not return it. The ebony eyes had instead fixed on hers and held them until she was almost relieved when it was time for him to move on to his next partner. As the dance ended, her heart still pounded furiously and she returned to her group of friends, who now spectated as some of the men, Antonis among them, reeled before them like human gyroscopes. It was a dizzying display. Their boots cleared the ground by several feet as they leapt into the air, and the perfectly synchronised bowing of the three-stringed lyre and the plucking of the lute urged them on, giving the dance a breathless energy right to the very end.

The married women and the widows watched the acrobatics even though the performance was not being staged for them, but for the nubile beauties who observed from the corner of the square. As Antonis rotated and the music and the drum beat built to a climax, Anna was certain that this handsome warrior was dancing for her alone. The whole audience clapped and cheered as they finished and the band, with hardly a moment's pause, launched into the next tune. A group of slightly older men now took the dusty centre stage.

Anna was bold. She broke away from her circle of friends and approached Antonis, who was pouring himself a glass of wine from a huge clay jug. Although he had seen her many times at his home, he had barely noticed her before tonight. Before the occupation Anna had seemed just a little girl; now a shapely, voluptuous woman had taken her place.

'Hello, Antonis,' she said boldly.

'Hello, Anna.'

'You must have been practising your dancing while you were away,' she said, 'to be able to do those steps.'

'We saw nothing but goats up in the mountains,' Antonis

replied laughingly. 'But they're pretty nimble on their feet, so maybe we learnt a thing or two from them.'

'Can we dance again soon?' she asked, over the noisy strains of the lyre and the beat of the drums.

'Yes,' he said, his face now breaking into a smile.

'Good. I'll be waiting. Over there.' she said, and returned to her friends.

Antonis had the feeling that Anna had offered herself to him for more than a *pentozali*. When a suitable dance began, he went up to her, took her by the hand and led her into the circle. Holding her round the waist, he now inhaled the indescribably sensual smell of her sweat, an essence of more intoxicating sweetness than anything he had ever breathed in before. Crushed lavender and rose petals would not compare. When the dance finished, he felt her hot breath in his ear.

'Meet me behind the church,' she whispered.

Anna knew that a stroll to the church, even during such wild celebrations, was perfectly normal on a saint's day, and besides, Agios Konstandinos shared his day with his wife, Agia Eleni, making it a special moment to remember her mother. She made her way swiftly to the alleyway behind the church and within a few moments Antonis was there too, fumbling to find her in the darkness. Her parted lips immediately sought his.

Not since he had been paying good money had he been kissed like this. In the last months of the war he had been a regular in the brothels of Rethimnon. The women there loved the *andarte* and gave them a special rate, particularly when they were as handsome as Antonis. Theirs had been the only business that had thrived during the occupation as men sought comfort after long absences from their wives, and young men took the opportunity to develop sexual experience that would never be tolerated under the watchful eyes of their own community. It had, however, been loveless. Here in his arms was a woman who kissed like a prostitute but was probably a virgin and, most importantly, Antonis could feel real desire. There was no mistaking it. Every part of his being craved for this lascivious kiss to continue. His mind was working swiftly. Here he was back for good and expected to marry and settle down in the community, and here was a woman eager for love who had been waiting quite literally on his doorstep, just as she had been since childhood. She had to be his. It was meant to be.

They separated from their embrace. 'We must get back to the square,' said Anna, knowing that her father would notice her absence if she was away for much longer. 'But let's go separately.'

She slipped out of the shadows and into the church, where she spent a few minutes lighting a candle before an image of the Virgin and Child, her lips, still wet from Antonis's, moving silently in prayer.

As she returned to the square there was a slight commotion in the street. A large saloon car had drawn up, one of few on an island where most people still travelled on their own two feet or on the back of a four-legged beast. Anna paused to watch the passengers as they climbed out. The driver, a distinguished man in his sixties, was immediately recognisable as Alexandros Vandoulakis, the head of the wealthy landowning family that lived on a sprawling farm near Elounda. He was a popular man, and his wife Eleftheria was liked too. They employed a dozen or so men in the village – Antonis included – several of whom had only just returned after long absences with the resistance, and had welcomed them back with open arms. They were generous with the men's wages, though some said, sarcastically, that they could afford to be. It was not just the thousands of hectares of olive groves that were the source of their wealth. They owned a similar amount of land on the fertile Lasithi plateau, where they grew huge crops of potatoes, cereals and apples, providing them with an all-year round income, and a guaranteed one at that. The cool climate of the plateau, 800 metres up, rarely failed and the green fields were verdant with moisture provided by the melting snows of the mountains that encircled it. Alexandros and Eleftheria Vandoulakis often spent the months of high summer in Neapoli, twenty or so kilometres away, where they had a grand town house, leaving the estate in Elounda to be managed by their son Andreas. Theirs was a fortune of rare magnitude.

It was, however, no surprise that such a well-to-do family should turn out to celebrate with fishermen, shepherds and men who worked the land. It was the same all over Crete. Every village member would turn out to dance and feast and the wealthy landowning families who lived on nearby farms or estates would come to join them. They could not throw a better party, however great their fortune, and they wanted to share in its exuberance. Both rich and poor had suffered and all had equal cause to celebrate their liberation. The soulful sentiment of the *mantinades* and the excitement of the energetic *pentozali* were the same whether your family owned ninety olive trees or ninety thousand.

From the back seat of the car emerged the two Vandoulakis daughters and finally their older brother, Andreas. They were immediately welcomed by some of the villagers and given a good table with the best view of the dancing. Andreas, however, did not sit for long.

'Come on,' he said to his sisters. 'Let's join in with the dancing.'

He grabbed them both and pulled them into the circle, where they blended in with the crowd of dancers, dressed as they were in the same costumes as the village girls. Anna watched. Some of her friends were in the group and it struck her that if they were going to have the opportunity to link arms and dance with Andreas Vandoulakis, then so was she. She joined the next *pentozali* and, just as she had done with Antonis not an hour earlier, fixed Andreas in her gaze.

The dance soon came to an end. The lamb was now roasted and being cut into thick chunks, platters of which were passed round for the villagers to feast on. Andreas was back with his family but his mind was elsewhere.

At the age of twenty-five, he was being pressurised by his parents to find a wife. Alexandros and Eleftheria were frustrated by his rejection of every single one of the daughters of their friends and acquaintances. Some were dour, some were drippy and others were simply dim, and although all of them would have been more than generously dowried, Andreas refused to have anything to do with them.

'Who's that girl, the one with the amazing hair?' he asked his sisters, gesturing towards Anna.

'How should we know?' they chorused. 'She's just one of the local girls.'

'She's beautiful,' he said. 'That's what I'd like my wife to look like.'

As he got up, Eleftheria gave Alexandros a knowing look. Her view was that, given the lack of impact any dowry would have on Andreas's life, what did it really matter whom he married? Eleftheria herself had come from a considerably humbler background than Alexandros, but it had not significantly affected their lives. She wanted her son to be happy, and if that involved flying in the face of convention, then so be it.

Andreas had walked right up to the crowd of girls, who were sitting in a circle eating pieces of the tender meat with their fingers. There was nothing particularly remarkable about Andreas, who had inherited his father's strong features and his mother's sallow complexion, but his family background lent him a bearing that set him apart from all the other men at the gathering, except for Alexandros Vandoulakis. The young women were embarrassed when they realised Andreas was approaching them and hastily wiped their hands on their skirts and licked the fatty juice from their lips.

'Anyone care to dance?' he asked casually, looking directly at Anna. His was the attitude of a man confident of his superior social situation and there was only one response. To get up out of her seat and take the hand which was being offered to her.

The candles on the tables had guttered and burned out, but by now the moon had risen and cast its bright glow in the otherwise sable-black sky. Both raki and wine had flowed and the musicians, emboldened by the atmosphere, played faster and faster until the dancers once again appeared to fly through the air. Andreas held Anna close. It was the time of night when the tradition of swapping partners during the dance could be ignored, and he decided he was not going to exchange her for some matronly type with few teeth and two left feet. Anna was perfect. No one else would do.

Alexandros and Eleftheria Vandoulakis watched their son courting this woman, but they were not the only ones to do so. Antonis sat at a table with his friends, drinking himself into a stupor as he realised what was unfolding in front of him. The man he worked for was in the process of seducing the girl he desired. The more he drank the more miserable he became. He had felt less dejected when he was sleeping on an open hillside during the war, lashed by storms and stinging winds. What hope did he have of keeping Anna for himself when he was in competition with a man who was heir to a sizeable chunk of Lasithi?

In the far corner of the square Giorgis sat playing backgammon with a group of older people. His eyes darted back and forth from the board to the square, where Anna continued to dance with the most eligible man this side of Agios Nikolaos.

The Vandoulakis family eventually rose to leave. Andreas's mother knew instinctively that her son would not want to come home with them, but in the interests of respectability and the reputation of this village beauty he had taken such a liking to, it was important that he should. Her son was no fool. If he was going to break away from tradition and have the liberty to select his own wife rather than be manoeuvred into accepting some choice of his parents, he needed them to be on his side.

'Look,' he said to Anna, 'I have to go now, but I want to see you again. I'll have a note delivered to you tomorrow. It'll tell you when we could meet next.'

He spoke like a man used to issuing orders and expecting them to be carried out. Anna had no objection to that, for once realising that acquiescence was the right response. It could, after all, be her route out of Plaka.

Chapter Eleven

'HEY! ANTONIS! HERE a minute!'

The summons was perfunctory, the voice of a master to his servant. Andreas had stopped his truck some distance from where Antonis was hacking down some old and now barren olive trees and was waving him over. Antonis paused from his work and leaned on his axe. He was not yet used to being at the beck and call of his young master. The roamings of the past few years, though endlessly tough and uncomfortable, had had a joyful freedom about them, and he was finding it hard to get used to both the daily routine and the idea that he must jump to attention every time the boss issued an order. If that was not enough, there was also a specific cause for resentment between himself and this man who stood shouting at him from the driving seat of his vehicle. It made him feel like planting his axe into Andreas Vandoulakis's neck.

Antonis glistened. His brow was beaded with droplets of perspiration and his shirt clung to his back. It was only the end of May but already temperatures were soaring. He would not jump to attention, not quite yet anyway. Nonchalantly he pulled the cork from the hollow gourd at his feet and took a swig of water.

Anna . . . Before last week Antonis had scarcely noticed her, and he had certainly not given her a moment's thought, but on that saint's day night she had roused in him a passion that would not let him sleep. Over and over again he relived the moment of their embrace. Ten short minutes it had lasted, perhaps even less, but to Antonis every second had been as long and lingering as a whole day. Then it was all over. Right in front of him, the possibility of love had been snatched away. He had watched Andreas Vandoulakis from the moment he had arrived and seen him dance with Anna. He knew then, even before the battle lines were drawn up, who had won the war. The odds had been heavily weighted against him.

Antonis now sauntered over to Andreas, who was oblivious to the nuances of his manner.

'You live in Plaka, don't you?' Andreas said. 'I want you to deliver this for me. Today.'

He handed over an envelope. Antonis did not need to look at it to know whose name was written on the outside.

'I'll take it some time,' he said with feigned indifference, folding the letter in two and stuffing it into the back pocket of his trousers.

'I want it delivered *today*,' said Andreas sternly. 'Don't forget.'

The engine of his truck started up noisily and Andreas hurriedly reversed out of the field, whipping the dry earth into a filthy cloud that lingered in the air and filled Antonis's lungs with dust.

'Why should I take your bloody letter?' Antonis yelled as Andreas disappeared from sight. 'God damn you!'

He knew this letter would seal his own misery but he also knew he had no choice but to make sure it was safely handed over. Andreas Vandoulakis would soon find out if he had failed in his task and there would be hell to pay. All day long the crisp envelope sat in his pocket. It crackled whenever he sat down and he tortured himself with thoughts of ripping it up, crushing it into a tight ball and hurling it into a ravine, or of watching it burn slowly in the small fire he had made to dispose of some of the debris from his day's wood-cutting. But the one thing he had not been tempted to do was open it. He could not bear to read it. Not that he needed to. It was perfectly obvious what it would say.

Anna was surprised to find Antonis standing on her doorstep early that evening. He had knocked on the door, hoping not to find her in, but there she was, with that same broad-mouthed smile that was so indiscriminately flashed at whoever crossed her path.

'I have a letter for you,' said Antonis before she had time to speak. 'It's from Andreas Vandoulakis.' The words stuck in his throat but he found a perverse satisfaction in disciplining himself to say them without betraying the slightest emotion. Anna's eyes widened with unconcealed excitement.

'Thank you,' she said, taking the now limp and crumpled envelope from him, careful not to meet his gaze. It was as though she had forgotten the fervour of their embrace. Had it meant nothing to her? wondered Antonis. At the time it had seemed like a beginning, but now he could see that the kiss which for him had been so full of expectation and anticipation had for her been merely the grasping of a moment of pleasure.

She shifted from one foot to the other and he could see that she was impatient to open the letter and wanted him gone. Taking a step back, she said goodbye and closed the door. As it banged shut it was as though he had been slapped in the face.

Inside the house, Anna sat down at the low table and with trembling hands opened the envelope. She wanted to savour the moment. What was she going to find? An articulate outpouring of passion? Words that exploded on the page like fireworks? Sentiments as moving as the sight of a shooting star on a clear night? Like any eighteen-year-old girl anticipating such poetry, she was bound to be disappointed by the letter on the table in front of her:

Dear Anna,

I wish to meet you again. Please would you come to lunch with your father on Sunday next. My mother and father look forward to meeting you both.

Yours,
Andreas Vandoulakis

Though the content excited her, taking her one step closer to her escape from Plaka, the formality of the letter chilled her. Anna thought that because Andreas had enjoyed a superior education he might be masterful with words, but there was about as much emotion in this hastily scribbled note as in the dreary books of ancient Greek grammar that she had been happy to leave behind with her school days.

* * *

The lunch duly took place, and many thereafter. Anna was always chaperoned by her father in accordance with the strict etiquette observed by people both rich and poor for such situations. On the first half-dozen occasions, father and daughter were collected at midday by a servant in Alexandros Vandoulakis's car, taken to the grand porticoed town house in Neapoli and returned home again at three-thirty precisely. The pattern was always the same. On arrival they would be shown into an airy reception room where every piece of furniture was covered with throws of intricate, ornately embroidered white lace and a huge dresser gleamed with a display of fine, almost translucent china. Here Eleftheria Vandoulakis would offer them a small plate of sweet preserve and a tiny glass of liqueur, waiting to receive the empty plates and glasses on a tray once they had finished. Then they all processed into the gloomy dining room, where oil paintings of fierce moustachioed ancestors glared down from panelled walls. Even here the formalities continued. Alexandros would appear and, crossing himself, would say, 'Welcome,' to which the visitors replied in unison with the words: 'I am fortunate to be with you.' It was the same on each occasion, until Anna knew, almost to the minute, what would happen when.

Visit after visit they perched on elaborately carved high-backed chairs at the dark overpolished table, politely accepting every course that was brought to them. Eleftheria did all she could to make her guests feel relaxed; many years earlier she had been through the same ordeal when she was vetted by the previous generation of the Vandoulakis family for her suitability as Alexandros's wife, and she remembered the unbearable stiffness of it all as though it was yesterday. In spite of the woman's kind efforts, however, conversation was stilted and both Giorgis and Anna were painfully conscious that they were on trial. It was to be expected. If this was a courtship, and no one had yet defined it as such, there were terms of engagement that needed to be established.

By the time of the seventh meeting, the Vandoulakis family had decamped to the sprawling house on the large estate in Elounda which was where they spent the months between September and April. Anna was now growing impatient. She and Andreas had not been alone together since the dance they had had in May, and, as she moaned one evening to Fotini and her mother, 'That was hardly being on our own, with the whole village watching us! Why does it all take so long?'

'Because if it's the right thing for both of you and for both families there is no need to hurry,' answered Savina, wisely.

Anna, Maria and Fotini were at the Angelopoulos house, supposedly being instructed on their needlework. In reality they were all there to chew over the 'Vandoulakis situation', as it was referred to. By now Anna was feeling like an animal at the local market being sized up for her suitability. Perhaps she should have kept her sights lower after all. She was determined not to let her enthusiasm wane, however. She had turned eighteen, her school days were long past and she had only one ambition: to marry well.

'I'll just treat the next few months as a waiting game,' she said. 'And anyway, there's Father to look after in the meantime.'

It was Maria, naturally, who was really taking care of Giorgis and who knew that she would remain in the home for some while longer, putting aside her own remote dream of becoming a teacher. She bit her tongue, however. It wasn't a good idea to seek confrontation with Anna at the best of times.

It took until spring of the following year for Alexandros Vandoulakis to satisfy himself that, in spite of the differences in their wealth and social situation, it would not be a mistake if his son made Anna his bride. She was, after all, exceedingly handsome, bright enough and clearly devoted to Andreas. One day, after yet another lunch, the two fathers returned to the reception room alone. Alexandros Vandoulakis was blunt.

'We are all aware of the inequality of this potential union but we are satisfied that it will not cause repercussions on either side. My wife has persuaded me that Andreas will be happier with your daughter than with any other woman he has ever met, so as long as Anna performs her duties as wife and mother we can find no real objections.'

'I can't offer you much of a dowry,' said Giorgis, stating the obvious.

'We are perfectly aware of that,' replied Alexandros. 'Her dowry would be her promise to be a good wife and to do all she can in helping to manage the estate. It's a significant job and needs a good woman in the wings. I'll be retiring in a few years and Andreas will have a great deal on his shoulders.'

'I am sure she'll do her best,' Giorgis said simply. He felt out of his depth. The scale of this family's power and wealth intimidated him, reflected as it was in the size of everything with which they surrounded themselves: the big dark furniture, the lavish rugs and tapestries and the valuable icons that hung on the walls were all a manifestation of this family's significance. But it did not matter whether he felt at home here, he told himself. What mattered was whether Anna could really become accustomed to such grandeur. There was no evidence that she felt anything but perfectly at ease in the Vandoulakis home, even though it was, to him, as alien as a foreign country. Anna could sip delicately from a glass, eat daintily and say the right things as though she had been born to do it. He, of course, knew that she was simply acting a role.

'What is as important as anything is that her basic education has been a good one. Your wife taught her well, Kyrie Petrakis.'

At the mention of Eleni, Giorgis maintained his silence. The Vandoulakis family knew that Anna's mother had died a few years earlier, but more than that he did not intend them to find out.

When they returned home that afternoon, Maria was waiting for them. It was as if she knew that this meeting had been a crucial one.

'Well?' she said. 'Has he asked you?'

'Not yet,' replied Anna. 'But I know it's going to happen, I just know it.'

Maria knew that what her sister wanted more than anything in the world was to become Anna Vandoulakis, and she wanted it for her too. It would take her out of Plaka and into the other world she had always fantasised about where she would not have to cook, clean, darn or spin.

'They're not under any illusions,' said Anna. 'They know what sort of house we live in and they know that I'm not bringing a fortune with me, just a few pieces of jewellery that were Mother's, that's all—'

'So they know about Mother?' interrupted Maria with incredulity.

'Only that Father is widowed,' Anna retorted. 'And that's all they're going to know.' The conversation was closed, as if it was a box with a sprung lid.

'So what happens next?' asked Maria, steering them both away from danger.

'I wait,' said Anna. 'I wait until he asks me. But meanwhile it's torture and I'm going to *die* if he doesn't do it soon.'

'He will, I'm sure. He obviously loves you. *Everyone* says so.'

'Who's everyone?' Anna asked sharply.

'I don't know really, but according to Fotini everyone on the estate seems to think so.'

'And what does Fotini know?'

Maria knew that she had said too much. Though there had been few secrets between these girls in days gone by, over the past few months this had changed. Fotini had confided in Maria about her brother's infatuation with Anna and how it aggravated him to hear all the estate workers talk of nothing but the impending engagement between their master's son and the girl from the village. Poor Antonis.

Anna bullied Maria until she told her.

'It's Antonis. He's obsessed with you, you must know that. He tells Fotini all the estate gossip and everyone's saying that Andreas is about to ask you to marry him.'

For a moment Anna basked in the knowledge that she was the focus of discussion and speculation. She loved to know she was the centre of attention and wanted to know more.

'What else are they saying? Go on, Maria, tell me!'

'They're saying he's marrying beneath him.'

It was not what Anna expected and certainly not what she wanted to hear. She responded with vehemence.

'What do I care about what they think? Why *shouldn't* I marry Andreas Vandoulakis? I certainly wouldn't have married someone like Antonis Angelopoulos. He doesn't own more than the shirt he stands up in!'

'That's no way to talk about our best friend's brother – and anyway, the reason he has nothing is that he was away fighting for his country while other people stayed at home and lined their own pockets.'

Maria's parting shot was one barbed comment too many for Anna's liking. She hurled herself at her sister, and Maria, as ever when she became embroiled in an argument with the unrestrained Anna, chose not to retaliate. She fled from the house and, being a faster runner than Anna, was soon out of sight in the maze of little streets at the far end of the village.

Maria was a mistress of restraint. Unlike her volatile sister, whose feelings, thoughts and actions were simultaneously played out for all to see, she was thoughtful. Generally she kept her feelings and opinions to herself, observing that outbursts of emotion or careless words were often regretted. In the past few years she had learned to control her feelings better than ever. In this way she kept up the appearance of being contented, largely to protect her father. Sometimes, however, she would allow herself the luxury of a spontaneous outburst, and when it came, it could have the impact of a clap of thunder on a cloudless day.

In spite of the opinions of the estate workers and the residual misgivings of Alexandros Vandoulakis, the engagement took place in April. The pair had been left alone in the gloomy drawing room after dinner, which had been an even stiffer event than usual. The anticipation of the engagement had been such that when the moment finally came and Andreas asked for her hand, Anna felt little emotion. She had played the scene through in her mind so often that when it actually took place it was as though she were an actress on a stage. She felt numb, unreal.

'Anna,' said Andreas. 'I have something to ask you.'

There was nothing romantic, imaginative or even remotely magical about the proposal. It was as functional as the floorboards they stood on.

'Will you marry me?'

Anna had reached her goal, winning a bet with herself and cocking a snook at those who might have thought she was not up to marriage into a landed family. These were her first thoughts as she accepted Andreas's hand and kissed him fully and passionately on the lips for the first time.

As was customary during a period of engagement, gifts were then lavished on Anna by her future in-laws. Beautiful clothes, silk underwear and expensive trinkets were purchased for her so that, although her own father could provide very little, she would not be lacking for anything by the time she finally became a Vandoulakis.

'It's as though every day is my saint's day,' Anna said to Fotini, who had come to view the latest array of luxury items that had been delivered from Iraklion. The small house in Plaka overflowed with the scent of extravagance, and in this post-occupation period, when a pair of silk stockings was out of reach for all but the wealthiest women, Anna's trousseau was a spectacle that all the girls queued up to see. The oyster-coloured satin camisoles and nightgowns that sat in boxes between layers of crinkly tissue paper were the stuff of Hollywood movies. When she lifted some of the items out to show her friends, the fabric ran between her fingers like water spilling into a pool. They were beyond even her own wildest dreams.

A week before the wedding itself took place, work began in Plaka on the traditional crown of bread. Leavened seven times, a large circle of dough was decorated with intricate patterns of a hundred flowers and fronds, and in the final stage of its baking was glazed to a golden brown. The unbroken circle symbolised the bride's intention to stay with her husband from beginning to end. Meanwhile, at the Vandoulakis home, Andreas's sisters began work on decorating the nuptial quarters at the couple's future home with silk cloth and wreaths of ivy, pomegranates and laurel leaves.

A lavish party had been thrown to celebrate the engagement, and for the wedding itself in March of the following year, no expense was spared. Before the service, which was to take place in Elounda, the guests arrived at the Vandoulakis home. They were a curious mix. Wealthy people from Elounda, Agios Nikolaos and Neapoli mixed with the estate workers and dozens of folk from Plaka. When they caught sight of Anna, the people from her old village gasped. Enough gold coins to fill a bank vault jangled across her chest and heavily jewelled earrings hung from her ears. She glittered in the spring light, and in the rich red of her traditional bridal gown she could have stepped from the *Tales of the Arabian Nights*.

Giorgis looked at her with pride and some bemusement, marvelling that this was his own daughter. She was almost unrecognisable. He wished at this more than any other moment that Eleni was here to see their firstborn looking so beautiful. He wondered what she would have thought about Anna moving into such an important family. So much of his elder daughter reminded him of his wife, but there was also a part of her that was completely unfamiliar. It seemed an impossibility that he, a humble fisherman, could have anything to do with this vision.

Maria had helped Anna get ready that morning. Her sister's hands trembled so violently that she had to do up every button for her. She knew this was what Anna wanted and that she was achieving her ultimate goal. She was confident that her sister had rehearsed being the *grande dame* so often in her daydreams that she would have no trouble adapting to the reality.

'Tell me it's really happening,' Anna said. 'I can't believe I'm actually going to be Kyria Vandoulakis!'

'It's all real,' Maria reassured her, wondering as she spoke what the reality of going to live in a grand house would be like. She hoped it would mean more than fine jewellery and smart clothes. Even for Anna such things might have their limitations.

The mix of guests made this an unusual event, but even more unconventional was that the pre-nuptial feast was held in the groom's house rather than the bride's, as was the tradition. Everyone understood the reasons for this. They did not need to be articulated. What kind of feast would have been on offer at the house of Giorgis Petrakis? The smart ladies of Neapoli tittered at the very thought, just as they had done when they heard that the Vandoulakis boy was marrying a poor fisherman's daughter. 'What on *earth* is the family thinking of?' they had sneered. Whatever anyone thought of the marriage, everyone was there to enjoy the fine lunch of roast lamb, cheese and wine from Vandoulakis's own crops, and when all two hundred stomachs were full it was time for the marriage service. It was a motley procession of cars, trucks and donkeys pulling carts that finally made its way down to Elounda.

For Cretans both rich and poor the rituals of the marriage ceremony were the same. Two *stephana*, the simple marriage crowns made from dried flowers and grasses and linked by a ribbon, were placed on the heads of the couple by the priest, and then exchanged three times to cement their union. These crowns would be framed later on by Anna's mother-in-law and hung high above the couple's bed so that, as the saying went, no one could tread on the marriage. For much of the time, the words of the sacred ritual were lost in the chatter of the congregation, but when the bride and groom finally joined hands with the priest, a hush spread around the church. Now they performed a sedate dance around the altar, the Isaiah Dance, and the guests knew that soon they would be outside in the sunshine.

Following the bride and groom, who rode in a carriage, everyone trooped back to the Vandoulakis home where trestle tables were laid out for another feast. People ate, drank and danced into the night, and just before the sun rose a volley of gunshots was fired to mark the end of the celebrations.

* * *

After the wedding, Anna more or less vanished from life in Plaka. She visited once a week to see her father, but as time went on she began to send a car down to collect him instead, so her appearances in Plaka became very few and far between. As the wife of the future head of the estate, she found her social position much altered. This was, however, not a problem for her. It was exactly what she wanted – a disconnection from her past.

Anna threw herself into her new role and soon found that her duties as daughter-in-law were as weighty as those of being a wife. She spent each day in the company of Eleftheria and her friends, either calling on them or receiving them at their home, and just as she had hoped, they all enjoyed a level of leisure that bordered on idleness. Her main duty was to help manage the domestic aspects of the Vandoulakis household, which largely involved ensuring that the maid had laid on a great spread of food for the menfolk when they returned in the evening.

She longed to make changes to the two family homes, to relieve them of their dark drapes and sombre furnishings. She nagged Andreas until he took his mother aside to ask for permission, and Eleftheria in turn consulted the real head of the household. This was the way in which everything had to be done.

'I don't want the big house altered too much,' said Alexandros Vandoulakis to his wife, referring to the house in Elounda. 'But Anna can give the house in Neapoli a lick of paint if she'd like to.'

The new bride threw herself into the task and was soon carried away on a wave of enthusiasm for fabrics and wallpapers, making endless trips to an importer of fine French and Italian goods who had a smart shop in Agios Nikolaos. It kept her busy and absorbed and Andreas benefited, finding her in a lively and buoyant mood at the end of each day.

Another of her duties was to manage the *panegyria* celebrations which the Vandoulakis family threw for their workers. Anna excelled at putting on a show. At these feasts she would sometimes feel the eyes of Antonis Angelopoulos on her and she would look up to meet his steely glare. Occasionally he would even speak to her.

'Kyria Vandoulakis,' he would say with exaggerated deference, his bow rather too low. 'How are you?'

His manner made Anna flinch and her reply was appropriately curt.

'Well, thank you.'

With that she turned her back on him. Both his look and his manner challenged her right to be there as his superior. How *dare* he?

Anna's marriage brought a change not only to her own status; her departure also meant a change in Maria's. The younger sister now clearly had the role of mistress in her own household. Much of Maria's energy had gone into pleasing and pacifying her sister, and the fact that Anna was no longer there meant a lightening of her load. She put renewed energy into running the Petrakis home and now often went with her father to make deliveries to Spinalonga.

For Giorgis, who could not lay flowers on her grave, each visit to the island was an opportunity to remember Eleni. He continued to go to and fro with Dr Lapakis in both fair and stormy weather, and on these journeys the doctor talked about his work, confessing to Giorgis how many of the lepers were now dying and how much he missed the visits of Dr Kyritsis.

'He brought a hint of good things to come,' said Lapakis wearily. 'I don't believe in very much myself, but I saw how belief can be a good thing, an end in itself. For some of the lepers, having the faith that Kyritsis might be able to cure them was enough to stop them wanting to die. Many of them feel there's nothing left to live for now.'

Lapakis had received some letters from his old colleague, explaining and profusely regretting his absence. Kyritsis was still involved in putting back together the damaged hospital in Iraklion and at present could not be spared to continue his research. Privately, Lapakis began to despair and poured out his heart to Giorgis. Most people would have prayed to God on bended knee, but in the absence of faith, Lapakis leant on his loyal boatman, whose suffering would always be greater than his own.

Although people continued to die of the disease, for those with the less virulent strain life on Spinalonga was still full of the unexpected. Since the war finished, there had been two film showings every week, the market was better than ever and the newspaper thrived. Dimitri, who was now seventeen, had already begun to teach the five- and six-year-olds whilst a more experienced teacher took charge of the older children; he continued to live at the Kontomaris house, an arrangement which brought great happiness on both sides. As far as it could do, a general sense of contentment pervaded the island. Even Theodoros Makridakis no longer had the will to make trouble. He liked a good debate in the bar but had long since given up the idea of taking over the position of ultimate authority. Nikos Papadimitriou did the job far too well.

Maria and Fotini were engaged in a pattern of daily tasks that took them through the next few years like a dance, with an endlessly repeated sequence of steps. With three sons, Savina Angelopoulos needed the help of her fit and capable daughter to keep the men in the house fed and looked after, so Fotini, like Maria, had domestic duties that tied her to Plaka.

Even if Eleni might have wished for better things for her daughter than remaining in the village, she would not have wished for a more conscientious child than Maria. There was no question in the girl's mind that she should be doing anything other than looking after her father, even if she had once entertained fantasies of standing, chalk in hand, at the front of a class, as her mother had done. Like the printed pattern on their old curtains, all such aspirations had long since faded.

The two girls shared the joys and the limitations of this existence for several years, and in all the time they performed their duties it did not occur to them that they had any real cause for complaint. There was water to fetch from the village pump, wood to be collected for their ovens, sweeping, spinning, cooking and the beating of rugs. Maria would regularly collect honey from her hives on the thyme-covered hillside overlooking Plaka; it yielded such intense sweetness that for several years she had no need to buy even one gram of sugar. In the courtyards at the back of their homes old olive oil cans overflowed with basil and mint and *pithoi*, huge urns once used to store water and oil, provided a perfect home for carefully tended geraniums and lilies, when they became cracked and no longer of practical use.

The girls were heiresses to a millennium of secretly evolved folklore and were now considered old enough to be taught the crafts and skills that had been handed down through generations without written record. Fotini's grandmother was a great source of such lore and showed them how to dye wool with extracts of iris, hibiscus and chrysanthemum petals, and how to weave coloured grasses into elaborate baskets and mats. Other women passed on to them their knowledge of the magical benefits of locally grown herbs, and they would walk far into the mountains to find wild sage, cistus and camomile for their healing powers. On a good day they would return with a basket of the most precious herb of all, *origanum dictamus*, which was said to heal wounds as well as cure sore throats and stomach problems. Maria would always have the right potion to minister to her father if he was sick, and soon her reputation for mixing useful remedies spread round the village.

While they were on their long walks into the mountains they would also gather *horta*, the iron-rich mountain greens that were a staple part of every diet. The childhood games they had played on the beach when they fashioned pies out of sand were now replaced by the more adult pastime of making them out of pastry and herbs.

One of Maria's most important jobs between late autumn and early spring was to keep the home fire burning. It not only provided the warmth which kept them sane while winter winds howled outside; it also kept the spirit of the house alive. The *spiti* – the Greeks used the same word for both 'house' and 'home' – was a divine symbol of unity, and theirs, more than most, needed constant nurturing.

However onerous Maria's domestic tasks might have seemed to anyone living in a city – or indeed to Anna, who now lived in some luxury – there was always time for chatter and intrigue. Fotini's house was a focal point for this. Since idleness was considered a sin, the serious business of gossip was conducted in the innocent context of sewing and embroidery. This not only kept the girls' hands busy but also gave them the opportunity to prepare for the future. Every pillowcase, cushion, tablecloth and runner in the house of a married woman had been woven or embroidered by herself, her mother or her mother's mother. Anna had been an exception. Over the few years she had sat in a sewing circle with women older and wiser than herself, she had completed just one small corner of a pillowcase. It had been symptomatic of her continuous state of rebellion. Her stubbornness was subtle. While the other girls and women sat talking and sewing, her fingers remained idle. She would wave her needle around, gesticulating and making patterns in the air with her thread, but rarely pricked the cloth. It was just as well that she had married into a family where everything was provided.

At certain times of year, the girls turned their hands to the seasonal tasks which demanded they should be outside. They would join the fray at grape harvest and would be the first into the troughs to tread the copiously juicy fruit. Then, just before autumn turned to winter, they would be among the crowd who would beat the olive trees to make the fruit cascade down into the open baskets below. Such days were full of laughter and flirtation, and the completion of these communal tasks would be marked with dancing and merrymaking.

One by one, members of this carefree but duty-laden coterie of young women moved out of the group. They found husbands, or, as was more generally the case, husbands were found for them. On the whole they were other young men from Plaka or one of the neighbouring villages such as Vrouhas or Selles. Their parents had usually known each other for years and had sometimes planned the match between their offspring before they could even count or write their own names. When Fotini announced her own engagement Maria saw her world coming to an end. She displayed only pleasure and delight, however, quietly castigating herself for her feelings of envy as she anticipated the rest of her life spent on doorsteps with the widowed crones, crocheting lace as the sun went down.

Fotini, like Maria, was now twenty-two years old. Her father had supplied the fish taverna on the seafront for many years, and the owner, Stavros Davaras, was a good friend, as well as being a reliable customer. His son, Stephanos, was already working for his father and one day would take over the business, which had a gentle flow of customers on weekdays and a torrent of them on saints' days and Sundays. Pavlos Angelopoulous regarded Stephanos as a good match for his daughter, and the already established mutual dependence of the families was considered a desirable grounding for the marriage. The pair had known each other since childhood and were confident that they could develop feelings for each other which would add sparkle to what was, after all, just an arrangement. A modest dowry was negotiated, and once the engagement had run its usual course, the wedding took place.

The great consolation for Maria was that Fotini would be living no further away from her now than she had been before. Although Fotini now had different, more onerous duties – working in the taverna as well as running the home and negotiating the minefield of living with her in-laws – the women would still see each other every day.

Determined not to betray her dismay at finding herself the last of a diminishing group, Maria threw herself more enthusiastically than ever into her filial duties, accompanying her father with increasing frequency on his trips to Spinalonga and ensuring that their home was always immaculately tidy. For a young woman it was far from fulfilling. Her devotion to Giorgis was admired in the village, but at the same time her lack of a husband reduced her status. Spinsterhood was perceived as a curse, and to be left on the shelf was daily public humiliation in a village like Plaka. If she got any older without finding a fiancé, respect for her dutiful behaviour could quickly turn to scorn. The problem now was that there were few eligible men in Plaka, and Maria would not consider a man from another village. It was unthinkable that Giorgis should uproot himself from Plaka and therefore unimaginable that Maria would ever move either. There was, she reflected, as much chance of marriage as there was of seeing her beloved mother walk through the door.

Chapter Twelve

1951

Anna was now four years married and thriving on her new status. She loved Andreas dutifully, and willingly responded to his passion for her. To everyone around her, Anna seemed a faultless wife. She was aware, however, that the family was awaiting the announcement of a pregnancy. The lack of a baby did not bother her at all. There would be plenty of time for children and she was enjoying this carefree time far too much to want to lose it to motherhood. Eleftheria had broached the subject one day when they were discussing the decor for one of the spare bedrooms in Neapoli.

'This used to be the nursery,' she said, 'when our girls were little. What colour would you like to paint it?'

Eleftheria thought she was providing the perfect opportunity for her daughter-in-law to say something about her plans and aspirations for becoming a mother, and was disappointed when Anna professed a liking for pale green. 'It'll complement the fabric I've ordered to cover the furniture,' she said.

Anna and Andreas, along with his parents, lived for some

of the time during the summer months in the family's grand neoclassical villa in Neapoli, which Anna had now extensively refurbished. Eleftheria considered its fine drapes and fragile furniture very impractical, but it appeared she could not stand in this young woman's way. In September the family started to move back to the main house in Elounda, which Anna was also gradually transforming to her own taste in spite of her father-in-law's penchant for the sombre style favoured by his generation. She often had herself taken into Agios Nikolaos to shop, and one day in late autumn she arrived back from one of these trips to see her upholsterer and check up on the progress of her latest pair of curtains. She rushed into the kitchen and planted a kiss on the back of the head of the figure seated at the table.

'Hello, darling,' she said. 'How was the press today?'

It had been the first day of olive pressing, a significant date in the calendar, when the press was used for the first time in many months and it was always touch and go whether the machinery would perform. There were thousands of litres of oil to be extracted from the countless baskets of olives that sat waiting to be crushed and it was crucial that everything went smoothly. The golden liquid that poured from press to *pithoi* was the basis of the family's wealth and, as Anna saw it, each jar was another metre of fabric, another tailored dress to be hand-fitted to her curves, with tucks and darts that moulded the garment around her body. These clothes, more than anything, illustrated her separation from the village women, whose shapeless gathered skirts were no different now from those that their grandmothers had worn a hundred years before. Today, to keep the biting November winds at bay, Anna wore an emerald-green coat which hugged her breasts and hips like an embrace before falling away almost to the ground in extravagant swirls of fabric. A fur collar rose up her neck to warm her ears and stroke her cheeks.

As she walked across the room, the silk lining of her coat rustling against her legs, she chattered about the minutiae of her day. She was putting water on to prepare herself some coffee when the man at the table rose from his chair. Anna turned round and let out a scream of surprise.

'Who are *you*?' she asked in a strangulated voice. 'I . . . I thought you were my husband.'

'So I gathered.' The man smiled, clearly amused by her confusion.

As the two stood face to face, Anna saw that the man she had greeted so affectionately, though clearly *not* her husband, was in every way very like him. The breadth of his shoulders, his hair and, now that he was standing, even his height seemed to match Andreas's exactly. The strong and distinctive Vandoulakis nose was the same and the slightly slanted eyes bore an uncanny resemblance. When he spoke, Anna's mouth went dry. What trick was this?

'I'm Manoli Vandoulakis,' he said, holding out his hand. 'You must be Anna.'

Anna knew of the existence of a cousin and had heard Manoli's name mentioned a few times in conversation, but little more than that. She had never pictured him as this carbon copy of her husband.

'Manoli.' She repeated the name. It was pleasing. Now she needed to regain control of the situation, feeling foolish that she had made such a mistake and carelessly embraced a total stranger. 'Does Andreas know you're here?' she asked.

'No, I arrived an hour ago and decided to give everyone a surprise. It certainly worked with you! You look as though you've seen a ghost.'

'I feel as though I have,' answered Anna. 'The similarity between the two of you is uncanny.'

'I haven't seen Andreas for ten years, but we were very alike. People were always mistaking us for twins.'

Anna could see that, but she could also see many other things that actually made this version of her husband very different from the original. Though Manoli had the same broad shoulders as Andreas, he was actually thinner and she could see his bony shoulder blades protruding under his shirt. He had laughter in his eyes and deep lines around them. He thought it was a terrific joke that she had mistaken him for his cousin and she realised quite quickly that he had set the moment up. Life was there to be enjoyed, you could see it in his smile.

At that moment, Andreas and his father returned and there were exclamations of delight and amazement when they saw Manoli standing there. Soon the three men were sitting round a bottle of raki and Anna excused herself to make arrangements for dinner. When Eleftheria arrived an hour or so later, a second bottle of raki was already drained and both she and Manoli wept tears of joy as they embraced. Letters were immediately sent off to Andreas's sisters, and the following Sunday a great reunion party was held to mark Manoli's return after his decade of absence.

Manoli Vandoulakis was a free-spirited youth who had spent

the past ten years, largely on mainland Greece, squandering a sizeable inheritance. His mother had died in childbirth and his father had passed away five years later at the age of thirty, of a heart attack. Manoli had grown up hearing dark murmurings of how his father had died of a broken heart and whether or not this was true, it made him resolve to live as though each day might be his last. It was a philosophy that made perfect sense to him, and even his uncle Alexandros, who since the death of Yiannis Vandoulakis had been his guardian, could not stop him. As a child Manoli had noticed that everyone around him carried out a relentless round of tasks and duties, apparently only enjoying themselves when they were given permission on saints' days and Sundays. He wanted pleasure every day of his life.

Though the memory of his parents dimmed by the day, he was often told that they had lived good and dutiful lives. But what real good had their exemplary behaviour done them? It had not kept death away, had it? Fate had snatched them like an eagle plucking its defenceless prey from a bare rock face. To hell with it, he thought; if destiny could not be outwitted, he might as well see what else life had to offer him other than a few decades of living on a Cretan hillside before burial beneath it.

Ten years earlier, he had left home. Apart from the occasional letter to his aunt and uncle – some from Italy, some from Yugoslavia, but mostly from Athens – to reassure them that he was still alive, he had had little contact with his family. Alexandros was aware that if his older brother Yiannis had not died so young, it would be Manoli who would now be in line to inherit the Vandoulakis estate, rather than his own son. But such thoughts were hypothetical. Instead of the promise of land, when he had reached the age of eighteen Manoli had come into a small cash fortune. It was this money that he had largely squandered in Rome, Belgrade and Athens.

'The high life had a high price,' he confided to Andreas soon after his return. 'The best women were like good wine, expensive but worth every drachma.' Now, however, the women of Europe had cleaned him out of everything he owned and all he had left were the coins in his pocket and a promise from his uncle that he would employ him on the estate.

His return caused a great stir, not just with his uncle and aunt, but also with Andreas himself. With only six months' difference between them, the two were virtually twins. As children they had almost known each other's thoughts and felt each other's pain, but after their eighteenth birthdays their lives had taken such divergent paths that it was hard to imagine how things would be now that Manoli was back.

It was, however, timely. Alexandros Vandoulakis was due to retire the following year, and Andreas could really do with a helping hand in managing the estate. They all felt it would be better for Manoli to take on the role than for them to employ an outsider, and even if Alexandros had some doubts about whether his nephew would really buckle down to it, he would put those doubts aside. Manoli was family, after all.

For several months, Manoli lived in the house on the Elounda estate. There were plenty of rooms that were never used so his presence inconvenienced no one, but in December Alexandros provided him with a house of his own. Manoli had enjoyed this taste of family life and being part of the dynasty from which he had chosen for ten years to absent himself, but his uncle expected him to get married in the future and for this purpose insisted that he should live in his own home.

'You'll be lucky to find a girl who's prepared to live in a house where there are already two mistresses,' he said to his nephew. 'A third woman in a house is asking for trouble.'

Manoli's house had belonged to the estate manager in the days when Alexandros had paid an outsider to perform the role. It was set at the end of a short driveway a kilometre from the main house, and with its four bedrooms and large drawing room was considered a substantial home for a bachelor. Manoli, however, continued to be a regular visitor at the main house. He wanted to be fed and pampered, just like Alexandros and Andreas, and here were two women to do just that for him. Everyone loved his lively conversation and welcomed him there, but Alexandros always insisted that eventually he should go home.

Manoli had lived his life in a state of impermanence, flitting like a butterfly from one place to the next. And wherever he went he left a trail of broken promises. Even as a child, he had stretched things to the limit. Just for a dare, he once held his hand in a flame until the skin began to melt and another time he jumped off the highest rock on the Elounda coast, scraping his back so badly the sea around him turned scarlet. In the foreign capitals of Europe he would gamble until he was down to his shirt and then make a spectacular comeback. It was just the way he was. In spite of himself he found he was playing the same game in Elounda, but the difference here was that he was now obliged to stay.

He could no longer afford to fly away, even if he had wanted to.

To Alexandros's surprise, Manoli worked quite hard, though he did not have the same commitment as his cousin. Andreas would always take his lunch to the fields to save the time it took to return home, but Manoli preferred to get away from the harsh sunshine just for a few hours and had taken to coming in to eat his lunch at the spacious table in the Vandoulakis kitchen. Anna had no objection. She welcomed his presence in the house.

Their interaction was not so much conversation as flirtation. Manoli made her laugh, sometimes until tears streamed down her face, and her appreciation of his teasing humour and the way the enlarged pupils of her eyes sparkled when she held his gaze were enough to keep him from the olive groves well into the afternoon.

Sometimes Eleftheria was there rather than in Neapoli and feared that her nephew was not really pulling his weight on the estate. 'Men shouldn't hang around the house in the day,' she once remarked to Anna. 'It's a woman's territory. Theirs is outside.'

Anna chose to ignore her mother-in-law's disapproving comment and welcomed Manoli more effusively than ever. In her view, the closeness of the kinship between them sanctioned their friendship. It was the custom that a woman enjoyed much greater freedom once married than she had been allowed as a single woman, so at first no one questioned Anna's liberty to spend an hour a day, sometimes even more, with her 'cousin'. But a few people began to notice the frequency of Manoli's visits, and tongues started to wag.

One lunchtime that spring, Manoli had lingered even longer than usual. Anna sensed his recklessness and for once shuddered at the danger she was putting herself in. Nowadays when he left he would hold on to her hand and kiss it in an absurdly histrionic way. She could have passed it off as a frivolous gesture, but the way in which he pressed his middle finger into the very centre of her palm and held it there made her shiver. More significantly, he touched her hair. It was dead matter, he said laughingly, and anyway she had started it, he teased, by kissing a total stranger . . . on the hair. And so it went on. He had picked some meadow flowers that day, and presented her with a bouquet of bright, if wilting, poppies. It was a romantic gesture and she was charmed, especially when he pulled one from the bunch and carefully placed it in the front of her blouse. His touch was subtle and there was a moment when she was not entirely certain whether the contact of his rough hand with her smooth skin was accidental, or whether he had, very deliberately, brushed her breast with his fingers. A moment later, when she felt his gentle touch on her neck, the doubt was gone.

Anna was an impetuous enough woman, but something held her back. My God, she thought, this is the threshold of insanity. What am I doing? She pictured herself standing in this huge kitchen almost nose to nose with a man who, though he looked so very like him, was not her husband. She saw the situation as it would appear to someone looking in through the open window, and however hard she tried to convince herself, she knew it would not seem ambiguous. She was one second away from being kissed. She still had a choice.

Her marriage to Andreas lacked nothing. He was warm,

adoring and gave her free rein to make changes in their homes when she wished; she even got on tolerably well with her in-laws. They had, however, quickly settled into a pattern, as happened in such marriages, and life had a predictability that made it unlikely that the next half-century would hold any real surprises. After all the anticipation and excitement at starting a new life, Anna was discovering that it could be just as dull as her old one. What it lacked was the thrill of the clandestine, the frisson of the illicit. Whether such things were worth risking everything for, she did not quite know.

I ought to stop this, she thought. Otherwise I could lose everything. She addressed Manoli with her usual haughtiness. It was their game, how she always talked to him. While he was extravagantly flirtatious, she treated him as her inferior.

'Look, young man,' she said. 'As you know, I'm spoken for. You can take your flowers elsewhere.'

'Can I indeed?' Manoli answered. 'And exactly where shall I take them?'

'Well, my sister isn't yet spoken for. You could take them to her.' As if the true Anna was somewhere very distant, she heard a voice saying: 'I shall invite her to lunch next Sunday. You'll like her.'

The following Sunday was the feast of Agios Giorgis, so it was a perfect excuse for inviting Maria and her father to visit. It was a duty rather than a particular pleasure to see them both; she felt she had nothing in common with her tedious little sister and little to say to her father. For the rest of that week Anna dreamed of Manoli's lingering touch and looked forward to the next time they could be alone, but before that happened, she mused, the dull family luncheon had to take place.

There were still shortages of many kinds of food in Crete at that time, but these never seemed to affect the Vandoulakis household, especially on a saint's day, when it was conveniently considered a religious duty to feast. Giorgis was delighted to receive the invitation.

'Maria, look! Anna has invited us to lunch.'

'That's kind of her ladyship,' said Maria with uncharacteristic sarcasm. 'When?'

'On Sunday. In two days' time.'

Maria was secretly pleased that they had been invited. She yearned to strengthen the bond with her sister, knowing that this would have been what their mother wanted, but nevertheless she felt some trepidation as the day approached. Giorgis, however, who was finally emerging from his long state of grief, was happy at the prospect of seeing his elder daughter.

Anna cringed as she heard the spluttering sound of her father's newly acquired truck in the driveway and with little enthusiasm made her way slowly down the big staircase to greet them. Manoli, who had already arrived, had got to the front door well before her and thrown it open.

Maria was not at all what he had expected. She had the biggest brown eyes he had ever seen and they looked at him with wide-eyed surprise.

'I'm Manoli,' he said, striding towards her with outstretched hand, adding: 'Andreas's cousin.'

So negligent was Anna in her correspondence that Maria and Giorgis had known nothing of the arrival of the long-lost relative.

Manoli was always in his element with a pretty girl, but never more so than with one like this, who added innocence to such sweet beauty. He took in every detail: a slim waist, a neat bosom and muscular arms built up by years of hard physical work. She was at once fragile and strong.

At one o'clock they all sat down to eat. With Alexandros, Eleftheria, their two daughters and their respective families, there were at least a dozen. Chatter was noisy and animated.

Manoli had decided in advance that he would flirt with Anna's younger sister. A practised lothario such as he was did so out of habit. What he had not expected was that Maria would be so pretty and so eminently easy to tease. Throughout lunch he dominated her with his playful talk, and although she was unused to such flippancy, she parried his witty remarks. Her unaffected personality made her so different from most of the women he was used to meeting that he eventually found himself toning down his banter and asking her questions about herself. He discovered that she knew about mountain herbs and their healing powers, and they talked earnestly about their place in a world where the boundaries of science were being pushed forward by the day. Maria and Anna were as unalike as a raw pearl and a polished diamond. One had natural lustre and its own unique, irregular shape. The other had been cut and polished to achieve its glittering beauty. Manoli loved both such jewels, and this soft, gentle-eyed girl who was so clearly devoted to her father appealed strongly to him. She was without artifice and had a naïvety that he found unexpectedly alluring.

Anna watched as Manoli drew Maria into his magnetic field, telling her stories and making her laugh. She saw her sister melt in his warmth. Before the meal was over, Anna realised what she had done. She had given Manoli away, handed him like a gift-wrapped parcel to her sister, and now she wanted him back.

Chapter Thirteen

FOR THE NEXT week, Manoli was vexed. This was unusual for him. How could he pursue Maria? She was quite unlike most of the women he had met on his travels. Besides which, the accepted patterns and modes of behaviour between men and women in Plaka were very different from those governing such relationships in the cities where he had lived. Here in rural Crete, every move, every word was subject to scrutiny. He had been perfectly aware of this when he had visited Anna on all those occasions, and though he had always been careful to ensure that certain boundaries were never crossed, he had known that he was playing with fire. In Anna he had seen a bored, isolated woman who had separated herself from the village where she had grown up and achieved her ambition of being in a position where other people were paid to do those tasks which would otherwise have kept her busy and occupied. She had improved her position, but now floated in a friendless social vacuum, one in which Manoli had been happy to entertain her. A woman with eyes that so hungrily sought his and lips that spread themselves into such a generous smile: it would have been rude to ignore her.

Maria was quite different. Not only did she lack her sister's ambition to marry outside the village, she seemed without desire to marry at all. She lived in a small house with her widowed father, apparently content and yet so exceptionally marriageable. Manoli would not have admitted it to himself, but it was largely her lack of interest that attracted him. He had all the time in the world, though, and would be patient, certain that sooner or later she would be won over. Confidence was not lacking in the Vandoulakis male. It rarely occurred to them that they would not get what they wanted. Manoli had much on his side. Perhaps the most important factor was that Fotini had protected Maria from the gossip about Manoli and Anna. The source of the endlessly flowing fountain of stories was Fotini's brother Antonis. It was more than five years since that kiss which had meant nothing to Anna and far too much to Antonis, but the sense of having been cast aside still rankled. He despised Anna and had watched with malicious satisfaction the comings and goings of her husband's cousin, which had increased in regularity now that Eleftheria and Alexandros Vandoulakis were spending more time in Neapoli and less in Elounda. Antonis gave reports to Fotini whenever he called in for supper at the waterfront taverna which was now her home.

'He was there for at least two hours one lunchtime last week.' he gloated.

'I don't want to hear your stories,' Fotini said brusquely to Antonis as she poured him a raki. 'And above all, I don't want Maria to hear them either.'

'Why not? Her sister is a tart. Don't you think she knows that already?' snapped Antonis.

'Of course she doesn't know that. And nor do you. So

what if her husband's cousin comes to visit her? He's family, why shouldn't he?'

'Just the occasional visit would be one thing, but not virtually every day. Even family don't bother to visit each other that often.'

'Well, whatever you think, Maria mustn't know – and nor must Giorgis. He has suffered quite enough. Seeing Anna married to a wealthy man was the best thing that could have happened to him – so you're to keep your mouth shut. I mean it, Antonis.'

Fotini did mean it. She slammed the bottle down on the table in front of her brother and glared at him. She was as protective of Giorgis and Maria Petrakis as she would have been of her own flesh and blood, and wanted to keep these vicious and damaging rumours from them. Part of her could not believe them in any case. Why would Anna, whose whole life had turned around the night she met Andreas, risk throwing it all away? The very thought of it was baffling, ridiculous even, and besides, she held out hope that Manoli, the subject of Antonis's scurrilous rumour-mongering, might one day notice Maria. Since the lunch on the feast of Agios Giorgis, Maria had chatted incessantly about Andreas's cousin, repeating every detail of their encounter at the Vandoulakis house.

Manoli had been seen a few times in the village. With his connection to Giorgis he had found a warm welcome among the men of Plaka and soon became a regular fixture at the bar; he was found there as often as anyone, playing backgammon, passing around strong cigarettes and discussing the politics of the island beneath a thick pall of smoke. Even in this small village on a road that led only to even smaller villages, the pressing issues of world politics were high on the agenda. In spite of their remoteness from them, events on mainland Greece regularly aroused both passion and fury.

'The Communists are to blame!' exclaimed Lidaki, banging his fist on the top of the bar.

'How can you say that?' answered another voice. 'If it wasn't for the monarchy, the mainland wouldn't be in half the mess it is,' and so they went on, sometimes into the small hours. 'Two Greeks, one argument', the saying went, and here, on most nights of the week, there were twenty or more villagers and as many arguments as there were olives in a jar.

Manoli had a broader world view than others in the bar – many had been no further than Iraklion and most had never got as far as Hania – and he brought a new perspective to argument and conversation. Though he was careful not to brag of the casual conquests that had been a recurring theme of his travels, he entertained them all with stories of Italians, Yugoslavians and their brothers on mainland Greece. His was a light touch and everyone liked him, enjoying the gaiety that he brought to the bar. Whenever there was a pause in the argument Manoli would have an anecdote or two to tell and the assembled company were happy to indulge him. His tales of the old Turkish quarter in Athens, the Spanish Steps in Rome and the bars of Belgrade were mesmerising and while he spoke there was silence, except for the occasional clack of worry beads. He did not need to embroider the facts to entertain. The stories of his brief imprisonment, being adrift on a ship in the middle of the Mediterranean, and fighting a duel in the back streets of a Yugoslavian port were all true enough. They were the tales of a man who had travelled without responsibilities and initially without cares. They showed him to be a wild but not uncaring man, but as he spoke, Manoli was conscious that he did not wish to be perceived as an unsuitable match for Giorgis's daughter and accordingly toned down his stories.

Even Antonis, who had ceased to skulk in the corner whenever his boss's rakish cousin appeared, now greeted him warmly. Music was their common bond, plus the fact that they had both spent a few years away from this province; though decades younger than the grizzled men they drank with, they were in some ways more worldly-wise than their elders would ever be. As a child, Manoli had learned to play the lyre and during his travelling years it had been both a companion and his security, at one point the only thing that stood between him and starvation. Often he had found himself singing and playing for his supper, and his lyre was the only possession of any value that he had not gambled away. This precious instrument now hung on the wall behind the bar, and when the raki was low in the bottle he would remove it from its hook and play, the bow sending the sound of its vibrating strings shuddering through the night air.

Likewise, Antonis's wooden flute, his *thiaboli*, had been his constant companion during his years away from home. Its mellow sounds had filled a hundred different caves and shepherds' huts, the notes soothing the hearts and souls of his companions and, more prosaically, helping them while away all those hours they had spent watching and waiting. As different as Manoli and Antonis were, music was a neutral space where wealth and hierarchy played no part. The two of them would play in the bar for an hour or so, their haunting melodies casting a spell over their audience and over those whose open windows captured the escaping sounds as they drifted through the stillness.

Though everyone was aware of the great wealth that Manoli's parents had enjoyed and of the fortune that he himself had frittered away, most of the villagers now accepted him as someone just like themselves, who needed to work hard for a living and who, quite naturally, aspired to having a wife and a family. For Manoli, the simplicity of this more settled life had its own rewards. Even without the possibility of seeing Maria, which had been his original motivation in visiting Plaka, he found much in this village to love. The bonds between childhood friends, the loyalty to family and a way of life that had not needed to change for centuries, all had great appeal. If he could secure a woman like Maria, or perhaps even one of the other village beauties, it would complete his sense of belonging. Apart from saints' day celebrations in the village, however, there were few legitimate occasions for him to meet her.

The formalities still observed in villages like Plaka drove him mad. Though he found the enduring traditions part of the attraction, the obscurity of the courting rituals he found nothing less than ridiculous. He knew he could not mention his intentions to Anna, and anyway, he was not visiting her so much now. It was a pattern he knew he needed to break if he wanted to achieve his planned conquest of Maria. Anna had been predictably brittle with him when he last visited.

'Well, thanks for coming to see me,' she said tartly.

'Look,' said Manoli, 'I don't think I should come at

lunchtime any more. People are beginning to mutter about me not pulling my weight.'

'Suit yourself,' she snapped, her eyes full of angry tears. 'You've obviously finished your little game with me. I assume you're now playing it with someone else.'

With that she marched out of the room, and the door slammed behind her like a thunderclap.

Manoli would miss their intimacy and the sparkle in Anna's eyes, but it was a price he was prepared to pay.

Since there was no one at home preparing him meals, Manoli often ate in one of the tavernas in Elounda or in Plaka. Each Friday he went to Fotini's taverna, which she and Stephanos had now taken over from his parents. One visit in July, he sat there looking out to sea towards Spinalonga. The island, shaped like a large, half-submerged egg, had become so familiar to him that he scarcely gave it a second thought. Like everyone else, he occasionally wondered what it must be like over there, but he did not dwell on such thoughts for long. Spinalonga was simply there, a lump of rock inhabited by lepers.

A plate of tiny *picarel* fish sat on the table in front of Manoli, and as he stabbed each one with his fork, his eye was caught by something. In the dusky half-light a little boat was chugging its way from the island, creating a broad triangular wake as it cut through the dense water. Two people were in it, and as the boat came into the harbour, he saw that one of them looked very like Maria.

'Stephanos!' he called. 'Is that Maria with Giorgis? You don't usually see a woman out fishing, do you?'

'They haven't been fishing,' replied Stephanos. 'They've

been making one of their deliveries to the leper colony.'

'Oh,' said Manoli, chewing slowly and thoughtfully. 'I suppose someone has to.'

'Giorgis has been doing it for years. It's better money than fishing – and more guaranteed,' said Stephanos, putting a plate of fried potatoes down on Manoli's table. 'But he mostly does it for—'

Fotini, who had been hovering in the background, saw where this conversation might lead. Even if he did not intend to, she knew that Stephanos was likely to forget Giorgis's desire to keep the facts of Eleni's tragic death from leprosy a secret from the Vandoulakis family.

'Here you are, Manoli!' She dived forward with a plate of sliced aubergines. 'These are freshly cooked. With garlic. I hope you like them. Would you excuse us a moment?'

She grabbed her husband's arm and led him back to the kitchen.

'You must be careful!' she exclaimed. 'We *all* have to forget that Anna and Maria's mother was ever on Spinalonga. It's the only way. We know it's nothing for them to be ashamed of, but Alexandros Vandoulakis might not see it that way.'

Stephanos was shamefaced.

'I know, I know. It slips my mind sometimes, that's all. It was really stupid of me,' he muttered. 'Manoli comes in here so often, I forget that he's connected with Anna.'

'It's not just Anna's position I'm thinking of,' admitted Fotini. 'Maria has feelings for Manoli. They met only once, up at Anna's house, but she hasn't stopped talking about him, at least not to me.'

'Really? That poor girl needs a husband, but he looks a

bit of a rogue to me,' replied Stephanos. 'I suppose there's not much choice around here, is there.'

Stephanos only saw things in black and white. He understood what his wife was getting at and realised that he and Fotini had a role to play in bringing these two together.

It was precisely a week later that the opportunity to engineer a meeting between Maria and Manoli presented itself. When Manoli appeared that Friday, Fotini slipped out of a side door and ran to the Petrakis house. Giorgis had eaten and gone to the bar to play backgammon and Maria now sat in the fading light, straining to read.

'Maria, he's there,' Fotini said breathlessly. 'Manoli is at the taverna. Why don't you come down and see him.'

'I can't,' said Maria. 'What would my father think?'

'For heaven's sake,' replied Fotini. 'You're twenty-three. Be bold. Your father needn't even know.'

She grabbed her friend by the arm. Maria resisted, but only feebly; in her heart she yearned to go.

'What do I say to him?' she asked anxiously.

'Don't worry,' Fotini reassured her. 'Men like Manoli never allow that to be your concern, at least not for long. He'll have plenty to say.'

Fotini was right. When they arrived at the taverna, Manoli was immediately in charge of the situation. He did not question why Maria was there, but invited her to join him at his table, asking her what she had been doing since they had last met, and how her father was. Then, more boldly than a man normally did in these situations, he said, 'There's a new cinema opened in Agios Nikolaos. Would you come there with me?'

Maria, already flushed from the excitement of seeing Manoli

again, blushed even more deeply. She looked down into her lap and could hardly reply.

'That would be very nice,' she said eventually. 'But it's not really the done thing around here . . . going to the cinema with someone you hardly know.'

'I tell you what, I shall ask Fotini and Stephanos to come as well. They can act as chaperones. Let's go on Monday. That's the day the taverna shuts, isn't it?'

So before she knew it and had had time to be anxious and think of all the reasons against it, the date was agreed. In a mere three days from now they would all go to Agios Nikolaos.

Manoli's manners were impeccable and their outings became a weekly event. Each Monday, the four of them would set off at about seven in the evening to spend an evening watching the latest movie, followed by supper.

Giorgis was delighted to see his daughter being wooed by this handsome and charming man, someone he had liked for many months even before his daughter had got to know him. Though it was a very modern approach – all this going out before there was any kind of formal agreement – they were, after all, moving into a more modern era, and the fact that Maria had an escort helped to contain the mutterings of disapproval from the older ladies of the village.

The four of them enjoyed each other's company and the trips out of Plaka changed the texture and pattern of their otherwise routine lives. Laughter characterised their times together, and they were often bent double with amusement at Manoli's jokes and antics. Maria began to allow herself the luxury of a daydream and to imagine that she could spend the rest of her days looking at this handsome, lined face, aged by life and laughter. Sometimes when he looked straight into her eyes she felt the invisible hairs on her neck stand on end and the palms of her hands dampen. Even on a warm evening she would feel herself shudder involuntarily. It was a new experience to be so flattered and teased. What light relief Manoli was from the colourless backdrop of the rest of her life! There were moments when she wondered if he was actually capable of taking anything seriously. The bubbles of his effervescence spread to everyone around him. Maria had never enjoyed such carefree happiness and began to think this euphoria was love.

Always weighing on her conscience, however, was what would become of her father if she should marry. With most marriage arrangements, the girl left her own family and moved in with her new husband's parents. Clearly that would not happen with Manoli since he had no parents, but equally impossible was the idea that he might move into their small Plaka home. With his background, it was inconceivable. The problem went round and round in her mind, and not once did it seem absurd that Manoli had not yet even kissed her.

Manoli was on his best behaviour and had long since decided that the only way he would win Maria was by conducting himself faultlessly. How absurd it sometimes seemed to him that in another country he might have taken a girl to bed when they had scarcely exchanged names, and yet here he had spent many dozens of hours with Maria and had not yet touched her. His desire for her was intense but the waiting had a delicious novelty. He was sure his patience would be rewarded and the wait only made him want her all the more. In the early months of this courtship, when he gazed at her pale oval face framed by its halo of dark plaited hair, she would look down bashfully, afraid to meet his eye. As time went on, however, he watched her grow bolder and stare back. If he had looked closely, he would have had the satisfaction of seeing a quickening pulse on her pretty neck before her fine features broke into a smile. If he took this virgin now he knew he would be obliged to leave Plaka. Though he had deflowered dozens of girls in his past, even he could not disgrace the lovely Maria and, more importantly, a voice inside urged him to hold back. It was time to settle down.

From a distance, Anna smouldered with envy and resentment. Manoli had hardly been to visit her since Giorgis and Maria had come for lunch, and on some occasions when there were family gatherings he had stayed away. How *dare* he treat her that way? Soon she learned from her father that Manoli was wooing Maria. Was this just to provoke her? If only she could show him that she really did not care. There was no such opportunity, however, and therefore no such catharsis. She desperately tried not to think about them together, and irritably threw herself into increasingly extravagant projects about the home to distract herself. All the while she knew that in Plaka events were inexorably unfolding, but there was no one in whom she could confide, and the fury built up inside her like steam in a pressure cooker.

Andreas, dismayed by her strange mood, repeatedly asked her what was wrong and was told not to bother her. He gave up. He had sensed for a while that the halcyon days of early marriage, with its loving looks and kind words, were over, and he now busied himself more and more on the estate. Eleftheria noticed the change too. Anna had seemed so happy and vivacious just a few months before and now she seemed permanently angry. For Anna, concealing her emotions like this was the antithesis of everything that came naturally to her. She wanted to scream, shout, yank her hair in handfuls from its roots, but when her father and Maria visited her from time to time, Manoli was not even mentioned.

By some instinct, Maria felt that her friendship with Manoli might have strayed into her sister's territory and that perhaps she regarded the Vandoulakis family as her own domain. Why make things worse by talking about it? She had no idea of the scale of Anna's anguish and assumed that her air of vagueness was something to do with the fact that she had so far failed to conceive a child.

One February evening, six months after the weekly nights out had begun, Manoli went to find Giorgis in the bar. The old man was sitting alone, reading the local newspaper. He looked up as Manoli approached, a plume of smoke curling above his head.

'Giorgis, may I sit down?' Manoli asked politely.

'Yes,' Giorgis replied, returning to the paper. 'I don't own the place, do I?'

'There's something I want to ask you. I'll get to the point. I would like to marry your daughter. Will you agree to it?'

Giorgis folded the newspaper carefully and placed it on the table. To Manoli it seemed an age before he spoke.

'Agree to it? Of course I'll agree to it! You've been courting the most beautiful girl in the village for over half a year – and I thought you might never ask. It's about time!'

Giorgis's blustering response concealed his absolute joy at the request. Not just one, but now two of his daughters were to become part of the most powerful family in the province. There was no snobbery at the heart of his sentiment, just sheer relief and pleasure that both their futures were now secure. It was the best a father could possibly hope for on behalf of his children, especially a father who was a mere fisherman. Behind Manoli's head he could see the twinkling lights of Spinalonga through the half-shuttered window of the bar. If only Eleni could share this moment.

He put out his hand to seize Manoli's, momentarily lost for words. His expression said enough.

'Thank you. I will look after her, but between us we will look after you too,' said Manoli, fully aware of the lonely situation Maria's marriage could put her father in.

'Hey! We need your best *tsikoudia*!' he called out to Lidaki. 'We have something to celebrate here. It's a miracle. I'm no longer an orphan!'

'What are you talking about?' said Lidaki, sauntering over with a bottle and two glasses, well used now to Manoli's verbal stunts.

'Giorgis has agreed to be my father-in-law. I am to marry Maria!'

There were a few others in the bar that evening, and even before the girl in question knew anything about it, the menfolk of the village were toasting her future with Manoli.

Later that night when Giorgis returned home, Maria was getting ready to retire to bed. As her father came in through the door, shutting it quickly to keep the February wind outside and the warmth of the fire in, she noticed an unfamiliar expression on his face. It was suffused with excitement and delight.

'Maria,' he said, reaching out to grab her by both arms,

'Manoli has asked for your hand in marriage.'

For a moment she bowed her head, pleasure and pain somehow mixed in equal measure. Her throat contracted.

'What answer did you give him?' she asked in a whisper.

'The one you would have wanted me to. Yes, of course!'

In all her life Maria had not felt this unfamiliar mingling of emotions. Her heart felt like a cauldron of ingredients that declined to blend. Her chest tightened with anxiety. What was this? Was happiness meant to feel so like nausea? Just as she could not imagine someone else's pain, Maria did not know what love felt like for anyone else. She was fairly certain she loved Manoli. With his charm and wit, it was not hard to do so. But her whole future with him? A host of worries began to gnaw at her. What would happen to her father? She voiced her anxieties immediately.

'It's wonderful, Father. It's really wonderful, but what about you? I can't leave you here alone.'

'Don't worry about me. I can stay here – I wouldn't want to move out of Plaka. There's still too much for me to do here.'

'What do you mean?' she asked, though she knew exactly what he meant.

'Spinalonga. The island still needs me – and as long as I'm fit to take my boat there I'll keep going. Dr Lapakis relies on me, and so do all the islanders.'

There were as many comings and goings to and from the leper colony as ever. Each month there were new arrivals and supplies to be delivered, as well as building materials for the government-funded refurbishment that was being carried out. Giorgis was an essential part of the whole operation. Maria understood his attachment to the island. They rarely spoke about it now, but it was accepted between them that this was his vocation and his way of maintaining a connection with Eleni.

Both father and daughter slept fitfully that night, and morning could not come too soon. That day, Giorgis was to take Maria to Manoli's house on the Vandoulakis estate. It was a Sunday, and Manoli was there to greet them on the doorstep. Maria had never even seen his house before, and it was now to become her home. It took her no time at all to calculate that it was four times the size of their house in Plaka and the thought of living there daunted her.

'Welcome,' Manoli said, warming her with a single word. 'Come in, both of you. Come out of the cold.'

It was indeed the coldest day they had yet had this year. A storm was brewing and the winds seemed to come from several directions, stirring up eddies of dead leaves and sending them spiralling around their ankles. Maria's first impression when they went into the house was of a lack of light and a general untidiness that she was unsurprised to find in a house that might have had a maid but did not have a mistress. Manoli took them into a reception room which was slightly tidier and more cared for, with its embroidered lace cloths and a few photographs on the walls.

'My aunt and uncle are due to arrive shortly,' he explained, almost nervously, and then to Maria he said: 'Your father has consented to my asking for your hand. Will you marry me?'

She paused a moment before answering. To both of them it seemed an age. He looked at her with pleading eyes, momentarily doubtful.

'Yes,' she said, finally.

'She says yes!' roared Manoli, suddenly regaining his confidence. He hugged her and kissed her hands and spun her round until she pleaded for mercy. There would always be surprises with Manoli, and his exuberance took her breath away. The man was a human *pentozali*.

'You're going to be my wife!' he said excitedly. 'My uncle and aunt are so looking forward to meeting you again, Maria. But before they get here we must talk about the important matter of you, Giorgis. Will you come and live with us here?'

Manoli had, typically, waded in. Asking Giorgis to live with them was the closest they could approximate to re-establishing a traditional pattern where parents were ultimately taken care of by their children. Manoli had not discussed the matter with Maria and was unaware of the sensitivities, though he knew that she would want to have her father close by.

'It's very kind of you. But I couldn't leave the village. Maria understands, don't you, Maria?' he said, appealing to his daughter.

'Of course I understand, Father. I don't mind, as long as you come to see us as often as you can – and anyway we'll be down in Plaka to see you most days.'

Giorgis knew Maria would be true to her word and that he could look forward to her visits without fear of disappointment. She would not be like Anna, whose letters and visits had virtually dried up now.

Manoli could not really understand his future father-in-law's attachment to his old house in the village, but he was not going to pursue the point. At that moment the sound of tyres could be heard on the stony track outside, and then car doors slamming shut. Alexandros and Eleftheria were at the door and Manoli ushered them in. Warm handshakes were exchanged. Although the Vandoulakis and Petrakis paths had not crossed for several months, they were pleased to see each other. Alexandros, as head of the family, had a duty to speak.

'Giorgis and Maria. It will be a pleasure, once again, to welcome you into our family. My brother and his wife, Manoli's dear late parents, would have felt as we do that Maria will make our nephew very happy.'

The words came from his heart and Maria flushed with embarrassment and pleasure. Alexandros and Eleftheria were as aware as they had been with Anna that there was no dowry attached to this bride, no more than a trousseau of embroidery and lace to soften the harsh lines of their nephew's spartan home. They would not dwell on this, however, since there was more to be gained than lost from having Manoli settled down and attached to a local girl. The match would fulfil their promise to Manoli's father to ensure his son's well-being. When the boy had disappeared to Europe, Alexandros had felt a terrible sense of failure. Everything he had promised Yiannis had been unfulfilled. Most of the time during that period of his absence Alexandros had not even known if his nephew was dead or alive, and rarely which country he was in, but once Manoli was married to Maria he would be anchored to Elounda, and would always be there to support Andreas in the management of the great Vandoulakis estate.

The five of them drank to each other's health.

'*Iassas!*' they chorused as glasses clashed together.

There was soon talk of when the wedding might take place.

'Let's get married next week,' said Manoli.

'Don't be ridiculous!' retorted Eleftheria with alarm. 'You don't realise how much goes into the preparation of a good wedding! It'll take at least six months.'

Naturally Manoli was joking, but he continued to tease.

'Surely we could do it sooner than that. Let's go and see the priest. Come on, let's go now and see if he'll marry us today!'

Part of him meant it. He was now as impatient as a tiger, eager for his prey. His mind raced forwards. Maria, beautiful, pale and firm, her hair strewn across a pillow, a shaft of moonlight cutting across the bed to illuminate a perfect body. Waiting for him. Six whole months. My God, how could he possibly wait that long?

'We must do everything as your parents would have wanted,' said Alexandros. 'Properly!' he added, fully aware of Manoli's impetuous side.

Manoli shot him a glance. He knew that his uncle thought he needed a firm hand, and he, though he had great affection for Alexandros, loved to play up to his anxieties about him.

'Of course we'll do everything properly,' he said, now with genuine sincerity. 'We'll do everything by the book. I promise.'

As soon as she could, Maria rushed to tell Fotini the news.

'There's just one thing that worries me,' she said. 'My father.'

'But we'll be around to keep an eye on him, and so will my parents,' Fotini reassured her. 'Come on, Maria. It's time for you to marry. Your father understands that, I know he does.'

Maria tried not to feel uneasy, but her concern for Giorgis always seemed to stand between her and a sense of absolute joy.

Chapter Fourteen

THE ENGAGEMENT BETWEEN Manoli and Maria was cemented with a party to which the whole of Plaka was invited. It took place just a month after Manoli's proposal. Both of them felt as if they had been blessed by good fortune. So many of Maria's childhood friends had been married off by their fathers to men they did not love and with whom they were expected to develop some kind of affection as though they were cultivating geraniums in an urn. Matches were mostly made these days for the sake of convenience, so Maria was surprised and thankful to find herself marrying for love. She felt a certain gratitude to her sister for this, but the right moment and the right opportunity to express this never presented itself, since they rarely saw each other. To everyone's amazement and concern, she did not even appear at the engagement party. She sent her excuses with Andreas, who came to join in the celebrations with his parents.

Manoli loved the idea of marriage. He felt his life as a wandering libertine was well and truly over and now relished the prospect of being looked after and even, perhaps, of having children. In contrast to Maria, who thanked the God she spoke to in church each week, he attributed his luck to various gods, mostly Aphrodite, who had delivered this beautiful girl to him on a gilded platter. He would rather not have married at all than marry where there was no love and no beauty, and he was relieved to have found both in such equal measure.

The engagement party was in full swing and the village square teemed with merrymakers. Stephanos carried round huge trays of food and Maria and Manoli mingled with the crowd.

Manoli took his cousin to one side.

'Andreas,' he asked, almost shouting to be heard above the din of the band and the singing, 'would you agree to be our wedding sponsor?'

The wedding sponsor, the *koumbaros*, was a key figure in the marriage. In the ceremony itself his role was almost as significant as the priest's and, God willing, in due course he would become the godparent of the first child.

Andreas had expected the invitation. He would have been wounded if they had not asked him, so obvious a candidate was he. Manoli and he were more than brothers, closer than twins, and he was the perfect choice to be the person who would help bind these two in marriage, particularly with the added dimension of his already being Maria's brother-in-law. His expectation of being asked, however, did not diminish the pleasure.

'Nothing would delight me more, cousin! I'd be honoured,' he said.

Andreas felt strangely protective towards Manoli. He remembered well when his uncle had died and the period that followed when Manoli had been brought into their household. Andreas, always a steady and rather serious child, and Manoli, a wilder, less disciplined boy, could not have been more different. They had rarely squabbled as children, unlike most siblings, and there had never been any jealousy between them. Five years into their lives, they were each presented with a ready-made brother and playmate. Andreas benefited from the adventurous, less responsible influence of his cousin, and there was little doubt that Manoli needed the firm hand that his uncle and aunt could provide. Andreas, six months the older, naturally assumed the protective role, though Manoli had been the one to lead his older cousin astray, and to invite him to be bolder and more daring in their escapades around the estate as they grew into the years of early adolescence.

Maria received the first of many gifts for her trousseau, and the merrymaking continued into the small hours, after which the village became the quietest place on Crete. Even the dogs would be too tired to bark until the sun was well over the horizon.

When Andreas arrived home everyone was asleep. Alexandros and Eleftheria had returned before him and the house was eerily silent and dark. He crept into the bedroom and heard Anna stir.

'Hello, Anna,' he whispered quietly, in case she was still asleep.

The truth was that Anna had not had a wink of sleep that night. She had tossed and turned, crazed with anger at the thought of the merrymaking down in Plaka. She could picture her sister's beaming smile and Manoli's dark eyes fixed on her, his hands around her waist perhaps as they lapped up the compliments from all the well-wishers.

When Andreas switched on the bedside light she rolled over.

'Well,' she said. 'Was it fun?'

'It was a great celebration,' he answered, not looking at his wife as he undressed and so failing to take in the look on her tear-stained face. 'And Manoli has asked me to be *koumbaros*!'

The issuing of such an invitation had been inevitable but Anna had still not really braced herself for the blow. Andreas's role in the lives of Manoli and Maria would now be a significant one and would bind them all together, condemning her to an eternity of having her nose rubbed in her sister's happiness. In the shadows, her eyes pricked as she rolled over to bury her face in the pillow.

'Goodnight, Anna. Sleep tight.' Andreas climbed into bed. Within seconds the bed vibrated with his snores.

The crisp-aired March days passed quickly, spring arrived with an explosion of buds and blossom, and by summertime plans for the wedding were well under way. The date was set for October and the marriage would be toasted with the first wines from the season's crops. Maria and Manoli continued their weekly outings, still in the company of Fotini and Stephanos. A girl's virginity was an unspoken prerequisite of the marriage contract and the powers of temptation were well recognised; it was in everyone's interest that a girl should not be alone with her fiancé until the wedding night.

One May evening when the four of them were sitting over a drink in Agios Nikolaos, Maria noticed that Fotini looked slightly flushed. She could tell that her friend had something she wanted to say.

'What is it, Fotini? You look like the cat that's got the cream!'

'That's exactly how I feel . . . We're having a baby!' she blurted out.

'You're pregnant! That's such wonderful news,' said Maria, grasping her friend's hands. 'When's it due?'

'I think in about seven months – it's very early days.'

'That's only a few months after our wedding – I'll have to come back to Plaka to see you every other day,' Maria said, bubbling with enthusiasm.

They all toasted the good news. To both girls it seemed only moments since they had been making castles in the sand and, now, here they were discussing marriage and maternity.

Later that summer, concerned by the length of time that had elapsed since she had seen Anna, and rather bemused by her sister's complete lack of interest in her forthcoming nuptials, Maria decided that they should call on her. It had been one of August's hottest days, when even night-time brought little relief from the soaring temperatures, and rather than their customary outing to Agios Nikolaos with Fotini and Stephanos, Manoli and Maria would instead go alone to see Anna. It was a bold move. No invitation had been issued and no word received that the rather grand and elusive Anna wanted to see them. The message was clear to Maria. Why else would her sister be behaving in this way unless she was trying to express disapproval? Maria wanted to get to the bottom of it. Several letters she had written – one describing the engagement party that Anna had missed, supposedly because of illness, and another telling her about the beautiful lingerie she had been given for her trousseau – had gone unanswered. Anna had a telephone but Maria and Giorgis did not, and communication between them had ground to a halt.

As Manoli drove up the familiar road just beyond Elounda that led to the imposing Vandoulakis home, taking the bends as would any young man who had negotiated them a thousand times, Maria was nervous. Courage, she told herself. She's only your sister. She could not understand why she felt in such a needless state of anxiety about calling on someone who was such close flesh and blood.

When they drew up, Maria was the first to get out of the car. Manoli seemed slow, fiddling to get his key out of the ignition, and then combing his hair in the rear-view mirror. Maria stood waiting for him, impatient for this encounter. Her fiancé twisted the great round door handle – this was, after all, a sort of home from home for him – but it failed to budge, so he seized the knocker and banged hard three times. Eventually the door was opened. Not by Anna, but by Eleftheria.

She was surprised to see Manoli and Maria. It was rare that anyone should call unannounced, but everyone knew that Manoli was not the type to bother about etiquette, and she embraced him warmly.

'Come in, come in,' she fussed. 'It's so nice to see you. I wish I had known you were coming, then we could have had dinner together, but I'll get us something to eat and some drinks . . .'

'We've really come to see Anna,' said Manoli, interrupting.

'How is she? She's been rather out of touch – for months.'

'Has she? Oh, I see. I didn't realise. I'll go up and let her know you're here.' Eleftheria bustled out of the room.

From her bedroom window, Anna had seen the familiar car draw up. What should she do? She had managed to avoid such a confrontation for as long as she possibly could, believing that if only she could keep away from Manoli her feelings for him might gradually fade. Each day of the week, however, she saw him. She saw his reflection in her husband when he came in from the estate, and on the nights when Andreas made love to her, Manoli was easily conjured through half-closed eyes. The intensity of her passion for this vivacious version of her husband was as strong as it had been the day he had tucked a flower between her breasts, and the merest thought of him was enough to arouse her. She longed to see that sparkling smile which ignited her passion and sent shudders down her spine, but any such meeting would now be with Maria, and that would mean a reminder that Manoli could never be hers.

She had pretended to be in control. Until this evening. Now she was cornered. The two people she loved and loathed most in the world were downstairs waiting for her.

Eleftheria tapped gently on her door.

'Anna, your sister and her fiancé are here!' she called, without entering. 'Will you come and see them?'

Without ever having been taken into her confidence, Eleftheria had harboured her suspicions about Anna's feelings for Manoli. She had been the only person who had known quite how often he had called on her, and the only person who had known full well that Anna was not ill on the day of her sister's engagement party. Even now she could feel her daughter-in-law's reluctance to leave her bedroom. It could not possibly take that long to walk across the room. It was all beginning to make sense. She stood patiently for a few moments before knocking again, this time with more insistence. 'Anna? Are you coming?'

From behind the closed door, Anna delivered a sharp retort. '*Yes* I *am* coming. I'll be down when I'm ready.'

A few moments later, her vermilion lipstick freshly applied and her glossy hair shining like glass, Anna threw open her bedroom door and went downstairs. She took a deep breath and pushed open the door to the reception room. Looking every inch the *grande dame* of the house, even though Eleftheria was its real mistress, she swept across the room to greet her sister and pecked her politely on the cheek. Then she turned to Manoli, holding out a pale, limp hand to shake his.

'Hello,' she said, smiling. 'This is such a surprise. Such a nice surprise.'

Anna had always been able to act. And in so many ways it *was* nice to see this man, this obsession of hers, in the flesh; but it was also much more than that. She had thought of him each and every day for months and now here he was standing in front of her, even more rugged, more desirable than she had remembered. What seemed many minutes later to Anna but was only a second or two, she found she was still holding his hand. Hers was damp with sweat. She pulled away.

'I felt it had been such a long time since I saw you,' said Maria. 'Time is moving on so quickly and you know we are getting married in October, don't you?'

'Yes, yes, that's marvellous news. Truly marvellous.'

Eleftheria bustled in now with a tray of glasses and a row of little plates piled with olives, cubes of feta cheese, almonds and warm spinach pies. It was a miracle that she had produced such an array of *meze* in a matter of moments, but nevertheless she apologised for not being able to honour them with a more elaborate feast. She continued to bustle about as she removed an elaborate decanter of ouzo from the sideboard and poured everyone a drink.

They all took a seat. Anna perched on the edge of hers; Manoli sat back, comfortable, totally at ease. The room was filled with a warm orange light cast through the lace curtains by the setting sun and though conversation was stilted, Anna kept some sort of dialogue going. She knew it was her role in this situation.

'Tell me about Father. How is he?'

It was hard to tell whether Anna really cared, but it had certainly never occurred to Maria that she did not.

'He's fine. He's very pleased about our wedding. We asked him to come and live with us afterwards, but he is adamant about staying where he is in Plaka,' she said.

She had always made plenty of excuses for her sister's apparent lack of concern: her distance from Plaka, her new role as a wife, and other duties that Maria presumed she must have on an estate such as this. She knew now that similar changes were going to affect her. It would be a great help if Anna would begin to play more of a role with their father, and at least try to see him more often. She was about to broach the subject when there were voices in the hallway.

Alexandros and Andreas had returned from an inspection of their land up on the Lasithi plateau, and though the cousins saw each other regularly to discuss the affairs of the estate, they embraced now like long-lost friends. More drinks were poured and the two men of the house sat down.

Maria detected a tension but could not put her finger on the cause. Anna seemed perfectly happy making conversation, but she could not help noticing that most of her comments were directed at Manoli rather than her. Perhaps it was just the positions in which they were seated. Manoli was opposite Anna, while Andreas and Maria sat to one side on a long upholstered bench with Eleftheria between them.

Manoli had forgotten the strength of his attraction to Anna. There was something so gloriously coquettish about her, and he recalled those lunchtime trysts with something approaching nostalgia. Even though he was now an officially engaged man, the old rogue in Manoli still lurked close to the surface.

Eleftheria could see a difference in Anna. So often she could be sulky and monosyllabic, but tonight she was animated, her cheeks flushed, and even in this half-light she could see that there was a breadth to her smile. Her appreciation of everything that Manoli said was almost fawning.

As usual, Manoli dominated the conversation. Anna tried not to be infuriated when he kept referring to Maria as his 'beautiful fiancée', concluding that he was doing it deliberately to annoy her. He was still teasing her, she thought, still playing with her as he had done all those months ago, and making it obvious that he had not forgotten their flirtation. The way he was looking at her now, leaning forward to speak to her as though there was no one else in the room, made that quite plain. If only there *was* no one else in the room.

This hour she had spent in the company of Manoli was both heaven and hell.

It was mostly wedding talk. When the service was going to be, who was to be invited, and Andreas's role as *koumbaros*. It was almost dark by the time Maria and Manoli rose to go. Their eyes had adjusted to the gloaming, and only now did Eleftheria put on one of the dim table lamps so that they could make their way from the room without tripping on rugs or bumping into side tables.

'There is just one thing, Anna,' Maria said, determined not to leave without achieving her mission. 'Would you come and visit Father soon? I know you are busy, but I think he would really appreciate it.'

'Yes, yes, I will,' said Anna with unusual deference to her younger sister. 'I've been neglectful. Very naughty of me. I'll come down to Plaka in a few weeks' time. What about the third Wednesday in September? Would that be convenient?'

It was a casual, throwaway question, but somehow full of malice. Anna knew perfectly well that a Wednesday in September was the same for Maria as a Wednesday in April, June or August, or, for that matter, a Monday or a Tuesday. She was engaged in the same pattern of domestic activities for six days every week and, apart from Sundays, it didn't matter in the slightest when Anna came. Also, Maria had expected Anna to suggest something a little sooner. She was impeccable in her reply, however.

'That would be lovely. I shall tell Father,' she said. 'And I know he will look forward to it. He's usually back from Spinalonga by five o'clock with Dr Lapakis.'

Damn her for mentioning the island! thought Anna. She

felt they had all done well over the past five years to make sure that the full extent of their connection with the leper colony had not reached the ears of the Vandoulakis family. She knew too that it was now as much in Maria's interest to keep their past quiet as it was in hers. Why couldn't they all just forget about it? Everyone knew that Giorgis made his deliveries to Spinalonga and ferried the island's doctor. Wasn't that shameful enough, without it being constantly referred to?

There were final embraces and Manoli and Maria eventually drove away. Even if Anna had seemed edgy at times, Maria felt that perhaps the ice had begun to thaw. She always tried not to judge her sister, and to contain her criticisms, but she was not a saint.

'It's about time Anna came to Plaka,' she said to Manoli. 'If I'm leaving Father there on his own, she'll have to start visiting him a bit more often.'

'I'll be amazed if she does,' said Manoli. 'She's rather a law unto herself. And she certainly doesn't like it when things don't go her way.'

Such knowledge of Anna puzzled Maria. He spoke of her sister as someone he understood. Anna was not a complex person, but even so it surprised her that Manoli could make such an accurate observation.

Maria was now counting the days until her marriage. There were only four weeks to go. She wished they would pass more quickly, but the fact that she would be leaving her father still weighed heavily on her mind and she resolved to do everything she possibly could to ease the transition. The most practical step she could take would be to tidy up the house for when Giorgis would be there alone. She had put this task off during the summer months when the air both outside and inside shimmered in the soaring temperatures. It was much cooler now, the perfect day to do such a job.

It was also the day that Anna had promised to visit. There were still some of her possessions in the house and she might want to take them when she went home again. Some were her childhood toys. Perhaps Anna would need them soon, mused Maria. Surely there would be a baby in the Vandoulakis home before long.

A spring-clean in autumn-time. The small house was generally tidy – Maria always saw to that – but there was an old dresser stuffed with bowls and plates that were rarely used but could do with a wash, furniture that needed a polish, candlesticks that looked tarnished and many picture frames that she had not dusted for months.

As Maria worked, she listened to the radio, humming along to the music that crackled over the airwaves. It was three o'clock in the afternoon.

One of her favourite Mikis Theodorakis songs was on the radio. Its energetic bouzouki made an ideal accompaniment to cleaning, so she turned the volume up as high as it would go. The music drowned out the sound of the door being opened, and with her back turned, Maria did not see Anna slip in and take a seat.

Anna sat there for some ten minutes watching Maria work. She had no intention of helping her, got up as she was in a dress of finest white cotton embroidered with tiny blue flowers. What perverse satisfaction she derived from seeing her sister toil in this way, but how she could seem so happy and carefree, singing while she scrubbed shelves, made no real sense to Anna. When she thought of the man Maria was about to marry, however, she understood perfectly. Her sister must be the happiest woman in the world. How she hated that. She shifted in her seat, and Maria, suddenly hearing the scrape of wood on the stone floor, started.

'Anna!' she shrieked. 'How long have you been sitting there? Why didn't you tell me you were here?'

'I've been here for ages,' said Anna languidly. She knew it would annoy Maria to know that she had been watching her.

Maria climbed down from the chair and took off her apron.

'Shall I make us some lemonade?' she asked, instantly forgiving her sister's deception.

'Yes please,' Anna said. 'It's quite hot for September, isn't it?'

Maria busily halved a few lemons, squeezing them hard into a jug, and diluted the juice with water, vigorously stirring in sugar as she did so. They both drank two glasses before either of them spoke again.

'What are you doing?' asked Anna. 'Don't you ever stop working?'

'I'm getting the house ready for when Father is on his own here,' answered Maria. 'I've cleared out a few things you might need.' She indicated a small pile of toys: dolls, a flute, even a child's weaving loom.

'You might need those just as soon as me,' snapped Anna defensively. 'No doubt you and Manoli will be hoping to continue the Vandoulakis name once you're married.'

She could barely contain her jealousy of Maria and this single sentence carried all her resentment. Even she no longer relished her childlessness. The abandoned lemon skins which lay crushed and dry on the table in front of her were no less barren and bitter than she.

'Anna, what's the matter?' There was no avoiding such a question, even if it meant treading closer than Maria felt she ought. 'Something is wrong. You can tell me, you know.'

Anna had no intention of confiding in Maria. It was the last thing she planned to do. She had come to see her father, not to have a tête-à-tête with her sister.

'There's nothing the matter,' she snapped. 'Look, I might call on Savina and come back a bit later when Father returns.'

As Anna turned to leave, Maria noticed that her sister's back was damp, the fine fabric of her tightly fitting dress transparent with sweat. That there was something troubling her was as crystal clear as the water in a rock pool, but Maria realised that she was not going to find out. Perhaps Anna would confide in Savina and Maria could find out indirectly what the problem was. For so many years her older sister's emotions had been easy to read; they were like the posters that went up on every tree and building advertising the time and date of a concert. Nothing had been hidden. Now everything seemed so tightly wrapped up, so swaddled and secret.

Maria continued cleaning and polishing for an hour or so longer until Giorgis returned. Perhaps for the first time, she did not feel anguished about leaving him. He looked strong for a man of his age and she knew for sure that he would survive without her being there. Nowadays he did not seem too bowed down with the world's worries, and she knew the companionship of his friends in the village bar meant that lonely evenings were thankfully rare.

'Anna came by earlier,' she said chattily. 'She'll be returning quite soon.'

'Where has she gone then?' Giorgis asked.

'To see Savina, I think.'

At that moment Anna walked in. She embraced her father warmly and the two sat down to chat as Maria made drinks for them both. Their conversation skimmed all the surfaces. What had Anna been doing? Had she finished all the work on her two houses? How was Andreas? The questions Maria wanted to hear her father asking – Was Anna happy? Why did she so rarely come to Plaka? – went unasked. Not a word of Maria's forthcoming wedding was mentioned, not the slightest reference was made to it. The hour went quickly and then Anna rose to go. They said their farewells and Giorgis accepted an invitation to visit the Elounda house for Sunday lunch in just over a week's time.

After supper, when Giorgis had gone to the *kafenion*, Maria decided to do one last task. She kicked off her shoes to climb on to a rickety chair so that she could reach into the back of a tall cupboard and, as she stepped up, she noticed a strange mark on her foot. Her heart missed a beat. In some lights it might scarcely have been visible. It was like a shadow but in reverse, a patch of dry skin that was slightly paler than the rest. It almost looked as though she had burned her foot in the sun and the skin had peeled off to leave the lighter pigment underneath. Perhaps it was nothing at all to worry about, but she felt sick with anxiety. Maria usually bathed at night, and in the dim light such a thing could have gone unnoticed for months. She would confide in Fotini later, but she did not plan to worry her father about it yet. They all had quite enough to think about at the moment.

That night was the most troubled Maria had ever endured. She lay awake almost until dawn. She could not know for certain and yet she entertained little doubt about this patch. The hours of darkness passed with aching slowness as she tossed and turned and fretted with fear. When she finally fell into a brief and fitful sleep, she dreamt of her mother and of huge stormy seas which wrecked Spinalonga as though it was a great ship. It was a relief when day broke. She would go and see Fotini early. Her friend was always up by six o'clock, tidying away dishes from the night before and preparing food for the following one. It seemed she worked harder than anyone in the village, which was especially tough on her given that she was now in the third trimester of her pregnancy.

'Maria! What are you doing here so early?' Fotini exclaimed. She could see that there was something on her friend's mind. 'Let's have some coffee.'

She stopped working and they sat down together at the big table in the kitchen.

'What *is* the matter?' asked Fotini. 'You look as though you haven't had a wink of sleep. Are you getting nervous about the wedding or something?'

Maria looked up at Fotini, the shadows under her eyes as dark as her untouched coffee. Her eyes welled with tears.

'Maria, what is it?' Fotini reached out and covered her friend's hand with her own. 'You must tell me.'

'It's this,' said Maria. She stood up and put her foot on the chair, pointing to the faded patch of dry skin. 'Can you see it?'

Fotini leaned over. She now understood why her friend had looked so anxious this morning. From the leaflets regularly distributed in Plaka, everyone round here was familiar with the first visible symptoms of leprosy, and this looked very like one of them.

'What do I do?' Maria said quietly, tears now pouring down her cheeks. 'I don't know what to do.'

Fotini was calm.

'For a start, you mustn't let anyone round here know about this. It could be nothing and you don't want people jumping to conclusions, especially the Vandoulakis family. You need to get a proper diagnosis. Your father brings that doctor home from the island nearly every day, doesn't he? Why don't you ask him to have a look?'

'Dr Lapakis is a good friend of Father's, but he's almost too close and someone might get to hear of it. There was another doctor. He used to come over before the war. I can't even remember his name but I think he worked in Iraklion. Father would know.'

'Why don't you try and see him then? You've plenty of excuses for going to Iraklion with your wedding round the corner.'

'But it means telling my father,' Maria sobbed. She tried to wipe the tears from her face, but still they flowed. There was no avoiding this. Even if it could be kept secret from everyone else, Giorgis would *have* to know, and he was the one Maria would most have liked to protect.

Maria returned home. It was only eight o'clock but Giorgis was already out, and she knew she would have to wait until the evening to speak to him. She would distract herself by continuing with the work she had begun the day before, and she threw herself into it with renewed vigour and energy, polishing furniture until it gleamed and picking the dust with her fingernail from the darkest corners of every cupboard and drawer.

At around eleven o'clock there was a knock at the door. It was Anna. Maria had already been awake for seven hours. She was exhausted.

'Hello, Anna,' she said quietly. 'Here again so soon?'

'I left something behind,' Anna answered. 'My bag. It must have got tucked down behind the cushion.'

She crossed the room and there, sure enough, concealed beneath a cushion, was a small bag in the same fabric as the dress she had been wearing the day before.

'There, I knew it would be there.'

Maria needed a rest.

'Would you like a cold drink?' she asked from her elevated position on a stool.

Anna stood looking at her, transfixed. Maria shifted uncomfortably and climbed down from the stool. Her sister's eyes followed her but they were trained on her bare feet. She had noticed the sinister mark and it was too late for Maria to conceal it.

'What's that patch on your foot?' she demanded.

'I don't know,' said Maria defensively. 'Probably nothing.'

'Come on, let me see it!' said Anna.

Maria was not going to fight with her sister, who now bent down to have a closer look at her foot.

'I think it's nothing, but I am going to have it checked,' she said firmly, standing her ground.

'Have you told Father about it? And has Manoli seen it?' Anna asked.

'Neither of them knows about it yet,' answered Maria.

'Well, when are they going to know? Because if you're not going to tell them, then I'm going to. It looks like leprosy to me,' Anna said. She knew as well as Maria what a diagnosis of leprosy would mean.

'Look,' said Maria, 'I shall tell Father tonight. But no one else is to know. It may be nothing.'

'You're getting married in less than a month, so don't leave it too long to find out. As soon as you know the truth, you're to come and let me know.'

Anna's tone was distinctly bullying, and the thought even crossed Maria's mind that she was relishing the thought of her sister being leprous.

'If I haven't heard from you within a fortnight or so, I'll be back.'

With that, she was gone. The door banged shut behind her. Apart from Maria's pounding heart, a faint whiff of French perfume was the only evidence that Anna had ever been there.

That night, Maria showed Giorgis her foot.

'It's Dr Kyritsis we ought to go and see,' he said. 'He works at the big hospital in Iraklion. I'll write to him straight away.

He said little more than that, but his stomach churned with fear.

Chapter Fifteen

WITHIN A WEEK of writing, Giorgis had received a reply from Doctor Kyritsis.

Dear Kyrie Petrakis,

Thank you so much for writing to me. I am sorry to hear of your concern about your daughter and would be very pleased to see you both for an appointment. I shall expect you on Monday 17th September at midday.

I would also like to express my sorrow that your lovely wife Eleni passed away. I know it was some years ago, but I only recently heard the sad news from Dr Lapakis, with whom I am once again in contact.

With kind regards.
Yours sincerely,
Nikolaos Kyritsis

The appointment was only a few days away, which was a relief to both father and daughter as they were both, by now, thinking of little else other than the mark on Maria's foot.

After breakfast on that Monday morning, they set off on

the three-hour trip to Iraklion. No one thought it strange that the two of them should be going on such a long journey together and assumed it was on some kind of business connected to the forthcoming wedding. Brides-to-be had to buy gowns and all sorts of other finery, and what smarter place to go than Iraklion? chattered the women on their doorsteps that evening.

It was a long and often windswept journey along the coast, and as they approached the city, and the mighty Venetian harbour came into view, Maria wished more than anything that they had no cause to be here. In her entire life she had not seen such dust and chaos, and the noise of trucks and construction work deafened her. Giorgis had not visited the city since the war, and apart from the hefty city walls, which had stubbornly withstood German bombardment, most of it had changed beyond recognition. They drove around in a state of confusion, catching glimpses of spacious squares with fountains playing in their centre, only to pass the same point some time later and realise to their irritation that they had been going round in circles. Eventually they spotted the newly built hospital and Giorgis pulled up outside.

It was ten minutes before midday, and by the time they had negotiated the labyrinthine corridors of the hospital and found Dr Kyritsis's department, they were late for their appointment. Giorgis, particularly, was flustered.

'I wish we had allowed more time,' he fretted.

'Don't worry, I'm sure he will understand. It's not our fault that this city has been turned into a maze – or that they've built this hospital like one as well,' said Maria.

A nurse was there to greet them and took some details as

they sat in the stifling corridor. Dr Kyritsis would be with them shortly. The two of them sat in silence, breathing in the unfamiliar antiseptic smells that characterised the hospital. They had little conversation to make but there was plenty to watch as nurses bustled about in the corridor and the occasional patient was wheeled by. Eventually the nurse came to escort them into the office.

If the war had transformed the face of Iraklion, it had left an even greater mark on Dr Kyritsis. Though his slim figure was unchanged, the thick black hair had turned silver-grey and the previously unlined face now bore clear signs of age and overwork. He looked every one of his forty-two years.

'Kyrie Petrakis,' he said, stepping from behind his desk and taking Giorgis's hand.

'This is my daughter Maria,' said Giorgis.

'Despineda Petrakis. It's over ten years since I saw you but I do remember you as a child,' said Dr Kyritsis, shaking her hand. 'Please, do sit down and tell me why you have come.'

Maria began, nervously at first, to describe her symptoms.

'Two weeks ago, I noticed a pale mark on my left foot. It's slightly dry and a little numb. With my mother's history I couldn't ignore it, so that's why we are here.'

'And is it just this one area? Or are there others?'

Maria looked across at her father. Since the discovery of the first mark, she had found several others. No one ever saw her undressed, and she had had huge difficulty craning her neck to examine her own back in a small bedroom mirror, but even in the dim light she had made out several other blemishes. The patch on her foot was no longer the only one.

'No,' she replied. 'There are some others.'

'I will need to examine them, and if I think it necessary we will have to take some skin smears.'

Dr Kyritsis got up and Maria followed him into his surgery, leaving Giorgis alone in the office to contemplate the anatomical drawings that lined the walls. First of all Kyritsis examined the lesion on her foot and afterwards those on her back. He then tested them for sensitivity, first using a feather and then a pin. There was no doubt in his mind that there was some impairment to nerve endings, but whether it was leprosy he was not one hundred per cent certain. He made detailed notes and then sketched on an outline of the body where the patches had been found.

'I am sorry, Despineda Petrakis, I will have to take some smears here. It won't take long, but I am afraid it will leave your skin a little sore afterwards.'

Maria sat in silence as Kyritsis and a nurse prepared slides and gathered the required instruments. Only a month ago she had been showing off the latest items from her trousseau to her friends, some silk stockings which floated across their hands, lighter than air, as transparent as dragonfly wings. She had tried them on and they slipped over her skin, so gossamer fine it was as though her slim legs were still naked; the dark seam that traced the back of her leg was the only clue to their existence. She had then tried on the shoes she was to wear on her wedding day, and now the same foot that had slipped into that delicate shoe was to be cut open.

'Despineda Petrakis, I need you to lie on the couch, please.' Dr Kyritsis's words broke into her reverie.

The scalpel was razor sharp. It penetrated her skin by no more than two millimetres but in her mind the incision was magnified. It felt as though she was being sliced apart like meat as the doctor gathered enough tissue pulp from below the surface of the skin to put on the slide and examine under a microscope. She winced and her eyes watered with pain and fear. Kyritsis then took a smear from her back, and the nurse quickly applied some antiseptic ointment and cotton wool.

Once the bleeding had stopped, Maria was helped from the couch by the nurse and they returned to Dr Kyritsis's office.

'Well,' said the doctor. 'I will have the results of those smears within a few days. I shall be examining them for the presence of the Hansen bacillus, which is the only definitive proof of the presence of leprosy. I can write to you or, if you prefer, you can come and see me again and I can tell you in person. Personally, I think it's better for all parties if a diagnosis can be given face-to-face.'

In spite of the long journey involved, both father and daughter knew that they did not want to receive such news by post.

'We'll come to see you,' said Giorgis on behalf of them both.

Before they left the hospital, another appointment was made. Dr Kyritsis would expect them at the same time the following week. His professionalism was absolute and he had given no hint of what he expected the result to be. He certainly did not want to worry them unnecessarily, nor did he wish to give them false hope, and his manner was therefore neutral, almost indifferent.

It was the longest week of Maria's life. Only Fotini knew

that her friend was living on the edge of a precipice. She tried to occupy herself with as many practical tasks as possible, but nothing was enough to distract her from what might happen the following Monday.

The Friday before they were due to return to Iraklion, Anna called on her. She was eager to know: had Maria been to have tests? What were the results? Why did she not know? When were they going to hear? There was no implied sympathy or concern in her questions. Maria answered her sister in monosyllables and eventually Anna went on her way.

As soon as her sister was out of sight, Maria rushed off to see Fotini. She had been disturbed by the almost vindictive note of enthusiasm she had detected in Anna's reaction to the situation.

'I suppose she's eager for information because it could affect her one way or the other,' said Fotini holding her friend's hand tightly. 'But we mustn't dwell on that. We must be optimistic, Maria.'

For a few days Maria had hidden herself away. She had sent a message to Manoli that she was unwell and would not be able to see him until the following week. Fortunately, he did not question it, and when he saw Giorgis at the bar in Plaka, his future father-in-law supported her story and assured Manoli that his daughter would be better before long. Not being able to see Manoli made Maria miserable. She missed his gaiety and felt leaden with misery at the prospect that their wedding might now be in jeopardy.

Monday arrived, eventually. Maria and Giorgis repeated the journey to Iraklion, but this time found the hospital more easily and were soon sitting outside Kyritsis's office once again.

It was his turn to be late. The nurse came out to see them and apologised for the delay. Dr Kyritsis had been detained but would be with them within half an hour, she said. Maria was nearly beside herself. So far she had managed to contain her anxiety, but the thirty minutes she now had to wait took her beyond the limits of endurance, and she paced up and down the corridor to try and calm herself.

Eventually the doctor arrived, profusely apologetic that he had made them wait, and ushered them straight into his office. His entire demeanour seemed so different from the last visit. Maria's file was on his desk and he opened it and shut it again, as though there was something he needed to check. There was not, of course. He knew exactly what he had to say and there was no reason to keep these people waiting any longer. He came straight to the point.

'Despineda Petrakis, I am afraid that there are bacteria in your skin lesions to indicate that leprosy is present in your body. I am sorry it's bad news.'

He was not sure for whom the news was more devastating, the daughter or the father. The girl was the spitting image of her late mother, and he was keenly aware of this cruel repetition of history. He hated these moments. Of course there were emollient phrases that he could use to soften the blow, such as: 'It's not too advanced so we may be able to help you', or 'I think we've caught it early'. The announcement of bad news, however it was delivered, was still just that: bad news, catastrophic and cruel.

The pair sat in silence, their worst fears realised. In their minds they both pictured Spinalonga, knowing for certain now that this was to be Maria's final destination, her destiny.

Although she had initially made herself ill with worry, over the past few days Maria had tried to persuade herself that all would be well. To imagine the worst would have been unbearable.

Kyritsis knew that he must fill the gaping silence that had opened up in the room, and while the terrible news sank in, he gave them some reassurance.

'This is very hard news for you and I am terribly sorry to deliver it. You must be reassured, however, that great advances have been made in the study of leprosy. When your wife was ill, Kyrie Petrakis, the only methods of relief and treatment were still, in my view, extremely primitive. There has been good progress in the past few years and I very much hope you will benefit from it, Despineda Petrakis.'

Maria stared at the floor. She could hear the doctor speaking but he sounded as though he was a very long distance away. It was only when she heard her name that she looked up.

'In my opinion,' he was saying, 'it could be eight or ten years before your condition develops. Your leprosy type is, at present, neural, and if you remain in otherwise good health it should not progress to the lepromatous type.'

What is he saying? thought Maria. That I am effectively condemned to death but that it will take me a long time to die?

'So,' her voice was almost a whisper, 'what happens next?'

For the first time since she had entered the room, Maria looked directly at Kyritsis. She could see from his steady gaze that he was unafraid of the truth, and that whatever needed to be told, he would not fail to tell her. For her father's sake, if not her own, she must be brave. She must not cry.

'I shall write a letter to Dr Lapakis to explain the situation, and within the next week or so you will have to join the colony on Spinalonga. It probably goes without saying, but I would advise you to say as little as possible to anyone, except those who are closest to you. People still have very out-of-date ideas about leprosy and think you can catch it just by being in the same room as a victim.'

At this point Giorgis spoke up.

'We know,' he said. 'You can't live opposite Spinalonga for long without knowing what most people think of lepers.'

'Their prejudices are completely without scientific basis,' Kyritsis reassured him. 'Your daughter could have caught leprosy anywhere and at any time – but most people are too ignorant to know that, I'm afraid.'

'I think we should go now,' Giorgis said to Maria. 'The doctor has told us what we need to know.'

'Yes, thank you.' Maria was now completely composed. She knew what she had to do and where she would be spending the rest of her life. Not with Manoli near Elounda, but alone on Spinalonga. For a moment she had an urge to get on with it all. During the last week she had been in limbo, but now she knew what was to happen. It was all so certain.

Kyritsis opened the door for them.

'Just one final thing,' he said. 'I have been in regular correspondence with Dr Lapakis and I shall be resuming my visits to Spinalonga at some time in the future. I will, therefore, be involved with your treatment.'

They both listened to his words of comfort. It was kind of him to be so solicitous, but it did not help.

Maria and Giorgis emerged from the hospital into the bright mid-afternoon sun. All around them people went about their business, oblivious to the grief of the two individuals who stood there. The lives of all those going to and fro were the same now as they had been when they got up that morning. This was just another ordinary day. How Maria envied them the trivial tasks of their routine that in a few days would be lost to her. In the space of an hour, her life and her father's had changed totally. They had arrived at the hospital with a scrap of hope and had left it with none at all.

Silence seemed the easiest place to hide. For a while at least. An hour or so into the journey, however, Maria spoke.

'Who do we tell first?'

'We have to tell Manoli, and then Anna and then the Vandoulakis family. After that there will be no need to tell anyone. They will all know.'

They talked about what needed to be done before Maria left. There was little. With her wedding imminent, everything was already prepared for her departure.

When they arrived back in Plaka, Anna's car was parked outside their house. She was the last person in the world Maria wanted to see. She would much rather have sought comfort from Fotini. Anna, however, still had a key and had let herself into the house. It was almost dark by now and she had been sitting in the twilight waiting for their return. There was no mistaking that their news was bad. Their downcast faces as they walked through the door said it all, but Anna, insensitive as ever, shattered their silence.

'Well?' she said. 'What was the result?'

'The result was positive.'

Anna was momentarily confused. Positive? That sounded good, so why the glum faces? She was in a quandary, and realised that she hardly knew herself what the best result would be. If her sister did *not* have leprosy she would marry Manoli. For Anna that would be an unwelcome outcome. If Maria *did* have leprosy, it would immediately affect Anna's status in the Vandoulakis family. They would inevitably discover that Maria was not the first Petrakis to inhabit the island of Spinalonga. Neither was a desirable outcome, but she could not decide which was the lesser of the two evils.

'Which means what?' Anna found herself asking.

'I have leprosy,' her sister replied.

The words were stark. Even Anna now let the silence linger. All three of them standing in this room knew exactly what this meant, and there was no need for questions.

'I will go and see Manoli tonight,' said Giorgis decisively. 'And Alexandros and Eleftheria Vandoulakis tomorrow. They all need to know as soon as possible.'

With that he left. His daughters sat on together for a while, though they had little to say to each other. Anna would see her parents-in-law later that evening and fretted over whether she should say anything to them before Giorgis had the opportunity. Would it soften the blow if she told them the news herself?

Although it was now late, Giorgis knew Manoli would be at the bar in the village. He strode in and spoke directly, bluntly even.

'I need to talk to you, Manoli. Alone,' he said.

They withdrew to a table in the corner of the bar, out of earshot of everyone else.

'I have bad news, I'm afraid. Maria will not be able to marry you.'

'What's happened? Why not? Tell me!' There was sheer disbelief in Manoli's voice. He knew Maria had not been well for a few days, but had assumed it was something minor. 'You have to tell me what's wrong!'

'She has leprosy.'

'Leprosy!' he roared.

The word thundered round the room, silencing everyone in it. It was a word that most here were used to, though, and within a few minutes conversations around the room had resumed.

'Leprosy,' he repeated, more quietly this time.

'Yes, leprosy. The day after tomorrow I will be taking her to Spinalonga.'

'How did she get it?' Manoli asked, immediately worried for his own health.

What should Giorgis tell him? It could take many years before the symptoms of leprosy made themselves evident, and it was very possible that Maria had been infected by her mother all that time ago. He thought of Anna and the implications this might have for her. The chances of her having leprosy as well were infinitesimally small, but he knew that the Vandoulakis family might need some persuasion of that.

'I don't know. But it's unlikely that anyone will have caught it from her,' he answered.

'I don't know what to say. It's such terrible news.'

Manoli moved his chair away from Giorgis. It was an unconscious gesture, but one full of meaning. This was not a man who was about to give comfort, nor one who needed any himself. Giorgis looked at him and was surprised by what he saw. It was not the crumpled figure of a broken-hearted man just given the news that he could not marry the woman of his dreams. Manoli was shocked, but by no means destroyed.

He felt very sad for Maria, but it was not the end of his world. Though he had loved her, he had also passionately loved a dozen other women in his life, and he was realistic. His affections would sooner or later find another object; Maria had not been his one and only true love. He did not believe in such an idea. In his experience, love was a commodity, and if you were born with it in ample supply, there was always plenty left for the next woman. Poor Maria. Leprosy, as far as Manoli knew, was the most terrible fate for any human being but, in heaven's name, he might have caught the same disease if she had discovered it any later. God forbid.

The two men talked for a while before Giorgis took his leave. He had to be up very early to call on Alexandros and Eleftheria. When he arrived at the Vandoulakis house the following morning the four of them were already waiting for him. A nervous-looking maid led Giorgis in to the gloomy drawing room where Alexandros, Eleftheria, Andreas and Anna all sat like wax-works, cold, silent, staring.

Knowing that it was only a matter of time before the truth of her family history came out, Anna had confessed to Andreas that her mother had died on Spinalonga. She calculated that her honesty might appear to be a virtue in this situation. She was to be disappointed. Even though Alexandros Vandoulakis was an intelligent man, his views on leprosy were no different from those of an ignorant peasant. In spite of Anna's protestations that leprosy could only be transmitted through close human contact, and that even then the chances of catching it were small, he seemed to believe the age-old myth that the disease was hereditary and that its presence in a family was a curse. Nothing would deter him from this.

'Why did you keep Maria's leprosy secret until the eleventh hour?' he demanded, incandescent with rage. 'You have brought shame upon our family!'

Eleftheria tried to restrain her husband, but he was determined to continue.

'For the sake of our dignity and the Vandoulakis name, we will keep Anna within our family, though we shall never forgive the way you have deceived us. Not just one leper in your family, but two, we now discover. Only one thing could have made this situation more serious and that is if our nephew Manoli had already married your daughter. From now on we would be happy if you would keep your distance from our home. Anna will visit you in Plaka, but you are no longer welcome here, Giorgis.'

There was not one word of concern for Maria, not a moment's thought for her plight. The Vandoulakis family had closed ranks, and even the kindly Eleftheria sat silently now, afraid that her husband would turn his wrath on her if she spoke in defence of the Petrakis family. It was time for Giorgis to go, and he left his daughter's home for the last time, in silence. On the drive back to Plaka, his chest heaved with sobs as he lamented the final fragmentation of his family. It was now as good as destroyed.

Chapter Sixteen

WHEN GIORGIS ARRIVED home, he found that Fotini was already there helping Maria. They both looked up from their conversation as he walked in, and knew without asking that the encounter with the Vandoulakis family had been difficult. Giorgis looked even more pale and battered than they had expected.

'Have they no pity?' Maria cried out, leaping up to comfort her father.

'Try not to be angry with them, Maria. In their position they have a lot to lose.'

'Yes, but what did they say?'

'They said that they were sorry that the marriage is not to take place.'

In its way, what Giorgis said was true. It just missed a great deal out. What was the point of telling Maria that they never wanted to see him again, that they would deign to keep Anna within the family but as far as they were concerned her father was no longer part of it? Even Giorgis understood the importance of dignity and good name, and if Alexandros Vandoulakis felt that the Petrakis family was in danger of besmirching his, what option did he have?

Giorgis's neutral words almost matched Maria's state of mind. There had been a dreamlike quality to the past few days, as though these events were not really happening to her but to someone else. Her father described to her Manoli's reaction to the news and she had no trouble reading between the lines: he was sad, but not demented with grief.

Giorgis left the two women to get on with their preparations for Maria's departure, though there was little to do. It was only a few weeks ago that she had been preparing her trousseau, so boxes already stood in the corner of the room packed with her possessions. She had been careful not to take anything that Giorgis might need himself, but she had anticipated that the place where Manoli lived lacked much of what made a house a home, and there were many items of a domestic kind carefully stowed into the boxes: bowls, wooden spoons, her scales, scissors and an iron.

What she had to decide now was what to remove from the boxes. It seemed unfair to take the things that people had given her when she was going to a leper colony rather than her marital home in an olive grove, and what use on Spinalonga were those presents of nightwear and lingerie that had been given to her for her trousseau? As she lifted them out, all these frivolous luxury items seemed to belong to another life, as did the embroidered cloths and pillowcases that she had spent so long working on. As she held these in her lap, Maria's tears dripped on to the finely stitched linen. All those months of excitement had come to an end, and the cruelty of the turnaround stung her.

'Why don't you take them?' said Fotini, putting her arm

around her friend. 'There's no reason why you shouldn't have fine things on Spinalonga.'

'You're right, I suppose; they might make life more bearable.' She repacked them and shut the box. 'So what else do you think I should take?' she asked bravely, as though she was getting ready to go on a long and agreeable journey.

'Well, your father will be delivering several times a week, so we can always send you anything you need. But why not take some of your herbs? It's unlikely they all grow on the island and there's bound to be someone there who would benefit from them.'

They spent the day going over what Maria might need on the island. It was an effective distraction from the impending catastrophe of her departure. Fotini kept up a gentle flow of conversation that lasted until it was dark. Neither of them had left the house all day, but now the moment came for Fotini to depart. She would be needed at the taverna, and besides, she felt that Maria and her father should be alone that evening.

'I'm not going to say goodbye,' she said. 'Not just because it hurts, but because it isn't goodbye. I shall be seeing you again, next week and the week after.'

'How come?' asked Maria, looking at her friend with alarm. For a fleeting moment she wondered whether Fotini was also leprous. That could not be, she thought.

'I'll be coming with your father to do the occasional delivery,' Fotini said matter-of-factly.

'But what about the baby?'

'The baby isn't due until December, and anyway Stephanos can take care of it while I come across and see you.'

'It would be wonderful to think that you might come and see me,' said Maria, feeling a sudden surge of courage. There were so many people on the island who had not seen a relative for years. She at least would have a regular chance to see her father, and now her best friend too.

'So that's that. No goodbyes,' said Fotini with bravado. 'Just a "see you next week then".' She did not embrace her friend for even she worried about such proximity, especially with her unborn child. No one, not even Fotini, could quite put to one side the fear that leprosy could be spread by even the most superficial human contact.

Once Fotini had gone, Maria was alone for the first time in several days. She spent the next few hours rereading her mother's letters, from time to time glancing out of the window and catching sight of Spinalonga. The island was waiting for her. Soon all her questions about what it was like on the leper colony would be answered. Not long now, not long. Her reverie was disturbed by a sharp knock on the door. She was not expecting anyone, and certainly no one who would knock quite so forcefully.

It was Manoli.

'Maria,' he said breathlessly, as though he had been running. 'I just wanted to say goodbye. I'm terribly sorry it's all had to end like this.'

He did not hold out his hands or embrace her. Not that she would have expected either. What she would have hoped for was a greater sense of sorrow. His demeanour confirmed to Maria what she had half suspected, that Manoli's great passion would soon find another recipient. Her throat tightened. She felt as though she had swallowed broken glass and was no more able to speak than cry. His eyes would not meet hers. 'Goodbye, Maria,' he mumbled. 'Goodbye.' Within moments he had gone and once again the door was closed. Maria felt as hollow as the silence that once again filled the house.

Giorgis was yet to return. He had spent the last day of his daughter's freedom engaged in normal humdrum activities, mending his nets, cleaning his boat and ferrying Dr Lapakis. It was on his return journey with the doctor that he told him the news. He said it so casually that Lapakis did not, at first, take it in.

'I will be bringing my daughter over to Spinalonga tomorrow,' Giorgis said. 'As a patient.'

It was perfectly usual for Maria to accompany her father on the occasional delivery, so Lapakis did not react at first, and the last few words were lost in the wind.

'We went to see Dr Kyritsis,' Giorgis added. 'He will be writing to you.'

'Why?' asked Lapakis, taking more notice now.

'My daughter has leprosy.'

Lapakis, though he tried to conceal it, was aghast.

'Your daughter has leprosy? Maria? My God! I didn't realise . . . That's why you are bringing her to Spinalonga tomorrow.'

Giorgis nodded, concentrating now on guiding the boat into Plaka's small harbour. Lapakis stepped out of the boat. He had met the lovely Maria so many times and was shocked by the news. He felt he had to say something.

'She will receive the best possible care on Spinalonga,' he said. 'You are one of the few people who knows what the place is really like. It's not as bad as people think, but still, I am so terribly sorry that this has happened.'

'Thank you,' said Giorgis, and tied the boat up. 'I will see you tomorrow morning, but I might be a little late. I have promised to take Maria over very early but I'll do my best to be back for you at the usual time.'

The elderly fisherman sounded preternaturally calm, as normal as if he was making arrangements for any other day. This was how people conducted themselves in the first few days of bereavement, thought Lapakis. Perhaps it was just as well.

Maria had made supper for her father and herself, and at about seven in the evening they sat down opposite each other. It was the ritual of the meal that mattered tonight, not the eating, since neither of them had any appetite. This was to be their last supper. What did they talk about? They spoke of trivial things, such as what Maria had packed in her boxes, as well as more important ones like when she would next see her father on the island and how often Savina would expect him for supper at the Angelopoulos house each week. Anyone eavesdropping would have thought that Maria was simply moving out to live in another house. At nine in the evening, both exhausted, they retired to bed.

By six-thirty the following morning, Giorgis had carried all of Maria's boxes down to the quayside and loaded them on to his boat. He returned to the house to collect her. Still vivid in his mind, as though it had happened only yesterday, was Eleni's departure. He remembered that May day when the sun had shone on the crowd of friends and school children as his wife had waved goodbye to them. This morning there was deadly silence in the village. Maria would simply disappear.

A cold wind whipped through the narrow streets of Plaka and the chill of the autumnal air encircled Maria, paralysing her body and mind with a numbness that almost blocked her senses but could do nothing to alleviate her grief. As she stumbled the last few metres to the jetty she leaned heavily on her father, her gait that of an old crone for whom every step brought a stab of pain. But her pain was not physical. Her body was as strong as any young woman who had spent her life breathing the pure Cretan air, and her skin was as youthful and her eyes as intensely brown and bright as those of any girl on this island.

The little boat, unstable with its cargo of oddly shaped bundles lashed together with string, bobbed and lurched on the sea. Giorgis lowered himself in slowly, and with one hand trying to hold the craft steady reached out with the other to help his daughter. Once she was safely on board he wrapped her protectively in a blanket to shield her from the elements. The only visible indication then that she was not simply another piece of cargo were the long strands of dark hair that flew and danced freely in the wind. He carefully released his vessel from its mooring – there was nothing more to be said or done – and their journey began. This was not the start of a short trip to deliver supplies. It was the beginning of Maria's one-way journey to start a new life. Life on Spinalonga.

Chapter Seventeen

AT THE MOMENT when Maria wanted time to stand still it seemed to move faster than ever, and soon she would be dumped in a cold place where the waves broke on the shore. For once she had willed the boat's engine to stall, but the gulf between mainland and island was covered in moments and there was no turning back. She wanted to cling to her father, plead with him not to leave her stranded here, alone apart from two crates into which her life was now packed. But her tears had been spent. She had saturated Fotini's shoulder many times since her initial discovery of the mark on her foot, and her pillow was limp from the tears she had shed over the past two unhappy nights. Now was not the time for weeping.

For a few minutes they stood there alone. Giorgis was not going to leave her until someone came. He was now as familiar with the routine for new arrivals on the island as the islanders themselves, and knew that in due course they would be met.

'Maria, be brave,' said Giorgis quietly. 'I'll be back tomorrow. Come and see me if you can.'

He held both her hands in his. He was bold these days, and particularly so with his daughter. To hell with it if he got leprosy. Perhaps that would be the kindest solution because he could then come and live with Maria. The real problem if that happened would be the deliveries to Spinalonga. They would be hard pushed to find anyone else to make them, and that would cause untold hardship and misery on the island.

'Of course I'll come if it's allowed,' she answered.

'I'm sure it will be. Look,' said Giorgis, pointing to the figure emerging through the long tunnel which passed through the old fortress wall. 'Here is Nikos Papadimitriou, the island leader. I sent him a note yesterday to say I'd be bringing you today. He's the man to ask.'

'Welcome to Spinalonga,' Papadimitriou said, addressing Maria. How he could have such levity in his tone baffled her, but it distracted her for a moment. 'Your father sent me a note yesterday telling me to expect your arrival. Your boxes will be carried to your home shortly. Shall we go?'

He indicated that she should follow him up the few steps into the tunnel. Only a few weeks earlier, in Agios Nikolaos, she had been watching a Hollywood film where the heroine had swept up in a limousine and was led along a red carpet into a grand hotel while a porter dealt with her luggage. Maria tried to imagine herself in that very scene.

'Before we go,' she said hastily, 'can I ask permission to come and see my father when he brings Dr Lapakis and does his deliveries?'

'Why, certainly!' boomed Papadimitriou. 'I assumed that would be the arrangement. I know you won't try to escape. At one time we had to prevent people coming through to the quayside in case they tried to get away, but nowadays most people don't want to get off the island.'

Giorgis wanted to put the moment of parting behind him.

'I know they'll be kind to you,' were the words of reassurance he heard himself saying to her. 'I know they'll be kind.'

One or other of them had to turn away first, and Giorgis waited for his daughter to make that move. He had always regretted his hasty departure when Eleni arrived on the island fourteen years ago. So great had been his grief that he had set off in his boat before they had even said goodbye, but today he must have more courage, for his daughter's sake. Giorgis knew so much about the island now, whereas all those years ago his visits there had been just a job, a functional trip once or twice a week to drop boxes off on the quayside and then make a hasty retreat. In the intervening years his view of it all had been given a human dimension, and he had followed developments on the island as no other man outside it ever had.

Nikos Papadimitriou had been island leader ever since the election in 1940 when Petros Kontomaris had finally stood down, and he had now held the position for even longer than his predecessor. He had achieved great things on Spinalonga and the island had gone from strength to strength, so few were surprised when he was re-elected by an almost unanimous vote each spring. Maria recalled the day her father had transported the Athenians to Spinalonga. It had been one of the most dramatic episodes of that era, in a life rarely punctuated by much excitement. Her mother had written a great deal about the handsome, dark-haired island leader and all he did to change the island. Now his hair was grey, but he still had the same curled moustache that Eleni had described.

Maria followed Papadimitriou into the tunnel. He walked slowly, leaning heavily on his stick, and eventually they saw the light at the other end. Maria's emergence from the darkness of the tunnel into her new world was as much of a surprise for her as for any new arrival. In spite of her mother's letters, which had been full of description and colour, nothing had prepared her for what she now saw. A long road with a row of shops, all with freshly painted shutters, houses with window boxes and urns full of late-flowering geraniums, and one or two grander homes with carved wooden balconies. Though it was still too early for many people to be up, there was one early riser. The baker. The fragrance of freshly baked bread and pastries filled the street.

'Despineda Petrakis, before I show you to your new home, come and meet my wife,' said Papadimitriou. 'She has made breakfast for you.'

They turned left into a small side street, which in turn led into a courtyard with houses opening off it. Papadimitriou opened the door of one of these and ducked to get inside. They had been built by the Turks, and anyone of Papadimitriou's stature was more than a head taller than the original inhabitants.

The interior of the house was bright and ordered. There was a kitchen off the main room and stairs that led up to another floor. Maria even caught a glimpse of a separate bathroom beyond the kitchen.

'Let me introduce my wife. Katerina, this is Maria.'

The two women shook hands. In spite of everything that Eleni had told her to the contrary in her many letters, Maria had still expected the place to be inhabited by the lame and the deformed, and she was surprised at the woman's elegance and beauty. Katerina was younger than her husband and Maria surmised that she must be in her late forties. Her hair was still dark, and she had pale, almost unlined skin.

The table was set with embroidered white linen and fine patterned china. When they were all seated, Katerina lifted a splendid silver pot and a steady stream of hot black coffee filled the cups.

'There is a small house next door which has recently become vacant,' said Papadimitriou. 'We thought you might like that, or, if you prefer, there is a room free in a shared flat up the hill.'

'I think I would rather be on my own,' said Maria. 'If it's all right with you.'

There was a plate of fresh pastries on the table and Maria devoured one hungrily. She had eaten very little for several days. She was hungry for information too.

'Do you remember my mother, Eleni Petrakis?' she asked.

'Of course we do! She was a wonderful lady and a brilliant teacher too,' replied Katerina. 'Everyone thought so. Nearly everyone anyway.'

'There were some who did not?' Maria said.

Katerina paused.

'There was a woman who used to teach in the school before your mother arrived who regarded her as an enemy. She is still alive and has a house up the hill. Some people say that the bitterness she feels for what happened to her almost keeps her going,' said Katerina. 'Her name is Kristina Kroustalakis and you need to be wary of her – she'll inevitably find out who your mother was.'

'First things first, though, Katerina,' said Papadimitriou, displeased that his wife might be unsettling their guest. 'What you need before any of this is a tour of the island. My wife will take you round, and this afternoon Dr Lapakis will be expecting to see you. He does a preliminary assessment of all new arrivals.'

Papadimitriou stood up. It was now after eight o'clock in the morning and it was time for the island leader to be in his office.

'I shall no doubt see you again very soon, Despineda Petrakis. I shall leave you in Katerina's capable hands.'

'Goodbye, and thank you for making me feel so welcome,' responded Maria.

'Shall we finish our coffee and start the tour,' Katerina said brightly when Papadimitriou had left. 'I don't know how much you know about Spinalonga – probably more than most people – but it's not a bad place to live. The only problems come from being cooped up with the same people for your whole life. Coming from Athens I found that hard to get used to at first.'

'I've spent my whole life in Plaka,' said Maria, 'so I'm quite accustomed to that. How long have you been here?'

'I arrived on the same boat as Nikos, fourteen years ago. There were four women and nineteen men. Of the four women there are two of us left now. Fifteen of the men are still alive, though.'

Maria tightened her shawl about her shoulders as they left the house. When they turned into the main street, it was a very different scene from the one she had first seen. People came and went about their business, on foot, with mules or with donkey and cart. Everyone looked busy and purposeful. A few people looked up and nodded in Katerina and Maria's direction, and some of the men lifted their hats. As wife of the island leader, Katerina merited special respect.

By now the shops were open. Katerina pointed them all out and chatted busily about the people who owned them. Maria was hardly likely to remember all this information, but Katerina loved the details of their lives and relished the intrigue and gossip that circulated. There was the *pantopoleion*, the general store that sold everything for the house, from brooms to oil lamps, and had many of its wares displayed in profusion at the front of the building; a grocer whose windows were piled high with cans of olive oil; the *mahairopoieion*, the knife-maker; the raki store; and the baker, whose rows of freshly baked golden loaves and piles of coarse Cretan rusks, *paximithia*, drew in every passer-by. Each shop had its own hand-painted sign giving the owner's name and what he offered inside. Most important of all, for the men of the island at least, was the bar, which was run by the youthful and popular Gerasimo Mandakis. Already a few customers sat in groups drinking coffee, whilst their tangled mounds of cigarettes smouldered in an ashtray.

Just before they came to the church, there was a single-storey building which Katerina told Maria was the school. They peered in through the window and saw several rows of children. At the front of the class, a young man stood talking.

'So who is the teacher?' asked Maria. 'Didn't that woman you mentioned get the school back after my mother died?'

Katerina laughed. 'No, not over St Pantaleimon's dead body. The children did not want her back and neither did most of the elders. For a while one of my fellow Athenians took over, but he then died. Your mother had trained another teacher, however, and he was waiting in the wings. He was very young when he started but the children adore him and hang on his every word.'

'What's his name?'

'Dimitri Limonias.'

'Dimitri Limonias! I remember that name. He was the boy who came over here at the same time as my mother. We were told that it was he who had infected her with leprosy – and he's still here. Still alive!'

As occasionally happened with leprosy, Dimitri's symptoms had hardly developed since he had first been diagnosed, and now here he was, in charge of the school. Maria felt a momentary pang of resentment that the dice had been so heavily loaded against her mother.

They would not go in and interrupt the class. Katerina knew there would be another opportunity for Maria to meet Dimitri.

'There seems to be a large number of children,' commented Maria. 'Where do they all come from? Are their parents here too?'

'On the whole they don't have parents here. They're children who contracted leprosy on the mainland and were sent here. People try not to have children at all when they come to Spinalonga. If a baby is born healthy it's taken away from the parents and adopted on the mainland. We've had one or two such tragic cases recently.'

'That's desperately sad. But who looks after these children, the ones who are sent here?' asked Maria.

'Most of them are adopted. Nikos and I had one such child until he was old enough to move out and live on his own. The others live together in a house run by the community, but they're all well cared for.'

The two women continued on up the main street. High up above them on the hill towered the hospital, the biggest building of all.

'I'll take you up there later on,' said Katerina.

'You can see that building from the mainland,' said Maria. 'But it looks even bigger close to.'

'It was extended quite recently, so it's larger than it used to be.'

They walked round to the north side of the island, where human habitation ran out and eagles soared in the sky above. Here Spinalonga took the full blast of the wind from the north-east and the sea crashed on the rocks far below them, sending its spray high into the air. The texture of the water changed here, from the usual calmness of the channel that divided Spinalonga from Plaka to the galloping white horses of the open sea. Hundreds of miles away lay the Greek mainland and, in between, dozens of small islands, but from this vantage point there was nothing. Just air and sky and birds of prey. Maria was not the first to look over the edge and wonder, just for a moment, what it would be like to hurl herself off. Would she hit the sea first or be dashed against the serrated edges of the rocks?

It began to drizzle now and the path was becoming slippery.

'Come on,' Katerina said. 'Let's go back. Your boxes will have been brought up by now. I'll show you your new home and help you unpack if you like.'

As they descended the path, Maria noticed dozens of separate, carefully cultivated areas of land where, against the odds created by the elements, people were growing vegetable crops. Onions, garlic, potatoes and carrots were all sprouting on this windswept hillside and their neat weed-free rows were an indication of how much effort and attention went into the process of nursing them out of this rocky landscape. Each allotment was a reassuring sign of hope and showed that life was tolerable on this island.

They passed a tiny chapel that looked across the huge expanse of sea and finally reached the walled cemetery.

'Your mother was buried here,' Katerina said to Maria. 'It's where everyone ends up on Spinalonga.'

Katerina had not meant her words to sound so blunt, but in any case Maria did not react. She was keeping her emotions in check. It was someone else who was walking around the island. The real Maria was far away, lost in thought.

The graves were all unmarked, for the simple reason that they were shared. There were too many deaths here to allow anyone the luxury of solitude in the afterlife. Unlike most graveyards, which were situated around the church so that all who worshipped were constantly reminded that they would die, this one was secluded, secret. No one on Spinalonga really needed a memento mori. They all knew too well that their days were numbered.

Just before they came full circle they passed a house that was the grandest Maria had seen on the island. It had a large balcony and a porticoed front door. Katerina paused to point it out.

'Officially that's the home of the island leader, but when

Nikos took over he didn't want to push the previous leader and his wife out of their home, so they stayed where they were and so did Nikos. The husband died many years ago now, but Elpida Kontomaris is still there.'

Maria recognised the name immediately. Elpida Kontomaris had been her mother's best friend. The harsh fact was that her mother seemed to have been outlived by nearly all around her.

'She's a good woman,' added Katerina.

'I know,' said Maria.

'How do you know?'

'My mother used to write about her. She was her best friend.'

'But did you know that she and her late husband adopted Dimitri when your mother died?'

'No, I didn't. When she died I didn't really want to know about the details of life here any more; there was no need.'

There had been a long period after Eleni's death when even Maria had resented the amount of time that her father spent going to the colony; she had no interest in it once her mother had gone. Now, of course, she felt some remorse.

From almost all points on her walk the village of Plaka had remained in sight, and Maria knew that she would have to start disciplining herself not to glance over there. What good would it do to be able to see what activities people were engaged in across the water? From now on nothing over there had anything to do with her, and the quicker she got used to that, the better.

By now they had returned to the small cluster of houses where they had begun. Katerina led Maria towards a rust-coloured front door and took a key from her pocket. It seemed as dark inside as out, but with the flick of a switch the room was cheered up just a little. There was a dampness about it, as though it had been uninhabited for some time. The fact was that the previous incumbent had languished in the hospital for several months and never recovered, but given the sometimes dramatic recovery that could take place after even the most virulent lepra fever, it was island practice to retain people's homes until there was no further possible hope.

The room was sparsely furnished: one dark table, two chairs and a 'sofa' against the wall which was made of concrete and covered with a heavy woven cloth. Little other evidence of the previous inhabitant remained, except a glass vase containing a handful of dusty plastic flowers and an empty plate rack on the wall. A shepherd's hut in the mountains would have been more hospitable.

'I'll stay and help you unpack,' said Katerina bossily.

Maria was determined to hide her feelings about this hovel and could only do so if she was left her on her own. She would need to be firm.

'That's very kind of you, but I don't want to impose any more on your time.'

'Very well,' said Katerina. 'But I'll pop back later this afternoon to see if there is anything I can do. You know where I am if you need me.'

With that she was gone. Maria was glad to be alone with her own thoughts. Katerina had been well-meaning but she detected a hint of fussiness and had begun to find her twittering voice faintly irritating. The last thing Maria wanted was for anyone to tell her how to arrange her house. She would turn this miserable place into a home and she would do so herself.

The first thing she did was to pick up the vase of pathetic plastic roses and empty it into the bin. It was then that despondency overtook her. Here she was in a room that smelt of decay and the damp possessions of a dead man. She had held herself in check until this moment but now she broke down. All those hours of self-control and false good cheer for her father, for the Papadimitrious and for herself had been a strain, and the awfulness of what had happened now engulfed her. It was such a very short journey that had marked the end of her life in Plaka and yet the greatest distance she had ever travelled. She felt so far from home and everything that was familiar. She missed her father and her friends and lamented more than ever that her bright future with Manoli had been snatched away. In this dark room she wished she was dead. For a moment it did occur to her that perhaps she *was* dead, since hell could not be a gloomier or less welcoming place than this.

She went upstairs to the bedroom. A hard bed and a straw mattress covered with stained ticking were all the room contained, except for a small wooden icon of the Virgin clumsily nailed to the rough wall. Maria lay down, her knees pulled in towards her chest, and sobbed. How long she remained so she was not sure, since she eventually fell into fitful, nightmarish sleep.

Somewhere in the profound darkness of her deep underwater dream, she heard the distant sound of booming drums and felt herself being pulled to the surface. Now she could hear that the steady percussive beat was not a drum at all but the insistent sound of someone knocking on her door downstairs. Her eyes opened and for several moments her body seemed unwilling to move. All her limbs had stiffened in the cold and it was with every ounce of her will that she raised herself off the bed and stood upright. This sleep had been so profound that her left cheek bore the clear impression of two mattress buttons and nothing would have woken her except for what she now realised was the sound of someone almost battering down the door.

She descended the narrow staircase and as she drew back the latch and opened the door, still in a state of semi-consciousness, she saw two women standing there in the twilight. One of them was Katerina; the other was an older woman.

'Maria! Are you all right?' cried Katerina. 'We were so worried about you. We have been knocking on the door for nearly an hour. I thought you might have . . . might have . . . done yourself some harm.'

The final words she blurted out were almost involuntary, but there was a strong basis for them. In the past there had been a few newcomers who had tried to kill themselves, some of them successfully.

'Yes, I'm fine. Really I am – but thank you for worrying about me. I must have fallen asleep . . . Come in out of the rain.'

Maria opened the door wide and stepped aside to let the two women in.

'I must introduce you. This is Elpida Kontomaris.'

'Kyria Kontomaris. I know your name so well. You were my mother's great friend.'

The women held on to each other's hands.

'I can see so much of your mother in you,' said Elpida. 'You don't look so very different from the photographs she had of you, though that was all long ago. I loved your mother, she was one of the best friends I ever had.'

Katerina surveyed the room. It looked exactly as it had done many hours ago. Maria's boxes stood unopened and it was obvious that she had not even attempted to unpack them. It was still a dead man's house. All Elpida Kontomaris saw was a bewildered young woman in a bare, cold room at just the time of day when most people were eating a warm meal and anticipating the familiar comfort of their own bed.

'Look, why don't you come and stay with me tonight?' she asked kindly. 'I have a spare room, so it will be no trouble.'

Maria gave an involuntary shudder. Chilled by her situation and the dampness of the room, she had no hesitation in accepting. She remembered passing Elpida's house earlier that day and with her womanly eye for detail recalled the elaborate lace curtains that had covered the windows. Yes, that was where she would like to be tonight.

For the next few nights she slept in Elpida Kontomaris's house and during the day would return to the place which was to become her own home. She worked hard to transform it, whitewashing her walls and recoating the old front door with a bright, fresh green that reminded her of the beginning of spring rather than the tail-end of autumn. She unpacked her books, her photographs, and a selection of small pictures which she hung on the wall, and ironed her embroidered cotton cloths, spreading them on the table and on the comfortable chairs that Elpida had decided she no longer needed. She put up a shelf and arranged her jars of dried herbs on it, and made the previously filthy kitchen a hostile place for germs by scrubbing it until it gleamed.

That first dark day of despondency and despair was left behind, and though she dwelt for many weeks on what she had lost, she began to see a future. She thought much of what life with Manoli would have been like and began to question how he would have reacted in difficult times. Although she missed his levity and his ability to make a joke in any situation, she could not imagine how he would ever have tolerated adversity if it had come their way. Maria had only tasted champagne once, at her sister's wedding. After the first sip, which was full of fizz, the bubbles had disappeared, and she reflected on whether marriage to Manoli would have been rather like that. She would never know now and gradually she gave him less and less thought, almost disappointed in herself that her love seemed to evaporate by the day. He was not part of the world that she now occupied.

She told Elpida about her life from the day her mother had left: how she had looked after her father, about her sister's marriage into a good family, and about her own courtship and engagement to Manoli. She talked to Elpida as though she was her own mother, and the older woman warmed to her, this girl she had already known from her mother's descriptions all those years before.

Having overslept and missed it on the first afternoon, Maria went later that week for her appointment with Lapakis. He noted her symptoms and drew the location of her lesions on a diagrammatic outline of the body, comparing his observations with the information that Dr Kyritsis had sent him and noting that there was now an additional lesion on her back. This alarmed him. Maria was in good general health at present, but if anything happened to change this, his original hopes that she had a good chance of survival might come to nothing.

Three days later Maria went to meet her father. She knew that he would have set off punctually at ten to nine to bring Lapakis across, and by five minutes to she could just about make out his boat. She could see that there were three men aboard. This was unusual. For a fleeting moment she wondered if it was Manoli, breaking all the rules to come and visit her. As soon as she could distinguish the figure in the boat, however, she saw that it was Kyritsis. For a moment her heart leapt, for she associated the slight, silver-haired doctor with the chance of a cure.

As they bumped gently into the buoy, Giorgis threw the rope to Maria, who tied it expertly to a post as she had done a thousand times before. Though he had been anxious about his daughter, he was careful to conceal it.

'Maria . . . I am so pleased to see you . . . Look who is here. It's Dr Kyritsis.'

'So I can see, Father,' Maria said good-naturedly.

'How are you, Maria?' enquired Kyritsis, stepping nimbly from the boat.

'I feel absolutely one hundred per cent well, Dr Kyritsis. I have never felt anything else,' she replied.

He paused to look at her. This young woman seemed so out of place here. So perfect and so incongruous.

Nikos Papadimitriou had come to the quayside to meet the two doctors, and while Maria stayed to talk to her father, the three men disappeared through the tunnel. It was fourteen years since Nikolaos Kyritsis had last visited, and the transformation of the island astonished him. Repairs to the old buildings had been started even then, but the result had exceeded his expectations. When they reached the hospital, he was even more amazed. The original building was just as it had been, but a huge extension, equal in size to the whole of the old building, had been put up. Kyritsis remembered the plans on Lapakis's office wall all those years ago and saw immediately that he had fulfilled his ambition.

'It's astonishing!' he exclaimed. 'It's all here. Just as you wanted it.'

'Only after plenty of blood, sweat and tears, I can assure you – and most of those from this man here,' he said, nodding his head towards Papadimitriou.

The leader left them now and Lapakis showed Kyritsis proudly around his new hospital. The rooms in the new wing were lofty, with windows that reached from floor to ceiling. In the winter, the sturdy shutters and thick walls shielded patients from battering rains and howling gales, and in the summer the windows were thrown open to receive the soothing breeze that spiralled up from the sea below. There were only two or three beds to each room and the wards had been designated for either men or women. Everywhere was spotlessly clean, and Kyritsis noticed that each room had its own shower and washing cubicle. Most of the beds were occupied but the atmosphere in the hospital was generally still and quiet. Only a few patients tossed and turned, and one moaned softly with pain.

'Finally I've got a hospital where patients can be treated as they should be,' said Lapakis as they returned to his office. 'And moreover a place where they can have some self-respect.'

'It's very impressive, Christos,' said Kyritsis. 'You must have worked so hard to achieve all this. It looks exceptionally clean and comfortable – and quite different from how I remember it.'

'Yes, but good conditions aren't all they want. More than anything they want to get better and leave this place. My God, how they want to leave it.' Lapakis spoke wearily.

Most of the islanders knew that drug treatments were being worked on, but little seemed to have come their way. Some were sure that within their lifetime a cure would be found, though for many whose limbs and faces were deformed by the disease it was no more than a dream. A few had volunteered to have minor operations to improve the effects of paralysis on their feet or to have major lesions removed, but more than that they did not really expect.

'Look, we've got to be optimistic,' said Kyritsis. 'There are some drug treatments under trial at the moment. They don't work overnight, but do you think some of the patients here would be prepared to try them?'

'I'm sure they would, Nikolaos. I think there are some who would try anything. Some of the wealthy ones still insist on doses of hypnocarpus oil, in spite of the cost and the agony of having it injected. What do they have to lose if there's something new to try?'

'Actually quite a lot at this stage . . .' replied Kyritsis

thoughtfully. 'It's all sulphur-based, as you probably know, and unless the patient is in generally good health the side-effects can be disastrous.'

'What do you mean?'

'Well, anything from anaemia to hepatitis – and even psychosis. At the Leprosy Congress I've just been to in Madrid, there were even reports of suicide being attributed to this new treatment.'

'Well we'll have to think very carefully about which, if any, of our patients act as guinea pigs. If they have to be strong in the first place, there are plenty who would not be up to it.'

'Nothing has to be done straight away. Perhaps we could start by drawing up a list of suitable candidates and I can then discuss the possibility with them. It's not a short-term project – we probably wouldn't begin to inject for several months. What do you think?'

'I think that's the best way forward. Having a plan at all will seem like progress. Do you remember the last time we compiled a list of names here? It seems so long ago, and most of the people on it are dead now,' said Lapakis gloomily.

'But things are different today. We weren't talking about a real, tangible possibility of a cure in those days; we were simply trying to improve our methods of preventing contagion.'

'Yes, I know. I just feel I've been treading water here, that's all.'

'That's perfectly understandable, but I do believe there's a future to look forward to for some of these people. Anyway, I shall be back in a week, so shall we have a look at some names then?'

Kyritsis took himself back to the quayside. It was now midday and Giorgis would be there to collect him as arranged. A few heads turned to look at him as he made his way back down the street, past the church, the shops and the *kafenion*. The only strangers these people ever saw were newcomers to the island, and no newcomer ever walked with such purpose in his stride as this man. As the doctor emerged from the tunnel and the choppy late October sea came into view, he saw the little boat bobbing up and down a hundred metres or so off the shore, and a woman standing on the quayside. She was looking out to sea but heard his step behind her and turned. As she did so, her long hair blew up in wisps around her face and two large oval eyes gazed at him with hope.

Many years earlier, before the war, Kyritsis had visited Florence and seen Boticelli's captivating image of the Birth of Venus. With the grey-green sea behind her and her long hair caught by the wind, Maria strongly evoked the painting. Kyritsis even had a framed print on his wall at home in Iraklion, and in this young woman he saw the same shy half-smile, the same almost questioning incline of the head, the same just-born innocence. Such beauty in real life, however, he had never seen. He was stopped in his tracks. At this moment he was not regarding her as a patient but as a woman, and he thought her more beautiful than anyone he had ever seen.

'Dr Kyritsis,' she said, rousing him from his reverie with the sound of his own name. 'Dr Kyritsis, my father is here.'

'Yes, yes, thank you,' he blustered, suddenly aware that he must have been staring.

Maria held the boat fast for a moment as the doctor climbed in, and then she released it and tossed him the rope. As Kyritsis caught it he looked up at her. He needed one more glimpse, just to make quite sure he had not been dreaming. He had not. The face of Venus herself could not have been more perfect.

Chapter Eighteen

AUTUMN IMPERCEPTIBLY TURNED to winter and the musky smell of wood smoke pervaded the air on Spinalonga. People went about their daily business wrapped from head to foot in every woollen layer they possessed to defend themselves from the cold, for whichever way the wind blew this small island caught its full force.

In Maria's house the spirits of past inhabitants had been banished. Every picture, cloth and piece of furniture was now hers, and a glass dish of lavender and rose petals in the middle of the table scented the air with its sweet fragrance.

To Maria's surprise, her first few weeks on the island passed quickly. There was one moment alone that left her with a distinct sense of unease. She had just moved out of Elpida's warm and rather grandly furnished home into her own more familiar surroundings. As she turned the corner from the small alleyway into the main street to buy some groceries she physically collided with another woman. She was much smaller than Maria, and as they stepped away from each other Maria saw that she was considerably older too. Her face was furrowed with deep lines and so gaunt that her ear-lobes, which were greatly enlarged by leprosy, were monstrously accentuated. The old woman's walking stick had gone flying halfway across the street.

'I'm so sorry,' said Maria breathlessly, holding the woman's arm and helping her to regain her balance.

Dark beady eyes glared into Maria's.

'Just be more careful,' the woman snapped, grabbing her stick. 'Who are you anyway? I've not seen you before.'

'I'm Maria Petrakis.'

'*Petrakis!*' She spat the name out as though it had all the sourness of an olive eaten straight from the tree. 'I once knew someone called Petrakis. She's dead now.'

There was a note of triumph in her voice, and Maria immediately realised that this bent crone was her mother's old enemy.

The two women went their separate ways. Maria continued up the hill to the bakery, and when she glanced back to see where Kyria Kroustalakis had gone, she saw that she was standing at the bottom of the street by the old communal tap, staring up at her. Maria quickly looked round again. She shuddered.

'Don't worry,' said a voice behind her. 'She's pretty harmless really.'

It was Katerina, who had seen the collision between Maria and her mother's old enemy.

'She's just an old witch marinaded in her own bitter juices, a viper who's lost her venom.'

'I'm sure you're right, but she does a good impression of a snake who could still bite,' said Maria, her heart beating slightly faster than usual.

'Well, believe me, she can't. But what she is good at is

spreading bad feeling – and she's certainly succeeded at that with you.'

The two women continued up the street together, and Maria decided that she would give Kristina Kroustalakis no further thought. She had already seen that many people on Spinalonga accepted their situation, and the last thing any of them needed was someone who undermined this.

A more welcome encounter with part of her mother's past was her first meeting with Dimitri Limonias. Elpida invited them to her home one evening and both approached the meeting with some trepidation.

'Your mother was extremely kind to me,' Dimitri began, once drinks were poured and both were seated. 'She treated me like her own son.'

'She loved you like her own son,' said Maria. 'That's why.'

'I feel I should apologise in some way. I know that everyone thought I was responsible for giving her the disease,' said Dimitri hesitantly. 'But I've talked to Dr Lapakis about this at length and he thinks it is highly improbable that the bacteria were passed from me to your mother. The symptoms are so slow to develop that he thinks we contracted it quite independently from each other.'

'I don't believe any of that matters now,' said Maria. 'I'm not here to blame you. I just thought it would be a good idea to meet. You're almost like a brother after all.'

'That's a very generous thing to say,' he said. 'I don't feel as though I have much of a family any more. My parents have both died and my brothers and sisters were never exactly in the habit of writing letters. No doubt they're all ashamed. God knows, I do understand that.'

Several hours passed as the two talked about the island, the school and Eleni. Dimitri had been lucky. During his time on Spinalonga he had enjoyed the loving care of Eleni and then Elpida. One was an experienced mother and the other had treated him as the precious child she had always yearned for, giving him love and attention that sometimes almost swamped him. Maria was glad to have met this quasi-half-brother and the pair would often meet for coffee or even for supper, which she would cook while Dimitri enthused about his work. He currently had fourteen children in the school and aimed to get them reading by seven years old. Spending time with someone who was driven by his working life made Maria realise that being a leper was not going to dominate her every waking hour. A fortnightly appointment at the hospital, a compact house to keep neat and tidy, a small allotment to tend to. Along with the meetings with her father, these were the cornerstones of her single, childless existence.

To start with, Maria was nervous about telling her father that she had struck up a friendship with Dimitri. It might seem like a betrayal, as the family lore had always been that it was this boy who had infected Eleni. Giorgis had spent enough time with Lapakis to know that this was not necessarily the case, so when Maria made her confession that she was now Dimitri's friend, her father's reaction was unexpected.

'What's he like then?' he asked.

'He's about as dedicated as Mother was,' she answered. 'And he's good company too. He's read every book in the library.'

This was no mean feat. The library now had over five hundred books, most of them sent from Athens, but Giorgis was unimpressed by this. There were other things he wanted to know.

'Does he talk about your mother?'

'Not much. He probably thinks that would be insensitive. He did once tell me that his life was better here than it would have been if he hadn't had to come to Spinalonga.'

'That's an odd thing to say,' exclaimed Giorgis.

'I get the impression life was really hard for his parents and he certainly would never have become a teacher . . . Anyway, how's Anna?'

'I don't know really. I suppose she's all right. She was supposed to come and see me on the feast of Agios Grigorios but she sent a message saying she wasn't well. I really don't know what's wrong with her.'

It was always the same story, Maria thought. Promised meetings and last-minute cancellations. It was a pattern Giorgis expected now, but from afar Maria continued to be annoyed by her sister's callous disregard for the man who had struggled so hard to bring them up.

Within a month Maria knew she needed something to occupy her and picked a battered notebook off her shelf. It contained all her handwritten instructions on the use of herbs. *For healing and cure*, she had written on the title page in her neat, schoolgirl script. In the context of leprosy, those words looked so naïve, so optimistic, so entirely far-fetched. There were, however, plenty of other ailments that people suffered from on Spinalonga, from stomach disorders to coughs, and if she could relieve them of those as she had done so successfully in her old life, then it would be a worthwhile contribution.

Maria was bubbling over with news of her plans when Fotini came to visit her one day, telling her how she planned to scour the uninhabited, rocky part of the island for herbs as soon as spring came.

'Even on those limestone cliffs with the salt spray there's apparently plenty of sage, cistus, oregano, rosemary and thyme. Those will give me the basic means of providing remedies for general ailments and I'll try to cultivate other useful plants on my allotment. I'll need to get approval from Dr Lapakis, but once I've done that I'll advertise in *The Spinalonga Star*,' she told Fotini, who, on this chilly day, was warmed to see her dear friend so full of fire and enthusiasm.

'But tell me what's going on in Plaka,' Maria asked, never one to keep the conversation one-sided.

'Not much really. My mother says that Antonis is as grumpy as ever and it's high time he found himself a wife, but Angelos met a girl last week in Elounda that he seems very keen on. So who knows, perhaps one of my bachelor brothers might be married before long.'

'And what about Manoli?' asked Maria quietly. 'Has he been around?'

'Well, Antonis hasn't seen him on the estate quite so much . . . Are you sad about him, Maria?'

'It probably sounds awful, but I don't miss him as much as I thought I would. I only really think about him when we're sitting here talking about Plaka. I almost feel guilty about not feeling more. Do you think that's strange?'

'No, I don't. I think it's probably a good thing.' Since Fotini had been on the receiving end of Antonis's gossip about Maria's fiancé all those months ago, she had never entirely trusted

Manoli, and she knew it would be better in the long term if Maria could put him to the back of her mind. After all, there was no chance that she would ever marry him now.

It was time for her to go. Maria looked down at her friend's swollen belly.

'Is it kicking?' she asked.

'Yes,' replied Fotini. 'All the time now.'

Fotini was nearing the end of her pregnancy and beginning to worry about the rough waters she had to cross to see her friend.

'Perhaps you shouldn't be coming across now,' said Maria. 'If you're not careful you'll be giving birth in my father's boat.'

'As soon as I've had the baby I'll be straight back,' Fotini reassured her. 'And I'll write. I promise.'

By now Giorgis had established a firm routine for seeing his daughter on Spinalonga. Though Maria was comforted by the idea that her father came and went sometimes several times a day, it made no sense for her to see him each time. She knew it would be wrong for both of them to meet so often; it would be to pretend that life was going on just as it had before, simply in a different location. They decided to limit themselves to three encounters a week, on Mondays, Wednesdays and Fridays. These days were the high points of her week. Monday would be Fotini's day once she had resumed her visits, Wednesday was the day Dr Kyritsis visited, and on Fridays she saw her father alone.

In mid January Giorgis brought the exciting news that Fotini had given birth to a son. Maria wanted all the details.

'What's his name? What does he look like? How much does he weigh?' she asked excitedly.

'Mattheos,' replied Giorgis. 'He looks like a baby and I've no idea what he weighs. About the same as a bag of flour, I suppose.'

By the following week, Maria had embroidered a tiny pillowcase with the baby's name and date of birth and filled it with dried lavender. *Put it in his cradle*, she wrote in a note to Fotini. *It'll help him to sleep.*

By April, Fotini was ready to come and see Maria again. Even with her new responsibilities as a mother, she still knew the minutiae of everything that happened in Plaka and her antennae were well tuned to the comings and goings of its inhabitants. Maria loved to hear the gossip but also listened intently as her friend described the trials and pleasures of her new state of motherhood. For her part she shared all that took place on Spinalonga, and their talks always lasted for well over an hour, with hardly a pause for breath.

The Wednesday encounters with Dr Kyritsis were a very different matter. Maria found the doctor a little disconcerting. It was hard to disassociate him from the moment when the diagnosis had been delivered, and his words still echoed in her mind: '. . . leprosy is present in your body.' He had condemned her to a living death and yet he was also the man who now held out a tenuous promise that one day she might be free of the disease. It was confusing to link him with the worst and possibly the best of all things.

'He's very aloof,' she said to Fotini one day when they were chatting, sitting together on the low stone wall that surrounded one of the shade-giving trees by the quayside. 'And a bit steely, like his hair.'

'You make it sound as though you don't like him,' Fotini responded.

'I'm not sure I do,' answered Maria. 'He always seems to stare at me, and yet it's as though he's looking through me as if I'm not really there. He seems to make my father cheerful, though, so I suppose that's a good thing.'

It was strange, reflected Fotini, how Maria kept bringing this man into the conversation, especially if she didn't really like him.

Within a few weeks of Kyritsis's first visit, the two doctors had short-listed the cases that they would monitor for suitability for drug treatment. Maria's name was among them. She was young, healthy, newly admitted and in all ways an ideal candidate, and yet for reasons that Kyritsis could not explain even to himself, he did not want her to be in the first group that they would begin to inject several months from now. He struggled against this irrationality. After years of delivering unwelcome diagnoses to people who deserved so much better, he had trained himself to limit his emotional involvement. This objectivity made him imperturbable, even expressionless sometimes. Though Dr Kyritsis cared about humankind in a general sense, people tended to find him cold.

Kyritsis decided to cut the list from twenty to fifteen and these cases he would monitor closely over a period of months to decide on dosage and suitability. He omitted Maria's name from the final list. He did not need to justify this decision to anyone but he knew it was the first action he had taken in perhaps his entire career which was not governed by reason.

He told himself it was in her best interest. Not enough was known about the side-effects of some of these drug doses and he did not want her to be in the front line of an experiment. She might not be up to it.

One morning early that summer, during the journey over from the mainland, Kyritsis asked Giorgis whether he had ever been further than the great gateway of Spinalonga.

'Of course not,' replied Giorgis with some surprise. 'I've never even thought of it. It wouldn't be allowed.'

'But you could visit Maria in her own home,' he said. 'Almost entirely without risk.'

Kyritsis, now familiar with Maria's symptoms, knew that the chances of Giorgis Petrakis contracting leprosy from his daughter were a million to one. There were no bacteria on the surface of Maria's flat skin patches, and unless Giorgis came into direct contact with any broken skin there was virtually no chance at all of him being infected.

Giorgis looked thoughtful. It had never occurred to either him or Maria that they could spend any time together in Maria's house. It would be infinitely more civilised than seeing each other on the quayside, windswept in winter and sun-scorched in summer. Nothing would be more wonderful.

'I shall speak to Nikos Papadimitriou about it and seek Dr Lapakis's opinion, but I see no reason why it should not happen.'

'But what would they think back in Plaka if they knew I was going into the colony rather than just delivering goods on to the quayside?'

'If I were you I would keep quiet about it. You know as well as I do what visions people over there have of life here.

They all think leprosy is spread in a handshake, or just by being in the same room as a sufferer. If they thought that you were drinking coffee in the same house as someone with the disease I think you know what the consequences of that might be.'

Giorgis knew better than anyone that Kyritsis was right. He was all too familiar with the prejudices against lepers and for so many years had been obliged to listen to the ignorant views – even of men who called themselves his friends – on the subject. What a dream, however, to sit and share a pot of coffee or a glass of ouzo once again with his lovely daughter. Could it really happen?

That day Kyritsis spoke to the island leader and solicited the views of Lapakis. When he saw Giorgis that night he was able to give him official approval for his visits.

'If you wish to invite yourself through that tunnel,' he said, 'you may.'

Giorgis could hardly believe his ears. He could not remember feeling such excitement for a very long time and was impatient to see Maria so that he could tell her what Kyritsis had suggested. That very Friday morning, as soon as he stepped off the boat, she knew something was up. Her father's face gave it away.

'I can come to your house!' he blurted out. 'You can make coffee for me.'

'What? How? I don't believe it . . . are you sure?' Maria said with incredulity.

It would be such a simple thing, but so precious. Like his wife and daughter before him, Giorgis entered with trepidation the dark tunnel which led through the heavy fortified wall. When he emerged into the bright light of the leper colony it was as much of a revelation to him as it had been to them. The early June day was already warm, and though the clear light would later dissolve into a haze, the sharp colours of the scene that confronted Giorgis almost dazzled him. A profusion of crimson geraniums cascaded out of huge urns, a candy-pink oleander gave shade to a litter of tortoiseshell kittens and a deep green palm waved gently next to the sapphire door of the hardware store. Shiny silver pans hung down in a string and glinted in the sunlight. Huge pots of bright green basil stood outside almost every door ready to give flavour even to dull dishes. No, it was not as he had imagined it.

Maria was as excited as her father, but at the same time slightly nervous about his presence. She did not want him wandering too far into the leper colony, not just because he would invite stares and curiosity but because his presence could cause jealousy and resentment among the other lepers. She wanted to keep her father to herself.

'It's this way, Father,' she urged, leading him off the main street and into the little square where her house was situated. She unlocked her front door and led the way in. Soon there was an aroma of coffee in the small house as it bubbled up through the percolator on the stove, and a plate of baklava stood on the table.

'Welcome,' Maria said.

Giorgis did not really know what he had expected, but it was not this. It was a replica of his house in Plaka. He recognised photographs, icons and pieces of china which matched his own at home. Dimly he recalled that Eleni had asked for some plates and cups from the family set so that she would be eating from the same crockery as her family. After that, those pieces had gone to Elpida, who had kept some of his wife's possessions when she died, and now they were in Maria's hands. He also saw the cloths and throws which Maria had spent so many months embroidering, and a wave of sadness passed over him when he thought of Manoli's house in the olive grove where she should have been living, had things worked out as originally planned.

They sat down at the table and sipped their coffee.

'I never thought I would sit at a table with you again, Maria,' he said.

'Neither did I,' Maria answered.

'We have Dr Kyritsis to thank for this,' said Giorgis. 'He's got some rather modern views, but I like this one.'

'What will your friends in Plaka say when you tell them that you have started coming into the colony?'

'I shan't tell them. You know what they'd say. They're as stuck in their views about Spinalonga as they ever were. Even though there's a strip of water dividing them from here, they're convinced leprosy will be carried across on the air to infect them. If they knew I was coming into your house, they'd probably ban me from the bar!'

The last comment may have been flippant, but Maria still expressed concern.

'It's probably best that you keep it to yourself then. No doubt it worries them enough that you come over here as often as you do.'

'You're right. You know some of them even think that I somehow managed to carry germs across from here to infect you back in Plaka.'

Maria was horrified at the idea that her leprous state might be used to fuel such fears on the mainland and it alarmed her that her father might be faced with prejudice even from his oldest friends, men he had grown up with. If only they could see them now: a father and his daughter sitting at a table, eating the sweetest pastries that money could buy. Nothing could have been further from the conventional image of a leper colony. Even her irritation at the thought of all the ignorant talk on the mainland could not spoil this moment.

When they had finished their coffee, it was time for Giorgis to go.

'Father, do you think Fotini would come one day?'

'I am sure she would, but you can ask her when she comes on Monday.'

'It's just that . . . this is so like normal life. Sharing a drink with someone. I can't tell you what it means to me.'

Maria, usually so steadfast at controlling her emotions, had a catch in her voice. Giorgis stood to go.

'Don't worry, Maria,' he said. 'I am sure she will come – and so will I.'

The two of them walked back to the boat and Maria waved him goodbye.

As soon as he returned to Plaka, Giorgis wasted no time in telling Fotini that he had been into Maria's house, and without even hesitating, his daughter's oldest friend asked whether she would be able to do the same. Some people would have considered this reckless, but Fotini was more enlightened about the way in which leprosy could be spread than others, and on her next visit, as soon as she got off the boat, she seized Maria's arm.

'Come on,' she said. 'I want to see your home.'

A broad smile spread across Maria's face. The two women sauntered through the tunnel and were soon at the door of Maria's house. The coolness of the interior was welcome, and instead of strong coffee they drank *kanelada*, the chilled cinnamon drink they had both loved as children.

'It's so kind of you to come here to see me,' said Maria. 'You know, I never pictured anything but loneliness here. It makes so much difference having visitors.'

'Well it's much nicer than sitting on that wall in the heat,' said Fotini. 'And now I can picture where you really live.'

'So what's new? How's little Mattheos?'

'He's wonderful, what more can I say? He's eating a lot and growing very big.'

'It's just as well he likes his food. He does live in a restaurant after all,' commented Maria with a smile. 'And what's happening in Plaka? Have you seen my sister lately?'

'No. Not for a long time,' Fotini said thoughtfully.

Giorgis had told Maria that Anna came to see him quite regularly, but now she wondered if that were really true. If Anna had turned up in her shiny car, Fotini would have known about it. The Vandoulakis family had been angry in the extreme when they learned of Maria's leprosy and it had not surprised her at all that Anna had not written since she came to Spinalonga. Neither would it really surprise her if her father had lied about her sister's visits.

Both women were silent.

'Antonis sees her from time to time, though, when he's working,' Fotini said at last.

'Does he say how she looks?'

'Fine, I think.'

Fotini knew what Maria was really asking. Was her sister pregnant? After all those years of marriage, it was high time that Anna had a child. If not, there must be a problem. Anna was not expecting a baby, but there was something else happening in her life that Fotini had thought long and hard about telling Maria.

'Look, I probably shouldn't tell you this, but Antonis has seen Manoli coming and going from Anna's house.'

'That's allowed, isn't it? He is family.'

'Yes, he is family, but even members of your family don't need to visit every other day.'

'Perhaps it's to discuss estate business with Andreas,' Maria said matter-of-factly.

'But he doesn't go when Andreas is there,' said Fotini. 'He goes during the day, when Andreas is out.'

Maria found herself being defensive.

'Well it sounds to me as though Antonis is spying.'

'He isn't spying, Maria. I think your sister and Manoli have grown rather close.'

'Well if they have, why doesn't Andreas do something about it?'

'Because he has absolutely no idea that it's going on,' said Fotini. 'It wouldn't even occur to him. And what he doesn't see or think about, he need never know about.'

The two women sat in silence for a moment, until Maria got up. She pretended to busy herself with washing their glasses but nothing took her mind away from what Fotini had just told her. She was thoroughly agitated, suddenly remembering her sister's rather edgy behaviour all those months ago when she and Manoli had visited. It was perfectly feasible that there might be something going on between them. She knew her sister was more than capable of such infidelity.

With sheer vexation she twisted the cloth round and round inside the glasses until they squeaked. As ever her thoughts were with her father. She felt keenly, even in anticipation, his ever-deepening shame. As for Anna, was she not the only one of the three Petrakis women who still had the possibility of a normal, happy life? Now it sounded as though she was doing everything she could to throw it all away. Maria's eyes pricked with tears of anger and frustration. She would hate Fotini to think that she was jealous. She knew Manoli would never be hers but it was hard nevertheless to bear the idea of him being with her sister.

'You know, I don't want you to think I care about Manoli any more, because I don't, but I do care about my sister's behaviour. What's to become of her? Does she really think that Andreas will never find out?'

'She obviously thinks he won't. Or if she does, it doesn't bother her. I'm sure the whole thing will just fade out.'

'That's probably optimistic, Fotini,' Maria said. 'But there's nothing we can do about it, is there?'

The two sat in silence for a moment before Maria changed the subject.

'I've started using my herbs again,' she said, 'with some success. People are beginning to come to me now and the *dictamus* worked almost immediately for an elderly gentleman with a stomach disorder.'

They continued to chat, though Fotini's revelation about Anna weighed heavily on their minds.

* * *

The relationship between Anna and Manoli did not, as Fotini predicted, fade out. On the contrary, the spark between them was rekindled and a fire soon smouldered. Manoli had been entirely faithful to Maria while they were engaged to be married. She was perfect, a virgin, his Agia Maria, and undoubtedly she would have made him a happy man. Now she was a fond memory. The first few weeks after Maria had gone to Spinalonga he had been listless and unhappy, but the period of mourning the loss of his fiancée soon passed. Life had to go on, he had thought to himself.

Like a moth to a flame he was drawn back to Anna. She was still there in that house, so close, so needy and somehow so gift-wrapped in her tightly fitted ribbon-trimmed dresses.

It was around lunch time one day, his old habitual visiting time, when Manoli let himself into the kitchen at the big house on the estate.

'Hello, Manoli.' Anna greeted him without surprise and with enough warmth to melt the snows on Mount Dhikti.

His confidence that she would be pleased to see him was matched by her arrogance. She had known that he would come, sooner or later.

Alexandros Vandoulakis had recently handed the entire estate over to his son. This gave Andreas huge responsibilities and less and less time at home, and soon Manoli was seen leaving his cousin's house more often than just on alternate days. He was now there every day. Antonis was not the only person aware of this. Many of the estate workers knew about it too. There was a double safety net that Anna and Manoli relied on: Andreas was too busy to notice anything himself, and it was worth more than any man's job to approach their boss with tales about his wife. For these reasons they could enjoy each other with impunity.

There was nothing that Maria could do and the only influence Fotini had was to urge her brother to keep it to himself. If Antonis mentioned it to their father, Pavlos, then it was bound to reach Giorgis, since the two men were great companions.

Between Fotini's visits, Maria tried to put her sister to the back of her mind. Her inability to influence the situation was not determined only by the distance between them. She knew that even if she was still on the mainland, Anna would have been doing just what she liked.

Maria began to look forward to the days when Kyritsis came across, and always made sure she was at the quayside to meet her father and the silver-haired doctor. One fine summer day Kyritsis stopped to talk. He had heard from Dr Lapakis of Maria's skills with herbal cures and tinctures. A firm believer in modern medicine, he had long been sceptical about the power of the sweet, gentle flowers that grew on the mountainsides. What strength could they possibly have when compared with twentieth-century drugs? Many of the patients he saw on Spinalonga, however, talked of the relief they had experienced through some of Maria's concoctions. He was prepared to relax his cynicism, and told her so.

'I know conviction when I see it,' he said. 'I've also seen some real evidence on this island that these things can work. I can hardly continue to be a sceptic, can I?'

'No, you can't. I'm glad you admit it,' said Maria, with a note of triumph. It gave her huge satisfaction to realise that she had successfully persuaded this man to change his views. Even greater was her satisfaction when she looked at him and saw his face break into a smile. It transformed him.

Chapter Nineteen

THE DOCTOR'S SMILE changed the climate around him. Kyritsis had not been given to smiling in the past. Other people's misery and anxiety were the cornerstones of his life and rarely gave him cause for levity or pleasure. He lived alone in Iraklion, working long days in the hospital, and the few waking hours he had outside it were spent reading and sleeping. Now, at last, there was something else in his life: the beauty of a woman's face. To the hospital staff in Iraklion and to Lapakis and the lepers who were now regular patients he was just the same as he always had been: a dedicated, single-minded and unnervingly serious – some would say humourless – scientist. For Maria he had become a different person. Whether he would be her salvation in the long term she did not know, but he saved her in a small way every time he crossed the water by making her pulse quicken. She was a woman again, not just a patient waiting on this rock to die.

Though the temperatures began to drop during those first days of autumn, Maria felt an increasing warmth in Nikolaos Kyritsis. When he arrived on the island each Wednesday he would stop to talk to her. First of all it would be just for five minutes, but as time went on it was for longer on each occasion. Eventually, meticulous about punctuality and the need to be on time for his hospital appointments, he began to arrive earlier on the island to allow himself enough time to see Maria. Giorgis, who always rose at six o'clock in the morning, was perfectly happy to bring Kyritsis over at eight-thirty rather than nine and observed that the days when Maria had come to talk to him on Wednesdays were over. She still met the boat, but not to see her father.

Usually a man of few words, Kyritsis talked to Maria about his work back in Iraklion and explained the research with which he was involved. He described how the war had interrupted everything and told her what he had been doing during those years, painting a detailed description for her of a war-blasted city where every last trained medical person was required to be on duty almost round the clock to care for the sick and wounded. He told her about his travels to international conferences in Egypt and Spain where the world's experts on leprosy treatment gathered to share their ideas and to give papers on their latest theories. He told her about the various cures that were currently being tried out and what he really thought of them. Occasionally he had to remind himself that this woman was a patient and might eventually be a recipient of the drug therapy that was being trialled on Spinalonga. How strange, he sometimes found himself thinking, to have found such friendship on this small island. Not only his old friend, Christos Lapakis, but this young woman too.

For her part Maria looked at him and listened, but offered very little of her own life in return. She felt she had little to share. Her existence had become so small, so limited, so narrowly focused.

As Kyritsis saw it, people on Spinalonga were living a life that he might almost have envied. They came and went about their business, sat in the *kafenion*, saw the latest films, went to church and nurtured friendships. They lived in a community where everyone knew each other and had a common bond. In Iraklion he could walk the length of the bustling street every day for a week and not see a familiar face.

As vital to Maria as the conversations with Dr Kyritsis were her weekly meetings with Fotini, but these she anticipated half with dread these days.

'So has he been seen leaving the house this week?' she asked as soon as Giorgis was out of earshot.

'Once or twice,' answered Fotini. 'But only when Andreas was there too. The olive harvest has started so he is around more. Manoli and Andreas are supervising the presses and apparently they both go back to the big house for dinner.'

'Perhaps it was all in your brother's imagination, then. Surely if Manoli and Anna were lovers he wouldn't go for dinner there with Andreas?'

'Why not? It would be *more* likely to arouse suspicion if he stopped going there.'

Fotini was right. Anna was spending many an evening perfectly coiffed, manicured and poured into immaculately well-fitted dresses, playing the twin roles of good wife to her husband and welcoming hostess to his cousin. It was no more than Andreas expected of her. She carried the situation off effortlessly and the chances of her fluffing a line or casting a giveaway glance were almost non-existent. For Anna the under-currents only added to the frisson of being on an imaginary stage, and on the days when her parents-in-law were there it created additional tension, increasing her excitement and the sublime thrill of concealment.

'Did you enjoy our evening?' she would ask Andreas later in the blank darkness of their ample bed.

'Yes, why?'

'I was just asking,' she would say, and as they began to make love she felt the weight of Manoli's body and heard his deep groans. Why should Andreas question such pleasure? Afterwards, he lay silent and breathless in the dark shuttered room, the unsuspecting victim of her passion for another man, a man with whom she had only made love in broad daylight.

For Anna there was no conflict in this situation. Since she had no choice in the matter of her passion for Manoli, her infidelity was almost justified. He had appeared unannounced in her life and her reaction had been spontaneous. Free will played no part in her response to him and it had never occurred to her that it could. Manoli's presence electrified her, aroused every hair on her body and made every square centimetre of her soft, pale skin yearn to be touched. It could never be any other way. I can't help it, she said to herself as she brushed her hair in the morning on the days when Andreas had left for the furthest area of the estate and she expected Manoli to appear in her kitchen at lunchtime. There is nothing I can do. Manoli was her husband's blood relative. With all the will in the world she could not have driven him away. She was a trapped but uncomplaining victim, and even though it was happening under his own roof Andreas had not the slightest inkling that Anna was betraying him in his own bed, with the framed *stephana*, the marriage crowns, witnessing her act of perfidy.

Andreas did not spend much time thinking about Manoli. He was glad that he had returned from his travels but he left any worrying about him to his dear mother, who fretted that her nephew was in his thirties and not yet married. Andreas was sorry that the marriage to his wife's sister had encountered such an insurmountable obstacle, but he supposed that sooner or later his cousin would find another suitable woman to bring into the family. As for Eleftheria, she was sorry that her nephew's sweet bride had been snatched away but was even sorrier to have a nagging suspicion that some affinity existed between Manoli and her daughter-in-law. She could not quite define it and indeed sometimes told herself it was in her imagination. It was as fleeting as a shape in a cloud.

Maria shuddered to think of how Anna might be behaving. Her sister had never bothered with caution and nothing would change that now. Her real concern, however, was not Anna herself but the impact of her behaviour on their father. There was not one secure element in that poor dear man's life, she thought.

'Has she no shame?' she muttered

'I'm not sure she has,' said Fotini.

The women tried to talk of other things, but conversation always began and ended with talk of Anna's infidelity and speculation on how long it would be before Anna cast a careless glance in Manoli's direction that might just make Andreas pause for a moment and wonder. Little by little, any residual feelings Maria might have had for Manoli evaporated. The only certainty she had was that there was nothing she could possibly do.

It was now late October. The winter winds were gaining

strength and would soon penetrate the thickest overcoats and the heaviest of woollen wraps. It seemed to Maria that it was uncivilised to stand here in the perishing cold talking to Dr Kyritsis, but the thought of giving up their conversations was unbearable. She loved talking with this man. They seemed never to run out of things to say, even though she felt she had so little of interest to tell him. She could not help comparing the way he spoke to her with the way Manoli had talked. Her fiancé's every sentence had been full of playful banter, but with Kyritsis there was not a flicker of flirtation.

'I want to know what it's really like to live here,' he said to her one day as the wind gusted around them.

'But you see the island every week. You must be as familiar with how it looks as I am,' she said, rather puzzled by his statement.

'I look at it, but I don't see it,' he said. 'I see it as an outsider passing through. That's very different.'

'Would you like to come to my house and have some coffee?' Maria had quietly practised saying these words for some time, but when they finally came out she hardly recognised her own voice.

'Coffee?' Kyritsis had heard her clearly enough, but repeated the word for want of something to say in response.

'Would you?'

It was as though she had disturbed him from a reverie.

'Yes, I think I would.'

They walked together through the tunnel. Though he was the doctor and she the patient, they walked side by side, like equals. Both of them had passed through the Venetian walls a hundred times, but this was a different kind of journey.

Kyritsis had not walked a street like this in the company of a woman for years, and Maria, walking along with a man who was not her father, felt self-conscious in a way she thought she had left behind with childhood. Someone might see her and jump to the wrong conclusion. 'It's the doctor!' she wanted to shout, desperate to spare herself from gossip.

Quickly she showed the way into the small alleyway close to the end of the tunnel and they entered her house. Maria began making coffee. She knew Kyritsis did not have long and would want to be punctual for his first appointment.

While Maria busied herself finding sugar, cups and saucers, Kyritsis looked about the room. It was much more comfortable and colourful than his own small apartment in Iraklion. He noticed the embroidered cloths, the picture of the young Kyria Petrakis with Maria and another girl on the wall. He saw a neat row of books, a jug containing leafy sprigs from an olive tree and bunches of lavender and herbs hanging to dry from the ceiling. He saw order and domesticity and felt warmed by them both.

Now that they were on Maria's terrain, he felt he could get her to talk about herself. There was one burning question he wanted to ask. He knew so much about the disease, its symptoms, its epidemiology, its pathology, but of course he did not know what it really *felt* like to have leprosy and until now he had never thought of asking one of his patients.

'How does it feel . . .' he ventured, 'to be a leper?'

The question seemed so personal, but Maria did not hesitate to answer.

'In some ways I feel no different now than I did a year ago, but I *am* different because I've been sent here,' she said. 'It's a bit like being in prison, for someone like me who's not affected by the disease day to day. Except there are no locks on the door, no bars.'

As she said this, her mind went back to that cold autumn morning when she had left Plaka to come to Spinalonga. Life on a leper colony had certainly not been what she had wished for, but she paused for a moment and wondered what it would have been like had she married Manoli. Would that have been another kind of prison? What sort of man would betray his own family? What Judas would abuse the kindness and hospitality that had been shown him? She had been taken in by his charm but realised now that circumstances might have spared her. This was a man with whom she had not once had a conversation that touched anything deeper or broader than the olive harvest, the music of Mikis Theodorakis or whether to attend the saint's day celebrations in Elounda. Such *joie de vivre* had attracted her at first but she realised that perhaps there was no more to him than that. Life with Manoli might have been just another kind of life sentence, no better than the one she was condemned to on Spinalonga.

'There are lots of good things, though,' she added. 'Wonderful people like Elpida Kontomaris and the Papadimitrious and Dimitri. They have such spirit and, do you know something, even though they've been here an awful lot longer than I have, they never, ever complain.'

When she had finished speaking, Maria poured coffee into a cup and passed it to Kyritsis. She noticed, too late, that his hand trembled violently, and when he took the coffee, the cup clattered to the ground. A dark puddle spread across the stone floor and there was an awkward silence before Maria rushed to the sink to get a cloth. She sensed his profound embarrassment and was keen to relieve him of it.

'Don't worry, it's fine,' she said, mopping up, collecting the pieces of patterned china in a dustpan as she did so. 'As long as you didn't burn yourself.'

'I'm terribly sorry,' he said. 'I'm terribly sorry to have broken your cup. It was so clumsy of me.'

'Don't worry about it. What's a cup?'

It was, in fact, a special cup, one of the set that her mother had brought from Plaka, but Maria realised that she did not mind at all. It was almost a relief that Kyritsis was not so perfect, not as impeccable in every way as he outwardly appeared.

'Perhaps I shouldn't have come,' Kyritsis mumbled. In his mind, it was a sign that he should not have broken the rules of professional etiquette in which he believed so strongly. By coming into Maria's house for social reasons he had crossed a boundary with a patient.

'Of course you should have come. I invited you and I would have been miserable if you hadn't.'

Maria's outburst was spontaneous, and more enthusiastic than she had really intended. It surprised Dr Kyritsis, but it also surprised her. Now they were even. Both had lost their composure.

'Please stay and have some more coffee.'

Maria's eyes looked into the doctor's so imploringly that he could do nothing but accept. She took another cup from the rack, and this time, once the coffee was poured into it, she left it on the table for him to pick up safely.

They both sipped without speaking. Sometimes there is

awkwardness in silence, but not this time. Eventually Maria broke the spell.

'I hear a few people have started some drug treatment. Is it going to work?' It was a question she had been longing to ask.

'It's quite early days, Maria,' he answered. 'But we have to hold out a little hope. We are aware of some contraindications to the treatment, which is why we have to be cautious at this stage.'

'What kind of drug is it?'

'Its full name is diphenyl sulphone, but it's generally known as dapsone. It's sulphur-based and potentially toxic. The key thing, though, is that any improvement generally takes place over the very long term.'

'So it's no magic potion then,' said Maria, trying not to sound disappointed.

'No, I'm afraid it's not,' said Kyritsis. 'It'll be a while before we really know if anyone will ever be fully cured. I'm afraid no one will be leaving quite yet.'

'So that means you might be able to come for coffee another time?'

'I very much hope so. You make such good coffee.'

Dr Kyritsis knew his answer was somehow gauche and that it implied he was only interested in coming because of the quality of her coffee. That was not at all how it was meant to sound.

'Well, I had better be going now,' he said, trying to cover his embarrassment. 'Thank you.' With that rather stiff farewell, Kyritsis left.

As she cleared the cups and swept the floor to remove the

last shards of the broken cup, Maria heard herself humming. The sensation could only be described as a lightness of heart, an unfamiliar feeling in a grey place, but she would enjoy it and hope against hope that it would remain with her. All day she felt as though her feet did not quite touch the ground. She had much to do but each task felt a pleasure. As soon as she had tidied up, she bundled some of her herb jars into a rough basket and set off to see Elpida Kontomaris.

The elderly woman rarely locked her door, and Maria let herself in. She found Elpida in bed, pale but propped up on her pillows.

'Elpida, how are you feeling today?'

'I am actually feeling much better,' she said. 'Thanks to you.'

'It's thanks to nature, not to me,' Maria corrected her. 'I'm going to make another infusion for you. It's obviously working. You're to have a cupful of this now, one in about three hours, and then I will come back this evening to give you a third.'

For the first time in weeks, Elpida Kontomaris was beginning to feel well again. The griping stomach aches she had been suffering from finally seemed to be on the wane, and there was no doubt in her mind that her improvement was due to the soothing herbal medicines that Maria had been preparing for her. Though the skin on her elderly face sagged and her clothes hung off her like limp rags, her appetite was beginning to return and she could now imagine a time when she might eat properly again.

As soon as she had made sure that Elpida was comfortable, Maria was gone. She would return that evening to ensure that her patient took her next dose, but meanwhile she would spend the day at 'the block', as it was unaffectionately known. The large apartment building situated at the end of the main street was still unpopular. It felt lonely and desolate up there at the top of the hill. People preferred the cosiness of the small Turkish and Italian houses. The proximity of the older houses to each other helped promote a sense of community which mattered more to them than bright strip lighting and modern shutters.

Today Maria went there because four of the apartments were home to lepers who could no longer fend for themselves. These were the cases whose ulcerated feet had led to amputation, whose claw-like hands rendered them incapable of even the simplest domestic tasks and whose faces were deformed beyond recognition. In any other situation, the lives of these disfigured individuals would have been abjectly miserable. Even now several of them lived on the very brink of despair, but the efforts of Maria and a few other women like her never allowed them to go over it.

What these people cherished more than anything was their privacy. For one young woman, whose nose had been destroyed by leprosy and whose eyes were held permanently open through facial paralysis, the stares of her fellow colonists were insupportable. Occasionally she went out at night and crept into the church, alone with the dark icons and the comforting smell of melted candlewax, but otherwise, she would never go out, except for the very short monthly walk to the hospital, where Lapakis would chart any changes to her lesions and prescribe drugs to help lure her mind and body from an almost permanently wakeful state into one of short but blissful sleep. Another, slightly older woman had lost one of her hands. She was paying the highest price for the severe burns she had inflicted on herself while cooking for her family only a few months before coming to the island. Dr Lapakis had done everything he could to try and heal the ulcerated wounds, but the infection had got the better of both of them and his only choice had been to amputate. Her remaining hand was fixed in a claw. She could just about hold a fork, but she could not open a tin or do up a button.

Every one of the dozen or so extreme cases who lived here was hideously scarred. Most of them had arrived on Spinalonga in an acute state of decrepitude, and in spite of the hospital's best efforts to ensure that no long-term damage was done to them by the numbing effects of the disease, it was not always possible to control it. They matched the biblical image of the leper and were as far along the hellish road to disfigurement as anyone could be while still being perceptibly human.

Maria shopped and cooked for these end-stage cases. She hardly even noticed their deformities any more, as she served them lunch and, in some cases, helped to feed them. Always in her mind was the thought that her mother might well have been like this. No one had ever really told her, but as she lifted spoons of rice to their lips, she hoped that Eleni had never suffered as these people did. She regarded herself as one of the lucky ones. Whether or not the new drug treatment worked successfully, these people's broken bodies could never be mended.

Most people on the mainland imagined that all lepers were as ravaged by the disease as these extreme cases and the very thought of their proximity repulsed them. They feared for themselves and for their children and had no doubt that the bacillus that had infected the people on this island could be airborne into their own homes. Even in Plaka there were people with such misconceptions. In the past few years, a secondary reason for resenting the colony had brewed. Greatly exaggerated stories of the Athenians' wealth had whipped people up into a state of increasing rancour, particularly in the poorer hillside communities of Selles and Vrouhas which did not enjoy the reliable income of fishing villages such as Plaka. One minute they feared the idea that they too might end up on Spinalonga; the next they seethed with envy at the idea that the colonists might be living more comfortable lives than they were themselves. Their fears were both ill-founded and deep-rooted.

One day in February a rumour began to circulate. It was sparked by the idle comment of one man, and like a forest fire from a single carelessly dropped match it spread with frightening speed and soon rampaged through every nearby village from Elounda in the south to Vilhadia on the northern coast. It was said that the mayor in Selles had taken his ten-year-old son to hospital in Iraklion. He was to have tests for suspected leprosy. Perhaps the disease was spreading from the island to the mainland. Within a day, the storm clouds of crowd overreaction had gathered. A ringleader in each village and the long-incubated feelings of fear and loathing were all it took for anger to boil over, and people began to descend on Plaka, intent on the island's destruction. Their cause was an irrational one. If Spinalonga was sacked, they reasoned, no further lepers could be sent there and the Greek government would be forced to relocate the colony. They also imagined that once threatened, the influential Athenians would insist on being taken somewhere safer. Either way, it would rid them of this filthy blot on their landscape.

The mob planned to take every fishing boat they could lay their hands on and land under cover of darkness. By five o'clock that Wednesday afternoon there was a gathering of two hundred, mostly men, on the Plaka quayside. Giorgis saw the first trucks arrive and heard the commotion as people spilled out of them and made their way down to the quayside. Like the other villagers of Plaka, he was aghast. It was time for him to go over to collect Kyritsis, but first he had to force his way through the crowd to find his boat. As he did so, he caught snatches of conversation.

'How many can we fit into a boat?'

'Who's got the petrol?'

'Make sure there's plenty!'

One of the ringleaders spotted the old man getting into his boat and addressed him aggressively.

'Where do you think you're going?'

'I'm going across to collect the doctor,' he answered.

'What doctor?'

'One of the doctors who works over there,' answered Giorgis.

'What good can doctors do for lepers?' the ringleader sneered, playing to the crowd.

As the group laughed and jeered, Giorgis pushed his boat away from the quay. His whole body quaked with fear and his hand trembled violently on the tiller. The little boat fought hard against the choppy sea, and never had the journey seemed longer. From some way off he could see the dark silhouette of Kyritsis, and eventually he was bringing the boat close to the stony wall.

The doctor did not bother to tie the boat up, but instead climbed straight in. It had been an arduous day and he was eager to get home. In the half-light, he could hardly see Giorgis's face under his hat, but the old man's voice was unusually audible.

'Dr Kyritsis,' he almost choked, 'there's a crowd over there. I think they're planning to attack Spinalonga!'

'What do you mean?'

'Hundreds of them have arrived. I don't know where from, but they're getting some boats together and they've got cans of petrol. They could be on their way any time now.'

Kyritsis was dumbstruck both by the stupidity of these people and by fear for the islanders. There was little time. He had a very swift choice to make. It would be wasting valuable minutes if he went back inside the great walls to warn the lepers. He had to get to the mainland to talk these lunatics out of their plan.

'We need to get back – *fast*,' he urged Giorgis.

Giorgis swung the boat around. This time the wind was behind him, and the caique covered the distance between island and mainland in no time at all. By now the people on the quayside had lit their torches, and as the small boat reached the shore another truckload of men was arriving. There was a ripple of excitement as Giorgis brought the boat in, and when Kyritsis disembarked the crowd parted to make way for a tall, broad-shouldered man who was clearly their spokesman.

'So who are *you*?' he mocked. 'Coming and going from the leper colony as freely as you like?'

The noisy crowd fell silent to listen to the exchange.

'My name is Dr Kyritsis. I am currently treating a number of patients on the island with new drug therapy. There are signs that this could lead to a cure.'

'Oh!' the man laughed sarcastically. 'Listen, everybody! Do you hear that? The lepers are going to get better.'

'There is a very strong chance of it.'

'Well supposing we don't believe that?'

'It doesn't matter if *you* don't believe it.' Kyritsis was dramatic in his emphasis. He focused on the ringleader. He could see that this bully would be nothing without his mob.

'So why is that then?' the man said with scorn, surveying the crowd who stood expectantly on the quayside, their faces lit by the flickering torches. Now he was trying to whip them up. He had misjudged this slight man who seemed to command more attention than he would have expected for someone of his stature.

'If you lay so much as a finger on a single one of those lepers out there,' said Kyritsis, 'you will find yourself in a prison cell darker and deeper than your worst nightmares. If even *one* of those lepers dies, you will be tried and convicted for murder. I will personally see to it.'

There was a stir amongst the crowd and then it fell silent again. The leader could sense that he had lost them. Kyritsis's firm voice penetrated the silence.

'Now what do you plan to do? Go home quietly or do your worst?'

People turned to each other and small huddles formed. One by one, torches were extinguished, plunging the quayside almost into darkness. One by one the crowd walked quietly to their vehicles. All their resolve to destroy Spinalonga had evaporated.

As the leader made his way alone back to the main street, he cast a backward glance at the doctor.

'We'll be looking out for that cure,' he shouted. 'And if it doesn't come, we'll be back. You mark my words.'

Giorgis Petrakis had remained in his boat during this confrontation, watching first with fear and then with admiration as Dr Kyritsis diffused the mob. It had seemed so unlikely that a lone individual could deter the force of this gang of thugs that had appeared hell-bent on destroying the leper colony.

Kyritsis had seemed to be completely in control, but inwardly he had feared for his own life. Not just that. He had feared for the life of every leper on the island. Once his heart ceased to feel that it would burst from his chest, he realised there was something specific that had given him the courage to stand up to the crowd: it was the possibility that the woman he loved had been in danger. He could not deny it to himself. It was Maria he had been desperate to save.

Chapter Twenty

IT DID NOT take long for word to get around Spinalonga that an uprising against the island had been quelled. Everyone soon knew that Dr Kyritsis had single-handedly dispersed a rowdy mob and for that he was the hero of the hour. He returned the following Wednesday as normal, and his anticipation at seeing Maria was more intense than ever. The realisation that he had such strong feelings for her had taken him by surprise, and he had thought of little else all week. She was on the quayside to meet him, a familiar figure in her green coat, and today a broad smile stretched across her face.

'Thank you, Dr Kyritsis,' she said, before he had even stepped off the boat. 'My father told me how you stood up to those men and everyone here is so grateful for what you did.'

By now Kyritsis was on dry land. Every part of him wanted to take her in his arms and declare his love, but such spontaneous behaviour went against a lifetime of reticence and he knew that he could not do it.

'Anyone would have done the same. It was nothing,' he said quietly. 'I did it for you.'

Such unguarded words. He knew he should be more careful.

'And for everyone on this island,' he added hastily.

Maria said nothing and Kyritsis had no idea whether she had even heard him. As usual they walked together through the tunnel, their feet crunching on the gravelly surface, and neither of them spoke. There was a silent acknowledgement that Kyritsis would come to her home for coffee before going on to the hospital, but as they reached the bend in the tunnel he saw immediately that today something was different. It was dark at the exit, and the usual view of Spinalonga's main street was obscured. The reason for this soon became clear. A huge crowd of perhaps two hundred had gathered there. Nearly every inhabitant of the island who was fit enough had made his or her way from home to greet the doctor. Children, young people and the elderly with their sticks and crutches had all turned out that chilly morning, hats on, collars up, to express their gratitude. As Kyritsis emerged, applause broke out all around him and he stopped in his tracks, taken aback to be the centre of attention. As the clapping died down, Papadimitriou stepped forward.

'Dr Kyritsis. On behalf of every inhabitant of this island, I would like to thank you for what you did last week. We understand that you saved us from invasion and in all likelihood from injury or death. Everyone here will be eternally grateful to you for that.'

Expectant eyes gazed at him. They wanted to hear his voice.

'You people have as much right to life as anyone on the

mainland. As long as I have anything to do with it, no one will destroy this place.'

Once again applause broke out, and then the islanders gradually drifted away and went about their daily business. Kyritsis had been overwhelmed by the ovation and was relieved when he was no longer the centre of so much attention. Papadimitriou was now at his side and walking along with him.

'Let me accompany you to the hospital,' he said, unaware that this deprived the doctor of precious moments with Maria. With the milling crowd Maria already knew that she could not expect Kyritsis to come to her house. It would be entirely inappropriate. She watched his receding figure and returned to her home. Two cups sat in the middle of her small table, and as she filled one and sat down to drink the coffee which had been brewing on her stove she addressed an imaginary figure sitting across the table.

'Well, Dr Kyritsis,' she said. 'You're a hero now.'

Meanwhile, Kyritsis thought of Maria. How could he possibly wait until the following Wednesday to see her? Seven days. One hundred and sixty-eight hours. There was, however, plenty to distract him. The hospital was under pressure. Dozens of the lepers were in need of urgent attention, and with only two people running the entire place, Lapakis and Manakis were more relieved than ever to see him.

'Good morning, Nikolaos!' cried Lapakis teasingly. 'The finest doctor in Crete, and now the Saint of Spinalonga!'

'Oh come on, Christos,' replied Kyritsis, slightly abashed. 'You know you would have done the same.'

'I'm not sure, you know. By all accounts they were pretty rough.'

'Well all that was last week,' said Kyritsis, brushing the episode to one side. 'We need to get on with today's issues. How are our test patients doing?'

'Let's go into my office and I'll put you in the picture.'

On Lapakis's desk was a tower of files. He picked them up one by one and gave his friend and colleague a brief description of the current state of each patient receiving the drug treatment. Most of the fifteen were showing signs of a positive reaction, though not all.

'Two of them are in a severely reactive state,' said Lapakis. 'One of them has had a temperature of around 104 degrees since you last came, and Athina just told me that the other kept the whole island awake last night with her screams. She keeps asking me how she can have no sensation in her arms and legs and yet feel such terrible pain. I haven't got an answer for her.'

'I'll take a look at her in a minute, but I think the best thing now would be to withdraw the treatment. There's a good chance that there might be some spontaneous healing and the sulphone could do some damage if that's the case.'

When they had taken a brief look through the notes, it was time for the two doctors to do the ward rounds. It was a grim business. One of the patients, who was covered with pus-filled swellings, wept in sheer agony as Lapakis applied a solution of trichloracetic acid to dry the lesions. Another listened quietly as Kyritsis suggested that the best way of dealing with the dead bones in his fingers would be amputation, a simple operation which could be done without anaesthetic, such was the absence of physical sensation in that part of the body. For another there was a visible surge of optimism as Lapakis described the tendon transplant he planned to do on his foot to enable him to walk again. At each bedside, the doctors agreed with the patient what the next stage would be. For some it was the prospect of pain-relieving injections, for others it might be the excision of lesions.

The first of the outpatients then began to arrive. Some merely needed new dressings for their ulcerated feet, but for others the treatment was more gruelling, particularly for a woman who required the excision of a lepromatous growth in her nose and the application of a dozen adrenaline swabs in order to stem the bleeding.

All of this took until mid-afternoon, and then it was time to see the patients who were receiving the new treatment. One thing was becoming clear. Several months into the trial, the new doses of drug therapy were producing encouraging results and the side-effects which Dr Kyritsis had been wary of had not materialised among most of these cases. Each week he had been on the lookout for symptoms of anaemia, hepatitis and psychosis, all of which had been reported by other doctors involved in the administration of dapsone, but he was relieved that none of these were present here.

'We've taken all our guinea pigs up from twenty-five to three hundred milligrams of dapsone twice a week now,' said Lapakis. 'That's the most I can give them, isn't it?'

'I certainly wouldn't recommend anything higher, and if that's giving us these results I think we should regard it as the upper limit, especially given the length of time they'll all be having the injections. The most recent directive is that we should continue to prescribe dapsone for several years after the patient's leprosy has ceased to be active,' said Kyritsis, adding after a pause: 'It's a long haul, but if it leads to a cure I don't think any of them will complain.'

'What about starting the treatment with the next group?'

Lapakis was both excited and impatient. No one would be bold enough to claim that these lepers had been cured, and it would be a few months until they actually ran tests to see whether the leprosy bacillus had been eliminated from their systems. He had a gut feeling that after all these years of talk, false starts and no real faith in a cure, a turning point had been reached. Resignation, even despair, could now be replaced with hope.

'Yes, there's no point in waiting. I think we should select the next fifteen as soon as possible. As before, they should be in good general health,' said Kyritsis.

With every bone in his body, he wanted to make sure that Maria was among the list of names, but he knew it would be unprofessional to exert his influence. His mind had drifted from discussion of the new treatment to thoughts of when he would see Maria again. Each day would seem an age.

The following Monday, Fotini arrived on the island as usual. Maria wanted to tell her about the hero's welcome Dr Kyritsis had received the previous week, but she could see that Fotini was bursting with news. She had hardly got inside Maria's door before she came out with it.

'Anna's pregnant!'

'At last,' Maria said, unsure whether this news was good or bad. 'Does my father know?'

'He can't do, otherwise he would have said something to you, surely?'

'I suppose he would,' she said thoughtfully. 'How did you find out?'

'Through Antonis, of course. By all accounts the estate has been buzzing with speculation for weeks!'

'Tell me then. Tell me what they've been saying,' said Maria, impatient for detail.

'Well, for weeks and weeks Anna wasn't seen outside the house and there were rumours of ill-health, and then one day last week she finally reappeared in public – having put on a very noticeable amount of weight!'

'But that doesn't necessarily mean she's pregnant,' exclaimed Maria.

'Oh yes it does, because they've announced it. She's three and a half months gone.'

In her first few months of pregnancy, Anna had been racked by sickness. Every morning and throughout the day she heaved and retched. Nothing she ate stayed inside her, and for several weeks her doctor was doubtful that the baby would survive at all. He had never seen a woman so ill, so reduced by pregnancy, and once the vomiting subsided there was a new problem. She began to bleed. The only way she might save this baby now was to have complete bed-rest. It seemed, however, that the child was determined to cling on, and in her fourteenth week of pregnancy everything stabilised. To Andreas's great relief Anna then rose from her bed.

The gaunt face that had stared back at Anna from the mirror only a month before was now rounded once more, and as she turned sideways she could clearly see a bump. Her trademark slim-fitting coats and dresses had been put in the back of the wardrobe and she now wore more voluminous clothes, under which her belly slowly swelled.

It was an excuse for celebration on the estate. Andreas threw open his cellar, and early one evening under the trees outside the house all his workers came to drink the best of the previous year's wine. Manoli was there too, and his was the loudest voice among them as they toasted the forthcoming child.

Maria listened in disbelief as Fotini described these recent events.

'I can't believe she hasn't made a point of going to see Father,' she said. 'She never thinks of anyone but herself, does she? Do I tell him, or wait until she gets round to it?'

'If I were you, I would tell him. Otherwise he's bound to hear it from someone else.'

They sat in silence for a while. The expectation of a child was normally a cause for great excitement, especially among women and close relations. Not this time, though.

'Presumably it's Andreas's?'

Maria had said the unsayable.

'I don't know. My hunch is that even Anna doesn't know, but Antonis says that gossip is still rife. They were all happy to drink to the new baby's safe arrival, but behind Andreas's back there was plenty of whispering and speculation.'

'That's not really surprising, is it?'

The two women talked for a while longer. This significant family development had swept other events aside and temporarily diverted Maria's thoughts from Kyritsis and his gallant behaviour the week before. For their first meeting in many weeks, Fotini found she was not listening to Maria's continual chatter about the doctor. 'Doctor Kyritsis this,

Doctor Kyritsis that!' she had teased Maria who had turned the colour of a mountain poppy when Fotini pointed out this slowly growing obsession.

'I'll have to tell Father about Anna as soon as I can,' said Maria. 'I'll tell him as though it's the best news ever and say Anna has been too sick to come and see him. It's half true anyway.'

When they got back to the quayside, Giorgis had offloaded all the boxes he was delivering and was sitting on the wall under the tree, quietly smoking a cigarette and surveying the view.

Though he had sat here a thousand times, weather and light combined together to produce a different picture every day. Sometimes the barren mountains that rose up behind Plaka would be blue, sometimes pale yellow, sometimes grey. Today, with the low clouds across the landscape, they were not visible at all. Parts of the sea's surface were whipped up by wind, creating areas of light spray that swirled about across the water like steam. The ocean was masquerading as a seething cauldron of boiling water, but in reality it was as cold as ice.

The sound of the women's voices disturbed him from his reverie, and he stood up to get the boat ready to go. His daughter hastened her step.

'Father, don't rush away. There's some news. Some really good news,' she said, doing her best to sound enthusiastic. Giorgis paused. The only good news he ever hoped for was that Maria might one day say she could come home. It was the only thing in the world he prayed for.

'Anna is having a baby,' she said simply.

'Anna?' he said vaguely, as though he had almost forgotten

who she was. 'Anna,' he repeated, staring at the ground. The truth was that he had not seen his elder daughter for over a year. Since the day that Maria had started her life on Spinalonga, Anna had not visited even once, and as Giorgis was *persona non grata* at the Vandoulakis home, contact had ceased. Initially this had been a source of great sadness, but with the passage of time, though he knew the paternal tie would always remain, he began to forget about his daughter. Occasionally he would wonder how two girls born of the same mother and father and treated the same way from the day they were born could turn out so differently, but that was about all the thought he had given to Anna of late.

'That's good,' he said at last, struggling to find a response. 'When?'

'We think it's due in August,' replied Maria. 'Why don't you write to her?'

'Yes, perhaps I should. It would be a good excuse to get in touch.'

What reaction should he have to hearing about the impending arrival of his first grandchild? He had seen several of his friends in a state of high exuberance when they became grandfathers. Only the previous year his greatest friend Pavlos Angelopoulos had celebrated the birth of Fotini's baby with an impromptu session of drinking and dancing, and it seemed that the entire population of Plaka had descended on the bar to celebrate with him. Giorgis did not picture himself making merry on *tsikoudia* when Anna's baby arrived, but it was, at least, an excuse to write to her. He would ask Maria's help in composing a letter later that week, but there was no hurry.

Two days later it was time for Kyritsis's visit. When he came to Spinalonga he had to rise at five a.m., and after his long journey from Iraklion the last few miles were full of anticipation for the taste of strong coffee on his lips. He could see Maria waiting for him, and today he inwardly rehearsed the words he was going to say to her. In his head he saw a version of himself that was articulate but full of passion, calm but fired with emotion, but as he got off the boat and was confronted by the face of the beautiful woman he loved, he knew that he should not be so hasty. Though she looked at him with the eyes of a friend, she spoke to him with the voice of a patient, and as her doctor he realised that his dreams of confessing his love were but that. Dreams. It was out of the question to cross the barrier created by his position.

They walked through the tunnel as normal, but this time, to his relief, there was no one cheering him at the end of it. As usual the cups were on the table, and Maria had saved time by making the coffee before he arrived.

'People are still talking about the way you saved us,' she said, taking a pot off the stove.

'It's very nice of them to be so appreciative, but I am sure they'll forget about it soon. I just hope those troublemakers keep away in future.'

'Oh, I think they will. Fotini told me it was all sparked by the rumour that a local boy had been taken to Iraklion for leprosy tests. Well, the child and his father returned last weekend. They'd been on a trip to see the boy's grandmother in Hania and decided to stay there for a few days. He wasn't ill at all.'

Kyritsis, listening intently to Maria, resolved to keep his

feelings under control. To do otherwise would be wrong, a transgression of his position.

'We've had some very encouraging results from the drug testing,' he said, changing the subject. 'Some of the patients are really showing an improvement.'

'I know,' she said. 'Dimitri Limonias is one of them, and I was talking to him yesterday. He says he can already feel a change.'

'Much of that could be psychological,' said Kyritsis. 'Being put on any kind of treatment tends to give patients a huge boost. Dr Lapakis is compiling a list of people from whom we will select the next group. Ultimately, we hope almost everyone on Spinalonga will be given the new drugs.'

He wanted to say that he hoped she would be on that list. He wanted to say that all his years of research and testing would be worthwhile if she was saved. He wanted to say that he loved her. None of those words came.

Much as he would have loved to linger in Maria's pretty home, he had to leave. It was hard to face yet another seven days before seeing her again, but he would not tolerate bad time-keeping in himself or others and knew that they would be waiting for him up at the hospital. Wednesdays were like a shaft of sunlight in the darkness of a strenuous, overworked week for Dr Lapakis and Dr Manakis, and this made Kyritsis's assiduous punctuality even more important. The extra workload that had been created for these two doctors in administering the drug therapy was taking them over the edge of endurance. Not only did they have to treat the patients who were in lepra reaction, but they also now had people who were suffering from the side-effects of the drugs. On many nights now, Lapakis was not leaving the island until ten o'clock, sometimes returning again at seven in the morning. Soon Kyritsis would have to consider increasing the frequency of his visits to Spinalonga to twice or even three times a week.

Within a couple of weeks, Dr Lapakis had shortlisted his next group of candidates for treatment. Maria was one of them. One Wednesday in mid-March, when the wild flowers were beginning to spread across the slopes on the north side of Spinalonga and the tight buds on the almond trees were bursting into blossom, Kyritsis went to find Maria in her house. It was six o'clock and she was surprised to hear a knock on the door at that time. She was even more amazed to see the doctor standing there, when she knew he was usually hurrying to meet her father in order to begin his long journey back to Iraklion.

'Dr Kyritsis. Come in . . . What can I get for you?'

The evening light glowed burnt amber through the gauze curtains. It was as though the village outside was going up in flames, and for all Kyritsis cared at this moment, this could have been the case. To Maria's surprise, he took both her hands.

'You're going to start treatment next week,' he said, looking directly into her eyes and, with absolute certainly, he added, 'one day you're going to leave this island.'

There were so many words he had rehearsed, but when the moment came he declared his love with a soundless gesture. For Maria, the cool fingers that grasped hers and lightly pressed them were more intimate, more articulate, than any arrangement of words about love. The life-giving sensation of flesh on flesh almost overwhelmed her.

In all those hours of discussion when she and Kyritsis had sat together talking of abstract things, she had been aware that even in the chinks where silence crept in she felt complete and content. It was just like the feeling she got when she found a lost key or a purse. After the frantic search and then the discovery, there was a sense of peace and wholeness. That was what being with Dr Kyritsis was like.

She could not help comparing him with Manoli, whose flamboyant talk and flirtatious behaviour flowed out of him unchecked, like water from a burst pipe. On their very first meeting at the Vandoulakis home, he had grabbed her by the hands and kissed them as though he was passionately in love. Yes, that was just it: she knew with absolute certainty that Manoli had not been passionately in love with her, but with the *idea* of being passionately in love. And here was Kyritsis, who gave every indication of not recognising his own feelings. He had been much too busy and preoccupied with his work even to acknowledge the signs or the symptoms.

Maria looked up. Their eyes and hands were now locked together. His was a look that overflowed with kindness and compassion. Neither of them knew how long they stood like this, though it was enough time for one era of their lives to end and another to begin.

'I will see you next week,' Kyritsis said finally. 'By then I hope Dr Lapakis will have given you a date for starting treatment. Goodbye, Maria.'

As he left her house, Maria watched Kyritsis's slight frame until it disappeared round the corner and out of sight. She felt she had known him for ever. It was in fact more than half her life ago that she had first set eyes on him, when he came to visit Spinalonga in the days before the German occupation. Though he had made little impression then, she now found it hard to remember what it had felt like *not* to love him. What had lived in that great space that Kyritsis now occupied?

Though no recognisable words of love had been spoken between Maria and the doctor, there was still plenty to tell Fotini. When she arrived the following Monday, it was patently obvious to her that something had happened to her oldest friend. Theirs was a friendship that could pick up a subtle sign of mood change; the merest hint of unhappiness or ill-health was always betrayed in hair that seemed dull, skin that was sallow or eyes that lacked their usual sparkle. Women noticed these things in each other, just as they noticed a gleam in the eye or a lingering smile. Today Maria was radiant.

'You look as though you have been cured,' Fotini joked, putting her bag down on the table. 'Come on, tell me. What's happened?'

'Dr Kyritsis—' Maria began.

'As if I couldn't have guessed,' teased Fotini. 'Go on . . .'

'I don't know what to tell you, really. He didn't even say anything.'

'But did he *do* anything?' urged Fotini, with the fervour of a friend eager for detail.

'He held my hands, that's all, but it meant something. I'm sure of it.'

Maria was conscious that hand-holding might sound insignificant to someone who was still part of the great outside world, but even on mainland Crete a certain formality between men and women was still the norm for unmarried people.

'He said that I would be starting treatment soon and that I might one day leave this island . . . and he said it as though he cared.'

All of this might have seemed feeble evidence of love. Fotini had never even met Kyritsis properly, so who was she to judge? In front of her, though, she had the sight of her greatest friend suffused with happiness. That much was very real.

'What would people here think if they knew there was something between you and the doctor?' Fotini was practical. She knew how small-town people talked, and Spinalonga was no different from Plaka, where a relationship between a doctor and his patient would keep the gossips on their doorsteps well into the small hours.

'No one must be allowed to know. I'm sure that a few people have noticed him coming out of my house on Wednesday mornings, but nobody has said anything. At least not to my face.'

She was right. A handful of people with vicious tongues had tried to spread the word, but Maria was well liked on the island, and malicious talk only tended to stick when someone was already halfway to being unpopular. What concerned Maria more than anything was that people might think she was getting preferential treatment; first place in a queue for injections, for example, or some other kind of perk, however meagre, would be enough to spark jealousy. That would reflect badly on Kyritsis and she was determined to ensure that no criticism attached itself to him. People like Katerina Papadimitriou, who had proved rather interfering, had seen Kyritsis leave her house on many occasions, and for someone who wanted to be in control of everything around her, this was disturbing. The leader's wife had done all she could to find out from Maria why Kyritsis came, but Maria had been deliberately unforthcoming. She had a right to her privacy. The other source of trouble was Kristina Kroustalakis, the unofficial town-crier, whose attempts to discredit Maria in some way had continued relentlessly for the past year. She went into the *kafenion* every evening and, on the basis of no evidence at all, dropped hints to anyone she met that Maria Petrakis was not to be trusted.

'She's carrying on with the specialist, you know,' she would say in a stage whisper. 'You mark my words, she'll be cured and off the island before any of us.'

It kept her going, this mission to stir up anger and discontent. She had tried – and failed – to do the same with Maria's mother; now she would do her best to destabilise the daughter's peace of mind. Maria, however, was strong enough to withstand such behaviour and enough in love with the doctor to make her happiness untouchable.

Maria's course of treatment began that month. Her symptoms had been slow to develop since she arrived on the island, with the anaesthetic patches on her skin spreading only marginally during the past eighteen months. Unlike so many of her fellow islanders, she had not experienced numbness in the soles of her feet and the palms of her hands, which meant she was unlikely to be vulnerable to the sores and ulcers which had cost so many of her fellow lepers the ability to walk and fend for themselves. If a sharp stone found its way into her shoe she soon knew about it, and her lithe hands curled around the handles of the big cooking pots she used at the 'block' as readily as they had ever done. This made her one of the lucky ones, but there was, nevertheless, an extraordinary relief in the sense that, finally, something was being done to combat the disease. Though it had not yet devastated her body, it had already done plenty of damage to her life.

The springtime wind, the Sokoros, blew from the south, finding its way between the mountains to the Gulf of Mirabello, where it whipped the sea into a white frenzy. Meanwhile on land the trees, now full of leaves in bud, began to whisper. How much better a sound than the rattle of dry, barren branches. Now that it was nearly May, the sun came out strongly and reliably each day and drenched the landscape in colour. Monochrome sky and rock had vanished and the world now put on its blue, gold, green, yellow and purple. Throughout early summer, birdsong was noisily exuberant, and then came two months when nature stood still in the breathless air and the scent of roses and hibiscus hung heavily on the air. Leaves and flowers had strained to emerge from dormant winter trees and plants and remained perfect through June and July before curling, scorched and dry, in the heat of the sun.

Dr Kyritsis continued to visit Maria at home once a week. They continued to say nothing of their feelings towards each other and there was an element of magic in their silence. It had the perfect fragility of a soap bubble rising into the sky, so visible, so multicoloured, but best left untouched. Maria one day found herself wondering how much her mother and father had ever spoken about love. She guessed correctly that they rarely had; in their happy marriage, there had seemed no need to mention something so certain, so unequivocal.

Throughout these summer months Maria, and now over half the population of Spinalonga, continued with the dapsone treatment. They knew it did not mean an overnight cure – or, as the more sardonic of them called it, 'reprieve from the gallows' – but at least it gave them hope, and even those still waiting for their treatment bathed in reflected optimism. Not everyone thrived, however. In July, having started her course only two weeks earlier, Elpida Kontomaris went into lepra reaction. Whether or not it was a consequence of the drug treatment, the doctors could not be sure, but they stopped giving her the injections straight away and did what they could to relieve the agony she was in. Her temperature raged out of control and for ten days did not drop below 105 degrees. Her body was now covered in ulcerated sores and every nerve felt tender; there seemed to be no position in which she was comfortable. Maria insisted on visiting her and, against all the rules of the hospital, Dr Lapakis allowed her into the small ward where the old lady lay, sobbing and sweating by turns.

Through her half-closed eyes, she recognised Maria.

'Maria,' she whispered hoarsely, 'they can't do anything for me.'

'Your body is fighting the disease. You mustn't give up hope,' Maria urged. 'Especially now! For the first time ever, they are so confident of a cure.'

'No, listen to me.' Through a burning, uncontrollable wall of pain, Elpida pleaded with Maria. 'I've been ill for so long. I just want to go now. I want to be with Petros . . . Please tell them to let me go.'

Sitting on an old wooden chair by her bed, Maria took

the woman's limp hand. Was this, she wondered, the same death that her own mother had suffered? The same violent battle where a weary body found itself under attack with no means of defence? She had not been there to say farewell to her mother, but she would stay with Elpida until the end.

At some point during that hot night, Athina Manakis came to relieve her.

'Go and get some rest,' she said. 'You won't do yourself any good if you sit here all night without anything to eat or drink. I'll stay with Elpida for a while.'

By now, Elpida's breathing was shallow. For the first time, it seemed that she was out of pain. Maria knew she might not have long and did not want to miss the moment of her going.

'I'll stay,' she said firmly. 'I must.'

Maria's instincts were right. A short while later, in the quietest hour of the night, between the very last moments of human activity and the first stirring of the birds, Elpida gave a final sigh and was gone. At last she was released from her ravaged body. Maria wept until her body was drained of tears and energy. Her grief was not just for the elderly woman who had given her so much friendship since she had arrived on the island, but for her own mother, whose last days might have been as agonising as Elpida's.

The funeral was an event which brought everyone on the island pouring down to the little church of St Pantaleimon. The priest conducted the service in the doorway so that the hundred or so who stood outside in the sun-baked street could share it with those who were crammed into the cool interior. When the chanting and prayers were over, the flower-covered coffin was carried at the head of a long procession which made its way slowly up the hill past the hospital and the 'block' and round to the unpopulated side of the island, where rocks fell away into the dark Stygian waters. Some of the older people sat on their wooden-saddled donkeys to make this long journey; others took each step carefully and slowly, reaching the cemetery long after the body had been lowered into the ground.

It was the last week of July and the saint's day for St Pantaleimon was on the twenty-seventh of the month. It seemed both a good and a bad time for such a celebration. On the one hand, with one of the most beloved members of the community so recently buried, the patron saint of healing seemed not to have been doing his job. On the other, many people on Spinalonga who had been receiving the drug treatment were showing early signs of recovery. For some, their lesions no longer seemed to be spreading; for others, as blood returned to tissue, paralysis appeared to be reversed. At least for a few it seemed as though a miracle might be about to take place. St Pantaleimon's birthday party must go ahead, even if people thought they should be in mourning for a lost friend.

Special breads and pastries were baked the night before, and on the day itself people filed through the church to light their candles and say a prayer. In the evening there was dancing and the singing of *mantinades*, and the half-heartedness which had characterised some recent festivals was absent. When the wind gusted in their direction, the people of Plaka could hear the occasional strains of lyre and bouzouki as they drifted across the water.

'People need a future,' Maria remarked to Kyritsis when he was sitting at her table the following week. 'Even if they're unsure about what it's going to bring.'

'What do you hear them saying?' he asked. She was his earpiece in the real world of the leper colony.

'No one talks about leaving yet,' she said. 'I think we all realise it's still early days. But the mood has changed. The people who haven't started their treatment are getting restless too. They know it matters.'

'It does matter. It might seem slow, but I promise you it really is going to make a difference.'

'How slow will it be?' she asked. The question of how long it was all going to take had never really been broached.

'Even when the disease has ceased to be active, we would need to continue with treatment for one or two years, depending on the severity of the case,' he replied.

In the timescale of this ancient disease, the oldest known to mankind, one or two years was the blink of an eye. But as Kyritsis looked at Maria, he realised that it seemed an eternity to him. It did to her too, though neither of them was likely to say so.

As if to balance death with birth, news came at the end of August that Anna's baby had been born. Giorgis arrived one Friday morning to tell Maria. He had not yet seen the child, a girl, but Antonis had come hotfoot to Plaka the previous day to tell him. It had not been an easy birth. Anna had been ill for some weeks at the end of the pregnancy and the labour had been difficult and protracted. Though she was still weak, the doctor assured her she would make a quick recovery, ready to have another. Nothing was further from her mind. The baby, fortunately, was healthy and now thriving.

The birth of a child in the family had softened Alexandros Vandoulakis towards Giorgis Petrakis and he now felt that it was an appropriate moment for reconciliation. The old man had had sufficient time out in the cold. A few days later an invitation arrived for him to attend the baptism. This would take place the following week and would be followed by feasting and merrymaking, for which Cretans needed little excuse. The arrival of a child in the Vandoulakis family after nearly a decade of waiting was a reason for great thanksgiving and celebration in both the family and the community beyond it. No one welcomed the disruption of the natural order which occurred when the people who owned the land and provided jobs failed to produce children. Now that Anna Vandoulakis had given birth to one child, none doubted that she would produce another and that the next time it would be a boy. That would ensure, once and for all, that the old patterns would continue for the next generation.

The baptism took place in the same church in Elounda where Anna and Andreas had been married nine years earlier. How much had changed since then, reflected Giorgis as he sat on a hard wooden seat at the back of the church waiting, along with dozens of others, for his daughter and her husband to arrive with the baby. He had arrived as late as he could and now sat hunched inside his jacket, keen to avoid conversation with other members of the Vandoulakis family, whom he had not seen for nearly two years now. Alexandros and Eleftheria were already at the front of the church when he arrived, and next to them was Manoli, who was talking animatedly to the people in the row behind him, his hands waving about as he told some anecdote that left his audience helpless with laughter. He was as handsome as ever, his dark hair slightly longer than Giorgis remembered it and his teeth gleaming white against his tanned skin. He must miss Maria, he mused, to have still not found another girl to be his wife. Then the congregation rose. The priest had entered and was processing down the aisle, followed by Andreas and Anna. She carried a tiny bundle of white lace.

Giorgis was immediately struck by the appearance of his daughter. He expected to see the radiance of motherhood, but instead it was an almost gaunt figure who wafted past him. He thought back to how Eleni had looked after the birth of their two children and remembered how she had maintained a healthy fullness that seemed natural to someone who had been carrying a child all those months. Anna, however, was as slim as a young vine and looked as fragile. It was a long time since he had seen her, but her physique was not as he had expected. Andreas looked just the same, thought Giorgis, rather stiff and upright and as aware as ever of his place in the world

The buzz of lively chatter stopped and a hush descended on the congregation, as though no one wanted to wake the baby. Though she was blissfully unaware of anything but the warmth of her mother's arms around her, it was a significant moment for the child. Until baptised, Sofia, as she was to be named, was exposed to the 'evil eye', but once the ritual had taken place her spiritual safety would be guaranteed.

As the rest of the gathering once again took their seats, Manoli stepped forward. Aside from the priest and the baby, he was the key figure at the baptism: the *nonos*, the godfather. In accordance with Cretan tradition, a child was given one godparent, who was the most important person in his life after his mother and father. As the congregation watched and listened to the priest's incantations and saw the waters washing away the baby's nonexistent sins, the spiritual bond between Manoli and Sofia was forged. He was handed the baby and now kissed her forehead. As he did so, the indescribably sweet essence of newborn infant enveloped him. Nothing seemed more natural than to treasure this tiny weightless being.

In the final stage of the ritual, a pure white ribbon was hung round Manoli's shoulders by the priest and knotted to create a symbolic circle embracing both man and child. Manoli looked down at the baby's sweet face and smiled. She was awake now, and her dark, innocent eyes gazed unfocused into his. On his face she would have seen a look of pure adoration, and no one doubted for a second that he would forever love and cherish his godchild, his precious *filiotsa*.

Chapter Twenty-one

AFTER THE BAPTISM, Giorgis hung back as the crowd made their way out of the church's great double doors and into the sunshine outside. He wanted to see his granddaughter up close but also he wanted to speak with her mother. Until now Anna had not even been aware that her father was there, but as she turned to leave the church she spotted him and waved enthusiastically across the sea of people who were now making their way past him, resuming the conversations they had started before the service began. It seemed like an age before she reached him.

'Father,' she said brightly, 'I'm so pleased you could come.'

She spoke to him as though he were some old friend or distant relative with whom she had long since lost touch but with whom she was quite pleased to resume an acquaintance.

'If you really are so pleased I came, why haven't you been to see me for over a year? I've not been anywhere,' he said, adding pointedly: 'Except Spinalonga.'

'I'm sorry, Father, but I wasn't well at the beginning or end of the pregnancy, and these summer months have been so hot and uncomfortable.'

There was no point in being critical of Anna. There never

had been. She had always managed to twist criticism round and make the accuser feel guilty; the disingenuity of her manner was only what he had expected.

'Can I meet my granddaughter?'

Manoli had lingered at the front of the church while a group gathered around him to admire his god-daughter. She was still bound to him within the white ribbon and he appeared to have no intention of letting her go. It was loving, but also proprietorial, the way in which he held her so close. Finally he made his way up the aisle towards the man who had so nearly become his father-in-law. They greeted each other and Giorgis studied what he could see of his little granddaughter, who was buried deep in many layers of lace and once again fast asleep.

'She's beautiful, isn't she?' said Manoli, smiling.

'From what I can see of her she is,' replied Giorgis.

'Just like her mother!' continued Manoli, glancing up at Anna with laughter in his eyes.

He had not really given Maria a second thought for months but felt he ought to enquire after her.

'How is Maria?' he asked, his voice sufficiently full of concern and interest to fool anyone who might overhear into thinking that he still cared for her. It was the question Anna should have asked, and she now stood quietly to hear the answer, wondering after all whether Manoli still carried a flame for her sister. Giorgis was more than happy to talk about his younger daughter.

'She is quite well and her symptoms haven't really got worse since she's been there,' he said. 'She spends most of her time helping the lepers who can't look after themselves. If they need a hand with their shopping and cooking she does it for them, and she still does a lot with her herbal cures as well.'

What he did not mention was that most of the islanders were now undergoing treatment. There was no point in making too much of it, because even he did not know what it really meant. He understood that the injections they were having could alleviate symptoms, but more than that he did not know. He certainly did not believe in a cure for leprosy. It was pure fantasy to imagine that the oldest disease in the world could be eradicated, and he would not let himself indulge in such a dream.

As he finished speaking, Andreas came over.

'Kalispera, Giorgis. How are you?' he asked rather formally. The appropriate niceties were exchanged and then the moment came for them all to leave the church. Alexandros and Eleftheria Vandoulakis hovered in the background. Eleftheria was still embarrassed by the gulf that existed between themselves and Giorgis Petrakis, and privately she felt a great deal of pity for the old man. She did not, however, have the guts to say so. This would have been to defy her husband, who felt as keenly as ever the shame and stigma of having such a close connection with the leper colony.

The family were the last to leave the church. The bearded priest, magnificent in his gilded crimson robes and tall black hat, stood laughing in the sunshine with a group of men. All around him women in bright floral dresses chattered and children ran about, dodging the adults and squealing as they gave chase to each other. There was to be a party tonight and a sense of excitement hung in the air like an electric charge.

The wall of shimmering heat that met Giorgis when he

emerged from the marble coolness of the church of Agios Grigorios made him feel light-headed. He blinked in the glare and beads of perspiration rolled down his cheeks like cool tears. The collar of his woollen jacket prickled uncomfortably at his neck. Was he to stay with this crowd and make merry through the night? Or should he return to his village, where the familiarity of every winding street and worn front door gave him comfort? As he was about to try and slip away unnoticed, Anna appeared at his side.

'Father, you must come and have a drink with us. I insist on it,' she said. 'It'll bring the baby bad luck if you don't.'

Giorgis believed as much in the influence of fate and the importance of trying to ward off evil spirits and their malicious power as he did in God and all his saints, and not wishing to bring any misfortune to this innocent baby he could not refuse his daughter's invitation.

The party was already in full swing when he parked his truck under a lemon tree at the side of the long driveway that led to the Vandoulakis home. On the terrace outside the house, a group of musicians was playing. The sounds of lute, lyre, mandolin and Cretan bagpipe wove in and out of each other, and though the dancing had not yet begun, there was a keen sense of anticipation. A long trestle table was laid out with rows of glasses, and people helped themselves from barrels of wine and took platefuls of *meze*, small cubes of feta cheese, plump olives and freshly made *dolmades*. Giorgis stood for a while before helping himself to some food. He knew one or two people and for a while engaged in polite conversation with them.

When the dancing began, those who wished to do so joined

in, while others stood around to watch. Glass in hand, the old man looked on as Manoli danced. His lithe figure and energetic steps made him the centre of attention, as did his smile and the way in which he shouted instructions and encouragement. In the first dance he whirled his partner round and round until it made onlookers dizzy to watch. The regular thump of the drum and the passionate insistence of the lyre had the power to mesmerise, but what held the audience spellbound was the spectacle of someone entirely transported by the rhythmic beat of the music. They saw in front of them a man with the rare ability to live for the moment, and his sheer abandon showed he did not give a damn what people thought.

Giorgis found his daughter standing by his side. He could feel the heat from her body, even before he saw she was there, but until the music stopped there was no purpose in speaking. There was too much noise. Anna folded her arms and unfolded them and Giorgis could sense her agitation. How desperately she seemed to want to be among the dancers, and when the music stopped and new people filtered into the circle and others bowed out, she quickly slipped in to take her place. Next to Manoli.

A different tune struck up. This one was more sedate, more stately, and the dancers held their heads high and rocked backwards and forwards and to left and right. Giorgis watched for a few moments. As he caught sight of Anna through the forest of arms and spinning bodies he could see that she had relaxed. She was smiling and making comments to her partner.

While his daughter was immersed in the dance, Giorgis took the opportunity to leave. Long after his small truck had bumped its way down the track and out on to the main road, he could still hear the strains of music in the air. Back in Plaka, he stopped at the bar. It was where he would find the easy camaraderie of his old friends and a quiet place to sit and think about the day.

It was not Giorgis who described the baptism to Maria the following day but Fotini, who had been given a detailed description by her brother, Antonis.

'Apparently he hardly put the baby down for a minute!' raved Fotini, outraged at the man's audacity.

'Do you think that annoyed Andreas?'

'Why should it?' asked Fotini. 'He clearly doesn't suspect a thing. Anyway, it left him free to circulate with his neighbours and the other guests. You know how focused he is on everything to do with the estate – he loves nothing more than talk of crop yields and olive tonnage.'

'But don't you think Anna wanted to hold her?'

'I don't honestly think she's that maternal. When Mattheos was born I couldn't bear him to be out of my arms. But everyone is different and it really doesn't seem to bother her.'

'And I suppose Manoli had the perfect excuse to monopolise her. Everyone expects it of the godfather,' said Maria. 'If Sofia *is* his child, it will have been the one day of his life when he could make a fuss of her like that without anyone questioning it.'

Both women were silent for a while. They sipped their coffee and finally Maria spoke.

'So do you *really* think Sofia is Manoli's child?'

'I have absolutely no idea,' answered Fotini. 'But he certainly feels a strong bond with her.'

Andreas had been delighted by the birth of Sofia, but became anxious about his wife during the next few months. She looked ill and tired but seemed to perk up when Manoli came to call. At the time of the baptism Andreas had been unaware of the strong current that flowed between his wife and cousin, but in the months that followed he began to question the amount of time that Manoli spent in their home. His position as a member of the family and now *nonos* to Sofia was one thing, but his frequent presence in the house was another. Andreas began to observe how Anna's mood could change the minute Manoli left, from frivolous to frowning, from gay to grumpy, and noticed how her warmest smiles were reserved for his cousin. He tried to put these thoughts from his mind for much of the time, but there were other things to arouse his suspicion. One evening he returned from the estate to find the bed unmade. This happened several more times, and on two other occasions he noticed that the sheets had only been roughly straightened.

'What's wrong with the maid?' he asked. 'If she's neglecting her duties, she ought to be sacked.'

Anna promised to talk to her, and for a time there was no more cause for complaint.

Life on Spinalonga continued just as before. Dr Lapakis came and went each day and Dr Kyritsis got approval from the hospital in Iraklion to increase his visits from once to three times each week. One particular autumn evening as he made his journey from Spinalonga to Plaka, something struck him forcibly. Dusk had already fallen; the sun had dropped behind the mountains, depriving the whole strip of coastline of its light and plunging it into near darkness. When he looked round, however, he saw that Spinalonga was still bathed in the golden glow of the last of the sun's rays. It seemed to Kyritsis the right way round.

It was Plaka that had many of the qualities you would expect of an island – insular, self-contained and sealed against the outside world – whereas Spinalonga hummed with life and energy. Its newspaper, *The Spinalonga Star*, still edited by Yiannis Solomonidis, carried digests of world news along with comment and opinion. There were also reviews of films which were due to be shown in forthcoming months, and extracts from the writings of Nikos Kazantzakis. Week by week they serialised his visionary book *Freedom and Death* and the inhabitants of the colony devoured every word, waiting each week for the next instalment, which they would then discuss in the *kafenion*. When the Cretan writer was awarded the World Peace Prize in June that year, they even reprinted his acceptance speech. 'If we do not want to allow the world to sink into chaos, we must release the love which is trapped in the heart of all humans,' Kazantzakis had said. The words resonated with readers on Spinalonga, who were all too aware of the mayhem and suffering that they had been protected from both in Greece and further afield by being incarcerated on the island for so long. Many of them relished the chance to stretch their intellects, and they would sit for hours chewing the cud over the latest sayings of this literary and political Goliath, as well as other contemporary authors. Several of the Athenians had books sent out each month to augment the sizeable library already on the island which was free for everyone to use. Perhaps because they dreamed of leaving, they continually looked outwards, beyond the place where they lived.

The *kafenion* and the taverna overflowed with customers in the evening and now even had competition in the form of a second small taverna. The allotments round the back of the island all looked as though they would yield good crops that summer, and there was plenty to buy and sell in the twice-weekly market. The island had never been in such good shape; not even when the Turks first built their homes had conditions been so comfortable.

Occasionally Maria allowed herself a moment of frustrated outburst with Fotini.

'It's almost more agonising now that I know there's a chance we might be cured,' she said, gripping her hands together. 'Can we dream or should we just be happy with the present?'

'It's never a bad thing to be content with the present,' said Fotini.

Maria knew her friend was right. She had nothing to lose if the here and now could be enough. One thing that did prey on her mind, however, was the consequence for her of being cured.

'What would happen then?' she asked.

'You'd be back with us in Plaka, wouldn't you? Just as you were before.'

Fotini appeared to be missing the point. Maria stared down at her hands and then looked up at her friend, who was crocheting the edge of a baby's coat as they talked. She was pregnant again.

'But if I was no longer on Spinalonga, I would never see Dr Kyritsis again,' she said.

'Of course you would. If you weren't living here he'd no longer be your doctor and things might be different.'

'I know you're right, but it fills me with dread,' said Maria. She pointed at the newspaper which lay on her table, open at the serialised extract from Kazantzakis's book. 'See that,' she said. '*Freedom and Death*. It sums up my situation exactly. I might get my freedom, but when I do it'll be no better than death if I can't see Dr Kyritsis any more.'

'Has he still not said anything to you?'

'No, nothing,' Maria confirmed.

'But he comes to see you every week. Doesn't that say enough?'

'Not quite,' Maria said bluntly. 'Though I do understand why he can't say anything. It wouldn't be the right thing to do.'

Maria betrayed none of her anxiety when she saw Kyritsis. Instead she used the time with him to ask for advice in helping the cases she looked after in the 'block'. These were people who needed immediate relief from the aches and pains they endured on a daily basis. Some of their problems were irreversible, but others could be alleviated with the right physiotherapy. Maria wanted to make sure she was advising them correctly on exercising, since some of these cases rarely got to see a doctor. More vigorously than ever she threw herself into her work. She was not going to dwell on what she regarded as the remote possibility of leaving Spinalonga. Repatriation would bring such mixed feelings, not just for her but for so many others. Spinalonga was a safety net for them, and the thought of leaving it was bittersweet. Even

'We have been given permission to release you from the colony.'

Dimitri knew what he was supposed to feel, but it was as though the numbness that used to afflict his hands had returned and this time taken his tongue. He remembered little of life before Spinalonga. It was his home and the colonists were his family. His real family had long since stopped communicating with him and he would have no idea how to find them now. His face had become very disfigured on one side, which was not a problem here, but in the outside world it would single him out for attention. What would he do if he left, and who would teach in the school?

A hundred questions and doubts whirled around in his mind and a few minutes went by before he could speak.

'I would rather remain here while I have a function,' he said to Kyritsis, 'than leave all of this behind and go into the unknown.'

He was not alone in his reluctance to leave. Others also feared that the visible legacy of the disease would always remain with them and mark them out, and they needed reassurance that they might be able to reintegrate. It was like being a guinea pig all over again.

In spite of the misgivings of these few, it was a momentous occasion in the island's history. For more than fifty years lepers had come but never gone, and there was thanksgiving in the church and celebration in the *kafenion*. Theodoros Makridakis and Panos Sklavounis, the Athenian who had set up the thriving cinema, were the first to leave. A small party gathered by the entrance to the tunnel to bid them farewell, and both of them fought back tears, with little success. What weight of mixed feelings burdened them as they shook hands with the men and women who had been their friends and companions for so many years. Neither of them knew what life over that strip of water held for them as they boarded Giorgis's waiting boat to pass from the known into the unknown. They would travel together as far as Iraklion, where Makridakis would try to pick up the threads of his former life, and Sklavounis would take the boat to Athens, knowing already that his former career as an actor could not be resumed. Not the way he looked now. Both men would keep a tight hold on the medical papers which declared them 'Clean'; there would be several occasions over the following few weeks when they would be obliged to show them in order to verify that they were officially free of the disease.

Months later, Giorgis brought letters to Spinalonga from the two men. Both described the great hardship of trying to fit back into society and told how they were treated as outcasts by anyone who identified them as men who had once lived in the leper colony. Theirs were not encouraging tales, and Papadimitriou, who was the recipient, shared them with no one. Others from the first treatment group had also now left. They were all Cretan and had been welcomed by their families and found new work.

The pattern of recovery continued during the following year. The doctors kept meticulous records of everyone's date of first treatment and how many months the test had shown up as negative.

'By the end of this year we'll be out of a job,' said the sardonic Lapakis.

'I never thought that unemployment would be my aim in

life,' replied Athina Manakis, 'but it is now.'

By late spring, save for a few dozen cases who had reacted so badly against the treatment that they had been obliged to stop undergoing it, and some who had not responded at all, it was clear that the summer could bring a widespread clean bill of health. By July there were discussions on Spinalonga between the doctors and Nikos Papadimitriou regarding how all this should be managed.

Giorgis, who had ferried that first batch of cured men and women away from Spinalonga, now counted the days until Maria might be on his boat once again. The inconceivable had now become a reality and yet he feared there might be some hitch, some unforeseen problem that had not yet been envisaged.

He kept both his excitement and his anxieties to himself and many times had to bite his tongue when he overheard the usual tactless banter in the bar.

'Well I for one shan't be putting up the bunting to welcome them back,' said one fisherman.

'Oh, come on,' responded another. 'Have a bit of sympathy with them.'

Those who had always been more openly resentful of the leper colony remembered with some shame the night when plans to raid the island had nearly got out of hand.

In Lapakis's office early one evening, the island leader and the three doctors were discussing how the event should be marked.

'I want the world to know that we're leaving because we're cured,' said Papadimitriou. 'If people leave in twos and threes and steal off into the night it gives out the wrong message to everyone on the mainland. Why are they sneaking away? they'll ask. I want everyone to know the truth.'

'But how do you suggest we do that?' asked Kyritsis quietly.

'I think we should all leave together. I want a celebration. I want a feast of thanksgiving on the mainland. I don't think it's too much to ask.'

'We have those who aren't cured to think about too,' said Manakis. 'There's nothing for them to celebrate.'

'The patients who are facing longer-term treatment,' said Kyritsis diplomatically, 'will also be leaving the island, we hope.'

'How's that?' asked Papadimitriou.

'I am currently awaiting authority for them to be transferred to a hospital in Athens,' he answered. 'They will receive better care there, and in any case the government won't fund Spinalonga once there are too few people here.'

'In that case,' said Lapakis, 'can I suggest that we allow the sick to leave the island before the cured. I think it would be easier for them that way.'

They were all in agreement. Papadimitriou would have his public display of this new freedom, and those who were yet to be cured would be tactfully transferred to the Hospital of Santa Barbara in Athens. All that remained now was to make the arrangements. This was to take several weeks, but a date was soon set. It was to be 25 August, the feast of Agios Titos, the patron saint of all Crete. The only one among them who harboured any misgivings about the fact that Spinalonga's days as a leper colony were now numbered was Kyritsis. He might never see Maria again.

Chapter Twenty-two

1957

As they would have done in any normal year, the residents of Plaka made preparations for the saint's day feast. This year would be different, however. They would be sharing the celebrations with the inhabitants of Spinalonga, their close neighbours who had existed only in their imaginations for so many years. For some it would mean welcoming home almost forgotten friends; for others it would mean confronting their own deep prejudices and trying to suppress them. They were to sit down at a table and share food with their hitherto unseen neighbours.

Giorgis was one of very few people who had known the reality of the colony. Many others on the mainland had for years enjoyed the financial benefits of having such an institution across the water, supplying them with much of what they consumed, and for them the prospect of the colony's closure meant a loss of business. Others admitted to themselves that they felt a certain relief at the thought of Spinalonga's demise. The sheer volume of sick men and women over the water had always worried them, and in spite of the knowledge that this disease was less contagious than many others, they still feared it as they would bubonic plague. These people kept their minds closed to the fact that leprosy could now be cured.

There were some who keenly anticipated the arrival of their guests for this historic night. Fotini's mother, Savina Angelopoulos, still cherished the memory of her friend Eleni whose loss she had grieved for many years, and to see Maria free again would be pure joy. It would mean only one tragedy, not two. Apart from Giorgis, Fotini rejoiced more than anyone. She was to be reunited with her best friend. No longer would they need to meet in the semi-darkness of Maria's house on Spinalonga. Now they would be able to sit on the bright restaurant terrace chewing over the events of the day while the sun went down and the moon came up.

In the steamy heat of this August afternoon, in the taverna kitchen, Stephanos was cooking up great metal dishes of goat stew, swordfish and rice pilaff, and the *zakaroplastion*, the patisserie, was baking trays of honeysweet *baklava* and *katefi*. This would be the feast to end all feasts in its lavish offerings of food.

Vangelis Lidaki relished such an event. He enjoyed the emotional temperature created by a day so out of the ordinary, and also knew what it must mean to Giorgis, one of his most regular if least talkative customers. It occurred to him too that some of the inhabitants of Spinalonga might become new citizens of Plaka, swelling the population and increasing his own business. Success for Lidaki was judged by the number of empty beer and raki bottles that rattled around in his old crates at the end of each day, and he hoped that the volume of these might swell.

Feelings among the lepers were as mixed as the feelings of the people about to receive them. Some of the members of the colony dared not admit even to themselves that their departure filled them with as much dread as had their arrival. The island had given them undreamt-of security and many dreaded losing that. Some of the islanders, even though there was not a mark, not a blemish, to indicate that they had been leprous, were full of trepidation that they would never be able to live a normal life. Dimitri was not the only one of the younger islanders to have no memory of anywhere other than Spinalonga. It had been their world, with everything outside it no more real than pictures in a book. Even the village they looked at across the water each day seemed little more than a mirage.

Maria had no problem remembering life on the mainland, although it seemed that the past she looked back on was someone else's, not her own. What would become of a woman who had lived the best part of her twenties as a leper and who would be considered an old maid back on the mainland? All she could really see as she looked across the continually churning, undulating waters was the uncertainty of it all.

Some people on Spinalonga had spent the month before departure carefully packing each and every possession to take with them. There were several who had received a warm response from their families when they had written to tell them the good news of their release and who expected a kind welcome. They knew they would have somewhere to unpack their clothes, their china, their pots, their precious rugs. Others ignored what was about to happen, carrying on the routine of daily life until the very last minute as though it was never going to change. It was a hotter than ever August, with a fierce Meltemi that blew the roses flat and sent shirts flying from washing lines like giant white gulls. In the afternoons, everything but the wind was subdued. It continued to bang doors and rattle windows while people slept in shuttered rooms to escape the heat of the sun.

The day for departure came, and whether people had prepared themselves or not, it was time to leave. This time it was not only Giorgis who went to the island, but half a dozen other village fishermen who finally believed they had nothing to fear and would help ferry people away from Spinalonga with all their worldly possessions. At one o'clock in the afternoon on 25 August, a small flotilla could bc seen approaching from Plaka.

A final service had been held in the tiny church of St Pantaleimon on the previous day, but people had filed through the church to light candles and mumble their prayers for many days before that. They came to give thanks, and as they took deep breaths to calm their unsteady nerves, inhaling the heady, treacle-thick scent of the candles that flickered around them, they prayed to God that He would give them the courage to face whatever the world across that narrow strip of water brought them.

The elderly and those still sick were helped on board first. Donkeys worked hard that day, plodding back and forth through the tunnel bearing people's possessions and pulling carts piled high with boxes. A great mountain of goods built up on the quayside, turning a long-held dream into the tangible reality of departure. It was only now that some of them really believed this old life was ended and a new one was to begin. As they made their way through the tunnel they imagined they could hear their own heartbeats drumming against its walls.

Kyritsis was officiating on the quayside in Plaka, ensuring that those who were still sick and being taken back to Athens to continue treatment were carefully dealt with.

Among the last few left on the island were Lapakis and Maria. The doctor had needed to clear up the final pieces of paperwork and had packed all the necessary folders in a box. These medical records gave his patients a clean bill of health and would be in his own safe-keeping until everyone had crossed the water. Only then would he distribute them. They would be the islanders' passports to freedom.

Leaving the little alleyway from her house for the final time, Maria looked up the hill towards the hospital. She could see Lapakis making his way down the street, struggling with his cumbersome boxes, and set off to help him. All around her were signs of hasty departure. Until that final hour, a few had refused to believe that they were really leaving. Someone had failed to fasten a window and it now banged in the breeze; several shutters had come loose from their catches and curtains flapped around them like sails. Cups and saucers sat abandoned on tables in the *kafenion*, and in the school room an open book lay on a desk. Algebraic formulae were still scratched in chalk on the blackboard. In one of the shops a row of tins remained on a shelf as if the shopkeeper had imagined he might open it up again some day. Bright geraniums planted in old olive oil drums were already wilting. They would not be watered that night.

'Don't worry about me, Maria,' said the doctor, red in the face. 'You've got plenty to think about.'

'No, let me help you. There's no reason why you should break your back for us any more,' she said, taking one of the smaller record boxes. 'We're all healthy now, aren't we?'

'You certainly are,' he replied. 'And some of you can go away and put this whole experience behind you.'

Lapakis knew as soon as he had said it how hard this would probably be, and was embarrassed at his own thoughtlessness. He fumbled his way towards the words that he thought would give greatest comfort.

'A new beginning. That's what I mean . . . You'll be able to have a new beginning.'

Lapakis was not to know it, but a new beginning was exactly the opposite of what Maria wanted. It suggested that everything of her old life on the island would be swept away. Why should he know that the most precious thing of all was something she would never have found but for her exile on this island and that, far from wanting to leave everything of her life on Spinalonga behind, Maria wanted to take the best of it with her?

As she took a last look up the main street, acute feelings of nostalgia almost made her swoon. Memories rolled one after the other into her mind, overlapping and colliding. The extraordinary friendships she had formed, the camaraderie of laundry days, the merrymaking on feast days, the pleasure of seeing the latest films, the satisfaction in helping people who really needed her, the unwarranted fear when fierce debates raged in the *kafenion*, mostly between the Athenians and usually on subjects that seemed to have little relevance to their own day-to-day lives. It was as if no time at all had elapsed between the moment she had stood on this spot for the first time and now. Four years ago she had been full of hatred for Spinalonga. At the time, death had seemed infinitely preferable to a life sentence on this island, but now here she was, momentarily reticent about leaving. In a few seconds, another life would begin, and she did not know what it would hold.

Lapakis read all this in her face. For him, as well, life was to bring new uncertainties now that his work on Spinalonga was over. He would travel to Athens to spend a few months with the lepers who were going to the Santa Barbara hospital and still needed treatment, but after that his own life was as unmapped as the moon.

'Come on,' he said. 'I think we should go. Your father will be waiting for us.'

They both turned now and walked through the tunnel. The sound of their steps reverberated around them. Giorgis was waiting at the other end. Drawing deeply on a cigarette, he sat on the wall in the shade of a mimosa tree watching for his daughter to emerge from the tunnel. It seemed as though she would never come. Apart from Maria and Lapakis, the island was now evacuated. Even the donkeys, goats and cats had been ferried across in a scene reminiscent of Noah's Ark. The last boat, except for this, had departed ten minutes earlier and the quayside was now deserted. Close by, a small metal box, a sheaf of letters and a full packet of cigarettes had been dropped, all testimony to the hurried departure of the final group. Perhaps there had been a hitch, Giorgis thought in a panic. Maybe Maria could not leave after all. Perhaps the doctor had not signed her papers.

At the moment when these rogue thoughts had taken on an uncomfortable reality, Maria emerged from the black semicircle of the tunnel and ran towards him, her arms outstretched, all second thoughts and doubts about leaving the island forgotten as she embraced her father. Wordlessly he basked in the sensation of her silky hair against his rough skin.

'Shall we go?' Maria asked, eventually.

Her possessions were already loaded on board. Lapakis got on first and turned to take Maria's hand. She put one foot on the boat. For a fraction of a second the other remained on the stony ground, and then she lifted it. Her life on Spinalonga was over.

Giorgis untethered his old caique and pushed it away from the quayside. Then, nimbly for a man his age, he jumped aboard and swung the boat around so that it was soon heading away from the island and out towards the mainland. His passengers faced towards the front of the boat. They watched the sharp point of the prow which, like an arrow, sped swiftly towards its target. Giorgis was wasting no time. His view of Spinalonga was still all too clear. The dark shapes of the windows looked at him like hollow, sightless eyes and their unbearable emptiness made him think of all those lepers who had ended their days afflicted by blindess. Suddenly he had a vision of Eleni as she was the last time he ever saw her, standing on that quayside, and for a moment the joy of having his daughter close by him was forgotten.

It was only a matter of minutes now before they were to land. The little harbour in Plaka was crowded with people. Many of the colonists had been greeted by family and friends; others simply hugged each other as they touched their native land for the first time in as many as twenty-five years. The noisiest contingent were the Athenians. Some of their friends and even colleagues had travelled all the way from their city to celebrate this epoch-making day. There would be no time for sleep tonight, and tomorrow morning they would all make their way back to Iraklion for the return journey to Athens. For now they would teach Plaka a thing or two about the art of making merry. Some of them were musicians and had already practised that morning with the locals, forming an impressive orchestra of every instrument, from lyre and lute and mandolin to bouzouki, bagpipe and shepherd's flute.

Their new baby, Petros, in arms, Fotini and Stephanos were there to greet Maria, along with Mattheos, their little brown-eyed boy, who danced about with excitement in the heady atmosphere, not at all aware of the significance of the day but delighted by the suggestion of carnival in the air.

'Welcome home, Maria,' said Stephanos. He had stood back as his wife embraced her best friend, waiting his turn to greet her. 'We are so glad that you are back.'

He began to lift Maria's boxes and load them on to his pick-up truck. It was only a short distance to the Petrakis house, but too far to carry everything by hand. The two women crossed the square, leaving Giorgis to tie up the boat. They would go on foot. Trestle tables were already set up and chairs were laid out in groups. Bright little flags traced the four sides of the square and fluttered gaily across its diagonals. It would not be long before the party began.

By the time Maria and Fotini arrived at the house, Stephanos had already unloaded the boxes, which now sat inside the door. As she went in, Maria felt a pricking sensation on the back of her neck. Nothing had changed since the day she left. All was immaculately in place just as it always had been: the same embroidered sampler with its welcoming '*Kali Mera*' – 'Good Morning' – that her mother had completed just in time for her marriage hung on the wall opposite the door to greet visitors, the same collection of pans hung near the fireplace and the familiar set of flower-sprigged china plates was ranged on the rack. Inside one of her boxes Maria would soon find some matching ones and the parts of the service would be united once again.

Even on such a luminous day, it was gloomy in this house. All the old familiar objects might still be in their places, but the walls themselves seemed to have absorbed the profound misery that had been endured within them. They exuded the loneliness of her father's previous few years. Everything appeared to be the same, but nothing was as it had been.

When Giorgis walked in a few moments later, he found Stephanos, Fotini, Petros and Mattheos, who was clutching a small posy of flowers, and Maria all crowded into the little house. At last it seemed that some fragments of his life were fitting back together. His beautiful daughter was standing in front of him, one out of the three women in the framed photograph he looked at each and every day. In his eyes, she was lovelier than ever.

'Well,' said Fotini. 'I shouldn't stay too long – there's food still to be prepared. Shall we see you back in the square?'

'Thanks for everything. I'm so lucky to be coming back to old friends like you – and a new friend as well,' she said, looking towards Mattheos, who now plucked up the courage to step forward and give her the flowers.

Maria smiled. They were the first flowers she had been given since Manoli had presented her with some four years earlier, only a week before she had gone to be tested for leprosy. The little boy's gesture touched her.

It was more than half an hour later, changed into a different dress and with her hair brushed until it gleamed more brightly than the mirror itself, that Maria felt ready to go out and face the curiosity of the inhabitants of Plaka. Despite the welcome that some of her neighbours would give her, she knew that others would be scrutinising her and looking for signs of the disease. They would be disappointed. Maria did not bear the slightest trace. There were several on whom the disease had taken a greater toll. Many would hobble for life on their crippled feet, and the unlucky few who had lost their sight would forever be reliant on their families. For the majority, however, lesions had vanished, ugly skin pigmentations had faded to invisibility, and feeling had returned to the places where anaesthesia had numbed them.

Maria and her father walked together towards the square.

'I won't believe it until I see it,' said Giorgis, 'but your sister has said she might come tonight. I got a note from her yesterday.'

'Anna?' said Maria, astonished. 'With Andreas too?'

'So she said in her letter. I suppose she wants to welcome you back.'

Like any parent, he yearned for reunion and assumed that Anna thought it a good moment to make up for her negligence over the past few years. If he could have two daughters back instead of one that would make him happier than ever. For

Maria, on the other hand, a meeting with Anna tonight was a prospect that she did not relish. Celebration not reconciliation was the purpose of today: every last leper on Spinalonga was finally to be given his liberty.

In her Elounda home, Anna was preparing herself for the party in Plaka, carefully pinning her hair and meticulously applying her lipstick so that it followed precisely the curve of her full lips. Sitting on her grandmother's lap, Sofia watched intently as her mother painted her face until her cheeks were as highly coloured as a doll's.

Ignoring both his mother and his daughter, Andreas marched in.

'Aren't you ready yet?' he asked Anna coldly.

'Almost,' she replied, adjusting her heavy turquoise necklace in the mirror and lifting her chin to admire the effect before spraying herself with a storm cloud of French perfume.

'Can we go then?' he snapped.

Anna seemed oblivious to her husband's icy tones. Eleftheria was not. She was discomfited by the way her son addressed his wife. She had not heard this coolness of tone before, nor seen him give her such glaring looks, and she wondered whether Andreas had, at last, woken up to the familiarity that now existed between his wife and Manoli. She had once mentioned her concerns to Alexandros. It was a mistake. He was angry and swore to boot out 'that good-for-nothing Don Juan' if he crossed any boundaries. After that, Eleftheria had kept her worries to herself.

'Night-night, sweetheart.' Anna turned to her little daughter, whose chubby arms reached out towards her. 'Be good.'

And with that she planted a perfect imprint of her lips on Sofia's forehead and left the room.

Andreas was already waiting in the car, the engine revving. He knew why his wife was taking such meticulous care with her appearance, and it was not for him.

It was something extraordinarily small that had finally made Andreas face the fact that his wife was being unfaithful to him: an earring under his pillow. Anna was always meticulous about removing her jewellery and carefully laying it inside a velvet-lined drawer in her dressing table before she went to bed, and Andreas knew he would have noticed if she had come to bed wearing her gold and diamond earrings the previous night. He said nothing when he saw the glint of gold against the white linen as he climbed between his otherwise immaculate sheets, but his heart turned to ice. In that instant, his *philotemo*, the very sense of honour and pride that made him a man, was mortally wounded.

Two days after that he came home in the early afternoon, parking his car some distance away and walking the last fifty metres to his house. He was not surprised to see Manoli's truck parked outside. He had known it would be there. Opening the front door quietly, he stepped into the hallway. A clock ticked but otherwise the house was deadly quiet. Suddenly the silence was shattered. A woman wailed. Andreas gripped the banister, repulsed, sickened by the sound of his wife's ecstasy. His instinct was to leap the stairs two at a time, burst into his bedroom and tear them both limb from limb, but something stopped him. He was Andreas Vandoulakis. He had to act in a more measured way and he needed time to think.

⋆ ⋆ ⋆

As Maria approached the square there was already an immense crowd gathered there. She spotted Dimitri standing at the centre of a small group along with Gerasimo Vilakis, who had run the colony's *kafenion*, and Kristina Kroustalakis, who was smiling. It made her almost unrecognisable. All around was the buzz of excited talk and the faint strain of music as someone strummed a bouzouki at the far end of the street. Greetings were called from left and right as she came into the open space. She met many boisterous families and friends from Athens and was introduced by them as *Agia* Maria or 'the herbal magician'. The latter pleased her, though being sanctified most definitely did not.

The last few hours had been so momentous that she had given little thought to Dr Kyritsis. There had been no goodbye, so she was sure they would meet again. It could not be soon enough. Coming into the thick of the crowd, Maria felt her heart lurch as though it might dislodge itself from her chest. There he was, sitting at one of the long tables with Lapakis. In the mêlée he was the only person she saw, his silver hair almost luminous in the fading light. The doctors were deep in conversation, but eventually Lapakis looked up and noticed her.

'Maria!' he exclaimed, getting to his feet. 'What a great day for you. What is it like being home after all this time?'

Fortunately it was not a question she was really expected to answer and if it had been she would not have known where to begin or where to end. At this moment, Papadimitriou and his wife approached, with two men who bore such a close resemblance to Papadimitriou that it went without saying that they were his brothers. The island leader wanted his family to meet the men who were responsible for giving them a new life. There would be a thousand toasts later, but they wanted to be the first to say thank you.

Kyritsis stood back but Maria could feel the pressure of his gaze, and as Lapakis talked to the Papadimitrious, he drew Maria to one side.

'Can I have a moment of your time?' he asked politely, but loudly enough to be heard above the noise. 'Somewhere quieter than here,' he added.

'We could walk down to the church,' she answered. 'I want to go in and light a candle.'

They left the packed square where the cacophony of excited voices had reached a deafening pitch. As they walked the length of the empty street towards the church, the crowd sound became little more than a background hum. A sense of impatience determined Kyritsis's next action. Enough of this woman's life had been taken away by the disease and every second seemed one too many lost. His restrained bedside manner left him for a moment and boldness took over. By the entrance to the church door, he turned to face her.

'I have something to say. It's very simple indeed,' he said. 'I would like you to marry me.'

It was a statement, not a question. And it was as if no reply was required. For some time now, there had been no real doubt in Maria's mind that Kyritsis loved her but she had forced herself to stop imagining that this might have some kind of resolution. She had found it safer in the past few years to banish daydreams as soon as they had started to take shape and to live in the here and now where disappointment could not lay waste her fantasies.

For a moment she said nothing, but looked up at him as he held her by the shoulders, his own arms outstretched. As though she needed persuasion that he meant it, he filled her silence.

'There has never been anyone who has affected me as you have. If you don't wish to marry me, I shall go away and you need never think of me again.' His hands had tightened their grip on her shoulders. 'But either way, I need to know now.'

So it *was* a question. The moisture had drained from her mouth and a supreme effort was required to regain control of her tongue.

'Yes,' was the single, husky syllable that she was capable of expelling. 'Yes.'

'You will?' Kyritsis seemed astounded. This dark-haired woman, this patient of his whom he felt he knew so well and yet still knew so little about, was agreeing to be his wife. His face broke into a smile and Maria's mirrored it, dazzlingly. Uncertainly at first, and then with increasing passion, he kissed her, and then, suddenly aware of how they must look in the deserted street, they pulled apart.

'We must return to the celebrations,' said Kyritsis, speaking first. His sense of duty and correctness was even more keenly developed than her own. 'People might wonder where we are.'

He was right: they needed to return because it was a night for everyone to share before they went their separate ways. By the time they got back to the square, the dancing had begun. A huge circle had formed and a slow *pentozali* dance was in progress. Even Giorgis had joined in. The man who so often sat in the shadows at any event had come forward and now wholeheartedly joined the merrymaking.

Fotini was the first to spot her friend's return in the company of the doctor, and she knew beyond a shadow of a doubt that Maria, at last, had the opportunity for happiness. The pair had chosen not to say anything tonight – they wanted Giorgis to be the first to know, and the heady atmosphere of this *panegyri* was not where they wanted to tell him their news.

When Giorgis came to find them at the end of the dance, he had only one question on his lips for Maria.

'Have you seen Anna? Is she here?'

In the past few years, he had more or less abandoned hope of his family ever being together, but today there was a chance of it. He was puzzled by Anna's continuing absence, though; she had, after all, promised to be here.

'I am sure she will come, Father, if she said she would,' Maria reassured him, though the words sounded hollow to them both. 'Why don't we have another dance,' she suggested. 'You seem to have the energy.' She led her father back to the fray and they joined in as a new dance began.

Fotini was busy carrying plates of food to the table. She noticed the doctor observing Maria dancing and felt happier than ever that her dearest friend had found such a fine man. By now it was dark, the wind had dropped and there was not a ripple in the sea. The temperature seemed not to have fallen even by one degree since that airless afternoon, and when people came to sit out between dances, they thirstily gulped back tumblers of sharp wine, slopping much of it in the dust. Maria returned from her dance, found her place at

Kyritsis's side and they simultaneously lifted their glasses. It was a silent toast.

Anna and Andreas were nearly in Plaka now. Neither had spoken throughout the journey. Both were lost in their own thoughts. It had occurred to Andreas that Manoli might resume his engagement to Maria now that she was back, and as they approached the village and could see the thronging crowd he broke the silence, taking pleasure in provoking his wife with the suggestion.

'*Manoli?* Marry *Maria*? Over my dead body!' she screamed with a passion he had never seen in her before. The barriers were down now. 'What makes you say that?' Anna could not let it drop.

'Why shouldn't he? They were engaged and about to get married before,' he taunted her.

'Shut up. Just shut up!' She lashed out at him as he parked the car.

The violence of Anna's response had shocked Andreas.

'My God!' he roared, defending himself from the hard blows that rained down on him. 'You love him, don't you!'

'How *dare* you say that!' she screeched.

'Go on, why don't you admit it, Anna! I'm not a complete fool, you know,' he said, trying to regain control over his voice.

Anna was silent, as though her fury had momentarily subsided.

'I know it's true,' said Andreas, almost calm now. 'I came home early one day last week and he was there with you. How long. . . . ?'

Anna was now crying and laughing at the same time, hysterical. 'Years,' she spluttered. 'Years and years . . .'

It seemed to Andreas that Anna's scarlet lips smiled as though even now she was lost in some kind of ecstasy. Her denial would have given him a place to retreat, the possibility that he was wrong after all, but her admission was the greatest mockery of all. He had to wipe that rictus grin from her face.

In one deft movement he reached inside his jacket pocket and drew out his pistol. Anna was not even looking. Her head was tilted back, the round beads of her necklace vibrating with her laughter. She was delirious.

'I've never . . .' she gasped, now completely crazed with the excitement of telling him the truth, 'I've never loved anyone as much as Manoli.' Her words lashed out like a whip, cracking the air around him.

In the main square, Kyritsis watched as the first of the fireworks was let off into the limpid sky. Rockets would be sent into the air every hour until midnight, each one exploding with a violent bang and a shower of sparks that were reflected like gems in the still sea. As the first volley of fireworks came to an end there was a moment's quiet before the band thought it worthwhile striking up again. Before they could do so, however, there were two more loud and unexpected bangs. Kyritsis turned his face upwards, expecting to see a shower of glittering sparks descending from the sky, but it was immediately apparent that there would be none.

A commotion had broken out around a car parked near the square. It had been seen drawing up only a few minutes earlier and now a woman lay sprawled in the passenger seat. Kyritsis started to run towards it. For a moment it seemed as though the rest of the crowd was petrified into inactivity. Disbelief that such an act of violence could intrude on this merrymaking almost paralysed them, but they cleared a path to let him through.

Kyritsis felt the woman's pulse. Although it was weak, there was still a sign of life.

'We need to move her,' he said to Dr Lapakis, who was now at his side. Rugs and pillows had miraculously appeared from a nearby house and the two men carefully lifted the woman down on to the ground. At their request, the crowd of onlookers moved to a respectful distance to let them do their work.

Maria had worked her way to the front to see whether there was anything she could do to help. As they laid the woman down on the blanket, she realised who it was that they held in their blood-stained embrace. Many in the crowd now recognised her too and there was a collective gasp of horror.

There was no mistaking her. Raven haired, full-bosomed and clad in a dress now soaked with blood that no one else at this gathering could have afforded in a month of feast days, it was, without any doubt at all, Anna Vandoulakis. Maria knelt down beside her on the rug.

'It's my sister,' she whispered through her sobs to Kyritsis. 'My sister.'

Someone in the crowd was heard to shout: 'Find Giorgis!' and seconds later Giorgis was kneeling by Maria's side, weeping silently at the sight of his elder daughter, whose life was ebbing away before them all.

In a few minutes it was all over. Anna never regained consciousness, but her dying moments were spent with the two people who loved her most, praying fervently for her salvation.

'Why? Why?' repeated Giorgis through his tears.

Maria knew the answer but she was not going to tell him. It would only add to his grief. Silence and ignorance were what would help him more than anything at this moment. He would learn the truth soon enough. What would haunt him always was that in a single evening, he had celebrated the return of one daughter and lost the other for ever.

Chapter Twenty-three

WITNESSES SOON EMERGED from the crowd. One bystander had heard a couple arguing through the open window of the car when he had passed it a few minutes before the gunshots, and a woman claimed to have seen a man running off down the street immediately afterwards. This information sent a group of men off in the direction of the church, and within ten minutes they had returned with their suspect. He still held the weapon in his hand, and made no attempt to resist arrest. Maria knew his identity before she was told. It was Andreas.

There was a profound sense of shock in Plaka. It had always promised to be a memorable night, but not quite in this way. For a while people stood around in small groups and talked in low voices; it had not taken long for word to pass around that it was Maria's sister who had been shot dead, and that Anna's husband had been arrested for the crime. An extraordinary party had come to an untimely end and there was no choice but to wind up the evening and go their separate ways. The musicians dispersed and the remains of the food were put away; muted goodbyes were said as the Athenians began to leave, taken by their families and friends to start a new life.

Those with shorter distances to go had been offered beds by local people for the night and were to stay until the following day, when they would start their journeys back to their villages and towns in other parts of Crete. Andreas Vandoulakis had been taken away under police escort to spend the night in an Elounda cell and Anna's body was carried to the small chapel by the sea, where it was to remain before burial.

The daytime temperature had not dropped. Even now, when night was almost giving way to breaking day, there was a breathless warmth in the air. For the second time in twenty-four hours, Giorgis's small house was overcrowded. Last time his visitors had been looking forward to a celebration. This time they prepared for a great lamentation. The priest had visited but when he could see that little comfort was to be given in such tragic circumstances, he left.

At four o'clock in the morning Giorgis climbed, exhausted, to his room. He was numb and did not know whether this was grief or perhaps a sign that he was no longer capable of feeling at all. Even Maria's long-awaited return felt like nothing now.

Kyritsis had stayed for an hour or so, but there was no more he could do tonight. Tomorrow, which was already today, he would help them make arrangements for the funeral, but meanwhile he would snatch a few hours' sleep in a spare room above Fotini and Stephanos's taverna.

At the least interesting of times the villagers loved to gossip, but now they scarcely had time to draw breath. It was Antonis who was able to shed some light on the events leading up to Anna's killing. In the early hours of the morning, when a few of the men still sat around a table in the bar, he related what he had observed. A few weeks before, he had noticed that Manoli always seemed to slip away for several hours in the middle of the day. It was circumstantial evidence, but even so it might go some way towards explaining what had driven Andreas to murder his own wife. During this period, Andreas's mood had darkened by the day. He was ill tempered with everyone with whom he came into contact and his workers had begun to live in fear of him. A gathering thunderstorm rarely brought such tension. For so long Andreas had been kept in the dark, blissfully unaware of his wife's behaviour, but once he had emerged blinkingly into the daylight and seen the truth, there had been only one course of action. The drinkers in the bar were not unsympathetic, and many agreed that being cuckolded would drive them to murder. A Greek's manhood would not stand such ignominy.

Lidaki seemed to be the last one to have seen Manoli, who had now disappeared without trace, though his precious lyre still hung on the wall behind the bar.

'He came in here about six o'clock last night,' he said. 'He was his usual cheerful self and he certainly gave the impression he was going to stay for the celebrations.'

'No one seems to have seen him after that,' said Angelos. 'My hunch is that he felt awkward about seeing Maria.'

'Surely he doesn't still feel under obligation to marry her?' chipped in another voice.

'I doubt it, knowing Manoli, but it might have kept him away all the same,' said Lidaki.

'Personally I don't think it has anything to do with Maria,' said Antonis. 'I think he knew that his time was up.'

Later that morning Antonis went up to Manoli's home. He held nothing against this charming but feckless individual; he had been a good companion and drinking partner, and even the passing thought that he could be lying in his house in a pool of blood could not be ignored. If Andreas had killed his wife, it might not have been beyond him to kill his cousin too.

Antonis peered through the windows. Everything looked just as normal: the unruly mess of a bachelor home, with pots and plates piled up in no apparent order, curtains half drawn, a trail of crumbs across the table and an uncorked, two-thirds-empty bottle of wine; all of this was what he would have expected to see.

He tried the door and, finding it open, ventured inside. Upstairs in the bedroom, in a scene which might well have simply been further evidence that the person who lived here had no regard for tidiness, there were signs of a hasty departure. Drawers were pulled open and items of clothing spilled out like a volcanic eruption. Wardrobe doors gaped to reveal an empty rail. The unmade bed with its skewed sheets and flattened pillow was as Antonis might have expected, but what really gave him the clue that the feeling of emptiness in the house was possibly a permanent one were the picture frames that lay face down on the surface of a chest of drawers in the window. It looked as though they had been knocked over in haste, and two of the frames were empty, their contents hurriedly ripped out. All the signs were there. Manoli's truck had gone. He could be anywhere in Greece by now. No one would be looking for him.

* * *

Anna's funeral was not to take place in Plaka's main church, where Andreas had sought shelter, but in the chapel on the outskirts of the village. This small building overlooked the sea and had an uninterrupted view of Spinalonga. Nothing but salt water lay between the chapel's burial plot and the lepers' final resting place where the remains of Anna's mother lay in the ground.

Less than forty-eight hours after the death, a small, darkly clad group gathered in the damp chapel. The Vandoulakis family was not represented. They had remained firmly within the four walls of the Elounda house since the murder. Maria, Giorgis, Kyritsis, Fotini, Savina and Pavlos stood with their heads bowed as the priest prayed over the coffin. Wafts of incense billowed from the censer as lengthy intercessions were said for the forgiveness of sins before the comforting words of the Lord's Prayer were uttered almost inaudibly by them all. When it was time for the interment, they moved outside into the relentless glare of the sun. Tears and perspiration mingled to flow down their cheeks. None of them could quite believe that the wooden box soon to disappear into the darkness contained Anna.

As the coffin was lowered into the ground, the priest took some dust and scattered it crosswise over the remains.

'The earth is the Lord's,' he said, 'and all who dwell on it.' Ash from the censer floated down to mix with the dust, and the priest continued: 'With the spirits of the righteous made perfect in death, give rest to this the soul of thy servant . . .'

The priest's delivery had a singsong lilt. These words had been spoken a thousand times, and they held the small congregation spellbound as they poured from his scarcely parted lips.

'O pure and spotless Virgin, intercede for the salvation of your servant's soul . . .'

Fotini contemplated the notion of a pure and spotless Virgin interceding on Anna's behalf. If only Anna herself had remained a little more spotless, they might not be standing here now, she thought.

By the time the service was drawing to a close, the priest was in competition with an army of a thousand cicadas, whose unrelenting noise reached a climax as he came to the closing words.

'Give her rest in the bosom of Abraham . . . May your memory be everlasting, our sister, and worthy of blessedness.'

'Kyrie Eleison, Kyrie Eleison, Kyrie Eleison.'

A few minutes passed before anyone could bring themselves to move. Maria spoke first, thanking the priest for conducting the ceremony, and then it was time to walk back into the village. Maria went home with her father. He wanted sleep, he said. That was all he wanted. Fotini and her parents would return to the taverna to find Stephanos, who had been minding Petros and playing with the carefree Mattheos on the beach. It was the quiet mid-afternoon hour. Not a soul stirred.

Kyritsis would wait for Maria on a shady bench in the square. Maria needed to get away from Plaka just for a few hours and they planned to drive to Elounda. It would be the first journey she had made in four years, apart from the short one which had brought her from Spinalonga to the mainland. She yearned for an hour or so of privacy.

There was a small *kafenion* she remembered by the water's edge in Elounda. Admittedly it had been somewhere she used to go with Manoli, but that was all in the past now. She would not let thoughts of him follow her. As they were shown to a table where the sea lapped gently on the rocks below them, the events of the past forty-eight hours already seemed distant. It was as though they had happened to someone else, somewhere else. When she looked across the water, however, she could clearly see Spinalonga. From here the empty island looked just the same as it ever had, and it was hard to believe it was now completely devoid of human life. Plaka was out of sight, concealed behind a rocky promontory.

It was the first opportunity Maria and Kyritsis had had to be alone since the moment outside the church on the night of the feast. For perhaps one hour her life had held such promise, such a future, but now she felt that this great step forward had been counteracted by several back. She had never even addressed the man she loved by his Christian name.

When he looked back on this moment some weeks later, Kyritsis blamed himself for rushing in. His overexcitement at the prospect of their future together bubbled over into talk of his apartment in Iraklion and how he hoped it would be adequate for them.

'It isn't very spacious, but there is a study and a separate guest room,' he said. 'We can always move in the future if we need to, but it's very convenient for the hospital.'

He took her hands across the table and held them. She looked troubled. Of course she did. They had just buried her sister, and here he was, impatient as a child, wanting to talk about the practicalities of their life together. Clearly Maria needed more time.

How comforting, the sensation of his hands clasping hers, full of such warmth and generosity, she thought. Why couldn't they just remain here at this table for ever? No one knew where they were. Nothing could disturb them. Except her conscience, which had followed them here, and now nagged at her.

'I can't marry you,' she said suddenly. 'I have to stay and look after my father.'

The words seemed to Kyritsis to have come out of the clear blue sky. He was shocked. Within minutes, though, he saw it made perfect sense. How could he have expected everything to continue on its former path, given the dramatic events of the past two days? He was a fool. How could this woman, whom he had been drawn to as much by her integrity and selflessness as by her beauty, be expected to leave her bereaved and distressed father? For his whole life rationality had ruled him, and the one moment when he had denied it to let his emotions take their turn, he had stumbled.

One part of him wanted to protest, but instead he held on to Maria's hands and gently squeezed them. He then spoke with such understanding and forgiveness that it almost broke her heart.

'You're right to stay,' he said. 'And that's why I love you, Maria. Because you know what's right and then you do it.'

It was the truth, but even more so was what he said next.

'I shall never love anyone else.'

The owner of the *kafenion* kept his distance from their table. He was aware that the woman had broken down in tears and he did not like to intrude on his customers' privacy. There had not been any raised voices, which was unusual for a row, but it was then that he observed the sombre way in which the couple were dressed. Except for old widows, black was unusual for a summer's day, and it dawned on him that perhaps they were in mourning.

Maria eased her hands away from Kyritsis's grasp and sat with her head bowed. Her tears flowed freely now and ran down her arms, her neck and between her breasts. She could not stop them. The restrained grief at the graveside had only temporarily held back the overwhelming sorrow that now burst its dam and would not abate until every last drop of it had poured out and drained away. The fact that Kyritsis was so reasonable made her weep all the more and made her decision all the more lamentable.

Kyritsis sat looking at the top of Maria's bowed head. When the shaking had subsided, he touched her gently on the shoulder.

'Maria,' he whispered. 'Shall we go?'

They walked away from their table, hand in hand, Maria's head resting on Kyritsis's shoulder. As they drove back to Plaka, in silence, the sapphire-blue water still sparkled, but the sky had begun to change. It had started its subtle transition through azure to pink, and the rocks took on the same warm tones. At last this terrible day was beginning to fade.

When they reached the village, the doctor spoke.

'I can't say goodbye,' he said.

He was right. There was too much finality about the word. How could something that had never really begun come to an end?

'Neither can I,' said Maria, now perfectly in control.

'Will you write to me and tell me how you are? Tell me what you're doing? Tell me how life is for you in the free world?' asked Kyritsis with forced enthusiasm.

Maria nodded.

It was pointless prolonging the moment. The sooner Kyritsis went, the better it would be for both of them. He parked outside Maria's house and got out to open the passenger door. Face to face they stood, and then for a few seconds they held each other. They did not so much embrace as cling to each other, like children in a storm. Then, with great strength of will, they simultaneously released each other. Maria immediately turned away and went into her house. Kyritsis climbed back into his car and drove away. He would not stop until he got back to Iraklion.

The unbearable silence inside the house quickly drove Maria back out into the street. She needed the sound of the cicadas, a dog barking, the buzz of a scooter, squeals of children. All of these greeted her as she walked towards the centre of the village where, in spite of herself, she glanced up the street to check whether Kyritsis's car was still in sight. Even the trail of dust his wheels sent into the air had already settled.

Maria needed Fotini. She walked quickly to the taverna, where her friend was spreading the tables with paper cloths, snapping lengths of elastic around them to keep them from blowing away in the wind.

'Maria!' Fotini was pleased to see her friend, but dismayed at the sight of her ashen face. Of course, it was not surprising she looked so pale. In the past forty-eight hours she had returned from exile and seen her sister shot and buried. 'Come and sit down,' she said, pulling out a chair and guiding Maria into it. 'Let me get you something to drink – and I bet you haven't eaten all day.'

Fotini was right. Maria had not eaten for over twenty-four hours, but she had no appetite now.

'No, I'm fine. Really I am.'

Fotini was unconvinced. She put the list of things that needed to be done before the first evening customers arrived to the back of her mind. All of that could wait. Drawing up another chair, she sat down close to Maria and put her arm around her.

'Is there anything I can do?' she asked tenderly. 'Anything at all?'

It was the note of kindness in her voice that sent Maria shuddering into sobs, and through them Fotini could make out a few words that gave away the reason for her friend's ever-deepening misery.

'He's gone . . . I couldn't go . . . couldn't leave my father.'

'Look, tell me what happened.'

Maria gradually calmed down.

'Just before Anna was shot, Dr Kyritsis asked me to marry him. But I can't leave now – and that's what I would have to do. I would have to leave my father. I couldn't do that.'

'So he's gone away, has he?' asked Fotini gently.

'Yes.'

'And when will you see him again?'

Maria took a very deep breath.

'I don't know. I really don't know. Possibly never.'

She was strong enough to mean it. The fates had been vengeful so far, but with each blow Maria became more resistant to the next.

The two friends sat for a while, and eventually Stephanos came out and persuaded Maria to eat. If she was going to make such a sacrifice for her father, then she might as well be strong enough to be useful. It was all completely pointless if she made herself ill.

As night fell, Maria rose to go. When she reached her house, it was still shrouded in silence. Creeping up to the spare bedroom, which would now be hers again, she lay down on the bed. She did not wake until late the following morning.

Anna's death left a trail of other disrupted and destroyed lives. Not just her sister's, her father's and her husband's, but her daughter's too. Sofia was not yet two years old, and it was not long before she noticed the absence of her parents. Her grandparents told her that they had both gone away for a while. She cried at first, and then began the process of forgetting. As for Alexandros and Eleftheria Vandoulakis, in one evening they had lost their son, their hopes for the future and the reputation of the family. Everything that had ever worried them about Andreas marrying beneath his class had been fulfilled to the letter. Eleftheria, who had been so willing to accept Anna Petrakis, had to face the bitterest disappointment. It was only a short time before Manoli's absence was brought to their attention and they worked out for themselves what had led to the horrifying events of the feast of Agios Titos. That woman had brought the deepest shame on them all, and the thought of their son languishing in his prison cell was a daily torture.

Andreas's trial in Agios Nikolaos lasted three days. Maria, Fotini and several other villagers were called as witnesses, and Dr Kyritsis came from Iraklion to testify, remaining afterwards only briefly to speak to Maria. Eleftheria and Alexandros sat impassively in the gallery, both of them gaunt with anxiety and shame at being on such public display. The circumstances of the murder were hung out and aired for the whole of Crete to salivate over, and the daily newspaper ran every last sensational detail. Giorgis attended throughout. Though he wanted justice for Anna, he was never in any doubt that it was his daughter's behaviour that had triggered Andreas's violent reaction, and for the first time in fourteen years he was glad that Eleni was not there.

Chapter Twenty-four

1958

FOR SEVERAL MONTHS there was no communication between the Vandoulakis and Petrakis families. There was Sofia to consider, however, and for her sake this ice age had to pass. Eleftheria would have come round to a point of reconciliation more speedily than her husband, but even Alexandros, given time to reflect, began to see that it was not only his own family who had suffered. He realised that the damage sustained had been heavy on both sides and, with an almost mathematical precision that was strictly in character, he weighed up their respective losses. On the Vandoulakis side: one imprisoned son, one disgraced nephew, one family name brought to ruins. On the Petrakis side: one dead daughter, a family depleted by murder and before that by leprosy. By his powers of reckoning, the equation balanced. The person who stood in the middle was Sofia, and it was the responsibility of all of them to knit some kind of a life together for the little girl.

Alexandros eventually wrote to Giorgis.

We have had our differences, but it is time to end them. Sofia is growing up without her parents and the best thing we can offer her is the love and companionship of the remaining members of her family. Eleftheria and I would be very happy if you and Maria would join us for lunch next Sunday.

Giorgis did not have a telephone in his home, but he hurried straight to the bar and used the one there. He wanted to let Alexandros know immediately that they accepted the invitation and would both be happy to come, and he left a message with the Vandoulakis housekeeper to say so. Maria, however, had mixed feelings when she read the letter.

'"Our *differences*"!' she said mockingly. 'And what does he mean by that? How could he describe the fact that his son killed your daughter as "our differences"?'

Maria was incandescent with rage.

'Does he accept no responsibility? Where is the remorse? Where is the apology?' she screamed, waving the letter in the air.

'Maria, listen. Calm down. He doesn't accept responsibility because he bears none,' said Giorgis. 'A father can't be responsible for all the actions of his child, can he?'

Maria reflected for a moment. She knew her father was right. If parents did carry the burden of their child's mistakes, it would be a different world. It would mean that it was Giorgis's fault that his elder daughter had driven her husband to shoot her through her own reckless and unfaithful behaviour. That was clearly absurd. She had to concede the point, if reluctantly.

'You're right, Father,' she said. 'You're right. The only thing that really matters is Sofia.'

Some kind of rapprochement was forged between the families after this, with unspoken acknowledgement that there was fault on both sides for the catastrophe that had damaged them all. Sofia, from the very beginning, was well cushioned. She lived with her grandparents but every week she would go down to Plaka and spend a day with her other grandfather and Maria, who would dedicate themselves to her entertainment. They would go out on boat trips, catch fish and crabs and sea urchins, paddle in the sea and go for short walks along the cliff path. At six o'clock, when they delivered Sofia back to her grandparents' house near Elounda, they would all be tired out. Sofia had the adoring attention of three grandparents. In some ways, she was lucky.

As spring turned into early summer, Kyritsis counted that two hundred days had passed since Anna's burial and the day he had driven Maria to Elounda and realised that their future was not going to be spent together after all. Every day he struggled to stop himself thinking of what might have been. He lived the same disciplined existence he had always lived: into the hospital on the dot of seven-thirty in the morning and out again at nearly eight at night, with a solitary evening of reading, studying and letter-writing ahead of him. It occupied him thoroughly, and many envied his dedication and his apparent absorption in what he did.

Within weeks of the patients' exodus from Spinalonga, news that the island was no longer in use as a leper colony had spread across Crete. It meant that many who had feared to reveal potential leprosy symptoms emerged from their villages and came to seek help. Now that they knew treatment would not mean incarceration in the leper colony, they were unafraid to reveal themselves and came in waves to see the man who was known to have brought the cure for leprosy to Crete. Though modesty prevented Dr Kyritsis from basking in this glory, his reputation spread. Once diagnosis had been confirmed, sufferers would come to him for regular injections of dapsone, and usually, in the space of a few months, as doses were gradually raised, improvements would begin to show.

For many months Kyritsis continued his work as head of department in the bustling main hospital of Iraklion. There should have been nothing more rewarding than seeing his patients walk away from him cured of the disease and discharged for good. All he felt, however, was a terrible emptiness. He felt this in the hospital and he felt it in his home, and each day became more of an effort than the last as he dragged himself from his bed and back to the hospital. He even began to question whether he really had to administer the drugs himself. Could someone else not take his place? Was he really needed?

It was during this time of feeling dispensable inside the hospital and empty outside it that he received a letter from Dr Lapakis, who, since Spinalonga had closed, was now married and had taken up the post of head of dermatovenereology at the general hospital in Agios Nikolaos.

My dear Nikolaos,

I wonder how you are. Time has gone so quickly since we all left Spinalonga and in all those months I fully intended to get in touch with you. Life is busy back here in Agios Nikolaos and the hospital has greatly expanded since I was here full time. Do come and see us if you would like a break from Iraklion. My wife has heard so much about you and would love to meet you.

Yours,
Christos

It set Kyritsis thinking. If someone he respected as much as Christos Lapakis found fulfilment working in Agios Nikolaos, then perhaps the choice was his. If Maria was not able to come to him, he would have to go to her. Every Tuesday, Crete's daily newspaper carried advertisements for hospital vacancies and each week he would scan them, hoping to find work closer to the woman he loved. The weeks passed and several suitable jobs were advertised in Hania, but these would take him even further from his desired destination. Disenchantment set in, until one day he received another letter from Lapakis.

Dear Nikolaos,

I hope all is well with you. You'll think me henpecked I am sure, but I am planning to give up my job here. My wife wants to live closer to her parents in Rethimnon so we shall be moving in the next few months. It just occurred to me that you might be interested in taking over my department. The hospital is expanding rapidly and there could be a bigger opportunity later on. Meanwhile, I thought I should let you know of my plans.

Yours,
Christos

Although nothing had ever been said, Lapakis knew that his colleague had formed a bond with Maria Petrakis, and he had been dismayed to learn that Kyritsis had returned to Iraklion alone. He surmised that Maria had felt obliged to stay with her father and regarded the whole situation as a terrible waste.

Kyritsis read and reread the letter before putting it into the top pocket of his white coat, where he reached for it several times during the day and ran his eyes over the words again and again. Although a job in Agios Nikolaos would close all kinds of doors in his career, there was one door in his life which would open: the opportunity to live closer to Maria. That night he wrote to his old friend and asked him how he should pursue this opportunity. There were formalities to be attended to, other candidates to be interviewed and so on, Lapakis replied, but if Kyritsis could write a formal letter of application within the week, then it was likely that he would be considered for the post. The truth of it, as both of them well knew, was that Kyritsis was overqualified for the job. Moving from the headship of a department in a city hospital to the same position in a smaller hospital meant that no one doubted he could do the job, and the hospital was delighted, if slightly mystified, that someone of his calibre and reputation should have applied. He was summoned for interview and it was only a matter of days before he then received confirmation that they would like to award him the post.

Kyritsis's plan was to establish himself in his new life before he contacted Maria. He did not want her to raise any objections to the apparent turnaround in his career and planned simply to present the situation as a fait accompli. Less than a month later, now established in a small house not far from the hospital, he set off to Plaka, which was only twenty-five minutes' drive away. It was a Sunday afternoon in May, and when Maria opened her front door to see Kyritsis standing there, she paled with surprise.

'Nikolaos!' she gasped.

A small voice then piped up. It seemed to come from Maria's skirt, and a face appeared from behind her at not much higher than knee level.

'Who is it, Aunt Maria?'

'It's Dr Kyritsis, Sofia,' she replied in a scarcely audible voice.

Maria moved aside and Kyritsis stepped over the threshold. She looked at his back as he passed her, the same neat, straight back that she had watched so many times when he had left her home to walk up the main street of Spinalonga to the hospital. Suddenly it seemed only a moment since she had been on the island, day-dreaming of a future.

Maria trembled as she laid out cups and saucers, and they clattered noisily. Soon she and Kyritsis were as comfortably seated as they could be on the hard wooden chairs, sipping their coffee just as they used to on Spinalonga. Maria struggled in vain to think of something to say. Kyritsis, however, came straight to the point.

'I've moved,' he said.

'Where to?' Maria asked politely.

'Agios Nikolaos.'

'Agios Nikolaos?'

She almost choked on the words. Astonishment and delight

mingled in equal measure as she struggled to imagine the implications of his announcement.

'Sofia,' she said to the little girl, who was sitting at the table, drawing, 'why don't you go upstairs and find that new doll to show Dr Kyritsis . . .'

The little girl disappeared upstairs to fetch her toy, and now Kyritsis leaned forward. For the third time in her life Maria heard the words: 'Marry me.'

She knew that Giorgis was able to look after himself now. They had come to terms with Anna's death and Sofia had brought pleasure and distraction into their lives. The distance to Agios Nikolaos meant that Maria could visit her father several times a week and still see Sofia as well. It took less than a second for all of this to go through her head, and before she took her next breath she had given him her answer.

Giorgis returned soon after. He had not been as happy since the day he learned that Maria was cured. By the next day, news had travelled all around Plaka that Maria Petrakis was to marry the man who had cured her, and preparation for the wedding began immediately. Fotini, who had never lost hope in the prospect of Maria and Kyritsis marrying, threw herself into the plans. She and Stephanos were to host the party before the wedding service and their friends would all crowd into the taverna for a great feast afterwards.

They set a date with the priest for two weeks hence. There was no reason to wait any longer. The couple had a house to move into, they had known each other for some years and Maria already had a trousseau, of sorts. She also had a dress, the one she had bought for her wedding with

Manoli. For five years it had lain in the bottom of a chest, wrapped in layers of tissue. A day or two after Kyritsis's second proposal, she unfolded it, shook out the creases and tried it on.

It still fitted as beautifully as it had done on the day it was purchased. She was physically unchanged.

'It's perfect,' said Fotini.

On the eve of the wedding the two women were together at Fotini's, planning how Maria should wear her hair.

'You don't think it's bad luck marrying in the same dress I was to have worn for a different wedding? A wedding that never took place?'

'Bad luck?' replied Fotini. 'I think you've run out of bad luck now, Maria. I must confess I think Fate did have it in for you, but not any more.'

Maria was holding the dress up to herself in front of the long mirror in Fotini's bedroom. The frothy tiers of its full, lacy skirt cascaded around her like a fountain and the fabric swished about her ankles. With her head thrown back, she began to twirl around like a child.

'You're right . . . you're right . . . you're right . . .' she chanted rhythmically, breathlessly. 'You're right . . . you're right . . . you're right . . .'

Only when she was dizzy did Maria stop spinning and throw herself backwards on to the bed.

'I feel,' she said, 'like the luckiest woman alive. No one in the whole world could be as happy as I am.'

'You deserve it, Maria, you really do,' replied her oldest friend.

There was a knock on the bedroom door and Stephanos put his head into the room.

'Sorry to disturb you,' he said jokingly. 'We've got a wedding happening here tomorrow and I'm trying to prepare the feast. I could really do with a hand.'

The two women laughed, and Maria jumped off the bed, throwing the dress across a chair. Both of them raced downstairs after Stephanos, giggling like the children they had once been, their excitement at the prospect of Maria's big day filling the air.

They woke up to a clear May day. Every last inhabitant of the village emerged to follow the bridal procession the short distance from Maria's home to the church at the other end of the village. They all wanted to be sure that the beautiful dark woman in white was safely conducted to the ceremony and that nothing, this time, would get in the way of her and a happy marriage. The doors of the church were left open during the ceremony and the crowd craned their necks to catch a glimpse of the proceedings at the far end of the aisle. Dr Lapakis was the best man, the *koumbaros*. He was a familiar figure in Plaka – people remembered his daily comings and goings to Spinalonga – but fewer villagers remembered Kyritsis. His presence had been a fleeting one, though they were all well aware of his significance in the evacuation of the leper colony.

As the pair stood at the altar, the priest crowned them with the woven halos of flowers and grasses. There was absolute silence in the church and the crowd standing in the sunshine outside were hushed as they strained to hear the words.

'The servant of God, Maria, is crowned to the servant of

God, Nikolaos . . . In the name of the father and of the son and of the Holy Spirit, now and ever unto the ages. O Lord our God, crown them with your glory.'

They all then listened as the priest read from the familiar marriage texts, St Paul's letters to the Ephesians and to St John. There was nothing hurried or perfunctory about the service. This was the most solemn and binding of ceremonies and its duration reinforced its significance to the two who stood at the altar. Over an hour later, the priest drew the proceedings to a close.

'Let us pray for the groom and the bride. That they may have mercy, life, peace, health and salvation. May Christ, our true God, who by his presence in Cana of Galilee approved the dignity of marriage, have mercy upon us, O Lord Jesus Christ, have mercy upon us.'

A resounding 'Amen' reverberated through the church and finally the deed was done. Sugared almonds were distributed to everyone in the congregation and all of those who had stood outside. They were a symbol of the abundance and joy that everyone hoped Maria and Kyritsis would now enjoy. There was not a soul who wished them anything else.

Giorgis had sat in the front pew of the church with Eleftheria and Alexandros Vandoulakis. It was a public symbol of their reconciliation, and between them sat little Sofia, charmed and excited by the pageantry and colour of the wedding. For Giorgis there was a strong sense of a new beginning and a certainty that all the woes of the past were firmly behind him. It was the first time in years that he had felt at peace.

When Maria emerged, crowned, with her silver-haired

groom, the crowd cheered and then trailed after them in the sunshine to the taverna, where the merrymaking would begin. The feast that Stephanos laid on for all the guests that night was munificent. Wine flowed and corks popped from bottles of *tsikoudia* long into the night. Under the stars, the musicians plucked and bowed until the dancers' feet were numb. There were no fireworks.

They spent the first two nights of their marriage in a grand hotel overlooking the harbour in Agios Nikolaos but were both eager to begin the next stage of their lives. Maria had been to the house which was to be their marital home on several occasions in the two weeks leading up to the wedding. It would be the first time she had lived in a big bustling town and she relished the prospect of this change. The house was on a steep hill close to the hospital and had a wrought-iron balcony and floor-to-ceiling windows, as did all the others in the street. It was a tall, narrow house with two flights of stairs, and the paintwork was the palest aquamarine.

Dr Kyritsis himself was new to the town, so it did not attract gossip when he brought home his bride, and the place was sufficiently far from Maria's old home for her to be able to start afresh. No one knew of her medical history here, except her husband.

Fotini was the first to visit, with Mattheos and baby Petros, and Maria proudly showed her round.

'Look at these huge windows!' exclaimed Fotini. 'And you can see the sea over there. And look, boys, there's even a little garden!'

The house was grander and more spacious than any in Plaka and the furniture less rough and ready than the village style which most people still had at that time. The kitchen too was a good deal more sophisticated than the one Maria had been brought up with: for the first time in her life she had a fridge, a modern cooker and an electricity supply that did not suddenly shut down with no notice.

For a few months, life could not have been more perfect. Maria loved her new home on the hill near the hospital, and soon it was decorated to her taste and hung with the samplers she had embroidered as well as framed photos of her family. One morning in early September, however, she heard the bell of their newly installed telephone. It was Giorgis, who rarely rang her, so she knew immediately that something was amiss.

'It's Eleftheria,' he said in his usual blunt manner. 'She passed away this morning.'

In the past few months Giorgis had grown close to the Vandoulakis couple, and Maria could detect the sorrow in his voice. There had been no warning of illness and no signs of the stroke which had taken the elderly woman so suddenly and unexpectedly. The funeral was held a few days later, and it was only at the end of the ceremony, when Maria saw her little niece hand in hand with her two grandfathers, that the reality of the situation dawned on her. Sofia needed a mother.

She could not shake the thought off. It followed her, stuck to her like the spines of a thistle clinging to wool. The little girl was only just three years old – what was to happen to her? Suppose Alexandros died too? He was at least ten years older than Eleftheria had been so it was perfectly possible that this could happen, and she knew Giorgis would never manage to look after her on his own. As for her father, in spite of

Andreas's plea for leniency at the trial, the judge had passed a harsh sentence that ensured he would not be out of prison until Sofia was at least sixteen.

As they sipped their glasses of wine in the semi-darkness of the Vandoulakis drawing room in Elounda, a room that seemed purpose-made for mourning, with its forbidding family portraits and heavy furniture, the solution seemed more and more perfect. This was not the time to discuss it with anyone, although she now ached to share it. It felt as though the walls themselves murmured as people adopted the low, restrained tones of those who felt that even the clink of a glass might ruin the strict sobriety of the atmosphere. All the while Maria wanted to stand on a chair and make an announcement about what she wanted to do, but she had to wait an hour or so until it was time to leave before confiding in Kyritsis. Before they were even in their car she seized his arm.

'I've had an idea,' she blurted out. 'It's about Sofia.'

There was no need for her to say any more. Kyritsis had been mulling over the very same possibility.

'I know,' he replied. 'The little girl has lost two mothers now, and who knows how long Alexandros will live after this?'

'He was devoted to Eleftheria and he's heartbroken. I can't imagine how life will be for him without her.'

'We need to think about this carefully. It might be the wrong time to suggest that Sofia comes to live with us, but being with her grandfather won't be a long-term solution, will it?'

'Why don't we go and talk to him about it in a few days' time?'

Only two days later, having telephoned ahead to let him

know they would like to come, Maria and Nikolaos Kyritsis found themselves once again in Alexandros Vandoulakis's drawing room. The once statuesque man seemed to have shrunk since the funeral, when he had held his head high and proud throughout the service.

'Sofia has already gone to bed,' he began, pouring them both a drink from a bottle which stood on the sideboard. 'Otherwise she would be here to say hello to you.'

'It's about Sofia that we've come,' began Maria.

'I thought it might be,' said Vandoulakis. 'The matter scarcely warrants discussion.'

Maria paled. Perhaps they had made a terrible faux pas in coming.

'Eleftheria and I had a discussion a few months ago on this very subject,' Vandoulakis began. 'We talked about what would happen to Sofia if one of us died – though of course we were assuming it would be me who would go first. What we agreed was that if one of us were left on our own, the very best thing for our granddaughter would be for her to be taken care of by someone younger.'

Alexandros Vandoulakis had spent decades being in command, but even so it astonished them that he had so completely taken charge of the situation. They did not have to say another word.

'The finest solution for Sofia would be if she went to live with you,' he said, addressing them both. 'Would you consider it? I know you are very fond of her, Maria, and as her aunt you are the closest of all her blood relations.'

For a few moments Maria struggled to speak, but Kyritsis managed to say everything that was necessary.

The next day, when Kyritsis had finished work at the hospital, he and Maria returned to the Vandoulakis home and between them began to prepare Sofia for the next stage of her life. By the end of the following week she had moved to the house in Agios Nikolaos.

At first Maria was nervous. Within a year of leaving Spinalonga she had become a wife and now, almost overnight, the mother of a three-year-old. She need not have feared, however. Sofia led the way and adapted happily to being with a couple who were so much younger and more energetic than her grandparents. In spite of her traumatic start in life, she was an apparently carefree child and loved the company of other children, which she soon found in abundance in their very own street.

Kyritsis had also been anxious about becoming a parent. Although he had always numbered a few children among his patients, his contact with anyone as young as Sofia had been limited. The little girl was wary of him too, at first, but then realised that with the slightest provocation she could make his serious face crease into a smile. Kyritsis began to dote on her and was soon frequently castigated by his wife.

'You do spoil her,' wailed Maria, when she saw how Sofia ran rings around Nikolaos.

As soon as Sofia went to school, Maria began to train to work in the hospital dispensary. It seemed a perfect complement to her work with natural herbs, which she also continued to practise. Once a week Maria, who had learned to drive since her marriage, took Sofia to her paternal grandfather's house, where she would spend the night in the bedroom that was kept for her there. The next day, when Maria collected her, they would usually continue to Plaka, where they saw Giorgis. Almost every visit they would see Fotini too and Sofia would play on the beach below the taverna with Mattheos and Petros while the two women caught up on the minutiae of each other's lives.

Life continued in this happy and settled way for a while. Sofia enjoyed the routine of seeing both her grandfathers once a week and the excitement that growing up in a busy harbour town offered a child. Eventually the knowledge that Maria and Nikolaos were not her real parents slipped out of memory's reach. The house where they lived in Agios Nikolaos was all she would ever be able to recollect of early childhood. The only gap in any of their lives was a sibling for Sofia. It was a subject they rarely spoke about, but it weighed heavily on Maria that she had not produced a child of her own.

When Sofia was nine, Alexandros Vandoulakis died. He passed away peacefully in his sleep having tied up every last detail of his will, leaving the estate to be split between his two daughters and their families and a generous lump sum of money in trust for Sofia. Three years later, Giorgis became bed-ridden after a chest infection and moved to the house in Agios Nikolaos to be cared for by Maria. Over the next two years, his teenage granddaughter spent hours each day sitting on his counterpane playing backgammon with him. One autumn day, just before Sofia's return from school, he died. Both the women in his life were inconsolable. Their only real comfort was to see the throng that gathered for his funeral. It was held in Plaka, the village where he had spent almost his entire life, and the church was filled with well over a hundred villagers, who remembered with great affection the taciturn fisherman who had borne so much misfortune so uncomplainingly.

One chilly morning, early the next year, a typed envelope bearing an Iraklion postmark arrived. It was addressed to 'The Guardians of Sofia Vandoulakis'. Maria's stomach lurched when she saw the name. It was not one that Sofia had ever known she possessed and she snatched the letter up from the doormat and immediately stashed it at the back of a drawer. There was only one source for a letter addressed in such a way and Maria was full of trepidation; she planned to wait until her husband returned before finding out whether her fears were justified.

At about ten that night, Nikolaos arrived home from a long day at the hospital. Sofia had gone to bed an hour earlier. With some formality, Nikolaos slit the envelope with his silver opener and drew out a stiff sheet of paper.

To Whom It May Concern

They were together on the settee, their legs touching, and Nikolaos's hand quivered slightly as he held the letter out for both of them to read.

We regret to inform you that Andreas Vandoulakis passed away on 7th January. The cause of death was pneumonia. Burial will take place on 14th January. Please confirm receipt of this letter.

Yours faithfully,
Governor, Prison of Iraklion

For a few moments, neither of them spoke. But they read, and re-read, the perfunctory note. Andreas Vandoulakis. His was a name which had carried such connotations of wealth and promise. It was hard to believe, even after the dreadful events over a decade earlier, that the life of such a privileged individual had finally ended in a damp prison cell. Without speaking, Nikolaos got up, returned the letter to its envelope and crossed the room to lock it in his bureau. There was no chance that Sofia would ever find it there.

Two days later, Maria was the only mourner as Andreas's coffin was lowered in to a pauper's grave. Neither of his sisters attended. They would not even have considered it. As far as they were concerned, their brother had been as good as dead for a very long time.

By now it was the late 1960s and the first wave of tourists began to arrive in Crete, many of them visiting Agios Nikolaos, which became a magnet for northern Europeans beguiled by the sunshine, the warm sea and the cheap wine. Sofia was fourteen and becoming wilful. With parents who were so conventional and such pillars of the community, she soon found that an effective way to rebel was to hang around in the town with boys from France and Germany who were only too pleased to keep the company of a beautiful Greek girl with a gloriously buxom figure and waist-length hair. Although Nikolaos hated to be in any conflict with Sofia, in the summer months battles became an almost daily occurrence.

'She's inherited her mother's looks,' despaired Maria late one night when Sofia had failed to return home. 'But it now looks as though she might have her character too.'

'Well, I think I finally know which side of the nurture versus nature debate I'm on,' said Kyritsis ruefully.

Though she was rebellious in other ways, Sofia worked hard at school, and when she reached the age of eighteen it was time to consider university. It was an opportunity that had never been open to Maria and was one that both she and Nikolaos wanted for her. Maria assumed that Sofia would go to Iraklion for her studies, but she was disappointed. From childhood Sofia had watched large boats coming and going from mainland Greece. She knew that Athens was where Nikolaos had studied, and this was where she wanted to go. Never having left Crete herself, Maria was filled with trepidation at Sofia's ambition to go further afield.

'But the university in Iraklion is as good as any on the mainland,' she said, appealing to Sofia.

'I'm sure it is,' Sofia replied. 'But what's wrong with going somewhere further away?'

'Nothing's wrong with it at all,' Maria replied defensively. 'But Crete seems a big enough place to me. It has its own history and its own customs.'

'That's precisely the point,' snapped Sofia, showing a steely determination that nothing could bend. 'It's too wrapped up in its own culture. It seems almost sealed off from the outside world sometimes. I want to go to Athens or Thessalonika – at least they connect with the rest of the world. There's so much happening out there and we're never even touched by most of it here.'

She was displaying a desire to travel that was only natural for a girl at her stage of life. Nowadays everyone of her age seemed keen to go off and see more of the world. Maria dreaded it, though. As well as her own fears at losing Sofia, it raised in her mind the question of Sofia's paternity. Manoli would have talked like that, about Crete being a small island on a very large planet and how exciting the possibilities were beyond it. There was something strangely familiar about this wanderlust.

By the time June came, Sofia had made her decision. She was going to Athens and her parents would not stand in her way. At the end of August she would be sailing away.

The night before their daughter was to take the boat to Piraeus, Maria and Nikolaos were sitting in their garden under an ancient vine which dripped with ripening bunches of purple-hued grapes. Sofia was out. Nikolaos nursed the last few drops of a large balloon of Metaxa.

'We have to tell her, Maria,' he said.

There was no reply. During the past few months the two of them had gone over and over the arguments for telling Sofia that they were not her true parents. It was when Maria had eventually admitted the possibility that Manoli might have been Sofia's father that Kyritsis had finally made up his mind. The girl had to know. Now there was a chance that her father could be living and working in Athens, or anywhere else for that matter, she had to be told the truth. Maria knew that Nikolaos was right and that Sofia must be told before she left for Athens, but every day she deferred the moment.

'Look, I don't mind doing the talking,' said Nikolaos. 'I just think the time for procrastination is over.'

'Yes, yes. I know you're right,' Maria said, taking a deep breath. 'Let's tell her tonight.'

They sat in the warmth of the summer night, watching moths twirl like ballerinas in the candlelight. Occasionally the silence would be disturbed by the rustle of a lizard, its tail catching a dry leaf before it made its vertical dash up the wall of the house. What did those bright stars have in store for her family? wondered Maria. They seemed always to be watching, knowing the next chapter before she did. It grew late and still Sofia did not return, but they were not going to give up and retire to bed. They could not postpone what they had to do for yet another day. By a quarter to eleven the temperature had dropped and Maria was shivering.

'Shall we go inside?' she said.

Time dragged its heels for the next fifteen minutes, but eventually they heard the front door slam. Sofia was back.

Part 4

Chapter Twenty-five

As Fotini reached this point in the story, she was suddenly overwhelmed by the responsibility of describing the emotions of someone who was more than capable of telling her own tale. Although Fotini knew as well as anyone else alive how Sofia must have felt, who could tell the story better than she who had taken the blows of truth first hand? It was Sofia who, on that August night, had tried and repeatedly failed to catch her breath when her parents revealed that they were not really her parents at all; she who had had to face the fact that her real mother was no longer alive, and that there was no certainty about the identity of her natural father. She could never be sure of anything ever again. If the earth had undulated beneath her feet and the island of Crete been shaken by a great seismic movement she could not have felt more insecure.

Fotini realised there was only one thing to do, and all it would take was a phone call to Sofia in London. She slipped away, leaving Alexis to contemplate the now familiar view of Spinalonga.

As soon as she picked up the telephone, Sofia knew who it was who was calling.

'Fotini! Is that you?'

'It is me. How are you, Sofia?'

'Very well, thank you. Has my daughter Alexis been to visit you? I gave her a letter for you.'

'She most certainly has been to see me and she's still here now. We've had a very rewarding time together and I've done almost everything you asked.'

There was a moment's hesitation at the other end of the line. Fotini felt a sense of urgency.

'Sofia, how long would it take for you to get here? I've told Alexis all I can, but there are some things that I don't feel right about telling her. She has to leave soon to meet up with her boyfriend, but if you could get here before she goes, we could all have a couple of days together. What do you think?'

Again, silence at the other end.

'Sofia? Are you still there?'

'Yes, I'm still here . . .'

It was such a spontaneous invitation. There were a thousand reasons why Sofia could not drop everything and fly out to Greece, but there were enough very good reasons why she should, and almost instantly she decided to put the objections to one side. She would get herself to Crete by the following day, come what may.

'Look, I'll see if I can get a flight. It would be lovely to come to Plaka after all this time.'

'Good. I shan't tell Alexis, but I'll keep my fingers crossed you'll be able to get here.'

Sofia had no problem getting a seat on a flight to Athens. At this stage of the season there was little demand and there was a plane leaving Heathrow that afternoon. She hurriedly packed a small bag and left a message on Marcus's answer phone to explain where she was going. Take-off was on time, and by eight o'clock that night she was speeding in a taxi towards Piraeus, where she caught the night boat to Iraklion. As the ferry tilted this way and that on its southward course, Sofia had plenty of time to become anxious about what she was going to face when she arrived. She could not quite believe she had made this decision. Going to Plaka would be a journey so laden with memories that she was surprised at herself, but Fotini had sounded so insistent. Perhaps it really was about time she faced her past.

The following morning, less than twenty-four hours since the telephone conversation between the two women, Fotini saw a car drawing up in the side road near the taverna. A well-rounded blonde woman stepped out. Though it was twenty years since she had seen her and her fair hair could have thrown her off the scent, Fotini realised immediately who it was. She hurried out to meet her.

'Sofia, you're here. I can't believe it!' she exclaimed. 'I wasn't sure you'd come!'

'Of course I've come. I've wanted to come back for years but there just never seemed the right moment. And anyway, you never invited me,' she added teasingly.

'You know you don't have to wait for invitations to come here. You could have come any time you liked.'

'I know.' Sofia paused and looked around her. 'It all looks just the same.'

'Nothing much has changed,' Fotini said. 'You know what these villages are like. The local shop paints its shutters a different colour and there's an outcry!'

As she had promised, Fotini had not breathed a word to Alexis about her mother's impending arrival, and when the younger woman appeared on the terrace, bleary-eyed with sleep, she was astounded to see her mother, and wondered at first whether the previous evening's brandy was responsible for giving her hallucinations.

'Mum?' was all she could say.

'Yes, it is me,' replied Sofia. 'Fotini invited me and it seemed a good opportunity to come over.'

'It's such a surprise!' her daughter replied.

The three women sat around a table and sipped cold drinks in the shade of an awning.

'How has your trip been?' asked Sofia.

'Oh, so-so,' said Alexis with a noncommittal shrug of her shoulders. 'Until I got here. And then it became much more interesting. I've had a fantastic time in Plaka.'

'Is Ed here with you?' Sofia asked.

'No. I left him in Hania,' Alexis said, looking down at her coffee. She had scarcely given him a thought in the past few days and suddenly felt a pang of guilt that she had abandoned him for so long. 'But I plan to go back tomorrow,' she added.

'So soon?' exclaimed Sofia. 'But I've only just got here.'

'Well,' said Fotini carrying more drinks to the table, 'we haven't got much time then.'

All three of them knew that there was an agenda. Why else would Sofia have come? Alexis's head was still spinning from everything that Fotini had told her over the past few days, but she knew there was a final chapter. This was what her mother was here to provide.

Chapter Twenty-six

IT WAS THE night before Sofia was to leave for Athens to begin her life as a student at the university. Her trunk only had to be transported a few hundred metres down the road to the port and loaded on to the ferry, and its next stop, like hers, would be the capital of Greece, three hundred kilometres away to the north. Sofia's resolve to spread her wings was balanced by an equal amount of anxiety and fear. Earlier that day she had fought the temptation to unpack each and every item and put them back where they had always belonged: clothes, books, pens, alarm clock, radio, pictures. Leaving the known for the unknown was hard, and she perceived Athens as a gateway to either adventure or disaster. The eighteen-year-old Sofia could not imagine a middle ground. Every bone in her body ached with the anticipation of homesickness, but there was no going back now. At six o'clock she went out to meet her friends, to say goodbye to the people she was leaving behind. It would be a good distraction.

When she returned, on the stroke of eleven, she found her father pacing up and down the room. Her mother sat on the edge of a chair, her hands clasped tightly together, her knuckles white with tension. Every muscle in her face was taut.

'You're still up! I'm sorry I'm so late,' Sofia said. 'But you didn't have to wait up.'

'Sofia, we wanted to talk to you,' said her father gently.

'Why don't you sit down,' suggested her mother.

Sofia immediately felt uncomfortable.

'This all seems a bit formal,' she said, throwing herself into a chair.

'There are one or two things we feel you ought to know before you go off to Athens tomorrow,' said her father.

Now her mother took over. After all, most of it was her story.

'It's hard to know where to begin,' she said. 'But there are a few things we want to tell you about our family . . .'

That night they told her everything, just as Fotini had related it to Alexis. Not the slightest suspicion or unguarded word had given Sofia any forewarning, and she was totally ill equipped to deal with such revelations. She saw herself standing on a high mountain where layers of secrecy had been laid down over the millennia, each stratum of rock and stone hardening across the previous one. They had kept every last detail from her. It seemed like a conspiracy. When she reflected on it, there must have been dozens of people who knew about her mother's murder, and each and every one of them had maintained their silence for all those years. And what about the speculation and gossip that must have ensued? Perhaps people who knew her still whispered behind her back as she passed: 'Poor girl. I wonder if she ever found out who her father was?' And she could imagine the malicious susurration, the mutterings about leprosy: 'Fancy that,' they must have said. 'Not just one, but two cases in her family!' All those stigma that she had blithely carried about with her for years and years but not been in the least bit aware of. A disfiguring disease, an immoral mother, a murderer for a father. She was utterly repulsed. Her ignorance had been nothing less than bliss.

She had never questioned that she was the product of these two people who sat in front of her. Why should she? She had always imagined that her looks were a mixture of Maria's and Kyritsis's. People had even said so. But she was no more a blood relation of the man she had always called father than of any man she might meet in the street. She had loved her parents unquestioningly, but now that they were not her parents, were her feelings for them different? In the space of an hour, her entire life history had changed. It had dissolved behind her and when she looked back, there was a void. A blank. A nothingness.

She received the news silently and felt sick. Not for a moment did she think of how Maria and Kyritsis might be feeling or what it had cost them to tell her the truth after all this time. No. This was *her* story, *her* life that they had falsified, and she was angry.

'Why didn't you tell me all this before?' she screamed.

'We wanted to protect you,' said Kyritsis firmly. 'There seemed no need to tell you before.'

'We have loved you as your own parents would have loved you,' interjected Maria pleadingly.

She was desperate enough to be losing her only child to university, but even more distressed that the girl who stood in front of her and looked at her as though she was a stranger would no longer regard her as her mother. Months and years had gone by when the fact that Sofia was not their own flesh and blood had had no relevance, and they had loved her all the more perhaps because they had been unable to produce children of their own.

At this moment, however, Sofia just saw them as people who had lied to her. She was eighteen, irrational, and resolved now in her desire to invent a future for herself where she would be in command of the facts. Her anger gave way to a *froideur* that brought her emotions under control but chilled the hearts of the people who loved her most in the world.

'I'll see you in the morning,' she said, getting up. 'The boat leaves at nine.'

With that, she turned on her heel.

The following morning Sofia was up at dawn doing her final packing, and at eight o'clock she and Kyritsis loaded her luggage into the car. Neither of them spoke. All three of them drove down to the port, and when the moment came, Sofia's farewells were perfunctory.

She kissed each of them on both cheeks.

'Goodbye,' she said. 'I'll write.'

There was a finality about her adieu that gave no promise of short-term reunion. They trusted her to write, but they knew already that there was no purpose in watching for letters. As the ferry pulled away from its moorings, Maria was certain this was the worst that life could bring. People standing beside them were waving a loved one a fond farewell, but of Sofia there was no sign. She was not even on deck.

Maria and Kyritsis stood watching until the boat was a speck on the horizon. Only then did they turn away. The emptiness was unbearable.

For Sofia, the journey to Athens became a flight from her past, from the stigma of leprosy and the uncertainty of her parentage. A few months into her first term, she was ready to write.

Dear Mother and Father (or should I call you Uncle and Aunt? Neither seems quite right any more),

I am sorry things were so difficult when I left. I was terribly shocked. I can't even begin to put it into words and I still feel sick when I think about it all. Anyway, I am just writing to let you know that I am settling in well here. I am enjoying my lectures, and though Athens is much bigger and dustier than Agios Nikolaos, I am getting used to it all.

I will write again. I promise.

Love,
Sofia

The letter said everything and nothing. They continued to receive notes that were descriptive and often enthusiastic but gave away little of how Sofia was feeling. At the end of the first year, they were bitterly disappointed, if not entirely surprised, when she did not return for the vacation.

She became obsessed with her past and decided to spend the summer trying to trace Manoli. At first the trail seemed warm and she followed a few leads around Athens and then other parts of Greece. Then her sources became imprecise, phone books and tax offices for example, and she simply knocked on the door of any stranger who happened to be called Vandoulakis; the two of them would then stand there awkwardly before Sofia briefly explained herself and apologised for troubling them. The trail, such as it was, went stone cold, and one morning she woke up in a hotel in Thessalonika wondering what on earth she was doing. Even if she found this man, she would not know for sure if he were her father. Would she, in any case, prefer her father to have been a murderer who had killed her mother, or an adulterer who had abandoned her? It was not much of a choice. Should she not turn away from the uncertainty of her past and build a future?

At the beginning of her second year, she met someone who turned out to be a much more significant figure in her life than her father, whoever he might have been. He was an Englishman by the name of Marcus Fielding and he was on sabbatical at the university for a year. Sofia had never met anyone quite like him. He was big and bearish with a pale complexion that tended to blotchiness when he was embarrassed or hot, and he had very blue eyes, which were a rare thing to see in Greece. He also looked permanently crumpled in a way that only an Englishman could.

Marcus had never had a real girlfriend. He had generally been too wrapped up in his studies or too shy to pursue women, and he had found the sexually liberated London of the early 1970s intimidating. Athens during the same period was well behind in this revolution. In his first month at the university he met Sofia in a whole group of other students and thought her the most beautiful woman he had ever seen. Though she seemed quite wordly, she was not unapproachable, and he was astonished when she accepted an invitation from him.

Within weeks they were inseparable, and when it was time for Marcus to return to England she made the decision that she would forgo the rest of her course in order to go with him.

'I have no ties,' she said one night. 'I'm an orphan.'

When he protested, she assured him it was true.

'No, really, I am,' she said. 'I have an uncle and aunt who brought me up but they're in Crete. They won't mind me going to London.'

She said no more about her upbringing and Marcus did not pursue it, but what he did insist was that they should marry. Sofia needed no persuasion. She was completely and passionately in love with this man and knew beyond a shadow of a doubt that he would never let her down.

One chilly February day, the kind when frost lingers until midday, they married in a south London registry office. The invitation, an informal one, had stood on the high shelf above Maria and Nikolaos's fireplace for a few weeks. It would be the first time they had seen Sofia since the day she had sailed out of their lives. The searing pain of abandonment that they had felt so keenly at first gradually eased and gave way to the dull ache of acceptance. They both approached the wedding with a mixture of excitement and trepidation.

They liked Marcus instantly. Sofia could not have found herself a kinder, more dependable man, and to see her so content and secure was as much as they could have wished for, even if it was tainted by the fact that there was little likelihood now that she would ever return to settle in Crete. They enjoyed the English wedding, though it seemed to lack all the ritual and tradition that they were used to. It was just like an ordinary party except there were a few speeches, and what was strangest of all was that the bride did not really stand out from the other guests, dressed as she was in a red trouser suit. Maria, who spoke no English at all, was introduced to everyone as Sofia's aunt, and Nikolaos, who spoke excellent English, as her uncle. They remained at each other's side throughout, Kyritsis acting as translator for his wife.

Afterwards they stayed in London for two nights. Maria, particularly, was baffled by this city where Sofia had now chosen to live. It was another planet to her, a place that throbbed incessantly with the sound of car engines, monstrous red buses and heaving crowds filing past windows of slim mannequins. It was a city where, even if you were a resident, the chances of bumping into anyone you knew were non-existent. It was the first and last time Maria ever left her native island.

Even with her husband Sofia had explored the no-man's-land between secrets and lies. She convinced herself that concealment, the act of *not* telling something, was very different from telling something that was untrue. Even when her own children were born – Alexis, the first of them, only a year after the wedding – she vowed never to speak to them of her Cretan family. They would be guarded from their roots and forever protected from the deep shame of the past.

In 1990, at the age of eighty, Dr Kyritsis died. Several short obituaries, no more than a dozen or so lines long, appeared in British newspapers, praising him for his contribution to leprosy research, and Sofia carefully cut them out and filed them away. In spite of an age gap of nearly twenty years, Maria survived him by only five years. Sofia flew out to Crete for a perfunctory two days for her aunt's funeral and was overwhelmed by guilt and loss. She realised that her eighteen-year-old self had shown nothing but self-centred ingratitude in the way she had left Crete all those years before, but it was too late now to make amends. Far, far too late.

It was at this point that Sofia decided she would finally erase her background. She disposed of the few keepsakes of her mother's and her aunt's that lived in a box at the back of her wardrobe, and one afternoon, before the children returned home from school, a stack of yellowing envelopes with Greek stamps was burned on the fire. She then removed the backing from the framed photograph of her uncle and aunt and discreetly tucked the newspaper cuttings précising Kyritsis's life to a few sentences behind the picture. This record of their happiest day now lived by Sofia's bedside and was all that remained of her past.

By destroying the physical evidence of her history, Sofia had tried to shrug off her background but the fear of its discovery ate into her like a disease and, as the years passed, the guilt over how she had treated her aunt and uncle intensified. It sat in the pit of her stomach like a stone, a regret that sometimes made her feel physically sick when she realised there was nothing she could do to make amends. Now that her own children had left home, she felt more keenly than ever the agony of remorse and knew for certain that she had caused unforgivable pain.

Marcus had known better than to ask too many questions and went along with Sofia's desire to avoid any reference to her past, but as the children grew up, the Cretan characteristics were unmistakable: in Alexis the beautiful dark hair and in Nick the black lashes that framed his eyes. All the while Sofia feared that her children might one day discover what sort of people their ancestors had been, and her stomach churned. Looking at Alexis now, Sofia wished she had been more open. She saw her daughter scrutinising her as though she had never seen her before. It was her own fault. She had made herself a stranger both to her children and to her husband.

'I am so sorry,' she said to Alexis, 'that I've never told you any of this before.'

'But why are you so ashamed of it all?' Alexis asked, leaning forward. 'It's your life story, sort of, but at the same time you played no part in it.'

'These people were my flesh and blood, Alexis. Lepers, adulterers, murderers—'

'For goodness' sake, Mum, some of these people were heroic. Take your uncle and aunt – their love survived everything, and your uncle's work saved hundreds, if not thousands, of people. And your grandfather! What an example he'd be to people nowadays, never complaining, never disowning anyone, suffering it all in silence.'

'But what about my mother?'

'Well, I'm glad she wasn't *my* mother, but I wouldn't blame her entirely. She was weak, but she'd always had that rebellious streak, hadn't she? It sounds as though she always found it harder than Maria to do what she was meant to. It was just the way she was made.'

'You're very forgiving, Alexis. She was certainly flawed, but shouldn't she have fought harder against her natural instincts?'

'We all should, I suppose, but not everyone has the strength. And it sounds as though Manoli exploited her weakness as much as he possibly could – just as people like that always do.'

There was a pause in their exchange. Sofia fiddled anxiously with her earring as though there was something she wanted to say but she could not quite spit it out.

'But you know who behaved worse than anyone?' she eventually blurted out. 'It was me. I turned my back on those two kind, wonderful people. They'd given me everything and I rejected them!'

Alexis was stunned by her mother's outburst.

'I just turned my back on them,' Sofia repeated. 'And now it's too late to say sorry.'

Tears welled up in Sofia's eyes. Alexis had never seen her mother cry.

'You mustn't be too hard on yourself,' she whispered, drawing her chair up close and putting an arm around her mother. 'If you and Dad had dropped a bombshell like that on me when I was eighteen, I would probably have done just the same. It's totally understandable that you were so angry and upset.'

'But I still feel so guilty about it, and I have done for so many years,' she said quietly.

'Well, I don't think you need to now. It's the past, Mum,' said Alexis, holding her closer. 'From everything I've heard about Maria, I think she probably forgave you. And you wrote letters to each other, didn't you? And they came to your wedding? I'm sure Maria wasn't bitter – I don't think she had it in her.'

'I hope you're right,' said Sofia, her voice muffled as she struggled to suppress her tears. She looked away towards the island and slowly regained her composure.

Fotini had listened quietly to this exchange between mother and daughter. She could see that Alexis was making Sofia look at the past from a new perspective, and decided to leave them alone together for a while.

The Vandoulakis tragedy, as it was known, was still chewed over in Plaka, and the little girl who had been left without a father or mother had not been forgotten by those who had witnessed the events of that memorable summer night. Some of those people still lived in the village. Fotini strolled into the bar and had a quiet word with Gerasimo, who then gesticulated frantically to his wife. They would drop everything and come; their son could serve behind the bar for a while. All three of them hastened to the taverna.

At first Sofia did not recognise the small group who had appeared at a table close to where she and Alexis were sitting but as soon as she was aware that the elderly man was mute, she realised who it was.

'Gerasimo!' she cried. 'I remember you now. Weren't you working in the bar here when I used to come and visit?'

He nodded and smiled. The fact that Gerasimo was dumb had intrigued the little Sofia. She remembered being slightly afraid of him, but also recollected how much she enjoyed the iced lemonade he made specially for her whenever she and Maria called in at the bar, which was where they usually went to meet her grandfather. She had more difficulty remembering Andriana. Though she was now plump and terribly afflicted with varicose veins, which were ill concealed by her thick stockings, Andriana reminded Sofia that she had been a teenager when Sofia used to come to Plaka. Sofia dimly remembered a beautiful but rather languid girl who would usually be sitting outside the bar chatting to her friends while groups of teenage boys hung around, leaning nonchalantly on their mopeds. Fotini had found the brown envelope of photographs again, and once more they were spread out on the table and the family likenesses between Sofia, Alexis and their ancestors marvelled over.

The taverna was closed that night, but Mattheos, who was soon to take over his parents' business, now arrived. He had grown into a mountain of a man, and Sofia and he embraced enthusiastically.

'It's so good to see you, Sofia,' he said warmly. 'It's been such a long time.'

Mattheos began to lay a long table. One more guest was still to arrive. Fotini had telephoned her brother Antonis earlier that day, and at nine o'clock he arrived from Sitia. He was now very grey and quite stooped, but he still had those dark, romantic eyes that had drawn Anna to him all those years ago. He sat between Alexis and Sofia and after a few drinks he lost his shyness about talking English after so many years without practice.

'Your mother was the most beautiful woman I ever saw,' he said to Sofia, adding as an afterthought, 'apart from my own wife, of course.'

He sat quietly for a moment before he spoke again.

'Her beauty was a gift as well as a curse, and a woman like her will always drive some men to extreme behaviour. It wasn't all her fault, you know.'

Alexis watched her mother's face and could see that she understood.

'*Efharisto*,' Sofia said quietly. 'Thank you.'

It was well past midnight, and the candles had long since guttered to extinction, before everyone round the table got up to leave. Only a few hours later both Alexis and Sofia needed to be on the road, Alexis to retrace her steps to Hania to meet up with Ed, and her mother to catch the ferry back to Piraeus. For Alexis it was as though a month had passed since she had arrived, even though it was actually only a few days. For Sofia, in spite of the fact that her visit had been fleeting, its significance was immeasurable. Embraces as warm as the day itself were exchanged, and fond promises made to return the following year for a longer and more peaceful stay.

Alexis drove her mother to Iraklion, where Sofia was to catch the night ferry back to Athens. There was not a moment of silence on the journey as their conversation flowed. Once she had dropped her mother, who would happily spend the day in the city's museums before catching the ferry that night, Alexis carried on towards Hania. She had resolved the mystery of the past; today the future would be her concern.

Nearly three hours later she arrived back at the hotel. It had been a long, sweaty journey and she was desperate for a drink, so she crossed the road to the closest bar, which overlooked the beach. Ed was there, sitting alone and gazing out to sea. Alexis moved towards him quietly and took a seat at his table. The scrape of her chair alerted him to her presence and he looked round, startled by the noise.

'Where the *hell* have you been?' he shouted.

Apart from the message she had left for him four days earlier to say that she would be staying in Plaka for a couple of nights, she had not contacted him. Her mobile phone had been switched off.

'Look,' she said, knowing she had been wrong to be so out of touch, 'I'm really sorry. It all got very involved and somehow I lost track of time. Then my mum came over and—'

'What do you mean, your mum came over? So you were having some kind of family reunion or something and just forgot to tell me about it! Thanks a lot!'

'Listen . . .' Alexis began. 'It was really important.'

'For God's sake, Alexis!' he groaned with sarcasm. '*What* is more important? Buggering off to see your mother, who you can visit any day of the week when you're at home, or having this holiday with me?'

Ed did not expect an answer to this. He had already sauntered across to the bar to get himself another drink, his back turned to Alexis. She could see the anger and resentment in the line of his shoulders, and while they were still turned she slipped quickly and silently away. It took her a matter of minutes at the hotel to stuff all her clothes into a bag, grab a couple of books from the bedside table and scribble him a note.

Sorry it's ended like this. You never did listen.

There was no 'Love Alexis', no row of kisses. It was the end. She could admit it to herself now. There was no love left.

Chapter Twenty-seven

Alexis was soon back on the road to Iraklion. It was already four in the afternoon and she would have to put her foot down to reach it by seven o'clock, in time to return the hire car and catch the ferry which left at eight.

As she drove along the smooth road, which hugged the coastline and gave her a continuous and spectacular view of the sea, a feeling of euphoria swept over her. To her left there was nothing but blue: azure sea and sapphire sky. Why were feelings of misery called 'the blues'? she wondered. This bright sky and sparkling water seemed integral to her ecstatic sense of wellbeing.

With the windows wound down and warm air blowing through, her hair flickered behind her like a dark stream and she sang along loudly and passionately to 'Brown-Eyed Girl' as the cassette whirred round in the car's cheap tape deck. Ed hated Van Morrison.

This exhilarating journey lasted a little more than two hours, and as she rattled along, fear of missing the boat kept her foot firmly pressed on the accelerator. There was nothing quite like the sense of abandon she got at the wheel of a car.

With only moments to spare, she dealt with the irritations

of dispensing with the hired car, purchased her ticket for the ferry and climbed the ramp which brought her into the bowels of the ship. She was all too familiar with the stench of fumes that greeted passengers boarding a Greek ferry but knew that in an hour or two she would acclimatise. Cars were still being driven on, and freight was being loaded on to the deck, along with plenty of commotion and shouting from a crowd of dark-haired men yelling at each other in a language that she was still ashamed she knew so little of. In this particular situation, it was probably just as well. She saw a door marked 'Foot passinjers' and disappeared gratefully through it.

Somewhere on this boat, she knew she would find her mother. There were two lounges, one for smokers, another much emptier one for non-smokers. A group of American students occupied the latter, while in the former there were several dozen big family groups returning to mainland Greece after their holidays to relatives in Crete. They were vociferous and all appeared to be haranguing each other, though in truth they were probably simply discussing whether to have toasted sandwiches now or later on in the journey. Alexis could not find her mother on this level so she went up on deck.

In the fading light she saw Sofia at the far end, towards the prow. She was sitting alone, her small travel bag at her feet, looking across at the twinkling lights of Iraklion and the vaulted arches of the great arsenal built by the Venetians. The pristine walls of the solid sixteenth-century fortress which stood guard over the harbour could have been built yesterday.

A day earlier it was Alexis who had been amazed to see her mother. This time it was Sofia's turn to be surprised by the sight of her daughter.

'Alexis! What are you doing here?' she exclaimed. 'I thought you were going back to Hania.'

'I did.'

'But why are you here then? Where's Ed?'

'Still in Hania. I left him there.'

There was little need to explain, but Alexis wanted to talk.

'It's all over. I realised how pointless it was, how half-hearted,' she began. 'When I sat listening to Fotini describe your family and what they went through, what really struck me was how powerfully they loved each other. It was through sickness and health, thick and thin, until death parted them . . . I knew I didn't feel like that about Ed – and I certainly wouldn't feel like that about him in twenty, or even ten years' time.'

In the decades since Sofia had turned her back on the people and the place that had nurtured her into adulthood, she had never perceived it all so clearly. Her daughter had made her look at these ancestors of hers as though they were characters in a drama. At last she saw not humiliation but heroism, not perfidy but passion, not leprosy but love.

Everything was in the open now, the wounds were exposed to the air and at last there was the possibility of healing. There was no shame in any of it. She no longer had anything to hide and for the first time in twenty-five years her tears flowed unchecked.

As the cumbersome ferry moved slowly out of the harbour and blasted its horn into the still night air, Alexis and Sofia stood against the railings, catching the breeze on their faces. Arms entwined, they looked back across the pitch-black water until, gradually, the lights of Crete faded into the distance.

Leprosy – A Continuing Problem in the 21st Century

Leprosy is one of the world's oldest diseases. If left untreated, it can disfigre and result in permanent disability. In the 1980s an effective cure became available in the form of multi-drug therapy (MDT).

There is no preventative vaccine and much is still unknown about the disease and why some people are naturally immune while others are not.

Every two minutes one more person is diagnosed and starts treatment for leprosy. Many of these are already disabled by the time they are diagnosed.

What this means is that today, although it is entirely curable, millions of people around the world are still disabled by the consequences of leprosy. Many are still being subjected to discrimination and social exclusion because they, or members of their families, have had the disease.

Lepra's work

Lepra is an international charity fighting disease, poverty and prejudice. The charity focuses on people affected by some of the world's oldest and most neglected diseases, including leprosy. They not only ensure that health needs are met but also support people to improve their lives and livelihoods.

As the world's first leprosy prevention organisation the charity Lepra has been at the forefront of prevention, treatment and management of leprosy since 1924.

On average it costs £25 for Lepra to change the life of someone living with the consequences of cured leprosy.

In addition to working with leprosy affected people to fight prejudice and reduce their poverty, Lepra's past successes mean that governments are now able to deliver simple leprosy services. The charity also publishes academic research on leprosy and promotes sharing of best practise in the field.

Reaching more than one million people per year who are affected by disease, poverty and discrimination Lepra's work is just scratching the surface of need. With greater financial support they can do more.

Further information can be found online: www.lepra.org.uk or from Lepra, 28 Middleborough, Colchester, Essex CO1 1TG
T: 01206 216700

lepra

Fighting disease, poverty and prejudice

March 2013

the Return

For Emily and William, with love

With thanks to: Ian Hislop, David Miller, Flora Rees,
Natalia Benjamin, Emma Cantons, Professor Juan Antonio Díaz,
Rachel Dymond, Tracey Hay, Helvecia Hidalgo,
Gerald Howson, Michael Jacobs, Herminio Martinez,
Eleanor Mortimer, Victor Ovies, Jan Page, Chris Stewart,
Josefina Stubbs and Yolanda Urios.

FRANCE
Coruña
Oviedo
Santander
Bilbao
Guernica
Durango
San Sebastián
Pamplona
ANDORRA
St Cyprien
Argelès
Cerbère
León
Burgos
Figueres
Girona
Valladolid
Zaragoza
Barcelona
Tarragona
Salamanca
Segovia
Jarama
Ávila
Guadalajara
El Escorial
Brunete
Madrid
Teruel
Menorca
Mallorca
PORTUGAL
Cuenca
Toledo
Cáceres
València
Mérida
Ciudad Real
Albacete
Ibiza
BALEARIC ISLANDS
Badajoz
Alicante
Murcia
Córdoba
Jaén
Huelva
Sevilla
Granada
Almería
Málaga
Cádiz
Marbella
Algeciras
Ceuta
Melilla
N
0
150 miles
0
250 km
SPANISH MOROCCO

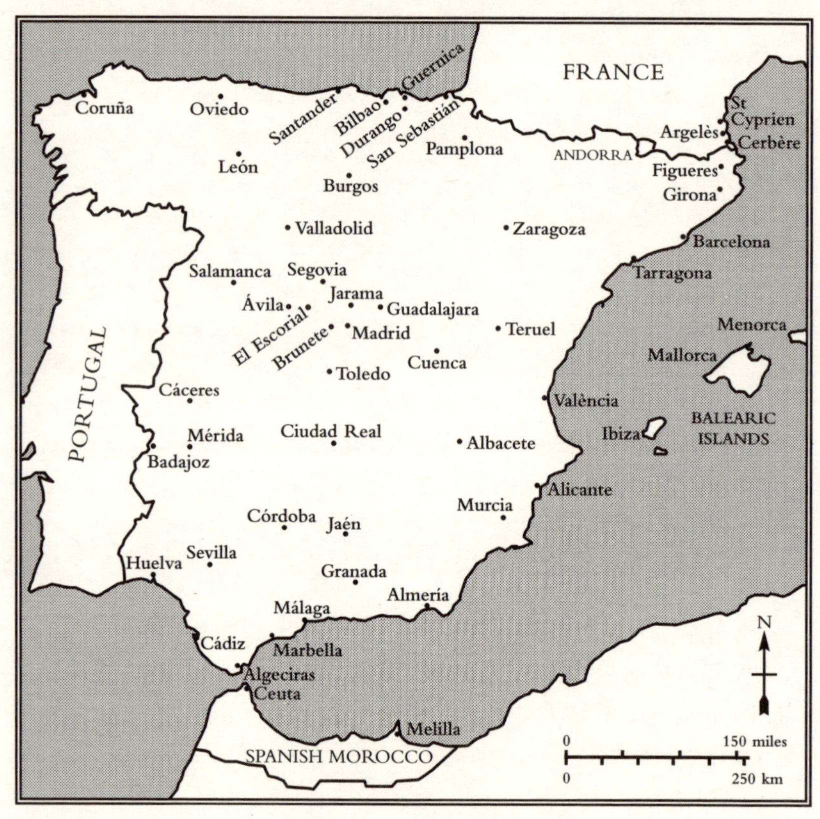

Spain, 1931

Granada, 1937

In the shuttered nocturnal gloom of an apartment, the discreet click of a closing door penetrated the silence. To the crime of being late, the girl had added the sin of trying to conceal her surreptitious homecoming.

'Mercedes! Where in the name of God have you been?' came a harsh whisper.

A young man emerged from the shadows into the hallway and the girl, who was no more than sixteen, stood facing him, her head bowed, hands concealed behind her back.

'Why are you so late? Why are you doing this to us?'

He hesitated, suspended in the uncertain space between total despair and uncompromising love for this girl.

'And what are you hiding? As if I couldn't guess.'

She held out her hands. Balanced on her flattened palms was a pair of scuffed black shoes, the leather as soft as human skin, their soles worn to transparency.

He took her wrists gently and held them in his hands. 'Please, for the very last time I am asking you . . .' he implored.

'I'm sorry, Antonio,' she said quietly, her eyes now meeting his. 'I can't stop. I can't help myself.'

'It's not safe, querida mia, *it's not safe.'*

Part 1

Chapter One

Granada, 2001

JUST MOMENTS BEFORE, the two women had taken their seats, the last of the audience to be admitted before the surly *gitano* slid the bolts decisively across the door.

Voluminous skirts trailing behind them, five raven-headed girls made their entrance. Tight to their bodies swirled dresses of flaming reds and oranges, acid greens and ochre yellows. These vibrant colours, a cocktail of heavy scents, the swiftness of their arrival and their arrogant gait were overpoweringly, studiedly dramatic. Behind them followed three men, sombrely dressed as though for a funeral, in jet black from their oiled hair down to their hand-made leather shoes.

Then the atmosphere changed as the faint, ethereal beat of clapping, palm just brushing palm, seeped through the silence. From one man came the sound of fingers sweeping across strings. From another emanated a deep and plaintive wail that soon flowed into a song. The rasp of his voice matched the roughness of the place and the ruggedness of his pock-marked face. Only the singer and his troupe understood the obscure patois, but the audience could sense the meaning. Love had been lost.

Five minutes passed like this, with the fifty-strong audience sitting in the darkness around the edge of one of Granada's damp *cuevas*, hardly daring to breathe. There was no clear moment when the song ended – it simply faded away – and the girls took this as their cue to file out again, rawly sensual in their gait, eyes fixed on the door ahead, not even acknowledging the presence of the foreigners in the room. There was an air of menace in this dark space.

'Was that it?' whispered one of the latecomers.

'I hope not,' answered her friend.

For a few minutes, there was an extraordinary tension in the air and then a sweet continuous sound drifted towards them. It was not music, but a mellow, percussive purring: the sound of castanets.

One of the girls was returning, stamping her feet as she paced down the length of the corridor-shaped space, the flounces of her costume brushing the dusty feet of the tourists in the front row. The fabric of her dress, vivid tangerine with huge black spots, was pulled taut across her belly and breasts. Seams strained. Her feet stamped on the strip of wood that comprised the dance floor, rhythmically *one*-two-*one*-two-*one*-two-three-*one*-two-three-*one*-two . . .

Then her hands rose in the air, the castanets fluttered in a deep satisfying trill and her slow twirling began. All the while she rotated, her fingers snapped against the small black discs she held in her hands. The audience was mesmerised.

A plaintive song accompanied her, the singer's eyes mainly downcast. The dancer continued, in a trance of her own. If she connected with the music she did not acknowledge it and if she was aware of her audience they did not feel it. The expression on her sensual face was one of pure concentration and her eyes looked into some other world that only she could see. Under her arms, the fabric darkened with sweat, and watery beads gathered at her brow as she revolved, faster and faster and faster.

The dance ended as it had begun, with one decisive stamp, a full stop. Hands were held above her head, eyes to the low, domed ceiling. There was no acknowledgement of the audience's response. They might as well not have been there for all the difference it made to her. Temperatures had risen in the room and those close to the front inhaled the heady mix of musky scent and perspiration that she spread in the air.

Even as she was leaving the stage, another girl was taking over. There was an air of impatience with this second dancer, as though she wanted to get it all over with. More black dots swam in front of the audience's eyes, this time on shiny red, and cascades of curly black hair fell over the gypsyish face, concealing all but the sharply defined Arab eyes, outlined in thick kohl. This time there were no castanets, but the endlessly repeated, rattling of feet: *clack*-a-tacka tacka, *clack*-a-tacka tacka, *clack*-a-tacka tacka . . .

The speed of movement from heel to toe and back again seemed impossibly fast. The heavy black shoes, with their high, solid heels and steel toecaps vibrated on the stage. Her knees must have absorbed a thousand shockwaves. For a while, the singer remained silent and gazed at the ground, as though to catch this dark beauty's eyes might turn him to stone. It was impossible to tell whether the guitarist kept up with her stamping or whether he dictated its pace. The communication between them was seamless. Provocatively she hitched up the heavy tiers of her skirt to reveal shapely legs in dark stockings and further showed off the speed and rhythm of her footwork. The dance built to a crescendo, as the girl, half whirling dervish, half spinning top, rotated. A rose that had clung precariously to her hair, flew out into the audience. She did not stoop to collect it, marching from the room almost before it had landed. It was an introverted performance and yet the most overt display of confidence they had ever seen.

The first dancer and the accompanist followed her out of the cave, their faces expressionless, still indifferent to their audience in spite of the applause.

Before the end of the show, there were another half-dozen dancers, and each one conveyed the same disturbing keynotes of passion, anger and grief. There was a man whose movements were as provocative as a prostitute's, a girl whose portrayal of pain sat uncomfortably with her extreme youth, and an elderly woman in whose deeply furrowed face were etched seven decades of suffering.

Eventually, once the performers had filed out, the lights came up. As the audience began to leave, they caught a glimpse of them in a small backroom, arguing, smoking and drinking from tall tumblers filled to the brim with cheap whisky. They had forty-five minutes until their next performance.

It had been airless in the low-ceilinged room, which reeked of alcohol, sweat and long-ago smoked cigars, and the crowd was relieved to emerge into the cool night air. It had a clarity and purity that reminded them they were not far from the mountains.

'That was extraordinary,' commented Sonia to her friend. She did not really know what she meant, but it was the only word that seemed to fit.

'Yes,' agreed Maggie. 'And so tense.'

'That's exactly it,' agreed Sonia. 'Really tense. Not at all what I imagined.'

'And they didn't look particularly happy, those girls, did they?'

Sonia did not bother to answer. Flamenco clearly had little to do with happiness. That much she had come to realise in the past two hours.

They walked back through the cobbled streets towards the centre of Granada and found themselves lost in the old Moorish quarter, the Albaicín. It was pointless to try to read a map; the tiny alleyways hardly had names and sometimes even petered out in sets of narrow steps.

The women soon got their bearings again when they turned a corner and were confronted with a view of the Alhambra, now gently floodlit, and though it was already past midnight the warm amber glow that bathed the buildings almost convinced them that the sun was still setting. With its spread of crenellated turrets that stood out against a clear black sky, it looked like something from *The Arabian Nights*.

Arms linked, they continued their walk down the hill in silence. The dark and statuesque Maggie reduced the length of her stride to match Sonia's. It was a habit of almost a lifetime between these two close friends, who were physical opposites in every way. They did not need to talk. For now, the crisp sound of their feet on the cobbles, percussive like the claps and castanets of the flamenco dancers, was more pleasing than the human voice.

It was a Wednesday in late February. Sonia and Maggie had arrived only a few hours earlier but even as they were driven from the airport, Sonia had fallen under Granada's spell. The wintry sunset illuminated the city with a sharp light, leaving the snow-capped mountains that were its backdrop in dramatic shadow, and as the taxi sped into the city along the freeway, they caught their first glimpse of the Alhambra's geometric outline. It seemed to keep watch over the rest of the city.

Eventually their driver slowed to take the exit into the centre and now the women feasted their eyes on regal squares, palatial buildings and occasional grandiose fountains before he turned off to take a route through the narrow cobbled streets that spread through the city.

Even though her mother had been from Spain, Sonia had visited this country only twice before, both times to the coastal resorts of the Costa del Sol. There she had stayed on the slick stretch of sparkling coast, where all-year sun and all-day breakfasts were marketed to the British and Germans who came in droves. Nearby plantations of matching villas, with ornate pillars and fancy wrought-iron railings, were so close and yet a million miles away from this city of confused streets and buildings that had been built over many centuries.

Here was a place with unfamiliar smells, a cacophony of ancient and modern, cafés overflowing with local people, windows piled high with small, glossy pastries, served by serious men proud of their trade, tatty shuttered apartments, glimpses of sheets hung out on balconies to dry. This was a real place, she thought, nothing ersatz here.

They swung this way and that, left and right, right and left and left again, as though they might end up exactly where they had started. Each of the small streets was one-way and occasionally there was a near miss with a moped that was going the wrong way up the street and approaching them at speed. Pedestrians, oblivious to the danger, stepped off the pavement into their path. Only a taxi driver could have negotiated his way through this complex maze. A set of rosary beads suspended from the rear-view mirror clattered against the windscreen and an icon of the Virgin Mary watched demurely from the dashboard. There were no fatalities on this journey, so she seemed to be doing her job.

The sickly, boiled-sweet smell of air-freshener combined with the turbulence of the journey had made both women feel nauseous, and they were relieved when the car eventually slowed down and they heard the grating sound of the handbrake being yanked into position. The two-star Hotel Santa Ana was in a small, scruffy square, flanked by a bookshop on one side and a cobbler on the other, and along the pavement was a row of stalls now in the process of being packed up. Smooth golden loaves and hefty tranches of flat, olive-studded bread were being wrapped, and the last remaining segments of some fruit tarts originally the size of wagon wheels were being stowed away in waxed paper.

'I'm ravenous,' said Maggie, watching the stallholders loading up their small vans. 'I'll just grab something from them before they disappear.'

With typical spontaneity, Maggie ran across the road, leaving Sonia to pay off the taxi driver. She returned with a generous section of bread that she was already tearing into pieces, impatient to satisfy her hunger.

'This is delicious. Here, try some.'

She thrust some of the crusty loaf into Sonia's hand and they both stood on the pavement by their bags, eating and scattering crumbs liberally on the stone slabs. It was time for the *paseo*. People were beginning to come out for their evening saunter. Men and women together, women arm in arm, pairs of men. All were smartly dressed and though they enjoyed a stroll for its own sake they looked purposeful.

'It looks attractive, doesn't it?' said Maggie.

'What?'

'Life in this city! Look at them!' Maggie pointed at the café on the corner of the square, which was packed with customers. 'What do you think they talk about over their *tinto*?'

'Everything, I expect,' replied Sonia with a smile. 'Family life, political scandal, football . . .'

'Look, let's go and check in,' said Maggie, finishing her bread. 'Then we could go out and have a drink.'

The glass door opened into a brightly lit reception area that was given a sense of grandeur by a number of chocolate-boxy arrangements of silk flowers and a few pieces of heavy baroque furniture. A smiling young man behind a high desk gave them a registration form and after photocopying their passports, told them the time of breakfast and handed them a key. The full-size wooden orange attached to it was an absolute guarantee that they would never leave the hotel without handing it in for replacement on the row of hooks behind reception.

Beyond the lobby, everything else in this hotel was tawdry. Nose to nose, they went up in a tiny box of a lift, their luggage balanced in a tower, and on the third floor emerged into a narrow corridor. In the darkness they clattered along with their suitcases until they could make out in large, tarnished figures the number '*301*'.

Their room had a view of sorts. But not of the Alhambra. It looked out onto a wall and, specifically, onto an air-conditioning unit.

'We wouldn't spend much time looking out of the window anyway, would we?' commented Sonia, as she drew the thin curtains.

'And even if there was a balcony with gorgeous furniture and far-reaching views over the mountains we wouldn't use it,' added Maggie, laughing. 'It's a bit early in the year.'

Sonia quickly threw open her suitcase, squashed a few T-shirts into the small bedside drawer and hung the rest of her things in the narrow wardrobe; the scrape of metal coat hangers on the rail set her teeth on edge. The bathroom was as economically sized as the bedroom, and Sonia, though petite, had to squeeze behind the basin to shut the door. Having cleaned her teeth she tossed her brush into the single glass provided and reappeared in the bedroom.

Maggie was lying on top of the burgundy bedspread, her suitcase on the floor, still unopened.

'Aren't you going to unpack?' enquired Sonia, who knew from experience that Maggie would probably spend the week living out of a suitcase that frothed over with bits of flirtatious lace and tangles of ruffled blouses, rather than actually hang anything up.

'What's that?' Maggie asked distractedly, engrossed in reading something.

'Unpack?'

'Oh, yes. I might do that later.'

'What's that you're reading?'

'It was with a pile of leaflets on the table,' Maggie replied from behind a flyer, held close to her face in an attempt to make out the words.

The low-voltage lighting lifted the gloom of the dark beige room only a little and scarcely provided enough illumination to read. 'It's advertising a flamenco show somewhere called *Los Fandangos*. It's in the gypsy area, as far as my Spanish can tell, anyway. Shall we go?'

'Yes. Why not? They'll be able to tell us on reception how to get there, won't they?'

'And it doesn't start until ten thirty, so we could go and eat first.'

Shortly afterwards, they were out on the street, a map of the city in hand. They wound their way through a labyrinth of streets, partly following their noses, partly the orientation of the map.

Jardines, *Mirasol*, *Cruz*, *Puentezuelas*, *Capuchinas* . . .

Sonia remembered the meaning of most of these words from her schooldays. Each one held its magic. They were like brush strokes, painting the landscape of the city, each one helping to build up a picture of the whole. As they got closer to the heart of this city, the street names clearly reflected the dominance of the Roman Catholic religion.

They were making for the cathedral, the city's central point. According to the map, everything emanated from here. The narrow alleyways seemed an unlikely way to reach it but it was only when Sonia saw some railings and two women sitting begging in front of a carved doorway that she looked up for the first time. Towering above was the most sturdy of buildings. It filled the sky, a solid mass of distinctively fortress-like stone. It did not reach up to the light, like St Paul's, St Peter's or the Sacré-Coeur. From where she stood, it seemed to blot it out. Nor did it announce itself with a huge empty space in front of it. It lurked behind the workaday streets of cafés and shops, and from most places in these narrow streets was unseen.

On the hour, however, it reminded the world of its presence. As the two women stood there, the bells began to toll. The volume was enough to make them reel back. Resoundingly deep, metallic clangs banged inside their heads. Sonia cupped her ears with her hands and followed Maggie away from the deafening noise.

It was eight o'clock and the tapas bars around the cathedral were already filling up. Maggie made a speedy decision, drawn to the place where a waiter stood outside on the pavement, smoking.

Once they were perched on high wooden stools, the women ordered wine. It was served in small stubby tumblers with a generous plate of *jamon* and each time they ordered another drink, more tapas magically appeared. Although they had been hungry, these small offerings of olives, cheese and pâté slowly filled them up.

Sonia was perfectly happy with Maggie's choice of venue. Behind the bar, ranks of mighty hams hung from the ceiling, like giant bats suspended upside down in trees. Fat dripped from them into small plastic cones. Next to them were *chorizos*, and on shelves behind sat huge tins of olives and tuna. There were rows and rows of bottles just out of reach. Sonia loved this dusty chaos, the rich, sweet smell of *jamon* and the hum of conviviality that wrapped itself around her like a favourite coat.

Maggie interrupted her reverie. 'So, how is everything?'

It was a question typical of her friend. As heavily loaded as the cocktail stick onto which she had speared two olives and a cherry tomato.

'Fine,' answered Sonia, knowing as she said it that this response would probably not do. It sometimes annoyed her that Maggie always wanted to get straight to the heart of things. They had kept conversation quite light and superficial since they had met up at Stansted early that day, but sooner or later, she knew Maggie would want more. Sonia sighed. This was what she both loved and loathed about her friend.

'How's that dusty old husband of yours?' This more direct question could not be deflected with one single word, especially not 'Fine'.

Since nine o'clock, the bar had filled up rapidly. Earlier in the evening the clientele had been mostly elderly men, gathered in tight-knit groups. They were neat figures, Sonia observed, small and smartly jacketed, with highly polished shoes. After that, slightly younger people began to pack the place out and stood chatting animatedly, balancing wine and plates of tapas on the narrow ledge that ran around the room especially for this purpose. The volume of noise meant that conversation was more difficult now. Sonia drew up her stool so close to Maggie's their wooden frames touched.

'Dustier than ever,' she said in her ear. 'He didn't want me to come here, but I suspect he'll get over that.'

Sonia glanced over at the clock above the bar. Their flamenco show was beginning in less than half an hour.

'We really should go, shouldn't we?' she said, slipping down off her stool. Much as she loved Maggie, for the time being she wished to deflect her personal questions. In her best friend's view no husband was really worth having, but Sonia had often suspected that this might have been something to do with the fact that Maggie had never had one, at least not one of her own.

Coffee had just been served to them on the bar and Maggie was not going to leave without drinking it.

'We've got time for this,' she said. 'Everything starts late in Spain.'

Both women drained their rich cups of *café solo*, manoeuvred their way through the crowds and went outside. The throng continued into the street and almost all the way to the Sacromonte where they soon found a sign pointing to '*Los Fandangos*'. It was set into the hillside, a white-washed, roughly plastered building, the *cueva* where they were going to see flamenco. Even as they approached, they could hear the alluring sound of someone picking out chords on a guitar.

Chapter Two

THAT NIGHT, BACK in the hotel bedroom, Sonia lay awake staring at the ceiling. As is the way with cheap hotel rooms, it was too dark in the day and too light in the night. Through the unlined curtains a beam of light from the lamp outside illuminated the beige pattern of hallucinogenic swirls on the ceiling and her mind, still stimulated by caffeine, whirled. Even without the light and the coffee, the thin mattress would have been conducive to wakefulness.

Sonia contemplated her happiness at being in this city. Maggie's rhythmic breathing in the next bed only a few inches away was strangely comforting. She mulled over the evening and how she had deflected her friend's questions. Whatever she said, Maggie would get at the truth sooner or later and would simply know how things were with her in spite of any words. She could tell merely from a shadow that flickered across a face in answer to the question 'How are you?' what the answer should be. This was why James did not like her, and indeed why so many men shared his feelings. She was too perceptive, generally too critical of men and never gave them the benefit of any doubt.

James was, as Maggie so kindly put it, 'dusty'. It was not his age alone, but his attitudes. Dust had probably settled on him in the cradle.

Their wedding five years earlier, following a courtship of textbook romanticism, had been a vision of contrived but fairy-tale perfection. In this hard, narrow bed, so distant in every way from the expansive luxury of the four-poster where she had spent her wedding night, Sonia thought back to the time when James had appeared in her life.

They met when Sonia was twenty-seven and James was hurtling towards his fortieth birthday. He was a junior partner in a small private bank and for the first fifteen years of his career had worked an eighteen-hour day, ambitiously climbing his way up the corporate ladder. Though he might be in the office for eighteen hours a day, he was at the end of a phone for twenty-four if he was seeing through a deal. Occasionally he picked up a girl late at night in a wine bar, but these were women he would never introduce to his parents, and once or twice he had had relationships with kittenish, stiletto-heeled receptionists who worked in the bank. These never resulted in anything and sooner or later, these girls drifted off, usually to work as PAs in another bank.

Only weeks before his landmark birthday, as the Americans who owned his bank would have put it, James 'reprioritised'. He needed someone to take to the opera, to dinners, to have his children. In other words, he wanted to be married. Though she was unaware of it for several years, Sonia eventually realised that she had nicely fulfilled an entry in his Filofax 'to do' list.

Sonia remembered their first meeting very clearly. James's employer, Berkmann Wilder, had recently merged with another bank and had taken on the PR consultancy she worked for to rebrand them. Sonia always dressed provocatively for meetings with financial institutions, knowing that men who worked in the City usually had rather obvious taste, and when she was shown into the bank's boardroom, her attraction was not lost on James. Petite, blonde, with a pert bottom well outlined by a tight skirt, and a neat bosom cupped in a lace bra just visible through a silk blouse, she satisfied several male fantasies. James's stares made her feel almost uncomfortable.

'Peachy,' James described her to a colleague that lunchtime. 'And quite sparky too.'

The following week when she returned for a second meeting, he suggested a working lunch. The lunch led to a drink in a wine bar and within the week, they were what James called 'an item'. Sonia was being swept off her feet and she had no desire to feel the ground beneath them. As well as being quite handsome, he filled in all kinds of gaps in her life. He came from a large, terribly English, entirely conventional, Home Counties family. Such firm foundations had been lacking in Sonia's life and proximity to them made her feel secure. The two significant relationships she had been through in her twenties had ended disastrously for her. One had been with a musician, the other with an Italian photographer. Neither had been faithful to her and the appeal of James was his reliability, his public school solidity.

'He's so much *older* than you!' objected her friends.

'Why does that matter so much?' queried Sonia.

It was the very fact of this age gap that probably gave him the resources for lavishly extravagant gestures. On Valentine's Day, he did not send a dozen red roses, he sent a dozen dozen, and her small flat in Streatham was overwhelmed. She had never been so spoiled, or indeed so happy when, on her birthday, she found a two-carat diamond solitaire ring in the bottom of a glass of champagne. 'Yes' was the only possible answer.

Although Sonia had no intention of giving up a job she enjoyed, James offered her long-term security and in return she brought a dowry of childbearing potential and tolerance of a mother-in-law for whom no one was good enough for her son.

As she lay in her cramped Granada hotel room, Sonia thought of their glorious white wedding, the images of it still so clear; a video had been professionally done and was still occasionally replayed. The marriage had taken place, two years after their first meeting, in the Gloucestershire village close to James's family home. The dingy part of south London where Sonia had grown up would not have provided a picturesque enough backdrop for these nuptials. There was a rather obvious imbalance in the congregation (representation on the bride's side was noticeably thinner than on the groom's, which swelled with second cousins, fleets of small children and friends of his parents) but for Sonia the only really noticeable absence was her mother's. She knew that her father felt it too. Apart from that, everything was perfect. Sprays of freesias festooned pew-ends and scented the air, and there was a gasp as Sonia entered through the arch of white roses on her father's arm. In a full tulle gown that almost filled the width of the aisle, she floated down the strip of carpet towards her groom. Crowned with flowers, the sun creating a halo of light around her, the silver-framed photographs in her home reminded her that she had looked translucent, other-worldly on that day.

After the reception (a four-course dinner for three hundred in a pink candy-striped marquee), James and Sonia left in a Bentley for Cliveden and by eleven the following morning they were on their way to Mauritius. It was a perfect beginning.

For a long while, Sonia had loved being petted, cared for. She enjoyed the way that James opened doors for her, came home from business trips to Rome with satin lingerie in silk-lined boxes, from Paris with perfumes packaged in boxes within boxes layered like Russian dolls, and with airport scarves from Chanel and Hermès that were not quite her. The habit of clothing her and choosing how she might be fragranced was one he had copied from his father. Sonia's in-laws, Richard and Diana, had been together for nearly fifty years, so it was clearly a technique that women liked, James had evidently concluded.

They both had careers that absorbed them. Sonia had moved to a younger, smaller company that looked after the PR interests of manufacturing companies rather than City institutions. She felt she had enough bankers and lawyers in her private life. She did not mind the fact that James did not bother to change his working patterns. He would be disturbed at all times of day or night by a ringing phone and the need to deal with some international conference call between London, Tokyo and New York. This was the personal cost of a banker's salary. Sonia perfectly understood and never minded that, a few times a week, he had to have dinner with clients. On the evenings when he was at home, he had very little energy for anything much apart from a perusal of *Investors Chronicle* and a vacant stare at the television. The only exceptions were the occasional visits to the cinema and the very regular dinner parties that he and Sonia gave and attended.

On the surface of things, all looked rosy. They had everything:

good jobs, a Wandsworth house that was steadily increasing in value, and plenty of space to begin a family. They seemed a solid couple, just like their home and the street where they lived. The obvious next stage in their lives was to become parents, but to James's irritation something held Sonia back. She had begun to make excuses, both to herself and to James, usually to do with it not being the right moment to take a career break. Admitting, even to herself, the real reason was not easy.

Sonia could not put a date on when the drinking had seemed to become a problem. There probably was not an exact moment, a particular glass of wine, a specific bar or an evening when James had come home and she felt he had had 'too much'. Perhaps the moment had been at a business lunch, or even at a dinner party, possibly the one they had given the previous week when the large mahogany table had been laid with their best china and cut glass, all gifts at their perfect fairy-tale wedding five years earlier.

She could picture her guests standing around sipping flutes of champagne in their comfortable shades of ice-blue drawing room, making conversation that followed a predictable pattern. The men had been uniformly dressed in suits but the women had their own strict dress code too: floaty skirts and kitten heels and what at one time would have been called a 'twinset'. Some kind of diamond pendant was de rigueur, too, and a set of fine jangly bangles. It was the smart-casual dress style of their generation: feminine, slightly flirty but steering well clear of tarty.

Sonia recalled how conversation had followed its usual pattern: information had been exchanged about when to put children's names down for nursery, the flattening of property prices, the rumoured opening of a new deli-restaurant on the Common, brief reference to an awful road rage incident in the neighbouring street, and then the men told crude jokes that had been circulating on the internet to try to lighten the atmosphere. She remembered feeling almost at screaming point with the sheer predictability of the middle-class talk and with these people with whom she felt she had nothing in common.

That night, as usual, James had been eager to show off his huge collection of vintage clarets, and the husbands, tired after a long week in the city, had enjoyed knocking back a few bottles of 1978 Burgundy, though even after a glass and a half they began to get disapproving looks from their wives who now realised that it would be their job to drive home.

Cigars had made their appearance at midnight.

'Go on,' coaxed James, passing around a box of pure Havana cigars, 'guaranteed to have been rolled between a virgin's thighs!'

Though they had heard it said a thousand times before, the men all roared with laughter.

For conservative forty-six-year-old bankers like James, an evening such as this was perfect: safe, respectable and just as his parents would have enjoyed. In fact, it was no different from dinners that Mr and Mrs Cameron Senior had hosted. James once told Sonia that he remembered sitting on the landing peering through the banister rails and catching snippets of conversation that floated up from the dining room and the occasional burst of laughter as doors were opened and closed, his mother hurrying to and from the kitchen, delivering tureens of soup or casserole to her generously proportioned hostess trolley. His childhood spying on the staircase had always come to an end well before the guests left and the conviviality of it all lived on in his imagination. Sonia sometimes wondered if his parents had bickered over the debris of the evening, or how often his mother climbed wearily into bed at two in the morning beside a snoring husband.

That previous week, it had not been until well after midnight that the guests had all departed. Faced with the depressing aftermath of the dinner party, James had displayed a level of belligerence that had taken Sonia by surprise, given that it had been, as usual, his decision to fill their home with City colleagues and their shrill wives. It was not exactly her idea of fun either, dealing with glasses that were too fragile to go in the dishwasher, ashtrays full of smouldering dog-ends, tidemarks of soup now stuck to the bowls like green concrete, a tablecloth stained with splatters of claret, and white linen napkins covered with perfect lipstick kiss marks. Someone had spilled coffee onto the carpet and not mentioned it, and there was a splash of red wine on a pale armchair.

'What's the point of having a cleaner if we still have to scrub the dishes?' exploded James as he attacked a particularly resistant pan and sent a tidal wave of water flying over the edge of the sink. Even if his guests had limited the amount they had drunk, James had not.

'She only works during the week,' said Sonia, mopping up the lake of greasy water, which lapped against James's feet. 'You know that.'

James knew full well that the cleaner did not come on Friday nights, but it did not stop him from asking the same question every time he found himself at the sink doing battle with stubborn stains.

'Bloody dinner parties,' he swore, carrying in a third tray laden with glasses. 'Why do we give them?'

'Because we get invited to them and you like them,' Sonia replied quietly.

'It just goes round in bloody circles, doesn't it?'

'Look, we don't have to give another one for ages. We're owed lots of invitations.'

Sonia knew not to pursue this line of conversation. It would be much better to button her lip.

By one o'clock, the plates were filed in perfect order, facing right in the dishwasher like a row of soldiers. They had had their usual argument about whether or not the sauce should be rinsed off the plates before stacking them. James had won. The smart Worcestershire china already gleamed inside the now humming machine. The pans were spotless too and James and Sonia had nothing more to say to each other.

Retiring to bed in Granada was so different. She loved the solitude of this narrow bed and being alone with her own reflections. There was such peace in this. The only sounds she could hear were reassuring: a moped buzzing in the street below, a muffled conversation amplified by the acoustics of the narrow street and the faintly rasping breath of her oldest friend.

In spite of the light that still streamed in from the lamppost outside and even now a subtle brightening of the sky, suggestive of dawn breaking, her mind finally shut down, like a candle extinguished. She slept.

Chapter Three

ONLY A FEW hours later the women were woken by the insistent pulse of an alarm.

'Rise and shine,' said Sonia with mock cheerfulness, peering at the bedside clock. 'Almost time to go.'

'It's only eight,' groaned Maggie.

'You haven't changed your watch,' replied Sonia. 'It's nine and we're meant to be there at ten.'

Maggie pulled her sheet up over her head while Sonia got up, showered and dried herself with a rough, threadbare towel. By nine twenty she was dressed. She had come to Granada for a purpose.

'Come on, Maggie, let's not be late,' she said coaxingly. 'I'm going to nip down for some coffee while you get dressed.'

While she breakfasted on a limp croissant and tepid coffee, Sonia studied the map of Granada and located their destination. The dance school was not far away, but they would have to concentrate on taking the correct turnings.

As she sipped her coffee, Sonia mused on how things evolved. It had all begun with a film. Without that, the dancing would never have happened. It was like a board game – she had not known where the next move would take her.

One of the few things that James occasionally agreed to do on a weekday was to go to their local cinema, even if he was usually asleep well before the film's denouement. The local south London picture house resolutely refused to show blockbusters, but had enough local clientele wanting to see high-brow, art-house films, to half fill it most nights. It was only a mile or so from where they lived, but the atmosphere was much edgier this side of

Clapham Common: Caribbean takeaways, kebab houses and tapas bars competed with Chinese, Indian and Thai restaurants, all a contrast with the glassy metropolitan restaurants closer to their home.

The side street into which they emerged after the film matched the hauntingly gloomy Almodóvar film they had watched. As they walked along Sonia noticed something that she hadn't seen before – a brightly illuminated, flashing, Las Vegas-vulgar sign: 'SALSA! RUMBA!' it shrieked in neon. In the dimly lit street, there was something reassuringly cheerful about the sign.

As they approached, they could hear music and see a suggestion of movement behind the frosted windows. They must have walked past this building on their way to the cinema but not even given it a second look. In the intervening two hours, the prosaic-looking nineteen fifties hall, squeezed into the space where a bomb had fallen during the Blitz, had come to life.

As they passed, Sonia had taken in a smaller, illuminated sign:

Tuesday – Beginners
Friday – Intermediate
Saturday – All Levels

From inside came a scarcely audible but alluring Latin American beat. Even the faint suggestion of rhythm exerted a strong pull on her. The clipped sound of James's heels retreating down the street confirmed to her that he had not even noticed it.

Coming home from the office a few weeks later, she had, as usual, to force open the front door and push aside the embankment of paper that lay behind it. Leaflets clogged up the hallway as irritatingly as slush on winter roadsides – every type of takeaway and home delivery imaginable, catalogues for DIY shops that she had no intention of visiting, offers of carpet cleaning at half price, English lessons that she did not need. But there was one leaflet that she could not throw into the recycling bin. On one side was a photo of the neon sign that had winked at her all those weeks ago and the words: 'Salsa! Rumba!' On the reverse, were days and times for lessons and at the bottom of the page, rather endearingly, the following words: 'Lern to dance. Dance to live. Live to dance.'

As a little girl she had been taken to weekly ballet lessons and later on to tap dancing. She had given up dance school as a teenager but was always there until the bitter end at any school disco. Since they married, James had made it clear that dancing was not his 'thing' so the opportunity rarely arose. Now there was just the occasional black tie birthday party or a corporate event for James's bank, where there might be a small square of parquet flooring and a DJ who played a few desultory disco hits from the nineteen eighties. It was not the real thing. The thought that there was somewhere she could take dance lessons less than ten minutes' drive from where she lived kept coming back to her. Perhaps she would pluck up the courage to go one day.

That day came sooner than she had imagined. It was a few months later. They had planned to see a film and James had rung on her mobile just as she was arriving at the cinema to say that he was stuck in the office. Across the way, the neon lights of the dance school winked at her.

The hall was as seedy on the inside as it appeared on the outside. Paint peeled from the ceiling and there was a waist-height tide-mark all the way round the room as though it had once filled up with water like a giant fish tank. This might have explained the unmistakable smell of damp. Six bare light bulbs hung down from the ceiling on irregular lengths of flex, and a few posters advertising Spanish fiestas were intended to cheer up the walls. Their tattiness only reinforced the general sense of decay. Sonia's nerve almost failed her, but one of the instructors spotted her in the doorway. She was given a warm welcome, and was just in time for the start of a lesson.

She found that she soon picked up the rhythm. Before the end of the evening she discovered that the movement could turn into something as subtle as a twitch of the hips rather than a meticulously counted sequence of steps. Two hours later she emerged, flushed, into the chilly evening air.

For some reason that she could not have articulated to anyone, Sonia felt exhilarated. Even the music had filled her to the very top of her being. She was brimming – that was the only way she could describe it to herself – and without hesitation she signed up for a course. Each week the dancing thrilled her more. Sometimes she could hardly contain her exuberance. For an hour or so after it had finished, the mood of the dance class remained with her. There was an enchantment about dancing. Even a few minutes of it could leave her in a state of near-ecstasy.

She loved everything about her Tuesday evening engagement with Juan Carlos, the stubby Cuban with the shiny, pointy-toed dancing boots. She loved the rhythm and the momentum and the way the music reminded her of sunshine and warm places.

Whenever the instructor needed to, he would demonstrate the complex steps with his even tinier wife, Marisa, and whilst they did so their dozen or so pupils stood in silent, admiring rapture. It was the deftness of their steps and the ease with which they moved that reminded this small motley audience why they showed up each week. The truth was that, most of the time, women were dancing with women. The older of the only two men, Charles, had clearly been a good dancer in his youth. Now in his late sixties, his footwork was still feather light and he moved his partner firmly but with faultless rhythm. He never missed a beat and never failed to pick up the instructions they were given. Whenever Sonia danced with him, she knew that he dreamed of his wife who, she had gathered from a brief conversation, had died just over three years before. He was brave, sprightly, sweet.

The other, a recently divorced and slightly overweight man in his forties, had taken up dancing as a way of meeting women. In spite of the healthy ratio of women to men, he was already finding this class to be a disappointment as there was no one here who was going to take the slightest interest. Each week he asked a different woman out for a drink with him and, one by one, they declined. It might have been something to do with the way he sweated profusely even during the slow dances. The girls were much happier dancing with each other than finding themselves cheek to cheek with desperation and a large perspiring frame.

Over the following weeks, Sonia acknowledged that Tuesday was her favourite of all days, and her class the one unmissable commitment in her diary. What started as a distraction, grew into a passion. Salsa CDs littered the boot of her car, and on her journeys to work she mind-danced as she drove. Each week, she returned warm and flushed from the exhilaration of her lesson. On the occasions when he was already in, James would greet her with a patronising comment, bursting the balloon of her euphoria.

'Good time at your dancing class?' he enquired, glancing up from his newspaper. 'How were all the little girls in their tutus?'

James's tone, though it pretended to be teasing, had a distinctively sarcastic undertone. Sonia tried not to be provoked, but felt obliged to deflect his criticism.

'It's just like a step class. Don't you remember? I used to go to them all the time a couple of years ago.'

'Mmm . . . vaguely,' came the voice behind the newspaper. 'Can't see why you have to go every week, though.'

One day she mentioned this new interest of hers to her oldest school friend, Maggie. The two girls had been inseparable for the seven years they were at grammar school together, and two decades on they were still almost as close, meeting several times a year for an evening in a wine bar. Maggie was full of enthusiasm for Sonia's dancing. Could she come too? Would Sonia take her? Sonia was only too pleased. It could only make it more fun.

The bond between them had been forged when they were eleven and never broken. Initially all that had brought them together was the simple fact that they had gained places at the same grammar school in Chislehurst, wore the same navy blazer that chafed at their necks and stiff flannel skirts that crackled round their knees. On the very first day of school they had been thrown together in the fourth row by the proximity of their surnames in the register: pale, little Sonia Haynes and tall, chatty Margaret Jones.

From that day, they observed and admired the many differences in each other. Sonia envied Maggie's relaxed attitude to her schoolwork and Maggie looked admiringly at her friend's meticulous notes and neat annotated set texts. Maggie thought Sonia's colour TV the most amazing thing in the universe, but Sonia would have swapped it any day for the platform shoes her friend was allowed to wear. Sonia wished she had liberal parents like Maggie's, who let her stay out until midnight, while Maggie knew that she would have wanted to come home earlier if there was a dog curled up by a glowing fire. Whatever one of them had, to the other it seemed desirable.

In every way, their lives could not have been more contrasted: Sonia was an only child and her mother was already in a wheelchair by the time she started secondary school. The atmosphere in her tidy semi-detached house was subdued. Maggie, on the other hand, lived in a ramshackle house with four siblings and easy-going parents who never seemed to mind if she was in or out.

In their all-girls school, academic work absorbed little of their energy. Feuds, discos and boyfriends were their main preoccupations, and confessions and confidences were the oxygen of friendship. When Sonia's mother was finally beaten by the multiple sclerosis that had been slowly destroying her for years, Maggie was the person Sonia cried with. Maggie more or less moved in with her and both Sonia and her father appreciated her presence. She lifted the terrible gloom of their grief. This happened in the girls' lower sixth. In the following year, Maggie had her own crisis. She became pregnant. Her parents took the news badly and for the second time Maggie went to live with Sonia for a few weeks until they got used to the idea.

In spite of this closeness, they went very separate ways when they left school. Maggie's baby was born not long after – no one ever knew the name of the father, perhaps not even Maggie herself – and eventually she supported herself by teaching pottery part time in a couple of colleges and at night classes. Her daughter, Candy, was now seventeen, and had just started at art school. In a good light, with their big hoop earrings and quasi-bohemian style of dress, they could easily be mistaken for sisters. In a harsher one, some would look at Maggie and wonder why a woman her age was still dressing in Topshop. Though her long dark curls were almost identical to her daughter's, years of smoking had indented her sun-tanned face with lines that revealed her true age. They lived together on the borders of Clapham and Brixton, close to a row of pound shops and the best Indian vegetarian restaurants this side of Delhi.

Sonia's lifestyle, a career in PR, an expensively upholstered home, and James were all very alien to Maggie, who had never hidden her concerns about her friend marrying such a 'stuffed shirt'.

Their lives might have gone in very different directions, but geographically they had remained close, their south of the river homes being only a few miles apart. For nearly twenty years they had diligently remembered each other's birthdays and nourished their friendship with lengthy evenings over a few bottles of wine, when they told each other every detail of their lives until it was closing time, and then parted, not to be in touch again for weeks or even months.

For the first half of her introductory salsa class in Clapham, Maggie sat out and watched. All the time she was tapping out the beat with her foot and rocking gently on her hips, never for a moment taking her eyes off the instructors' feet as they demonstrated that night's steps. Juan Carlos had the music turned up loud that night, and the insistent beat seemed to make the floorboards themselves vibrate. After the five-minute break, when everyone sipped water from their bottles and Sonia introduced her old friend to the other dancers, Maggie was ready to try the steps. A few of the regulars were sceptical that someone who had not been to the class before could join halfway through a term and expect to catch up; they feared that their own progress would be delayed.

The Cuban took Maggie's hand and, in front of the mirror, led her through the dance. The rest of the class watched, several of them hoping that she would flounder. Her brow might have been furrowed with concentration but Maggie remembered every move and half-turn that they had been working on that night and was step-perfect. There was a ripple of applause as the dance finished.

Sonia was impressed. It had taken her weeks to get as far as Maggie had in half an hour.

'How did you manage that?' she asked Maggie over a glass of Rioja in the wine bar afterwards.

She admitted that some years ago she had done some salsa on a trip to Spain and had not forgotten the basic technique. 'It's like riding a bike,' she said nonchalantly, 'once learned, never forgotten.'

Within a few sessions, her enthusiasm surpassed even Sonia's and, with few other commitments in her life, Maggie began going to a salsa club, dancing in the darkness with hundreds of others until five in the morning.

In a few weeks it was to be Maggie's thirty-fifth birthday.

'We're going dancing in Spain,' she announced.

'That sounds fun,' said Sonia. 'With Candy?'

'No, with you. I've got the tickets. Forty pounds return to Granada. It's done. And I've booked us some dance classes while we're there.'

Sonia could imagine exactly how badly this would go down with James, but there was no question of refusing Maggie. She knew for sure that her friend would have little sympathy for any kind of vacillation. Maggie was a free spirit and never understood how anyone could give up their liberty to come and go as they pleased. But most importantly for Sonia, she did not want to refuse. Dance already seemed like a driving force in her life and she was addicted to the sense of release it gave.

'How fantastic!' she said. 'When exactly?'

The trip was in three weeks' time, to tie in with the day of Maggie's birthday.

James's *froideur* was no surprise. If James had disliked his wife's new interest in dancing, his antagonism intensified when she had announced this trip to Granada.

'Sounds like a hen party,' he had said dismissively. 'Bit old for that kind of thing, aren't you?'

'Well, Maggie did miss out on the whole wedding thing, so perhaps that's why she's making such a celebration of a big birthday.'

'*Maggie* . . .' As ever, James's contempt for Maggie was ill concealed. 'Why didn't she ever get *married*? Like everyone else?'

He could see what Sonia saw in her university friends, her colleagues and the various acquaintances she had made within sugar-borrowing distance of their home, but his attitude to Maggie was different. As well as being part of his wife's dim and distant schooldays, Maggie did not fit into any boxes and he could not begin to see why Sonia kept in touch with her.

Far away from her husband, under the sympathetic gaze of a cheaply reproduced Virgin Mary in the breakfast room of the Hotel Santa Ana, Sonia realised that she had ceased to care what James thought of her unconventional friend.

Maggie appeared, bleary-eyed at the doorway.

'Hi, sorry I'm late. Have I got time for coffee?'

'No, not if we're going to get there for the start of the class. We'd better go straight away,' instructed Sonia, keen to obstruct any further procrastination that Maggie might be dreaming up. In the daytime, Sonia felt she was in charge. At night, she knew they would swap roles. It had never been any different.

They went out into the street and were taken aback by the sharp air. There were few people about: a handful of elderly folk with small dogs on leads, and the rest sitting in cafés. Most shop fronts were still hidden behind metal grilles, with only bakeries and cafés showing signs of life, the alluring fragrance of sweet pastries and *churros* scenting the air. Many of the cafés were already densely fogged with the steam of coffee machines and cigarette smoke. Most of the city would only really stir itself in another hour. Until then, early risers like Sonia and Maggie would have the narrow streets almost to themselves.

Sonia hardly looked up from her map, following the twists and turns of the alleyways and passageways to steer them to their destination. Every step of the way was guided by the blue lettering of the ceramic street signs, the musical charm of the names – Escuelas, Mirasol, Jardines – taking them closer. They crossed a recently hosed-down square, sloshing through puddles of water, and passing by a glorious flower stall that was set up between two cafés, its huge fragranced blooms luminous. The smooth slabs of the marble pavement were soft underfoot and the fifteen-minute walk seemed like five.

'We're here,' announced Sonia triumphantly, folding the map into her pocket. 'La Zapata. This is it.'

It was a tatty building. Layers of small posters had built up over the years on the walls of its façade, one after the other stuck over the brickwork advertising flamenco, tango, rumba and salsa evenings taking place all over the city. Every phone box, lamppost and bus-shelter in the city seemed to have been used in the same way, informing passers-by of forthcoming *espectáculos*, one flyer plastered over another often before it had even taken place. It was a chaotic kind of collage but it represented the spirit of this city and the profusion of dance and music that was its lifeblood.

The inside of La Zapata was as scruffy as the exterior. There was nothing glamorous about it. This was not a place for performance but for practice and rehearsal.

Four doors led from the hallway. Two were open, two shut. From behind one closed door could be heard the sound of thunderous stamping. A herd of bulls charging down a street would not have made more noise. It stopped abruptly and was followed by the sound of rhythmic clapping, like the patter of raindrops after a thunderstorm.

A woman bustled purposefully past them and down an unlit corridor. Steel heel- and toecaps clip-clopped on the stone floor and music burst through a briefly opened door.

The two Englishwomen stood reading the framed posters advertising performances that had taken place decades earlier, slightly unsure what they should do. Eventually Maggie got the attention of a skeletally thin and tired-looking woman of about fifty, who seemed to run the place from a dark cubbyhole within the reception area.

'Salsa?' said Maggie, hopefully.

With a perfunctory nod, the woman acknowledged their presence. '*Felipe y Corazón – allí*,' she said, pointing emphatically to one of the open doors.

They were the first in the studio. They put their bags in the corner and changed their shoes.

'I wonder how many of us there will be,' mused Maggie, doing up her buckles. Her statement required no response.

A mirror ran across one end of the room and a wooden bar ran down another. It was a clinical space with high windows that overlooked a narrow street, and even if the glass had not been opaque with dirt, little daylight would have entered the room. A strong smell of polish seeped from the dark wooden floor worn smooth by years of wear.

Sonia loved the slightly musty smell of age and usage that emanated from the walls of this room, the way that the cracks between the boards had filled with dust, grime and wax. She noticed the way fluff had mounted up between the segments of the ancient old radiators and saw silvery cobweb threads wafting gently from the ceiling. In each layer of dust there was another decade of the place's history.

Half a dozen other people drifted into the studio. There was a group of Norwegian students (mostly girls) all doing Spanish Studies at university, and then a few additional men in their early twenties appeared, all of them locals.

'They must be what are called "taxi dancers",' Maggie whispered to Sonia. 'It said in the brochure that they hire them in to balance up the numbers.'

Eventually, their instructors appeared. Felipe and Corazón were both raven-haired and as lean as young calves, but their weathered skin betrayed that they were well into their sixties. Corazón had evenly spaced rows of deep lines on her bony face, not etched there just by the passing of time, but through expressiveness and the unashamed exaggeration of her emotions. Whenever she smiled, laughed and grimaced it took its toll on her skin. Both were dressed in black, which accentuated their slimness, and against the whiteness of the room, they stood out like silhouettes.

The group of twelve had spread themselves out, all of them facing their instructors.

'*Hola!*' they said in unison, smiling broadly at the group lined up expectantly in front of them.

'*Hola!*' chorused the group, like a class of well-disciplined six year olds.

Felipe carried a CD player, which he set down on the floor. He pressed 'play' and the space they shared was transformed. The joyful sound of a trumpet introduction pierced the air. The class automatically mirrored Corazón's movements. It did not take a word from her, it was simply obvious that this was her intention. For a while the class warmed up gently, turning wrists and ankles, flexing heels, stretching necks and shoulders, and rotating hips. All the while they kept their eyes fixed on their teachers, fascinated by their pipe-cleaner bodies.

Though they had grown up in the flamenco tradition, Felipe and Corazón had seen which way the wind was blowing. In teaching terms, the Cuban-originated dance of salsa was more commercial and would appeal to an audience who might not be drawn to the dramatic intensity of flamenco. Some dancers of their age still performed, but Felipe and Corazón knew that they could not make a decent living out of doing so. Their strategy had worked. They had mastered salsa and created new choreographies, attracting many Granadinos as well as foreigners to their classes. They liked salsa; it was more superficial, less emotionally draining than their true passion, like a light Jerez next to a full-bodied Rioja.

For a few years there had been a steady wave of people wanting to learn salsa and Felipe and Corazón, old and experienced as they were, had no difficulty in becoming experts. Given a short demonstration of the steps, the pair could have danced any dance in the world. Just as musicians with perfect pitch can listen to a complex tune and then repeat it back, note perfect, and then a second time with variations and inversions, so it was with these two. One day they might watch a series of moves and the very next they had mastered it, having observed the male and female parts just a single time.

Salsa instruction now began. It was Corazón who did most of the shouting. Her voice cut through the music and even the strident tone of jazz trumpet that blasted its way through the salsa tune.

'*Y un, dos, tres! Y un, dos, tres!* And! Clap! Clap! Clap! And! Clap! Clap! Clap! And . . .'

On she went. Repetition, after repetition, after repetition of the beat until it would haunt them and penetrate their dreams. Every turn their pupils mastered was greeted with huge encouragement and enthusiasm.

'*Eso es!*' That's it!

When it was time to move on, to try something new, Felipe would call out: '*Vale!*' OK! And a demonstration of the next turn, or *vuelta*, would commence.

'*Estupendo!*' the teachers would cry out, unashamed of the hyperbole.

Between attempts at each new move, the women would move round one partner, so that by the end of the lesson's first half, they had danced with all of the taxi dancers. Even if none of them could speak English, these young men were all fluent in the language of salsa.

'I love this,' said Maggie as she passed Sonia on the dance floor.

In dancing, mused Sonia, perhaps Maggie showed her true self. She certainly looked happy being passed across a man's body this way and that, her hand running down the back of his neck to an instruction given precisely by him. A dismissive flick of his hand was all that was required to tell her when to spin. She responded on the beat, without hesitation. Sonia watched her friend being used to demonstrate a complex sequence of steps and found it strange that Maggie seemed so attracted to a dance where the man played an entirely dominant role. The feisty feminist who wanted to be in charge seemed happy being twirled.

Maggie received praise from the teachers and an expression that Sonia remembered from schooldays passed across her face. It was a look of slight surprise, accompanied with a huge beam of pleasure.

There was a break when big jugs of iced water were brought in and poured into plastic cups. It had become stifling in the room and everyone drank thirstily while polite snippets of stilted conversation were exchanged between people of different nationalities.

When they had quenched their thirst, the two Englishwomen went off to the cloakroom. Sonia noticed huge quantities of graffiti, particularly several sets of initials heavily scored into the old wood. Some of the scratches had almost been polished away through the passing years, and others were freshly done, the recent carvings still the colour of naked flesh. One particularly ornate set of letters reminded her of a church carving, a work of art. It must have been a labour of love to have made such deep dents in these solid doors. Anyone who had bothered was not making a careless expression of short-lived passion but a declaration of real, lasting devotion. 'J – M' – the heavy doors would never shed this expression of affection until they were taken from their hinges and turned into firewood.

As they sauntered back into the corridor, they paused outside the studio, where the framed posters jostled with each other. Felipe and Corazón appeared on one of them. The style of type dated it to around 1975 and it was advertising a flamenco performance.

'Look, Maggie, it's a picture of our teachers!'

'God, so it is! Hasn't age been cruel!'

'They haven't changed that much,' said Sonia in their defence. 'Their figures are pretty similar.'

'But those crow's-feet – she didn't have them in those days, did she?' commented Maggie. 'Do you think they'd show us some flamenco? Teach us how to stamp our feet? Give us a bit of a clatter on the castanets?'

Maggie didn't wait for an answer. She was already back in the studio, explaining and gesticulating to the teachers what she wanted them to do.

Sonia watched her from the doorframe.

Finally, Felipe found some English words: 'Flamenco can't be taught,' he said gutturally. 'It's in the blood, and only in gypsy blood at that. But you can try if you like. I'll show you some at the end of the lesson.'

It was a statement designed to challenge.

For the next hour they repeated the movements from the first half of the lesson and then fifteen minutes before the end, Felipe clapped his hands together.

'Now,' he said. 'Flamenco.'

He strutted over to the CD player, flicked swiftly through his wallet of music, and carefully extracted what he wanted. Meanwhile, Corazón changed her shoes in the corner, to a pair with heavy heels and steel-capped soles.

The class stood back, quietly expectant. They heard palms against palms and low drums. It was dark and very different from the happy-go-lucky sound of salsa.

Corazón strode out in front of the group. It was as though she no longer knew they were there. As a guitar played, she raised one arm and then another, her sinuous fingers fanning out like daisy petals. For more than five minutes, she stamped her feet in a complex sequence of heel and toe, heel and toe, that accelerated to a thunderous vibration before it stopped dead, with a final, decisive 'BANG' of her hard shoe on the solid floor. It was a virtuoso display of strength and breathtaking technical prowess as much as a dance, somehow the more impressive because of her age.

On the very beat that she stopped, a wail emanated from the speakers and eerily wrapped itself around everyone in the room. It was a raw-throated male voice and seemed to express the same anguish that had shown on Corazón's face as she had danced.

Just before she finished, Felipe had begun and for a few seconds mirrored his wife's movements, proving to the audience that this dance was not pure improvisation, but a well-rehearsed piece of choreography. Now Felipe took her place centre stage. Narrow-hipped, his slim back arched into a 'C', Felipe briefly struck a pose before spinning himself around and beginning a series of floor-hammering steps. The sound of metal on wood bounced off the mirrored walls. His movements were even more sensual than those of his wife, and certainly more coquettish. It was as though he flirted with the class, his hands travelling up and down his body, his hips rocking one way and then another. Sonia was transfixed.

As though to compete with Corazón, he executed an ever more complex sequence of steps, time after time landing by some miracle on precisely the same spot, the music drowned out by the hammering of feet. The passion of it was extraordinary and it seemed to have come from nowhere.

Felipe's finishing pose, eyes to the ceiling, one arm wrapped around his back, the other thrown across his front was one of pure arrogance. From the back a quiet voice said '*Olé*'. It was Corazón; even she was moved by her husband's display, his total absorption in the moment. Then there was silence.

After a moment or two, Maggie broke it by applauding rapturously. The rest of the group clapped but with less enthusiasm.

Felipe's face broke into a smile, all traces of arrogance melting away. Corazón came out in front of the audience and challenged them.

'Flamenco? Tomorrow? You want?' she enquired, flashing her yellowing teeth.

Some of the Norwegian girls, slightly embarrassed by this display of naked emotion, turned to chat to one another; meanwhile the taxi dancers were looking at their watches to see whether their time as hired hands was nearly over. They did not plan to do overtime.

'Yes,' said Maggie. 'I want.'

Sonia felt uncomfortable. Flamenco was so very different from salsa. From what she had seen in the past twelve hours, it was an emotional state of being as much as a dance. Salsa was carefree, an emotional escape route and, moreover, it was what they had come to improve.

By now the rest of the class had dispersed and Sonia needed fresh air.

'*Adiós*,' said Corazón, packing up her bag. '*Hasta luego.*'

Chapter Four

IT WAS ONE o'clock. The dance studio did not have glamorous neighbours and the workaday side street in which they found themselves offered little more than a car parts depot and a key cutter. As they walked to the end of the shadowy street and turned into the main road the atmosphere changed and they were dazzled by the glare of sunlight and deafened by the crazed cacophony of lunchtime traffic, brought to a standstill.

The bars and cafés were now crammed with builders, students and anyone else who lived too far out of town to get home for their lunchtime siesta. All the other shops – greengrocers, stationers and the plethora of hairdressing salons – were firmly shut up again, having opened for just a few hours since Sonia and Maggie had last passed. Their slatted metal grilles would not be raised again until some time after four.

'Let's stop at this one,' suggested Maggie, outside the second bar they came to. La Castilla had a long, stainless-steel bar and several tables down the side of the room, all but one occupied. The two Englishwomen quickly went in.

The smells were intense and mingled together to form a distinctive aroma of Spanish café life: beer, *jamon*, stale ash, the slightly sour smell of goat's cheese, a whiff of anchovies and, wafting across it all, strong, freshly ground coffee. A row of uniformly blue-overalled manual workers sat up at the bar, oblivious to everything but the plates in front of them. They were intent on sating their hunger. Almost simultaneously they put down their forks, and clumsy hands reached for packets of strong cigarettes, generating a mushroom cloud of smoke as they lit up. Meanwhile the patron manufactured a row of *café solos*. It was a daily ritual for them all.

Only now did his attention turn to his new customers.

'*Señoras*,' he said, coming to their table.

Reading from the board behind the bar, they ordered huge crusty *bocadillos* to be filled with sardines. Sonia watched the bar owner preparing them. In one hand he wielded a knife, in the other a cigarette. It was an impressive juggling act and she marvelled as he ladled crushed tomatoes from a bowl and squashed them on to slabs of bread, fished sardines out of a bucket-sized tin and all the while took regular drags on his Corona cigarette. If the process seemed unconventional, the end result was by no means disappointing.

'What did you think of the lesson?' asked Sonia, between mouthfuls.

'The teachers are wonderful,' answered Maggie. 'I love them.'

'They're life-enhancing, aren't they?' agreed Sonia.

She had to raise her voice above the clatter of falling coins that erupted from a one-armed bandit next to their table. Since entering they had listened to the perpetual warbling of the fruit machine, and now one of the café's customers happily scooped a handful of coins into his pocket. He walked away whistling.

Sonia and Maggie both ate hungrily. They watched as the workmen left the bar, leaving behind them a pall of smoke and dozens of tiny screwed-up paper napkins carelessly scattered on the floor like a snow storm.

'What do you think James would make of it all?' asked Maggie.

'What? This place?' responded Sonia. 'Too grubby. Too earthy.'

'I meant the dancing,' said Maggie.

'You know what he'd think. That it's all self-indulgent nonsense,' replied Sonia.

'I don't know how you stand him.'

Maggie always went for the kill. Her open dislike of James almost drove Sonia to his defence but she did not really want to think about her husband today and quickly changed the subject.

'My father, on the other hand, used to love dancing. I only discovered that a few weeks ago.'

'Really? I don't remember anything about that when we were growing up.'

'Well, it was all over by then anyway, because of Mum's illness.'

'Of course it was,' said Maggie, slightly embarrassed. 'I forgot about that.'

'When I last went to see him,' continued Sonia, 'he was so enthusiastic about my salsa lessons it almost made up for James's cynicism.'

Sonia's visits to her elderly father were usually timed for when James was having a golf day. It seemed a good opportunity, given that the two men had very little to say to each other. Unlike James's parents, a visit to whom involved a three-hour drive out of London, the packing of green Wellington boots, occasionally evening wear and an obligatory overnight stay, Sonia's father lived a mere thirty-minute drive away, in the outer suburbs of Croydon.

It was always with a pang of guilt that she rang his doorbell, one of a set of twenty outside the characterless block of nineteen fifties flats. Each visit, it seemed to take even longer before the buzzer went and the outer door, which let visitors into the pale green, uncarpeted communal hallway, opened. It was then a disinfectant-scented climb up to the second storey of this building, and by that time Jack Haynes would be standing at his open doorway ready to welcome his only daughter in.

Sonia recalled that last visit and how the seventy-eight year old's round face had creased into a smile as she came into sight. She had embraced his stout frame and kissed the top of his liver-spotted head, making sure she did not disturb the few remaining strands of silver hair, which he had carefully combed back across his pate.

'Sonia!' he said warmly. 'How lovely to see you.'

'Hello, Dad.' She hugged him tighter.

A tray with cups and saucers, a jug of milk and a small plate of Rich Tea biscuits was already set out on a low table in the living room, and Jack insisted that Sonia took a seat while he went into the kitchen to fetch the teapot, which rattled noisily as he carried it through and set it down. Pale liquid slopped from the spout and splashed the rug but she knew not to ask him whether he needed any help. Such a ritual as this preserved the dignity of old age.

As her father held the tea strainer above the cup and the brown liquid streamed through, Sonia began the usual line of questioning.

'So how—'

Her question was interrupted by the rumble of a train going past, only a few feet from the back wall, causing enough of a vibration to send a small cactus plant on the window-ledge crashing to the floor.

'Oh, what a nuisance,' said the elderly man, struggling to his feet. 'I'm sure these trains are getting more frequent, you know.'

Once the dustpan and brush had been fetched and the scattering of gravel, dry soil and spiny cactus limbs had been patiently reassembled and pressed back into the plastic pot, their conversation resumed. It covered the usual ground: what Jack had been doing in the past couple of weeks, what the doctor had said about his arthritis, how long he would have to wait for a hip replacement, how he had been to Hampton Court on a recent outing along with some of the other people who went to the day-care centre, and a description of a funeral he had been to of an old National Service acquaintance. The latter seemed to have been the highlight of the month, the funeral wakes in village halls around the country providing welcome reunions for those who still survived, with hours of reminiscence and a slap-up tea.

Sonia gazed at her father as she listened to his cheerful tales. Seated in his electronically adjustable chair, a gift from her and James for his seventy-fifth birthday, he looked comfortable but out of place in this environment that had as much character as a station waiting room. Everything looked makeshift except for the incongruous Edwardian furniture, which he had refused to part with when he moved here from his previous house. These hefty pieces of dark mahogany were a link for him with the last place he had lived with Sonia's mother, and though they were totally impractical – a sideboard that monopolised the living room and a bureau that was so wide it blocked half the window in his already sombre bedroom – he would no more have parted with them than he would the forest of spider plants that cluttered their dusty surfaces.

Once her father had given her the headlines of his life in the past few weeks, it was Sonia's turn. She always found it hard. The machinations of the PR world would be incomprehensible to someone who had worked as a teacher all his life, so she kept talk of work to a minimum and tended to make it sound as though she was in advertising, which was a much easier world for an outsider to grasp. Her social life would have been equally alien to him. On that last visit, though, she had told him about the dance class she had begun to attend and his enthusiasm took her by surprise.

'What dances are you doing exactly? Who are your instructors? What sort of shoes do you wear?' he quizzed her.

Sonia expressed surprise that her father knew so much.

'Your mother and I used to dance a lot in our courtship and in our early married life,' he told her. 'In the fifties everyone did! It was as though we were all celebrating the end of the war.'

'How often did you go?'

'Oh, at least twice a week. Always on Saturdays and then usually another night or two.'

He smiled at his daughter. Jack loved it when she came to visit and knew it must be quite hard for her to fit these trips into her busy schedule. What he was always keen to avoid, though, was to talk too much about the past. It must be tiresome for children to have to listen to their parents reminiscing about days gone by and he had always been wary of it.

'But they always say that the best things in life are free, don't they?' he added, smiling at her, hoping that even with her lovely house and expensive car that she still knew that.

Sonia nodded. 'I just can't believe I never really knew,' she said.

'Well, I suppose we stopped soon after you were born.'

Although her mother had died when Sonia was sixteen, she was amazed that she had never known anything about this aspect of their lives. Like most children, she had not spent much time wondering what her mother and father did before she was there and her curiosity had never been much aroused.

'Don't you remember all the dancing you did yourself when you were little?' he asked. 'You used to go every Saturday afternoon. Look!'

Jack had rummaged in the bureau and found some pictures. On top of the pile was a photograph of Sonia, pale and self-conscious in a white, ribbon-trimmed tutu, standing by the fireplace of her childhood home. Sonia was more interested in the others, which were of her parents at various dance events. One showed the pair of them, her father looking not unlike he did today though with more of his pale hair, and her mother, erect, elegant, her black hair slicked tightly into a firm bun. They were holding a trophy and on the reverse of the picture, in pencil, was written: '1953: Tango, 1st.' There were several others, most of them taken at competitions.

Sonia held a picture in each hand. 'Is this really Mum?'

In her memory, she was frail, semi-bedridden and silver-haired. Here she was vibrant, strong and, most arrestingly for Sonia, upright. It was hard to revise the image of her mother that she had had for so long.

'We all danced properly in those days,' Jack assured his daughter. 'We were taught the right steps and we danced together, not like people do nowadays.'

These photos evoked such strong emotions for Jack and, as he gazed silently at this image of himself, memories of how he and Mary had not always performed according to the rule book returned to him. The rule of dancing is that the man leads, but for them this wasn't always the case. Within the subtlety of their movements, whether it was tango, rumba or paso doble, Jack had known where Mary wanted to be led and from the slightest pressure she exerted on his arm, they had developed a way of communicating this. She was totally in control of their movement. Having danced almost as soon as she could walk, until the moment when her legs began to lose the power to carry her, it could not have been any other way.

Jack found another envelope stuffed with photographs. Each one featured himself and his wife in a stiff pose and on the back, the date and the dance for which they had won a prize.

'What happened to all those beautiful gowns?' Sonia could not resist asking.

'I'm afraid they all went to a charity shop when she stopped dancing,' Jack answered. 'She couldn't bear to have them in the wardrobe.'

Though Sonia was amazed to have uncovered such a significant part of her father's life, and one that she had never been aware of, she knew without asking why they had really stopped dancing and why they had never talked about it. Her mother had developed multiple sclerosis during her pregnancy with Sonia, and within a short time was confined to a wheelchair.

Sonia would have liked to spend the rest of the day asking her father more, but could sense she might already have asked one question too many. He had already put the other photographs back in the envelope.

There was one stray picture that still lay face down on his coffee table and she turned it over before handing it back. It showed a group of children in hand-knitted cardigans. Two of them were sitting on top of a barrel and two others were leaning against it. They had stiff smiles. A group of tables in the background suggested it was taken outside a café and the cobbles suggested somewhere continental.

'Who are these children?' she asked.

'Some of your mother's family,' he answered, not volunteering any further information.

It was time for Sonia to go. She and her father embraced.

''Bye, sweetheart, it's been lovely to see you,' he said, smiling. 'Enjoy your dancing.'

As she had made her way home that afternoon, Sonia's imagination had been filled with images of her parents gliding around the dance floor. Perhaps the discovery of their interest shed light on why she already could not imagine life without her dance lessons.

Sonia had been silent for a few minutes, chewing her way through lunch in the Granada café, tomato paste and crumbs spraying onto the table around her. When she looked up, her eye was caught by a series of cheaply produced oil paintings of women in long, extravagantly ruffled dresses. They were the clichéd image of Spain but every restaurant and café in the city subscribed to the myth.

'Were you serious about wanting them to teach you flamenco?' Sonia asked Maggie.

'Yes, I was.'

'But didn't you think it looked tricky?'

'I'd just like to learn the basics,' said Maggie confidently.

'Whatever those are,' responded Sonia.

It seemed to her that there could be nothing 'basic' about flamenco. Surely it had an entire culture of its own, and she felt mildly irritated that Maggie had not recognised that.

'Why are you so down on it?' snapped Maggie.

'I'm not down on it at all,' replied Sonia. 'I'm just not entirely sure it isn't like being a Brit who comes on a cheap package holiday and asks whether he can learn how to be a bullfighter. It just doesn't look as though it can be done.'

'Fine. But if you don't want to do it, it doesn't stop me, does it?'

The two women were rarely out of tune like this and when it happened it took them both by surprise. Sonia could not explain to herself why she felt so irritated by Maggie's attitude and by her assumption that she could penetrate the outer layer of this culture, but she felt it showed disrespect.

They finished eating in a silence that Maggie eventually broke.

'Coffee?' she asked, wanting to clear the air.

'*Con leche*,' responded Sonia with a smile. They could not sulk with each other for long.

As the mid-afternoon sunshine was fading to an ochre glow, Sonia and Maggie returned to their hotel. The streets were now deadly quiet; the traffic had vanished and the shops remained firmly closed. They too would follow the Spanish pattern and take to their beds for a few hours of afternoon siesta. Sonia had slept very little the previous night and was now beginning to feel jaded.

Though the curtains filtered only a fraction of the light, nothing would have stopped Sonia falling into a deep sleep that afternoon. The sound of cars honking their horns, the wail of a police siren and the banging of doors in the corridor would normally have been enough to wake her, but for several hours she was in a state of blissful unconsciousness.

When they woke, it was dusk, and light no longer streamed in. This was the major flaw in the siesta habit, having to get out of bed just as the dying light was telling your body and mind that it was time to climb into it.

Now it was Sonia's turn to have difficulty stirring and Maggie who bounced out of bed.

'Come on, Sonia, time to go out!'

'Go out? Where?'

She was half asleep, bleary-eyed, confused and in a bemused state of semi-wakefulness in which she could not quite remember where she was.

'That's why we're here, isn't it? To go out dancing?'

'Dancing? Mmm . . .'

Her body was still heavy with a not-quite-fulfilled need to sleep. Her head throbbed. She could hear the sound of Maggie in the shower, singing, whistling, humming, her *joie de vivre* almost bursting through the bathroom wall. She could not face dancing tonight.

Maggie came back into the room, her hair wound up into a tall turban, a second towel tightly drawn across her breasts, her naked chest and shoulders dark against the whiteness. Sonia watched her. There was something majestic, even statuesque about this woman. Maggie continued to hum as she dressed, pulling on jeans and a white ruffled shirt, and fastening a wide, leather belt. Her face glowed from the warmth of the shower and the few hours of sunshine they had enjoyed earlier that day. She seemed lost in her own thoughts and it was as though she had forgotten Sonia was there.

'Maggie?'

She turned round and sat on the end of her bed, fiddling with a pair of hooped earrings. 'Yes?' she replied, her head tilted to one side.

'Would you mind if I didn't come out tonight?'

'Of course I wouldn't. But it seems a bit of a shame. We did come here to dance . . .'

'I know. I just feel completely wrung out. I'll come tomorrow, I promise.'

Maggie continued to get herself ready, spraying on perfume, outlining her eyes in inky black, accentuating her long lashes with layers of mascara.

'Are you sure you'll be all right going on your own?' Sonia added anxiously.

'What's the worst that can happen?' laughed Maggie. 'Everyone here is shorter than me. So I can always run away if I need to.'

Sonia knew that Maggie meant it, and that she was a match for anyone. There was no need to give a moment's thought to her safety. Maggie was the most independent woman she knew.

Sonia continued to doze. At nine thirty, Maggie was ready to leave.

'I'm going to have something to eat on the way. Are you sure you don't want to come out with me?'

'No, really. I just want to catch up on sleep. I'll see you in the morning.'

For a second night, Sonia enjoyed the tranquillity of her single bed. Though noises continued to float up from the street, there was a magical silence in the space of the room. She loved the knowledge that she was going to be here alone, that no one could dent her peace of mind.

It was so different from those nights when she went to bed early, tired out from a long day at the office and then lay, tense, wondering when James was going to arrive home. Perhaps once or twice a week he would stagger through the front door at three or four in the morning and the stained-glass panes in the front door would shudder with the impact as it was slammed shut. He would then stumble up the stairs and collapse, fully clothed, onto the bed, his mouth breathing out the foul fumes of his evening's excess. It was not the sex – fast, rough, and easily forgotten – that sometimes happened when he was in this state that repelled her most. It was the sour smell of stale alcohol that made her retch with disgust. It was a stench that revolted her more than any other in the world and she recoiled from this vast, dark hulk lying in the darkness next to her, rattling the stillness with his snores. On the mornings after these nights, there was no reference to his state of inebriation. James seemed to be able to rise at six without even a hangover, shower, dress in his City uniform and leave for work with the same punctuality as he did on any other day. It was as though he was unaware that anything out of the ordinary had even happened. No one else was aware either. In the picture book of marriage, they were the perfect married couple. It was a story told for an audience.

Now, as she lay in the semi-darkness, she felt her stomach contract with the recalled nausea of it all. She rolled over onto her side and soon felt the chill of tears on her pillow. This was meant to be a peaceful night, one where she caught up on her sleep. It was not intended to be a night in which she tortured herself with recollection of all that was wrong. Occasionally she fell into a fitful sleep and in the moments when she came to, she noticed that Maggie's bed was still empty.

At three o'clock in the morning, she was just dropping off to sleep when the sound of a key in the lock disturbed her.

'Are you still awake?' whispered Maggie.

'Yes,' grunted Sonia. Even if she had been asleep the noise of Maggie stumbling into the room would have woken her.

'I've had such a fantastic night,' enthused Maggie, switching on the overhead light, oblivious to her friend's mood.

'I'm glad for you,' Sonia answered, with ill-disguised annoyance in her voice.

'Don't be cross. You could have come with me!'

'I know, I know. I don't know why I didn't really, for all the sleep I've had.'

'You're just afraid of letting your hair down,' she said, tugging at the band that held her hair up and, as if to demonstrate her point, letting her thick, wavy locks tumble around her shoulders.

'We haven't got many nights here and you should come out. Why on earth didn't you?'

'There are hundreds of reasons why I didn't. I'm not good enough, for a start.'

'That's complete rubbish,' said Maggie. 'And even if you aren't, you soon will be.'

With this decisive statement she switched off the light and, now naked, threw herself onto her bed.

Chapter Five

DESPITE HER NIGHT of snatched, unsatisfactory sleep, Sonia rose early the next morning. The airlessness of the room had left her with a throbbing head and she yearned to get out. She was hungry too.

Their dance lesson was not until the afternoon and since Maggie was clearly going to be comatose for a while, Sonia dressed quietly and crept out of the room, leaving her friend a note.

Turning right out of the hotel, she wandered up to the main street that ran like a spine through the centre of the city. She soon realised that Granada was impossible to get lost in, so simple was the topography of this small city. Distant, towards the south, was a high wall of mountains, eastwards the streets climbed towards the Alhambra, westwards the roads sloped down towards a stretch of lowland. Even if she found herself in the maze of narrow alleyways that snaked around the cathedral, it would not be long before the gradient, a glimpse of mountain or sight of that monumental building would tell her which way to turn. There was something liberating about this aimless meander. She could lose herself in these streets and yet never be fearful of being lost.

Every few turns brought Sonia to a new square. Many of them had grand, ornamental fountains, and all had cafés, each serving a handful of customers. One leafy, open space had four shops selling an almost identical range of tourist paraphernalia, comprising fans, dolls in flamenco costume and ashtrays emblazoned with bulls. Outside another was a forest of a dozen postcard carousels. It seemed there were a million images of Spain that people would buy. Sonia chose quickly: a generic image of a flamenco dancer.

By the time she had wandered the streets for an hour her head was clear. She was in the Plaza Bib Rambla and the flower market filled it with vibrancy on this rather colourless February day. It was nine thirty, and although the place still had the peace and quiet of a city out of season, a few more people were now wandering about. Sonia passed two Scandinavians with huge backpacks, chilly and slightly ridiculous in their optimistically chosen shorts, and a group of East Coast students being given a guided tour by a fellow American whose voice filled the otherwise peaceful space. There were several cafés to choose from but one of them particularly appealed. Its tables were just catching the first rays of sunshine that were slanting across the rooftops, and standing outside it was a barrel overflowing with geraniums that had survived a cool winter.

Purposefully, she strode towards the sunniest table and sat down. She hastily scribbled the postcard to her father and then began to read her guidebook. It seemed that the city had much more to offer than the famed Alhambra and its gardens.

In what seemed like a matter of moments after taking her order, the elderly waiter served her with a creamy *café con leche*. As he did so he looked over her shoulder. Her book was open at the page on Federico García Lorca, 'the greatest of Spanish poets', as it described him. Sonia had been reading how he had been arrested in Granada at the beginning of the Spanish Civil War.

'He used to stay nearby, you know.'

The waiter's words penetrated her concentration and she looked up. Sonia was surprised not just that he had looked at what she was reading, but by the deeply serious expression on his handsome, lined face.

'Lorca?'

'Yes, he and his friends used to meet not far from here.'

Sonia had once seen *Yerma* at the National Theatre. Oddly enough she had gone with Maggie, because James had a last-minute business dinner, and she recalled her friend's verdict: 'dull and depressing'.

Sonia asked the man if he had ever met Lorca and the waiter told her that he remembered seeing him once or twice.

'Many people here believe that part of this city died with him,' he added.

The statement was both powerful and intriguing.

Sonia's knowledge of the Spanish Civil War did not extend much further than a couple of dimly remembered books by Ernest Hemingway and Laurie Lee; she knew that they had been involved, but little more than that. Her curiosity was aroused, given the way in which the disappearance of Lorca seemed to have touched this old man personally.

'What do you mean exactly?' she asked, aware that she must respond.

'When people realised what had happened to Lorca – that he had been shot in the back – it gave out the message to all liberal-minded people that it was not safe for anyone and that the war in Granada was as good as finished.'

'Forgive me, but I don't really know very much about what happened in your Civil War.'

'That's not surprising. Many people in this country don't know very much about it either. Most of them have either forgotten or been brought up in a state of near ignorance.'

Sonia could tell that the old man disapproved of this state of affairs.

'Why did it happen?' she asked.

The waiter, who was small in stature like many Spaniards of his age, leaned forward and gripped the back of the spare chair at Sonia's table. His dark eyes stared at the red tablecloth so intently it seemed as if he was examining its weft and warp. Several minutes went by and Sonia wondered if he had forgotten that she had posed a question. Though his hair was still predominantly dark, Sonia observed that the skin on his chiselled face and hands was as creased as an autumnal leaf, and she guessed he could be in his eighties. She noticed too that the fingers of his left hand were badly deformed, she assumed with arthritis. Her father's mind often wandered like this so she was quite used to such a silence.

'Do you know something?' he answered finally. 'I'm not sure I can tell you that.'

'Don't worry,' she reassured him, noticing that his eyes were red and watery. 'It was just idle curiosity.'

'But I do worry,' he said, mildly agitated, now looking directly at her.

She suddenly realised that she had misinterpreted his earlier remark. There was a clarity in his look that told her that this man was as lucid as he had ever been.

He continued: 'I worry that the whole terrible story will disappear, just like Lorca and so many other people.'

Sonia sat back. The man's passion took her aback. He was referring to an event of nearly seventy years ago, and yet it was as though it had taken place yesterday.

'I can't give you one single reason why war broke out. The beginning of it all was so confused. People didn't really know what was happening and they certainly had no idea at the time what it would lead to, or how long it would go on for.'

'But what triggered it all off – and why was Lorca involved? He was a poet, not a politician, wasn't he?'

'I know your questions sound so simple and I would like to give you simple answers, but I can't. The years leading up to the Civil War were not entirely peaceful. Our country was in turmoil some of the time and the politics were so complicated, most of us couldn't begin to understand them. People were going hungry, the left-wing government didn't seem to be doing enough and the army decided to take over. That's the quick way to explain it.'

'That sounds fairly black and white.'

'I can assure you it wasn't.'

Sonia sipped her coffee. Her interest was engaged and since he appeared to have no other customers, she was tempted to press the elderly man further.

A twelve-strong group of Japanese on a guided tour then arrived and were soon waiting expectantly for their orders to be taken. The elderly man moved away to attend to them and Sonia watched him writing things on his pad. Without his patience it might have been a tortuous business given their lack of both Spanish and English, a language which he spoke with great fluency but a thick accent. No wonder so many menus here were illustrated with garish photographs of unappetising-looking dishes and foaming milkshakes; at least that way foreigners could order just by pointing.

When he brought the drinks and pastries they had ordered, he also came out with another coffee for Sonia; she was touched that he had thought of her.

By now the café was filling up with people and she could tell that the moment had passed for him to devote all his attention to her.

'*La cuenta, por favor*,' she said, using most of the words she knew to ask for the bill.

The café owner shook his head. 'It's nothing,' he said.

Sonia smiled. It was a simple gesture and she was touched. She knew instinctively that he was not in the habit of giving away drinks.

'Thank you,' she said. 'It was really interesting talking to you. I might go and look at Lorca's house. Where is it from here?'

He pointed down the street and said she must turn right at the end of it. It would not take her more than ten minutes to reach La Huerta de San Vicente, the Lorca family's summer house in the south of the city.

'It's pretty,' he said. 'And it's got some good mementoes of the man and his family. It's a bit cold, though.'

'Cold?'

'You'll see.'

Sonia could not ask him any more questions. He was busy now and had already turned his back to take another order. She rose from her seat, gathered her book, her bag and her map, and edged her way past the other tourists.

As she walked away, the elderly man came after her, for a moment holding on to her arm. There was one more thing he was eager to tell her.

'You should go up to the cemetery as well,' he said. 'Lorca didn't die there but thousands of others were shot up on that hill.'

'Thousands?' she queried.

The old man nodded. 'Yes,' he said deliberately. 'Several thousand.'

It seemed a huge figure to Sonia, given the scale of this city.

Perhaps the old man was a bit soft in the head after all, and telling a tourist to go and look at a municipal graveyard was fairly bizarre too. She nodded politely and smiled. Even if the house of a dead poet exerted some fascination, she had no intention of visiting a burial place.

Sonia followed the directions he had given her, taking the long straight road, Recogidas, towards the edge of town. Shops were now open and snatches of music floated out onto the pavements that now began to fill with young women, arms linked, chattering, pristine carrier bags swinging at their sides. This was the street for youthful fashion, and alluring window displays of high boots, jewel-coloured belts and stylish jackets on blank-faced dummies drew these girls like children to sweetshops.

Walking down the sunny side of a street, which pulsated with a sense that life had never been so good, the café owner's portrayal of a strife-ridden Spain seemed hard to imagine. Though she was intrigued by what he had told her of the war, Sonia was puzzled that so little evidence of it remained. She had noticed neither plaque nor monument that recorded the events of that period, and the atmosphere all around her did not suggest that these young people were burdened by the past. The historical buildings of the Alhambra might have been what drew most visitors to Granada, but a street such as this showed a Spain that was pressing on into the future, transforming buildings from the previous centuries into futuristic palaces of glass and steel. A few old shop fronts remained with their ornate fascias and the owner's name etched in gold on black glass, but they were a curiosity deliberately preserved for the sake of nostalgia, not part of this modern Spain.

At the bottom of the street where the shops ended and anonymous blocks of flats were planted in crop-like rows, Sonia could clearly see beyond the city to the green plains of the Vega, the lush pastureland beyond the city. Consulting her city map she turned right and through some gates into a park. It extended over several acres and had been laid out in a style that was somewhere between dreary municipal and Elizabethan knot garden, with sandy pathways running between geometrically arranged borders and low box hedging. The plants had been recently watered. Moisture hung like crystal beads on velvety crimson petals and the heavy scents of rose and lavender mingled in the moist atmosphere.

As far as Sonia could see, the park was empty save for a couple of gardeners and two silver-haired men sitting on a bench, walking sticks propped against their knees. They were deeply engaged in conversation and did not even look up as she passed, nor were they remotely disturbed by the sound of a trumpet that pierced the air. The acoustics of the empty park amplified the sound of the lone musician, who was not busking (there would have been little point, given the paucity of passers-by) but using the space to practise.

According to the guidebook, La Huerta de San Vicente was in the middle of the park and through the dense foliage of a group of trees Sonia could now make out the shape of a white, two-storey dwelling. A few people were clustered outside waiting for the door to be opened.

The house was more modest than she had imagined for a place associated with such a grand name as Federico García Lorca. At eleven o'clock the deep green front door opened, visitors were permitted to file in and a smartly dressed middle-aged woman welcomed them in Spanish. Her manner was that of a housekeeper, thought Sonia, proprietorial yet reverential about the house she looked after. Visitors were expected to treat it like a shrine.

Sonia's Spanish allowed her to grasp a few things from the speech that the woman trotted out at the beginning of the tour: Lorca had loved this house and had spent many happy summers there – the house was as it had been the day he left in August 1936 to seek safety with his friends in the centre of the city – after his death, the rest of his family had gone into exile – visitors were requested not to use flash photography – they had thirty minutes to look round.

Sonia got the impression that she expected visitors to know about the man and his work, just as a guide in a cathedral would assume tourists might know who he meant by Jesus Christ.

The house was as stark as the information. The walls were white, the ceilings lofty and the floors tiled. For Sonia it had as little soul as the parkland that now surrounded it. It was difficult to imagine lively conversation around the dark wooden dining table, with its hard, high-backed chairs, or to picture Lorca at the cumbersome desk composing poetry. Some of his manuscripts were displayed in a cabinet, the fine, loopy writing illustrated with delicate, coloured drawings. There were interesting portraits on the walls and some of Lorca's theatre set designs but what it lacked was any sense of who this man was. It was a shell, an empty husk, and Sonia was disappointed. The old man in the café had spoken with such passion about him and she was slightly bemused by how little atmosphere remained in what had once been a family home. Perhaps it filled her with gloom because she had been brought here by the story of the poet's assassination.

She paused at the postcard display. Only here did something clarify itself. There were several dozen images of a man's face. Here was the man who had once filled this building with his presence. There was something astonishingly vivid and modern-looking about the face, chocolate-brown eyes meeting not just those of the photographer but of anyone who was standing at the postcard counter all these years later.

His hair was wavy, his brows thick, his skin slightly roughened by acne and his ears stuck out more than he must have liked. He adopted many different guises. In one picture he played the role of uncle, and a niece, who resembled him so closely she might have been his own little daughter, sat on his lap learning to read, a stubby forefinger pointing to a single word. In another he was a sibling, cheerfully posing with his brother and sister, all of them appearing to suppress their laughter for the picture. The warmth of both the day and the affection between them made the image glow. Other pictures showed family groups and glimpses of a long-gone world when children were dressed in cotton pinafores, and babies wore mobcaps, when women engaged in embroidery and men sat in striped deck chairs. There were plenty of pictures that showed a frivolous side to Lorca: in one he posed as a pilot behind a huge image of a bi-plane, and in another a smiling face poked out from behind a huge fairground cartoon of an overweight woman. There was childlike laughter in such photographs, but in others, with a group of intellectuals or with just one other young man, he looked highly serious.

Whatever he was doing – playing the piano, giving speeches, larking about, striking a pose – he was clearly a man who loved life, and a warmth and vitality emanated from these pictures that inspired Sonia in a way that the house itself had failed to. They provided glimpses of precious carefree moments in a life that had been wiped out not long after. For that reason alone they were absorbing.

At the end of the row of postcards, which were ranked along the counter in neat wooden sections, there was one where he stood outside the front door of this very house, with a sharp shadow of bright summer sunshine behind him. Sonia wondered if it had been taken the summer of his arrest and death.

Sonia moved along the row, picking out one each of every image.

'Can I help you?' asked the girl on the cash desk.

She had been slightly bemused by the length of time this visitor had hovered. Sometimes the stock in here was pilfered, but that only usually happened when school parties came in and this woman did not look remotely suspicious. When she saw the pile of cards in Sonia's hand, she leaned over towards a pile of books.

'If you want so many,' she said, 'it makes sense to buy this.'

Sonia took from her the little book she held out and flicked through its pages. All the postcard images and more were contained in it, along with captions and quotes. With a dictionary, she might be able to translate them.

Her eyes rested on the last image of Lorca where he sat, white-suited, at a café table with a stylish-looking woman who wore a beret. A carafe of wine stood on the table in front of them, sunlight streamed down through the branches of trees in full leaf and people sat back in their wicker seats at other tables. This was a portrayal of people at leisure, of Spain at peace.

Below the picture were a few words: '*Lo que más me importa es vivir.*' Sonia did not need a dictionary to translate them: 'What matters to me most is to live.'

The tragic irony of the words struck her forcibly. All these images of Lorca, in a turban, in an aeroplane, with friends, with family, showed him as a man with a huge appetite for life. It was unimaginable now that any poet could have been important enough to execute. The simple white-washed farmhouse was an image of innocence, frozen in time, a memorial that had been left alone while all in its immediate surroundings had been swept up in a new, forward-looking Spain. It was like a gravestone without a corpse.

She handed over some pesetas for the book and left.

Soon she was back in the hotel. As she pushed the button for the lift, Maggie stepped out of it, radiant after ten hours of uninterrupted dreams.

'Sonia,' she gushed, 'where have you been?'

'Just having a wander,' replied Sonia. 'I did leave you a note.'

'Yes, I saw it. I just wasn't sure when you'd be back.'

'I'm going up to grab my shoes,' Sonia said through the narrow gap between the closing doors of the lift.

In the claustrophobic box of the lift, she began to feel slightly faint and realised she should have had something to eat. In the glow of sepia light, she caught a glimpse of herself in the mirrored wall. Compared with the vision of Maggie's bright face, she felt hollow-eyed and sunken-cheeked. Half-moons of darkness hung like eclipses below her eyes and her hair looked mousy with grease. She acknowledged to herself that it did not matter to her what she looked like, but she knew she would still feel the age-old pangs of resentment when men cast admiring glances at Maggie and she became her invisible friend. Having spent years practising this role, it was an all-too-familiar feeling.

Back in their room, she swiftly brushed her hair, defined her eyes with kohl pencil and smeared on some lip gloss. In the descending lift, her spirits lifted slightly as she observed the improvement.

Soon they were outside in the street and the two women propelled each other along, both equally excited by the prospect of their dance lesson.

Sonia's enthusiasm for the lesson waned after only twenty minutes, and the harsh brass sound of the salsa band, slightly distorted by the CD player, began to grate. She was as stiff as one of the shop dummies she had noticed earlier in the day. Engaging her mind to absorb instructions, she counted out the beats like a child, repeating and holding the numbers in her head.

Felipe spotted her furrowed brow and tense arms. '*Señora,*' he reprimanded. 'Not like that. Please. More relaxed.'

She felt chastened. It was a sin to be unrelaxed here and to think, rather than feel. She was not sure she could do it any differently today.

It was a relief when the lesson finished at five o'clock sharp.

'I'm so bad at this,' she said under her breath, as she fiddled with a buckle, eventually pulling off her shoes without undoing them and aiming them furiously at her bag, which lay a few feet away.

'Don't be stupid,' said Maggie. 'You're just having a bad day. You're coming out with me tonight. You'll never improve otherwise, which was the whole point of coming here.'

'Was that the point?' asked Sonia grumpily, as they emerged from the building. 'I can't really remember.'

'And for my birthday.'

'Maggie! I'm so sorry. It's today! Happy Birthday! God! How awful of me, I'd completely forgotten which day it was. I'm really, really sorry.' She threw her arms around her friend and there in the sunny street hugged her with bone-crushing affection.

'Don't worry,' smiled Maggie. 'I do understand, honestly I do. You've got things on your mind, but the biggest favour you can do yourself is to try and think beyond them. You should let yourself go a bit more.'

Normally Sonia might have allowed her irritation at Maggie's instruction to show, but not today. It was Maggie's birthday.

'Yes. You're probably right,' she said.

'So will you come dancing tonight?'

'Of course I will. Is there somewhere particular you want to go?'

'There's a place quite near the dance school. It's really friendly and very unintimidating. You'll love it.'

Just before midnight, Sonia found herself ducking to enter a low stone archway and descending a narrow staircase into a dimly lit basement. There was a small bar at one end, with a row of stools in front of it and the two couples who were dancing were enjoying the luxury of having the whole dance floor to themselves. At this stage of the evening, the flamboyance of their twists and turns was almost acrobatic.

Sonia soon saw the reason for her old friend's insistence that they should come here. Hardly had they reached the foot of the stairway, when a handsome, stocky, figure emerged from the shadows near the bar and made his way towards them. Above the conversation-stifling noise of the music, Maggie introduced Paco, and although the three of them mimed frantically, little was communicated. The problem was not so much the relentlessly thudding beat as much as Paco's lack of English and theirs of Spanish. He did however show an attentiveness towards Sonia that allowed her to appreciate his charm, buying drinks for both women until, with a gesture of apology, he eventually led Maggie away to the dance floor. Sonia could see his appeal. Though she towered over him, there was something alluringly sexual about Maggie's new man.

Sonia watched, mesmerised by the way in which Paco's hand spread against the small of Maggie's back like a star, as he guided her firmly about the floor with deft, understated moves. She was perched on a stool, a glass of cold beer in her hand, and a strong sense of déjà vu overwhelmed her. How many times had she watched from the sidelines as Maggie danced? It happened when they were fourteen and it was still happening more than twenty years on.

No one was a spectator for long – the collective enthusiasm for dance meant that everyone was going to be involved. The club was now filling up and soon Sonia was approached. There was no question of saying no, even had she wanted to.

She recognised the music. It was one of the tracks that they had danced to that afternoon and the familiarity of its rhythm gave her confidence. It was neither too slow, nor too fast. The five minutes that followed were intimate, energetic, enlivening and physical. Almost immediately she felt the welcome synchronicity between mind and body as her feet began to move without instruction. It was as though the invisible ropes that kept her anchored to the ground had been severed. On the final beat of the music, the encounter was over. The dance was an end in itself. All she noticed was that her partner took her through the steps as if he had danced for his whole life. It was as natural to him as breathing.

On her third or fourth dance, each one with a new stranger, Sonia began to feel less inhibited. She was no longer telling her feet which way to point and her mind no longer counted a beat. She had experienced a fleeting sense of what this might be like once before, watching the Cuban instructors back in London and seeing the expression on their faces that showed they were dancing with their souls not their minds. Sonia recalled the way in which the hairs on her neck had stood on end. Now she knew what that felt like. The enchantment of dance had buried itself deep inside her.

Between dances, she had gravitated back towards the bar. Occasionally, Maggie and Paco stepped off the dance floor and came to find her. Maggie glistened. Her white shirt, luminous in the fluorescent lighting, was transparent with perspiration and tiny droplets beaded her hairline like a tiara.

'Are you OK, Sonia?' she asked. 'Are you having a good time?'

'Yes. I'm having a great time,' she responded, and there was no edge to her answer.

She had no idea at what hour her head finally sank into her pillow. It was another sleepless night but not, this time, because she was anxious about Maggie, whose bed in the twin room remained empty. Tonight, it was the endorphins coursing through her body that kept her spinning round till sunrise.

Chapter Six

NOT LONG BEFORE midday, Sonia turned the taps to 'cool' and gasped as the water sputtered from the showerhead, covering her in waves of shocking iciness. It was what she needed to feel fully awake and with the day. Her next thought was for coffee and for that there was only one destination. She slipped out of the lobby, knowing that she would be too late anyway for the paltry hotel breakfast of shrink-wrapped, long-life croissant, whose only chance of being brought to life was to be dipped into the weak coffee.

By some kind of homing instinct she retraced her route to the pretty square where she had been the previous day. It was not just the excellence of his *café con leche* that drew her back but the sense that some of her conversations with the kind waiter were yet to be concluded. It was chilly and none of the other tables outside was occupied when she arrived, so she went inside. For more than five minutes, she sat there and no one came. Her sense of disappointment was out of proportion to the situation. There were plenty of other cafés close by that would serve decent coffee, she told herself.

While she was waiting, she took the time to observe that the busier the café, the more it seemed to attract additional customers. She was about to follow the trend and take her custom elsewhere when she heard a friendly voice behind her.

'*Buenos días, Señora.*'

She turned. There was the café owner, smiling, evidently pleased to see her.

'I thought you must be closed.'

'No, no. I'm sorry, I was on the telephone. What can I bring you?'

'*Café con leche, por favor.* And something to eat? A pastry?'

Some minutes later, both arrived.

'You had a late night?' commented the man. 'If it's not rude to say it, you look very tired.'

Sonia smiled. She enjoyed the café proprietor's honesty and knew she must look terrible, with smudges of yesterday's mascara and all the other signs of sleep deprivation.

'Was it a good night?'

'Yes, it was,' she replied, smiling. 'I went dancing.'

'You liked that? You found some *duende*, perhaps?'

Sonia was unfamiliar with the word. It sounded rather like 'duet', so perhaps he was asking if she had found a partner. For the first time in the last twenty-four hours, her thoughts turned to James. How would he have liked it here? Would he have appreciated the jaded décor of the dance school? The relentless exertion of the dancing lessons? The decibel level in the nightclub? The answer to all of these questions was 'no'. Perhaps he might have enjoyed the grandeur of the architecture, she thought as she glanced at the upper storeys of the strong, rather magnificent buildings that comprised even this unimportant square. A spark of guilt passed through her when she realised that she had not even thought to ring James, but, on the other hand, he had not rung her either. He would be frantically involved in some deal at the bank, she was fairly certain of that, and would not be missing her.

'I had a fantastic time,' she answered simply. '*Fantástico.*'

'*Bueno, bueno,*' he said, as though he got some personal satisfaction from the fact that his customer had had a good night out. 'People will always dance. Even when we were living under a tyrannical regime, people continued to dance. For many of us, the priests had destroyed our religion, but many people simply had another one ready-made. Dancing became a new religion for a few people, a way of rebelling.'

'It was for dance classes that I came here, really,' said Sonia. 'I just enjoy it, but I don't really see it becoming my religion,' she added, laughing.

'No, I don't suppose it will. But things are different today. Granada is full of dance now and people do it freely.'

As on the previous day, the café owner seemed to have more time on his hands than customers to fill it, though Sonia could imagine that in the high season this would not be the case. She was in no hurry either, and this smiling elderly Spaniard clearly wanted to make conversation with her.

'Do you dance?' asked Sonia.

'Me? No,' he replied.

'So how long have you had this café?' she asked.

'Oh, for years now,' he replied. 'I took over in the mid nineteen fifties.'

'And you've been here all that time?'

'Yes, I have,' he said quietly.

To stay in one place, in one job, for all those decades was almost beyond the reach of Sonia's imagination. How could anyone tolerate the sheer tedium of such stubborn continuity?

'Things were still in a state of upheaval then. It was all to do with the Civil War. It changed everything.'

Sonia was embarrassed by her ignorance of Spanish history but she felt she had to give an adequate response.

'It must have been awful for—'

The man cut her off. She saw that he suddenly had no wish to pursue this line of conversation.

'But you really don't want to hear about it. It's such a long story and you've got dancing to do.'

He was right. There had not been any other customers since her arrival, so he was still in no hurry for her to leave, but she did have a dance class to go to. Even though she loved sitting here passing the hours in this café with its kind owner, she could not miss her dancing. She glanced at her watch and was amazed to realise how much time had passed – it was one thirty in the afternoon. The lesson was at two o'clock.

'I'm so sorry,' said Sonia. 'I have to leave soon.'

'Tell me before you go – did you go to Lorca's house?'

'I did. I saw what you meant about it being cold. It's hard to put your finger on it, isn't it? But somehow you can sense that it all ended badly there and that's the reason that no one has lived in it for all those years.'

'Did you like the park?'

He genuinely wanted her views and was interested in what she had to say.

'It was a bit formal for my taste. It's quite hard to make a garden gloomy, but they had managed.'

Sonia felt she had been inadvertently rude about this man's city and was relieved by his reaction.

'I completely agree with you. It's not a nice place. Lorca himself would have hated it. I know he would. It's just the kind of stiffness and lack of imagination that he was opposed to.'

The elderly man was suddenly aroused from his gentle state into one of ire. She could not help contrasting him with her father, in whom gentleness and patience was the entire man. Nothing budged Jack Haynes from his mood of quiet acceptance. The café owner, however, was different. She caught a glimpse of something steely in his look, a glint that suggested he was not a gentle old man through and through. There was another side to him. It made her reflect that the stereotype of the fiery Spanish personality had something in it after all. That hard look was very different from the kindness she had associated with him until now. It was a hint of anger, not with her, but with something that had gone through his mind. The creases around his mouth had hardened and his eyes had ceased to twinkle with the warm smile that she had already grown to recognise.

'I really must go,' she said. 'Thanks for my breakfast. Or was it lunch? I don't know really, but thank you.'

'I have enjoyed talking to you. Enjoy your dancing.'

'I'm not going home until the day after tomorrow,' she said. 'So I might come back for breakfast if you're open.'

'Of course I'll be open. Except for the occasional day off, I have been open every day since I can remember.'

'I'll see you tomorrow then,' said Sonia brightly.

Sonia smiled, partly at the prospect of seeing him again, but also at the evident pride he took in this café, which was clearly his life's work. There appeared to be no one else involved. No wife. No son to follow in his footsteps. She slung her bag over her shoulder and got up to leave. It was less than five minutes until the start of her dance lesson.

She arrived at the dance school slightly late, and walked into the studio where Felipe and Corazón were already in mid-demonstration. It was not salsa. The Norwegian girls had gone to one of the shows in the Sacromonte the night before and were keener than ever on learning some for themselves. Maggie had voiced no objections and the men in the class would go along with the plan as long as they could revert to salsa in the second half of the lesson. For the second time in as many days they could show this class what, in their view, was the greatest dance of all.

As soon as it ended, with a fired, machine-gun rattle of feet, Corazón cried out to her pupils: 'OK, *this* is how we start with flamenco.'

The music they now danced to was very different from the brash salsa sound whose beat had become almost second nature to them all. It was much harder for the ear to grasp or to find its way into the pulse; it nevertheless had a regular time signature, though confusingly it seemed to depart from it often. Along with the sound of a guitar could be heard clapping and counter-clapping, pulses that weaved in and out of each other with impossible complexity, but occasionally resolved and met in unison, ending on a final single beat. Sonia strained to hear the pattern.

By now Corazón had her hands held high. Her supple wrists allowed her hands to create perfect circles as her fingers splayed in and out, in time with the beat. Her loose hips swayed easily to the rhythm, and from time to time she accentuated the beat with a click of her tongue.

Soon, the women in the class were copying, some with a greater degree of success than others.

They warmed up like this for ten or fifteen minutes, feeling their way into the rhythm and occasionally Corazón would disturb their semi-hypnotised state with an exhortation.

'Listen! Can you hear?' she said, finding no difficulty speaking and swaying at once. 'The sound of the anvil? The beating of metal?'

The class looked at her blankly. She responded to their stupidity with a withering look and persisted with the comparison.

'Come on,' she cried, with increasing impatience. 'Listen! Ting! – Ting! – Ting! – Ting! Have you not walked into the Albaicín? Have you not noticed all that wrought iron? Do you not hear the sound of men working that metal? Can you not still hear it in those narrow streets?'

Someone sniggered but as far as Corazón was concerned, their inability to understand was their loss. She had run out of time and patience trying to explain.

Sonia began to hear the echo of the ironworkers' craft and even that brief pause between the beats made her think of the swing of the hammer before it struck metal. Corazón was not insane after all. She clapped and swayed to illustrate her point and those with imagination could hear the sound of the blacksmiths.

'Now! Follow me. Do this!'

Corazón seemed in her element, issuing instructions like a martinet. Salsa was a sideshow for her; it was clear that this was where her heart lay.

She tightened her fists, then slowly unfurled the fingers one by one, starting with the smallest and progressing to the thumb, repeating the movement, then with variations, starting with the forefinger and working towards the smallest, all the while twisting the wrists round and round, back and forward.

Sonia's wrists felt almost bruised with this unfamiliar movement and her arms ached. Simultaneously with the hands, Corazón wound her arms up and down like serpents, one minute above her head, the other down by her side. In a shambolic way, the class attempted to keep up.

'*Mira! Mira!*' she cried, with a mixture of frustration and boundless enthusiasm. 'Watch!'

Corazón knew that they could do much better, but it might take time. So far they had only worked on the upper half of the body and there was much more to come.

'OK, OK. *Muy bien.* Take a break.'

Gratefully, the class relaxed. It was not for long, though. Felipe, who had been sitting observing, leaped to his feet. It was his turn to be centre stage.

The class formed a horseshoe around him and watched.

'This is the basic footwork,' he said. One leg extended to the front, the knee slightly bent, he stamped down on the ball of his foot and then onto the heel. He did this several times and then speeded up to show how this simple movement formed the basis for the spectacular pattern of foot stamping that people associated with flamenco. They all tried it. There was nothing particularly complex about doing this in slow motion.

'*Planta!*' he shouted as he slammed his foot on the ground.

There was something perfectly onomatopoeic about the next word he shouted as the sharp sound of his heel drove down into the floor. '*Tacón! Ta-CON!*' he repeated.

For a while they practised the basic movement and then Felipe began to complicate things, moving from heel to toe in different sequences. Some of the pupils could keep up. Others who were less co-ordinated began to flounder. It was all proving to be so much harder than it had looked. Felipe was undeterred. He was so serious about flamenco that he did not even notice that some of the dancers were no longer with him.

'You must listen to the rhythms created by your feet,' he said. 'You are making your own music with them. Have nothing in your heads, but much in your ears.'

It almost makes sense, thought Sonia, concentrating intensely but trying to put into practice the idea that she should be doing this with her ear rather than her mind. She caught Maggie's eye and saw that for once her friend looked mildly bored.

Now it was Corazón's turn again.

'The most important thing of all I have left until last,' she said dramatically. 'And *that* is the very beginning.'

By now, most of the class stood sipping water from plastic bottles. It was all becoming more demanding than any of them had expected.

'*ActiTUD!*' she said, and in the very manner of delivering the word, she demonstrated what was expected. Her chin up, her nose pointing to the ceiling and with an arrogance of posture that reminded Sonia of the flamenco dancers they had gone to see three nights ago, they watched as Corazón showed them how they had to 'announce' themselves at the beginning of a dance.

'The entrance is the most important moment of all,' she told them. 'You can't come in quietly. You have to tell everyone you are here – with the language of your body. Tell people that you are now the most important person in the room.'

Corazón was the sort of woman who made herself noticeable by simply walking through a door. She had been born with presence. It had not occurred to Sonia that this was something that could be acquired and she had always assumed it had to come naturally. Twenty minutes later, though, when she caught sight of a woman in the mirror who was striking a convincing pose and realised it was herself, she decided that it was not beyond her reach. One arm stretched towards the ceiling, her fingers splayed, her body twisted at the waist and her other arm curved in front of her, she looked almost authentically flamenco.

With a sharp, double-clap of her hands, Corazón brought this section of the class to an end.

'*Bueno, bueno.* We will have you dancing in the Sacromonte by tomorrow,' she said, smilingly. 'Take a break and then we will get back to salsa.'

'Thank God for that,' muttered Maggie in Sonia's direction. 'I'm not sure that flamenco is really my bag.'

'But you seemed so keen a couple of days ago,' answered Sonia, trying to hide a slight note of 'I told you so' from her voice. 'Was it harder than you'd thought?'

Maggie threw her head back, sweeping her mane of hair away from her face. 'It's all so melodramatic, isn't it? So egocentric. Such a *performance*.'

'But isn't all dancing a performance?'

'No, I don't think so. At least, not when you're dancing with a partner. And if it is, then it's just a performance for that one other person.'

For the first time Sonia realised something about her friend: that for her, dancing had to be about another person. It was part of her search for the elusive perfect man. It was Maggie's life's quest.

'Two minutes, everyone!' shouted Corazón. 'Two minutes.'

Sonia slipped out of the room to go to the cloakroom. Through the main glass doors, she could see two of the Norweigian girls and all of the taxi dancers clustered outside on the pavement, a cloud of cigarette smoke swirling around them. Her attention was then caught by a sound coming through a slightly open door on the other side of the entrance hall. Feeling like a spy, she peered through the crack. What she saw transfixed her. A group of perhaps a dozen people sat around the edge of the room listening to a guitarist. They were all scruffy, pale with tiredness, hair straggly and unkempt, mostly in jeans, and T-shirts with long-since faded motifs. The oldest-looking man, his wavy, tar-black hair in a ponytail, was picking out a tune of such sweet soulfulness that Sonia felt a lump rising to her throat. It was this and the gentle clapping that accompanied him that had drawn her. No one made eye contact; their rhythms required the concentration that could only be sustained by staring into the void.

One girl, willowy, hollow-eyed, in black Lycra dance trousers and scoop-necked top, stood up. In one hand she held a voluminous froth of dark green fabric and she now stepped into it, for a moment struggling with a broken zip. She seemed in no particular hurry. Then she fastened the buckles on her shoes. They were pale with dust. Finally, she removed the clip that held the hair away from her face and ringlets fell around her shoulders. She refastened it, ensuring that all the strands were now firmly caught. The guitarist continued and the clapped accompaniment went on. The pattern made by these sounds was like hand-made lace. It was hard to see how individual groups of stitches were going to fit in with the whole but after a while they formed the most astonishing and symmetrical pattern.

The young woman was ready now. She began to join the clapping, as though tuning herself into the rhythm. Her hands held high, she moved seamlessly into a series of sensuous hand-movements, her hips swaying in counterpoint to the gestures of her arms. She danced in front of the guitarist, and he held her in an unerring gaze, reading every nuance of her dance, scrutinising every subtle flicker of her body and responding in rhythms and notes. One moment his fingers would caress the strings, another they would pluck them sharply to pick out a melody, anticipating rather than dictating. She leaned backwards, limbo-like, twisting her torso as she turned. It was a feat that was accomplished with gravity-defying balance. Sonia could not imagine how she had achieved this without falling to the ground, but the woman repeated the movement four, five, even six times to prove that it had been anything but a fluke, and each time her body curved itself into an even more impossible arc.

Now upright again, she performed a series of deft pirouettes, flicking her body round at such speed that Sonia wondered if she had actually turned at all. One blink, and the spectator might have missed these breathtaking spins entirely. All the while, her feet were hammering out angry patterns on the floor. Every limb, every sinew of her body was engaged in this display, even her facial muscles, which at times contorted her beautiful features into a gargoyle-like grimace.

Sonia was frozen to the spot. The energy of this woman and the flexibility of her body were impressive, but the sheer physical power locked inside that insubstantial frame was what really amazed her.

Once or twice, the dance seemed to reach a natural end, when the girl would pause and look away from the guitarist and towards the palmists, but then she herself would begin to clap and moments later her stamping and swaying would begin again, and her arms would resume their snakelike motion. Several times Sonia heard a quiet, encouraging '*Olé*', the acknowledgement that this woman was not just impressing her peer group but also stirring their emotions as they rocked and swayed in their seats.

When the dance did truly come to an end, the rhythmic claps immediately turned to rippling applause. Some of them stood up and embraced her, and there was astonishing beauty in her broad smile.

Sonia had pushed the door slightly more open at one point and now one of the accompanists strode purposefully towards it.

He had not seen her but she slunk guiltily away before he could spot her and disappeared into the cloakroom. It was not as though she had witnessed a crime, but she felt she had seen something illicit, an event that might never have been on public display.

That night, Sonia returned willingly to the salsa club. She had lost her anxiety about venturing into places where she knew so few people. Once she had relaxed and accepted a few invitations to dance, she enjoyed herself just as she had done the night before. Salsa was easy on the mind and the body, a far cry from the intensity of flamenco. She could not entirely put out of her mind the image of the girl she had seen that afternoon dancing with such consuming passion in front of her *gitano*, her gypsy.

Chapter Seven

THE NEXT MORNING, for the first time, Sonia understood why the nearby mountains were called the Sierra Nevada, the snowy mountains. Although the sky was bright there was an icy freshness in the air and when she pushed open the door of the hotel to leave, it was like stepping into a fridge.

Today was their last full day in Granada. Sonia was already feeling nostalgic about her visit, though it was not yet over. There was still one more dance lesson and one more chance to emerge from a nightclub as dawn was breaking.

The sun would struggle to appear above the pale turrets of the Alhambra today and would cast a golden glow only briefly on the squares before it sank behind the mountains. The owner of her favourite café, El Barril, as she had now noticed it was called, knew that few of his customers would be wanting to sit outside when the temperatures had plummeted so had not bothered to put any chairs out that day. Sonia entered the dark interior and gradually her eyes adjusted to the dimness.

The old man was behind the bar polishing glasses and he emerged to greet her. He did not need to ask what she wanted to drink and there was soon the shriek of the coffee grinder as he began to prepare her coffee with all the diligence of a scientist conducting an experiment.

Even he was finding it difficult to operate in the gloom and he crossed the room to switch on the lights. The place was transformed by the sudden illumination. It was much larger than Sonia had realised, a big square room, with perhaps thirty round tables, each with two or three chairs, and at the back of the room several dozen more piled up to the ceiling. The space was unexpected.

There was nothing remarkable about the furniture or the décor, but what caught Sonia's eye were the walls. Every square inch of them was covered.

On one wall were several dozen *corrida* posters. Sonia had seen something like these in the prints sold all over Spain, customised with the tourist's name, so that people could imagine themselves famed toreadors. The posters on the walls here were not souvenirs, though. They carried the patina of age and authenticity. Sonia rose to read them.

The fights advertised by these posters had taken place in bull-rings all over the country: Sevilla, Madrid, Málaga, Almería, Ronda . . . The list went on. The venues were all different, but one name was common to them all: Ignacio Ramírez.

Sonia walked slowly along the row of prints, taking in detail, like an art critic at a gallery opening. The posters eventually gave way to a montage of black-and-white pictures of a man, presumably Ignacio Ramírez. Some of the pictures were stiffly posed portraits and in each one he wore a different bullfighting costume: tight, embroidered breeches, a short, heavily brocaded bolero jacket and a tricorn hat. He glowered, violent, handsome, an arrogance burning through the picture. Sonia wondered whether this was the same look he gave the bull in order to terrify him into submission.

Another set of pictures showed him in action, apparently doing that very thing. There he was, facing the bull, only a few metres from five hundred kilograms of untamed fury. In several, the swish of his cape was a passing blur, just captured by the photographer's lens. In one picture, the animal passed close enough to brush the matador's body and his horns seemed wrapped up in the cape.

By now, a cup of the deepest black coffee, along with a jug of steaming white foam, had been set down on a table close to where Sonia stood. She stirred in a drop of milk and sipped slowly, hardly taking her eyes away from the pictures. The café owner stood next to her, almost poised to answer a question.

'So who was Ignacio Ramírez?' she asked.

'He was one of the boys who once lived here, and a star bull-fighter.'

'And was he eventually killed by a bull?' asked Sonia. 'He looks slightly too close for comfort here.'

'No, that wasn't how he died.'

They stood in front of a picture that showed the bullfighter with arms raised, sword held high and the bull only feet away. It captured the dramatic pause when the matador was ready to plunge his weapon between the animal's shoulder blades. Man and bull looked each other in the eye.

'That,' said the café owner, 'is "*la hora de la verdad*".'

'The hour of . . . ?'

'Well, you would translate it as "The moment of truth". It's the moment when the matador must make the kill. If he gets his timing wrong, or doesn't do it cleanly then that's the end of him. *Terminado. Muerto.*'

It was only when she had studied every single one of the pictures and gazed into the impenetrably dark eyes that stared out at her, that she noticed the massive head and shoulders of a bull on the wall at the far end of the bar. He was as black as coal tar, with shoulders nearly a metre across, and, even in death, a look of terrifying ferocity. Underneath, though almost too high to read, Sonia could make out a date: '3 de Septiembre 1936'.

'That was one of his best kills,' said the old man. 'It was here in Granada. The bull was a beast and the crowd went completely wild. It was a stupendous day. I can't even begin to describe to you the excitement in the bullring. Have you ever been to a *corrida*?'

'No,' said Sonia, 'I haven't.'

'You should,' said the old man with passion. 'Even if it's just once in your lifetime.'

'I'm not sure I could sit there. It looks so brutal.'

'Well, the bull usually dies, it's true. But there is much more to it than that. It's like a dance.'

Sonia was unconvinced but knew it was not the moment for a discussion on what she imagined to be a cruel sport. She wandered to the wall opposite, which was covered with equal density by dozens of photographs, mostly of young women in flamenco costume. In some of them, there was a man too.

At first glance they looked like a series of shots of different girls, but on closer examination Sonia saw that they were in fact one and the same person, metamorphosing from child to adult, from little girl with puppy fat in polka dots to glowering, voluptuous beauty in lace, from ugly duckling to elegant swan complete with feather fan. In each one her hair was different, coiled, plaited or knotted into a chignon, and in some an enormous comb stood up from the back. The outfits varied too. There were dresses with extravagant ruffled trains, sometimes a fringed shawl or a knee-length skirt and even one with trousers and a short jacket. She wore a different outfit in every photograph but in all of them she had the same provocative, fiery expression, what Corazón would have called '*actitud*'.

'That was Ignacio's sister,' said the old man, volunteering the information.

'What was her name?'

'Mercedes Catalina Concepción Ramírez.' He spoke the name slowly, as if reciting poetry.

'That's quite a name.'

'It's a fairly typical one here. Her family all called her "Merche".'

'She was beautiful, wasn't she?'

'Yes, she was . . .' For a moment he seemed lost for words. '. . . very beautiful. Her parents doted on her and her brothers nearly ruined her with the way they spoiled her. She was a rebellious child, but everyone adored her. She was a dancer, you see, a flamenco dancer – and a very good one, a very, very good one. She was famous in the region.'

The image of the dancer she had spied on that afternoon still lingered in Sonia's mind. The woman in these pictures was physically very different.

'Where did she dance?'

'She danced at all the local fiestas, at *juergas*, which are private parties, and sometimes in the bar. From about the age of three, she would amuse everyone by pretending to be a flamenco dancer, endlessly practising the moves as though she was a wind-up doll. On the day she turned five, Mercedes had her first proper lesson up there in the Sacromonte and for her birthday she was given her first pair of proper dancing shoes.'

Sonia smiled. She was touched by the formal manner in which the old man spoke. His was the careful English of an elderly foreigner, and she could tell he enjoyed recounting the minutiae of the past.

'She sounds very determined about it all. Did her mother dance?'

'No more than most women here,' replied the old man. 'Everyone around here grows up seeing people dancing flamenco. It's part of the city. You can't avoid it, at fiestas, at parties, up in the Sacromonte, and most girls at some point have a go, but not to the extent of that little girl.'

'Who accompanied her? Did her father play the guitar?'

'He did a little. But one of her brothers was very musical, so she always had someone willing to play for her. She gave her first performance when she was about eight years old, right here in the bar. Emilio, the musical brother, was playing and she got a fantastic reception, not just because everyone in the audience had watched her growing up – they weren't patronising her, I promise. It was more than that. When this little girl danced, she took on some other dimension. It was like magic. Even when people had got used to seeing her dance, she could still pull in a crowd every time she performed.'

The elderly man was silent for a few moments as he gazed at the photographs and Sonia thought she saw his old eyes water. He coughed, as if to clear his throat. She could tell that he had something else to say.

'She had *duende*.'

There was that word again. She remembered him using it the previous day and had not really understood it then, but today, in this context, she did. It was something otherworldly, as far as she could understand it, like the power that made hairs stand on end.

They both stood in front of the wall of photographs for a few minutes and Sonia looked at this woman. Yes, she could imagine that this woman had *duende*.

She said farewell and promised the café owner that she would come and see him if she ever returned to Granada. In their brief acquaintance, Sonia had grown fond of the old man and she kissed him on both cheeks as she left. How unlike Maggie she was. This was the closest she had come to a holiday romance. And she did not even know his name.

Chapter Eight

IT WAS THEIR final dance class that afternoon. As the week progressed, the late nights had begun to take their toll. The class was suffering from lack of sleep and it affected their ability to follow instructions.

Sonia and Maggie were no exception and their legs felt like lead as they tried to perform the moves they were being taught that day. Several times, Sonia found herself apologising to her partner and an audible cry of pain was heard from the usually patient taxi dancer who had been landed with Maggie. Corazón's patience was wearing thin.

'*Vamos, chicos!* Let's go, everyone!' she kept saying, to try to inject some energy into the class. Then she would issue cries of encouragement if they achieved anything that even remotely resembled the turn she had demonstrated. '*Eso es! Eso es!* That's it! That's it!'

Even the taxi dancers were jaded that day and it was clear that if they had not been getting paid they would have been anywhere but in this room. The energy and exhilaration of this joyful dance seemed to have evaporated for everyone and however hard they tried, Felipe and Corazón failed to lift the class. Eventually they gave up.

'*Vale, vale.* OK,' said Corazón. 'We will try something new. Have a break and then we will show you a new dance that even your grandmothers could do.'

A different rhythm now boomed from the sound system.

'Merengue!' cried Corazón, grabbing Felipe. 'If you can count up to *two* then you can do this.'

She was right: it was the simplest of dances and the clockwork, 'one-two, one-two' beat demanded nothing but the willingness for two people to fasten themselves together like limpets and rock from side to side. It was banal in its simplicity, but it did revive their spirits. After ten minutes or so, some simple turns were added and a new atmosphere pervaded the class. Faces lit up into smiles.

'That,' gasped Maggie, 'is about as intimate as you could get with your clothes on!'

'It's amazing that they even call it a dance,' agreed Sonia, laughing.

The two friends were bound together again in laughter. The mood of merengue was as far from the unsettling effect of flamenco as it could possibly be.

This was a dance that gave instant results and could be learned in a lesson rather than a lifetime. It sanctioned almost unholy communion with a partner, whereas flamenco required the utmost introspection and self-absorption. It was the diametric opposite of the gypsy dance, and few people were immune to its instant charm and energy; while it had none of the darkness of flamenco, it also had none of the depth.

It was time for the members of the class to disperse, to kiss each other extravagantly several times on both cheeks as though they had become lifelong friends, to exchange mobile phone numbers, make promises of reunions in salsa clubs, and commitments to visit each other's countries. Corazón told them all how wonderful they were and how she hoped they would all come back one day for more lessons. Felipe allowed his wife to speak for them both and stood there smiling in agreement. It was a weekly ritual for them both.

Once out in the street, their spirits heightened by the exhilaration of the lesson's conclusion, Sonia and Maggie linked arms.

'Let's go and celebrate our new dance careers,' trilled Maggie.

'Good idea. Where shall we go?'

It was an idle question. There were at least a hundred and one possibilities not far from this sunny patch on the pavement where they now stood.

'Let's just stroll until somewhere takes our fancy.'

They walked for ten minutes. The shops were still closed and few people were about. One or two elderly couples, diminutive, silver-haired, smart, took a mid-afternoon constitutional to stretch arthritic legs, perhaps en route stopping to take coffee and a cognac. Sonia and Maggie turned into the main street.

They almost missed Casa Enrique. It filled a small space between two shops. No sign swung outside, but an old barrel now used as a table stood on the pavement, almost blocking the entrance. Two distinguished-looking men, one in an olive-toned jacket, the other in a dark suit, talked companionably in the late afternoon glow, glasses of Rioja in one hand, cigars as thick as cucumbers in the other. They epitomised Granadino respectability and affluence.

Maggie steered Sonia into the dark interior and smiled at the two men as she passed. The bar was little more than a corridor and the space for customers scarcely a metre wide. They ordered glasses of wine and chose tapas from the blackboard above the entrance.

'Well,' said Maggie, clinking her glass against Sonia's, 'have you had a good time?'

'A wonderful time,' replied Sonia honestly. 'I've really enjoyed the dancing.'

'Yes,' agreed Maggie, hardly able to suppress her happiness. 'I've had a wonderful time too.'

'Not just because of the dancing,' teased Sonia.

'No, I suppose not . . .'

They finished their drinks and walked out into the street. Maggie caught the eye of one of the men as she passed and he touched her arm.

'*Señora* . . .'

She hesitated.

'Come on, Maggie. Let's go . . .' Sonia threw her arm around Maggie and guided her smartly away and up the street. For once, she felt that Maggie should be wary of the indiscriminate forwardness of the Spanish male.

Both women needed to sleep. Back at the hotel they undressed and climbed into their beds. Being in Spain was like being on a night shift, reflected Sonia as she set the alarm for eleven p.m. It was their last evening in Granada and they had no desire to miss it.

On the dance floor that night Sonia felt the air beneath her feet. It was as though they did not touch the ground. Everything she had learned that week fell into place. Some part of her had always struggled with the notion that the woman was meant to be in an entirely responsive role. But tonight the paradox made sense to her: being passive did not mean being subservient. Her power lay in how well she chose to respond. There was no subservience involved. It was subtle, and for a moment she thought of James and imagined how impossible he would find it to understand.

All night, she was whisked, whirled and wound like a spring. At four in the morning, she could finally dance no longer, but as she thanked her last partner her face beamed with pleasure. She had neither trodden on his feet, nor tripped him up, and she was dizzy with exhilaration.

It had not been such a satisfying evening for Maggie. Paco had not appeared and for the first time in a few days, she returned to the hotel with Sonia.

The streets were still full of life when they emerged from the nightclub, couples coiled together in doorways and youths engaged in furtive exchanges of drugs and money. Almost overpowered by cheap brandy, Maggie leaned heavily on her friend; as they staggered along the cobbled streets it took every ounce of Sonia's strength to hold her friend upright. She was considerably smaller than Maggie and several times they both nearly lost their balance. Sonia was reminded, once again, of their teenage years and how little distance they seemed to have come.

She managed to get her friend into bed, tucked the sheets firmly around her and set a glass of water on her bedside table. Maggie would wake up with a raging thirst.

The following morning, a thick head was the least of Maggie's troubles. She was inconsolable that Paco had turned out to be as unreliable as any other man she had ever met.

'But you were going home today anyway,' Sonia tried to reason with her.

'That's not really the point,' said Maggie nasally. 'He never said goodbye.'

On the journey to the airport, Maggie was silent, partly stupefied by the miniatures from the minibar that she had consumed in place of a more substantial breakfast. Sonia tried to lift her out of her despair.

'You really haven't changed since we were sixteen!' she teased gently.

'I know.' Maggie wept quietly into a sodden tissue and continued to stare out of the car window. Occasionally she made a kind of drowning noise as she gulped down her sobs.

Sonia rested her hand on her friend's arm as a gesture of comfort and she reflected on the irony of a supposedly cheerful birthday celebration that had begun with her own tears and ended with Maggie's. Perhaps women were hard-wired to weep.

The taxi travelled at terrifying speed along the motorway, dodging in and out between cars and huge pantechnicons that transported the products of Spain's now rich, poly-tunnelled farmland towards the markets of northern Europe. Both women were silent for the next half-hour, and eventually Maggie's outburst of grief and self-pity began to subside. She had exhausted herself.

'I should stop myself getting carried away,' she said eventually, tears welling up again in her eyes, 'but I'm not sure I can.'

'It's hard,' said Sonia comfortingly. 'It's so very hard.'

Their charter flight to Stansted was delayed by four hours, and by the time they landed and crossed London, it had gone eight o'clock in the evening. They shared a taxi from Liverpool Street to Clapham and before it dropped Maggie off, the women gave each other the warmest embrace.

'Take care, Maggie,' called Sonia out of the window.

'And you. I'll ring you.'

As the cab moved off, Sonia glanced out of the rear window and saw Maggie fishing in her bag for a key. Litter and leaves swirled together in the gutters. Two figures in hooded jackets loitered close by. The dimly lit Clapham street seemed nothing but forlorn.

Though it was only a further five minutes in the cab, Sonia's neat street, with its clipped hedging, perfect tessellated paths and polished door furniture was a world away from Maggie's where every house had a row of bells and a front garden crowded with bins.

Despite Maggie's misery, which she knew from experience would probably not last for ever, Sonia was determined to hold on to the sense of wellbeing that these past few days had given her. She rang the gleaming doorbell, but no one came, which struck her as odd since James's car was parked outside. After waiting a few more seconds, still expecting to see his shadowy outline appear behind the stained-glass panes, she began to rummage for her key.

Once inside, she dumped her bags on the hall floor and pushed the door shut with her foot. Amplified by the harsh acoustics of the hallway's high ceiling and polished tiles, the sound of it slamming shut was like the crack of pistol fire. She winced. It was a noise that James hated.

'Hello,' she called out. 'I'm back.'

Sonia could see through a crack in the door that James was in an armchair in the sitting room. He waited until she entered before answering.

'Hi,' he grunted as though she had just returned from work, rather than almost a whole week away.

The coolness of his tone suggested that he was not really interested in an answer. The flat monosyllable conveyed no enthusiasm and nothing was going to be added. She echoed his tone with her own crotchet-beat response.

'Hi.' And then with some hesitation: 'How have things been here?'

'Fine, thanks. Just fine.'

The newspaper, which had briefly been lowered, now moved up in front of him again like a sash window. Sonia could just see the top of his head and the shine of his just-beginning-to-be-bald pate.

The staccato delivery of James's last words carried more a hint of irritation, and the pages of his newspaper made a snapping sound as he pulled them straight and resumed his perusal of the previous day's share movements. Sonia turned to leave the room, desperately in need of something to quench her thirst, and heard James's sarcastic tone of voice calling out to her retreating back: 'Don't worry too much about dinner. I had a big lunch.'

The words brought Sonia's spirits crashing down hard. She was reminded of the feelings of despair that she had experienced in the hotel room only four days earlier. Granada already felt a million miles away.

I wasn't going to worry actually, she thought as she retreated to the kitchen. 'OK then,' were the words that came out. 'I'll see what I can knock up.'

James had evidently eaten out every night while she was away. Nothing in the fridge had been used up; the cheese was mouldy and the tomatoes bearded. At the back was some smoked salmon just past its sell-by date, which she was sure would not poison him, and a couple of free-range eggs. Enough to make a meal, of sorts.

As Sonia stood in her kitchen, which squeaked with antibacterial cleanliness, the sterility of the environment crawled over her like a damp sheet. An empty glass stood next to the sink, the ring of water around it the sole blot on the otherwise perfect landscape of the work surface. The oak kitchen cabinets with their glass insets were some kind of attempt to emulate an old cottage style, but these units would not weather with age. They would never even acquire a little characterful dust in the corners of the mouldings, such was the scrutiny of the cleaner's lightly dampened jiffy cloth.

It was James's house when they married, and somehow she still thought of it that way. It had already been gutted and decorated before she arrived and there had never been any question that anything should be modified to her taste.

At that moment James appeared, casting a cursory glance at the ingredients that sat on the kitchen worktop.

'I've had second thoughts,' he said. 'I'm going to turn in. Got an early meeting. 'Night.'

Before Sonia had had the opportunity to respond, James had gone upstairs. She ran the tap until it turned icy cold and filled her glass, drinking the water in one long draught until her head tipped back and her face was turned upwards to the ceiling. One of the spotlights had gone. The little black hole in the ceiling held her attention for a moment.

Once, her interest in the minutiae of her home would have driven her immediately to the cupboard under the stairs and the dead bulb would have been prised from its cavity and a new one put in. Not now. It no longer seemed to matter.

She had sometimes stood in this kitchen and asked herself the one question that really mattered: 'Is this really it?' She was less certain than ever before that it was.

James's coolness towards Sonia continued. He worked late at the office and so did she, catching up on various crises that had brewed in her absence.

Almost a week passed before they sat down and had a meal together, and when they did, conversation was stilted. What could they talk about? Sonia knew James would not want a detailed description of her time in Granada, and would certainly not want to hear that Maggie had fallen in love.

Conversation was kept very general until, halfway through a second bottle of wine, James said, 'I picked up one of your books while you were away.'

'Did you?' replied Sonia, rather surprised. 'Which one?'

'*The End of the Affair*,' stated James bluntly. 'By Graham someone.'

'Greene,' said Sonia. 'We went to see the film, don't you remember?'

James grunted.

'Did you like it?' she asked.

'I didn't read it. Well, not all of it, anyway.'

'But you started it?'

'I just read the underlinings. They were quite interesting.'

Sonia had never managed to drop her schoolgirl habit of making copious marks and notes in her books.

'They told me a lot about you.'

'What do you mean by that?' Sonia was mildly affronted that her textual markings had been studied by James. There was something mildly prurient about it. 'Why didn't you read the whole book?'

'Because I just wanted to read the bits that you'd highlighted. It seemed faster.'

James's tone was aggressive, and Sonia knew that they were heading for a fight. The half-dozen glasses of wine that he had drunk that evening were merely topping him up after a boozy lunch, and Sonia sensed that there was no avoiding a confrontation. Her heart thumped. James's lips looked purple, as if bruised with claret, and for the first time she noticed how stained his teeth were, as though he had been eating blackberries.

'It made me wonder whether you've been having an affair yourself. You certainly seemed very interested in the way that woman, Sarah Miles, did things.'

'James! That's outrageous! On the basis of a few underlined passages in a book?'

'Yes, it would help to explain why you steal off for your so-called "dancing class" each week and where you were last week!'

'I was with Maggie in Spain – for her thirty-fifth birthday!' protested Sonia.

'Oh, I know you were in sunny Spain,' he said sarcastically. 'You've had a postcard from some greasy dago.'

At this point James rose, staggered over to the kitchen dresser where they always left that day's post, and picked up a postcard. It was of the Alhambra.

'Dear Sonia,' he read aloud, 'I enjoyed our talks. If you ever come to Granada again, come and see me. Miguel.'

The postcard had been addressed to the hotel and forwarded to Sonia. It was a sweet gesture from an old man and she wondered how he had known her name.

James held out the postcard to Sonia as though it was burning his fingertips and she took it from him.

'I imagine it's from the waiter I talked to a few times,' she said. 'His name must have been Miguel.'

'I suppose it must,' snorted James with derision.

'I went to his café every morning. He told me a bit about Granada's history,' said Sonia defensively.

'I see,' said James, leaning back in his chair and emptying the last of the bottle into his glass. 'A *waiter*,' he added derisively.

'Surely you don't have a problem with that. He was ancient, James!'

'You expect me to believe that? You really expect me to believe that? For God's sake, Sonia, I'm not an *idiot*.'

He leaned towards her now and shouted this last comment into her face. She felt a droplet of red-wine spittle land on her mouth and was repulsed. Sonia did not want this argument, but she did want the last word.

'I'm not sure about that,' she said as she turned on her heel, leaving the room and the debris of their dinner still on the table.

She slept in the spare room that night and the ones that followed. As usual James left for work at the crack of dawn and returned when she had gone to bed. It was strange, Sonia realised, how easy it was to live in the same house as someone and never see him, and she wondered how long they could keep this up.

Even if some kind of confrontation had been inevitable, she would never have imagined that a slightly limping, elderly man, who lived a thousand miles away, would be the catalyst. That much had surprised her.

Chapter Nine

THE FOLLOWING TUESDAY, Sonia went back to her dance class in Clapham. She had spoken to Maggie a couple of times since their trip and had assumed that she would see her friend there.

After the scale of the Granada dance school, with its half a dozen studios and a hallway adorned with memorabilia, the south London venue seemed insignificant. The defining characteristics, though, were common to both establishments. They had a strong smell of dampness and a rundown air but, in spite of these, a vibrancy that seduced most people who came through their doors. The people who ran both these dance schools had more pressing concerns than repainting the walls and mending broken light fittings. Dance was always at the forefront of their minds.

Sonia was mildly surprised when her friend did not turn up but soon became absorbed in the lesson. After the intensity of the previous week, her dancing was noticeably improved and at the end of the class, Juan Carlos told her she was too good to stay with the beginners. Would she like to join the Intermediate Class?

'I would love to,' she replied. 'When is it?'

'Every Friday at eight,' he answered.

Excited and flattered as she was, she did realise that this could be the final straw for James. She swallowed hard and nodded.

'See you on Friday then,' said the dance teacher, smiling at her.

Sonia and James had not spoken for some days now. She was not naïve enough to expect an apology from him, especially as he still believed that the sender of the postcard was some kind of holiday romance, but she had desperately hoped for a thaw in the atmosphere. His attitude of stubborn self-righteousness and refusal to see any other position than his own was nothing new, but in the past she would always have made a movement towards rapprochement. She knew that marriage was about compromise but she was angry to be disbelieved and this anger in her gave her a new strength to contemplate, for the first time, the possibility of being without this man who had dominated her for the past seven years.

She knew that going to dance classes on Friday nights would do little towards appeasement. Friday was the focal point of their social life, when James would not be rising at the crack of dawn the following morning and no one would yet have gone away for the weekend. It was the night when dinner parties took place, though at this moment it was hard to imagine that they could ever act out the charade of being a happily married couple, eating off other people's best china and chattering about the price of property in SW12.

The moment to approach James did not arise. She had been asleep for several hours when he eventually came home.

Sonia rang Maggie the next day.

'Why weren't you at the class last night?' she demanded.

'I'll tell you later if you meet me for a drink,' she replied enigmatically. 'The Grapes at eight thirty?'

Maggie had only one thing she wanted to talk about that evening and Sonia guessed what it was going to be the moment she came through the door that evening. She radiated contentment. The last time she had seen her friend, her eyes had been swollen with tears. Tonight they shone with excitement.

'So, what's happened?' Sonia asked expectantly.

She had already bought a bottle of wine and now poured a glass for Maggie, who picked it up and clinked it against Sonia's.

'Well . . . Paco rang on Saturday. Apparently his car broke down that night and he couldn't get to the club . . . And he couldn't get a signal on his mobile. He was genuinely, really, really sorry.'

'That's good. So he should have been, given how upset you were.'

'But there's more than that. He wants me to go out there again – to stay with him this time.'

Sonia hesitated. Though she knew that good sense never played much of a part in Maggie's decision-making, she felt it was occasionally her role to suggest it, to voice caution.

'Do you really think that's such a good idea?'

Maggie looked slightly quizzically at her friend. 'I can't really think of a good reason why I shouldn't go,' she said. 'In fact I'm thinking of giving everything up and going out there to live. It's been on my mind for ages.'

'But what about Candy?'

'Candy wants to move into a flat with some friends from art school, so she won't miss me too much.'

'And your work?'

'It's all freelance. I could give it up tomorrow. And Spain is fantastically cheap to live in. I've got a bit saved up.'

'It all seems a bit speedy to me.'

'Yes, but let's face it, Sonia, what do I have to lose?'

Maggie was right. The boundaries of her life were fluid. Though Sonia might have been anchored down to the last detail, Maggie was tied by very little. Her daughter was already independent and she had no financial commitments.

'Even if things don't work out with Paco,' she said, swirling the wine round in her glass, 'at least I'll be in a country that I love.'

As far as Sonia was concerned, there were only two reasons for telling Maggie not to go: first, that she would miss her friend and second, that she doubted the sincerity of the Spaniard.

She voiced neither. At the end of the evening, it became clear that Maggie already had her flight booked, confirming what Sonia had half suspected, that her opinion was not being sought at all.

Maggie was so full of her own exciting plans that Sonia only got round to telling her about her problems with James at the end of the evening.

'So you fell out pretty much as soon as you came home? Because of some markings in a novel? And then he decided you'd been having an affair with some waiter?'

'That's about the sum of it,' admitted Sonia sheepishly.

'But it's so ridiculous. He really is an idiot, if you don't mind me saying so.'

'No, I don't mind. It's not as though you haven't always thought that,' laughed Sonia.

'So what are you going to do about the Friday dance class?' asked Maggie, as though this was the main concern.

'I'm dreading telling him. But I *have* to go. I can't just stop dancing, can I?'

'No, you can't. I shall ring you next week and I'll expect to hear that you have made the right decision.'

They drained the bottle of wine and finished the mean little bowl of olives that they had ordered to remind themselves of being in Spain.

On the pavement they hugged each other.

'Take care, Maggie,' said Sonia. 'You will keep in touch, won't you?'

'Of course I will. You'll be coming out to see me. If you don't visit, I'll come and drag you over there.'

Ten days later, the various threads of her life all tied up as neatly as they ever could be, Maggie left to pursue her infatuation.

Chapter Ten

SONIA COUNTED UP the weeks since she had visited her father. Nearly two months had passed since she had last seen Jack and a wave of the unshared guilt of the only child passed through her.

She wished he lived closer, but Jack had always assured her that he was perfectly happy and that he would not want to leave the familiar territory of the area where he had been born and lived for his adult life. Occasionally she wondered what would happen if he ever became infirm, and tried to picture him moving in with her and James. Somehow it was an image impossible to conjure up. As she left the leafy Wandsworth streets behind her, and drove through Balham, Tooting and Norwood, she told herself that she must not worry her father by letting slip her problems with James.

Croydon. If ever there was a place more antithetical to Granada, it was this grey suburb. Its lack of romance, magic and beauty must be unparalleled in the Western world, thought Sonia to herself. It hurt the very soul to drive down its grey streets. She wondered if the architects of the nineteen sixties ever came back to view the way their work had aged. Had they ever imagined the pale concrete streaked with jagged stains and the huge panes of dark, smoked glass opaque with dust? Why on earth would those who designed it ever return? It was, however, the place that her father loved, and even though he had seen it change beyond recognition, he saw only the ghost of how it once had been. It was where his heart was.

The ritual was the same as ever. That Saturday afternoon in his flat, Jack Haynes had set out some Nice biscuits on a plate decorated with now faded flowers.

'How is your dancing going?' he asked.

'It's going really well,' Sonia smiled. 'I'm so enjoying it.'

'That's good. I wish I could still do it,' he chuckled. 'I could have taught you some of our favourite steps. Though I expect you'd find them too old-fashioned now.'

'I'm sure I wouldn't,' responded Sonia kindly. 'Dance is dance, isn't it?'

'Well, I don't know about that. But anyway, I'm so pleased that you are still doing it.'

'I can't ever imagine giving it up.'

'And how was Spain?' he asked. 'I got your postcard. Did Maggie have a nice birthday?'

Sonia had rung her father just before she went, to tell him that she was going away with her old school friend.

'It was fabulous,' Sonia told him, sipping from the fine china cup. 'We took some dance lessons while we were there.'

'How lovely. And where did you stay?'

'Granada . . .'

Hardly had the word left her lips when she heard her father repeat it, softly under his breath.

'*Granada?* Your mother was born in Granada.'

'*Was* she?' exclaimed Sonia. 'I don't think I ever knew that. I *loved* it.'

After that came a barrage of questions from Jack. He wanted to know all about the city, what it looked like, what and where she had eaten, and whether she had visited any of the monuments. At the best of times, he was always interested in her life, but today he seemed hungry for information.

She described the networks of cobbled streets, the wonderful tree-filled squares, the grand boulevards and the way in which snow-capped mountains formed a backdrop of almost film-set unreality to the city. She enthused about the warm, red-hued Alhambra and the atmospheric Moorish quarter just below it, unchanged for centuries and still unspoiled by cars. He listened with rapt attention but, more than anything, he was eager to hear about the dancing.

She described the school, the teachers and the nightclub where they put it all into practice, and the kinds of dancing they had done.

'We did salsa, merengue and even a little flamenco,' she told him.

Jack poured himself some more tea. As usual, a goods train rumbled past and their cups rattled gently in their saucers.

'Granada is such a beautiful place. Why on earth did Mum leave?' asked Sonia.

Stirring in some sugar, Jack Haynes looked up at his daughter. 'It was something to do with the Civil War. Lots of people left about that time, I believe.'

'But didn't she ever want to go back?'

'I don't think so. Anyway, she met me,' he smiled, his old face creasing into as many wrinkles as his years.

'Of course she did,' responded Sonia. 'And I can't imagine you ever living in Spain.'

It was not easy to imagine her father in a foreign country. He was uncomfortable in the heat, disliked eating anything but plain food, and had no grasp of any language apart from his own.

'But didn't she have relatives to visit?'

'I don't believe there was any family left there.'

Her father sounded sufficiently vague for Sonia to realise that there was little point in asking too many questions, but they began to reminisce about Sonia's mother. Usually, Jack never dwelled on the subject of Mary for long. Though he had lived with her infirmity and nursed her for fifteen years, when death came it had been a shocking blow for him. Strangers who met him usually assumed that her mother had only recently died. It still seemed so raw. Today, though, she was emboldened to pursue the subject.

'I do have a vague memory of something from when I was about ten or eleven,' she mused.

'What was that?'

'That Mum was very disapproving when people started to go to Spain on holiday. And that when one of my friends from school came back and said how fantastic it was, she hit the roof.'

'Yes, I remember that too,' said Jack quietly.

'And one summer I asked if we could go there.'

Jack recalled it vividly. Though Mary Haynes was physically frail, her reaction to the suggestion had been violent. Occasionally she displayed traces of a fierce Mediterranean temper, and he could remember almost to the syllable the words she had used, each one spat out with venom.

'I would rather have my fingernails pulled out than set foot in that country . . . until that Fascist is dead and buried,' she had said.

At the time, Sonia had no comprehension of who her mother meant by 'that Fascist'. At first she wondered if she had simply been insensitive, asking for a trip to a faraway place when her parents could scarcely afford any kind of holiday at all. Later on, though, her father had explained the problem to her.

'Franco is still in charge,' he had told her when her mother was out of earshot. 'He brought about the Civil War that was the reason for your mother leaving Spain. She still hates him.'

It was 1974 and a year later Franco died. Even then Sonia's mother had shown no desire to return and never mentioned Spain again.

They drank more tea, and Sonia ate one of her father's sugary biscuits.

'It's so sad that she never saw Granada again,' reflected Sonia. 'Did she keep up her Spanish?'

'Not really, after a while. In the very beginning she couldn't speak a word of English but I remember the morning when she woke up and realised that she no longer dreamed in her native tongue. She wept.'

Jack Haynes did not want his daughter to dwell on the sadness of her mother's exile from her homeland. As far as possible, he wanted her to have a positive image of her mother and he pulled himself up sharply.

'Look,' he said, 'I have a few pictures of your mother from when she was in Granada.' He opened the heavy desk drawer and burrowed under some papers before finding a dog-eared envelope.

As he settled himself back into his armchair, a few pictures fell out onto his lap and he passed them to Sonia. There was one picture of Mary taken outside a church, perhaps at her first communion, but it was the second and third that arrested her. In one her mother was wearing traditional flamenco costume. The eyes were playful, teasing, flirtatious, but nearly half of her face was tantalisingly concealed behind a fan. If she had not known this was Mary Haynes, it would have been difficult to identify her. What was hard to imagine was that the woman in this picture could really be one and the same person as the frail woman of her memory. In this photograph she was raven-haired, majestic, unmistakably Andalucian.

Then Sonia looked at the next. For a moment she simply stared. Her mouth went dry. In this one Mary was totally unrecognisable as her mother, but she reminded Sonia of someone else. She bore a striking resemblance to the girl in the pictures in the bar. It was a notion that Sonia knew she should dismiss as absurd but one she could not entirely put out of her mind.

She could tell that these pictures were well thumbed and she always suspected that her father spent more time leafing through his past than he would ever have allowed her to know about. The last thing she wanted to do was to upset him with more unnecessary questions.

The woman behind the fan could have been any girl with characteristic Granadino features, she told herself sternly, but when her father went to the kitchen to refill the teapot, Sonia slipped a couple of photographs into her handbag. She stayed for one more cup of tea and then kissed her father goodbye.

The stalemate with James could not continue. Sooner or later they had to speak.

Sonia knew that it would be her job to instigate some kind of rapprochement, as James was even more stubborn than she. She left him a note on the kitchen table one night before she went to bed, suggesting they had supper together the following day, but the following morning when she came down to breakfast she saw that the note had not even been touched. She went up to their bedroom. Though James always neatly made the bed, she could tell he had not made it that morning. The laundered shirts that their cleaner had left in a pile on the middle of the bed the previous day had not been moved. James had not been home.

That evening, Sonia met him in the hallway. She said nothing about his absence the previous night.

'I think we should eat together tonight,' she said.

'OK. If you want.'

'I'll do some pasta,' she offered as James brushed past her into the bathroom.

They never got as far as eating the *tagliatelli putanesca*. Before Sonia had even finished preparing the sauce, James was draining the first bottle of wine. The touchpaper had already been ignited.

As she poured herself a glass from a second bottle, which was already uncorked and standing on the table, she could sense James's aggression.

'So, been dancing lately?' he slurred.

'Yes,' Sonia replied, trying to keep herself calm, neutral.

'You must be a bloody professional by now.'

She sat down, playing with the stem of her glass and took a deep breath. A glass of wine had emboldened her too.

'I'm starting lessons on Fridays now,' she said.

'Fridays . . . That's kind of the weekend, isn't it?'

In spite of herself, she began to trickle oil onto the flames. 'It's the day that they hold intermediate lessons. I'm not really a beginner now,' she continued.

'Yeah, but Fridays will be a pain in the arse. It'll bugger up Friday nights, Sonia.'

James's tone to her now was friendly but slightly mocking, and she found this strange mix mildly threatening.

James poured himself another glass and slammed the bottle down on the table.

'It's a fucking *nuisance*, Sonia!'

'You don't need to put it like that, James.'

'Well, tough! That's the way I see it,' he slurred. 'This dancing thing just doesn't fucking well fit with our life, Sonia.'

Our life, thought Sonia, turning this pair of words over in her head. *Our* life?

The words sounded alien to her. She couldn't identify with them any more than she could picture an existence without dance. There was a degree of menace in a six-foot drunk, even sitting at his own kitchen table in a pinstripe suit. He rocked back on his chair and glared at Sonia. Wine splashed onto his yellow silk tie and she watched the spreading stain. At all costs she wanted to avoid confrontation.

The pasta was cooked. Sonia switched off the gas and just as she lifted the pan she heard James roar, '*WELL?* Are you going to give it up or not?'

The volume of his voice almost made her drop the pan. Scalding water splashed across the floor and, realising that her hands were shaking violently, she put the pan down on the draining board.

'Look, I don't really feel like eating at the moment,' she said. 'I'm going to have an early night.'

She had genuinely lost her appetite and left the room, nauseous with fear and shocked by the realisation that she was married to someone who now instilled such terror in her.

It looked as if the new 'normality' of sleeping in separate rooms would continue. A knot tightened in her stomach. She had never imagined it would get to this.

The next afternoon an envelope icon appeared on her mobile phone. It was a text from Maggie asking her to come out to Spain for a few days. It took Sonia less than a second to write her three letter answer. There was nothing pressing in her diary and another trip to Granada would be a welcome escape. She could do with a few days to mull things over, and she would visit the old man at the bar. It was just the opportunity she had wanted.

Chapter Eleven

NEAT ROWS OF olive trees, strong vines and ripening vegetables chequer-boarded the fields. High in the mountains, snows had gently melted through the last few weeks of March and into April, supplying steady streams of moisture for germination, and now the rich soils were dense with crops. Sunshine, growing in intensity almost by the day, began to ripen strawberries and tomatoes from green to scarlet. Craggy mountains, rolling hills, smudges of white-washed pueblos dotted amongst them and great spreads of cultivation – through the murky aeroplane window, Sonia peered at this landscape, transformed since she last saw it by the early summer warmth.

The air-conditioned aircraft left her unprepared for the blast of heat that greeted her as its doors were opened. She blinked as she emerged into the late afternoon sunshine, gusts of warm air circling round her on the tarmac as though a giant hair dryer was targeting her with its hot blast. In that moment, she felt herself begin to thaw. The icy English weather of the past few months had chilled her to the core.

A taxi whisked Sonia into Granada's city centre, giving her a glimpse of the Alhambra as she passed. The driver was in a hurry, swerving between other cars in the rush-hour traffic, impatient to return to the airport for another flat-fare passenger.

'I can't take you there,' he had told her grumpily when she showed him the address. He had the manner of someone who thrived on the pleasure of being unhelpful. 'It's not possible.'

Maggie was living in the Albaicín, the old Arab quarter where the winding cobbled streets were barely wide enough for pedestrians, let alone cars, and the taxi driver peremptorily dropped Sonia off in the Plaza Nueva.

She stood in the square and looked about her. One side was lined with cafés, all of them now crowded with people, mostly tourists refreshing themselves with soft drinks and ice creams in a forest of colourful umbrellas advertising beer or Coke. Following Maggie's directions, she walked up to the church at the far end and climbed some broad stone steps to the side of it.

A group of dreadlocked travellers lay across her path, one strumming a guitar, another playing a flute, while a third tossed a ball for his mangy dog. Struggling with her heavy bag, Sonia knocked over one of their cans of beer, spilling its contents down the steps. The guitarist leaped up.

Before she had time to react, he wrested the bag from her hands and began to run. Her stomach somersaulted with panic. She started after him, only to find that, at the top of the steps, he stopped dead.

'Please . . .' he said, with a heavy accent. To her relief and surprise, he carefully set the bag down on the smooth stones.

'*Gracias*,' she said, covered with confusion, realising now that his intentions were entirely noble.

'*De nada*,' he said, his handsome, bearded face suffused with a smile.

Sonia noted that he could have been little more than eighteen. The bristles hid angelic, almost childlike features.

It was only another twenty metres to her destination and the wheels of her bag rattled noisily on the cobbles as she made her way along the Calle Santa Ana, hugging a slim strip of shade. She rang the doorbell to flat 8, at number 32. Beyond the ornate ironwork and the glass of the outer door she could see a hallway tiled from floor to ceiling with bright blue and white tiles. High above her she heard her name. She stepped away from the doorway and looked up.

Almost dazzled by the brightness of an azure sky, she saw a silhouette. It was Maggie, leaning precariously over a balcony.

'Sonia!' she called. 'Here! Catch!'

A bunch of keys landed noisily on the stones.

'It's the silver one! I'm on the fifth floor!'

Sonia let herself in and began to climb the stairs. There was no cherubic boy here.

By the time she reached the right floor, she was panting. Maggie stood in the doorway, smiling, exotic in a bright printed kaftan, eyes luminous in her tanned face.

'Sonia! It's lovely to see you,' she cried, taking her friend's suitcase. 'Come in.'

After the brightness of the tiled stairwell, the flat seemed dark. A low-voltage light bulb in the hallway gave out a dim glow and Sonia's eyes struggled to adjust to the gloom.

Maggie's sitting room was kitted out in Moorish style, with rugs and throws, Arabic lanterns and mobiles of coloured glass that jangled in a breeze that blew lightly through the apartment. Sonia was as charmed by it as by the view out of the huge floor-to-ceiling windows of the River Darro, which ran just below the building, carving a divide between the clustered buildings of Granada's oldest *barrio*.

'It's heavenly,' said Sonia. 'How on earth did you find a place like this?'

'Through a friend of a friend of this gorgeous man I met when I went into the estate agency to find somewhere to rent.'

'Gorgeous man?' enquired Sonia, immediately picking up on something in Maggie's tone of voice.

'Oh, yes, Carlos,' she replied, not quite blushing. 'He owns the estate agency.'

'But what about Paco?'

'I'm sure you can guess. He came to meet me at the airport when I arrived and we spent a couple of nights together. And then after that it was excuses, excuses, excuses. But really, in the end I didn't mind,' she said philosophically. 'I sort of owe it to him for making me come out here.'

'So it's OK, is it?' Sonia said cautiously.

'OK?' exclaimed Maggie breathlessly. 'It's so much more than OK. They really know how to live life here. It's quite exhausting, though, going to bed at three every night when you have to get up to work. But I love it. I absolutely love everything about it.'

'And what about this Carlos?' asked Sonia teasingly.

'Well, he seems quite keen. We've seen quite a lot of each other. And he likes dancing . . .' Maggie mentioned the latter as though it was the most important of all.

For several hours they lounged on low, bright cushions and drank mint tea. They had so much to tell each other, having spoken only once on the telephone since Maggie had moved to Granada. Sonia mentioned James's worsening drink habit and his resentment of her dancing, but she did not reveal how fragile things had become.

The sun had gone down by the time they went off into the city in search of tapas.

Later that evening, leaving Maggie to meet her new boyfriend, Sonia went to El Barril. She hoped to catch Miguel before he closed for the night. She smiled to herself as she thought of the conclusion James had jumped to when she had received that postcard all those weeks ago.

It was almost eleven thirty when Sonia turned up there, and she decided to go inside to find him. She could see on his face an immediate flash of recognition.

'Yes, yes!' he exclaimed. 'You are the beautiful English lady. You have come back!'

'Of course. And thank you for the postcard.'

'It reached you!'

'How did you know my name?' she said, holding out her hand for him to shake, which he did with great enthusiasm.

'I caught a glimpse of your signature when you were writing a postcard,' he admitted guiltily. 'It stuck in my mind.'

'Oh!' she said, rather surprised.

He seemed to have slowed down a little in the weeks since she had been there. She was warmed by his welcome and settled herself on to a stool at the bar. All the other customers had gone.

'Are you here to do more dancing?' he asked. 'You must want coffee – and a brandy?' Before Sonia had replied to either question, steam was gurgling noisily through a jug of milk and conversation was temporarily precluded.

While Miguel was busy, she got up and strolled as nonchalantly as she could towards the display of pictures on the wall. There they were, just as before, the proud bullfighter and, next to him, the dancer. Sonia went up close and stared into the girl's eyes. No, she could not be absolutely certain. The features were similar to those of the woman in the photo she had squirrelled away in her wallet but they did not appear identical. The dress in her own photo was reminiscent of those in the framed pictures, and yet not exactly the same.

Miguel came up behind her with her coffee and handed it to her.

'You like these pictures, don't you?' he said.

Sonia hesitated. 'Like' wasn't really adequate to describe the effect they had on her, but she couldn't tell Miguel the truth. It would sound so far-fetched.

'I'm fascinated by them,' she said. 'They're real period pieces.'

'They are certainly that,' agreed Miguel.

'Perhaps it's because they're in black and white,' she said hastily. 'It makes them seem from a distant era. They couldn't have been taken last week, could they?'

'No, that's right. They capture a particular time,' responded Miguel. 'A very specific moment in history.'

His statement seemed heavily loaded and Sonia sensed that the pictures meant as much to Miguel as they might to her. She could not help pursuing the conversation.

'So,' she said casually, concerned not to betray the depth of her interest, 'tell me how Granada has changed.'

She was sitting at the bar. She picked up a slender sachet of sugar from a glass dish and poured it into her coffee. Miguel was polishing glasses and lining them up neatly.

'I took the bar over in the nineteen fifties,' he began. 'It was quite run down then, but in the late twenties and early thirties it had been a great focal point. Everyone from workmen to university professors came here. People didn't invite each other into their homes; they met in bars and cafés instead. There weren't many tourists to speak of in those days, just the occasional intrepid Englishman, perhaps, who had heard stories of the Alhambra.'

'You make it sound like a golden age,' commented Sonia.

'It was,' he said, 'throughout the whole country.'

Sonia then noticed a picture at the end of the wall. 'They look like the Ku Klux Klan,' she exclaimed. 'They're really sinister!'

The image showed a group of several dozen figures clad in white robes, with small round eyeholes cut out of their pointed, witch-like headdresses. They were processing down a street, some of them engaged in the labour of carrying a cross.

'That's a typical Holy Week procession,' said Miguel, folding his arms.

'It's very dramatic,' said Sonia.

'That's right. It's just like theatre. Today you're spoiled for entertainment, but we didn't have very much in those days and we loved it. I still do. Every day in the week before Easter these huge icons of the Virgin or Christ are carried around the town. Have you ever been in Spain for that week?'

'No, I haven't,' replied Sonia.

'It's in a few weeks' time. It's an unforgettable experience, if you haven't seen the *pasos* before. You should stay.'

'That's a lovely thought,' said Sonia, 'but I'll have to come back for Easter another year.'

'The icons are huge and it takes over a dozen men hidden underneath to carry each one through the streets. They're accompanied by the brotherhood from their church and a band.'

Sonia peered at the photograph. '*Semana Santa 1931*,' she read aloud. 'Was that a special year?'

The old man paused.

'Yes. The King abdicated just after Easter of that year and the country got rid of its dictatorship. The Second Republic was declared.'

'That sounds like a major event,' said Sonia, now more ashamed than ever of her ignorance of Spain's history. 'Was it violent?'

'No,' said Miguel. 'It was bloodless. There had been plenty

of unrest beforehand, but for most people this marked a new beginning. There had been eight years of dictatorship under Miguel Primo de Rivera, and throughout that time we had retained the monarchy. It was the worst of all worlds. As far as most people were concerned, the dictatorship had done nothing to benefit ordinary people. All I can really remember is my parents moaning about some of the laws they passed, like banning crowds and making cafés close early.'

'I can imagine that was unpopular!' interjected Sonia. It was hard to imagine Spain without its bars and cafés being open all hours.

'And anyway,' continued Miguel, 'the dictatorship had done nothing to help the poor, so when King Alfonso XIII abdicated and the Republic began, millions of people knew life would improve. There were big celebrations that day and the bars and cafés were overflowing with people.'

The excitement in Miguel's voice could not have been greater if these events had happened only the day before. The memory of them was vivid.

It was almost poetic, Sonia thought, the way he talked about it.

'It was a magical moment,' Miguel said. 'Everything seemed full of promise. Even at the age of sixteen I sensed that. We were breathing the fresh air of democracy and from then on there would be many more people who would have a say in how the country should be governed. The power of the landlords who had subjected millions of peasants to a life of poverty was reduced at long last.'

'I can't believe those things were still going on in the nineteen thirties!' exclaimed Sonia. 'It sounds so primitive – peasants . . . landlords!'

'That's a good word for it,' said Miguel. 'Primitive.'

He had poured two generous brandies, explaining he always had one at the end of each day and was happy to have company.

'There's one thing I remember very vividly. Everyone seemed to be smiling. They were so happy.'

'Why would that have stuck in your mind?'

'I think some people had gone through a time of great hardship and anxiety. As children we probably just accepted the way things were, but I think our parents' lives had been tough.'

Miguel glanced at the clock and registered some surprise. 'I'm so sorry,' he said apologetically. 'I hadn't realised the time. I really should be closing up.'

Sonia felt panic rising inside her. Perhaps she had missed the moment to ask him more questions about the pictures on the wall and might never be given another opportunity to solve her nagging doubt about the photograph tucked away in her bag. She said the first thing that came into her head, anything to detain the old man for a little longer.

'But you still haven't really explained what happened,' she said quickly. 'Why did you end up taking over the café?'

'The shortest answer I can give you is this: the Civil War.' He held his glass to his lips but, before taking another sip, lowered it again and his eyes met her expectant gaze. 'But if you like, I'll give you a longer version.'

Sonia beamed at him. 'Would you?' she said. 'Do you have time?'

'I'll make time,' he said, nodding in affirmation.

'Thanks. I'd love you to tell me more. And will you tell me more about the Ramírez family?' she asked.

'If you like. Most people just aren't interested in the old days. But I'll tell you what I can. My memory is better than most.'

'And will you tell me about the dancer and the bullfighter?' she asked, trying to conceal her enthusiasm.

'I could even take you round the city if you'd like. I do sometimes close on Wednesdays at this time of year. I need the occasional day off at my age,' he chuckled.

'It's really kind of you,' said Sonia, now slightly hesitant. 'But are you sure?'

'Of course. I wouldn't have offered if I didn't mean it. Why don't you meet me, *mañana* . . . ? Tomorrow at ten. Outside here.'

It was an enchanting prospect, to be shown the city by someone who knew it so well. She knew that Maggie had no interest in Granada's history or culture, even if she now had encyclopaedic knowledge of its tapas bars.

Sonia said good night to Miguel and went back to Maggie's flat. She needed a good night's sleep.

Sonia was there to meet Miguel at precisely ten o'clock the next morning. It was strange to see him out of context and without his apron. Today he was dressed in a smart olive-green jacket and highly polished leather shoes. She looked at him slightly differently and realised for the first time that he must once have been extremely handsome.

'*Buenos días*,' he said, kissing her on both cheeks. 'Let's go somewhere for a coffee before I take you on a tour. I have a favourite place.'

A few minutes' walk away was a small square, dominated by the statue of a woman.

'It's Mariana Piñeda,' explained Miguel. 'I'll tell you about her later, if you are interested. She was a feminist heroine.'

Sonia nodded.

The café where Miguel took her was much bigger than his own and more crowded but he was warmly welcomed by the rival patron and teased for being with a '*señora guapa*'. Most of the other tables were occupied by dapper elderly men chatting with each other while several businessmen stood at the bar, all of them perusing copies of *El País*. Strong cigarettes smouldered in a row of ashtrays. The bar staff worked earnestly and swiftly, preparing *tostadas* with olive oil, tomatoes or jam, or noisily drying cutlery. Fresh *churros* gleamed beneath a glass dome.

Two well-dressed women, mid-fifties, chestnut hair stiffly coiffed, were getting up to leave as Miguel and Sonia arrived and they slipped quickly into their seats. It was a busy café and space was at a premium. While clearing away two brandy glasses, their rims red with lipstick, the waiter took Miguel's order and within moments they were served; his speed and efficiency were as pleasing as a dance.

'Where shall I begin?' asked Miguel rhetorically.

Sonia leaned forward expectantly. She knew he was not waiting for an answer.

'I think I'll tell you a little more about the time just before the Civil War,' he said. 'There was the half-decade I mentioned between the end of the Dictatorship in 1931 and the beginning of the Civil War in 1936. It was known as the Second Republic and there was relative content for the Ramírez family during those years. Yes, I think that would be a good place to start.'

Part 2

Chapter Twelve

Granada, 1931

Monumental fountains played in Granada's squares and elegant nineteenth-century buildings dominated the centre of the city. Their tall windows and graceful wrought-iron balconies contrasted with the ramshackle irregularity of the older Arab quarter, whose red-roofed buildings, with their confusion of triangular and trapezoid tiles, nestled into a tight space at the foot of the hill. The entire city was dominated by the Alhambra, its majestic towers watching over the city from the top of the hill.

Many of the roads were rough and stony, and, in spring, rain turned them into rivers of mud. Beasts of burden were used to carry goods around the city and live animals were herded through the streets. In winter, there was always a whiff of dung in the air and on a hot day in summer, the whole city reeked. The River Genil would sometimes burst its banks when the snows on the mountains high above Granada began to melt, but by August might almost have dried up. Its bridges were meeting places for friends and lovers throughout the year.

The Ramírez family lived above El Barril. It had been in the family for three generations and Pablo Ramírez had been born in the same bedroom where his wife had given birth to their children. Pablo had married his wife, Concha, when she was eighteen and their first child, Antonio, was born a year later. By the time she was twenty-six, they had four children, and the once curvaceous Concha was lean with hard work and worry. Her beautiful face was still rounded but she looked more than her age. Pablo, who was several years older than his wife, was small and dark, a typical Granadino.

Though they rarely had a moment of relaxation, it was a secure existence and a comforting sense of continuity more than made up for their limited income. Always there was someone coming or going through the bar and into the apartment above it, and though Pablo and Concha were usually busy, the family still managed to eat together every day at three. It was a ritual that they both insisted on, and all the children made sure they were there. When they were younger, they had all felt their father's slipper for being late. Love and respect for their parents was the one thing they all had in common.

El Barril sat at a meeting point between Granada's various different cultures. Living on the edge of the Albaicín, the children were equally at ease in the atmosphere of the Arab quarter, where the air rang with the rhythms of blacksmiths beating on metal, as in the Sacromonte, where the gypsies lived in their homes hollowed out of the hillside. And the plaintive wail of *gitano* song was as much a part of everyday life as the deep tones of the cathedral bells and the calls of stallholders in the flower market. From the rooms on the top floor they could see the green meadows outside the boundary of the city, and the Sierra Nevada beyond.

Like all Granadino children, Antonio, Ignacio, Emilio and Mercedes Ramírez had grown up playing in the streets and socialising in the squares. They mostly stayed quite close to the Plaza Nueva where their parents' café was situated and, when they were small, amused themselves with games of pitch and toss, and paddled in the River Darro beneath the Albaicín. The latter was an area where many of their friends lived, and though it was one of the poorer *barrios*, its poverty did not prevent it from being one of the most cheerful and lively.

Brothers, sisters, parents and classmates were the population of their world. They were friends with whole groups of siblings, so if Concha Ramírez was curious about where one of her children might be, the information was never hard to find.

'Oh,' she would be told, 'Emilio is playing with Alejandro Martínez – his brother just told me.' Or, 'Paquita's mother told me to tell you that Mercedes is going to the fiesta with them tonight.'

In that way, the city seemed a very small place. They were free to wander about and there was more danger from being trodden on by an irritable mule carrying firewood in from the countryside than being knocked down by one of the few cars that drove about in the city. In daylight hours, Pablo and Concha Ramírez never gave a second thought to their children's whereabouts. It was a city without danger, somewhere impossible to get lost in, and the influence of the outside world remained firmly at bay. They had very little experience of anywhere but this city. Once, a long time back, there had been a visit to the seaside, but it was never repeated. The only journey they made on a regular basis was to a village up in the mountains north of Granada where Concha's sister, Rosita, lived.

In 1931, when the Second Republic began, Antonio was twenty, Ignacio eighteen, Emilio fifteen and Mercedes twelve. Pablo and Concha Ramírez loved them all equally and unreservedly.

Antonio, the eldest, was broader than his father, and like everyone in his family he was dark. Behind his spectacles glittered earnest chestnut eyes. He had been a serious child and the fully grown young man was no different from the boy. Listening to adult conversation had always been his favourite pastime, and growing up in a café had exposed him to plenty. Pablo and Concha were always nagging him to play with his peers, but he lost interest in childish games at an early age. He did, however, have two very close friends, both known to him since early childhood.

One of them was Francisco Pérez, whose family lived on the corner of Calle Elvira and Plaza Nueva. In this confined world of theirs, the Ramírez and Pérez families were as close as blood relatives. Luis and María Pérez lived above their locksmith business, which had been set up many generations before, with their two sons, Julio and Francisco. When he was not behind the counter in his shop, Luis was always in El Barril, and in more than four decades of friendship he and Pablo had never run short of conversation.

The second of Antonio's close friends was Salvador. 'El Mudo' they called him, unabashed by the bluntness of the nickname. The mute boy. Over the years, Salvador's good friends had become fluent in sign language and the three of them would sit for hours engaged in discussion. Naturally Salvador, who had been both deaf and dumb since birth, was the most eloquent and graceful of them all in the way he communicated: crocheting the air with his hands, making patterns that built into expressions of humour, joy, anger and concern. Some of the time, his feelings would be greatly exaggerated, and at other times a subtle shrug or movement of his fingers would be all that was required.

When the Second Republic was declared, one of the new government's priorities was to make sure that everyone had the opportunity to learn to read and they launched a campaign to stamp out illiteracy. Antonio had just qualified as a teacher, which had always been his ambition, so the aim of the Second Republic to provide education for all met with his approval. He relished being part of something bigger than just the day-to-day work in a classroom. He saw that illiteracy made slaves of people and that every '*analfabeto*' taught to read was one less person to be an underpaid servant to the capitalists. He knew that education was a powerful liberating force.

After 1931, Señora Ramírez tried to persuade him not to go to political meetings. She regarded them as more dangerous than bullfights. It was ironic really, but she was not entirely wrong. At least in a bullfight, the struggle is occasionally balanced and the fighter and the animal have an equal chance. In politics this was not always the case.

Ignacio was the most colourful of them all. Although he was the most conceited person imaginable, he was also exciting company to be in. With ebony hair and eyes, he had a bewitching effect on people, particularly women. They could not leave him alone and that often made his life complicated. He only had to look in their direction and they were smitten. It was often like that for many men in this macho world of the *torero* – they were put on the same pedestal as movie stars.

The bullfighting obsession had begun very early. From the age of three, a café tablecloth had doubled as a cape while Ignacio practised his turns, his *verónicas*. Before he could even form sentences he knew what he wanted to do when he grew up.

Ignacio often performed his miniature *corrida* in front of a willing audience in the café, where drinkers would cheer and gasp as he killed his imaginary bull. When cajoled, both friends and brothers would take the bull's part for him. It was done with reluctance, given they knew it would probably mean feeling the bruising thrust of his wooden sword between their shoulder blades. For Ignacio, there was no acknowledgement of the boundary between fantasy and violence.

'*La hora de la verdad!*' he would cry in triumph, a bloodthirsty grin on his face. He was emulating 'the moment of truth', when the matador is poised to plunge the blade into the bull. With the charging animal now close, he had no time for hesitation and he knew, even as a child, that the cleaner the kill, the safer the man and the more impressed the spectators. As he held the toy sword aloft, it was as though he heard the crowd's collective intake of breath and the uncanny hush of a vast mass of humanity held in pure suspense. Who knows how many times he performed this dress rehearsal for what would become reality so many years later? When he was five, his grandmother had made him a little costume for his birthday and he wore it until all the seams frayed and finally split.

At the age of fifteen, Ignacio had left school. He had kicked his heels and just about everything else since he was born, and his parents found him hard to control. The classically perfect measurements between oval eyes, strong nose and a mouth such as only a painter would devise, made him seem untouchably divine. His behaviour was far from godlike, though. It was not even human some of the time. As a child he often acted like an animal and indeed he had the strength of an ox, making him a good match for the bull when he eventually went into the ring to fulfil his inescapable destiny.

Sturdy but slim-hipped, he could not have had a more perfect form for the bullfighter's costume: the jewelled jacket known as a *traje de luces*, and the leg-skimming hose that clung to buttocks, thighs and calves. He had earned the title 'El

Arrogante' by the time he was nine and it would follow him into adulthood and around the *corridas* of Spain. He had spent the past three years almost continuously shadowing one of Granada's matadors, watching him fight and observing him rehearse his turns with an imaginary bull, just as he had done himself as a child.

If he had ever had a nickname, Emilio's might have been 'El Callado', the silent one. He could not have been more different from his swaggering, self-aggrandising older brother, Ignacio, but occasionally when he did break his long silences, there was no mistaking the strength of his passions. His horizons were the nearby meadows of Granada's Vega in one direction and the Sacromonte in another, and he felt no need to know what was happening beyond them. His world was contained within the smooth and shapely body of his prized possession: a honey-coloured flamenco guitar.

Emilio was taller than his brothers. He was also the palest and the frailest. Like a tree reaching upwards to find the light, Emilio outgrew the other men in his family in height if not in width or weight.

Unlike Ignacio, who had been constantly out in the street, playing football and occasionally disappearing until very late at night with his friends, Emilio was usually in the attic room of the apartment. There he would sit for hours at a time, his back grazing the roof tiles, doubled like a hunchback over his guitar, his strong fingers picking out the notes of some forlorn tune. There was no question of him needing the light to read the notes on a printed page. The music was entirely in his head and in the gloom of that attic room, he would shut his eyes tight to block out any remaining chinks of light.

If anyone was drawn by his playing to the top of the narrow staircase, he rarely noticed their presence. He would carry on plucking his strings, enveloped by the enchanting waves of sound, locked inside his own rapturous music-making. He needed no one. Anyone who did eavesdrop would soon slope away, feeling guilty that they had intruded on his private world.

Emilio was not ambitious like Antonio and Ignacio, which was just as well really, as his parents were eventually going to need someone to work in the bar and he had anticipated doing that job since he had been able to see over it. He wanted nothing more than to stay in Granada. The guitar was his real passion. He had been taught by one of the customers in the bar, an old gypsy type called José, and though the old man died before Emilio was even twelve, the boy had already learned the basic techniques of flamenco. He worked on those until he was nearly as good as the stars of the Sacromonte.

He was already playing for his sister quite a bit when her parents allowed her to perform. Indeed, the only person Emilio acknowledged when they climbed the laddered stairway was his little sister. Mercedes could not keep away from the sound of her brother's playing and he tolerated the girl's interest in a way he would not have done with anyone else.

Like many little girls, Mercedes could dance flamenco from the age of five. Before this, it was discouraged as a child's bones were considered too soft to cope with the heavy pounding. So at a very early age, she would steal up to the attic and in the claustrophobic darkness beneath the sloping roof, she would find the rhythm with her palms, at first sitting down on the floor by Emilio's feet. Later she would rise to her feet and begin to stamp and twirl and by now Emilio might even open his eyes to show her that he did not mind her being there. These were their private fiestas.

It was common to see little girls, knee-high to their fathers, performing in private homes at local *juergas* and their precocious brilliance was a spectacle that quickly drew an audience. Even if her mother worried about those soft bones, Mercedes was not a child to be told what to do. In that tiny space she learned to snap her fingers, twist her body and click the castanets. There was no one teaching her, she simply emulated the *señoritas* that she had seen, picking up their haughty demeanour, watching their steps and absorbing the sound and the fury of their movements. It seemed to come completely naturally to her, even if she was not of gypsy blood.

Concha was always surprised that Emilio did not find Mercedes' presence an irritation and then, one night when she stood at the bottom of the stairs listening, she realised why. Mercedes added to his music. The beat of her heels on the wooden flooring and the clapping together of palms gave it percussion.

People in the street below sometimes heard the quick pattering of her feet and they would look up to see if they could detect the source of the sound. It was as fast and as smooth as the sound of someone rolling their Rs, as rapid as the vibration of a tongue against the roof of the mouth.

At the age of twelve, there was a strength and sturdiness about Mercedes that within a few years would bloom into voluptuousness. She had the same heart-shaped face as her mother, with dimples in her cheeks and chin, and the furrow on her brow was beginning to deepen. The glossy waves of black hair that flowed down her back were long enough for her to sit on.

She had a best friend, Paquita Maneiro, who lived in the Albaicín. The pair of them were often to be found sitting in a courtyard watching Señora Maneiro spinning and weaving. The woman's fingers did not stop from morning until night, and even then she seemed able to see in the dark, working on her rugs in the flickering candlelight. It looked a hard way to make a living, but it had been a conscious choice. Her husband had died five years earlier and she could easily have taken to the streets to earn her living. It would have been a quicker way to make a few pesetas than the back-breaking work she now did. While she wove, the two girls would dance in front of her, their steel toecaps catching the edges of the rounded cobbles. Like Mercedes, Paquita loved flamenco but she struggled to dance with the same fluency.

As the only girl in the family, Mercedes was doted on by her brothers to the point of being spoiled. She always seemed to get what she wanted and none of them liked to provoke her bad temper, which could be easily stirred. The haughty expression of the flamenco dancer came naturally to her.

The Ramírez family lived a relatively contented existence, even if peace did not always reign domestically. Their children were very individual and this was something their parents celebrated, but on the days when doors slammed and arguments raged it was something they bemoaned. Ignacio was usually at the centre of the troublemaking and did not seem to be happy unless he was arousing one of his brothers' anger. He loved to provoke his generally patient older brother, Antonio, and to wrestle with him to prove his own superior strength, and there was nothing that entertained him more than to goad the retiring Emilio to a fight. Ignacio never fought in any way with Mercedes. He teased and danced and flirted with her. Only she could diffuse the poisonous atmosphere that sometimes existed between her brothers.

Though their lives had been happy and contented even during the nineteen twenties, the Ramírez family celebrated when the Second Republic arrived. It was like a sweet springtime breeze for Spain. Someone had found the key, unlatched the door and thrown open the windows. Fresh air coursed through, lifting the dust and blowing the cobwebs away. Though most in the city had been well enough fed, many people in the countryside around it had been living hand to mouth. Landowners had kept their labourers on the breadline, feeding them just about enough to ensure that they were capable of working the land for them. Some of the customers at El Barril came in from outside and told stories of the hardship that people were enduring in rural areas. Concha's own sister had relatives who had been subjected to this harsh regime.

Concha was thrilled by the new liberty that the Second Republic was bringing, especially to women. Though Pablo would never have used it to suppress her, the repeal of the *código civil*, the civil code that gave men precedence over their wives, was of huge significance. There were many women, less fortunate than Concha, who were treated like chattels.

'Listen to this, Merche!' Concha said with excitement. Though her daughter was only twelve she could see how much impact some of the changes being made could have on her future. She was reading out of the newspaper. 'This is what it used to say:

> "The husband owes protection to the woman and the wife obedience to her husband . . . The husband is the representative of the wife. She cannot, without his permission, appear in court."'

Mercedes looked rather blankly at her mother. With such devoted parents as hers, it was unsurprising that the child failed to see the implications. The old law effectively precluded women from divorcing their husband.

'And this is what it says now,' Concha continued, excitedly.

> '"The family is in the safekeeping of the state. Marriage is based on equal rights for both sexes and can be dissolved by mutual agreement or by demand of either party."'

This was not legislation that directly affected the Ramírez family, but a new equality in marriage was emblematic of the kind of changes taking place under the Republic. Now there was education for all and culture of all kinds flourished, with élitism looking as though it might be a thing of the past.

As well as the excitement of these political developments, the other huge event for the Ramírez family in 1931 was Ignacio's first venture into the bullring. He was one of the banderilleros, the team of men who, with the use of their capes and sharp blades, goad and wound the bull before the matador arrives to make the final kill.

After all his years of childish play and fantasy, it was time for Ignacio to feel the heat of the bull's breath.

Bullfighting was popular in Granada and for a while there were even two bullrings in the city, the old and new, both of them in use. The Ramírez family had all been to the Plaza de Toros many times, but to see one of their own emerging into the ring would be a historic event for them. They were all there to witness the moment, except Emilio, who was disgusted by the whole idea of an innocent animal being murdered in front of a cheering crowd. For Mercedes it was the first time she had been permitted to go. She could hardly contain her excitement.

It was a hot June day, the kind that gives everyone a glimpse of what the summer will hold, teasing everyone with an early blast of the intense heat that will be the average in July and August. The atmosphere was one of excitement, of fiesta.

'Why do you keep fanning yourself?' asked Mercedes. 'We're in the shade.'

For the first time since they could remember, the family were in the better seats, out of the glare of the sun.

'I didn't realise I was,' said her mother, flicking her fan back and forth. 'I just wish they would start.' Clearly she was agitated.

There was a trumpet fanfare and the crowd fell silent for a moment. Then began the parade. From the gateway marched the three matadors and their teams of mounted lancers – the picadors – banderilleros and a *mozo de espada*, the sword bearer.

'Is that really our son?' whispered Concha into her husband's ear. Tears pricked her eyes.

A group of uniformly movie-star handsome young men paraded around the ring, dazzling the audience in the late afternoon sunshine with the sparkle of metallic embroidery that embellished their costumes. The shameless femininity of their rhinestone-encrusted, candy-coloured outfits in mauve, pink, pistachio green and ochre yellow made them appeal more than ever to the adoring crowds of women. For this day of days, Ignacio had picked a vibrant turquoise that made him stand out from the crowd and, with the skin-tight knickerbockers, the unashamedly vivid outfit only accentuated his glorious masculinity.

Their hats deferentially held in the right hand and their heavy pink capes supported in their left, they bowed low in front of the dignitaries in the presiding box. Already they enjoyed the adulation of the crowd. The matador who was at the top of the bill that day acknowledged the cheers of his fans with a grand sweep of his arm and then the entire troop processed out again. Ignacio's matador was the second on the bill.

The first kill was a dull affair. The bull was slow and presented little challenge to anyone in the *cuadrilla*. As his corpse was dragged around the ring by the team of horses, there was little reaction, just a desultory ripple of applause.

Moments later there was another trumpet blast. The gates swung open and a bull thundered in. He was a massive animal. Deep, chocolate brown with a thick neck and wide shoulders, his curved horns appeared needle sharp.

'What a beauty,' breathed Pablo Ramírez.

'He's huge!' exclaimed Mercedes with excitement.

Usually the best of the six bulls to be killed that day was kept until last. It was hard to imagine that any would be finer than this.

For the initial stage, the second of the matadors and his banderilleros, which included Ignacio, toyed with the bull, testing his grit with their capes, confusing him, twisting him this way and that to start the process of trying to tire him out. At this stage, bull and man seemed on equal terms. The bull was not yet maddened, but as they continued to play with him the animal began to sense their contempt and his anger grew. He could lower his head and charge faster than a man can run. For one moment at least, he was king of the ring.

Unlike most, this bull could almost pivot, and seemed agile, given his weight. The matador had to work out how best to challenge him, noting if he charged by instinct to left or right. Once he had done this, they all withdrew from the ring. Concha breathed a sigh of relief. Ignacio was still alive. She gripped Mercedes' hand and the girl felt the clammy chill of her mother's anxiety.

Next, the picador entered the ring, his horse weighed down with padding, its eyes blinkered. Within seconds, the man's job was done. His lance had been plunged deep down into the muscle that stood erect on the bull's neck. Blood oozed until the crimson had spread across his back like a blanket.

The bull was to have his revenge, though. His head bowed low, he barged into the horse and lifted it up with his horns, goring the unprotected part of its stomach. He tossed it aloft as if it weighed less than air and the picador struggled to keep his balance as his mount tumbled beneath him. Its vocal cords severed, the wounded creature was unable to make a sound.

'The poor horse!' squealed Mercedes, horrified. 'Will he die?'

'I think he probably will, darling,' replied her mother. This was no place for anything other than realism.

The Ramírez family watched as Ignacio re-entered the ring with the other banderilleros to lure the bull away from the dying horse and the stranded picador. It seemed to Concha the most dangerous and unprotected role on the stage, and the eyes of twenty thousand spectators would be on her son as the banderilleros stood with just a length of pink cloth and no other weapon to defend themselves against six hundred kilograms of confused and angry beast.

As the first of the banderilleros in this group, Ignacio left his cape and now had his longed-for opportunity with his knives. He wanted to show the crowd that he could provide more excitement than the matador himself and was determined to bring them right to the edge of their seats. His aim was to be the one whose name was celebrated in the bars that night.

Legs straight, arms stretched up with the two blades held aloft, he stood his ground against the bull, which charged at him from one side of the ring to the other. At the moment when the horns seemed only a hand's width from his chest, he sprang into the air to get the trajectory he desired for his daggers. In one seamless movement he plunged the sharp points of the banderillas deftly into the neck muscle and jumped from the bull's path. The knives had dug deep into the shoulder muscles and their tasselled ends waved in the air. Ignacio had aimed close to the wound already inflicted by the picador, and blood now seeped out to form a shiny saddle of red.

Ignacio's split-second timing could have been construed as simple folly, but the crowd were excited now. They gasped and cheered in one breath. This was exactly the sort of entertainment they wanted: a strong sense of risk and the chance to see human blood.

Ignacio had fulfilled his ambition. He had thrilled the crowd and won their adulation by making them marvel at his bravery and gasp at how close to the edge he had come.

No one who saw Ignacio would ever doubt the link between this sport and the bull-leaping of ancient Crete. For the briefest moment this lithe banderillero appeared to take off. Another few centimetres and he might have jumped right over the charging animal. It was pure acrobatics. At this point, he stood without cape, without sword, without dagger, and there was nothing between him and the bull, which now turned round to look at his assailant.

'I can't even look,' said Concha, burying her head in her hands, convinced of her son's imminent death.

Antonio gently took his mother's arm and held it. 'He'll be fine, Mother.'

Antonio was right. Ignacio could walk across the ring in front of the bull now and come to no harm. The bull's energy was flagging. The danger had passed. Within a moment he had retreated into the *callejón*, the passage that ran behind the ring's wooden barricade.

This bull was finished off by the matador but the important work had been done by the three banderilleros. Perhaps they had been over-efficient since the bull was virtually on his knees by the time the matador appeared with his red cape. The animal scarcely had the energy to follow the sweep of the scarlet *muleta* as the gold-clad figure of the matador executed his turns. The final moment when the sword pierced his heart thrilled no one.

The animal's finale was a farewell lap around the ring, dragged by the horse team. They used him like a brush to paint a perfect circle of crimson in the sand. It was his final humiliation.

Ignacio's second outing that afternoon was as impressive as the first. El Arrogante's career had been magnificently launched. The *aficionados* had noticed him.

For days after, the menus in the city's restaurants were dominated by stew made from *rabo de toro* – oxtail – and platters of braised cuts from these delicious beasts who had spent their innocent lives in rich pastures. The meat market in Granada was full of *toro* and everyone in the Ramírez family enjoyed it, with the exception of Emilio, who would not have it near his plate.

Concha realised then that watching her son in the ring was not going to get any easier, and that, however many times she did it, she would always have a premonition of her beautiful slim-hipped son being gored to death. She tortured herself with this. Occasionally Pablo attempted to reassure her with statistics on how few fighters were ever killed in the ring, but he could not allay her fears.

Chapter Thirteen

A FEW MONTHS after the arrival of the Republic, a certain amount of disillusion began to set in. Conversation in El Barril soon turned to the rumours that divisions on the left were beginning to develop and there were mutterings that the socialist-dominated Republican government were not bringing the swift end to poverty that they had promised. Even before the end of 1931 there were clashes between security forces and protesting workers who felt their interests were not being represented.

There were plenty who yearned for a return to rule by the wealthy and privileged, and many loathed the new liberalism, blaming it for a wave of permissive behaviour that they found hard to stomach. Over the next few years they opposed the Republic at every possible opportunity. The new government had swiftly made itself unpopular among conservatives by interfering with the Catholic Church, and restricting its religious processions and celebrations. This was seen as a severe threat to a traditional way of life. The power of the Church had also been weakened by the opening of new schools that were not religiously affiliated. The Church united with the landed and the wealthy in resenting the new regime, bemoaning the removal of their unchallenged power.

Even within the government itself divisions began to open up, a situation exploited by those who were keen to bring it down. At the beginning of 1933, as part of a wave of violence in the province of Cádiz, a group of anarchists besieged the Civil Guard post in the town of Casas Viejas and declared the arrival of libertarian communism. Inevitably, fighting broke out.

'But aren't these people meant to be on the same side?'

commented Concha. 'I don't understand it. If they start fighting each other, we might as well go back to a dictatorship!' She was looking over Antonio's shoulder at that day's newspaper headlines.

'That's the theory,' he responded. 'But I'm sure these workers don't feel as though the government is on their side. Most of them have been unemployed for a year.'

Antonio was right. These starving 'revolutionaries' had been living on the edge of desperation, eking out a living by begging, poaching and hoping for the occasional hand-out. The announcement of an increase in bread prices had finally spurred them to action.

Within days the news worsened. Civil Guard and Assault Guard reinforcements arrived from Cádiz to put down the insurrection. They surrounded the house of a six-fingered anarchist known as Seisdedos, and orders were eventually given for the building to be burned down. As well as those who died in the flames, other anarchists who had previously been arrested were shot in cold blood.

'That's brutal!' commented Ignacio, when he saw the report that a dozen men had died in this repression. 'What does the government think it's doing?'

Ignacio was not someone who naturally sided with peasants and revolutionaries, but for those like him who did not support the Republican-Socialist government that was in power, it was an opportunity to criticise the Prime Minister, Manuel Azaña. The incident had shocked the country, and the right wing saw a situation that could be exploited to its own advantage, quickly accusing the government of barbarism.

'I think the days of the coalition might be numbered,' Ignacio said in the innocent but knowing tone that he knew would annoy his older brother.

'We'll see, shall we?' responded Antonio, determined not to lose his temper.

The two brothers were often at loggerheads, and politics became a growing source of contention. In Antonio's view Ignacio had no firm political beliefs. He just liked trouble. Sometimes he was just not worth arguing with.

In elections held late in 1933, Antonio desperately hoped that the liberals would stay in power. To his dismay, a conservative government was elected and any reforms that the left had brought in were now threatened. Rumblings of anger erupted into explosions of discontent. Strikes and protests were staged. Both the socialists and Fascists had burgeoning youth movements and the highly politicised young men of Antonio's generation were in the vanguard, on both sides.

The situation worsened the following year and in October 1934, there was an abortive attempt by the left to stage a general strike. It failed but an armed rebellion in Asturias, the northern coal-mining area, continued for two weeks, with far-reaching consequences. Villages were bombed and coastal towns shelled.

The centre of the action was a long way from Granada, but the Ramírez family followed events closely.

'Listen to this,' said Antonio, his tone one of outrage as he read that day's newspaper. 'They've executed some of the ringleaders!'

'Why does that surprise you?' Ignacio responded. 'They can't have that sort of thing happening.'

Antonio decided not to react.

'Serves those leftists right for burning down churches!' Ignacio continued, determined to provoke his brother.

The Spanish foreign legionaries brought in to deal with the situation had not only executed some of the leaders, they had also killed innocent women and children. Large areas of the region's principal towns of Gijón and Oviedo were bombed and burned out.

'Mother, look at these pictures.'

'I know, I know, I've seen them. They say everything . . .'

The destruction of the buildings was not the last revenge. The people were now brutally repressed. Thirty thousand workers were imprisoned and torture was commonplace in the gaols. The socialist presses were silent.

The atmosphere in the country changed. Even in El Barril, where Pablo and Concha did what they could not to seem biased towards any political party, they could feel distrust between people beginning to set in. Some of their customers openly supported the socialists, others clearly welcomed the conservatives into government and at times there was animosity between them. There was a subtle shift of ambience in the bar. The halcyon days of the Republic seemed to be coming to an end.

Whatever the changes and upheavals going on in politics, Concha was concerned that any of the privileges that had been won for ordinary people were being eroded. Most importantly of all, she would lament the disappearance of any improvements for women. For the first time in Spain's history, women had been getting into public office and participating in politics. Thousands of them were now going to university too, and taking part in sport, even bullfighting.

Concha and her friends flippantly called the new freedoms for women 'liberation and lingerie' because of the exciting new undergarments that they now sometimes saw advertised in the newspapers. Having moved out of rural poverty herself when she married Pablo, she wanted to see Mercedes improve her life too, and had been pleased at the prospect of her daughter growing up in a society full of opportunity. With women now in the professions and reaching positions of power and influence, Concha hoped that life for Mercedes would have more to it than polishing glasses and lining them up neatly along the bar. Though Mercedes seemed to think of nothing but dance her mother regarded it as something of a childish pastime.

She did not worry about her sons. They had already-evolving careers and their futures looked promising.

'Granada is full of opportunities,' she said to Mercedes, 'so imagine what it must be like in the rest of Spain!'

Mercedes had only a limited idea of what the rest of her country was like but she nodded with agreement. It was usually the best thing to do with her mother. She knew that Concha did not take her dancing seriously enough. As the months and years passed by, she knew it was all she would ever want to do, but it was hard to convince her parents. All of her brothers appreciated this ambition of hers. They had watched her dancing from the days of her first flamenco shoes, the smallest anyone made, to the present time when she was a match for anyone in Granada, and Mercedes knew that they understood her desire.

When tales had begun to filter through from Concha's family in the countryside that landless farm workers were once again being ill-treated, she lectured her family on the unfairness of it all.

'This is not what the Republic was meant to stand for!' she would rant. 'Is it?'

She expected a response from her children even if her husband remained studiedly neutral. Pablo found this by far the best position to take, given that his business relied on the need to welcome anyone who cared to come in the door. He did not want El Barril to be too firmly identified with politics of any colour, unlike several bars in Granada that had become meeting places of very specific cliques.

Antonio muttered in agreement. He was more keenly aware of the political shifts taking place than anyone else in his family. He was following events in the Spanish parliament, the Cortes, closely, and read the newspapers voraciously and retentively. Though the city of Granada had a strongly conservative bias, Antonio, like his mother, was naturally drawn towards the left. The family could have remained unaware of this, but for the fights he used to have with Ignacio. The two boys lived on the edge of conflict.

As children they had fought over practically everything from toys and books to who should have the last piece of bread in the basket. Ignacio would never acknowledge that age and precedence should have any connection. Now the disagreement between them extended into the more serious business of politics and, though with fewer physical bruises and scratches than before, it was with hatred that they fought.

Emilio always remained silent when his brothers argued. He did not want to get drawn in, knowing that Ignacio was more than likely to pick on him. Mercedes occasionally interjected. The vehemence of their arguments upset her. She wanted them to love each other and for her this dislike seemed an unnatural state of affairs between brothers.

Another reason for their current polarisation was Ignacio's entrenchment in the bullfighting crowd. The people who were drawn to this sport – or, rather art, as so many people thought of it – tended to be the most conservative of Granadinos. They were the landowners and the wealthy, and Ignacio happily adopted their attitudes. Pablo and Concha accepted these inclinations and hoped that maturity might make him see that reason lay more in the middle ground. Meanwhile, Antonio found Ignacio's swaggering hard to stomach and never bothered to conceal it.

The household seemed to be relaxed only when Ignacio was away for a *corrida*. His days as a banderillero were behind him now and he had completed his apprenticeship as a *novillero*, a period during which he could fight only young bulls. He was now a fully fledged *matador de toros* and at his *alternativa*, the ceremony where this transition was formalised, the experts noted his precocious talent. Wherever he went, not just in Granada, but in Sevilla, Málaga and Córdoba too, Ignacio's reputation grew with every appearance.

As Emilio grew up, he began to develop an antipathy to his brother that surpassed even Antonio's. They were instinctively polarised on all matters. Ignacio taunted Emilio on several counts: for his passion for the guitar, for his lack of interest in women, and that he was not, as his older brother described it 'a real man'. Unlike Antonio, who could spar with words even better than Ignacio, Emilio would retreat into silence and then into his music. His lack of desire to retaliate and to fight back with Ignacio in one of the ways he understood, through fists or a clever turn of phrase, infuriated his brother all the more.

Although she was a much more sociable creature than her brother, Mercedes was immersed in the solipsistic world of music and dance. Nothing much had changed for her from the age of five to fifteen. She still spent much of her time in the attic listening to her brother or visiting her favourite shop behind the Plaza Bib Rambla, which made the best flamenco dresses in the city, talking to the owner, fingering the fabrics and feeling their folds, letting the extravagant ruffles run through her fingers, as though she was a soon-to-be-bride selecting her trousseau.

The shop, run by Señora Ruiz, was her private paradise. Racks of dresses hung from the ceiling in both adult and child sizes, and there were even tiny costumes for babies who could not yet walk, let alone dance. All of them were made with the same attention to detail, and their tiers of ruffles edged with ribbon or lace were all meticulously starched. Every single one was different and no two fabrics repeated. There were simple skirts for lessons and plain white shirts, embroidered shawls with silky tassels, hair combs and rows of shiny castanets. Boys were not forgotten and there were suits in every size, from toddler to adult, with black hats to complete the outfit.

Mercedes' favourite dresses were those with wired lower hems that would move in perfect wave motion as a dancer rotated. These were the ones she yearned to own, but they cost many thousands of pesetas and she had to make do with fantasy. Though she had three costumes sewn by her mother, she still wanted what she called a 'real' dress and the shopkeeper never tired of discussing quality and cost of fabric with her. For her sixteenth birthday, her parents had promised to grant her wish.

People had been marvelling at the way she performed since she was eight. It was common for girls to start dancing in public at that age and it was never considered unsuitable or precocious. From the age of eleven, she had been going up the hill into the Sacromonte, which was where the gypsies lived in their dank homes hollowed out of the hillside. Though she had several friends in the area, the real reason she went to the Sacromonte was to see an old *bailaora* known as 'La Mariposa'.

Most people thought her a mad old witch. Indeed, María Rodríguez had lost some of her reason, but she still had the memories of her great dancing days. They were as clear to her as if they had been yesterday. She saw in Mercedes a glimpse of her younger self, and perhaps in her elderly mind she thought that she and the child were one and the same as she relived her dancing through the adolescent girl.

Mercedes did have friends of her own age but it was at this woman's crumbling home that her mother would always look for her first. It was her retreat and the place where her obsession grew.

Señora Ramírez was worried about Mercedes' schoolwork and

reports from her teachers were unimpressive. She wanted to see her daughter take advantage of what this changing world might offer.

'Merche, when are you going to stay at home to do your studying?' she demanded. 'You can't spend your entire life spinning around. It'll never make you a living.'

She tried to make it sound light-hearted but she was serious and Mercedes knew that. The girl bit her tongue to prevent herself from answering back.

'There's no point arguing with Mother,' Emilio told her. 'She will never see your point of view. Like she never sees mine.'

Concha's view was that without gypsy blood Mercedes could never be a 'proper' dancer. She believed that the *gitanos* were the only ones who could dance, or play flamenco guitar, for that matter.

Even Pablo disagreed with her. 'She's as good as any of them,' he would say defensively to his wife when they watched her at a fiesta.

'Even if she was,' responded Concha, 'I would rather she was doing something else. That's how I feel.'

'And she "feels" that dancing is the right thing for her to be doing,' interrupted Emilio bravely.

'This is nothing to do with you, Emilio, and we'd rather you didn't egg her on quite so much,' snapped Concha.

Her father had always encouraged Mercedes' love of dancing but he was now beginning to worry about it, though not for the same reasons as his wife. Since the conservative government's win in the elections and the unrest in the north, the Civil Guard were beginning to tighten the screws on those who were not seen to conform. Anyone who fraternised with the gypsies, for example, was now regarded as a subversive. The amount of time Mercedes spent in the Sacromonte was beginning to worry even him.

One afternoon Mercedes came running back from La Mariposa's and burst through the door of El Barril. The place was empty except for Emilio, who was behind the bar drying cups and saucers. He was working almost full time in the café now. His parents were resting in the apartment, Antonio was at school teaching his last lessons for the term and Ignacio was away in Sevilla for a *corrida*.

'Emilio!' she said breathlessly. 'You have to take the evening off. You've got to come out with me!'

She came up to the bar and he could see droplets of perspiration on her forehead. She must have been running hard and her chest was heaving from the exertion. Her long hair, sometimes neatly plaited for school, was dishevelled and hanging loose about her shoulders.

'Please!'

'What for?' he asked, continuing to dry a saucer.

'A *juerga*. María Rodríguez just told me that Raul Montero's son is coming to play. Tonight. We are invited to go – but you know I can't go on my own . . .'

'What time?'

'About ten o'clock. *Please*, Emilio! *Please* come with me.' Mercedes gripped the edge of the bar, wide-eyed, pleading with her brother.

'All right. I'll ask our parents.'

'Thanks, Emilio. Javier Montero is meant to be nearly as good as his father.'

He could see that his sister was excited. The old lady had told her that if Javier Montero was even a fraction as handsome as his father or one tenth as accomplished on the guitar, then he was worth going to see.

Javier Montero was not exactly a stranger because many of the *gitanos* knew of him. He had come at their invitation from his home in Málaga. Musicians often came in from the outside but this one had excited local anticipation more than most. Both his father and his uncle were among the biggest names in flamenco, and that summer night in 1935 'El Niño', as he was known, was to play in Granada.

When they entered the long windowless room, a seated figure was already quietly playing a *falseta*, a variation on the piece that he would eventually open with. All they could see of him was the top of his head and a mass of glossy black hair that hung down and entirely screened his face. Bent lovingly over his guitar, he appeared to be listening, as though he believed it was the instrument itself that would give him his melody. Someone was subtly rapping out the rhythm on the table top nearby.

For ten minutes, while people were still coming into the room, he did not look up. Then he raised his head and gazed into the middle distance towards a point that only he could see. It was an expression of pure concentration, the pupils of his dark eyes just registering the outlines of the few figures already seated. With the light behind them, their faces were in the shadows, their silhouettes haloed.

The young Montero was spot-lit for all to see. He looked younger than his twenty years and his dimpled chin gave him an unexpected innocence. There was something almost feminine about him, with his copious, glossy tresses and features that were finer than most gypsy men.

From the moment she saw him, Mercedes was transfixed. She thought he was extraordinarily beautiful for a man and when his face disappeared once again behind the shroud of his mane it was like losing something. She willed him to look up so she could resume studying him. He continued idly moving his fingers across the strings, vain enough to want a bigger crowd and clearly not planning to start his performance until the room was filled to capacity.

More than half an hour later, and without apparent warning, he began.

The effect of his playing on Mercedes was physical. At that very moment, it was as though her heart expanded. The powerful beating that resounded in her ears as loudly as a drum was entirely involuntary. On the low uncomfortable stools on which they sat, she hugged herself in an attempt to still her shaking body. In her life, she had not heard anyone play like this. Even the older men who had been playing for half a century did not produce such an exquisite sound.

This *flamenco* was at one with his guitar, and the rhythms and melodies that he could draw from it passed through the audience like an electric current. Chords and melody emanated from his instrument along with percussive taps on the *golpeador*. It was as though a third invisible hand was at work and the sureness of his technique and the originality of the music astounded them all. The rise in room temperature was palpable and the murmured utterance of '*Olé*' was passed around the room like a hat.

Beads of sweat streaked Javier Montero's face and for the first time, as he tipped his head back, the audience could see that his features were distorted with concentration. Rivulets of moisture coursed down his neck. The drummer took over for a few minutes, allowing him to rest and once again he stared out blankly across the heads of the audience. He did not engage with them even for a moment. From where he sat, they were a single, amorphous mass.

There was one further piece and then, twenty minutes from the start of the performance, he gave a brief nod of his head, rose from his seat and edged his way past the applauding crowd.

Mercedes felt the edge of his jacket brush her face as he went past and caught the sweet-sour scent of him. Something akin to panic seized her now. It was as strong as pain and her heart resumed its earlier violent beating. In one thunder-clap instant, the postured gestures of love and grief that she had copied from other flamenco dancers over the years became something real. The play-acting had been a dress rehearsal for this moment.

The anguish, the despair that she might never again set eyes on this man almost made her forget herself and shout aloud: 'Stop! Don't go!' Reason and reticence could not hold her back, and she got up and slipped away, leaving Emilio discussing with others in the *cueva* what they had all just witnessed.

Such heightened atmosphere was not uncommon in these performances but even so, the player had been a cut above the best of them, they all agreed, and their slightly rivalrous envy of his brilliance gave way to admiration.

As the fresh air hit Mercedes, she nearly lost courage. Just outside the door, in the shadows, was the figure of the *guitarrista*. The fiery glow from a cigarette gave away his presence.

Suddenly her boldness seemed almost shameful.

'*Señor*,' she whispered.

Montero was used to such advances. The allure of a masterful player invariably proved irresistible to someone in the audience.

'*Sí*,' he replied. The lack of depth in his voice was a surprise.

Mercedes was set on a course of action and, in spite of a very reasonable fear of rejection, she continued. She was on a tightrope with an obligation to move forwards or backwards. Having come this far she had to speak the words she had rehearsed in her head.

'Will you play for me?' Overwhelmed by a sense of her own audacity, she braced herself for rejection.

'I *have* just played for you . . .'

There was a weariness in his voice. For the first time he bothered to look at her. He saw her features picked out in the lamplight. So many women approached him like this, seductive, available, aroused by his playing, but when he saw them in the light he could see they were old enough to be his mother. Sometimes, though, high on the adrenalin of his performance, it did not deter him from an hour or so of intimacy with them. Being the object of worship never failed to have some appeal.

This girl was young, though. Perhaps she genuinely wanted to dance. That would make a change.

'You'll have to wait,' he said roughly. 'I don't want a crowd.'

He had done enough performing for the day but the thought of seeing what this girl wanted from him was quite intriguing. Her audacity was enough to persuade him, even without her pretty face. He lit another cigarette and remained in the shadows. The minutes passed and the crowd drifted away.

Mercedes, hovering out of sight, saw the willowy figure of her brother slope down the narrow cobbled street and out of sight. He would assume that she was already at home. Only the *cueva* owner remained, eager to lock his doors for the night.

'Could we have just a moment inside?' Javier asked him.

'All right,' he said, recognising Mercedes. 'If you like. But I need to go in ten minutes. No more.'

Mercedes switched the light back on. Javier resumed his position, head bent, listened to the intervals between the strings, adjusted two of the pegs and then looked up. Now he was ready to engage with this *señorita*.

Until this moment, he had taken in little about her, merely her youth, but now, poised and ready to dance, he saw that she was no coy child. She had everything of the haughty madam about her: the poise, the 'attitude', a sense of drama.

'So what do you want? Some *alegrías*? *Bulerías*?'

In a simple full-skirted summer dress and flat shoes, she was not properly attired for dancing but this did not deter her.

'A *soleá*.'

She amused him, this girl. He smiled at the confidence she displayed in front of him. It flowed out of her before she had uncoiled so much as a fingertip.

Now his attention was fully on her like a beam of light. She tapped her palms together to take up his beat and once she could feel that his rhythm and hers were perfectly synchronised she began to move. She hammered out a pattern of beats on the floor, quite slowly at first, then raised her arms above her head and coiled her hands, folding them back almost flush against her wrists.

Then her feet began to move, faster and faster until they began to purr. There was not a breath between them, one step followed on so swiftly after the other. To begin with, Mercedes danced shyly, a respectful distance between herself and accompanist. He watched her closely, skilfully reflecting her movements in his playing, just as Emilio always did.

This dance continued for five or six minutes and she twirled and stamped, always returning to the same spot with her feet. The outline of her muscular body was visible to Javier through the thin cotton of her dress. Dancers tended to move the folds of their dresses as part of the choreography, but the fabrics were often heavy and Mercedes found the flimsiness of her frock a liberation. On the final beat she stopped, breathless, and her body continued to sway from the exertion.

'*Muy bien*.' He smiled for the first time. 'Very good. Very, very good.'

She had not so much as glanced at him during the dance, but he had not taken his eyes off her. It seemed to him that she had undergone a transformation between the opening and closing bars.

He had forgotten the pleasure it could be to accompany a

dancer. For some years he had avoided it. He so rarely came across a dancer that he wanted to be with. They were rarely good enough.

Now it was his turn to choose the music.

'Next the *bulería*,' he announced.

Mercedes found this a much harder dance but she had no trouble picking up his rhythm. The moment he began she sensed the beat and the pace, and her feet moved almost automatically. The dance was just for him now and it was her task to respond. She turned slowly through three hundred and sixty degrees, her pale, extended fingers reaching out but never touching him.

It was a longer piece and she gave everything this time. There would not be another after this. As she turned, her black curls flew out like a blanket and her hair clip clattered to the floor. Her arms seemed both to lead and to follow her rotations until, like a gyroscope, she finally slowed and ended the dance in one last stamp that timed with his final chord.

She was breathless and soaked with perspiration, strands of damp hair trailed across her face. She looked as though she had been running through the rain.

Pulling a chair towards her, Mercedes sat down. The silence was overpowering, unnerving after the noise they had been making. To break the tension, she busied herself by leaning down to retrieve her hairpin.

A few minutes passed. Javier studied this young woman who had turned into someone else while she danced. Quite unexpectedly, she had moved him. Perhaps once before in his life, he had been ignited by a *bailaora* but more often he had felt like a pack horse bearing a burden. A long time ago he had made the decision not to be an accompanist. With this girl it had been a duet.

'Well . . .' said Javier ambiguously, watching her as she fastened her hair back.

She felt uncomfortable in the spotlight of his gaze. Trying to hold her breath to hear what he might say next, while still panting, made her feel as though she might burst.

'. . . was that what you wanted?'

His question was not what she had anticipated, but she had to answer.

'It was more than I had hoped for,' was all she could think of to say.

The *cueva* owner had returned and was jangling his keys. This musician might be fêted in other places, but that did not stop the proprietor wanting to lock up and go home.

Javier replaced his guitar in its case and snapped it shut.

Outside he turned towards Mercedes. The temperature had dropped and in her sweat-soaked dress she shivered with cold. He could see her shaking and it seemed natural to take his jacket off and put it round her shoulders.

'Look, you take this. I'll come and get it in the morning before I leave,' he said gently. 'How will I find you?'

'My father's café. El Barril. Just off the Plaza Nueva. Anyone will direct you.'

Under the flickering light of the gaslamp he took a long look at this creature and was puzzled by his own reaction to her. She was a curious mix of child and adult, an adolescent on the brink of adulthood, naïve and yet worldly. He had seen many young flamenco dancers like her, virginal and yet lacking in innocence. Usually their extravagant sexuality vanished the moment they stopped dancing but with this girl it was different. She exuded a sensuality, the memory of which would keep him awake that night.

Mercedes arrived home and could immediately sense she was in trouble. Emilio had returned an hour before, expecting her to be there, and was now sitting at a table in the bar with his parents. Girls were never allowed out at night unaccompanied, and Concha and Pablo were furious, both with their son, for not performing his role of chaperon, and also with their daughter. She knew that it was not worth explaining that she had been dancing. It would only provoke the usual lecture on how dancing was going to get her into trouble one day. It was something she did not want to hear.

'And what exactly are you wearing?' demanded Pablo. 'That's not yours, is it?'

Mercedes absent-mindedly fingered the lapels of Javier's jacket.

'What do you think you are doing, going around wearing a man's jacket?' There was indignation in her father's voice.

She drew the jacket around her. It was suffused with the smell of the *flamenco* and she breathed deeply to take its intoxicating fragrance into her lungs. Her father held out his hands, expecting her to remove the offending item of clothing, but she darted past him and ran to her room.

'Merche! Come out at once!' Concha had pursued her up the stairs and now banged furiously on her door.

The girl knew that she could safely ignore her mother's summons. Everyone was tired and soon they would retire to bed. They could argue again in the morning.

Though it was a warm night, she slept with the jacket wrapped around her, inhaling deeply on the memory of the man who owned it. If she never saw him again, at least she would have this. She would never let it go.

The next morning Javier strolled into the café. It was Saturday so there was no school and Mercedes had been hanging out of her window since she woke up, hoping he might come.

He had lain awake almost the entire night. He could not stop thinking about that young dancer. When he shut his eyes she was there and when he opened them she stayed with him. Such sleeplessness was unusual for him. Most nights he retired to bed exhausted, full of whisky and cigars.

Unless he was actually in the company of women, he did not spend much time thinking about them. But this girl haunted him. He was glad of the excuse to go and find her again the next day.

He rather hoped that, in the daylight, she might not be as he remembered. He was mildly irritated with himself. He certainly did not need his life complicated by love. Perhaps the half-light of the previous evening had helped create a fantasy. In either case, he had to get his jacket back. It was his best.

A young man was making coffee at the bar when he went in. It was Emilio. Before Javier had time to speak to him, Mercedes rushed in. She was holding out his jacket. In the daylight, her charm seemed all the greater. Any trace of shyness that had been there the previous night had gone, replaced with the most open and enchanting smile he had ever seen.

Emilio observed them. He had recognised Javier.

'Thank you for lending me this,' Mercedes said, holding out the jacket.

How could she keep him there for a moment longer? She was desperate for inspiration.

'Was my dancing all right?' she asked impulsively.

'You are the best non-*gitana*, the best *payo*, that I have ever seen,' he answered truthfully.

It was a statement of such extravagance that she found it hard to believe. She blushed, not knowing whether he was teasing or telling the truth.

'If I ever come back, will you dance for me again?'

Her words dried in her throat. The question needed no reply.

They stood, a metre apart, breathing each other's air.

'I have to go now.'

Though the desire was there, he could not peck her on the cheek or touch her arm. He knew that such actions were unacceptable and, in any case, he was aware of the watchful gaze of Emilio, who was noisily piling up plates behind the bar.

A moment later, Javier was gone. To her own surprise, Mercedes found that she was not sad. She knew with absolute certainty that she would see him again.

For weeks she waited, thinking of nothing else, and trying to retain the memory of his smell.

Eventually a letter arrived. Javier had written to Mercedes via her teacher, La Mariposa. He was returning to Granada and wanted her to perform with him. They could rehearse at the old *bailaora*'s house.

Mercedes agonised. This man was a total stranger to her family, he was half a decade older than her, and most unacceptably of all, he was a *gitano*, a gypsy. She knew what her parents would say if she asked them. For her there was only one course of action and that was to do all of this behind their backs. She was prepared to take any risk to dance with Javier again.

Mercedes confided in Emilio, knowing that he would not betray her. He continued to play while she sat on his bed, bubbling over with news of this invitation.

'I will tell our parents,' she promised. 'But not straight away. I know they'd only stop me.'

Emilio did his best to conceal his resentment. He knew he was being left behind.

Mercedes was insensitive to the implications for her brother and carried on excitedly: 'You will come and see us perform, won't you? Even if I can't ask our mother and father, it won't be the same unless you come . . .'

The first time she took her dancing shoes up the hill to María Rodríguez's house to meet Javier, her trembling legs could hardly carry her. How was she going to dance when they shook so much she could scarcely walk?

She reached the old woman's house and, as she always did, lifted the latch without knocking. The interior was dark, as usual, and it would take her eyes a few minutes to adjust. María normally appeared a few moments later, alerted to her arrival by the sound of the door.

Mercedes sat on the old chair by the door and began to change her shoes. Out of the shadows came a voice.

'Hello, Mercedes.'

She almost jumped out of her skin. Assuming that she would be the first there, she had completely failed to notice that Javier was already in the room.

She did not even know what to call him. 'Javier' seemed too familiar. 'Mr Montero' seemed absurd.

'Oh, hello . . .' her voice said quietly. 'Did you have a good journey?'

It was the kind of neutral conversation that she had heard adults having so many times.

'I did, thank you,' he replied.

Just then, as if to diffuse the awkwardness of the moment, María came into the room.

'Ah, Mercedes,' she said, 'you're here. So shall we see some of this dancing? It sounds as though Javier was quite impressed with you last time he came to Granada.'

They repeated the *soleá* and the *bulería* from their first meeting, and then Javier played a sequence of other dances for Mercedes.

As the hour went by, almost without a break, she relaxed. They almost entirely forgot the presence of María Rodríguez. Occasionally she quietly joined in with the *palmas* but she did not want to distract them.

Eventually Javier stopped.

'I think that's probably enough for today, isn't it?' the old woman said.

Neither of them seemed to have anything to say.

'So I think another rehearsal, same time next week, and you should be ready to perform together. I'll work on a few things with you, Mercedes, meanwhile. Thank you,' she said to Javier, smiling. 'I'll see you both next week.'

'Yes . . .' said Mercedes. 'See you next week.'

She looked across at Javier, who was packing away his guitar. His eyes met hers and he seemed to hesitate. There was no doubt that he was on the point of saying something but he changed his mind.

A moment later he was gone. Within minutes, having changed her shoes, Mercedes too was outside on the cobbled street, but Javier had already disappeared. Their contact had been so intimate and yet so distant.

Mercedes' stomach churned with anxiety and confusion. She thought of nothing but Javier and counted not the hours but the minutes until she would see him again. She confided in her friend Paquita.

'Of course he isn't going to think of you in that way,' said Paquita. 'He's five years older than you! He's nearly Ignacio's age!'

'Well, I don't think of him as a brother,' said Mercedes.

'Just be careful, Merche. You know the reputation of those *gitanos* . . .'

'You don't know anything about him,' answered Mercedes defensively.

'But neither do you really. Do you?' teased Paquita.

'No. But I know how I feel when I am dancing with him,' she said very seriously. 'It is as though the whole world is contained in María's small house. Nothing outside it exists or matters.'

'And when will you see him again?'

'He's coming back in a week's time. I can't sleep. I can't eat. I can't think of anything else. There *is* nothing else.'

'Has he kissed you?' asked Paquita inquisitively.

'No!' exclaimed Mercedes, almost affronted. 'Of course he hasn't!'

They were in the courtyard of Paquita's home. Both sat silently for a while. Paquita could not doubt her friend's sincerity. She had never heard her talk in this way. They had both spent many hours of their lives hanging about in the city's squares exchanging flirtatious words and glances with boys of their age, but these feelings Mercedes had for Javier Montero appeared to have nothing to do with such childish crushes.

For Mercedes, the days passed with agonising slowness until the next rehearsal. Concha noticed the dark shadows beneath her daughter's eyes and her listless manner. She also became concerned about the uneaten food on her plate.

'What's the matter, *querida mia*?' she asked. 'You look so pale!'

'It's nothing, Mother,' she replied. 'I had to finish some school work last night.'

It was an explanation that satisfied Concha. She had, after all, been nagging Mercedes to take her studies more seriously.

The day for the second rehearsal arrived. Mercedes was almost overcome with nausea when she woke that morning. At five o'clock she went to La Mariposa's house. She was not due there until six, but she wanted to be the first there this time.

Mercedes put on her shoes and warmed her wrists by rotating them round and round and back again, tapping her feet as she sat there to create a rhythm: *one* two, *one* two, *one* two, one two *three*, one two *three*, one two . . .

Still María had not appeared. Mercedes stood up and her feet resumed the rhythm of the *seguiriya*. She began to turn and her steel heelcaps hammered on the floorboards of this tiny house. There was only just enough room for her hands to stretch upwards without touching the ceiling, and the walls could scarcely contain the volume of noise that she was making. As she twirled, Javier's playing filled her imagination.

Though Mercedes was oblivious to the racket she was making, it was audible in the street outside. For a few moments, Javier stood watching her through the window. What he could see was a young woman entirely lost in her own world, almost hypnotised by the rhythm of her own movements. What he could not see was the vision of himself that filled Mercedes' imagination.

In her mind he sat on the low chair in that room almost shredding his fingers with the passion of his playing.

Perhaps five or six minutes went by as she performed her private, solemn dance. He was transfixed not merely by the sight of the raw emotion she expressed so openly and so unreservedly; it was a lack of inhibition that was only possible in one who was dancing unobserved. What also held his attention was this combination of technical virtuosity with something that seemed almost wild. As she spun round and round and round again, she was like a creature possessed. Javier knew that to make those disciplined, precisely practised steps appear improvised was almost impossible. This girl was achieving it and watching her thrilled him to the core of his being. Such *duende* was so rare. It was like an electric current passing through him.

A moment before Mercedes stopped dancing, he felt a tap on his shoulder. María Rodríguez. He had no idea how long she had been standing there and whether she had observed him spying on Mercedes. He did not ask. He felt like a voyeur.

'Let me take that from you,' he said, taking her basket of shopping to cover his embarrassment. 'It looks heavy.'

'Thank you,' said the old woman, acknowledging his gesture.

'I don't know where she gets this fury from. It just rages up from inside her. And then she channels it into her dancing. You clearly recognise that this girl is exceptional.'

He nodded. Her comments were enough to indicate to Javier that María knew he had been watching her young protégée.

When María opened her door, Mercedes was still panting from the exertion of the dance. She was virtually steaming. She gave a shy smile, which for Javier seemed at odds with the overt sexuality that he had witnessed through the windowpane.

Mercedes had thought obsessively of this *guitarrista* in the past week, and it seemed natural that he should be back there, sitting on the low chair tuning his guitar. It was as though neither of them had moved from this very room in seven days.

They exchanged a few polite words of greeting and María Rodríguez took a seat in the corner of the room, ready to listen and observe.

'What would you like me to play?' asked Javier.

'A *seguiriya*,' she said firmly.

Javier bent his head low over his guitar and smiled to himself.

Mercedes picked up the rhythm from his introductory chords and soon she was dancing.

Whenever Mercedes glanced at Javier he was utterly absorbed in his playing and when he looked up to watch her, she seemed far away. They were unaware of each other's interest.

This time, as Javier looked up to observe, he noted that her movements were crisp and her timing exact. Her *zapateado*, the quick toe, sole and heel movements, were as faultless as before but she held something back this time. She seemed more reserved, shy like her smile. When he glanced across to where María had been sitting, he saw that she had disappeared from the room. He stopped playing, emboldened by the absence of their chaperone.

'Come and sit down,' he instructed her gently, indicating the empty chair next to his.

Mercedes was surprised by the sudden cessation of his playing and his invitation. They had never sat so close to each other before. She did not hesitate for a moment. Even if she did not always do what she was told, she was used to being given instructions by adults.

Once she was sitting down, he reached out and took her hand. It trembled violently against his own. He suddenly realised that he had nothing in particular that he wanted to say and that it was purely for the opportunity to hold her hand that he had stopped her dancing.

'You dance so beautifully, Merche.'

It was all he could think of to say.

He held her hand tightly and then, in a moment that seemed one of madness even to himself, he brought it to his lips and kissed not the back of it but the palm. Even for someone who had bedded dozens of women, it was a gesture of surprising intimacy.

Instinctively, Mercedes gave him her other hand and Javier held them both in his. They sat like this for a moment, their eyes meeting for the first time, and nothing needed to be said.

When María came back into the room, Mercedes got to her feet. Javier resumed his playing and within the hour they had gone their separate ways once again. In spite of his gypsy blood, Javier knew where the boundaries lay.

Their first performance together was the following week, but in the meantime there was an important date in Mercedes' diary.

Three days before she was due to meet Javier again, it was her sixteenth birthday. Her family celebrated and as she had been long promised, a large, soft parcel was waiting for her on the café table at breakfast time that day.

She tore the paper open and as she did so, folds of a magnificent flamenco dress billowed out. It was a classic design, black spots on a red background, exactly the one she had always dreamed of having, and she held it up to herself and twirled round. For a moment after she had come to a stop, the wired tiers seemed to have a life all of their own and continued to bounce from side to side and up and down.

'Thank you, thank you!' she cried in appreciation, hugging both her mother and the dress.

It was warming to see and feel her daughter's excitement but Concha silently rued Mercedes' passion for her dancing. She had noticed that her daughter was spending even more time than ever with María Rodríguez.

Before their first performance, Mercedes and Javier were to meet at María's house. It was a few steps from the *cueva* where a crowd was already gathering. Most of them were drawn by the *tocaor*'s reputation but some of them were intrigued by the combination of the great man from Málaga with this local girl.

As Javier arrived, Mercedes appeared from María's back room where she had been changing.

The dress fitted perfectly around every curve of her body, closely following the contours of breasts and hips. It was a stunning transfiguration and she was fully aware of the impression she made on Javier as she entered the room swathed in scarlet, her cheeks flushed with excitement.

'You look . . . wonderful,' he said.

'Thank you,' she replied, knowing that it was true.

She came up close to him now, full of courage and eager anticipation for their performance.

Without hesitating he reached out and stroked her hair, and as she took another step towards him, she felt his fingers touch her chin. Instinctively, she tilted her head upwards.

Javier's kiss shocked her with its strength and intensity. Mercedes had been kissed only once before on the mouth, and it had been a disappointment. This was an embrace that surged through her, body, mind and soul. Whether it lasted for minutes or only seconds had no relevance. It was powerful enough to feel as though her life now divided into two: before and after the feel of his soft lips on hers.

It was time for them to go. María Rodríguez, who had known what had to happen between these two before they did, walked up towards the *cueva* with them.

No one was disappointed. Mercedes danced with more intensity than ever before. The *guitarrista* and *bailaora* were perfectly paired.

At a second performance, the *cueva* overflowed. Emilio was there to see them this time and even he, predisposed to criticise this man who had usurped his role, could see that this was a remarkable partnership. At times, the spark between Mercedes and Javier could almost have ignited a blaze. Emilio slipped away before the applause died down. The last thing he wanted was for his sister to notice he had even been there, and even less so for her to see his reaction.

While Pablo and Concha thought their daughter was in her room finally getting round to doing some school work, she was dancing with Javier Montero in the Sacromonte. It was only a matter of time before someone mentioned it to them and sure enough they did.

'You are only just *sixteen*!' shouted her father, when she returned that night. She had hoped her parents would already be in bed, but she found them sitting waiting for her. Pablo's anger made all the more impact because it was so rare.

'All I'm doing is *dancing*!' she defended herself.

'But how old is this man? He should know better,' continued Pablo.

'You've been very deceitful,' reprimanded Concha.

'You're a disgrace!' Ignacio, who had arrived home moments earlier, joined in. 'Dancing with a bloody *gypsy*!'

Mercedes knew it was pointless trying to defend herself. She was under attack from all sides.

Emilio was the only person who understood this compulsion of hers, but he had sensed the brewing storm and withdrawn to his room. Having been displaced by an outsider, his own resentment had continued to brew. Filial love had been swept aside by the infatuation that now dominated his sister's every waking moment.

'Just go to your room. And don't come out,' ordered Pablo.

Without argument, Mercedes did exactly as she was told. Javier had travelled back to Málaga that night so there was nothing she wanted to leave it for.

For two days Mercedes stayed upstairs and Concha left meals outside her door. An hour later she would return to find them untouched.

Eating was the very last thing Mercedes felt like doing. She lay on her bed and wore herself out with weeping. In one move, her parents had taken away the two things that were at the centre of her life: dancing and Javier. If she could not dance with her *gitano* she was not going to dance at all. And if she could not dance, she could not bear to live.

Emilio knocked at her door late one afternoon and went in. Mercedes sat up when she saw him. Her eyes were swollen with crying.

He stood at the end of her bed, his arms folded. 'Look,' he said, 'I understand how you feel.'

Mercedes blinked at him. 'Do you?' she asked quietly.

'Yes,' he said. 'And I am going to talk to our parents. I've seen you dancing with Javier and that sort of performance doesn't happen every day.'

'What do you mean?'

'It was . . . um . . .' Emilio struggled. He suddenly felt awkward in front of his sister.

'It was what?'

'It was . . . perfection. Or something close to it. Between you and . . . him.'

Mercedes did not know how to react to her brother's clumsy compliment. She could see how much it had cost him to say it.

Emilio was true to his word. He took his father to one side, knowing that, of the two of them, Pablo was less vehemently against Mercedes' dancing than Concha.

'You can't just put a stop to something like this,' he said to his father. 'Nothing can stand in its way.'

Emilio's representations on Mercedes' behalf made Pablo reconsider. Even his description of the way Mercedes danced made her father proud and, within a few days, Concha, albeit reluctantly, had agreed to meet Javier.

Chapter Fourteen

DURING THE FEW weeks while these negotiations were going on, Mercedes' obsession with dance had increased. There was nothing else in life that she wanted to do.

Letters were exchanged, and one day Javier arrived at El Barril. For an hour he talked with Pablo.

In spite of himself, Señor Ramírez warmed to this young man. There was no doubt that he was a serious member of the flamenco scene and Pablo's view of the situation began to shift. Javier Montero had played not just in Granada and Málaga, but in Córdoba, Sevilla and Madrid. He even had forthcoming engagements in Bilbao, the home of his celebrated *guitarrista* uncle.

Eventually Concha appeared and introductions were made. She was not predisposed to liking Javier, but it was impossible to do otherwise. There was a sincerity in his manner that shone out and, sometime later, when she eventually heard him performing, she knew that it was this same quality that gave his playing such power.

Mercedes was not allowed to leave her room while Javier was there. Maternal fury was not so easily dispelled.

Javier was bold. He made it clear that he wished to continue playing for Mercedes in Granada but he wanted more than that. He wanted to take her to other cities. He did not tell Mercedes' parents as much, but he felt his whole life was held in limbo. As far as he was concerned, his future was in their hands, dependent on whether or not Mercedes could continue to dance for him, and he to play for her.

After an hour or so, their meeting came to an end. Pablo

spoke for himself and his wife, in agreeing to consider Montero's request.

Concha was very concerned. Having Mercedes dancing with Emilio was safe but this was another matter altogether.

'How do we know where all this will lead?' she said to Pablo. 'She's only just sixteen and he's almost five years older!'

Having met Javier, Pablo's views had changed. He smiled.

'And what is the age difference between *us*?' he enquired wryly.

Concha did not reply. It was at least a decade.

'What is the subject of this conversation?' asked Pablo. 'Are we just talking about dance? Or do you think there is something more?'

Concha thought of her daughter's hollow eyes and uneaten meals. Hard as she tried, she found it difficult to attribute these things to a ban on dancing. She was not a heartless woman and had once known that same intense, all-consuming love herself, even if it had grown quieter with the years.

'What is it that worries you more?' asked Pablo. 'Our daughter's love of dancing or the possibility of her falling for this man?'

'Well, we can't ask her that,' said Concha flatly.

'And anyway, the two things might be bound up together,' mused Pablo.

'You know I wanted her to expand her horizons,' lamented Concha, 'but not quite in this way.'

'Is there really a choice? If we don't let her dance with Javier, what else do you think she is going to do? Sit in her room like a good student?'

Antonio had come in.

'What do you think?' Concha asked him.

'Are you sure you want my opinion, Mother?'

His mother nodded. He hesitated to take sides in a dispute between his parents, but clearly a casting vote was needed.

'My view is this. One of the reasons her dancing affects people is that they witness this extraordinary determination,' he said. 'And that same determination will never allow anyone to get between her and this *flamenco*. You're fighting a losing battle if you try to stop her.'

Her mother was silent for a while as she reflected on what Antonio had just said.

'Well, as long as you chaperon her, Pablo, I suppose I shall have to put up with it.'

A while later, Mercedes came downstairs. The girl was pale. She knew her future had been discussed that afternoon.

Her parents were both in the bar.

'We met Javier today,' said Pablo, telling her something she already knew. 'And we liked him.'

'But can I dance with him again?' she asked impatiently. It was all she wanted to know.

Mercedes was overjoyed when she heard of her parents' decision.

A week later, she packed her bag. A crisp new flamenco dress spilled out. Antonio had given her some money to buy it.

'I think you'll need a spare,' he had said, kissing her on the forehead.

Mercedes and her father travelled on a bus to Málaga. They were to be away for three days. It was the furthest distance she had ever travelled, the longest time she had ever been alone with her father, and the first time she had danced away from her home city. Even without the prospect of seeing Javier, everything about this trip to the bustling friendly city of Málaga was an adventure. They rented a room close to where Javier lived and on the first morning he collected them for a rehearsal, which was to be in the back room of the café where they were to perform that night.

Pablo was amazed by the transformation in his daughter's dancing. He sat, mesmerised, as they went through their repertoire of tangos, fandangos, *alegrías* and *soleares*. This was a different Mercedes from the one he had seen dancing at a fiesta only a few months before. The little girl had become a young woman.

They were on a stage set up in the café and the audience was receptive. Javier was familiar to them, as was his father, Raul, who played at the beginning of the evening.

Mercedes was more nervous than she had even been in Granada.

Everything was so unfamiliar and she was sure the audience would not like her, but the performance went as well as the rehearsal. No one failed to appreciate the grace and energy of her dancing, the fineness of her hand movements, the love, the fear and the fury that she expressed through them all.

Neither of them could stop smiling, an expression that was so at odds with the mood of much of the music and dancing. They could not stop themselves. Mercedes felt euphoric and, when she saw the pride on her father's face, was unafraid to show it.

At the end of the evening, a photographer wanted to take pictures of them, together and separately. The following morning when Javier came to meet Mercedes, he had a set of portraits for her.

'You can show them to your mother,' he said. 'You look beautiful in them!'

'But there isn't one of you!' she protested. 'I want a photograph of you!'

'I'm sure your mother doesn't!' he teased.

'It isn't *for* my mother,' she said.

'I'll swap you a photograph,' he said. 'I want one of you as well.'

In every photograph, the subjects beamed almost from ear to ear.

The second night's performance was in Málaga's movie theatre. It was a much bigger room than the café and the stage was higher. As she waited in the wings behind some thick red curtains, Mercedes' anxiety almost got the better of her.

Javier took her hand gently and lifted it to his lips.

'You will be fine, my sweet, you will be fine. Don't worry. They will love you.'

His tender concern gave her courage. After only a minute or so on stage, she heard a murmured '*Olé*' and knew that the audience was with her. There was no play-acting of emotion in her dancing. In her mind, she merely recreated the anguish of separation from Javier, and the passion she required to dance poured out of her.

It was another magnificent performance. The local paper described it as a 'triumph' and their photographs appeared on the front page.

Pablo was persuaded to travel with his daughter on some future engagements and Mercedes' career and reputation grew. As did her devotion to the *guitarrista*. Their love was absolutely mutual, as equal as their limelight on the shared stage. When they were apart, both of them meticulously counted the days until they would be reunited.

Emilio tried to hide his sense of rejection. He stayed at home playing his guitar much less now that he did not have his sister's encouragement. When he was not working, he did not want to hang around in El Barril, especially when Ignacio was about.

A favourite haunt of his was the Café Alameda in the Plaza Campillo, a place much frequented by artists, writers and musicians. Without ever having the nerve to join his table, Emilio and his friend Alejandro would sit on the periphery of Lorca's circle, a coterie known as 'El Rinconcillo', simply because it usually occupied the 'corner' of the room.

Lorca was a regular visitor to Granada. He spent as much time as he could with his family on the outskirts of the city and his arrival there was considered significant enough to be mentioned in the local papers. Drawn there by the anguish and mystery of Andalucian culture, Lorca embraced flamenco as an embodiment of everything the region stood for. He had friends who were flamenco dancers and *gitano* companions who were guitarists and taught him to strum in the gypsy style. For Lorca this place felt like home, and the way in which people lived there inspired his work.

Emilio's admiration of Lorca was little short of hero worship. He was happy to be in the shadow of his shadow, and on the occasions when Lorca cast a dazzling smile in his direction Emilio felt as though his glowing heart might burn right through his shirt. He loved everything Lorca produced, from his poetry and plays to his music and drawings. But perhaps what he admired above all was his openness about his sexuality.

Perhaps I shall have the same nerve one day, he thought to himself.

Ignacio used his brother's attachment to the Café Alameda as an excuse to goad him. During the long winter months when Ignacio had no cause to be away in other cities for bullfights, he would spend long nights of drinking with his banderillero friends and return belligerently drunk. With too little to occupy them, some of these boys became indolent in the winter months. Like a few of the others, Ignacio was waiting for his next chance in the bullring.

Emilio would wince when he heard the characteristic slam of the door, long after El Barril itself had closed. If he heard whistling too, it was a bad sign. It was his brother's way of feigning nonchalance before he made trouble and Ignacio was in the mood to do so on this particular night.

'How is "El Maricón" today then?' asked Ignacio, using a derogatory expression to refer to Lorca. In the snide way he phrased the question, he managed to call his brother a 'poofter' too, knowing that he would not retaliate.

This taunting of Emilio made Antonio hate Ignacio more than ever.

'Why don't you just leave him alone?' shouted Antonio. His anger was not only for the way he abused his brother. Ignacio's hatred of homosexuals represented a more general bigotry that was common to many on the right wing of politics. Theirs was a narrow, macho and intolerant vision.

The country's politics continued to be troubled and Antonio was glad when he heard that there was talk on the left wing of a coalition. The appalling events in Asturias eighteen months earlier had made the left realise they needed political unity to get back into power. They wanted to give themselves a fresh start and put social justice at the top of their agenda to appeal to the average voter. It had been a tense few months in the Ramírez household, not just because of the personality clashes between the brothers, but because of their political differences too.

Elections were held in February of 1936 and, across the country as a whole, the socialists gained the majority of votes. In Granada, things were not so simple. The right-wing party won, but following claims of intimidation and infringements of the law, the results were annulled. Clashes broke out between right-wingers and trade union members, and antagonism between the parties intensified. In Granada churches were gutted, newspaper offices were wrecked and the theatre was destroyed by fire. The way Ignacio reacted, anyone would have thought that Emilio had personally struck the match.

Concha tried to calm the storm that raged in her own household, but the situation both inside their home and in the wider world did not improve. That summer a sequence of events triggered an outbreak of widespread violence. After a police lieutenant was gunned down by four Fascists outside his house in Madrid, the leader of the right-wing monarchist party, Calvo Sotelo, was killed in revenge. A shoot-out followed between police Assault Guards and fascist militia near the cemetery in the capital city where both funerals were taking place and four people were killed. The political temperature was high and tensions even higher.

Mercedes was preoccupied with her next flamenco engagement and counting the days until she next saw Javier. Now that she had left school, their performances could have been more frequent, particularly with the number of requests that they received, but Pablo was only prepared to leave El Barril for a few days each month. She had ceased to notice the growing dissent between her brothers and was unaware of the turbulence in the country as a whole. A series of performances was scheduled in Cádiz for July and she was busy mastering some new steps, spending hours each day cocooned with María Rodríguez, enveloped in the warm anticipation of seeing Javier again in a week or so.

Alone in her room Mercedes would gaze at the photograph of her *guitarra* propped against her bedside lamp. His strong cheekbones and the shock of straight glossy hair, a slim strand of it across one eye, seemed more beautiful to her every time she looked at the picture. The camera lens had captured so well the directness of his gaze, and the power of those smiling eyes reached down into the depths of her.

Meanwhile the rest of her family watched the gathering storm. They had heard the distant rumbles, but none of them had foreseen its scale.

Chapter Fifteen

July 17 was a typical summer's day in Granada. The heat was blistering. Shutters were down to keep out heat, light and dust. There was listlessness in the air. No one knew what to do with themselves.

Concha and Mercedes sat outside the café under the shade of the awning.

'It's even warmer outside than it is indoors,' said Señora Ramírez. 'There's nothing cooling in that breeze.'

'It's just too hot to do anything,' responded Mercedes. 'I'm going to lie on my bed.'

As Mercedes rose, her mother noticed that her daughter's dress was transparent with sweat. She got up too and gathered their glasses onto a tray. There were no customers that afternoon. The square was devoid of life and even the leaves on the trees crackled listlessly in the breeze, so dried out in these oven-hot temperatures that some had already begun to fall.

The city's siesta was as deep as a coma. Mercedes was almost unconscious until well beyond six o'clock that evening, when the mercury fell for the first time since midday. Even for Granadinos these were soaring temperatures. In a feverish sleep, she had a vivid dream that Javier and she were dancing in the bar downstairs and when she awoke, there was a moment of sadness at realising he was a hundred kilometres away in Málaga.

The next day, customers coming into El Barril each reported a different version of the rumours that military movement was taking place across the water in North Africa. There was some confusion at the time, with one radio broadcast announcing one thing and another contradicting it, but the truth soon became apparent. A group of army generals were rebelling against the government and staging a *coup d'état*.

Under the leadership of General Francisco Franco, the Army of Africa, comprising foreign legionaries and a fighting force of Moroccan mercenaries, were to be transported across the strait from Spanish Morocco to mainland Spain. Once they had landed, generals in army garrisons across Spain were to stage a rising in their own towns and cities and proclaim a state of war.

Granada melted in forty degrees of heat, cobbles burned through shoe leather and the mountains disappeared in a shimmering haze. That morning, the local paper, *El Ideal*, had carried an announcement on the front page that they could not bring any general news 'owing to forces beyond our control'.

In the café, Pablo was agitated. 'Something's really wrong, Concha, I know it is,' he said, pointing to the headline.

'It's nothing, Pablo. Probably a strike or something. The government isn't going to lose control. Don't worry so much,' she tried to reassure him, but he was unconvinced.

Pablo's sense of ill-ease was well founded, as both of them really knew. The government's claim that on the mainland business was as usual, in spite of a military *pronunciamiento* in Morocco, did not reassure them.

It seemed at odds with the rumour that a certain General Queipo de Llano had seized command of the garrison in Sevilla and, with only one hundred or so soldiers, had swiftly taken over the city.

'So how can they tell us that everything is normal?' Pablo said to anyone listening.

Like those in many other towns, the people of Granada felt vulnerable. They demanded weapons from the government but, to everyone's concern, the Prime Minister, Casares Quiroga, had forbidden the distribution of arms to the people and was absolutely adamant that what had happened in Sevilla did not affect the rest of the country. He maintained that everywhere else, the army remained loyal to the government.

On a different radio wave, the voice of General Queipo de Llano could be heard shrieking his victorious message. Except for Madrid and Barcelona, he raved, the whole of Spain was now in the hands of Nationalist troops. Neither of these contradictory messages was accurate and they left the people of Spain in total confusion.

In Granada, there was considerable alarm. Rumours were spreading that, in Sevilla, people opposing army rule were being massacred and thousands more were being detained. Suddenly, neighbours who had seemed to support the Republic came out against it. Pablo and Concha could feel it in the café, even on the morning of the eighteenth. Customers did not know whether to trust each other, or even whether to trust Pablo and Concha themselves. The ground had shifted beneath their feet.

The fate of individual towns and cities seemed to depend on whether their army garrison remained loyal to the Republican government. In Granada, a new military commander had arrived in the city only six days earlier. General Campins was staunchly loyal to the Republic and firmly, if naïvely, believed his officers would not rebel and join Franco's cause. The workers were not so confident, but when they asked to be armed in case the army rebelled, their civil governor, Torres Martínez, followed government instructions and refused to distribute arms to the workers.

Most of the Ramírez family was still awake at two o'clock on the morning of the nineteenth. No one had any intention of sleeping, even if the stifling heat of the day had allowed them.

'But why won't they give us any weapons? Who's to say that those soldiers aren't going to turn on us?' Antonio demanded of his father.

'Come on, Antonio!' his father urged him. 'That's exactly the point. What good will it do to have all you young men running about in the city brandishing guns that you don't even know how to use? Eh? Tell me what good it would do!'

'Try not to be so anxious,' urged his mother. 'We must keep calm and just see what happens.'

'But listen!' bellowed Antonio, disappearing to turn up the dial on the radio they kept in the cramped office behind the bar. 'Listen to this!'

The voice of Queipo de Llano echoed around the bar, as he bellowed his list of towns where the Nationalists were already victorious.

'We can't just sit here and let this happen, can we?' Appealing to his parents for even the slightest sign of agreement or support, Antonio's eyes filled with tears of frustration.

'Perhaps Mother is right,' suggested Mercedes. 'It's probably best not to get too worked up about it. Everything seems to be all right here so far, doesn't it?'

Antonio's reaction was not just born out of the youthful desire to wield a weapon. He had heard that it was not only the military that should be causing anxiety to Martínez. There were two other key players in this unfolding drama: the blue-uniformed Assault Guard and the green-clad Civil Guard.

Though both of these gendarmeries theoretically owed allegiance to the civil authority, their loyalty to the Republic also turned out to be questionable. The disloyalty of the Civil Guard to the government in most places was unsurprising, but the loyalty of the Assault Guard, which had been formed and organised under the Republic, might have been expected. Antonio had heard that in Granada a conspiracy against the Republic was brewing in both these forces. In the Civil Guard, Lieutenant Pelayo was plotting, as was Captain Álvarez of the Assault Guard.

Even if Martínez and Campins had not fully grasped the situation, the workers sensed that something was afoot and, that night, a huge group gathered in one of the city's most central squares, the Plaza del Carmen. Granada was like a pressure cooker with its contents almost at boiling point. At any minute it seemed as if the lid could be thrown sky high by the force of an explosion.

They were mostly manual workers and, without the lethargy-inducing heat, their anger would have tipped them into earlier action. People were desperate for weapons. Anything would do. In order to arm themselves, men wiped dust from the oldest of pistols. Soon, the streets were full of boys and men ready to fight, and even those who had never given more than a passing nod to politics found themselves whipped up into a frenzy of sympathy for the Republic.

Antonio and his two friends Salvador and Francisco went to the Plaza del Carmen to see what was going on. Everywhere they looked they saw men brandishing weapons, even up on the rooftops. At this point the troops were still confined to their barracks. No one knew where the power lay or what was going to happen but the city was brimful of tension and fear.

In the early hours of 20 July, the plans for the rebellion in Granada were finalised. Captain Álvarez committed the support of his Assault Guards to the leader of the rebels within the army garrison.

Right up to that very afternoon, the members of the civil government had been unaware of what was brewing. Martínez was meeting with some of his supporters, including Antonio Rus Romero, Secretary of the Popular Front, and also the head of the Civil Guard. At some point a message came through to Romero that the troops were lining up in the barracks and getting ready to march. Campins received a phone call telling him the situation and was incredulous. He maintained that the troops had sworn they would be loyal, but he would visit the barracks immediately to see for himself. When he arrived, he was shocked to find that not only had the artillery troops rebelled but that the infantry regiment, the Civil Guard and the Assault Guard had also come out against the Republic.

Campins was now a prisoner and, worse, was forced to sign a document drawn up for him that declared a state of war. The papers also outlined the punishments for anyone who did not comply with the new regime, crimes ranging from possessing firearms to gathering in groups of more than three people.

The citizens of Granada had no real information, but late in the afternoon, when the city was quiet and all the shops were still shut for siesta, some trucks trundled through the sleepy streets, with stern-faced army troops, eyes focused neither to right nor left. Behind them came artillery. Some people misunderstood the reason for their presence in the street, believing them to have come out to fight against the Fascists, and a few naïvely saluted them.

It was the sound of these trucks and the grating of their gears that disturbed Concha's siesta. She was dozing in her darkened bedroom overlooking the street, and immediately awoke Pablo. They opened one of the shutters just enough to observe what was going on below their window and stood close enough to feel each other's hot breath in the dark room. If the soldiers looked up they would have seen them, though the roar of the engines would have drowned out the sound of Concha's voice.

'Holy Mary,' she whispered, her fingers tightening around her husband's arm. 'It's happening. It's really happening.'

Something was taking place in front of them that had been rumoured for days. Concha felt panic rise inside her.

'Where are the children? Where are they? We need to find them.'

Concha's immediate response was to gather her family together and her anxiety was scarcely concealed. The sight of these armed brigades, whoever they supported and whatever their orders, meant that no one's safety was guaranteed.

'Antonio is out somewhere – maybe Ignacio too. But the others are in their rooms, I think,' Pablo replied, running out onto the landing to begin checking the bedrooms.

Though the children were all stronger and sturdier than their parents, the need to know the whereabouts of their offspring was primitive and compelling for Pablo and Concha. They ran from room to room, waking both Mercedes and Emilio, before they found Ignacio's bed was empty.

'I can tell you where he is . . .' muttered Emilio sleepily, stumbling down the stairs from his attic room.

'Where? *Where* do you think he is?' asked his mother anxiously.

'With that Elvira woman probably.'

'I don't want to know that, Emilio. Now isn't the time for talking like that about your brother.'

Elvira was the wife of one of Granada's most celebrated matadors, Pedro Delgado, and Ignacio's long afternoons with her had been the subject of much gossip. According to Ignacio, the older man was as aware as anyone of the situation and, when he was out of town, he more or less left her to be taken care of by his protégé, the young Ramírez. This did not validate the situation. Before marrying, Elvira had been a prostitute, albeit a high-class one and, whatever else Concha Ramírez thought of her son's behaviour, this was what appalled her most.

'All right then,' answered Emilio snappily. 'But that's where you'll find him if you want to.'

Even with Fascist troops beginning to fill the streets, Emilio could not allow an opportunity to denigrate his brother to slip by.

Antonio was not at home either. No one had seen him that day.

They all gathered round the narrow gap between the long shutters in the master bedroom. Mercedes stood on the bed, a hand on each of her father's shoulders to balance, eager to catch a glimpse of what was happening down in the square. The last of the troops had gone by and now it seemed unnervingly still.

'What's going on, Emilio? Are they still out there?' Mercedes' voice was all too audible in the silence. 'I can't see. I can't see!'

'Ssh, Merche,' said her father, gesticulating that she should keep her mouth shut.

He had made out the sound of muffled voices only a few doors up the street from them, and now they all heard the unmistakable sound of gunshots.

One-two-three.

Inwardly, they all counted the rhythmic, even, bullet beats. At that moment, their world began to alter. The sound of firing would punctuate their waking hours and penetrate their sleep for a long time to come.

Voices came from down in the street right below them, outside the café itself, but unless they leaned out it was impossible to identify the speakers. Before long their curiosity was satisfied. Two men were marched out across the square, arms raised in the air.

'They've come from the Pérez house. It's Luis and one of the boys! It's Luis and Julio!' gasped Concha. 'My God. Look, they're taking them away. They're actually taking them away . . .'

Her voice trailed off. It was hard for all of them to take in the sight of innocent men under arrest and being led away by soldiers. It was with some disbelief that they faced the significance of this moment.

'They've done it, haven't they? The army have taken over,' said Emilio flatly.

It was a situation that those who had been unimpressed by the Republican government had long since hoped for, but for supporters of a democratically elected party it was almost beyond belief that the rule of law should have been overturned before their very eyes.

With horror, the Ramírez family watched their friends being marched away. Once they were out of sight, the family withdrew from the window and stood around in the semidarkness.

Concha closed the shutters and sank onto the bed. 'What are we going to do?' she asked, looking around at the silhouetted forms of her husband and children.

The question was rhetorical. There was no action they could sensibly take, apart from to stay in their home and wait to see what happened next.

Not long afterwards Antonio returned. He listened with disbelief as they described how Luis Pérez and his son had been taken away.

'But why have they taken them? On what grounds?'

'Who knows?' answered his father. 'But we had better go round and see María and Francisco later.'

'Are you sure that's wise?' asked Concha, a note of cautious self-preservation creeping in.

Antonio then told his family what he had seen out on the streets that day, and especially of the moment when he realised that the army had rebelled.

Along with Francisco and Salvador, he had been in the crowd that had amassed in the Plaza del Carmen. He described the moment of confusion when news had reached them that the troops were out of their quarters and marching towards the square.

'We assumed that the soldiers coming in our direction were there to ensure public order and defend the Republic,' he said. 'But we soon realised our mistake.'

The intentions of the military became all too clear. With a cannon and machine guns now in position in front of the town hall, the crowd had had two options: to disperse or to be fired on.

'We just weren't ready to face anything like that,' Antonio continued. 'Francisco thought we were a bunch of cowards running away, but we wouldn't have had a chance!'

'So what happened?' asked Mercedes.

'We fled down a side street and then all we heard was the sound of gunfire.'

'I think we probably heard it too,' Emilio said.

'And now,' concluded Antonio, 'there are artillery batteries occupying every strategic point around the town: the Plaza del Carmen, the Puerta Real and the Plaza de la Trinidad. And you didn't believe me this morning, Father! If only we'd been given some weapons, we could have stopped all this!'

Both his parents shook their heads.

'It's awful, it's awful,' said Pablo, looking at the floor. 'We just didn't think it could really happen.'

Antonio told them everything else that he had heard. Torres Martínez was apparently under house arrest – 'If he had been more on top of the situation,' grumbled Antonio, 'we might not be in this mess' – and Valdes had taken over the post of Civil Governor. All of this seemed to have been achieved without the slightest resistance. Antonio had also heard the rumour that the town hall had been taken over and the mayor, Manuel Fernandez-Montesinos, who was Lorca's brother-in-law, had been dramatically arrested during a meeting with fellow councillors and locked up.

They sat and puzzled over what the humble locksmith, Luis Pérez, and his son had in common with the well-connected socialist mayor of the city, but people from all walks of life were being marched from their homes for arbitrary reasons. Intellectuals, artists, workers and freemasons were among the six thousand or so of those arrested in the first week. Being a known left-wing supporter or a member of a trade union now put a person's life in danger. Antonio decided to keep to himself what he knew about the politics of Francisco's older brother, Julio. Even Luis himself might not have known of his son's membership of a communist organisation.

'The worst thing of all,' declared Pablo, 'is that both the Civil Guard *and* the Assault Guard are now on the rebels' side.'

'You keep saying that, Pablo, but I don't believe you,' Concha protested.

'I'm afraid he's right, Mother. I've seen a few of them out there in the street talking to groups of soldiers. They certainly didn't look as though they were on different sides,' confirmed Antonio.

Antonio now sought to reassure his mother about what seemed to worry her most of all: that Ignacio was safe.

'He'll be back soon,' he told them. 'I'm quite sure of that.'

At around midnight, when everyone but Concha had fallen into a fitful sleep, Antonio was proved right. Ignacio arrived home.

'You're back,' said his mother, appearing at her bedroom door. 'We've been so worried about you. You wouldn't believe what's been going on today – here in this very street.'

'Everything's going to be fine,' said Ignacio blithely, taking his mother into his arms and planting a kiss on her forehead. 'Really it is.'

Though he could not see it in the darkness, her face registered some confusion. Had Ignacio been so entwined with his lover that the events of the day had passed him by? She did not have the chance to ask him. He had taken the stairs two by two and closed his door behind him. There was always the morning, she thought to herself. Nothing would have changed by then.

Chapter Sixteen

NEXT MORNING, THE streets were deserted. Shops and cafés kept their doors locked and the tension inside every home spread eerily into the empty streets.

The takeover of Radio Granada gave the Nationalist cause a perfect medium to broadcast their version of the previous day's events. *El Ideal* reinforced the same news stories and gloated over the easily won success of the rebel army forces and the fact that so many middle-class citizens of Granada had come out in support of Franco.

The Ramírez family stayed indoors, the café doors firmly bolted and the wooden shutters fastened. They took it in turns to watch from the first-floor windows, and the day was broken up with the passing of truckloads of troops and the regular sound of a voice crying out: 'Long live Spain! Death to the Republic!'

Emilio sat on his bed strumming chords. Apparently indifferent to the events going on outside, his stomach nevertheless churned with fear. He played until his fingers were sore, drowning out the sound of gunfire with his passionate *seguiriyas* and *soleares*.

Even Antonio, usually patient with his brother, was dismayed by Emilio's convincingly feigned lack of interest in the military coup.

'Doesn't he know what this could mean?' he pleaded to his father as they toyed with lunch that day, a meagre meal of cheese and olives. They had decided not to risk a potentially fruitless and dangerous outing to find bread that day. Emilio was not hungry and had stayed in his room.

'Of course he doesn't,' sneered Ignacio. 'He's in his own little *fairy*-tale world as usual.'

Everyone in the family but Ignacio turned a blind eye to Emilio's homosexuality so no one reacted to his jibe. Just once, a few months before, Concha and Pablo had finally discussed their concerns with each other. Even in the more liberal climate of the early days of the Republic, attitudes to homosexuality had not changed in Granada.

'Let's just hope he grows out of it,' Pablo had said.

Concha had nodded. Her husband assumed this was in affirmation and the subject was never raised again.

Like everyone on the side of the Republic in the city, they had lost their appetite for food, if not for news. On the radio they picked up that the aerodrome at Armilla had been taken and that the big explosives factory on the road to Murcia was now in the hands of the Nationalists. Both were considered of huge strategic importance, and those who wanted life to revert to normal now began to resign themselves to the idea of a new regime in their city.

Mercedes opened her window at dusk that day and leaned out to catch a breath of air. Swifts crossed the sky in front of her and bats darted to and fro. The events of the previous night – the sounds of gunshots and the sight of their neighbours being taken away – lingered with her, but her thoughts were elsewhere.

'Javier, Javier, Javier,' she whispered into the night. The yellow light from the gaslamp below her window flickered with the gusts of warm air and a moth twirled in its momentary brightness. She yearned to dance and could think of nothing except when she might see her *guitarrista* again. If only this emergency could end so that they could be together, she thought.

Faintly, escaping through the roof tiles and into the creamy atmosphere, she could hear the sound of Emilio's playing. She climbed the stairs for the first time in a while, drawn to the comforting sound of his music. Only now did it occur to her that he might have felt abandoned when she had started dancing with Javier, and she was unsure whether he would welcome her intrusion.

He said nothing when she entered the room but he continued to play, which had always been his way when, as a little girl, she had first invaded his privacy. The hours passed. Dawn broke. Mercedes woke to find herself lying on Emilio's bed. Her brother was asleep in his chair, his arms still wrapped around his guitar.

Concha opened up the café the next day. After a day of having the doors and shutters tightly closed, it was a relief to throw them open again and replace the stale air.

There seemed no particular reason not to open up, and the bar became the focus of intense discussions about what might happen next. Stories abounded about people being brutalised in order to betray friends or neighbours, and everyone had seen arrests taking place. Arrests were being made for a huge range of so-called crimes. What was lacking was hard information and a dearth of knowledge about the bigger picture in the country as a whole. Uncertainty and fear mingled.

In Granada there was one area that was still resolutely holding out against Franco's troops – the Albaicín. From their café on the edge of this old quarter, the Ramírez family now had good cause to fear for the fabric of their own home and livelihood.

Theoretically, this *barrio* should have been able to defend itself. It occupied a steep hillside and even had a moat, in the form of the River Darro, running along its lower boundary.

Barricades had been erected to block entry into the Albaicín, and from their superior vantage point the inhabitants there were in a strong position to defend their 'castle' against the troops. For several days there was incessant fighting, and the Ramírez family watched many members of the Civil Guard and several Assault Guards being carried away wounded.

Radio Granada gave regular warnings that anyone resisting the Assault Guard would be fired on, but still the siege continued. There was no doubt in anyone's mind that the determination of those holding out in the Albaicín would win over.

They might have had a better chance if the army had not already occupied the Alhambra, which loomed above them. One afternoon, as Concha watched from her window, it was as though mortars rained from the heavens. Ammunition poured down on the Albaicín, blasting roofs and walls. After the rebel soldiers had wreaked this comprehensive destruction, the dust settled briefly.

Moments later, the low moan of an aeroplane was then heard and aerial bombardment began. The people of the Albaicín were sitting targets.

For some hours, resistance continued but then Concha saw a stream of people starting to emerge from the still-rising dust. Women, children, and elderly men, all with bundles of clothing and handfuls of possessions that they had rescued from their homes, began to descend the hill. It was hard to hear much above the noise of the machine-gun fire that now sprayed the rooftops, and the thud of artillery, but every so often between the silences could be heard the sound of children crying and the soft moan of the women as they hurried towards the barricades.

The last few men, as they ran out of ammunition and realised the game was up, climbed on to rooftops and waved white sheets to signal their surrender. They had put up a brave struggle but knew that the Fascists had enough ammunition to raze every home in their *barrio* to the ground.

The most fortunate managed to escape towards Republican lines, but the majority were caught.

Antonio appeared that afternoon, pale with anxiety, his hair peppered with the dust that seemed to hang in the still air.

'They're just shooting them –' he said to his parents – 'anyone from the Albaicín that they catch – just shooting them. In cold blood.'

Coming to terms with their own powerlessness was a terrifying moment for them all.

'They're completely ruthless,' said Concha, almost inaudibly.

'I think they've well and truly proved that,' agreed her husband.

Although the initial takeover had been accomplished with impressive stealth and bloodless efficiency, the days following it brought a wave of resistance and violence. There was continuous shooting that night and machine guns were in action from dawn till dusk.

Five days after the initial takeover of the garrison, and once the bombardment of the Albaicín had come to an end, it became quieter. The workers were now on strike, which was the only safe means to register immediate protest against events.

With bread and milk easy to obtain, no one was going hungry, and El Barril could be run reasonably normally. The Ramírez family stayed close to the café, with the exception of Ignacio, who came and went with a smile on his face.

Elvira Delgado's husband had been in Sevilla when the army had taken over there and his firmly held right-wing position made him fearful of moving across the territory in between, which was still held by the Republic. His absence from Granada made Ignacio even more jubilant about the military coup than ever. He had bought a copy of *El Ideal*, which now lay on a table in the bar and, with its references to 'Glorious General Franco', there was no doubting its politics. Emilio came down late morning and saw it there, its taunting headline an offence to anyone who supported the Republic.

'Fascist bastard!' he said, hurling it across the room, its pages separating out across the floor like a carpet.

'Emilio, please!' shouted his mother. 'All you do is make things worse.'

'They couldn't be worse than they already are, could they?'

'But once things settle down, General Franco might not turn out to be such a bad thing,' she responded. Emilio knew as well as she did that these were words neither of them believed.

'I'm not talking about Franco, Mother. I'm talking about my brother.' He picked up one of the loose sheets of newsprint and waved it in front of his mother's face. 'How dare he bring this filth into the house?'

'It's just a newspaper.' Even if it was looking unrealistic in the country as a whole, Concha's yearning for peace in her own family obliged her to try to be conciliatory. Emilio knew that his mother hated what Franco was trying to do as much as he did.

'It's not just a newspaper. It's propaganda. Can't you see that?'

'But it's the only one on sale now, as far as I know.'

'Look, Mother, it's about time you faced up to something about Ignacio.'

'Emilio!' said Pablo, drawn into the room by the sound of raised voices. 'That's quite enough. We don't want to hear any more . . .'

'Your father's right. There's quite enough fighting going on outside, without everyone in here shouting at each other too.'

By now Antonio had appeared too. He knew that the old-established dislike between his two younger brothers had intensified. It was linked with the conflict that was rumbling like an earthquake across their entire country. The divisions of politics had entered their home. The hard-line conservative attitudes of those who wished to take over the country were a serious personal threat to Emilio, and the hatred between these two young men was now as real as that between the Republicans and the Fascist troops that patrolled in the streets of Granada.

Emilio stormed out of the room and no one spoke until the sound of his feet thumping up the stairs to the attic had receded.

News reports on the radio and in the newspapers were often no more accurate than rumours on the street, but the overall picture was becoming clear: Franco's troops were not having the success they had hoped for throughout the region and though some towns had surrendered, many others were putting up fierce resistance and were able to remain loyal to the government. The country carried on in a state of uncertainty.

In Granada, as though to force men to declare which side they were on, the Nationalists now asked for people to sign up for guard duty. These volunteers wore blue shirts and became part of the tyranny. There were numerous other ways to show support and shirt colour indicated which particular right-wing group you were affiliated with – blue, green or white. The right wing loved the discipline and order of uniform.

By the end of July, Antonio could see it was effectively all over in Granada. The strike came to an end and for a short while it was as though nothing had happened. Taxis stood in their usual positions, shops opened, cafés rolled out their awnings. The sun still shone, and the heat was not as fierce as it had been the previous week.

Everything appeared the same, but everything had changed. Even if much of the country was fighting back, Granada was now undisputedly under martial law. Civilians were forbidden to drive vehicles, the right to strike was abolished and the possession of firearms was banned.

Concha was still in her nightgown one morning, sipping her early morning coffee, when Ignacio came in through the front door of the café.

'Hello, my darling,' she said, relieved to see him and refraining, as usual, from asking where he had been all night.

He bent down to kiss her on the top of her tousled hair and wrapped his arms around her neck. The unmistakable smell of a woman's perfume almost overwhelmed her. It was lily of the valley, or was it damask rose? She could not quite tell as it was all mixed up with the familiar smell of her son's body and perhaps a cigar or two that he had smoked the previous evening.

He pulled out the chair next to her, sat down and took her hands in his. For years, Concha had been the practice ground for her son's now famed charm. She did not have a favourite son, but she did have one whose ability to win her round far surpassed that of the other two.

Ignacio had been due to appear in a number of bullfights that summer; for a while at least, the season was suspended and this meant he was a man at leisure. He seemed positively at ease with life and with himself.

'It isn't going to be so awful, is it?' he said. 'What did I tell you?'

'I wish I believed it, Ignacio,' she said, holding him at arm's length and looking into his eyes. His dark, seductive pupils swam with affection.

A week or so of this conflict had been more than enough to fray her nerves right to the very edge, and even the sound of a door banging was enough to make her jump out of her skin. She was still haunted by the sight of their neighbours being dragged away from their home. The previous day they had heard that both Luis and Julio had been shot, and the Pérez home was looted on the same night. Poor María now lived in fear of her life and would not leave her home. Concha had visited every day since the arrests of her loved ones and that morning the woman had been beyond consolation. Francisco was too angry to be able to comfort his mother and Antonio spent the day with him trying to keep the lid on his friend's fury. Now Ignacio was trying to tell her that things were not going to be 'so awful'.

In some ways, their nerves had yet to be tested. First thing in the morning on 29 July, an aerial bombardment of Granada began that was to last on and off until the end of August. The worst thing about it was not the wanton destruction of their city. It was the fact that many of them were on the same side of this conflict as the Republican planes now bombing them.

Occasionally, the bombers' targets met the approval of those who still supported the legal government.

Antonio was out on the street one morning with his father and saw Republican planes flying overhead. They opened their machine-gun fire on the cathedral tower. Though it was the most beautiful and celebrated of holy places, the damage to Isabella and Ferdinand's great edifice and burial place did not stir either of them. Like most people who supported the rightful Republican government, they had long since stopped kneeling down in front of the altar, so disgusted were they with the collusion of the priests in this rebellion. Right from the beginning, the Catholic Church had sided with the army in this coup.

Newspapers continued to play their role in stirring up aggravation in the Ramírez household.

'It's that fascist rag again,' said Emilio, casting a disdainful look at the newspaper that lay on the bar. 'Why does he have to bring it here?'

On that morning it provided detailed coverage of a victory for the Nationalist troops. The Republicans had landed some of their planes at Armilla, not realising that it had already been taken by the army. When they descended from their planes they were taken prisoner and the Fascists gleefully celebrated the 'delivery' of some magnificent new aircraft.

'What a gift for Franco,' commented Antonio, under his breath.

Such stories did nothing for the morale of anyone who supported the Republic. Though they were battling to retain their ground, it seemed that things could still go either way.

For the next few days, Granada continued to be bombed from

the air and more innocent people died, their houses collapsing around them. Sirens sounded the alert, but even though the arrival of planes was advertised, there was no real place of refuge. Occasionally a member of the Civil Guard might be buried in the rubble, but it was mostly the innocent citizens of Granada who were terrorised by the daily routine of bombs that seemed to increase in destructive power as the day went on.

On 6 August, a bomb fell close to the café in the Plaza Nueva. One of the upstairs windows shattered, spraying the room with shards of glass, and everything in the building was violently shaken. Glasses fell off shelves in the bar and bottles crashed to the ground; brandy flowed across the floor in a dark river.

Concha cleared up the mess, helped by Emilio and Mercedes. For the first time in their lives they saw their mother weep and were disconcerted by the sight of her despair.

'I hate all this,' she began tearfully.

Her children exchanged glances. They could see that she was about to launch into one of her occasional tirades.

'Our country's a mess! Our city's a mess – and now our café . . . just look at it!' she cried.

There was no doubt that these catastrophes were all linked but the only one they could resolve was the one in front of them.

'Look, we'll all help clear this up,' said Emilio, balancing on his haunches to pick up the jagged remains of a dozen or so bottles. 'It's not as bad as it looks.'

Mercedes went to find a broom. For the first time in weeks, something had distracted her from thinking of Javier. He had occupied the central-most part of her mind for almost every waking moment since the coup but the proximity of the bomb had jolted her.

But as she swept the floor, even the musical jangling of the shards of glass brought her mind back to the man she loved. What had dominated her mind before she met him? She hated this wretched conflict for separating them.

Antonio had appeared and made his mother sit down. He was now pouring her a drink from the only surviving bottle.

'I don't know how long we can carry on . . .'

'What do you mean?' asked Antonio, anxious to calm his mother down.

'. . . running the café. It's all so . . .'

Antonio could tell his mother was tired, but they all needed to keep going. Each day everyone looked for signs that the situation in the city might be getting more stable and there was a determination on Antonio's part to ensure that some part of their lives continued without disruption. At this point, supplies of food were still relatively plentiful in the city so there was no difficulty feeding their customers; fish was the only thing that they could not get hold of as the city was cut off from the coast at present, but meat, bread, vegetables and fruit were easy to obtain.

'Look, we need to try and carry on as normal, otherwise they really have won, haven't they?' he coaxed his mother.

She nodded with weary resignation.

Bombs had fallen on the Plaza Cristo and on the Washington Hotel, close to the Alhambra, where people had taken refuge from machine-gun fire. Nine people died in the city that day, the majority of them women, and there were numerous serious casualties. At the same time as the deaths of these innocents, other equally blameless people were being tried. The rumble of Republican bombers passing overhead had only increased the resolve of the Fascists to pass sentence on those who still supported the government. Even before the ink dried on the signatures authorising these deaths, their executions were carried out.

The first people to stand trial were the Civil Governor, Martínez, the president of the local council, a lawyer named Enrique Martín Forero, and two trade unionists, Antonio Rus Romero and José Alcantara. From their appearance in front of a jury on 31 July to their court martial, sentence and execution at dawn against the cemetery wall, it was a mere four days. For these men and for their families and friends, these were days of fear and disbelief that such unlawful decisions could be happening in the name of justice.

In the days that followed, numerous other key figures in Granada faced the firing squad – politicians, doctors, journalists. The news of these deaths horrified the Ramírez family.

'It means that no one is safe,' said Pablo. 'Absolutely no one.'

'If they can justify killing those men, then you're right,' said Antonio, who had always sought to reassure his parents.

Even he had now lost hope that this conflict might reach a swift conclusion once the parts of the army that had remained loyal to the Republican government had retaliated and gained control. The ruthlessness of the troops who were carrying out Franco's orders was breathtaking and without compromise. Idealists like Antonio were only just beginning to realise the nature of their enemy.

By the second week of August, both the heat and the bombing had intensified, but the former now ceased to be a topic of conversation. It was strange how one day, a whole building could be devastated and everyone would emerge miraculously unscathed, and then the next day a single explosion could kill half a dozen people in the street. Such an ill-fated group were the women who died when the Calle de Real Cartuja was targeted. Their deaths were as random as the roll of dice.

For over a fortnight now, Granada had been an island of fascism in a sea of loyal Republicanism. Antonio had held on to the hope that this relatively small area of land could be taken back but he was losing faith. News began to drift in of Nationalist successes in various other places including Antequera and Marbella.

The Nationalist force had now organised its defence against air bombardment of Granada. German cannons were in strategic positions to deter Republican planes, so air raids stopped.

Once the bombs ceased to drop, the streets of Granada were again full of activity. There were more people around than was usual for the time of year. Many would normally have left the city for the duration of the summer but had been afraid to do so because of the uncertainty of the political situation. Combined with the influx of people from surrounding villages the population had swelled.

The atmosphere was clearly not one of celebration, but at

certain times of day, the teeming streets and squares were redolent of fiesta. The cafés were full. People sat close to share precious shade, and young women moved about between the tables collecting coins for Red Cross hospitals that had been set up around the city to treat the wounded.

Cinemas were open as usual but were obliged endlessly to repeat the few films that they had in stock, and entertainment-starved audiences had no choice but to tolerate the repetition and to watch the newsreels, which were alarming whichever side of the political spectrum the audience was on.

Ignacio continued to antagonise his family with his own reaction to events. About the total domination of the city and nearby villages by the Fascists, he did not bother to hide his triumphalism, but as time went on he would also rant and rave about atrocities reported to have been committed by those defending the Republic in towns such as Motril and Salobrena.

'They dragged women into the sea,' he shouted at Antonio and Emilio, who listened silently to their brother, 'and murdered their children!'

Whether this was true or merely rightist propaganda, they were not going to give Ignacio the satisfaction of a reaction.

'And you presumably know they've destroyed the harvest – and killed the flocks!' he added.

Their silence infuriated him. He came right up to his brothers and Antonio could feel the heat of Ignacio's anger as he spat his next words right into his face: 'If we all starve it won't be Franco's fault!' he said, almost nose to nose with Antonio. 'It'll be the fault of you Republicans! Can't you see it's all over? The Republic is *finished*!'

All over Granada people sat huddled around radios. Fingers were yellow with nicotine and nails were bitten down to the quick. Anxiety, tension and heat made the city rank with sweat. Rumours of mass executions in other parts of the country intensified the terror.

People feared those who lived in the same street and even those who lived under the same roof. Across the country, families were being torn apart.

Chapter Seventeen

IGNACIO'S REPORTS OF Republican troops abandoning their weapons and fleeing from their positions in the villages up in the hills had more substance than the rest of his family wanted to admit. The effectiveness of Franco's army in and around Granada had been swift and absolute.

'I just can't believe it!' said Concha one morning, ill-concealed disgust in her voice. 'Have you been out this morning?' Her question was addressed to Antonio and Emilio. 'Go down the street and look! Take a walk down to the cathedral. You won't believe your eyes.'

Emilio did not react, but Antonio got up and left the café. As he turned right, down Reyes Catolicos, he saw immediately what it was that had vexed his mother so much. Approaching the cathedral, the streets were decked in red and yellow bunting. It must have been put up very early that morning and now the city was dressed as for fiesta.

It was 15 August. In another year, the date might have meant something to him but now it was meaningless. It was the Feast of the Assumption, the celebration of the day that the Virgin Mary was taken up to heaven, and for the hundreds of faithful that gathered around the cathedral doors, trying to hear the Mass that was being sung inside, this was one of the most revered days of the Church calendar; there simply was not enough room inside to accommodate them all.

From within came the sound of clapping. The ripple of applause spread into the square and soon the crowd joined their hands in response. The appearance of the Archbishop's procession at the main door was greeted by the perfectly timed blast of a military fanfare.

Now blocked in by the dense-packed flock, Antonio struggled to extricate himself. He was sickened by this blatant display of military and ecclesiastical co-operation and pushed his way out of the square. As he turned back into the main street and up towards the Plaza Nueva he almost collided with a troop of legionaries, marching down towards the cathedral, their hard, chiselled faces streaked with sweat. His own step almost turned to a run as he sped back towards home. He was scarcely aware of the groups of elegantly dressed people standing on their flag-bedecked balconies, though some of them noticed him, a sole figure moving against the steady tide of soldiers.

When he arrived back at the café, his parents were sitting together at a table. Pablo smoked, gazing into space.

'Antonio,' said Concha, with a smile for her eldest son, 'you're back. What's happening out there now?'

'People celebrating, that's what,' he said, almost choked with disgust. 'Catholics and Fascists. It's awful. I can't stand it. That smug, fat-arsed Archbishop . . . God, I'd like to run him through like a pig!'

'Ssh, Antonio,' said his mother, noticing that a few people were now coming into the café. Mass was over and the bars would now fill with people. 'Keep your voice down.'

'But why, Mother?' he hissed. 'How can a man who is head of the Church here ignore all this killing . . . this *murder*? Where's his compassion?'

Antonio was right. Monsignor Agustin Parrado y García, Cardinal Archbishop of Granada, was one of many senior members of the Catholic Church who sided wholeheartedly with Franco. These people saw the insurrection of the army generals as a holy crusade and for that reason alone would not intervene to save the lives of anyone falsely imprisoned and sentenced by the Nationalists.

Concha had tied her apron and was soon behind the bar, followed by her husband, and by the time they had taken orders, Antonio had disappeared out of the door.

It may have been no real comfort to Antonio, but Franco soon began to make demands on those who supported him, to the tune of tens of thousands of pesetas. There were subscriptions for the army, the Red Cross and for the purchase of aircraft, and some even had to share their homes with senior army officials. The cost of war was not cheap for anyone and the banks themselves were in crisis. No one was depositing money. They were only making withdrawals and their vaults were being drained of their reserves.

Pablo and Concha listened to the grumbles of their few wealthy customers. The café had always had a mixed clientele and the couple had worked hard to maintain their image of absolute neutrality. Anything else would have been suicidal in this climate and atmosphere.

'They took away my husband's Chrysler last week,' said one well-coiffed woman of about fifty-five.

'How dreadful,' responded her friend. 'And when do you think you'll get it back?'

'I'm not sure I'd want it now,' she replied, the disdain evident in her voice. 'I saw it only this morning – crammed full of Assault Guards. You can imagine what a filthy mess they'll be making of it. It already has a big dent in its side!'

Both sides were feeling the cost of this conflict. Many people had relatives in other cities and for some time now communication between Granada and the outside world had been restricted. No amount of brandy that they served could fully calm the anxiety of people who sat in the café fretting about the wellbeing of sons or daughters, uncles and parents in Córdoba, Madrid or distant Barcelona, from whom they had received no word. Mercedes was becoming desperate for news of Málaga.

Now that Granada was firmly in their hands, the Nationalists were sending out troops to other towns. Antonio and his friends were heartened to hear that many of them were putting up strong resistance. Although the narrow passage between Sevilla and Granada was held by the Nationalists and heavily guarded, much of the rest of the region was still holding out against Franco's troops, and fierce combat went on even in small towns that they had assumed could be taken without a fight.

The sinister task of keeping watch over people in Granada was now shared with members of the fascist Falangist youth party, who happily participated in denouncing and persecuting anyone they suspected of being Republican. Crimes against the new regime could consist of anything from having communist propaganda daubed on your walls, which might even have been put there by the Falangists themselves to stir up trouble, to having voted for the socialist party in previous elections. The terror of arbitrary arrest and imprisonment was intense.

For Emilio, the day after the Feast of the Assumption, 16 August, was the worst of the conflict so far. Within twenty-four hours, both his close friend Alejandro and his hero, Lorca, were arrested. The poet had travelled to Granada to stay with his family just before the coup, but realising the danger he might be in because of his socialist sympathies, he left his home and took refuge with a Falangist friend. Even being with someone who supported the right did not protect him. His detention took place on the same day as the execution of his brother-in-law, the Mayor, Montesinos, who was shot against the cemetery wall.

The news of Lorca's arrest had got round quickly and for three days his family and all of those who loved him waited anxiously. He belonged to no political party so there was slim justification for his detention.

Emilio was working in the café when he overheard two customers talking. At first he thought he must have been mistaken, when he realised who they were talking about.

'So they shot him in the back, did they?' asked one of the men.

'No, in the backside . . .' the other murmured. 'For being a homosexual.'

They were unaware that Emilio was listening to their every word.

A moment before, Ignacio had come downstairs. He had caught the last words and could not resist joining in.

'Yes, that's exactly what happened – they shot him in the arse for being a queer, a *maricón*! There are too many of his type in this city.'

Everyone in the room went completely silent. Even the ticking clock sounded embarrassed, but Ignacio could not resist another stab. This captive audience was irresistible.

'We need *real* men in this country,' he challenged. 'Spain will never be strong while it's full of poofters.'

With those words he strode through the bar and disappeared into the street. His was a sentiment shared by many on the right. Manliness was a prerequisite for the true citizen.

For a while no one spoke. Emilio stood, frozen to the spot, tears flowing down his face. At one point he wiped them away with his cloth but still they came. When Concha appeared she took her son's arm, led him into the office behind the bar and shut the door. The muffled sound of sobbing was drowned out as customers resumed their discussions. Pablo appeared to take over at the bar. There had been no news of Alejandro, and for Emilio it was as though the situation could not get any worse.

The death of Lorca was a landmark event in this conflict. Any residual belief in fairness and justice was destroyed. People across Spain were horrified.

At the end of August, just when people in Granada were beginning to feel safe from airborne attack, Republican army planes reappeared. Some thirty bombs were dropped on the city, the anti-aircraft cannons doing absolutely nothing to prevent them. Although their action brought renewed fear and terror to everyone, including those who supported them, it showed that the Republican cause was not yet a lost one.

'You see,' said Antonio, appealing to his parents the next day, 'we can still fight to restore the Republic!'

'We all know that,' interrupted Emilio, 'apart from Ignacio, of course.'

Concha sighed. This bitterness between her sons, which had brewed for so many years, now wearied her. She had struggled so hard not to take sides and to be even-tempered and even-handed.

When the air strikes ceased, the city once again put on a display of normality.

One day, at the end of the month, Ignacio came in looking more satisfied with life than ever.

'There's going to be a bullfight next week,' he announced to the family. 'My first here as a *matador de toros*.'

Antonio could not resist a tart comment. 'It'll be good to see a bullring put to its proper use,' he said. They all knew to what he was referring.

Earlier in August, in the bullring at Badajoz, a town in the south-west, instead of the blood of bulls the huge ring of sand had soaked up the blood of thousands of Republicans, socialists and communists. They had been herded towards the neat white *plaza de toros* and through the gate where the parade usually entered, and into the ring. Machine guns were lined up for them and eighteen hundred men and women were mown down. Some of the bodies lay for days until they were dragged away and their blood turned black in the sand. Reports mentioned that passers-by had retched at the sickening smell of spilled blood and that the only thing the victims were spared was the sight of their town being ransacked and looted.

'Whatever happened in Badajoz,' retorted Ignacio defensively, 'those *rojos* probably deserved it.'

He pushed past Antonio and put his hands on his mother's shoulders.

'You will come, won't you?' he asked imploringly.

'Of course I will,' she said. 'I wouldn't miss it. But I'm not sure your brothers will be there.'

'I wouldn't expect them to be,' he said, spinning round to look at Antonio. 'Especially him upstairs.'

The mood in the bullring the following week was euphoric. The stands hummed with excitement as the spectators, dressed in their best finery, talked animatedly and waved to friends across the crowd. For the predominantly conservative *aficionados* of this sport, the reopening of the ring symbolised a return to some form of normality and they savoured the moment.

Pablo and Concha were there that afternoon to watch their son. Antonio, Emilio and Mercedes had chosen to stay at home.

From where they sat on this late afternoon, securely enclosed in the perfect circle of the Plaza de Toros, the devastation that had taken place in parts of their city was out of sight. What mattered to the majority of people there at that moment was that they could enjoy the resumption of their old way of life, a sense of their élite position, a re-establishment of the old traditions and hierarchy. Even the choice of seat, in the sun or the shade, *sol o sombra*, reflected social standing in the city.

'Whatever happens in the next few months,' went one conversation overheard by Concha, 'at least we've got rid of those awful lefties in the town council.'

After that she tried not to listen to the two elderly men next to her, who clearly had no idea how brutally and thoroughly some of the socialist town councillors had been eliminated, but snatches of conversation kept drifting across to her and they were hard to ignore.

'Let's pray that the nation will see the light and give in to General Franco,' said one of them.

'We live in hope,' responded the other. 'It would be much better for everyone. And the sooner it happens the better.'

'Try not to listen to them,' said Pablo, overhearing too. 'There's nothing we can do about the way these people think. Look! The parade is going to start . . .'

The pageantry seemed more scintillating than ever, the men more handsome, the costumes more vivid. For the past hour, Ignacio had been preparing himself in his dressing room. He was laced into his trousers and his hair was dressed and pinned before he put on the smooth felt *montera* hat. He admired himself in the mirror and lifted his chin. The gleaming white of his costume accentuated his dark hair and tanned skin.

As he emerged into the ring with the others and they bowed before the fight director and the local celebrities who sat in the box, he wondered how life could possibly get better than this.

And everything is yet to come, he reflected, basking in the sheer joy of anticipation.

Ignacio was the third of the matadors to make his entrance in the ring. Though they had been polite, the crowd had been unimpressed by the other fighters. The second had a false start when his first bull rammed the wooden barricade and smashed his horns.

The creature's carelessness earned him his freedom and a return to the rich pastureland where he had been reared. This matador played his next bull deftly before making a swift, clean kill, but there had been no showmanship, nothing that thrilled the crowd.

They hoped for more drama with Ignacio. Many of them had seen him perform before and his reputation for deliberately breathtaking near misses with the bull had received plenty of coverage in the pages of the local newspapers.

The crowd was ready for something that captured the imagination and they always expected the best to be last. For many, the amount of death and violence they had witnessed in the past month or so had merely whetted their appetite for more. They had seen plenty of blood spilled that afternoon but the twin pleasures of danger and catharsis had so far been lacking. These bulls had not so far presented any real risk to these young men.

The cruelty of the crowd was palpable. They did not want the bull to die too soon: the stages of his degradation before the final decisive blow must be slow and painstaking and his suffering must be drawn out.

Most of the arena was now in shadow and the day was finally cooling. A shaft of low, late afternoon sunlight caught the dazzling gold embroidery of Ignacio's jacket. This was the best time to fight.

The bull thundered towards him and, as his horns came into contact with the cape, its forelegs left the ground. Despite the wounds from the picador and the banderilleros, the animal still had plenty of energy. The *muleta* cape brushed its back as Ignacio executed a deft flick.

After he had executed his first few simple turns, Ignacio became more daring. He dazzled the crowd with the elegance of a 'butterfly' pass, sweeping the cape behind his back and then, to their astonishment, he knelt on the ground.

'What absolute gall!' they gasped. 'What confidence!' 'What nerve!'

The bull's head was lowered. Would Ignacio get away with such an audacious manoeuvre? Seconds later, the crowd would have their answer.

Ignacio got to his feet and acknowledged their applause. His back was turned to the bull now, a further demonstration of his supremacy over the animal. The gesture was almost contemptuous. If the bull had it in him, he might have gored the perfect, rounded buttocks of his pert derrière, but the beast was already losing his will.

The *faena* was nearly completed now. There were some more *verónicas*, when he twirled the cape above his head as he pirouetted. On the final one, the wounded bull brushed so close to Ignacio's body that his pure white jacket was painted crimson with the animal's blood.

'Now I understand why he wore that colour,' said Concha to herself.

Ignacio touched the left horn as he passed. It seemed almost affectionate, as if he was stroking the bull, thanking him for the opportunity to prove himself.

The build-up had all the grace and elegance of a dance seen in slow motion and now the bull came before him, almost on bended knee, worshipful. Ignacio raised the sword and plunged it deep, reaching the animal's heart. As they watched the last twitch of the defeated beast, the crowd were on their feet and waving their handkerchiefs. Ignacio's confrontation with the bull was as near perfection as a bullfight could be.

Apart from joining with the occasional gasps uttered collectively by the crowd, Ignacio's parents had remained silent for the duration of the fight. Once or twice Concha had gripped her husband's arm hard. It was difficult for a mother to see her son facing a charging bull and not experience a moment of pure terror. Only when the dead weight of the animal's corpse was being dragged on its final circuit by the team of horses could she allow herself to breathe again. Then Pablo was up with the rest, awash with pride at the sight of his son basking in the crowd's adulation.

The fanfare sounded. Ignacio returned, parading before the crowd, arms aloft to acknowledge the cheers. Sensual and provocative, these slim-hipped youths strutted a single circuit of the ring, dazzling in their purples, pinks and blood-stained white.

Concha rose to her feet. She too was proud of Ignacio but she hated this place, its atmosphere sickened her, and she was glad that they could now leave.

The bullfight seemed to bring about a brief renaissance of the old Granada. Everyone flooded out, the bars filled up, and into the small hours the streets thronged with people. Civil Guards kept a wary eye, alert for trouble, but anyone who felt uncomfortable about the underlying sense of right-wing triumphalism stayed indoors that night.

Ignacio was the man of the hour. In the smartest bar near the bullring he was fêted by his entourage and dozens of wealthy landowners and *aficionados* who queued up to shake his hand. There were dozens of women all keen to catch his eye too and the party went on late into the night. Everyone in this coterie shared similar views on the current situation in Spain and the drunken toasts and songs reflected this.

Lovely Lorca, what a bore!
NOW we bet your arse is sore!

They chanted the words over and over again, thrilled with the double entendre.

'You should have seen my brother when he heard about Lorca,' said Ignacio laughingly to the group he was standing with. 'Devastated!'

'So he's a poofter too, is he?' said one of the more vulgar men through a thick cloud of cigar smoke.

'Well, let's put it this way,' answered Ignacio conspiratorially, 'he doesn't share my taste for girls . . .'

One of the more voluptuous women in the bar had sidled up to Ignacio during this conversation and his hand had slipped round her waist as he carried on talking to his male friends. It was an almost unconscious gesture. At three in the morning when the bar would eventually shut, they would stroll together to the nearby Hotel Majestic, which always kept a few rooms back for the stars of the bullfight.

During the days that followed, Ignacio was irrepressible. He could scarcely contain his jubilation. The family were given the head of his magnificent kill. Somewhere in a dark corner of the café, it hung for some years, its staring expressionless eyes looking out at customers as they came in to El Barril.

But even while Ignacio was celebrating, the violence continued. Lorca was only one of hundreds who had disappeared.

About a month later, there was a horrendous banging on the glass panel of the El Barril's door at three o'clock in the morning. The violence of the knocking was almost enough to break it down.

'Who's that?' yelled the elderly Señor Ramírez out of his third-floor window. 'Who the devil is making all that noise?'

'Open up, Ramírez. Now!' It was a harsh voice and its owner, in using Pablo's name, clearly meant business.

By now, every inhabitant of the street was out of bed. Shutters were open, women and children leaned out of windows, and a few courageous men had come out onto the pavement and were now face to face with the dozen or so soldiers in the street. Dogs barked and the strident sounds of their yapping ricocheted off the walls, creating a deafening cacophony in the narrow streets. Even as the bolts were being pulled across, the hammering continued to rain down on the glass. Only when Pablo opened the door, did it cease, and then even the dogs were silent. Five of the soldiers pushed past him into the café and the door banged behind them. The others remained in the street, loitering, smoking, indifferent to the resentful glares of the civilians around them. The street was quiet. Perhaps two minutes or twenty passed. No one could say.

Eventually the door was thrown open. Silence was replaced by the sound of screams. It was Señora Ramírez.

'You can't take him away! You can't take him!' she wailed. 'He's done nothing wrong! You can't take him!'

There was a sense of desperation and helplessness in her voice. She knew that no protestation of hers could stop these men. The fact that they had no legal warrant to make an arrest mattered not a fraction of a peseta.

There were no streetlights so it was hard to see exactly what was going on in the shadows but everyone could see that it was Emilio who was standing in the street. He was still in a nightshirt, which glowed supernaturally white in the gloom, his hands were tied fast behind his back, his head was downcast and he was perfectly still. One of the uniformed men shoved him in the stomach with his rifle butt.

'Get going!' he ordered. 'Now.'

With that, Emilio seemed to come to life. He stumbled away from his home like a drunk, almost losing his balance on the uneven cobbles.

Then there was the sound of Señor Ramírez, trying to calm his wife: 'We will get him back, my dear. We will get him back. They have no right to take him.'

Half a dozen soldiers trooped down the street behind Emilio, two of them regularly jabbing him between the shoulder blades to steer him in the right direction. Soon they had disappeared round the corner and the metallic click of military footsteps had faded. Now the street was full of people, neighbours in huddles, women comforting Concha, men both furious and fearful.

Antonio and Ignacio stood nose to nose.

'Come on,' said Antonio. 'We have to follow them. Quick.'

It had been a long while since Ignacio had responded to any instruction from his brother, but for now at least they had a common purpose. Concern for their own flesh and blood, particularly their mother, briefly united them.

It was only a minute or two before they caught sight of the uniformed group and then followed them stealthily for half a mile, retreating into dark doorways and archways every time they paused. If they were spotted, it would do no one any good, least of all Emilio. The real surprise to Antonio was that their route took them to the government building. Less than a month earlier, Granada had been ruled from there to the benefit of the people.

There was another jab in the back for Emilio as he fell over the threshold, and then the door banged firmly shut. By now it was beginning to get light and the two brothers would not be able to hang around in the street for long without being seen. They squatted in a doorway, unable even to light a cigarette in case a burning match drew attention to them, and for ten minutes or so remained huddled like this, arguing over what to do. Stay? Go? Bang on the doors?

The decision was soon made for them. Shortly afterwards, a car rolled up to a side door and two soldiers got out. Some unseen figures admitted them into the building and within a few moments they re-emerged. This time, there was another figure between them. They were supporting him because he was unable to walk, but it was not a humane gesture. The man was bent double with pain and when they opened the door of the vehicle and bundled him in, it was obvious that there was no kindness intended. He was being treated like a package. As he fell into the car, both Antonio and Ignacio caught a glimpse of the still-gleaming white nightshirt and knew beyond doubt that the person they had seen was Emilio.

The car roared off into the night and they had to accept that they could not follow.

Antonio's heart was heavy. Men can't cry, Antonio repeated to himself. Men can't cry. His face was locked in a spasm of grief and disbelief, his hand held fast over his mouth to stifle the sound of his sobs, but his eyes overflowed with tears. For some time the brothers stayed crouched low in the doorway of some stranger, who even now slept soundly in his bed.

Ignacio was getting agitated. It was nearly light now and they had to get away from this place and back home. Their parents would be waiting for news.

'What are we going to tell them?' whispered Antonio, his voice choked.

'That he's under arrest,' said Ignacio bluntly. 'What's the point of telling them anything else?'

They walked in silence, slowly through the empty streets. Antonio longed for some comfort from his younger brother, but he would receive none. Ignacio's sang-froid about the situation puzzled him for a moment. He knew that Ignacio hated Emilio, but he could not allow himself to suspect that he was involved in his own brother's disappearance.

As the older brother, it would be his duty to tell their parents what had happened. Ignacio would remain in the background, his views of the matter as shadowy as the street.

It was more than a month since the Nationalists had taken over in Granada but the number of people being arrested daily and taken off in trucks to the cemetery to be shot was still rising. It seemed unbelievable that this could happen, least of all to someone so close to them.

'Perhaps they just want to question Emilio about Alejandro,' offered Mercedes helpfully, desperately clinging to a straw of hope. There had been no news of Emilio's best friend since his arrest.

Concha Ramírez's grief overwhelmed her. She could not contain it. An active imagination and the terror of the unknown filled her mind with visions of what might be happening to her son.

Pablo, however, refused to accept that he might never see Emilio again and talked as though his son might appear again at any moment.

Sonia and Miguel had long since drained their second and third coffees and, from time to time, the waiter approached to see if they needed anything more. Two hours had passed since they arrived.

'They must have been so distraught,' said Sonia.

'I think they were,' murmured Miguel. 'It meant that these terrible events were not just happening to other people but to them. And the arrest of one family member meant they were *all* in danger.'

Sonia looked around. 'It's getting quite smoky in here. Do you mind if we get some fresh air?' she asked.

They paid the bill and wandered out. Miguel continued to talk as they strolled across the square.

Chapter Eighteen

For days Concha prayed for her son's return. She knelt at his bedside, her hands clasped in supplication, muttering to the Virgin to have mercy. She had little faith that anyone was listening. The Nationalists had claimed God, and Concha was sure He could not be answering prayers on both sides of this conflict.

The room was in the same state as it had been the night Emilio was torn out of his bed. His mother had no plans to rearrange anything. The sheets were rumpled, swirled like cream on the surface of coffee, and the clothes he had been wearing the day before his arrest were carelessly slung across an old chair. His guitar lay on the other side of the bed, the sensuous curves of its lovely body so like a woman's. It struck Señor Ramírez as ironic that this might be the closest Emilio had ever got to having something so feminine and voluptuous in his bed.

On the second morning after Emilio's arrest, Mercedes found her mother in his room, crying. For the first time in weeks, she thought about something other than Javier and, possibly for the first time in her life, she began to emerge from her childish introspection.

Over eight weeks had now passed since Mercedes had seen Javier and she had not smiled since that day. As far as she knew, Javier had been at home in Málaga when the rebel soldiers took over Granada and there was no reason for him to risk his skin coming back. Even for her. So she was torn between anxiety that something terrible had happened to him and growing irritation that he had not contacted her. She did not know what to think. If he was safe and happy somewhere, why had he not contacted her? Why had he not come? For Mercedes, it was a curious state of uncertainty and made her sad and dissatisfied, and just about everything in between, but the sight of her mother's tears shocked her into the realisation that people around her might be suffering as much as she was.

'Mother!' she said, putting her arms around Concha.

Unaccustomed to such tenderness from her daughter, Concha wept all the more.

'He'll come back,' whispered the girl into her mother's ear. 'He'll come back.'

Feeling her mother's shuddering in her arms, Mercedes felt suddenly afraid. Perhaps the loving, gentle brother with whom she had shared so much was not going to return.

A few days passed in this state of unknowing. Pablo buried himself in the business of running the café. It was as busy as ever, and now he did not have Emilio helping him out. Though heavily weighed down with anxiety, a whole day would pass where he could keep his mind occupied with other things. From time to time, the sharp recollection of Emilio's absence came almost like a physical blow, and when this happened he could feel a lump rising in his throat and tears, such as his wife could shed so freely, had to be fought back.

On the fourth morning after Emilio's arrest, Concha decided that this stalemate in their lives could not continue. She had to know the truth. The people who might hold some records were the Civil Guard.

She had always regarded these sinister individuals, in their ugly patent leather hats, with great suspicion, and since the conflict had begun, her dislike of them had intensified. They always lurked on the edge of treachery and betrayal in this city.

She went alone to the Civil Guard offices. Tremblingly she gave Emilio's name and the guard on duty opened the ledger on his desk to find the log for the past few days. He ran his finger down the list of names and turned several pages. Concha's heart lifted. Her son's name was not there. Perhaps this meant he had been released. She turned to leave.

'*Señora!*' he called out in a tone that might have sounded friendly. 'What did you say your surname was?'

'Ramírez.'

'I thought you said Rodríguez . . .'

For Concha Ramírez, the world stood still at that moment. Her hopes had been held so high but now she knew by the tone in his voice that they had been in vain. It was almost an act of deliberate cruelty that he had raised them and now they were to be crushed, like an insect beneath his boot.

'There is an entry for a Ramírez. Yesterday morning. Sentence has been passed. Thirty years.'

'Where is he?' she asked in a whisper. 'Which prison?'

'I can't give you that information yet. Come back next week.'

In turmoil, she just managed to get to the door before she fell to her knees. The news had winded her like a physical blow. She gasped for air and it was some moments before she realised that the animal howls she could hear were her own cries. In the echoing vestibule of the Civil Guard offices, the sound of her anguish reverberated from the high ceiling. From behind the counter, a bespectacled man regarded her with total lack of concern. He had seen several other weeping mothers already that morning and their troubles elicited little sympathy from him. The only reaction they provoked was one of irritation. He did not like 'scenes' and hoped that this woman, like the others before her, would get out of here soon.

Once in the street, Concha had just one purpose: to make her way back home to share this news. Stumbling along, the familiar buildings provided her with much-needed support as she took each clumsy step towards her destination. Passers-by took her for a drunk woman and steered clear as she staggered from one shop doorway to the next. She hardly recognised the roads of her own city but, by instinct, through the haze of her own tears made her way to the familiar frontage of El Barril.

There was little need to tell Pablo what was wrong. He could see from the look on her face as she pushed open the café door that the news was bad.

For nine nights they lost sleep, and each day Concha sought confirmation of where Emilio had been taken. She was now a familiar figure at the government offices. Eventual confirmation that her son was in a prison close to Cádiz brought a strange sense of relief. The prison was more than two hundred kilometres away, but at least they knew something for certain.

Concha's first thought was to make the journey to see her son. If she could take him some food, at least he would not starve.

'But it's a ridiculous distance to travel,' said Ignacio. 'Particularly on your own.'

'I have no choice,' said Concha.

'Of course you have a choice!' insisted Ignacio.

'One day you will understand,' she responded patiently, 'when you have your own children.'

'Well, God help you. That's all I can say.'

The journey there took her two days. Despite the papers she had, which were meant to allow her safe conduct, the frequent checks by soldiers and Civil Guards were often carried out with aggression, and on several occasions she was certain she would have to turn back to Granada.

When she eventually arrived, Concha's request to see her son was denied.

'He is in solitary,' barked the officer on duty. 'He has currently lost all his privileges.'

Quite what those 'privileges' might be in this awful place, she could not imagine.

'How long will that last?' she asked, numb with disappointment.

'Could be two days, could be two weeks. Depends.'

She did not have the heart to ask what it depended on. In any case, she would not have any faith in the answer.

The basket of food was left. She had no idea if it would ever reach him. Inside one of the walnuts she had packed in the bag, she had concealed a note. It was just a mother's letter, with superficial news of family life and messages of love sincerely meant, but when it was found his time alone in a cell was increased by a week.

Tales of conditions inside prisons reached Pablo and Concha from many sources. Occasionally someone succeeded in escaping but the more common stories were of the daily firing squads and the arbitrariness of the lists of victims.

While Concha was preoccupied with the personal drama of her son's imprisonment, mothers were losing sons all over the country. Sons were losing mothers too.

By the autumn, Nationalist bombers were terrorising the defenceless people of Madrid and nobody was safe. Even mothers queuing for their children's milk were blasted to eternity. The capital city was Franco's real goal and Nationalist troops had reached the outskirts of the city. Leaflets had been dropped warning the population that unless they handed the city over, it would be wiped off the face of the earth. The relentless air raids were beginning to wear the population down. They were sitting targets.

Everyone, whether they supported the Republic or Franco, followed what was taking place in Madrid. What happened to the capital city could determine the outcome of this conflict for the whole country.

At the beginning of November, the first Russian planes arrived and counterattacks began. Though the Republic was now doing better in the air, the Nationalists began to have some success on the ground. That same month they took one of the city's suburbs, Getafe, which gave them hope that they were on their way to complete victory.

Antonio studied the newspapers more closely than ever and often read out extracts to his mother as she dried the glasses in the morning.

'"In spite of bombardment from Republican troops the Nationalist army has taken the area of Carabanchel and significant bridges have been gained, which could allow access to the inner city,"' Antonio read. '"Hand-to-hand combat has been taking place on the streets and losses run into thousands on both sides. Franco's troops have pushed through Republican lines into the University City."'

Antonio did not know that his mother was already well abreast of events from listening early each morning to a banned radio station broadcasting from Málaga.

'It could be the end of it all,' said Antonio. 'Perhaps Franco is about to get his way.'

Ignacio, who had come into the café and heard Antonio's

comment, saw the opportunity to comfort his mother. 'Well, Mother,' he said, 'as soon as Franco can declare victory, you might have your Emilio back.'

'That would be a relief,' she said, smiling at the thought. 'But doesn't it depend what the charges against him are?'

'I suppose it might. I'm sure they weren't serious, though.'

It sometimes suited Ignacio to take a conciliatory position with his mother. It assuaged his occasional pangs of guilt that his indiscreet talk over his brother's homosexuality might have led to his arrest. If he had anticipated the severity of his brother's sentence and the grief it would cause, he might have been more careful, however much Emilio sickened him.

Franco's victory in Madrid was not as imminent as Ignacio thought. The exhausted citizens of Madrid saw uniformed soldiers marching past them, and assumed these men were battalions of Nationalist troops. With some astonishment and much joy, they soon realised their error. The strains of their revolutionary songs and the distinctive tune of 'The Internationale' told them that these were *Brigadistas*, members of the International Brigades, who had come, as if by magic, to their rescue. Among them were Germans, Poles, Italians and English, and it was said that, to a man, they were going fearlessly to the frontline.

Members of the anarchist movement, who were strong believers in freedom, even if not always the most disciplined of fighters, were also arriving to help defend Madrid against Franco, and there was further fighting in the University City, including an attack on the hospital, held by the Nationalists. The area was soon back in Republican hands and the frontline once again redrawn.

Later in November 1936, Ignacio was browsing through that day's right-wing newspaper, getting the latest on what was happening in Madrid. Unlike the rest of his family, who could not bear to read the biased reports of the right-wing press, Ignacio ostentatiously did so, and his muttered remark that it was a pity that Franco had given up the fight for Madrid at this stage was too much for his normally phlegmatic father to take.

'Ignacio,' Pablo said, finally losing his temper, 'do you really think it's right for soldiers to kill innocent people?'

'Which innocent people?' Ignacio did not conceal his scorn. 'What do you mean by "innocent"?'

'The ordinary people of Madrid, of course! Women and children who are being blasted to bits. What have they done?'

'So what about all those prisoners then? They hardly deserved to die, did they? Don't talk to me about *innocence*! There's no such *thing*!' Ignacio slammed the table with a fist.

Ignacio was referring to the execution of a thousand Nationalist prisoners earlier that month. Madrid had been a city of mixed sympathies, both Republican and Nationalist, and when the army coup took place, many Nationalists who were trapped inside the city were forced to go into hiding. In spite of this, many had been flushed out and imprisoned. When it had looked as though the Nationalist army might be on the point of taking Madrid in early November, there was serious concern that the army officers now in prison might join the invading force. To prevent this from happening, several thousand prisoners were evacuated and shot in cold blood outside the city by Republican guards who were eager to join the defence of their capital.

Pablo was silenced. Even die-hard supporters of the Republic were ashamed of what had happened. He walked away. Sometimes this was easier than pursuing an argument with his son, and though he totally disagreed with him, Ignacio's final words rang almost too true. In this conflict it was sometimes hard to say who was completely without blame.

The horror continued in Granada. One afternoon in December, when the streets were dark by early afternoon and the cobbles shone like metal under the streetlamps, two Nationalist soldiers came into the bar. This time there was no need for them to hammer on the glass. The bar was open and still full of customers having coffee after their lunch.

'We'd like to take a look around,' one of the soldiers announced to Pablo, in a manner that was too friendly for comfort.

The café owner made no attempt to get in the way of their search, knowing that it would only incite them to unnecessary aggression.

Behind the bar was a small kitchen and, off that, a small office not much bigger than a cupboard where Pablo did his ordering and kept his chaotic inventory of goods in and out. As well as a desk, there was an old wooden chest of drawers that spewed out papers even before the Fascist vandals set to work ransacking it. They turned each drawer over until the contents of the chest emptied, not pausing to read even one piece of paper. They were like children, grinning to each other as the mess in the room worsened, enjoying the blizzard-like effect as they tossed papers in the air. It looked just like a game. They were not in the slightest bit interested in the bills for bread and ham.

Pablo continued to serve at the bar. 'Don't worry,' he said bravely to his wife. 'We'll clear the mess up later. We've got nothing to hide and I'm sure they'll soon be gone.'

Concha sliced carefully through a huge slab of *manchego*, arranging it with more than usual care on a plate, successfully making herself look busy and at ease. Inside, her stomach churned with fear. Silently she and Pablo agreed that a pose of complete innocence was the best approach to the situation.

Customers continued to drink and talk in quiet tones but the tension in the room was palpable. People in Granada were accustomed now to such intrusions, and though it was hard to talk naturally in this atmosphere, they were determined to hold on to the small routines of their lives, such as the ritual of visiting a bar or café at least once a day.

The two intruders were not really there to search. Once the room was blanketed in white, their attention turned to the real reason they had come. It was the radio that interested them. The rest had been a charade. With a triumphant look on his face, the taller of the two soldiers reached for the dial, turned it on and stood back. There was no need to tune it. A signal was already being picked up and a voice now filled the room. It was the unmistakable tones of the communist radio station that regularly broadcast its updates on the current state of events across the country. He turned up the volume so that the sound carried out of the room and into the bar. There was a definite smirk on the face of the younger soldier as he appeared in the café. The radio now blared around the room. Pablo and Concha immediately ceased their activities and behind the barrier of the bar, they clasped hands. All eyes focused on the Fascists who stood, arms folded, perfectly calm.

Concha always listened to the radio in the very early hours of the morning, when Pablo had cleaned up the last of the ashtrays and glasses and the rest of the family had retired to bed.

The higher ranking soldier cleared his throat. He would need to project his voice to make himself heard above the sound of the radio. Concha loosened her tight grip on her husband's hand and moved slightly forward. She would not give this pair the satisfaction of an interrogation. She would give herself up now and save everyone time. It was not to be so easy, however. She could feel her husband's hand locked around her upper arm and then, a moment later, he had pushed her almost roughly to one side and now stood in front, almost blocking her view of the soldiers.

There was a fraction of a second in which she might have protested, but then the moment had passed. Pablo held out both wrists, was handcuffed, and seconds later was being led out into the street and away. His look silenced his wife. She knew what it meant. If she spoke up then they would take not just him but her as well. This way they only got one of them.

She was racked with guilt, but shock allowed her to carry on with her day's work in a dream state.

Mercedes walked into the café about an hour after the soldiers had left with her father. She had spent the morning with Paquita and her mother, helping them to organise things in their new apartment. The fabric of her friend's home in the Albaicín had proved to be unstable after the summer bombardment, and for safety's sake they had been obliged to find somewhere else to live. For the first time in a while, Mercedes wanted to dance and she hoped to find Antonio at home. He could just about pick out a tune and her need was strong enough for her to overlook the fact that he was a poor substitute for Javier or Emilio.

Concha was in the office reordering the last of the strewn papers when her daughter appeared. She knew immediately that something was wrong. She had not seen her mother so pale since the night that Emilio was taken away. Moments later Antonio returned home from school and Concha calmly informed them both of what had taken place. They were distraught but there was nothing to be done.

Ignacio returned late that night, unaware that anything was amiss. His mother was locking up for the night and his reaction to his father's arrest was one of anger. It was not directed against those who had arrested him, but against his own family, in particular, Concha.

'But why did he have to listen to that radio?' he protested. 'Why did you let him?'

'I didn't let him,' she explained quietly. 'It wasn't him listening to it.'

'It was Antonio!' he shrieked, his voice cracking with anger. 'That *rojo* brother! The stupid bastard – he'll be the death of all of us, you know. He doesn't care – you do realise that, don't you? He doesn't care!'

His face was almost up against his mother's. She could feel his hatred.

'It wasn't Antonio,' she said quietly. 'It was me.'

'You . . . ?' His voice was quieter now.

She explained that it was she who had really committed the crime.

Ignacio was furious with both his parents. His father should have stopped her from listening in to subversive radio stations, and she should not have made herself an object of such suspicion by campaigning for Emilio's release.

'You should have kept a low profile,' he raged at her. 'This is already branded the "*café de los rojos*", even if Father didn't realise it!'

But there was nothing that could be done. Some days later they heard that Pablo Ramírez was in prison not far from Sevilla.

When first arrested, Pablo had been locked up, along with hundreds of others, in the cinema of a nearby town. Many prisons were makeshift at that stage. The Nationalists were arresting so many thousands of people that the ordinary prisons were overflowing. Bullrings, theatres, schools and churches all became places to lock up the innocent, and the irony was never lost on the Republicans that places of pleasure, entertainment, education and even worship now became venues for torture and killing.

In the cinema where Pablo found himself, afraid, disorientated and in the dark for twenty-four hours a day, people slept in the foyer, in the aisle and slumped in the uncomfortable wooden seats. This had lasted a few days before a group of them was transferred to a prison two hundred kilometres north. No one bothered to tell them its name.

The prison had been built for three hundred inmates but now held two thousand. At night they lay tightly packed in rows without so much as a finger's width in which to turn and with nothing to cushion them from the stone floors. It was a cold hell. If one man coughed the whole cell-full was woken, and their proximity to each other meant that a single case of tuberculosis could spread like a forest fire.

Pablo was moved to several different prisons during this period but the routine was the same in all of them. The day began even before dawn broke, with the menacing jangle of keys and the thunderous sound of metal bolts being slid across to release the prisoners from their cages. There was a breakfast of thin gruel, enforced attendance at religious services, the singing of fascist patriotic songs and long hours of pure tedium and discomfort in the icy, lice-ridden cells. Dinner was like breakfast but with a handful of lentils tossed into the liquid and it was at this stage of the day that fear began to stir their bellies.

After their evening meal, a few men began to mutter prayers to a God they hardly believed in. Sweat broke out on every temple and hearts palpitated. It was time for the execution list to be read out in the dull monotone of the prison governor. They were obliged to listen, dreading the sound of each first syllable in case it was the beginning of their own name. The condemned would be taken away that night and shot the following dawn. The list seemed arbitrary and appearance on it could be a matter of chance, as though the warders had sat around a brazier drawing lots to pass the time.

For most there was a mixture of nausea and relief at realising they would live another day. Always, one or two who had heard their names lost their self-control, and their raw, helpless grief jolted the others from complacency. It could easily be them tomorrow.

Occasionally Concha visited Pablo. She would leave early in the morning and return at midnight, racked with anxiety at the conditions he was living in, and her fear that Emilio would be facing the same horror. She still had not seen her son.

Apart from those visits, Concha's every waking hour was now spent running the café. Recognising that her mother was cracking beneath the strain, Mercedes now offered to help and learned that keeping busy was one way to take her mind away from the absence of so many people she loved.

They had been informed that Emilio had been moved to a prison near Huelva, which was an even more difficult journey than the one to Cádiz, but the following month Concha was finally able to visit him. She had packed a basket with food and supplies, and was half excited about seeing him and half fearful of the state he might be in.

When she arrived at the prison, the officer looked at her with disdain.

'Your rations for Ramírez won't be required,' he said icily.

She was handed the death certificate. It stated that Emilio had died of tuberculosis. For so long she had clung to a last shred of hope, but it was now replaced with the uncompromising certainty of death.

Concha had no recollection of her journey home. Numbness and shock allowed her to function mechanically for the many hours it took to get back to Granada.

Ignacio had become an increasingly rare presence. The fragmentation of his family should have concerned him but his main interest was one of self-preservation, so as usual only Antonio and Mercedes were there when their mother arrived home. The pallor of her skin and the colourlessness of her lips told them everything. They put her to bed and quietly sat with her through the night. The following day she silently showed them the death certificate. It told them only what they already knew.

When her mother was away visiting her father, Mercedes ran the café single-handedly but on other days, when she had some time, she went up to the Sacromonte. Dancing was the only part of her life that had any meaning now. She took a risk to do so, given that there were new restrictive rulings on behaviour in Granada. Women were obliged to dress with modesty, to cover their arms and to wear high collars but, more significantly, 'subversive' music was banned, as was dancing. The tight tourniquet of the regime made Mercedes want to dance all the more. It was an expression of freedom that she would not allow to be taken away.

María Rodríguez had limitless patience and an inexhaustible range of footwork sequences to show Mercedes, and she was the first to appreciate that this girl had added new layers to her dancing. The absence of Javier, the death of Emilio and the atmosphere of grief that saturated her home meant that little was required of her imagination when she had to express pathos and loss. It was as real as the floor beneath her feet.

In Antonio, preoccupied and distant, there was no trace of the smiling older brother that Mercedes remembered. He was now the acting head of the household and was always concerned about Mercedes' welfare, especially when she returned late from the Sacromonte. This was now a city where dancing was not considered desirable.

In the shuttered nocturnal gloom of the apartment, the discreet click of a closing door penetrated the silence. To the crime of being late, Mercedes had added the sin of trying to conceal her surreptitious homecoming.

'Mercedes! Where in the name of God have you been?' came a harsh whisper.

Antonio emerged from the shadows into the hallway and Mercedes stood facing him, her head bowed, hands concealed behind her back.

'Why are you so late? Why are you doing this to us?'

He hesitated, suspended in the uncertain space between total despair and uncompromising love for this girl.

'And what are you hiding? As if I couldn't guess.'

She held out her hands. Balanced on her flattened palms was a pair of scuffed black shoes, the leather as soft as human skin, their soles worn to transparency.

He took her wrists gently and held them in his hands. 'Please, for the very last time I am asking you . . .' he implored.

'I'm sorry, Antonio,' she said quietly, her eyes now meeting his. 'I can't stop. I can't help myself.'

'It's not safe, *querida mia*, it's not safe.'

Chapter Nineteen

ANTONIO AND IGNACIO were now firmly on opposing sides. Francisco Pérez, his close friend, had put it into Antonio's head that his brother might have had something to do with the betrayal of his father, Luis, and brother, Julio. It had seemed an outrageous accusation at the time, but Antonio had never been able to dismiss it entirely. Ignacio's close connections with the right-wing element that now held the power in the city certainly left no doubt in anyone's mind that he was in Franco's camp. He was a celebrity mascot of some of the city's most vicious perpetrators of injustice and violence.

Antonio knew he had to exercise the most extreme caution. In spite of their blood kinship, he was aware that his views and friendships with active socialists made him vulnerable with his brother.

Though Granada was in Nationalist hands, there remained a strong undercurrent of support for the legal Republican government, and there were many people prepared to resist the tyranny under which they were now forced to live. This meant that the atrocities of war were not only perpetrated by supporters of Franco. Murders of people suspected of collaboration with Franco's troops were commonplace and there were frequently signs of torture to be found on their corpses.

Some of these incidents began as little more than street brawls, with name-calling, pushing and shoving. Within moments they might turn into full-scale fights between young men who, in many cases, had grown up together kicking a ball in the street. The same maze of narrow streets, with their sweet-sounding names, Silencio, Escuelas, Duquesa, once the location for endless childhood games of hide and seek, became the scene of terrifying pursuit. Doorways, momentary hiding places in those happy times, might now provide refuge and the difference between life and death.

On a night late in January 1937, Ignacio and three of his friends had spent most of the evening drinking in a bar near the new bullring. It was in the area frequented by supporters of the new regime and a hang-out of the bullfighting crowd, so if Republican sympathisers showed their faces it was likely to lead to trouble. There was a small group of drinkers in the corner who were not known to most of the regulars, and a scent of trouble hung in the air. Even if no one turned to stare, they were all aware of the quartet of slightly scruffily dressed youths, and the barman served them with careful formality, not wishing to engage in conversation.

Around midnight, the strangers got up to leave. As they walked by, one of them gave the seated Ignacio a hard shove in the shoulder. In any other circumstances it might have been construed as a friendly gesture, but not in these times and not in this bar. It was Enrique García. He and Ignacio had been at school together and had not been the best of friends even then.

'How's Ignacio?' Enrique asked. 'How's Granada's number one matador?'

The last comment was taunting and Ignacio was quick to pick up the innuendo. García's insinuation that he was involved in the executions that had been taking place in the city infuriated him. For Ignacio, there was a distinction between what he regarded as being a casual informer and actually being an assassin. His own blood lust he saved for the bullring.

He knew that he should not react. If García was here to pick a fight this would give him just the excuse he needed.

García towered over Ignacio. Like a picador on horseback the man had a clear advantage. Rarely did Ignacio feel so vulnerable, and he hated this man's proximity and the menacing way in which he leaned over him as if poised to plunge a *pica* into his side. If Ignacio was to control his hot-blooded temperament he had better get out of here. Fast.

'Right,' he said quietly, looking round at his circle of friends. 'I think it's time for me to go.'

A murmur passed around the group. It was relatively early for them to be leaving, but they could see that Ignacio needed to be on his way. There was unspoken acknowledgement between them that if they accompanied him outside, it might be taken as a sign of aggression. It was clearly preferable for Ignacio to slip away. There was a chance that the situation might diffuse itself if he did so.

Within seconds he was on the street. In spite of the hour, there was no one else around. Hands in his pockets, he sauntered up San Geronimo towards the cathedral. It was a damp night and the cobblestones glinted in the light of the dim gaslamps. He was not going to hurry. Thinking he heard the sound of another footstep, he turned his head but there was no one to be seen and he walked on, stubbornly determined not to hasten his step. Close to the top, he turned a sharp right towards one of the city's busiest streets.

It was there on the corner that he felt a sharp pain in the side of his neck. Whoever delivered the blow had been waiting for him in a doorway, knowing that his victim would be taking this route to get home. The shock sent him reeling into the gutter. Bent double with pain, his vision blurred and his stomach churned with nausea. A second blow was dealt between his shoulder blades. With great trepidation, his greatest fear being that his handsome face might be struck, he raised his head and saw three more men approaching him. They had appeared from the street parallel to San Geronimo, Santa Paula, and he realised that he had walked into some kind of carefully laid trap.

There was only one course of action now, and that was to try to escape. Fuelled by a surge of adrenalin, Ignacio began to run. His fitness for the bullring had never been put to such good use. He turned blindly, left and right, losing himself in these streets that he had known so well since boyhood. His sight was still blurred but he kept his eyes to the ground, watching his feet so that he did not trip. In spite of the cool night, a sensation of dampness spread across his body.

To get his breath back, he crouched in a doorway. He saw that it was not sweat that saturated his shirt, but blood, copious and crimson. He had his own weapon, a bone-handled knife he always carried with him, and though he had not yet had the chance to use it, he now reached inside his jacket to check it was there. His only thought was to get home, but as he tried to get to his feet his legs gave way beneath him.

He knew now he was the hunted beast, with little chance of getting away unscathed from his adversaries, who were no doubt armed with sharper blades than his. Perhaps he could remain concealed until they called off the chase. In a moment of rare leniency the director of a bullfight will grant a reprieve if he thinks that the bull has showed an outstanding degree of bravery. Ignacio prayed that these *rojos* might think that he had succeeded in shaking them off and leave him be. Perhaps this was the optimism that a bull carried with him right through to that final moment with the matador: that there will be a last-minute chance of salvation.

When he had gone into the bar earlier that evening, he had been as unaware of what was to come as a bull entering the ring. Those lefties had planned it all, he now realised, and they thought they knew the outcome, like the ticket-holders at the *corrida*. The whole evening had taken him through the stages of the bullfight and, as he crouched in that dark doorway, his body was tensed to withstand the final blow that was surely to come. Those moments of truth for the beasts he had brought to their knees passed before him and he knew then the inevitability of his end. There had never been a shred of doubt about the result of this ritual. He had been as trapped as a bull in a ring from the moment of García's first passing shove to the wounds he had sustained.

Perhaps this was the last of Ignacio's coherent thoughts before he began to slide into unconsciousness, his body now slumped so a passer-by might have mistaken him for a sleeping beggar. Dimly, he saw two figures approaching. In his blurred vision of a now fast-fading world, their heads seemed haloed in the lamplight. Perhaps these were angels coming to his rescue.

In a street called Paz, García seized him by the jacket and swiftly delivered one last knife thrust. This final stab was an unnecessary gesture. You cannot murder a dead man.

They dragged him by the ankles into the middle of the road so that in the early hours of daylight his body would be discovered; such a killing was as important for its propaganda value as for being a specific act of revenge. From a niche in the wall of a nearby church, a saint gazed down at Ignacio's body. A broad red trail marked the route from where he had hidden and a trickle of blood found a course between the cobbles and wound its way through them. The rain would have washed it all away by morning.

Inside the church an effigy of Christ appeared to drip with blood through his neatly pierced side; outside, the life of a real man had ebbed swiftly away through a crude gash in his neck.

As it was getting light, a message arrived at El Barril. For Concha the sound of hammering on the door immediately evoked the terrible memory of Emilio's arrest. She had scarcely slept since that night almost six months before, and even when she did, she was roused by the slightest sound, the bang of a shutter in the next street, the stirring of one of her remaining children in his or her bed, a creak on the stair, a stifled cough.

Antonio was sent to identify the body. It was not as though there could be any doubt. Though he had been savaged with stab wounds, Ignacio's handsome face was unblemished.

Dressed in his finest *traje de luces*, Ignacio was taken from the morgue and driven by horse and carriage up to the cemetery on the hill overlooking the city. Antonio led the funeral cortège. His sister put what little strength she had into supporting her inconsolable mother, bearing her meagre weight against hers.

For Concha Ramírez, each step was an effort, as though she carried the burden of the coffin herself. At the approach to the cemetery gates she suddenly felt the full force of the irrefutable: that two of her sons were dead. Before this moment, she could cling to some small vestige of hope that none of this was real. It was not a destination she cared to reach. Friends walked silently behind them, heads bent, staring at dirty shoes on the damp road.

A sizeable crowd turned out for this funeral. Along with the family appeared every bullfighting *aficionado* within a hundred miles of Granada and the outlying areas. Ignacio's may not have been a long career but it was a distinguished one, and in a short time he had established a large following. This included a good number of women; some of them were simply nameless admirers in his crowd, but just as many were girls who had been loved by him, whether for a few days or just for one night. His mistress, Elvira, was there too, along with her husband, Pedro Delgado, who had come to pay his respects to one of Andalucía's finest young fighters. He tried to ignore the copious tears that rolled unchecked down his wife's cheeks but then noticed that she would have been alone among the women if she had not been crying.

A stone marked the spot. '*Tu familia no te olvida*.' There may only have been one corpse, but the grieving was more than enough for two. The Ramírez family shed bitter tears. Concha wept for the loss of not just one but two of her fine sons and mourned them fiercely and equally. Both Emilio and Ignacio had tested the limits of their parents' tolerance but none of that seemed important now.

The grief of losing Emilio was as raw on this cold January day as it had been on the day he had been taken from their home, and it seemed as though Concha's state of mourning might have no end without the presence of a body. This funeral served as a double ceremony for both second- and third-born.

Though both Antonio and Mercedes were devastated by the loss of their brothers, it was the scale of their mother's grief that had overwhelmed them. For days she did not eat, speak or sleep, and it seemed that nothing would bring her out of this catatonic state. For a long while she was beyond their reach.

To lose loved ones on both sides of this conflict was a double misfortune for the Ramírez family, and they were bewildered that they had been dealt this blow. They survived the following weeks in a state of numb disbelief, oblivious to the fact that similar events were now taking place all over their country. For the present it was no consolation that theirs was not the only family enduring such unforeseen horror.

Chapter Twenty

THE CRISP DAYS of January had now given way to the damp days of February that wrapped a grey blanket around the city. The sun scarcely penetrated the clouds and the Sierra Nevada had disappeared into the mist. It was as though Granada had no connection with the world outside.

Eventually, the acute grief in the Ramírez family lessened and the day-to-day business of surviving in a country at war with itself began to distract them. The café had begun to look neglected. Concha's attempts to keep the place clean and swept were woefully inadequate. Even if she could have managed all alone, anxiety for her husband exhausted her, and a lingering sense of loss over Ignacio and Emilio continued to sap her energy.

Food shortages were becoming increasingly common and it was a daily struggle to get supplies for her family as well as provisions for the café. El Barril was her children's inheritance and its survival was now her sole preoccupation. Concha tried not to resent the portly-girthed owners of the grand homes in the Paseo del Salón who always seemed to have plenty to eat when for many it was a period of queues and malnourishment.

Over the past few months, Mercedes had become progressively less self-centred and now helped her mother without needing to be asked. In her own mind, however, she felt overwhelmed by the futility of it all. Serving people with coffee and small glasses of fiery cognac sometimes seemed so utterly pointless, and occasionally she could not help expressing this to her mother.

'I agree with you, Merche,' said Concha. 'But it reminds people of normal life. Maybe that's enough for the present.'

Brief moments of social intercourse in a busy café were the

only link with earlier days of peace and what they would soon describe as 'the old days'. For Mercedes everything seemed bleak. Naked trees stood like skeletons in the streets and squares. The city was gradually being stripped bare of everyone she cared about. She had still not received any news from Javier.

One morning, Concha was watching her daughter sweep the café floor, slowly and meticulously moving crumbs, ash and scraps of paper napkin into the centre of the room. She observed how her daughter drew perfect invisible arcs on the floor and how her hips rolled in a circular motion as she worked. The sleeves of her knitted cardigan were rolled up and the muscles of her sinewy arms were taut as she gripped the broom. Concha had no doubt that, in her imagination, Mercedes was in some other place. Dancing no doubt. Listening to Javier.

Mercedes had lived in a dream world since she was a small child and now it was only her fantasies that made life bearable. Sometimes she wondered if it would be like that until she died. It was certainly the only way to survive these cursed times. She looked up, feeling her mother's gaze.

'Why are you staring at me?' she demanded sulkily. 'Isn't my cleaning good enough?'

'Of course it is,' replied her mother, feeling the strength of her resentment. 'You're doing a very good job. I do appreciate it, you know.'

'But I hate it. I hate every second, of every minute, of every hour of every day,' she retorted petulantly, sending the broom clattering across the room.

She pulled out one of the wooden chairs from a nearby table and for a moment her mother shrank back, thinking that she was about to throw that too.

Instead Mercedes sank down onto it, exhausted. She rested her elbows on the table and held her head in her hands. Even if Mercedes had dealt bravely with her losses during the last few months, her ability to hide her feelings suddenly left her.

The young woman had more than enough to weep about. Two of her beloved brothers had died, her father was in prison and Javier, the man who had ignited greater feelings of love than she had ever imagined possible, had vanished. Even Concha could not expect her daughter to dwell on what remained. This was the moment to lament what had been taken away. Gratitude and the counting of blessings could wait.

One of their regular customers appeared at the door and then retreated; he could see that it was not a good moment for his daily *café con leche*.

Concha drew up a chair close to her daughter and put her arm around her. 'My poor Merche,' she whispered. 'My poor, poor Merche.'

Mercedes scarcely heard her, so loud was her keening.

Though their circumstances were not of Concha's making, she felt profoundly guilty about the way her daughter's life was turning out. It was as though the essence of it had been ripped out and she sympathised with her frustration and sadness. Though they went about their lives as normally as possible, strain was etched on the faces of everyone who lived in Granada. Fear of the Civil Guard, of the Nationalist soldiers and even of the wagging tongues of their neighbours haunted them. The tension in this city was affecting them all.

Concha's instincts were to lock her daughter away and to protect her from everything outside this dark, wood-panelled room. Now that her husband and her son had been seized from these four walls, home no longer seemed to offer the same security they had once taken for granted. Both women knew that the warmth and safety it appeared to offer were merely an illusion. For this reason she found herself speaking words that were contrary to every ounce of maternal instinct.

'You must find him.'

Mercedes looked up at her with surprise and gratitude.

'Javier,' Concha said emphatically, as though there could be any doubt about who she meant. 'You must see if you can find him. I suspect he is waiting for you.'

It took Mercedes no time to prepare and, within minutes, she was ready to go. Her eagerness to see Javier again overcame any hesitation about setting off alone. Up in her room, she grabbed her coat and a scarf. She tucked the photograph of her *tocaor* into her purse and then, at the last moment, noticed her dancing shoes just poking out from under her bed. I can't go without those, she thought as she bent down to pick them up. When she found Javier, she was quite likely to need them.

As Mercedes came downstairs, Concha was in the bar finishing the cleaning.

'Look, I know your father would disapprove of me letting you go . . . and I'm not sure it's the right thing . . .'

'Please don't change your mind,' Mercedes appealed to her mother. 'I'll be back soon. So . . . wish me good luck.'

Concha swallowed hard. She could not show Mercedes her anxiety. She hugged her briefly and handed her some money, a lump of bread and some cheese wrapped in waxed paper, knowing that her daughter had not eaten yet today. Neither could bring herself to say the word 'goodbye'.

Just as the bells of the nearby church of Santa Ana were clanging twelve, Mercedes hastened out of the café.

Concha carried on. Anyone would have thought it was business as usual.

Concha had been so preoccupied with the mechanics of keeping the café running that she had ceased to monitor Antonio's comings and goings. With all her other anxieties, her first-born son seemed one of the few people about whom she did not need to worry. School was functioning again and Concha assumed that his late nights were being spent at school preparing lessons. In fact, all his free time was being spent with Salvador and Francisco, his close childhood friends.

Silence had never meant solitude for El Mudo. Expressive eyes and perfect features drew people to this boy. Young women drawn into his embrace were never disappointed by his love-making, and his gentle instincts for a woman's needs were all the more sensitive for his lack of speech and hearing. They adored him all the more for the fact that they never left his bedroom with declarations of love echoing in their ears, their hopes vainly raised in the heat of the night. His two friends were in awe of his success.

Often the trio felt itself the object of curiosity. Strangers were fascinated by the spectacle of their sometimes wild gesticulations. Outsiders, who mostly assumed that all three of them were unable to hear or speak, found the boys as entertaining as mime artists and were intrigued by the silent world they inhabited. To local people, the sight of Antonio, Francisco and Salvador all rocking with silent mirth in the corner of the café was part of an everyday scene. When only two of them were together, they always played a game of chess.

They met most days in the same café where they had licked ice creams as children, and had grown up to believe in similar ideals. Their socialist beliefs now bonded them more closely than ever. The blood loyalty they had sworn to each other when they were eight years old had never wavered and for all three of them, socialism was the only possible route to a fair society. They knew some of the radicals in the city, left-wing lawyers and a smattering of politicians, and they tended to go to the bars they frequented, hovering on the edge of any group where politics were being discussed.

That evening, they had already gone over the same old ground, discussing for the hundredth time what was happening in Granada, where supporters of the Republic were still being randomly arrested. Salvador suddenly gestured to his companions that they needed to be watchful of two men in the corner of the bar. Being deaf, he could read more than most into a minor change of facial expression, which had led some to suspect him of supernatural mind-reading powers. In truth, he did what anyone could do: he observed the finest nuances of facial expression and learned to detect the merest hint of discomfort. His judgement was unerringly accurate.

'Be careful,' he signed. 'Not everyone in here shares our views.'

Generally they could communicate with each other in complete privacy but occasionally Salvador would sense an unfriendly scrutinising stare. Now was one of those moments. He was not, after all, the only *sordomudo* in Granada and there were others who might know the language.

'Let's go,' said Antonio.

They would have to continue their planning elsewhere, and all three rose to leave, tucking a few pesetas under the ashtray for their beers.

Within minutes they were back in Salvador's apartment. With an ear pressed close to its heavy door, even a determined eavesdropper would have struggled to hear more than the occasional rustle. Salvador was currently living alone. His mother and grandmother had been at an aunt's *cortijo* outside the city when the coup had taken place and had not returned. His father had died when he was eleven.

Salvador cleared the table of a variety of cups and plates, and they sat down. He set a pan of water on the gas stove and found a small bag of coffee. Francisco was already using a dirty plate as an ashtray and the smoke coiled its way up to the high ceiling, clinging to the yellowing walls.

They were gathered at the table to make plans together but there was a sense of unease, not only because the neighbour, a thin-faced book-keeper, had opened his door to peer at them when they had passed, but because resentment was simmering between them. The air had to be cleared.

Like all of those who opposed Franco, the three of them had accepted that there had never been any real means of resistance to the coup in Granada. Nationalist troops had been received into this city's strongly conservative heartland with almost open arms and it was too late to do anything about it now, since to show yourself an enemy of the new regime was tantamount to suicide.

Though Franco's men were firmly in charge of Granada, it did not mean that all those who opposed the *alzamiento* – the uprising – were apathetic. Francisco had certainly not been idle. He now knew that the charges against his father and brother had been the mere possession of trade union cards and had lost no time in seeking revenge for their deaths. He did not care how. His only desire was for the sour smell of Nationalist blood. Although the Fascists held the city of Granada with a firm fist, their grip on many of the surrounding rural areas was still tenuous. Francisco had become part of a campaign of resistance and subversion. In some places, Civil Guard garrisons that had betrayed the Republic were easily overcome and once they were out of the way, there were plenty of young men like Francisco overflowing with anger to unleash against the landowners and priests who supported Franco.

Landworkers and trade unionists had then set about collectivising some of the great estates, and the storehouses of the landowners were broken open. Malnourished peasants waited outside, desperate for anything with which to feed their families. Bulls, that had been bred and grazed on the finest pastures, were slaughtered and eaten. It was the first meat that many of them had tasted in years.

It was not only the blood of the bulls that Francisco spilled. Violence was perpetrated against individuals too. Priests, landowners and their families paid the price that many of those who supported the Republic felt they deserved.

Antonio, who clung on to the ideals of justice and fairness, balked at these random and uncoordinated acts.

'It does more harm than good,' he said bluntly, churned up with a mixture of disgust and admiration at what his friend was capable of. 'You know what your priest-killings and your nun-burnings mean to the Fascists, don't you?'

'Yes. I do,' responded Francisco. 'I know exactly what they mean to them. They show them we mean business. That we're going to run them out of the country, rather than stand by and let them stamp all over us.'

'The Fascists don't care about those old priests and a few nuns – but you know what they do give a damn about?' he said.

For a moment Antonio had abandoned the use of sign language. He sometimes found it hard to express himself that way. Salvador put his finger to his lips, urging his friend to keep his voice down. There was every danger that someone could be listening at the door.

'What?' said Francisco, unable to contain himself to a whisper.

'They want support from outside Spain and they use your actions for propaganda. Are you too stupid to see that? For every priest that dies, they probably win a dozen more foreign troops. Is that what you want?'

Antonio's blood was raised as well as his voice. He could hear himself sounding like a schoolteacher, didactic, patronising even, and yet, just as when he was in the classroom, he was completely certain of his rectitude. He had to impress this on his friend. He sympathised with Francisco's thirst for blood and for action, but he wanted his friend to make good use of this passion, in a way that was not counterproductive. Reserving their energies for a united onslaught against the enemy was how Antonio felt it should be done. It was the only chance any of them had.

Francisco sat in silence and Antonio carried on haranguing him, ignoring the appeals of Salvador to leave him alone but reverting now to signing.

'So how do you think they react in Italy? What does the Pope say when they tell him what's happening to priests here? No wonder Mussolini is sending troops to support Franco! Your actions are giving us *less* chance of winning this war, not more! It's hardly winning sympathy for the Republic.'

For his part, Francisco had no regrets. Even if his friend Antonio was right and retribution followed, his sanity had been saved by the momentary release he felt when he pulled a trigger. The satisfaction of seeing the target of his well-directed bullet folding over and sinking slowly to the ground was immense. He had needed ten such moments to feel that his father and brother were avenged.

In spite of these words to one of his oldest friends, a small part of Antonio despised his own inaction. His family was fragmented, his brothers killed, his father imprisoned, and what had he done? Though he disapproved of the way in which Francisco had gone about it, he quietly envied that he had enemy blood on his hands.

Salvador added his support to Antonio's appeal. 'And the massacre of all those prisoners too,' he signed. 'They've hardly helped our cause either, have they?'

Even Francisco had to agree with this. The execution of the Nationalist prisoners in Madrid had been an atrocity and he conceded that it was not a moment for them to be proud of. Most importantly for Antonio's argument, the event had been used by the Nationalists to illustrate the barbarism of the left and had cost the Republicans dearly in terms of the support they so desperately needed.

Whatever the differences of opinion that might have existed between these three friends, there was one thing that now united them: they were all ready to break out of the prison that Granada had become, not to take part in isolated acts of barbarism, but to join a more co-ordinated campaign.

'Whatever we agree or disagree about, we can't hang around here, can we?' urged Francisco. 'It's too late for Granada, but that's not the whole of Spain. Look at Barcelona!'

'I know. You're right. And Valencia and Bilbao and Cuenca . . . And all the rest. They're resisting. We can't just sit here.'

In spite of everything, there was a wave of optimism sweeping across Republican territory trapped under Fascist control that this uprising could be crushed. The resistance met by Franco's troops was only just the beginning. Given time, they could organise themselves.

Salvador, listening, involved and gesticulating agreement, now signed the word that had not yet been stated: 'Madrid.'

Antonio had left this off his list. This was the place to which they must go. The symbolic heart of Spain that must be fought for at all costs.

Four hundred kilometres north of where they sat in the semi-darkness of Salvador's apartment, Madrid was effectively under siege and if anywhere needed to resist the Fascists, it was the capital city. A popular army had been established the previous autumn to unite the portion of the army that remained loyal to the Republic along with volunteer militia to form some kind of unified force with central command. All three friends yearned to join the action and to be part of the struggle. Unless they went soon it might be too late.

For some months, with the volume turned so low that the listener had to sit with his ear pressed up against it, Antonio had been using the radio in Salvador's apartment to pick up news of the situation in Madrid. The capital city had been suffering bombardment by Franco's troops since November but, with the help of Russian tanks, had held out. Madrid continued to put up stronger resistance than the Nationalists had expected, but there was now a rumour that another great battle was about to begin.

Antonio and his friends may have stood by and watched their own city fall into Franco's hands, but the significance of allowing Madrid to go the same way was not lost on any of them. This had to be the moment, and the compulsion to leave was now strong. Franco had to be stopped. They had heard that there were young men coming from all over Europe: England, France and even Germany, to help the cause. The notion of this war being fought for them by foreigners spurred them to action.

Throughout the previous few days Antonio had thought only of Franco's growing dominance in Spain and the way in which his troops seemed to be spreading unstoppably throughout the region. The fact that they were meeting substantial resistance in the north of the country gave those that supported the Republic some hope. If he and his friends did not join the fight against fascism, they might forever regret their inaction.

'We must go,' said Antonio. 'It's time.'

Resolute, he set off home to make preparations for departure.

Chapter Twenty-one

By the time Antonio went to tell his mother he was leaving, Mercedes had been on the road for some hours. From Granada, she took the mountain road rather than the main route south, thinking she would meet fewer people that way. Though it was February and the snow was still thick on the mountain tops around her, she had taken off her thick woollen coat. She walked for five hours that day and, but for the extremities of her gloveless fingers, she was almost too warm.

For a short distance between Ventas and Alhama a farmer gave her a lift on his cart. He had just sold two dozen chickens at market and now had space to accommodate a passenger. The smell of livestock hung heavily about him, and Mercedes tried hard not to show her revulsion at the odour of him and the mangy dog that sat between them. There was a comforting normality about riding along next to this weather-beaten man whose hands were raw with cold and crisscrossed with deep tears and scratches.

Mercedes had regularly spent part of her summertime in the countryside outside Granada, and visits to her aunt and uncle in the sierras had been a happy aspect of her childhood. She was familiar enough with the landscape when the trees were in leaf and the meadows flirtatious with wild flowers, but in winter it was chilled and bare. The fields were a greyish brown, waiting for spring crops to be sown, and the road was stony and rutted. The mule's hoofs regularly slipped on loose shale, which slowed its already lazy pace. The weak afternoon sunlight provided no warmth.

Mercedes knew to trust no one and made little conversation, answering the old man's questions in monosyllables. She came from Granada and was going to visit her aunt in a village outside Málaga. That was about all she volunteered.

He was no doubt equally untrusting of her, and gave little information about himself.

Once during the journey they were stopped by a Civil Guard patrol.

'Purpose of journey?' the interrogator demanded.

Mercedes held her breath. She had prepared herself for this but now that she was faced with the moment, her mouth dried.

'My daughter and I are on our way back to our farm in Periana. We've been to market in Ventas,' the farmer said cheerfully. 'Chickens were fetching a good price today.'

There was nothing to suggest that he was lying. An empty cage, the faint whiff of chicken excrement, a girl. They waved him on.

'*Gracias*,' she said quietly when the patrol was well out of earshot. She looked down at the pattern of the road's rough surface as it moved under the big wooden wheels. She told herself she must still not trust this man and should stick to her fictitious story even if he now appeared to be a friend and knew that she needed some protection.

They travelled on for another hour or so until it was time for the farmer to turn off. His farm was up in the hills; he indicated somewhere in the direction of a wooded area on the horizon.

'Do you want to stop with us for the night? There would be a warm bed for you and my wife makes a decent enough supper.'

In her exhausted state she was, for a moment, tempted. But what did that invitation convey? Though he had been kind to her, she had no idea who this man was and, wife or no wife, she suddenly felt the full force of her vulnerability. She must keep going towards Málaga.

'Thank you. But I should press on.'

'Well, have this anyway,' he said, reaching behind his seat. 'I shall be enjoying my wife's cooking in an hour or so. I won't be needing it.'

She now stood in the road beneath him and reached up to take a small hessian bag. She could feel the reassuring bulk of a small loaf inside and knew that she would be grateful for this the next day. She had nearly run out of the supplies she had stashed away in her pockets and was grateful for replenishments.

Clearly he had not been offended by her refusal of his invitation but she knew it had been better not to be open with him. Gone were the days when you could feel entirely sure of those you knew, let alone strangers. They wished each other well and in moments he had disappeared out of sight.

Once again she was alone. The farmer had said that she was about five kilometres from the main road that would lead her to Málaga, so she decided to keep walking until she reached it before having a rest. If she did not set herself these goals she might never reach her destination.

It was about six in the evening and dark by the time she got to the junction. Hunger was beginning to hammer at her stomach. She sat down by the roadside, leaned against a large stone and reached into the small sack. As well as the loaf there was a lump of cake and an orange.

She tore off a wedge of the now dry and crumbly bread and chewed it slowly, washing it down with swigs of water, for a while oblivious to her surroundings and absorbed entirely in sating her hunger.

Uncertain of the distance to the next village and whether she would able to buy anything to eat there, she hoarded the cake and the orange for later. Protected from the wind, she closed her eyes. Against the dark screen of her closed eyelids, an image of Javier appeared. He was perched on the edge of a low chair, his back curved over his guitar, his eyes cast upwards towards her through the dark mop of his fringe. In her imagination, she felt the warmth of his breath and daydreamed that he was only a few yards away, waiting for her to dance. The temptation to step into the dream began to seduce her. In spite of knowing that she should keep walking and that with each passing hour she might have less chance of finding the man she loved beyond measure, Mercedes lay down and slept.

When Antonio retured to the El Barril, there was one dim light still burning behind the bar. He leaned over to reach the switch and as he did so, a voice startled him.

'Antonio.'

Obscured in the inky shadows at the back of the café, he could make out the silhouette of a familiar figure. His mother was seated alone at a table. There was enough light filtering in from a gaslamp in the street for him to cross the room without stumbling into tables and chairs. Seeing Concha sitting there alone, his heart pounded with fear and sorrow at what he had to tell her. Could he deal her such a blow?

'Mother! What are you doing down here so late?'

Now that he was close, he could see a large glass on the table in front of her. This was very unlike Concha. It had always been his father's job to do the final clearing up in the bar and he knew that Pablo always sat over a drink at the end of the evening and usually a few cigarettes too. But not his mother. She was always so desperately tired in the late evening that she would simply bolt the door and ignore the last glasses on the tables, knowing that Mercedes would make it her first job to clear them away in the morning.

There was no reply from Concha.

'Mother – why are you still up?'

There would be a good reason for his mother's change of routine but he was fearful. Everyone lived on edge in this city.

'Mother?'

Though she was scarcely visible, he could see now that her arms were folded across her body and that she gently swayed. It was almost as though she were rhythmically rocking a baby.

By now Antonio was crouched down next to her, his hands on her shoulders, gently shaking her. Her eyes were closed.

'What is it? What has happened?' His voice was insistent.

Concha tried to reply, but her speech was cloudy with cognac and tears. The effort of speaking made her weep all the more. She was incomprehensible with grief. Antonio held her tight and when she was reassured by the firm embrace in which he now held her, the spasm of her crying subsided. Eventually when he let her go, she lifted her floral apron to her face and noisily blew her nose.

'I told her to go,' she said falteringly.

'What are you talking about? Who did you tell to go?'

'Mercedes. I told her to go and find Javier. She will never be happy unless she goes to him.'

'So you have sent her to Málaga?' responded Antonio with a note of disbelief.

'But if she can track down Javier they can go somewhere together. She couldn't stay here pining like that. I was watching her every day, ageing with grief. This war is awful for all of us but at least Mercedes has a chance of being happy.'

In the darkness, Concha did not see the colour drain from her son's face.

'But they're shelling Málaga,' he said, his mouth dry with anxiety. 'I just heard.'

Concha did not seem to hear her son.

He held his mother's hands between his own. It was pointless castigating her at this moment, though he knew his father would not have hesitated.

'We're forced to live with our enemy here,' she continued. 'At least she's given herself the chance of getting away from them.'

Antonio could not disagree. His own view matched hers, almost too closely. He knew that she was right about the sense of impotence that reigned in Granada. Though there had been considerable bloodshed and destruction in the days that followed the coup, the city had been taken over with relative ease and many of its inhabitants regretted that they had not been ready to fight back. Other towns and cities were putting up a much stronger defence.

'So when did she go?'

'She packed a few things this morning. She was gone by lunchtime.'

'And if she's challenged, what will her story be?'

'She'll say that she has an aunt in Málaga . . .'

'Well, that much is almost true, isn't it?'

'. . . and that the aunt is sick and she is planning to bring her back to Granada to nurse her.'

'It's plausible enough, I suppose,' said Antonio, wanting to reassure his mother that she had done the right thing in encouraging his sister to go, though he knew that the whole venture was fraught with potential danger.

In his current role as head of the family, he felt that he should express more anxiety, if not anger, over his sister's irresponsible behaviour. They sat in silence for a while and then Antonio went over to the bar and poured himself a generous tumbler of brandy. He tipped his head back and swallowed it in a single gulp. The sound of his glass landing on the bar startled his mother from her reverie.

'Will she come back if she can't find him? Did she promise?'

Antonio watched his mother's eyes widen with surprise.

'Of *course* she'll come back!'

He wanted to share Concha's optimism and now was not the time to fill her with doubt.

He put a protective arm around his mother and swallowed hard. Now was not the right time to reveal his own plans either, but he could not delay for long. He was going to need the protection of a dark night, and tonight's cloudy sky and new moon would have been perfect for their departure.

In the very early hours of the following day, woken by the cold dawn, Mercedes made some headway along the main road. It felt open and exposed but it was virtually a straight line to Málaga from here.

That afternoon, up ahead in the far distance, she saw a small cloud of dust on the horizon. It moved like a slow, small whirlwind. There had been nothing on the road going in the other direction for some hours and all she had seen was an occasional bare tree along the way.

As the distance between them diminished, Mercedes could make out human shapes. There were a few donkeys, some of them pulling carts, and their pace seemed painfully slow. They were moving no faster than the most cumbersome float in a Holy Week procession.

Their approach was inexorable though, and she began to wonder how she would pass. This human tide formed a barrier between herself and her destination. It was nearly an hour later, when the distance between them had diminished to a few hundred metres and she could hear the uncanny silence in which they walked, that she asked herself the question, 'Why?' Why were all these people on the road, on a chill February afternoon? And why were they so quiet?

It became clear that this was a convoy, a caravan train of people and carts on the move. It was mystifying; they were like a procession that had taken the wrong turning at the *feria*, or pilgrims making a religious journey from one city to another to carry a precious icon. And even as they neared, Mercedes' mind could not make sense of what she saw. It was as though a whole village full of families had decided to move house, all at once, and had piled themselves up with everything they owned: chairs, mattresses, pots, trunks, toys. Mules almost disappeared under the weight and bulk of it all.

Once she was face to face with the people who led the way their silence was unnerving. No one seemed to speak. They looked right through her as though she did not exist. They were like sleepwalkers. She stood aside to let them pass. One by one they went by, old, young, the lame, the wounded, children, pregnant women, eyes staring ahead or fixed to the ground. One thing they all shared, apart from a look of fear, was a sense of resignation. There was vacancy in their expression, as though all emotion had been wiped out of them.

For a while Mercedes watched them pass. It was strange to be unnoticed and it did not occur to her to stop anyone to enquire where they were going. Then she noticed a woman who was sitting on her haunches, resting by the side of the road. A child sat close by, mindlessly drawing circles in the dust with a stick. Mercedes saw her opportunity.

'Excuse me . . . can you tell me where everyone is going?' she asked gently.

'Going? Where they're going?' The woman's voice, though feeble, conveyed her incredulity that anyone could be asking this question.

Mercedes rephrased her enquiry. 'Where have you all come from?'

The woman answered without hesitation. 'Málaga . . . Málaga . . . Málaga.' Each time she spoke the word, her voice grew fainter until the final syllable disappeared into a whisper.

'Málaga,' repeated Mercedes. Her stomach contracted. She kneeled down beside the woman. 'What has happened in Málaga? Why have you all left?'

Now that they were on the same level, the woman looked at Mercedes for the first time. The quiet crowd continued to file past. No one gave the two women and the grubby child a second look.

'You don't know?'

'No, I've come from Granada. I'm on my way to Málaga. What's going on there?' Mercedes tried to suppress her anxiety and impatience.

'Terrible things. Such terrible things.' There was a catch in the woman's throat, as though she feared to recount them.

Mercedes was caught between the desire to know the truth and the dread of it too. Her first thought was for Javier. Was he still there? Was he in this vast crowd, making his way out of the city? She needed to know more, and after a few minutes of sitting in silence with this woman, she plied her with another question. She might be her only source of information, since nobody else seemed to be stopping.

'Tell me. What's happened?'

'Do you have any food?'

Mercedes suddenly realised that there was only one thing that preoccupied this woman. Neither the events of the past few days nor her unknown future interested her. It was the stomach-gnawing ache of hunger and the nagging whine of her little son desperate for something to eat that crowded her thoughts.

'Food? Yes, I do. When did you last eat?' Mercedes was already reaching into her bag to find the cake and the orange.

'Javi!'

The small boy glanced up and within a second was upon them, grabbing the cake from his mother's hand.

'Stop!' she snapped at him. 'Not all at once! Don't snatch!'

'It's all right,' said Mercedes calmly. 'I don't need it.'

'But I do,' said the woman weakly. 'I'm so hungry. Please leave some for me, Javi.'

Her appeal was too late. In his desperation, the child had consumed every last crumb and now his cheeks were almost bursting, leaving him unable to respond.

'It's been so hard for him to understand why we've been desperately short of food for a few weeks,' she said tearfully. 'He's only three.'

Mercedes felt annoyed with this little boy for being greedy. Now she held the orange firmly in her hand and handed it to his mother.

'Here,' she said. 'Have this.'

The woman peeled it slowly. Each segment was offered first to her child and then to Mercedes and when they declined she put it in her own mouth, maintaining the discipline to consume it slowly and carefully and to enjoy every drop of juice that trickled down her parched throat.

No one else stopped. The crowd just kept passing. The woman was visibly strengthened.

'I think we should move on now,' she said generally to the space around her.

Mercedes hesitated. 'But I don't think I am going your way,' she said.

'Which way are you heading then? Not to Málaga!'

Mercedes shrugged. 'That was my plan.'

'Well, if I tell you what has happened there, it might change your mind.'

They stood face to face at the edge of the road.

'Tell me then,' said Mercedes, trying to conceal her own distress.

'Málaga didn't have a chance,' the woman began, her face close up to Mercedes'. 'The port was being bombed, but that wasn't the worst bit. It was when they arrived in the city – thousands of them. Maybe twenty thousand, that's what they said.'

'Who? Who arrived?'

'Moors, Italians, Fascists, and more trucks and weapons than we had in the whole of our city. It's been smashed to bits – from the sea, from the air, on the ground . . . And there we were –

defenceless. No one had thought to dig any trenches! They were raping the women and hacking off their breasts; they were even killing our children.'

The horror of it all was almost too much for her to describe. The legionaries who arrived were the most vicious of all Franco's troops and contemptuous of death itself. Most of them had been brutalised by the war in Africa.

'There were thousands seized,' she continued. 'Innocent men like my husband were executed, their bodies left unburied. They mutilated the dead. There was no choice. We had to get out.'

The woman's description was delivered in rapid bursts and under her breath. She did not need to broadcast the information to those who filed past them. They had all been there and so had her son, who did not need a reminder of the horror of the past days.

There were further atrocities to catalogue and once the woman had begun she seemed determined to tell Mercedes the whole story. She told it without emotion, recounting the facts dispassionately, numb with shock.

Many of the legionaries were already fugitives and criminals when they were recruited and then, further dehumanised by the ferocity with which they were expected to fight, behaved like animals towards their victims. '*Viva la muerte!*' they chanted. 'Long live death!' Even among those who fought on the same side, they instilled fear and disgust.

'The city is on fire. Everything is under threat apart from the Fascists' houses, of course. There is nothing left for anyone there now. Many of these women are now widows. Look at them! Look at us! We have nothing but the clothes we're standing in – and the chance to escape.'

Mercedes surveyed the pitiable crowd as they passed. From where she sat at the side of the road, all she saw were countless legs and feet passing in front of her. She did not look at their faces but at the lines of boots, so worn and broken down they might have already walked a thousand miles. The disintegrating leather of old soles provided little protection for blistered flesh. Toes protruded from the remnants of threadbare, rope-soled shoes. One woman appeared to be shod in crimson shoes but when Mercedes looked closely she saw that they were just stained the colour of her own blood. It had saturated the canvas.

Mercedes gazed. She was mesmerised. Old calves bulged purple with varicose veins, young feet were horribly misshapen by swellings and blisters, and, from stumps of feet tightly bound, traces of blood seeped through the folds in bandages. And dozens had limping gaits, their weight supported by sticks or crutches.

She stood dry-mouthed. If she stayed with these people she would probably be safe. She wondered again if Javier might be somewhere in this great moving mass of people and convinced herself that she might find her beloved if she asked around enough and showed everyone she met his photograph. If she went to Málaga it sounded as though she would probably be killed. Her decision was made. With a deep intake of breath, Mercedes turned and faced east.

Night was beginning to fall, but people did not break their journey just because of darkness. They feared that the Fascists would not be content with driving them from their city, and would be pursuing them relentlessly even now.

The moonlight kept the road in front of them visible. There were another one hundred and fifty kilometres to go before they reached Almería, which was their destination, and even for the youngest and fittest, it would be many days before it would even be in sight.

Mercedes walked with the woman, who seemed grateful for some company.

'I'm Manuela,' the woman eventually told her. 'And my little one is Javi.'

The child's diminutive form of her lover's name had already endeared the little boy to her. He had ceased to grizzle now that he had eaten and, for a time, his mother took him on her shoulders. Mercedes was amazed at her strength, given that her clothes hung from her emaciated body like a shroud and her cheekbones almost pierced her colourless skin. After a while, seeing that Manuela was exhausted, Mercedes took a turn. Javi's mother had removed his worn boots and the child's soft feet bounced on her chest as she walked. Just as she remembered her father doing to her, she held them to make him secure and found much comfort in their warm little pads. She was happy when she realised that his head had slumped on top of hers. He was asleep.

That night, Concha was exhausted too, and desperate for the solace of her bed. The past twenty-four hours had exhausted her. The last of her customers had just gone home and briefly she had propped the door open to dissipate the dense pall of smoke that hung in the air. The temperature had plummeted that night and her breath came out in white plumes as she gave each table a swift, circular wipe.

With the door already open, she was unaware of her son's entrance and he had to cough to ensure that she was not taken by surprise.

'Antonio! You're home early . . .' Her voice trailed off as she saw the grave look on his face.

He came quickly to the point. 'Look, I have to go away, Mother. I'm hoping it won't be for long.'

All the things he had had in his mind to say about it being for his father's sake went unsaid.

'That's just what you should do,' Concha said, disarming her son with her immediate, measured response. 'I'm glad you told me. I always imagined that you might just slip away into the night.'

For a moment, Antonio was lost for words. His mother's strength astounded and inspired him.

'I could never have done that. How would you have known what had happened to me?'

'But that's what people are doing, isn't it?' replied Concha. 'It means that when the Guards come to interrogate the parents, they can say: "Gone? Has he? Well, I don't know where he has gone . . ." with complete innocence.'

Concha felt, as did anyone of Republican leanings, that a crucial point had been reached in this conflict and that Franco's advance had to be stopped.

Antonio was amazed by his mother's understanding but questioned whether it might just be the prospect of losing another of her sons that numbed her. Could she differentiate between departure and death, or were the two simply blurring into a general abyss of loss?

'I don't want you to tell me anything,' she pleaded. 'I don't want to know – then nothing can be forced out of me. I mustn't be made to betray you.'

'Well, I don't know where we will end up anyway.'

'We?'

'Francisco and Salvador are coming with me.'

'That's good. There's strength in numbers.'

Both of them weighed up the ambiguity of Concha's words. They both knew that it was not manpower where the Republicans lacked strength, but in weaponry. While substantial supplies of arms were coming in to Franco's forces from Germany and Italy, those fighting for the Republic were deficient in ammunition, not in men.

There was silence for a moment.

'When are you going?'

'Tonight,' he said almost in a whisper.

'Oh . . .' Her voice was small, her breathing shallow now. She tried to make light of her son's imminent departure. 'Can I pack you something to eat?'

It was a mother's natural first thought.

Half an hour later he was gone. The air in the room was now crisp and clear, and only then did Concha shut the door. She shivered with cold and dread. Though Antonio had kept it to himself, his mother had a good idea of his destination. She would, though, have endured the slow pulling out of her fingernails before revealing it.

Chapter Twenty-two

THE THIN SLIVER of moon cast little light on the trio as they left the city, allowing them to avoid the keen-eyed attention of the Civil Guard. Getting out of the city without being challenged required a degree of luck and had to be done at the dead of night. They carried just enough food to last until the end of the following day, and no keepsakes to undermine the pretence that they were farm labourers in search of work. If they were searched their story would have to be watertight and even the smallest token – a memento, a photograph – might be used against them. Spare clothes would certainly arouse suspicion and provide enough evidence for arrest.

For most of that night they walked, wanting to put as big a distance as they could between themselves and Granada before day broke; wherever they could, they branched off onto small roads where they were less likely to encounter Nationalist troops.

In the early hours of the following morning they hitched a ride with a truckload of militia; these men were fired up by the prospect of victory over Franco and were certain this could be achieved. The ragged crew they had joined amused themselves with Republican songs and to passers-by raised their clenched fists in salute. Within a few hours Antonio, Francisco and Salvador were being treated like brothers. Now they really felt they were on the move.

Like them, the militiamen were aiming to join the efforts to protect Madrid and had heard that a battle was being fought to the south-east of the capital at Jarama.

'That's where we want to be,' said Francisco. 'In the thick of things, not here in this truck.'

'We'll get there soon enough,' muttered Antonio, attempting to stretch his legs.

They trundled for one uncomfortable kilometre after another across the open, empty landscape. In some areas there was little to indicate that this was a country at war with anyone, least of all itself. The open sierra seemed undisturbed. Early crops had been sown by some farmers, who were all but oblivious to the political storm that raged around them, but there were other areas where landowners had not bothered and the naked soil lay uncultivated, germinating the hunger that would eventually bite back at them.

Salvador, buffered by Antonio and Francisco, lip-read the conversation around him but took no part in it. No one commented on his silence. Some of them in the truck were half dead with exhaustion. They had come from towns near Sevilla where they had been engaged for months in a campaign of heavy but fruitless resistance, and did not even register his presence, let alone that he was different. This was how Antonio and Francisco planned it; if anyone suspected Salvador was deaf he would not be allowed to fight but they knew how much it meant to him to be there.

For most of the other twenty-one men, there was palpable excitement at the idea that they might now have a purpose. They were riding into Madrid to lift a siege and they sang songs of victory before it had been won.

For a few hours each night, they climbed down from the back of the truck, limbs weary from inaction, aching from the discomfort and continual vibration on the unending, uneven road. Once the bottle had been passed around and the singing had faded, there were a few hours of fitful sleep with nothing between the gravelly earth and their heads but prayerful hands. They could not afford the luxury of using a jacket as a pillow. They needed every layer they had around them if the blood was not to freeze in their veins.

Francisco coughed incessantly in his sleep, but disturbed no one. At four thirty, Antonio rolled a cigarette and lay in the dark, watching the smoke curl away into the damp air. It was the clank of tin mugs and the faint whiff of something that resembled coffee that stirred them. Their necks stiff, their stomachs hollow with hunger, rested in neither body nor mind, they stretched their limbs. Some got up and wandered off to urinate in the nearby bushes. This was the low point of the day: the colourless dawn, a bitter chill that might not lift until midday, and the prospect of another day of discomfort and hunger. Only later on, as their bodies were warmed by the proximity of one another, did their spirits rise and the songs begin again.

Antonio and his friends were well on their way northwards when Mercedes began her second day's trek with the refugees from Málaga. Though people mostly walked in silence, there was the occasional frantic cry of a mother looking for a child. In this great crowd it was easy for people to become separated, and there were several children to be seen aimlessly wandering, their faces shiny with snot and tears and panic. Their distress always upset Mercedes and her grip on Javi's hand would tighten. No one wanted this unnecessary grief and great efforts were made to reunite those who were separated.

Though most continued to walk at night, exhaustion and hunger forced some to stop for an hour or so, and there were always small mounds at the side of the road. Families huddled together, a blanket pulled over them for warmth and protection, now making use of the mattress that they had dragged from their home to create a small private tent for themselves, a miniature home.

The chill of the night contrasted with the sudden intense flashes of sunshine that would beat down on them at midday. The warmth never lingered but for a brief while children would be bare-armed as though for a summer picnic.

In the vanguard of this procession, there were mostly women, children and the elderly, and these were the ones that Mercedes walked with. They had been the first to leave Málaga, desperate to escape from the city's captors. Further towards the back of the procession trudged the surviving men and exhausted, defeated militia who had stayed in the city to put up a final show of resistance. Even if they walked night and day, the journey to Almería could take five days. For the old, sick and injured it might be many more.

A few cars and trucks had set out at the beginning of this exodus, but almost all of them had now been abandoned by the wayside. Along with these was the scattered debris of domestic life. Household chattels hastily taken from kitchen cupboards to form the basis for a new life now lay by the roadside. There were other, more surprising objects: a sewing machine, an ornate but chipped dining plate, an heirloom clock, all now discarded and worthless, along with the optimism with which they had been carried out of their homes.

For the first half of the route, there were many donkeys piled high with bedding, buckets and even furniture, but most of these were eventually to buckle under the weight of their burden and their corpses became a common sight in the gutter. At first a few flies gathered round their eyes, but once their bodies began to decompose they arrived in swarms.

Though generally they walked in a silence punctuated only by the sound of their own footsteps and the gentle rattle of their belongings, from time to time Mercedes told Javi a story. Much of the day, she carried him and they both sucked on sugar cane pulled from the fields. It was all that remained to give them energy now that their food was gone, and when exhaustion overcame them, they would take a fitful nap by the roadside.

Mercedes noticed a trunk that lay open in the middle of the road, its contents spilling out. A few garments had blown into a nearby bush and were now caught on its thorns: a bright white communion dress, an embroidered baby's nightgown, a wedding mantilla. They were spread out on the bush like advertising posters, almost taunting those who saw them with reminders of when those items had last been worn, of a time when life had been peaceful and when baptism and marriage could take place. Everyone filing past had the same thought. Those rituals now seemed long-ago luxuries.

From time to time they passed through a small town or village that had been evacuated. Nothing remained. A few people ransacked empty homes – not for valuables, but for something useful, like a bag of rice that might sustain them for a few more days.

Though Mercedes and Manuela occasionally spoke, there was generally little conversation among the one hundred and fifty thousand that walked. The only sounds were the scrunch of a shoe on the loose surface of the road and the occasional whimper of a baby, some of them newly born by the roadside.

When they were close to Motril, the halfway point of their journey, the two women heard a low grumble. It was late in the afternoon. Mercedes mistook it for the sound of trucks, but Manuela immediately recognised it as aircraft noise and stopped to look up. Nationalist planes were passing low overhead, cumbersome, noisy and graceless.

People watched them and wondered. No one spoke. Then the bombardment began.

During the months since this conflict had begun, Mercedes had never experienced the feelings of absolute terror that gripped her now. Her mouth filled with the metallic taste of fear, and for a moment the sound of her heart pounding drowned out the cries of alarm that went up around her. Her instinct was to run as hard and fast as she could, but there was nowhere to hide – no cellars or bridges or underground train stations. Nowhere. There was Javi to worry about, in any case, and his mother. She stood rooted to the spot as the planes passed directly overhead, her hands over her ears against the deafening roar.

Mercedes grabbed Manuela, who clasped Javi. They stood locked in this embrace, eyes closed against the world and the horrifying scene unfolding around them. Mercedes could feel the woman's sharp bones through her clothes. It was as though she might snap. They had nothing to protect them and, like most of the inhabitants of Málaga, so recently traumatised by the horrors of shelling and machine-gun fire in their own city, Manuela was briefly paralysed by the fresh onslaught of fascist aggression.

'Let's get off the road,' shouted Mercedes. 'It's our only hope.'

The irony was that the only places to hide along this unwelcoming stretch of road were the craters left in the fields by bombs that had exploded earlier. Many people cowered in them, petrified. At least the bombers had supplied some shelter for their terrorised victims.

Soon bodies lay everywhere like broken dolls.

To the horror and disbelief of everyone on the road that day, there was an even more terrifying method of attack to come. When the bombers had finished their work, fighter planes appeared to claim their next wave of victims. In order to instil more terror, they strafed the roads and then the people themselves. There were blinding flashes all around as bullets drew two lines of flaming dots among the screaming crowd. It was not a challenge for the pilots of those planes; they could have blown their targets apart with their eyes shut.

Mothers whimpered like babies when they saw their own children toppled like skittles. Some were mothers of four or five, and there was no protection that they could offer. In any case, a careful aim could wipe out several people in a single burst.

On one occasion, a two-seater plane came so low that Mercedes caught a glimpse of the pilot and behind him the gunner. People scattered, thinking that they might outrun his bullets but their action was futile. The gunner could easily manoeuvre his machine gun to maximum devastation. The pilot's face dimpled into a smile as he mowed them down.

Then everything went quiet. The minutes went by and the aeroplanes did not return.

'I think they've gone now,' Mercedes said, trying to reassure Manuela. 'We need to be on our way. We don't know when they might come back.'

The air was filled with the moans of the injured and bereaved. The problem for many now was whether to make an attempt to bury their dead or to continue towards the sanctuary of Almería. The ground was hard and burial was not easy, but some made the attempt. Others just covered the bodies with the only blankets they had, and moved on, taking the guilt and the grieving with them. If it was a mother who had been killed, their children were immediately adopted by others and shepherded onwards and away from the gruesome sight of a parental corpse.

In the previous forty-eight hours, Mercedes had been preoccupied by thoughts of Javier. There had not been a moment when the man she loved did not occupy the central-most place in her mind. It was only when the bombs came crashing around her that she was jolted out of this reverie. Then, for the first time, he had been far from her mind. Even the possibility that the man she loved might be somewhere in this diminishing crowd temporarily seemed of no importance to her. Getting this fragile creature, Manuela, and her son to safety now became her main concern.

Many were maimed, not killed, and a fresh wave of walking wounded was added to those who had limped from Málaga. The journey had to continue and the direction remained the same. There was no turning back and they could not stand still.

Manuela did not speak. For a moment she seemed paralysed by fear, but Mercedes' firm arm and the feel of her son's hand pulling on hers brought her to her senses. They resumed their journey.

Where the route turned towards the sea, the waves could be heard bashing against the rocks. The rhythm of nature was oblivious, and once or twice Mercedes saw people lying on a beach and was uncertain whether they were dead or alive. Either way, the sea would sweep them away sooner or later if they did not move. Donkeys lay beside humans, also dying. Swollen tongues protruded from their mouths.

On the fifth day that she had been walking, there was a moment when the sun briefly blazed and the water sparkled. Mercedes found Javi tugging at her skirt and pulling her towards the sea. It seemed to him as though it must be time for play, to toss pebbles into the waves, to dabble his toes into the water.

His childhood would eventually resume, but not yet. It would be too macabre to play among corpses.

'No, Javi, not now,' Manuela snapped, picking him up.

'We'll go and play in the sea another day,' said Mercedes, 'I promise.'

On a day when even the distant sight of a bird aroused terror in her, evoking memories of the planes that had massacred so many of them, she had only one aim: to reach her destination. Her mind was once again turned towards Javier. The thought of him sustained her as they walked these last kilometres, but she needed a new plan to find him.

Some people never made it to Almería. There were the wounded who fell by the way, but also some who took their own lives. Those such as Mercedes, who had gradually slipped towards the back of the exhausted human flow, saw the bodies of those who had shot themselves, and others who had hanged themselves from the trees. They had come this far, but desperation had finally overcome them. Many times Manuela had to hide Javi's eyes.

On reaching Almería, at the sight of the buildings and the promise of refuge Mercedes was almost overwhelmed with tears of relief. They had all walked far enough to deserve a feast, and her first thoughts were of something to eat. She had daydreamed of fresh bread.

For many people, exhaustion now swept over them. The streets of Almería seemed such a safe place to sleep after the exposed unsheltered road, and the pavements were like mattresses after the rough terrain of the week before. Most people sank down gratefully with whatever family they had left, and some dozed in broad daylight, the buildings around cocooning them like the walls of a room.

As soon as they arrived, Mercedes and Manuela began queuing for bread.

'Why don't you go back to Granada to find your family?' asked Manuela as they were standing together in a queue. 'Javi and I don't want to lose you but if we had somewhere else to go, we would. You don't have to be here.'

Mercedes did not want to return to Granada. It was the least safe option of all. Her family was a marked one. And Javier was not in Granada. It was this single fact that determined her decision. Her only real chance of survival was to stay away, and the only possibility of happiness was to find the man she loved. There was every chance that he would have survived. Javier was younger and stronger than most of the people that she saw around her. If they had escaped from Málaga, would he not have done so too?

'Half of my family aren't even in Granada any longer,' Mercedes reminded Manuela, 'and I need to carry on looking for Javier. If I don't keep searching, I'll never find him, will I?'

Javi was scratching at the ground with a stick, making a zigzag pattern in the dust, oblivious to the conversation going on between them. Mercedes looked down at the top of his dark head and stroked his hair. All she could see from above were his long lashes and the little splayed cushion of his nose. She picked him up from the ground and stroked his soft cheek. Even after all these days without bathing, the child's skin had a sweetness about it. Holding him was an extraordinary comfort.

'Well, you know you're welcome to be with us, don't you?'

'I know, I know . . .'

She did not want to be blunt, but her only desire now was to find Javier. The woman whose corpse she had seen hanging from the tree a few miles back had run out of purpose. Mercedes had not.

Once she had helped to settle Manuela and Javi safely in the doorway of a boarded-up shop where they would all sleep at least for the coming night, she went off to explore.

She continually stopped people to ask them whether they had seen Javier, and her picture of him was retrieved from her pocket a hundred times. Once or twice she found someone who thought they had seen him. The *guitarrista* was well known in Málaga and several people were sure they had caught sight of him before they had fled, even if they had not seen him since. At one point her hopes were raised when someone helpfully offered that they had just seen a man with a guitar. Mercedes hastened off in the direction he indicated and soon saw the figure that had been described to her from the back. Her heart missed a beat. Seeing the slim outline of a man carrying a battered guitar case, she hastened after him. She called out and the man turned round. As he did so, she realised that this man bore not the slightest resemblance to Javier. She found herself face to face with a man of more than fifty. She apologised and let him walk away. Tears of disappointment almost choked her.

She retraced her steps to where her companions were. Even with their small number of possessions they had made a neat, open-fronted home around them. Javi was already asleep, sprawled across his mother's lap. Manuela dozed, her head leaning back against the wooden doorframe. They looked peaceful together.

Mercedes wandered off to see if she could find some more food for them all. She joined two queues, only to be disappointed when what was being sold had run out before she had reached the front. Procuring a few grams of lentils at the end of a third was a triumph.

Almería had once been a beautiful city but she was too tired to notice and was completely unaware of the route she had taken. By the time she had stood in a few queues she had lost track of time. She did not possess a watch, and the sunless afternoon sky gave her no clues. She had been away for perhaps two hours.

As she was beginning to retrace her steps towards the centre of the city, she heard the distant sound of a siren and shortly after that the thud of an explosion and then another, closer this time. A shiny silver aeroplane passed overhead. Surely not here too? Their safe haven had been a very short-lived one.

When she got closer to the main square she could smell burning and sense the chaos, and as she turned the corner she found herself going against the tide, just as she had on the day when she met the procession filing out of Málaga. This time she must fight her way through. Panic rose inside her. In all the time since she had left Granada, she had not felt such fear. She was even more terrified than when they had been bombed on the road. The fleeing crowd were pushing her away, back in the direction she had come from, but she fought against them, manoeuvring herself towards the edge of the street so that she could stop and wait for the stampede to go by.

Eventually this first wave passed and then came the casualties. Some were supported, others were carried, many were lifeless. It was an unnervingly silent parade. Eventually they all passed and, but for a few stragglers, dazed and dusty with particles of fallen masonry, the street was quiet again. Mercedes trembled with fear. Though she had pictured what she would see when she turned the corner into the square, her anguish was no less intense when she saw the reality.

One entire side was bombed to oblivion and every building had collapsed. Not a single wall or pillar remained standing. It was a jumble of angled metalwork, twisted frames and blackened wood. Everything was charred or razed to the ground. Mercedes recalled that the shop that had briefly been Manuela's home was in the far corner, and she could see the empty space that it once occupied.

'Holy Mary, Mother of God . . . Holy Mary, Mother of God . . .' she muttered through her tears. She crossed the square quickly and recognised, even from its charred remains, the fragments of the deep green shop front where she had last seen her friends. There was nothing there now except fallen masonry and twisted metal girders.

Mercedes stood motionless. The absence of the two people that she had briefly known but intensely cherished dug a huge hollow inside her.

Someone came up behind her and tapped her on the arm.

She started and swung round. Manuela!

But it was not. It was an old woman.

'I saw them. I'm sorry. They didn't have a chance when that beam came down.'

If their shelter had been close to the centre of impact – and the crater nearby suggested it – they might not have suffered. This was Mercedes' first thought. Javi at least might have been sound asleep. She desperately hoped that this had been the case.

'Were they your family?'

Mercedes shook her head. She was completely incapable of speech. There was nothing to say even if her contracted throat had allowed it. She simply stood there and stared numbly at the place where her friends had once been.

More than a dozen had been killed in this single raid. Very few of the victims were residents of Almería; the majority were those who, like Manuela and Javi, had trekked for two hundred kilometres, only to perish in a strange city. The Fascist bombers had been efficient. They knew that the streets would be swollen with refugees, sitting targets on the streets, defenceless.

Mercedes looked around. She saw a woman standing in the

wreckage of her home. She had watched it fall and now fruitlessly sifted for possessions in the remains of charred wood and snapped off banisters that had once been on the floor above. If she did not retrieve what she could now, it would not be there for long. There were plenty of the desperate and destitute ready to scavenge dangerous and derelict properties.

Mercedes had considered herself lucky to have avoided machine guns, shells and aerial bombs on the long walk. She wondered why she had been spared in this latest onslaught as well.

In the pockets of her coat were the only possessions she now had: a bag of lentils and half a loaf of bread in one, and in the other her dancing shoes.

Chapter Twenty-three

SEVERAL DAYS AFTER leaving Granada, Antonio and his friends reached the outskirts of Madrid, approaching from the eastern side where Republican militia were in control. The sight of what had happened to the capital was shocking and the hollow, bombed-out buildings stirred them to anger. As their truck passed by, small children looked up at them and waved and women raised the *puño*, the Republican fist. The arrival of every new Republican supporter refreshed the hope that the Fascists could be kept out of their city.

As they queued to sign up for the militia, along with the men with whom they had travelled, they learned more about the situation in the capital city.

'At least there's the promise of rations if we join up,' said one of their companions. 'I'm looking forward to some decent grub.'

'I wouldn't hold out your hopes,' said another. 'There might not be much going here . . .'

Since September, Madrid had been full of refugees. Many of the towns surrounding it had been captured, and their terror-stricken populations had descended on the capital, swelling the population to many times its usual size. It was encircled by the enemy, but the ring was not so tight knit that it could not be broken through, thus sustaining the citizens' belief in freedom. The people of Madrid and the thousands of refugees with their possessions tied in rag bundles hoped that this awful situation would soon be over. They could not live on bread and beans for ever.

In the previous November optimism in Madrid had wavered. More than twenty-five thousand Nationalist troops had planted themselves in the western and southern suburbs, and were reinforced within a few weeks by troops from Germany. The starving people of Madrid could feel the clamp around them tightening and, with food becoming scarcer by the day, belts were drawn in too.

Then rumours circulated that the Republican government had evacuated from Madrid to Valencia. In the abandoned government offices, papers fluttered at empty desks and portraits kept watch on empty corridors. Birds flew in through half-opened windows and drops of pale excrement were now splashed across dark leather chairs. The move was supposedly temporary. Filing cabinets remained half filled and walls of books were undisturbed, dust already gathering round their elaborate-tooled spines and along the fine beading of the wood-panelled walls. High windows prevented the population from seeing inside these silent rooms, but they could imagine them and some were full of despair.

The majority in Madrid realised, though, that the absence of their government did not mean that the city had to fall to Franco, and there was renewed determination among them. Men, women and children would join the fight and from the beginning that was what they did, with small children running errands to the front, and a few brave women swapping their brooms for guns.

The now departed government's fears that the Fascists were about to enter Madrid were not immediately realised. Franco was held up in Toledo, and meanwhile aid finally arrived from the Soviet Union, as did anti-fascist volunteers from all around the world. Along with the communists, who had been ready to take over the defence of the city when the government left, these International Brigaders helped in the city's defence.

'*Salud!*' they cried.

'*Salud!*' the foreigners replied.

There was no common language but this gesture of solidarity and a single word was understood by them all.

Antonio found himself in conversation with a man who was a father of seven children.

'Until recently, you could let the children play in the streets.

Sometimes things could seem quite normal for a few hours,' he said ruefully. 'That's all changing now.'

Antonio looked round and saw how the buildings were scarred from mortar-fire and pockmarked with bullets. Panic and disorder was instilled by the regular crack of gunfire and the crump of shelling. It was obvious to Antonio that the sweetness of normal life, when things could be taken for granted, had been snatched away and replaced by the constant, stomach-tightening sensation of fear. Morale-boosting propaganda posters were peeling away from the walls, as frayed as their hopes.

'And you can imagine how much the children enjoyed the first few days when they couldn't go to school,' the father continued.

The children already yearned for the old routine, as did their mothers. Their well-ordered lives were like neatly stacked carts of fruit that had been overturned, their contents spilled into the gutter.

Standing in the streets, anxious to fight for these people, Antonio could see how crucial the deceptive guise of normality had become. Between air raids, shoeshine boys could still make a meagre living. Mothers and grandmothers walked through the streets in their best winter clothes, their children in velvet-collared coats either lagging too far behind or running in front to vex their elders. Men in felt hats with scarves at their necks to keep away the February blasts sometimes still took their evening stroll. It might have been the hour of *paseo* on an ordinary day during peaceful times.

At the sound of the siren, women would tighten their grip on the hands of their children and if they had too many to keep an eye on, strangers would stop and help. The great temptation was to look upwards to the sky, to see the planes and even to watch the battle that might take place above them. This was the instinct of children and many were pulled reluctantly into the darkness of the subway, to be hidden before the bombs fell around them screaming. In former times, the subway had been a way of getting from one side of the city to the other. Now, for some, station platforms had become a place of refuge and for others even a permanent home.

Eventually, terrified of what was happening above them but fearful of remaining for too long below, people would come up into the light, emerging into a street where buildings had been dissected like cakes with a carving knife. Perfect cross sections of precious homes were revealed, their treasured interiors now on display for the world to see. Plates and dishes were stubbornly unbroken and waiting to be used, even though their owners might be dead.

Eyes looked up into the privacy of strangers' lives, to see clothes wafting in the breeze, neat beds unmade by the wind, a dining table teetering on the edge, its chequered cloth still held down with a bowl of artificial flowers, pictures askew, bookcases empty, their contents spewed across the floor, a ticking clock that measured the passing of time before the next bomb blast or the days until this apartment block would be demolished for safety's sake. A mirror often hung on the back wall, reflecting the destruction. In some places only the façades of buildings remained standing, as fragile as cheap movie sets.

On their first day in the city, the trio from Granada were caught up in the chaos of such an air raid and nearly choked on the dust of shattered masonry, which did not settle until long after they had emerged from the claustrophobia of the airless, underground shelter.

When they had arrived in Madrid, the very worst of that winter's chill was over but the hunger continued. The constant nagging of an empty stomach was enough to encourage some men to join up with the militia, since it meant at least the promise of rations, and as Antonio queued up with his friends to sign up, he realised that he too was looking forward to a decent plateful of food. It was days since they had eaten more than a bowlful of watered-down lentils.

The mood here in Madrid was very different from that in Granada, where there were so many restricting new rules. Here was an almost revolutionary atmosphere, relaxed, casual and even sensual by comparison. Hotels were taken over for the soldiers, many of whom had never seen such grand panelling and fine gilding. The buildings themselves were cracked like old china.

The foreigners were a novelty to the Granadinos. They enjoyed the camaraderie with strangers from countries they could not even picture but found it odd that their own private conflict was now being played out on an open stage.

'Why do you think they're here?' Francisco asked his friends, baffled by the foreigners' presence. 'They know as well as we do what will happen if Franco invades this city.'

'They hate fascism as much as we do,' answered Antonio.

'And if they don't help stop it in our country, it will only spread to theirs,' added Salvador.

'It's like a disease,' said Antonio.

International Brigaders were hungry for action and mostly unafraid of what might happen to them. The people of Madrid could not have wished for better friends.

It was Antonio and his friends' first night in the poster-daubed city, a bigger and more sophisticated place than the one they had grown up in. The three of them were sitting up at a bar in one of the old hotels, and Antonio caught sight of himself in the tarnished glaze of the old mirrors that lined the walls behind the bar. Though the reflection was murky, their faces seemed happy and relaxed, as though they were just three young men, out for the night, carefree, shirts slightly crumpled, their hair slicked back, a little the worse for wear. The dim, sepia glow of the room flattered them and obscured the cavernous shadows under their eyes, hollowed out by hunger and exhaustion.

Antonio lost interest in his own reflection. His attention was drawn away by a group of girls who stood talking by the door. While he was merely observing them in the mirror they remained unselfconscious, but he knew that would change as soon as they knew they were noticed.

He nudged Salvador and realised that he had been similarly mesmerised. After the days of being packed in a truck like livestock, and the prospect of battle, the allure of these women was almost irresistible.

These girls were among the few people in this city for whom life had improved with this conflict. From the arrival of the first militia regiment, and now all the young men from foreign countries as well, business had boomed. Demand greatly exceeded supply, and though there were women who in peaceful times would have died rather than sell their bodies, some were now hungry enough to compromise.

When the three girls sauntered towards the bar, Francisco turned and smiled. He too had been watching them. They carried with them the cloying smell of cheap scent that was more intoxicating to these young men than the best Parisian fragrance worn by the smart women of Granada. Conversation began and the women introduced themselves as dancers. Perhaps they had been once. Drinks were bought and the chatter continued, with all of them shouting above the sound of a hundred other voices and the insistent music of an accordion player who moved about between the tables. There was only one thing on all their minds, though, and within the hour they were in a rundown brothel a few streets away, drunk on cheap brandy and succumbing to the powerful anaesthetic of sex.

The following morning, renewed after the deepest of sleeps, the friends from Granada were dispatched to the front line. The battle at Jarama, north-east of Madrid, had been going on for ten days now. It was where these young men wanted to be and the reason they had come. Antonio did not dread the crack of gunshots, the thud of a shell landing close by, the deep groan of an imploding building. The Granadinos were now officially part of the untrained militia unit they had travelled up with from the south. The Republic had lost such a huge part of its trained army that it welcomed any willing fighters such as these. Their enthusiasm and innocence obscured even the thought of death – it had barely entered their heads – and they posed with the other soldiers for light-hearted photographs that were unlikely to reach home.

At Jarama, Nationalist troops were aiming to seize the highway that ran to Valencia and had surprised the Republicans with their attack on 6 February. With the support of German tanks and planes, forty thousand troops, including many foreign legionaries, who were the most ruthless of them all, Franco had begun his offensive. Before the Republicans had time to organise themselves, strategic hills and bridges had been seized. Soviet tanks slowed the advance a little, but the Nationalists had begun to move forward and huge losses had already been sustained when the Granadinos arrived.

When they reached the site of the battle, they expected to go into action immediately. They stood around the lorry that had brought them and surveyed the landscape. It hardly looked like a battleground. They saw neat vineyards and rows of olive trees, low hills and clumps of gorse and wild thyme.

'There doesn't seem to be much cover . . .' commented Francisco.

He was right and before they had the opportunity to use their guns they found themselves part of a team dispatched to dig trenches. A pile of old doors had been salvaged from the shattered remains of a nearby village and were to be used to strengthen the trench walls. Francisco and Antonio worked together, standing in the ditch while others passed the doors down to them. Many still had their smooth brass handles; some had the faded paint of a door number.

'I wonder what happened to the people who lived behind this one,' Antonio mused. It had once guarded the privacy of its owners but now their home must be standing open to the winds.

Dug down into the olive groves on the hillside above the River Jarama, they waited for their first taste of action. By now they had done more than their fair share of trench reinforcement and this conflict had provided nothing but boredom. The dampness of the ground was bad enough during the day, but at night it gave them no sleep, and here for the first time they picked up the lice that were to plague them for many months to come. The inescapable, continual need to scratch, both day and night was torture.

'How much longer do you think?' muttered Francisco.

'For what?'

'This. This sitting here. This waiting. This nothing.'

'God knows . . . but we can't make things happen.'

'But we've been doing *nothing* for days. I can't stand it. I was more useful in Granada. I'm not sure I want to hang around here.'

'Well, you'll have to. You'll get shot by our own men if you try and leave. So don't even think of it.'

Playing chess or writing letters to relatives kept them occupied only for a while.

'It seems a bit pointless writing letters,' said Antonio with uncharacteristic glumness, 'when the person you're writing to might not even be alive by the time the letter arrives.'

He was addressing his letter to his aunt Rosita, in the hope that she might keep it for Concha. It was too incriminating to send a letter directly to his mother. He hoped that she was safe and wondered whether she had managed to visit his father. He prayed that Mercedes would have found Javier, or made her way back home. It was not safe for a sixteen-year-old girl to be alone.

'I don't even know if my mother is alive,' Francisco said as he folded a sheaf of paper ready to post, 'and by the time she gets this I might have died. Of boredom.'

Antonio tried to cheer his friend, even though he was feeling equally frustrated. The tedium of the wait was maddening them all.

Even if periods of inactivity have a timelessness about them, they never go on for ever and, sure enough, fighting soon resumed. Within a day or so, they were on the front line, where the relentless rat-a-tat-tat of machine guns, the boom of cannon and the shouts of '*Fuego!*' soon replaced the ennui.

Suddenly they were ordered to try to take command of a nearby ridge. As they dug in at the bottom of the slope, several battalions of Nationalist soldiers swept over the brow of the hill and charged towards them. At the moment when they could almost see the whites of their eyes, the order to fire was given. Some turned and ran for cover, others were mown down. The machine guns went briefly silent as their belts were replaced but the volleys of gunfire from the Nationalists went on for some minutes. An order was given to several dozen of the Republican soldiers, including Antonio, to advance up the ridge where they could be in a position to fire at the Nationalists but heavy artillery drove them back. The soldier next to Antonio was blasted open. His blood sprayed everyone within a few metres and, through the smoke, Antonio tripped over another body that lay spread-eagled across his path. Uncertain whether he was dead or alive, Antonio carried him back to their base. Only half of the unit survived the day. It was a brutal introduction to the reality of this conflict. The image of the shattered bodies haunted him that night.

The Nationalists, determined to drive the Republicans out, continued their assault on some last key positions. There were huge numbers of casualties, including many among the idealistic bands of International Brigaders, some of whom had not held a rifle before. Theirs were often unreliable weapons, old and defunct, with catches that jammed or useless ammunition. Thousands of them would now never get much practice in using them as they were dead within hours. In one afternoon, Antonio counted dozens who had been killed in an assault not far from their own location. Their sacrifice seemed utterly futile.

The course of the battle changed when Soviet planes went into action and began to prevent the Nationalists from protecting their own forces. Nationalist bombers were now being driven off by Soviet fighters.

At the end of February, the battle was over. Both sides had suffered huge losses but the Nationalists had advanced only a few kilometres. Every centimetre of dust they had gained had cost them many lives. As a mathematical equation, it made no sense at all, but in terms of morale, the Republican confidence was boosted. It was a stalemate they regarded as a battle won.

Francisco failed to see it as a victory.

'We've lost thousands and so have they. And they've taken some ground,' he pointed out.

'But not much, Francisco,' signed Salvador.

'It just seems a bloody mess to me, that's all,' said Francisco angrily.

No one was going to disagree with him. A 'bloody mess' was precisely what it was.

They returned to Madrid for a short while. This was a place where they could still get a haircut, a shave, clean clothes, and even stay in a comfortable bed. Life there was continuing as normal in spite of the threat of air raids. Once or twice they heard that the legendary communist leader Dolores Ibarruri was in their neighbourhood and joined a throng already amassing to hear her. The tireless, black-clad figure of Ibarruri, known by everyone as 'La Pasionaria', 'The Passion Flower', was a common sight on the streets of Madrid. She never failed to rally those with flagging spirits.

When Antonio caught sight of the chiselled face for the first time it was as though he had inhaled pure air. They had all often heard her voice on the radio or when it was broadcast from the travelling loud-hailers that had toured the front line, but the real person had a majesty that the voice alone did not convey. The woman's physical presence was extraordinary and her immense power and charisma radiated around the square.

In an unconscious gesture that came so naturally to Spanish women, she clasped her hands together. First of all she addressed the women, reminding them of the sacrifice they must make.

'Prefer to be widows of heroes, rather than wives of cowards!' she exhorted them, the rich timbre of her voice booming above the heads of the quiet crowd.

The solid flesh and blood of the woman inspired them all. They needed, all of them, to be as strong as she.

'*No pasarán!*' she called out. 'They shall not pass!'

'*No pasarán!*' the crowd chanted. '*No pasarán! No pasarán!*'

Her pure conviction inspired them. While they were standing, ready to put up this resistance, the Fascists would never enter their city, and La Pasionaria's clenched fist punching the air reinforced their belief that this could never be. Many of these men and women were exhausted, disillusioned, fearful, but she made them believe that the fight was worth continuing.

Salvador absorbed her magnetism and the warm response of the crowd. Ibarruri had been too far away for him to read her lips, but she had held his attention nevertheless.

'It's better to die on our feet than live on our knees!' she exhorted them.

There was not a man, woman or child left unmoved.

When her speech came to an end, the people dispersed.

'She's inspiring, isn't she?' said Antonio.

'Yes,' replied Francisco, 'she's an extraordinary woman. She actually makes you think it's possible.'

'Well, she's right,' said Antonio. 'And you mustn't stop believing that.'

Chapter Twenty-four

FOR A FEW days Mercedes wandered aimlessly through the streets of Almería. She knew no one in this city now. Occasionally there was a glimpse of a half-familiar face but it was just someone that she had seen on the road from Málaga. They were not friends, just other people like her, all of them in the wrong place, still on their feet, trudging from one queue to another.

For those with families, staying in Almería was the only choice, since the effort of moving again was beyond the realms of possibility. For Mercedes remaining here was the option she favoured least of all. She stood in a street where many other refugees loitered, all strangers to each other and to this city. She could not imagine staying. It was the one thing she knew.

So she faced a choice. The easiest course of action would have been to return home to Granada. Anxiety for her mother grabbed her hard, and she felt a surge of guilt that she was not there with her. She missed Antonio too and knew that he would be doing what he could to comfort their mother. Perhaps her father had been released. If only there was some way of finding out.

She desperately missed the café and the homely apartment above it, where every dark stair and window-ledge was so familiar. She allowed herself the momentary self-indulgence of remembering some of the things she loved about home: the sweet, indefinable scent of her mother, the dim light that cast a faint yellow glow on the staircase, the muskiness of her own bedroom, the thickly layered brown paint on the doors and windowframes, her old wooden bed with its heavy green wool blanket that had kept her warm for longer than she could remember. A wave of intense longing descended. All the small comforting things seemed very far away in this shattered, unfamiliar place. Perhaps these details of life were what mattered most of all.

Then she thought of Javier. She remembered the first time she saw him and how her life had changed in that instant. Her recollection of the moment when he had looked up from his guitar and his dark-lashed, limpid eyes gazed out towards her in the audience was vivid. He had not seen her then but she remembered the effect of his look. It was as though his eyes transmitted heat and she had melted in their intensity. After her first dance for Javier, each subsequent encounter had been like a stepping stone across a river, each one taking them closer to the other bank where she had assumed they could never be apart. Their desire to be together had been mutual, passionate and absolute. Separation from Javier was like a dull, perpetual ache that would never go away. An illness.

One day, about a week after Manuela had been killed, across the street, the discreet doorway into a church caught Mercedes' eye. Perhaps the Virgin would help her decide which direction to take.

Behind the battered entrance lay an interior of baroque grandeur, but it was not this that surprised her, since many churches had almost unnoticeable side-street doors that belied the immensity of the church hidden within. What really astounded her were the numbers of people inside. It was not as though they had come here for safety. There had been no divine protection for religious buildings in these times of turmoil. Churches were as vulnerable as anywhere, whether they were destroyed from the air by Nationalists or burned down by supporters of the Republic. Many aisles and naves were now open to the elements, and pulpits and organ lofts had become the nesting places for birds.

In spite of losing their faith, men and women sought safety and warmth in this open church. Some memories of what religion had once meant returned to Mercedes and yet it seemed a lifetime ago that she had gone each week to confess her sins and decades since she had taken her first communion. Candles flickered before an icon of the Mary and the eyes of the Holy Virgin met Mercedes' gaze. The 'Hail Mary' was an incantation that used to flow out of her like water from a tap. Now she resisted the temptation to recite it all. It would be hypocrisy. She did not believe. Those eyes that caught hers were just oil on a canvas, a chemical compound. She turned away, the smell of wax lingering in her nostrils. She almost envied those who could find comfort in such a place as this.

Around the curve of the apse, layers of cherubs reached up to heaven. Some looked out at the congregation with a mischievous grin. Beneath them sat the Virgin, the limp Christ lying in her arms. Mercedes studied her, looking for some message or meaning, but realised that her expression did not begin to capture the pain of the woman she had seen on the road from Málaga a few days earlier: a mother who, like Mary, had been nursing the corpse of her child. It was obvious that the painter of this *pietà* had never seen the real thing. His depiction of pain was not even an approximation. The image seemed an insult to grief. In every small side chapel, she saw vulgar portrayals of suffering and anguish and from each ceiling corpulent angels looked down, smiling.

Walking away from the main altar she found herself face to face with an upright, life-size Mary made of plaster. Glass tears glistened on her smooth cheeks, the eyes were strong and blue, the mouth slightly downturned. She gazed out at Mercedes through the bars of the locked chapel, incarcerated along with a small vase of faded paper flowers. While others could project their hopes and dreams on these figures and believe they found comfort, if not always definite answers, Mercedes found their stagy symbolism absurd.

The pious knelt on the steps of every side chapel, or sat with their heads bowed in the main body of the church. Everyone seemed at peace and yet Mercedes was churned up with anger.

'What use has God been?' she wanted to cry out, to break the reverend silence that reigned in this lofty space. 'What has he done to protect us?'

In reality, the Church had acted against them. Many of the Nationalists' actions against the Republic had been done in the name of God. In spite of this, she could see that many of the citizens of Almería clearly still held on to their belief that the Virgin Mary would help them. For those whose lips moved in prayers of supplication but who did not really expect answers, this place clearly still provided comfort, but for Mercedes, coming in here to find guidance, it now seemed laughable. The saints and martyrs, with their painted-on blood and theatrical stigmata, had once been part of her life. Now she saw the Church as a sham, a cupboard full of redundant props.

She took a seat for a while, watching people come and go, lighting candles, muttering prayers, gazing at icons, and wondered what it was they felt. Did a voice reply when they prayed? Did it respond immediately, or was it heard the next day when they least expected it? Did these frozen-eyed figures of the saints really become flesh and blood to them? Perhaps they did. Maybe these people, with their tear-filled, pleading eyes, and hands so tightly locked that their fingers whitened, were really engaged with something beyond her understanding, something supernatural. She could neither grasp it with her mind, nor feel it with her heart.

There was no divine hand. Of that she was now certain. For a moment she wondered if she should pray for the souls of Manuela and her little boy. She thought of them, innocent, harmless, and their annihilation only added to her conviction of God's absence.

With the realisation that she had neither faith nor belief to help her, she knew that her decision would have to be taken alone. At that moment, an image of Javier, more beautiful than any of the handsome saints depicted in oils, came into her mind. It was rare for more than a few moments to pass when he was not in her thoughts. Perhaps for the devout, the huge space of the imagination was occupied by God. For Mercedes, it was Javier who filled it. She worshipped him body and soul and believed him worthy of it.

The warmth of the church, the semi-darkness and the strong, musky scent of candles held her in an embrace; she could imagine this physical comfort being enough to bring people in and keep them there. It would have been easy for her to sit there too, but the stuffiness had become overwhelming and she had to get out for air.

The street outside was silent. A desperate dog scavenged. Another one chased the pages of a newspaper that flapped like a dirty bird struggling to fly. They eyed Mercedes suspiciously and, for a moment, hungrily. These animals had probably not eaten for days. In former times they had survived on the generous leftovers from restaurant bins but now there was nothing for them, not even the occasional carcass.

She now knew with blinding certainty what anyone who had ever felt the compelling force of reciprocated love would understand: that she could not go back to Granada. She recalled the way in which her mother had encouraged her to leave and knew she could count her among those who would not condemn her for walking away from her home city rather than towards it. Mercedes believed that Javier was her one unique opportunity for love and so, whatever bitter end or consummation it might lead to, she had to find him. Even the activity of searching and the unerring belief that he could be found would alleviate the pain of separation.

With no idea of where her feet were taking her, she ambled along. It gave her time to reflect. Perhaps she was no different from the people in church. Perhaps this belief, this knowledge, was what they felt too. They 'knew' that God existed and their belief in the miracle of the Resurrection was unshakeable. Her faith was this: she knew that Javier was still alive. As she stood on the pavement, the decision made itself for her. She would head north, following her instinct and the only other information she had, which was that his uncle lived in Bilbao. Perhaps her loved one would be there, waiting for her.

Though she had little fear now, it was still undesirable for a woman to travel alone and she knew she would be safer in the company of others. Almería was bursting with refugees and there were plenty of them who would be making their way out of the city with whom she could travel. Having decided to make enquiries, she struck up a conversation with two women. Though they were planning to stay for a while themselves, they told her of a couple they knew who were about to set off with their daughter.

'I'm sure I heard that they intended to leave soon,' the younger woman said to her sister.

'Yes, that's right. They have family in the north somewhere and that's where they're aiming to go.'

'When we've got our bread, let's go and find them. You can't go on your own, and I'm sure they'll be happy for the company.'

In due course, hugging their segments of loaf, they made their way to a school on the edge of Almería where the two women, along with hundreds of others, were camped out. Mercedes found it strange to see classrooms where adults now outnumbered children and where chairs and desks had been piled in the corner and old blankets lay strewn across the floor. The walls still carried cheerful displays of children's drawings. They seemed incongruous now, a reminder of how the old order had been turned upside down.

The sisters found the place where they had left their few belongings, and in the same room sat a middle-aged woman. She appeared to be darning a sock, but on closer inspection Mercedes saw that she was trying to sew up her shoe. The leather was so soft and worn that it could be pierced with an ordinary needle. She was more or less remaking this battered footwear. Without it she could go nowhere.

'Señora Duarte, this is Mercedes. She wants to go north. Can she come with you?'

The woman carried on sewing. She did not glance up.

Mercedes fingered the rounded toes of her dance shoes, one in each pocket of her coat. Sometimes she forgot about them, but the comforting weight of them was always there.

'We aren't going yet,' Señora Duarte said, looking up now into Mercedes' face. 'But when we do you can come with us, if you like.'

The words were spoken without a trace of warmth, let alone a genuine welcome. Though it was stuffy here Mercedes felt herself shudder. She understood how people could be stripped of their ability to care about others. Many had seen terrible atrocities and she could see that in this woman's eyes. Here was someone beyond the stage where she could take an interest in strangers and perhaps even her own family.

Moments later, a young woman of about Mercedes' age appeared.

'Did you get any?' asked her mother, once again speaking without looking up.

'As much as they would give me,' replied her daughter. 'But it wasn't much. Hardly enough for one really.'

'But there are three of us, including your father – and four now if this girl is going to attach herself to us,' she said, indicating Mercedes with an upward movement of her head.

Mercedes stepped forward. The woman who had introduced them had gone now.

'Some acquaintances of yours said I might be able to come on the road with you, as we're all planning on going in the same direction. Would that be all right?'

Mercedes spoke with some hesitation, unsure of whether she might get the same cool reception from the daughter.

The girl eyed her up and down, not with suspicion but with interest. 'Yes, I'm sure it would.' She spoke with unmistakable warmth.

'Come and find somewhere to cook these with me,' she said, waving the pathetic package of lentils. 'I'm sure we can make them stretch – and I see you've got some bread.'

The two women then found themselves in a queue for a small kitchen. They were all used to standing in lines now. This was where acquaintances might become friends.

'I'm sorry my mother doesn't seem very friendly.'

'Don't worry. I'm a total stranger. Why should she be?'

'She didn't used to be like that.'

Mercedes looked into the girl's face and saw someone like herself. She had a girl's complexion with an old woman's eyes. They were full of grief as though she had already experienced enough suffering for a lifetime.

'It was my brother. Eduardo. He was walking with three friends. They were ahead of us in a group and we got separated. Mother's shoes had worn down to nothing and her heels were cracked and bleeding. She couldn't go very fast and Eduardo had grown impatient. In the air attack we had a lucky escape, but when the planes had gone and we carried on walking, we saw them. All four of them. Dead. Lying in a row. They'd been moved from the middle of the road so that people didn't have to walk round them. The other parents hadn't caught up with them yet, so we were the first to realise who they were.'

Mercedes felt she had been there and indeed it was perfectly possible that she might have passed the very spot a few moments earlier.

'We had missed them, by a moment. You know when you're late to meet someone and when you get there, someone says, "Oh, they've just gone," and you have that sense of loss and waste. Well, it was like that, but for good. Eduardo had gone. We had missed him by a moment. He was still warm. It was impossible to take in that he was no longer alive. His body was there, but he just wasn't in it any more.'

Tears coursed down her cheeks. Mercedes could feel the enormity of her loss. She was reminded of when she saw her own brother's lifeless body. Ignacio had been dead for many hours and she had been shocked by her own reaction. It was not her brother, and she remembered realising that there was a difference between a body and a corpse. The latter was like an empty shell on the beach.

Mercedes found herself bereft of useful words. There had been hundreds of mortalities on that road from Málaga, but an individual death, even in the overall scale of suffering, would never lose its impact.

'I'm so sorry. How terrible . . . how terrible.'

'They'll never recover, I know they won't. My father didn't speak for two days. My mother never stops crying. And I'm meant to be the strong one . . .'

For a few minutes they stood in silence. The girl herself looked as though she had been weeping for days. Eventually she spoke.

'My name's Ana, anyway,' she said wiping her eyes.

'And I'm Mercedes.'

No one else in the queue even listened to their conversation.

The story Ana had told was nothing out of the ordinary in times like these.

While Ana stirred the mean mixture of lentils and water, the girls continued to talk. Mercedes told her that she needed to get to Bilbao, and Ana explained that her parents were aiming for her uncle's village in the north. Her father's brother, Ernesto, had never supported the Republic and her father did not have firm political views, so he had persuaded her mother that they should set up a new home, closer to his family, where they might be safe. He was convinced that it was only a matter of time before Franco took Madrid, and following that it would only be a few days before the whole country was in Nationalist hands. It was a long distance to travel, but their apartment in Málaga had been destroyed and it was doubtful they would ever return now. Her father had never held membership of a trade union or any other workers' association so he reckoned he was free to shift his allegiance at will.

Mercedes' sole aim was to find Javier, whether he was in Nationalist or Republican territory. She knew that he was most likely to be in the latter, but decided to keep this to herself. Even now she could see that keeping politics a private matter with this family might stand her in good stead. It was enough for her that they shared the same broad destination.

'I'll be really glad if you come with us. My parents hardly speak and we've got a long way to go. I could really do with some company.'

By the time they had returned to Ana's mother, her father was also there. He had been queuing all afternoon and had an onion and half a cabbage to show for it. Introductions were made and Mercedes was welcomed politely by Señor Duarte.

Though he had no bandages or visible signs of injury, Duarte was like a wounded man; it was as if he might snap beneath the burden of his grief. He certainly did not want to make conversation. Mercedes realised that these people were much younger than she had at first thought. Señora Duarte could easily have been mistaken for Ana's grandmother, and Mercedes wondered if it was the death of their only son that had aged them so many decades beyond their years.

Señora Duarte was a little friendlier now, perhaps because of the additional loaf that Mercedes offered her, and they formed a tight circle before sharing the soup between four enamel bowls and dividing up the bread. There were other people in the room and it was considered bad manners to display what you were eating, however little it was.

'So, Mercedes, you want to come up to the north with us?' said Señor Duarte, breaking the silence when they had all finished their meal.

'Yes, I do,' she answered. 'As long as I'm not going to be in the way.'

'You won't be. But you will have to understand something.'

Ana looked nervously at her father. She did not want him to scare away her new friend.

'Let me do the talking when we get stopped,' he said brusquely to Mercedes, his cold eyes fixed on hers. 'As far as anyone is concerned you two are sisters. You do understand that, don't you?'

'Yes, I think so,' she said.

She felt uncomfortable with his manner but she would have to put this aside; the mother seemed kind enough and it would make sense to be part of a family. To get to Bilbao they needed to cross territory occupied by Nationalist troops. That did not seem to concern Ana, so Mercedes told herself she must not worry either.

After their meagre supper, the girls intended to go for a stroll in the street to get away from the overcrowded building but, as they were about to leave, they heard the unexpected sound of music coming from a classroom down the corridor. It drew them towards it. For the first time in weeks the sound of something other than conflict reached their ears. Even when the bombs were not falling, or when they were not being strafed or machine-gunned, the noise of it all had left a continual ringing in their ears. The delightful fluid sound of an arpeggio quickened their heartbeats and hastened their steps.

They soon found where the music was coming from. Already

encircled by people, the top of his shiny bald pate reflecting the light from a single bulb illuminating the room, they saw the *tocaor*. His whole body was curved as though to protect his guitar.

People streamed from every door in the corridor and gathered in the room and a crowd of children sat on the floor looking up at him. During the journey from Málaga they had lost the naïvety of childhood and now seemed to understand the tragic potency of this sound.

No one knew the *flamenco*'s name. He seemed not to have any family with him. By the time Mercedes and Ana arrived, several people were accompanying him with quiet *palmas*. His long, stained fingernails skimmed lightly and airily across the strings. He was playing for himself but he occasionally looked up and his eyes registered the growing crowd. Mercedes slipped back to her own classroom. There was something she might need.

As she returned, she heard a familiar sequence of notes that sent a shockwave through her. Just four notes played in a unique sequence and she could tell this *toque* apart from a million others. It was a melody that meant more to her than any other. A *soleá*. It was the first piece she had ever danced with Javier. The melancholy of the tune might have lowered her spirits, but instead she took it as a sign that she would see him again. The thought lifted her heart.

Other people recognised the *compás* too and clapped in time with the beat. For a while she held back and then, almost involuntarily, she found herself removing the shoes from her pocket and slipping them on to her feet, buckling them with shaking fingers. The soft leather felt so familiar, so warm. She did not hesitate to step round the children who were sitting just a few feet from the guitarist. Her steel heelcaps click-clacked on the parquet as she approached the *guitarrista*. The children gazed with rapt attention at this girl, who now blocked their view of the musician.

A year ago, it might have seemed audacious to present herself to a stranger, ready to dance, but such rules no longer mattered. What did she have to lose in front of an audience who knew neither her nor her family? They were all strangers to each other here, brought together by bitter circumstances.

The man looked up and gave her a broad, encouraging smile. He could tell from her attitude, her position and the way she held herself that she had danced many times and would know how to direct him.

She bent to whisper in his ear, 'Can we have the same again?'

As he listened to her, his fingers chased a tune up and down the strings, his nails flicking the strings with a virtuoso's dexterity.

The arrival of this girl by his side felt like a glimpse back to an old life where evenings might evolve with delightful spontaneity. He was often hired for *juergas* and the only guaranteed thing was the uncertainty of how the evening might unfold, who would play well, how the women would dance, whether the gathering would have any spirit, any *duende*.

He smiled up at her. For Mercedes and everyone else who caught a glimpse of his face at that moment, it was as if the sun had burst out on an otherwise dull day. Such glimpses of warmth had become a rare thing of late. Now, from the introductory passage, emerged the *soleá* that she so much wanted him to repeat. Mercedes began to clap her hands, just lightly at first, until she could feel that the audience had the rhythm running right through them and could not tell it from the beating of their own hearts. Some women joined their hands together with her, eyes fixed on this girl who had come from nowhere to take centre stage. As their *palmas* strengthened, she began to tap her right heel until she established a stronger and more forceful beat. A moment later she banged her left foot down hard and the dance began, her wrists and arms moving in fluid motion above her head, her long slim fingers so much thinner than they had been a month before.

For the first time in days, the profound sense of defeat that many of these people had carried about with them was lifted.

The *tocaor*'s playing echoed her movements, increasing in passion as the dance went on. It was almost violent now, the way in which his nails ripped through the strings and tapped on the plates on the front of the guitar. Slung across his back, this instrument had been carried for miles, withstanding several falls on the way. Though these accidents had done miraculously little damage, the way he was playing it now made it seem as though he was hellbent on its destruction.

He had complete confidence in the strength of its pinewood body to withstand this treatment and now he used his instrument to express not just his own anguish but that of his audience. The music echoed it.

For the duration of the dance this stranger became someone else for Mercedes. When she had danced for that first time in the *cueva* two years earlier, she and Javier had been equally unknown to each other. Her eyes shut tight with concentration, the music had transported her back to that same evening and once again she gave every part of herself.

After the *soleá*, with its strong, quiet control and an expression of feeling that ran unfathomably deep, the crowd was almost tense with its agony and pathos. They knew that this was a spontaneous performance. The mutterings of '*Olé*' were hushed. It was as if they did not want to break the spell.

The *tocaor* knew to relieve the atmosphere with the lighter mood of the *alegrías* and found his dancer more relaxed as she picked up the new beat and felt her way into the movements. The stiffness Mercedes had felt from all the weeks without dancing had gone, and now she was able to bend and twist her body with the same suppleness she used to have, and to click her fingers with their usual sharp precision.

The joy of this dance took everyone's mind away from shattered lives and burned-out homes, from the images of corpses and the cruel faces of the people who had driven them out of their own city. Many of them joined in, clapping the rhythm more enthusiastically as the minutes went by.

By the end, Mercedes was tired. Sweat ran down her neck and down her back; she could feel it trickle between her buttocks. She had given everything of herself, forgetting both where she was and almost who. Like the audience she had been transported away from the present. In her mind she had been at a fiesta, surrounded by family and friends. She eased her way through the applauding crowd to the edge of the room where she saw that Ana was standing. Her new friend's face was beaming in admiration at the way Mercedes had danced.

'*Fantástico*,' she said simply. '*Fantástico*.'

The guitarist had not missed a beat. There was not a breath between the final, closing stamp of Mercedes' *alegrías* and the quiet first chord of his next piece. His audience was entranced and he wanted to hold them in that state.

It was almost an impossibility that the music he was making came from only one guitar. The volume of sound and the depth and richness of the notes seemed to come from several instruments, and when the warm tone of the guitar's hollow body being tapped was added, it magnified into layers of rich velvet. With the sound of the *palmas* and now one or two people tapping the rhythms on their chairs and on table tops, music emanated from every corner. Everyone in that room was enraptured now, swept along by a fast-flowing river of notes.

Mercedes tapped her fingertips gently against her palm. She stood leaning against the wall with Ana, their shoulders touching.

A man emerged from the shadows. He was a bulky individual, a head above most of the men there. He had a mass of dense, dark curls that fell well below his collar and the texture of this hair was coarse. His pitted skin was only half concealed by the patchy stubble of an unshaven face. The audience cleared a path for him since his manner showed that he would not hesitate to push his way through. There was no warmth in his gruff face.

As the guitarist brought his piece towards a conclusion, the new arrival was drawing up a chair. The two men looked easy together, side by side, as though they had met before. For a moment they spoke under their breath though the *guitarra* never for a second lifted his fingers away from his strings, continuing to pick out a tune while they whispered, not for a second losing the attention of the crowd.

The audience could not locate the source of the first sound they heard. It seemed unconnected with the singer. Everyone who had watched this man take his place to perform had a preconceived idea of how he would sound, but the reality of it defied their expectations. From his lungs came a low, sweet note, quite unlike the gypsy rasp that they had expected. It was the soft sound of someone's soul. After an introductory passage to the song, a *taranta*, the voice began to climb and the gypsy *cantaor's* fingers and hands started to express the emotions that poured from him. In the low light of the room his big pale hands stood out against his black jacket and performed like puppets in a mime show. The characters they played were pity, anger, injustice and grief. It was the story of the gypsy ghettos that he had been telling his whole life, and the tragic essence of his words seemed more appropriate than ever before to the exiled Malagueños.

This audience understood him now. When they looked at themselves, they realised that the roughness of his demeanour only mirrored their own. This was how they all appeared now – coarse, dirty, hunted, sad.

Ana turned to Mercedes at the end of the first *cante*.

'I wonder if he always sings like this,' she said.

'Who knows?' responded Mercedes. 'But it's the most beautiful sound I've ever heard.'

The appreciation for the *gitano* was immense. He described their story and their lives. In his expression their own feelings were miraculously told.

'How does he *know*?' muttered Ana under her breath.

Before the evening ended, many others danced, some with such exuberance that the dark mood that hung over Almería seemed to lift. Another guitarist appeared, followed by an elderly woman with astonishing mastery over the castanets that she had kept in the pocket of her skirt since leaving home. Rather as a pair of shoes had been for Mercedes, these simple pieces of wood had brought great comfort to this old lady every time she felt the reassuring shape of their cool domes beneath her fingertips. For her they were the only continuity in this strange, awful nightmare of the new life suddenly thrust upon her.

It was a *feria* like no other. By four in the morning, almost every man, woman and child sheltering in the school had squeezed into the room. It was rarely hotter than this in August. People forgot their situation and smiled. It was only when the *tocaor* finally exhausted himself that the evening came to an end. Everyone had a few hours of the deepest sleep they had enjoyed for many days and even dawn's grey light did not stir them.

Mercedes and Ana shared a blanket on the same patch of hard floor. Friendships were formed quickly under these circumstances and when the girls woke, they remained huddled under the blanket, exchanging their stories.

'I am looking for someone,' Mercedes explained. 'That's my reason for going north.'

She could hear her own voice, so resolute and determined, but the look she saw on Ana's face made her realise how ridiculous this might sound.

'And who is it you are looking for?'

'Javier Montero. He has family near Bilbao. I think he might be trying to get there.'

'Well, we're all going in the same direction,' Ana said. 'And we'll do our best to help you. We'll be leaving later today. He'll be ready by then.' She nodded in the direction of her father, who still lay sleeping, a motionless shape under a blanket by the wall.

Mercedes already knew that she could not expect any warmth from Ana's father. The night before, when she had returned to the classroom to fetch her dancing shoes she had overheard a conversation that shocked her. Just before going in, she had heard raised voices and her own name.

'Look, we don't know anything about this Mercedes girl,' Señor Duarte was ranting to his wife. The classroom had been vacated by most of its occupants, who had gone to find the music that was drifting so irresistibly towards them. 'Supposing she's a communist?'

'Of course she isn't a communist! Why do you say things like that?'

Mercedes continued to listen at a crack in the door.

'Because there are communists everywhere. Extremists. People who have caused all of this.' With a sweeping arm movement, he indicated the chaos of miscellaneous possessions around them, all such potent symbols of deracination.

'How can you say it's their fault?' Señora Duarte asked. Her voice was raised. 'You're beginning to sound like your brothers.'

Mercedes was transfixed by the argument. Ana had said that her father was very angry with the Republican government, but she realised herself how careful she would have to be now.

'Without those *rojos*,' he spat out the word as though it was phlegm, 'none of this would be happening.'

'Without Franco it wouldn't even have begun,' she retorted.

Señor Duarte's fury now overcame him and he lifted his hand to strike his wife. This answering back of hers was intolerable.

She raised her arm to parry the blow. 'Pedro!'

He regretted his action immediately, but it could not be undone. He had never been roused to hit his wife before, perhaps because she had never stood up to him in this way.

'I'm sorry, I am sorry,' he whispered almost helplessly, full of remorse.

Mercedes was horrified to see a man striking his wife. She knew for certain that her father would never have laid a finger on her mother and wondered for a moment if she should intercede. Señor Duarte was obviously casting about wildly for somewhere to place the blame for his only son's death. In his view, everyone was guilty, not just the bombers, who had mown down his son, and the Nationalist troops, who had seized half the country, but also the Republicans for failing to put up a united front.

Señora Duarte was stirred to continue the argument: 'So you're saying that you'll live under the Fascists and just go along with them, rather than stand up for what you voted for?'

'Yes, I'd rather do that than die . . . yes, I would. Because dying is pointless. Think of our boy,' Señor Duarte retorted.

'Yes, I do think of our boy,' answered Señora Duarte. 'He was killed by the side that you now want to support.'

Grief and anger clashed within them both. There was no possibility of their discussion taking any rational course.

Señora Duarte tearfully left the room and Mercedes hid in the shadows as she passed. She had needed her shoes and seized the moment to run in to fetch them. Señor Duarte looked up. He would always wonder if they had been overheard.

That afternoon the four of them would be ready to leave. There was a bus departing for Murcia.

Chapter Twenty-five

THE GRANADINOS WERE leaving Madrid for the second time. La Pasionaria's rousing words would go with them to the front line.

For a while, the Italians had been withdrawing their troops from the Jarama area and now, in early March, they began a new offensive at Guadalajara, thirty miles north-east of Madrid. This was what the trio had been waiting for and their morale was high as they faced new action. The reality of the conditions they would be fighting in, however, was not what they had envisaged. With a huge armoury of tanks, machine guns, planes and trucks, Mussolini's men were about to commence a massive assault on Republican territory.

By the time Antonio, Francisco and Salvador arrived at the front, the Italians had already broken through and were in a position of dominance. With the strength of their artillery, it was looking bleak for the Republican forces. Then the weather changed. Sleet began to fall and from then on the elements played a role almost as significant as the guns.

Shivering in a sparse copse under leafless trees that afforded no protection, everyone began to stiffen with cold. Dampness extinguished their cigarettes.

'Jesus,' said Francisco, examining his palm. 'I can hardly see my own hand. How are we going to tell our own men from the Fascists?'

'It won't be easy,' said Antonio, pulling up his collar and folding his arms tightly to keep warm. 'Perhaps it will let up.'

He was wrong. During the day, the sleet turned to snow and then fog descended. As the Republicans began their counterattack on the ground, the Italians, in tropical gear, were suffering even more from the cold than they were. Arctic temperatures became the enemy of both sides and many died from hypothermia. To his satisfaction, Antonio learned that the Italians had been over-ambitious about the speed they could move at, and in the chaos of the fog and snow their units were losing communication with each other. Their fuel was beginning to run low, vehicles were getting stranded and aircraft were struggling to take off.

The Republicans were becoming more dominant by the hour.

'Luck seems to be on the right side for once,' Antonio signed to his friends.

'Perhaps it's because we're here,' quipped Salvador, with a smile. 'Franco's had it now.'

If the Italians had little communication with each other, for much of the time Antonio's militia band had an only marginally clearer idea of the whole picture. Action raged all around them but almost zero visibility allowed them to see little of it. In the cold chaos, Antonio could hear the agonising cries of dying men, some shot by their own side.

Antonio had kept as close as he could to Salvador when they advanced into battle. He had already proved his courage at Jarama, but nevertheless Antonio felt a great sense of responsibility towards his friend.

Salvador had already found certain advantages to being deaf in battle. He could hear neither the whine of bullets nor the screams of the wounded, but nor could he hear the warning cry of a friend. To the very moment of his death, Salvador experienced no fear. All he saw was a brief glimpse of the grimace that registered on his friend's face. The cry of anguish that then followed was not the victim's but Antonio's as he watched his oldest friend, the beloved El Mudo, fall to the ground.

The blood-soaked shirt was Antonio's. It turned red as he cradled his dying friend. And the ground about them changed to scarlet as it absorbed the rest.

On this battlefield there was no time for the self-indulgence of grief. Salvador had been killed at the end of the day's fighting so, unlike many whose bodies lay for hours where they had fallen,

Francisco and Antonio were soon able to bury him. The frost-hardened soil did not make it an easy task. As they hacked at the solid earth, they were warmer than they had been for days. It takes a sizeable space to bury a man's body, and the great mound of earth that lay to the side of the hollow seemed absurd next to Salvador's shrouded corpse.

The next day they were assigned to the task of gathering equipment left behind by the Italians. Others were given the task of guarding prisoners and Antonio was glad that they had been spared this duty. He would not have trusted Francisco to give them humane treatment. Nor himself for that matter.

Fury fuelled them from this moment. There was no need for any further reminder that they were fighting for the right cause. Though everyone knew it already, the abandoned weapons and other material they were gathering proved that Italy was breaching an agreement of non-intervention that was supposedly being observed in Europe. This policy, not to take sides in Spain's internal conflict, was already being flouted by several countries, and the documents the Republican militia seized were useful to the politicians as evidence of this. The equipment itself was a huge boost to the Republican cause, too. They needed every piece of artillery they could get.

When the battle at Guadalajara was over, they returned to Madrid. If their homes were close enough and they still had family to visit, men might go back to their villages on leave. For Antonio and Francisco, there was no question of visiting their home city. Granada was firmly in Nationalist hands and travelling there would have resulted in certain arrest.

They stayed behind in the capital to help strengthen the barricades. Though it was hard to defend the city from the air, the aim was to build a strong enough defence to turn the capital into a fortress. For many days Antonio and Francisco worked on building walls of rain-sodden sandbags, their bulbous shapes as smooth as huge rounded pebbles. Many of the city's buildings now looked like honeycomb, their windows blasted out with the force of explosives. They were a constant reminder of the need to protect Madrid, even if Franco had now moved the focus of his offensive elsewhere.

Antonio and Francisco missed Salvador sorely. Their friendship had depended on his moderating influence and his absence left a void at its heart. After caring for him for so many years, their sense of failure at not having protected him from the enemy bullet was immense. Combined now with a period of uncertainty over where the fighting would take them, disillusion began to set in. The left was becoming increasingly fragmented and Franco would take advantage of its lack of cohesion.

'The problem is that there is still no unity, no solid core,' said Antonio anxiously. 'So what hope have we got?'

'But if people have strong principles, Marxist or communist, why should they give them up?' asked Francisco. 'If they did, would they still fight?'

'There are plenty of people with passion around,' answered Antonio. 'Even if they aren't extreme in their politics. And lots of us are prepared to fight. But until the leaders agree on a few things . . .'

'. . . We won't get anywhere,' finished Francisco. 'It's beginning to look as though you're right.'

Though the militia brigades were now united into the Popular Army, there were factions growing within factions among those opposed to Franco. The struggle against Franco seemed to be intensifying but inside the ranks of communists, anarchists, Marxists and many other smaller groups, there was infighting, backbiting and disagreement. Antonio longed for the leaders of each group to see that the only way forward was unity, but each day seemed to bring new divisions and arguments.

Chapter Twenty-six

MERCEDES WAS NEARING the end of her bus journey to Murcia. She gazed out of the window and thought of her parents. Señor and Señora Duarte had not spoken for the entire duration of the six-hour journey, and she reflected that the hostility between them was something that would never have been possible between Concha and Pablo. Even when there might have been disagreements between them, the overriding atmosphere was always warm.

Ana had slept for most of the ride.

In Murcia, as in so many places, people were reduced to begging on the street but their hands were only held out to others in a similar state of need. As they descended the steps of the old rickety vehicle that had brought them, the girls caught sight of an elderly man playing a trumpet while his dog danced.

'Look, Mercedes!' Ana tugged Mercedes' sleeve with delight. For an instant the spectacle had some charm and brought the first moment of light relief to their day. 'It's sweet, but look how scrawny it is . . .'

The dog's eyes were as sad as his master's and the sight of this duet, initially so charming, now seemed pathetic. It was demeaning both for the animal and his owner. A couple of coins that were tossed into the hat in front of them probably more than made up for the degradation, but few people actually lingered to watch.

'I can't think of anything but my stomach,' complained Ana. 'It's the only part of my body that I can feel.' Her bottom and legs were numb from sitting most of the day. 'I wonder where we can eat.'

The shops here were not badly stocked, but the Duartes had

to make sure that their money lasted a while. Señor Duarte had withdrawn everything they had in the bank some weeks before and they had no way of telling how long this would have to last them. He was keeping the purse strings tight.

Though they seemed willing to share with Mercedes, her conscience often pricked her. Apart from her company and conversation (and she was aware that Ana depended on her completely for both) she had little to give in return. She had run out of money many days earlier.

Ana and Mercedes wandered off while Señor Duarte looked for somewhere to stay. As they walked along, the image of the dancing dog with its frilled collar remained with Mercedes. It suddenly seemed obvious what she must do, even though the idea of it filled her with trepidation. If she could find someone to play for her, she would dance and then, if someone paid, she could give something back to this family. In this way she would not be a burden.

They went first into one of the cafés in the square. Like the rest of the town at this hour, it had the air of abandonment. Many of the younger men had gone off to join the militia, so it was as though a whole layer of their society had vanished. The middle-aged man running the bar was jovial enough, though. He would still have plenty of customers that night and he was getting the place ready. Alcohol was still in reasonable supply and people were drinking plenty. Business was not bad. He smiled at the two girls as they walked in.

'Can I help you?' he asked.

'We would like to ask you something,' Ana said boldly. 'My friend wants to dance. Could she do that here?'

The barman stopped polishing the glasses. 'Dance? In this café?'

He reacted as though it was an extraordinary request even though these wooden floorboards had taken a hammering from some of the region's greatest dancers. On the wall behind the bar there was even a signed photograph of the celebrated *bailaora*, known as La Argentina.

In former times, dancing had been such a simple act: a natural response to music, enjoyed by everyone from child to adult.

Now even such an innocent activity as this had political undertones.

It had not surprised anyone that the sensual, free-spirited art of flamenco that had thrived in so many parts of Spain did not meet with the approval of Franco's strict and sanctimonious regime. What was more alarming was the sense of disapproval in some Republican areas where posters had begun to appear listing dance as nothing less than a crime. They had been put up by the anarchists, and instilled both guilt and fear. When Mercedes spotted one of these on a wall in Murcia she was chilled by it. How could dancing ever be outlawed?

'*GUERRA A LA INMORALIDAD*,' screamed the poster headline. Along with drinking in bars, visiting cinemas and going to the theatre, dancing was listed as an obstruction to the fight against fascism.

'*El baile es la antesala del prostitucíon*,' the poster continued – 'Dancing leads to prostitution.'

To connect dancers with prostitutes might have had some validity in the cities, but these innocent young women who stood in his bar seemed far too sweet and naïve. The café owner was a Republican and as appalled by the prospect of criminalising dance as Mercedes.

'And what would you want for it?' he asked, trying to put on a businesslike tone to conceal what was going through his mind.

'Payment of some kind,' said Mercedes, putting on her best act of confidence. It would be the first time she had ever specifically danced for money but life had changed and so had the rules.

'Payment . . . Well, I suppose if it attracted more people into the bar, then I could justify paying you. And if customers wanted to give you something, there'd be nothing wrong with that, I suppose. All right. Why not?'

'Thank you,' said Ana. 'And is there anyone around here who could play?'

'I should think so,' the proprietor said, rather amused now. Every village and hamlet around here had someone that could play well enough to accompany a dancer. He could have someone there at nine and they could practise a few things out in the courtyard before they performed.

'There's just one other thing,' he said. 'I think you should wear something more . . . um, suitable.'

Mercedes flushed, suddenly embarrassed by her appearance. She had been wearing the same skirt and blouse for several weeks now. There had been few opportunities to wash her clothes and she had grown used to the grime.

'But I don't have anything else,' she confessed. 'This is what I left home with. Just shoes, that's all I have.'

'María! María!' The man was already shouting up the stairs that led directly from the bar and a moment later a slight woman, his wife, appeared.

There were no introductions.

'She's going to dance tonight,' the man said pointing at Mercedes, 'but she needs a dress. Can you find something for her.'

The woman sized Mercedes up and turned her back.

'It won't take her long,' said the bar owner. 'Our daughter used to dance – she was a bit fatter than you, but something will fit.'

Moments later the wife returned. She had two dresses slung over her arm and Mercedes tried them on in the back room. It was strange to feel the weight of the ruffles again and the eloquent way in which they moved around her ankles. There was one, red with huge white polka dots, that fitted her better than the other. It gaped around the chest and the arms, but anything would be better for dancing in than her threadbare skirt.

The girls left, promising to return later that evening.

The guitarist was competent enough, a man of about fifty, who had played in many *juergas*, but was more contented as a soloist than an accompanist. They worked through a repertoire that pleased and distracted the audience for a few hours and from time to time there were a few mutters of '*Olé*'.

Mercedes was surprised by how mechanical it felt to dance just in order to earn money. It was so unlike the emboldening experience of the night in Almería. But coins were tossed into the cup that Ana took around, and the café owner took a handful of change from his till and handed it to her with a smile. His takings had been improved that night.

'It was so wooden,' Mercedes lamented to Ana as they went to sleep.

'Don't worry,' consoled Ana. 'The crowd didn't notice. They just loved the entertainment.You were better than the dog anyway!'

Mercedes laughed.'They would have been better off at a puppet show,' she said.

They repeated the formula in several towns as they journeyed slowly towards Bilbao. Mercedes learned what pleased the audience and what failed to stir them, and discovered a new way of dancing that was competent and functional. Only a few members of the audience noticed how little of herself she gave. She knew that she would never move anyone this way but it was a way of making a living and she was happy to share the money with Ana and her parents. Dance was saving her in a different way now.

During the hours when they were travelling by bus or in a farmer's truck, Ana's parents remained mostly silent, and Mercedes often found herself observing Señor Duarte and wondering how hard it was for him to pretend she was his daughter. By the middle of March they had crossed into Nationalist territory. Señor Duarte was even more tense than before. There were informers on every street corner.

'No more dancing now,' he said one night to the girls. 'We don't know how it will be received here.'

'But does it matter, Father?' exclaimed Ana. 'Everyone loves Mercedes' dancing, so what's the harm in it?'

'It means that people notice us. And we don't want that. We want to lie as low as possible.'

The nights of dancing had added so much colour to the journey. Mercedes had begun to enjoy the release of each performance and her enthusiasm for it had returned. She was sorry to give it up but understood why the Duartes felt the need to restrict it.

Señor Duarte trusted no one, and it was often difficult to tell where people's sympathies truly lay, even though they were now well inside Nationalist-held territory.

There were several episodes when they were challenged by the

Civil Guard during their journey. 'Where have you come from? Where are you going?' they barked, their polished patent hats perched on top of their heads. These men were experts at detecting the slightest sweat that might break out on an interviewee's brow, or the way that eyes did not meet their stern look. A shifty glance or a sense of discomfort immediately aroused suspicion and earned protracted questioning.

Señor Duarte could answer their interrogations honestly enough. He had taken his family out of Republican territory and his destination was his brother's house in San Sebastián. They correctly deduced that he supported Franco and some of them noticed the woman's expression, the scent of fear, her silence. It was puzzling but did not bother them. In their view, it did no harm for society if women lived in fear of their husbands. What they were looking for were subversive elements and this woman and her two daughters who feigned disinterest in everything around them seemed harmless enough.

After a month together, they finally reached the junction in the road where Ana and her parents would go towards her uncle's village and Mercedes would continue going north towards Bilbao, crossing once again into territory held by the Republicans. Mercedes and Ana tried not to contemplate the next stages of their journeys, which they would be making without each other.

Señor Duarte's farewell was perfunctory while the *señora*'s was warm.

Their daughter held on to Mercedes as though she might never let go. 'Promise me that we will meet again,' Ana urged.

'Of course we will. As soon as I am settled I shall write to you. I have your uncle's address.'

Mercedes was determined to control her emotions. Promises of a reunion relieved them from the unimaginable possibility that they might never see each other again. In those weeks they had not been separated for a moment, day or night. No sisters were ever closer.

Chapter Twenty-seven

IN GRANADA, CONCHA continued to run El Barril. It kept her occupied while the weeks passed with almost intolerable slowness. The routine provided her with the only structure she had in her life now that she had stopped going to see Pablo in prison. In the first months after his arrest, Concha had visited him as regularly as she could, but as the conflict continued, it had become increasingly hard. The roads were dangerous, she was always afraid of arrest, and the journey was taking its physical toll. Two weeks earlier, Pablo had made her promise not to come.

In the half-light, through a double layer of metal grilling, they had stood and looked at each other in shadowy outline. The distance between them precluded all conversation apart from a few remarks shouted above the din of other couples exchanging information. There could be no sharing of confidences or fears with the guards standing close by. Each visit Concha had observed how her husband seemed visibly diminished, but through the haze of metal she was unable to see how ill he really looked. It was just as well.

'Someone has to keep their strength, *querida mia*,' Pablo had said, almost inaudibly through the mesh.

'But it should be me who is locked up,' she replied.

'Don't say that,' scolded Pablo. 'I would rather be in here than have you in some awful place.'

Everyone knew what happened in the women's prisons, and Pablo would have spared his wife at any price. They were shaved and purged with castor oil, often raped and branded. No man would allow his wife to suffer these indignities if there was an option and Pablo never regretted having made this choice.

'Please don't come,' he begged. 'It's not doing you any good.'

'But what about the food parcels?'

'I'll survive,' he said.

Pablo did not like to tell her that very little usually remained in them by the time the light-fingered guards had checked their contents and handed them over. He knew that his wife would have made the most enormous sacrifices to get these packages of food and tobacco to him and it was better that she was not disillusioned.

Concha ceased her visits but was endlessly racked by guilt. It could so easily have been her that was tortured and half-starved in a cell, and she carried this thought around with her every minute of the day. She tried to distract herself from thinking too much about what had happened to Pablo, knowing that anger and despair would do nothing to alleviate her situation.

Another source of anxiety for Concha was the lack of news from her children. Salvador's mother, Josefina, was the only one with any news of the boys. She had returned to Granada a month after they had left for Madrid only to find a letter from the militia informing her of her son's death. There was no other information to be had, but she also received two funny and eloquent letters that he had written before his death, describing in detail what they had done. Salvador had a gift for writing and description. She shared these letters with Concha and María Pérez and the three women spent hours together poring over them.

Concha knew that Mercedes would never have reached Málaga and hoped that she was now somewhere with Javier but too afraid to return to Granada. She was sure that all this uncertainty would be over soon so that they could all be reunited, and she yearned for a letter from her daughter.

Mercedes realised how independent she had become. She missed her friend Ana, but solitude was something she had grown accustomed to. It seemed a lifetime ago that anyone had looked after her, and the memory of how her brothers had fussed over her was a distant one.

She was now in the Basque country, which was Republican-held territory, and she calculated that it might be only a few days before she reached Bilbao. Mercedes had her shoes and the dancing dress the café proprietor's wife had given her in a bag, as well as a few other spare items of clothing that she had been able to afford with the money she was earning. She had not planned to dance once she was on her own, but one night, in a small place that only just qualified as a town, the circumstances seemed right.

When the bus reached its final destination late that afternoon, Mercedes soon found somewhere to stay. Her room overlooked a side street leading down to the square and, by leaning as far as she safely could out of her window, she caught a glimpse of the activity going on in there. Something seemed to be happening, so she went down to get a closer look.

It was 19 March. Mercedes was oblivious to the significance of the day. In the small square people were congregating. Two small girls ran around, chasing each other, squealing, rattling their castanets and almost tripping over the flounces of their cheap flamenco skirts. This dusty square, with its gently trickling fountain in the middle, was the centre of their universe. It was the only place they had ever known and Mercedes envied them their oblivion to the events taking place not so far away. Their parents had worked hard to keep them from feeling the effects of the shortages that afflicted the urban areas, and the occasional quiet boom and flash in the night sky from a faraway bombardment seemed a world away to the children of this apparently self-contained community. One or two of them knew the terror of it – their fathers had disappeared in the night – but the community was still functioning as normal.

Mercedes saw girls sitting on a wall chatting, some plaiting each other's hair, others spinning around with their fringed shawls. A group of boys eyed them from a distance and occasionally were rewarded with a surreptitious sideways glance cast in their direction. There was a slightly older boy holding a guitar. He was strumming a few notes with the kind of nonchalance only ever achieved by the self-confidently handsome, and when he looked up he noticed Mercedes watching him. She smiled. He was probably not much younger than she, but she felt a hundred years older. She was fearless now and had no hesitation in approaching him.

'Will there be dancing later?' she asked.

The disdainful look he gave her provided the answer. With the small wooden stage erected close by, this village was clearly prepared for a fiesta. It would be the first that Mercedes had seen for many months and even if the religious connotations meant little, the ritual, music and dancing had their own vibrancy. She would not be able to resist it.

'It's the feast of San José!' he said. 'Didn't you know?'

Later on in the evening, she saw the young guitarist again, along with an older man, seated on chairs at the edge of the stage. It was around eight o'clock now, and it was the first evening of the year when there had been some warmth left in the air at this time. At which precise moment the stage of gently tuning up turned into the beginning of the *alegrías*, it was hard to tell, but applause rippled across the crowd.

The rhythms of the music seemed to come from opposing directions, working against each other and merging again like currents at the confluence of two rivers. Father and son made music that intertwined. They crossed over each other, blended and receded again, pulling back in their original direction. There were sublimely pleasing moments when the two instruments made the sound of one and then moved away from each other back to their own melody. Even the discords seemed harmonious, minor and major chords sometimes engaging in polite collision.

Mercedes sat close by, patting her knee as she caught the rhythm, and smiled. This music was something sublime. For a while the strife-ridden outside world ceased to exist.

When this heavenly performance finished, the father looked up to catch Mercedes' eye. It was her turn. When she had spoken to the older guitarist earlier in the evening, she had learned that he and his son were also outsiders. They had left Sevilla a few months earlier and were biding their time until they returned. It seemed too dangerous at present.

'They'll be pleased to see someone dancing true flamenco!' he had said smilingly, showing a huge gap between his front teeth.

On the small wooden stage, where both boys and girls and one or two older women had already performed, Mercedes' dance turned into something much more than the usual display of passion and strength that characterised flamenco. The primitive power of her gestures reached out to the audience. There were mutterings of '*Olé*' from both men and women, who were astonished by this magnificent dancer. The *guitarristas* may have made them forget, but Mercedes reminded them that their country was being torn apart. Her movements embodied the anguish they all felt when they thought of the guns and cannons that were being turned against them. After dancing for twenty minutes, she had no more to give. Her final stamp, planted with a mighty 'crack' on the wooden boards, was an unmistakable gesture of defiance. 'We will not submit' it seemed to say and the audience erupted into applause.

People were curious about her. Some of the people she talked to that night could not understand why she was making for Bilbao, which they imagined was full of danger.

'Why don't you stay here?' enquired the woman whose house she was staying in. 'You'd be much safer. You can keep that room for a while if you like.'

'You're so kind,' answered Mercedes, 'but I must keep going. My aunt and uncle have been expecting me for a long time.'

It was simpler to lie than to tell the truth. She had not lost faith in finding Javier even if, in her mind, the image of him was fading. She would wake up in the morning and search her imagination in vain for an image of his face, and sometimes there was nothing at all, hardly an outline. Sometimes she had to take the photograph of him out of her pocket to remind herself of his features, the liquid, oval eyes, the aquiline nose, the beautiful mouth. That perfect moment in Málaga when the picture was taken seemed so long ago, in another lifetime. The image of such a dazzling smile seemed something that would only exist in history books.

Being separated from everyone she knew, and everywhere that was familiar, had created a growing sense of emptiness. From the moment when the Duarte family had disappeared from view she had felt insubstantial and unconnected with the world. Was it for weeks or months that she had been away? She scarcely knew. There was nothing to measure time against. Its solid framework had turned to dust.

Perhaps the only thing she knew for certain now was that, having come this far, she had to push on to her destination. She ignored a new but persistent doubt that she would ever find the object of her quest.

She got up in the dark that morning to be sure of catching the bus that she had been told would take her to her destination. For a few hours the vehicle rattled towards Bilbao. Eventually it dropped her on the edge of the city and it was not long before Mercedes began to realise why her plan to go there had been met with such incredulous looks the previous night.

She was given a lift from the outskirts by a doctor, who left her in one of the city's main squares.

'I don't want to put you off,' he said politely, 'but you won't find things easy in Bilbao. Most people are trying to get out of here.'

'I know,' answered Mercedes, 'but here's where I need to be.'

The doctor could see that she would not be deterred and he did not ask questions. At least he had done what he could. Like this young woman, he would not be going to Bilbao unless he was compelled, and for him it was a hospital full of wounded that drew him.

'I honestly don't think it'll be long before this place falls, so take care of yourself.'

'I'll try,' she said, doing her best to raise a smile. 'Thanks for bringing me here.'

The place was in chaos. There were frequent air raids, and a sense of fear and desperation and panic. None of these were things that she had seen in Granada the previous summer, or even in Almería among the traumatised refugees from Málaga.

Bilbao seemed a world away from some of the small towns where she had stayed, which were physically if not mentally untouched by the conflict. This city was receiving a continual battering. Day and night it was bombarded from the sea and from the air. The port was blockaded and food shortages were at critical level. The diet was rice and cabbage, and unless you were prepared to eat donkey there was no meat. The sight of dead bodies was common. They lay in the streets, lined up like sandbags, and early each morning were ferried to the morgue in carts.

There was only one reason that she would have come to this hell and that was to follow up the final clue she had for finding Javier. On a small scrap of paper folded inside her purse was an address. It was where she might find him. Even the slimmest possibility filled her with a sense of excitement and she was now impatient to get there.

The first few people she asked were strangers to the city just as she was. A shopkeeper would be more likely to give her directions and she pushed open the first door she came to. It was a hardware shop but it displayed about as much stock as the average kitchen. Customers were non-existent, but the old shopkeeper still sat in a dark corner by his till, carrying on the pretence that business was as normal. When he heard the chime of the bell he peered over the top of his newspaper.

'Can I help you?'

Mercedes' eyes needed to get accustomed to the gloom but she followed the source of the voice, bumping into a table loaded with dusty pans as she did so.

'I need to find this street,' she said, unfolding the paper. 'Do you know where it is?'

The old man removed his glasses from his top pocket and carefully put them on. He ran a stubby finger across the address.

'Yes, I know it,' he said. 'It's in the north of the city.'

On the reverse side of the paper, using a blunt pencil, he drew a map. Then he opened the door of his shop and took Mercedes out onto the pavement, instructing her to follow the road they stood on as far as it went and then to take a series of turns before she met another main road that would lead her eventually to her destination.

'Ask again when you get closer,' he advised. 'It will probably take you half an hour.'

For the first time in weeks, Mercedes felt a surge of optimism and the smile she gave the old man was the first he had seen for a long time.

It seemed strange to him that this young woman was apparently so excited about visiting the most bomb-ravaged area of his city. He did not have the heart to warn her.

As Mercedes worked her way towards her destination, meticulously following directions, her smile gradually faded. In each street, the extent of destruction seemed greater than it had been in the previous one. At first, she noticed a few shattered windows, most of them boarded up, but within half an hour of setting out walking, the condition of the buildings was noticeably worsening. By the time she caught a glimpse of the sea and knew she must be close to her destination, many of these apartment blocks were just shells. At best, they comprised the four outside walls, with gaping cavities at the centre, like boxes without lids. At worst they had been razed to the ground. Miscellaneous possessions lay scattered among their ruins: broken furniture and a thousand personal effects left behind in the scramble to evacuate.

Mercedes had to ask a dozen times if she was going in the right direction. Eventually she found the street name, attached to the first block on the corner. Only this end-building was still standing, the rest of the street was badly damaged. It looked as though a bomb had landed right in the centre of the road and blasted everything within a fifty-metre radius. It was obvious even from where she stood that all the apartments must be empty. Their windows were black and dark, like eye sockets in a skull. She worked out in which block Javier's aunt and uncle had lived and it was clear that they could no longer be there.

The street was deserted, like every single one of these buildings, and she assumed that anyone who had been at home when the bomb landed must be either injured or dead. The last shreds of hope that she had clung to for all those weeks were gradually disappearing. She had wanted so much to find Javier in this city and the irony now was that she hoped he had never reached Bilbao at all. Mercedes felt herself trembling. She was ice-cold, numb with shock.

Her fist closed around the scrap of paper with Javier's address, moulding it into a hard ball. Later that day she would notice its loss without concern. She was now truly without direction.

The next few hours of Mercedes' stay in Bilbao were spent in a queue for bread. The length of this straggling line far exceeded any she had seen in Almería or any of the other towns in Republican territory. It snaked down one street and round the corner into another. Mothers with small children tried to deal with the whining of their offspring as best they could, but if they were hungry when they joined the queue, three hours of waiting only worsened the hunger pangs. Patience began to run out, as did the certainty that there would be anything for them at the end.

'There were nearly a hundred people in front of me yesterday,' moaned the woman in front of Mercedes, 'and then the shutters came down. Bang. Nothing.'

'So what did you do?' she enquired.

'What do you think we did?'

The woman's manner was aggressive and her speech coarse. Mercedes felt obliged to engage in conversation, though she could happily have stood in silence. She was totally preoccupied with thoughts of Javier and merely shrugged in reply.

'We waited, didn't we? There was no way we were going to lose our places, so we slept on the pavement.'

The woman was determined to continue, in spite of the fact that Mercedes did nothing to encourage her.

'And you know what happened then? When we woke up these other people had moved in front of us. Taken our places.'

As she spoke these last words she punched the clenched fist of one hand into the flattened palm of the other. Reliving the moment of finding herself usurped in the queue, she felt her anger returning.

'So you see, I have to get some of that bread. There's no choice.'

Mercedes had no doubt that this woman would stop at nothing to feed her family, and her threatening manner suggested that she would resort to violence to do so.

Mercedes was in luck herself that morning. Supplies did not run out before she reached the front of the queue, but she knew nevertheless that the woman resented her because of her admission that she had no dependants. Since strict rationing was not in force, those with children often felt they were inadequately supplied. This woman clearly felt that the world was against her and, worst of all, it was cheating her family. Mercedes could feel the woman's eyes boring into her as she picked up her loaf from the counter. Such sparks of hostility between people even on the same side was one of the worst aspects of this war.

Despite the feeling of growing desperation there, Mercedes decided not to leave Bilbao immediately. She had done enough travelling and felt there was nowhere else to go. In the days after she had seen the derelict wreck of Javier's uncle's home, she allowed herself to hope that he might be elsewhere in the city. It was pointless being in a rush to leave now, and each day she made new enquiries.

One of Mercedes' immediate needs was for a roof over her head, and she soon found herself in conversation with a mother she met in one of the food queues. María Sánchez was so beset with the grief of losing her husband that she was only too happy to accept the offer of help with her four children in return for accommodation. Mercedes shared a room with the two daughters and soon they were calling her '*Tía*', Aunt.

Chapter Twenty-eight

THE END OF the Battle of Guadalajara in March had marked a break in Franco's attempts to take the capital and the turning of his attention to the industrial north: the Basque area was still stubbornly resisting. Meanwhile, Antonio and Francisco were back in Madrid, which, though not the focus of Franco's campaign, still continued to need defence.

They had weeks of relative inactivity, during which they wrote letters, played cards and occasionally engaged in a skirmish. Francisco, as ever, was desperate to be at the centre of the action again, while Antonio tried to be more patient. He was always hungry, not just for bread but also for news of events in other parts of the country. He devoured the daily papers as soon as they appeared on the newsstands.

At the end of March, they heard of the bombing of the defenceless town of Durango. A church had been targeted during Mass and most of the congregation had been killed, along with some nuns and a priest. Worse still, German fighters had strafed fleeing civilians and about two hundred and fifty people were killed. There was another event, however, the destruction of the ancient Basque town of Guernica, that had greater implications for both Antonio and Mercedes, even though they were separated from each other by hundreds of kilometres, and both far from home.

The late April day when the news was broadcast that Guernica had been reduced to a blackened shell was one of the darkest moments in this conflict. Sitting in Madrid's spring sunshine, Antonio found his hands shaking so violently that he could hardly hold his newspaper. It was a place neither he nor Francisco had ever been to, but the description of its horrific destruction marked a turning point.

'Look at these pictures,' he said. There was a catch in his throat as he passed the paper across to Francisco. 'Look . . .'

The two men surveyed them with disbelief. Several photographs showed the twisted wreckage of buildings, and human and animal corpses strewn across the street; it had been market day. The most shocking image of all was the body of a lifeless child, a small girl. There was a label around her wrist, like a price tag on a doll. It recorded where she had been found, should her parents ever turn up to find her in the morgue. It was the most appalling image they had seen, either with their own eyes or reproduced in newsprint.

The town had been systematically attacked by wave upon wave of mostly German and some Italian bombers, which over several hours dropped thousands of bombs and machine-gunned civilians as they fled for their lives. An entire community had been wiped out, with whole families perishing in their flaming homes. There were reports of victims staggering through the smoke and dust to try to dig out their friends and relatives, only to be killed as another wave of bombers passed over. More than fifteen hundred people died in that single afternoon.

The massacre of innocents disgusted them more than the death of comrades whose lives had been lost in some kind of equal if unjust combat.

'If Franco thinks he'll win by destroying all these towns,' said Francisco, his hatred all the more intense with every Republican defeat, 'then he's wrong. Until he walks into Madrid, he has nothing . . .'

The obliteration of Guernica was keenly felt by Antonio and Francisco, and everyone else who supported the Republic, and reinforced the determination of the militia to stand against Franco.

If the massacre in Guernica strengthened resolve in Madrid, in Bilbao it instilled terror. The effect on the residents of this northern city, and on those who had gone there for refuge, was measured panic. If Franco could wipe out one town in this manner, then he would presumably not hesitate to do the same with another. The thoroughness of the bombing shocked even those who had been exposed to the relentless daily attacks in Bilbao, and in the streets and the queues no one talked of anything else.

'Did you hear what they did? They waited until it was four o'clock in the afternoon. Everyone was coming out of their houses to go to market, and they chose that moment to drop their bombs.'

'And they came again and again and again. For three hours . . . until everything was flattened and almost everyone was killed.'

'They say that there were fifty planes and that the bombs came down like rain.'

'There's nothing left of the place . . .'

'We have to try and get the children out,' said Mercedes, to Señora Sánchez.

'There isn't anywhere safe for them to go,' she responded. 'If there was, I would have sent them there a long time ago.'

Señora Sánchez had become so resigned to the state of affairs in Bilbao that her imagination could not look beyond the present. Survival, for her, was not a question of planning an escape route but of living day to day and praying for deliverance.

'I've heard there are some boats going, and that they'll be taking people to safety.'

'Where will they take them?'

'Mexico, Russia . . .'

There was a look of sheer horror on Señora Sánchez's face. She had seen a photograph of children arriving in Moscow by train. It looked so unfamiliar: banners in an alphabet she could not decipher, little communist children meeting them with flowers, the faces of the people waiting for them so different, so foreign . . .

'How can I even think of letting my children go to any of those places? How could you even suggest it?'

Outrage and fear made tears form in her eyes. She could not even contemplate the distances that they would have to travel and could not picture what was at the end of such a journey. Her instincts told her to keep her children close.

'It would only be for a while,' Mercedes assured her. 'It would keep them out of harm's way while all this is going on, and they wouldn't be starving.'

People were now lining up to apply for places on these boats for their children, and the queues were even longer than those for bread. The horrors of Guernica, the bombing of innocent people and the methodical destruction of an entire town had made everyone in Bilbao face the brutal truth: the same could happen to their own city.

Such complete annihilation could be perpetrated by land, sea or air, and there was no safe haven for them – not in Spain at least. Like so many other parents in Bilbao, in the past few days Señora Sánchez had faced the fact that the best thing for her offspring would be for them to leave for a safer place. After all, people were saying that it would only be for three months.

For more than eighteen hours, Mercedes waited with Señora Sánchez and her four children to be seen about their application for evacuation abroad. Everyone was nervous, occasionally glancing up at a bright, empty sky, and wondering how many minutes' grace they might have between the first glimpse of a bomber and the earthquake rumble of an explosion. They were queuing up for places on the boat that was to go to England, the *Habana*. Though Señora Sánchez had no image of it in her mind, she knew that Great Britain was much closer than some of the other places on offer and for that reason she would see her children again much sooner.

After all these hours of patience, it was finally María Sánchez's turn to make the case for her precious sons and daughters.

'Tell me the ages of your children, please,' demanded the official.

'They are three, four, nine and twelve,' she answered, indicating each one in turn.

The official scrutinised them.

'And what about you?' he asked, addressing Mercedes.

'Oh, I'm not one of her children,' she replied. 'I've just been helping look after them. My name isn't on the application.'

The man grunted, marking something on the form in front of him.

'Your two youngest are below the age requirement,' he said, addressing Señora Sánchez. 'We're only taking them between the ages of five and fifteen. Your older two might qualify but first I need you to answer a few questions.'

After that he barked out a list that demanded instant, truthful answers: father's occupation, his religion and the party he had belonged to. María answered them truthfully. There seemed no point in lying now. Her husband had been a trade union member and a member of the socialist party.

The official put down his pen and picked up a file that lay on his desk, opened it and ran his finger down a column, counting silently. For a few minutes, he continued to make notes. There had to be an allocation of children from parents of all the various political parties in proportion to the voting patterns in the most recent election. The children were signed up for one of three groups: the Republicans and Socialists, the Communists and Anarchists, and the Nationalists. It seemed that the boat was not quite full, and that there was space for some more from the Socialist party.

'And you,' said the official, looking at Mercedes, 'would you like to join the boat as well?'

Mercedes was completely taken aback. It had not occurred to her that she would be given a place. She was too old to qualify for one of the children's places and had resigned herself to staying in Bilbao. She had had no ambition to get herself onto one of the boats that took adults to faraway places. In her mind, such journeys would have been an admission to herself that she would never find Javier.

But she had to cling on to the ever-shrinking hope of finding him, given that the other option, to retrace her steps, was now ruled out.

'We need a certain number of young women to look after the younger ones and there is a space. If you have been taking care of children for a while, you might be just the sort of person we need,' said the official.

Mercedes could only dimly hear his voice, so filled was her mind with this new dilemma.

'Mercedes!' exclaimed María. 'You must go! What a chance!'

For the first time since she had known her, Mercedes saw the colourless expression of resignation melt away from the woman's face.

Mercedes felt as though a hand was being held out to her and it would be ungrateful of her not to take it. People were clamouring for spaces on these boats. She told herself she could be back in a few months' time, reunited with her family. But to abandon the search for Javier was unthinkable.

The two older children, Enrique and Paloma, whose fates had already been decided, stood looking at her, with pleading expressions. They badly wanted her to come with them to this unfamiliar destination and instinctively knew that their mother would be happier if she was on the boat with them. Mercedes looked at their wide, hopeful eyes. Perhaps for the first time she would do something really useful, and take responsibility for someone other than herself.

'Very well,' she heard herself say. 'I'll go.'

There were a few formalities. Firstly a medical. Mercedes took her two charges to the office of the *Asistencia Social* and they waited in line until the English doctor was ready to see them. There was not much conversation since neither spoke the other's language.

Paloma and Enrique were each given a clean bill of health. A hexagonal card with the words '*Expedición a Inglaterra*' and their own personal number was pinned to their clothing, and they were instructed to wear it at all times.

'What are you going to take?' Paloma asked Enrique excitedly, as though they were going on a pleasure trip.

'Don't know,' he said miserably. 'Chess set? Not sure. Don't know if there'll be anybody to play with.'

They were allowed only one small bag each, with a change of clothing and a limited number of possessions, the choice of which would have to be very carefully thought out. For Catholic children a small Bible had to be fitted in too.

'I'm going to take Rosa,' said Paloma decisively.

Rosa was her favourite doll and her imaginary friend. If Rosa came on this journey, Paloma knew everything would be fine.

Her older brother was not so confident. He was anxious about where they were going but his seniority in the family obliged him to put on a brave front.

Mercedes' only possessions already fitted into a small bag, so she had no decisions to make. The boat was leaving in two days' time, and in every one of those forty-eight hours there was always a chance that she might find Javier. In those two last days in Bilbao she scanned every crowd and every queue in case she caught a glimpse of his face.

At six o'clock on the evening of 20 May, thousands of people thronged at the railway station of Portugalete. Six hundred at a time, the children were taken on special trains to Santurce, Bilbao's main dock, where the *Habana* was waiting. Some of the parents had travelled no further than Pamplona in their entire lives, so seeing their children leaving for the unknown was almost unbearable. A few children clung to their mother's skirts but often the distress was more on the mother's side than on the child's. Some children were cheerful, happy and smiling and anticipating seeing their parents again soon; they viewed this as a boat trip with a picnic, a short holiday, an adventure, and for them the atmosphere seemed exciting and festive. President Azaña had even come to wave them off.

Enrique remained glum right until the moment of departure, unable even to raise a smile for his mother, who struggled to hold back her tears. Señora Sánchez was not going to accompany them on the train to the dock. Her farewell would be on the station platform.

By contrast with her brother, Paloma was full of excitement. She was sick of the sirens and the aching hunger. 'It's only going to be for a few weeks,' she kept saying to him. 'It's an adventure. It might be fun.'

As far as all the children were concerned, they were going on a journey to keep them safe. Many of them were smartly dressed: little girls wore ribbons in their hair, their best floral frocks and white ankle socks, and the boys looked neat in crisp shirts and knee-length shorts.

The *Habana* seemed huge to the children, looming darkly over their heads, ready to swallow them up like a whale. Some of the smallest of them could not even reach up to catch the rope that ran the length of the gangplank. Sailors took tiny hands in their own and, squeezing them tight, escorted the smallest children along the narrow strip of wood to stop them plunging into the canal of dark water between the dock and the ship.

The ship was big enough to take eight hundred passengers but they had made provision for nearly four thousand children and almost two hundred adults (twenty teachers, one hundred and twenty auxiliaries, of which Mercedes was one, fifteen Catholic priests and two doctors). They were all on board by nightfall and after a bigger meal than they had eaten in weeks, slept on board.

At dawn on 21 May, the moorings were loosened. There was the clanking of heavy chains and the passengers felt the first, slow movements of the ship as she began to slide away and move out of the port.

Mercedes felt her stomach lurch. She was immediately unsettled by the unfamiliar rocking (she had never before been on the water) but it was mostly her emotions that induced this nausea. She was leaving Spain. All around her small children were wailing, while the older ones stood by them, bravely holding their hands. Mercedes bit her lip, suppressing an almost overpowering need to howl with grief and loss. After days of anticipation and preparation, everything was happening too quickly. With every second the distance between herself and Javier increased.

A spray of salt water mingled with the tears that ran down her face. The knowledge that she was leaving behind every single person she loved and knew was unbearable, and the temptation to run to the bow of the boat and fling herself into the wash almost overwhelmed her. Only the fact that she had to keep a brave face for the children stopped her.

Enveloped by a feeling of utter bleakness, she watched first the figures at the dockside and then the buildings themselves diminish to pinpricks and disappear from sight. Her hopes of seeing Javier seemed to vanish with them.

'And that,' said Miguel, 'was the last Mercedes ever saw of Spain.'

'What?' Sonia could not conceal her shock. '*Ever?*'

'That's right. And she still couldn't write to her mother to explain where she was because it might be incriminating.'

'How awful,' Sonia said. 'So Concha probably didn't even know she had left the country.'

'No, she didn't,' affirmed Miguel. 'Not until a long time later.'

They had finished their lunch in a restaurant near the cathedral and were now strolling slowly back to El Barril. Sonia suddenly felt rather afraid. If Mercedes had left Spain once and for all, perhaps Miguel would have no more information on her. She was about to enquire further when Miguel picked up the story again.

'I want to tell you more about Antonio,' he said determinedly, increasing his stride as they crossed the square towards his café. 'We haven't yet reached the end of the Civil War.'

Chapter Twenty-nine

THROUGHOUT THE SPRING and early summer of 1937, Antonio and Francisco were kept in Madrid. The transition in the season that year was sudden, with the kind enveloping warmth of May suddenly swept rudely aside by the searing temperatures of summer. The air in the capital was almost unbreathable and a deep torpor lay heavily over them both.

They were both pleased when, at the beginning of July, there was renewed action and they were sent towards Brunete, twenty or so kilometres west of Madrid. The Republican army was aiming to drive a wedge into Nationalist-held territory. If they managed to break the line of communication linking the Fascists to their troops in the villages near Madrid and on the edge of the capital itself, it would end the encirclement of the city. Antonio and Francisco were among eighty thousand Republican troops being mobilised for this campaign, which was also drawing in tens of thousands of International Brigaders.

At first things seemed to go well for them. By nightfall on the first day they had penetrated Fascist territory, Brunete was captured and the village of Villanueva de la Cañada followed. Republican troops now moved on towards Villafranca del Castillo.

Some of the time, Antonio and Francisco were fighting the few small Fascist forces that still remained, or collecting munitions and food supplies that had been abandoned in their retreat. Once, their battalion found itself caught in a bombardment and for four hours shells rained down on them as they sought cover in the ditches on either side of a road. Nationalist planes were now coming over and bombing them too. Dust, heat, thirst and aching exhaustion affected them all but none of these things mattered when the scent of victory hung in the air. It had a sweetness that overpowered the pungent odours of blood, sweat and excrement.

Francisco was euphoric.

'This is it, I think,' he said to Antonio, with boyish enthusiasm. 'This is it.' He was shouting above the sound of artillery fire.

'Well, I hope you're right,' answered his friend, who was glad to see something other than anger and frustration pouring out of his companion.

During the first few days, the Republicans felt a strong sense of momentum with this battle. They knew that the Nationalists were aware of it too and would be preparing themselves for effective retaliation. This was crucial territory and, if the Republicans achieved their next aim and took the hills above Madrid, their objective would be won.

But having been initially unprepared for this offensive, the Nationalists now moved vast troop numbers into play, and began a vicious counterattack. The Republican air force had achieved supremacy in the air at the beginning of the battle but within a few days, the Nationalists were superior in the sky and now repeatedly bombed Republican lines.

Sitting in shallow trenches, the earth too hard and dry to allow them to be dug any deeper, Antonio and Francisco knew they were in trouble. After the initial wave of optimism they could see that victory was going to take longer to grasp than they had thought.

One after another the Nationalist aircraft came, bombing them with almost tedious regularity. The artillery fire was relentless and the noise of it crushed their morale. The heat began to intensify. Rifles' catches that had frozen up the previous winter were now too hot to touch, and the battlefield turned into a living hell.

There was little talking in the trenches, but occasionally some seemingly senseless instruction was barked out and passed between them.

'They want us over there,' said Antonio one day, indicating an area thinly planted with trees.

'What? Where there's no cover at all?' shouted Francisco above the noise of an exploding shell.

In the brief respite from aerial bombardment, a group including

Antonio and Francisco clambered out of the trench and ran for cover in the copse. There was the crackle of sniper fire but no one was hit. Most of Antonio's unit had been lucky so far during this conflict. Though they achieved little, they did not lose their lives.

Blackened corpses of Republican militiamen littered the landscape. Occasionally they were retrieved, but often they just lay there, cooking in the heat, food for the flies. It was a desolate area. The landscape of pale earth was becoming more bleached by the day. Stray wisps of grass caught in the firing line would ignite and go up in brief, bright flames, only adding to the heat for anyone standing close by.

The appalling inadequacy of the supply lines soon became a problem. It was not just ammunition the Republicans lacked, but food and water.

'We have a choice: drink this filthy muck that could give us typhoid, or die of thirst,' said Francisco, holding up a battered enamel mug. The water situation was critical. He took a swig of brandy from a flask, wishing more than anything that he could swap it for a mouthful of pure, clean water. 'You know there are dead animals lying upstream,' he added.

Some of the men around him tossed their water ration onto the earth and watched it disappear into the ground. They knew Francisco was right. They had watched one of their fellow soldiers die of typhoid in front of them the previous day.

Aerial bombardment increased and in this exposed landscape it was often mere good fortune to survive. When a bomb fell, dried earth flew into the sky. Huge stony clods landed on the soldiers' heads, sprayed into their faces and filled their ears. Neither skill with a rifle nor accuracy with the throwing of a grenade played a part. Bravery did not increase anyone's chances, but nor did cowardice.

'You know what we are,' said Francisco one night, when calm had descended, and there was a moment of peace to allow them to talk. 'Target practice for German planes.'

'You're probably right,' muttered Antonio. In spite of his habitually positive stance, he was feeling increasingly disheartened.

It appeared that the Republican leaders did not communicate with each other and were uncertain about basic directions and even less sure about their position. The initially firm and well-thought-out strategy was now obscured by dust and chaos.

In spite of huge numbers of Franco's infantry dying when their lines were bombarded, the Nationalists had continued to bomb Republican airfields and considerably weakened their capacity in the air. The Republicans found that they were now struggling to defend the territory that they had gained at the beginning of the campaign.

By the last week of July, with temperatures still unbearable, the air power of the Nationalists had become the dominant factor, and many Republicans tried to flee. Some were shot by their own side as they ran away. Eventually firing ceased. Ammunition was all but spent and burned-out tanks dotted the landscape.

It seemed that, because of bad communications, poor leadership, confusion about the geography of the area, a poor supply system and Nationalist air superiority, the initial Republican gains ultimately meant little. This victory did not have the sharp lines of certainty, and the mess of war allowed both sides to feel that they had won. Leaders on the left claimed Brunete a masterpiece of cunning, but with the gain of a mere fifty square kilometres at the expense of twenty thousand lives and at least as many wounded, it was a small advance won at a very high price.

'So this is winning,' said Francisco, stabbing his heel into the ground. 'And this is what it feels like to be the victors.'

His bitter words reflected the discontent among his fellow troops and the anger over the pointless losses of this battle.

Where was La Pasionaria now to rouse them and to remind them that they must not give up? With communist leaders telling them that this was a triumph, they knew they would be called on to continue the fight, but for now they were glad to return to Madrid for some rest. There would be other fronts to fight later.

For a few months, Antonio and Francisco were back in the capital, where everyday life would still carry on a masquerade of normality that could be suddenly shattered. Even when they were enjoying a cool drink in the sunshine, an air-raid siren would send them running for shelter, reminding them of the threat that continually lurked in this city. Antonio's thoughts often strayed towards Granada and he wondered what life was like in a city where the Fascists had taken over. There would be no bombs dropping, but he doubted whether his beloved mother would be sitting in the Plaza Nueva eating an ice cream.

A new offensive took place on the Aragón front that autumn, but Antonio and Francisco discovered that their unit would not be among those heading into battle.

'Why aren't we going?' moaned Francisco. 'We can't sit around here for the rest of our days.'

'Someone has to stay and defend Madrid,' said Antonio. 'And that campaign looks like complete chaos. Why do you want to be cannon fodder?'

Antonio believed in what they were doing but lives were being wasted now, and it angered him. He did not want to be an unnecessary sacrifice. The papers they read in Madrid carried the detail of internal divisions on the Republican side that were doing nothing to help them. The Marxist militia and the trade union groups were being deprived of weaponry by the communists, who were now determined to take charge, and disputes were breaking out in their own ranks that did nothing to further their cause.

Antonio could never understand why his friend desired action for its own sake, and, just as he expected, news of huge loss of life on the Aragón front began to filter through.

In December, though, they were on the move. Loaded into a lorry, at the beginning of the bitterest winter anyone could recall, Antonio and Francisco were taken towards the town of Teruel, east of Madrid. Teruel was held by the Nationalists, and the Republicans hoped that Franco would divert troops from Madrid if they made it their target. There were fears that Franco was planning a renewed assault on the capital and the Republican leaders knew that something had to be done in order to draw their forces away.

The attack on Teruel took the Nationalists by surprise and for a while the Republicans enjoyed the advantage, eventually capturing the garrison. Grounded by severe weather, German and Italian planes were initially unable to join the conflict, but even without them, the Nationalists had the advantage of more weaponry and more manpower. They proceeded to use both to the full, and subjected Teruel to a relentless battering.

The landscape itself was cruel: flat and barren, with bare, chiselled hillsides. Antonio and Francisco, who were positioned inside the town and almost dead with cold, watched as dozens of their comrades died on this wasteland. They were both so hardened to discomfort now that Antonio wondered if they would one day cease to feel pain. The only time that Francisco did not complain about the general state of this war and the inadequacies of Republican leadership, was when he was immersed in danger and death. Even a hacking cough did not appear to bother him, and often he seemed at his most contented when he was in the midst of machine-gun fire.

On Christmas Day they were camped out on the outside of town. Snow had been falling for days and the soldiers' clothes were sodden. There was no hope of drying anything out. With saturated boots more than double their usual weight, walking was more arduous than ever.

Francisco was wheezing badly now. He was holding a cigarette but it fell to the ground as he doubled up, his whole body racked by a fit of coughing.

'Look, why don't you sit down for a while, or even come in here?' suggested Antonio. He put his arm around his friend and guided him towards a makeshift tent that was being used for medical supplies.

'It's nothing,' protested Francisco. 'Just flu or something. I'm all right.' He brusquely shrugged off Antonio's guiding hand.

'Look, Francisco, you need some rest.'

'I don't,' came his voice in a rattling whisper, his throat full of phlegm.

Antonio looked Francisco in the eyes and saw they were full of tears. It could have been the cold that made them water in this way, but Antonio could see a man at breaking point. His friend's heaving chest and the exhaustion from fourteen sleepless nights in the damp had pushed even this tough individual beyond endurance. Pain or injury he might have borne with some fortitude but this was sickness and his body was failing him.

'I have to be strong,' he sobbed in desperation. To find his body placing such limitations on his desires and to encounter his own frailty were harder to endure than sickness itself. He felt so ashamed.

Antonio put his arm around Francisco and found himself supporting his entire weight. Through the thick cloth of his uniform he could feel his friend's raging fever. Francisco was steaming.

'I don't . . . I don't . . . I want to . . . Don't . . .' As he slid into a state of shivering delirium, his sentences became rambling. Within the hour he had slipped into unconsciousness and that night was taken away from the battlefield to a military hospital.

The enemy in this battle was as much the horizontal sleet that sliced into their faces as the strafing bullets. The dampness sat in their lungs. Many men died of the cold. They simply did not wake up in the morning. Some of them had used alcohol to anaesthetise themselves and it had relaxed them into such deep slumber that their hearts forgot to beat. At least in the snow their bodies would not immediately putrefy.

The campaign continued for another month into the New Year. With Francisco on sick leave back in Madrid, Antonio found he was able to detach himself from the horrors around him. Francisco was always angry with his own side as well as with the enemy, and his continual protests had merely exacerbated their disgruntlement.

Antonio survived these weeks on the Aragón front, but always felt less than heroic. Before the battle was over, along with many others, he fought in the streets of Teruel, engaged in hand-to-hand combat. Until now he had always fired abstractly into the distance but one day he saw his enemy face to face and knew the colour of his eyes.

In that fraction of a second, before the moment of no return, Antonio hesitated. There was a man in front of him, younger than himself, crinkly haired, sharp-boned; they could have been mistaken for cousins. The colour of his shirt was the only clue that told Antonio this man was on the Nationalist side. It was purely a matter of pigment in the dye that instructed him to end this man's life and if he refrained now, he would probably lose his own.

Antonio discovered that there was nothing more brutalising than to drive a bayonet into another human being, and in this killing he felt part of himself die too. He would never forget the way in which this boy's look of fear contorted into an expression of pain before petrifying into the gargoyle features of death. It took less than thirty seconds for Antonio to see his victim pass through these stages and to hear the thud of a body landing heavily on the ground in front of him. It was horrifying.

Returning to base that evening, a few men short, Antonio reflected on how arbitrary it all was. For the first time since he had become a fighting man he felt like a pawn on a chessboard. There were lives being sacrificed on the whim of someone most of them would never meet.

The tug of war over Teruel continued until February when the Nationalists took the town back from the Republicans. It had been another campaign with massive waste of life on both sides and little gain. Antonio tried not to see this as a turning point in the conflict, but the one chilling thing it seemed to prove was that Franco's resources were apparently limitless.

Chapter Thirty

ANTONIO, NOW FEELING very pessimistic, had a few months back in Madrid and was no longer so desperate to join the latest battle against Franco. A new offensive was launched by the Fascists in Aragón with the aim of slicing in half the broad north-south strip of Republican territory on the country's Mediterranean coast, and by the middle of April 1938, they had successfully made a passageway to the sea, splitting Republican territory into two. Catalonia in the north was now separated from the centre and south.

By mid-summer Francisco had recovered. The unit in which he and Antonio served was once more part of the defence of the city. Until Franco took the capital, the Republicans were determined to fight on.

Everyone now expected Nationalist troops to march north and take Barcelona, where the Republican government had moved in the previous October, but instead of this they turned south towards Valencia.

There were acute shortages of everything for soldiers and civilians alike in both sections of the Republic's divided territory: not just food and medical supplies, but morale too. There was also a growing sense of panic and fear at the isolation in the separate parts of their territory, and communication between the two areas could only be carried out with difficulty. In the cities, there were still people who had secretly supported the Nationalists since the beginning of the conflict, and these networks of informers added to the sinister threat of unease.

Antonio and Francisco were about to be involved in another battle. It was almost an act of desperation on the part of the Republicans. Their objective was to reunite the two parts of their territory.

'How do you rate our chances?' asked Francisco, as he laced up his boots before they went off to this new front on the River Ebro.

'Why bother to speculate?' answered Antonio. 'We've got fewer guns and fewer planes, so I'd prefer not to think about it.'

Though he felt pessimistic, they were strong in numbers if not in weapons. A huge Republican army of eighty thousand men had been deployed. Conscription had brought in thousands of boys aged only sixteen as well as middle-aged men. On the night of 24 July, thousands of them crossed the River Ebro from north to south and attacked Nationalist lines.

The surprise nature of the attack gave an initial advantage, but Franco coolly ordered reinforcements. He saw this as his opportunity to annihilate the Republican army.

One of his first actions was to open the dams in the upper reaches of the river in the Pyrenees. This raised the water enough to sweep away the bridges on which the Republican troops were relying in order to receive supplies, and thereafter Franco continued to bomb the bridges, destroying them as regularly as they could be repaired. As well as moving thousands of additional troops into the area, the Nationalists also brought in huge amounts of their air force and for the first few days, the complete absence of defending Republican aircraft allowed German and Italian planes to attack the Republican army.

Temperatures soared to extreme heights in the first month of this engagement, and created an inferno reminiscent of Brunete. The lack of cover was similar too, but the violence was even more intense. For weeks, the Republicans, increasingly dehydrated and starving, were relentlessly bombarded on the ground and from the air. German equipment, particularly aircraft, was limitless and Franco was happy to sacrifice as many of the hundreds of thousands of troops under arms as it took, in order to wipe the Republicans off the face of the earth.

On a blazing afternoon, attempting to find cover in a valley, with the Fascists occupying a ridge above them, Francisco successfully fired on several of the enemy who had proved to be sitting targets.

'We need to get a lot more of them than that,' shouted Antonio.

After weeks of anticipating a bullet at any moment, the expectation of it can diminish when it does not come. During those months on the Ebro, Francisco's sense of immortality grew. Antonio thought it was typically perverse of his friend that, as conditions and prospects had deteriorated, Francisco had become increasingly positive.

'We've come this far,' he said optimistically. 'I don't think anything will get us now.' Having survived near fatal illness he was not going to be beaten by anything else.

It had not been possible to dig trenches in the solid ground, and their unit had built up a small makeshift fortress from rocks and boulders. They were having an hour of rare respite from enemy shelling and there was welcome shade behind the wall that they had made for themselves. Five of them, leaning almost comfortably, sat smoking.

'Think of it this way, Antonio. Franco has to get the help of the Germans and Italians,' Francisco quipped. 'We're fighting them alone. A bit of Russian support maybe . . .'

'But look at what's happening to our numbers, Francisco . . . We're being systematically wiped out. Swatted like flies.'

'How do we know for sure?'

'Maybe you should believe some things you're told,' said Antonio wearily.

That afternoon, the Granadinos were separated when they were suddenly under attack. From a hill above, the enemy pounded them and for an hour or so shells poured down in a relentless storm. There was nowhere to take cover and the shriek of bullets drowned out any instructions they were given. In occasional moments of silence, cries of agony could be heard.

When Francisco's end came, he felt no pain. He was quite literally swept away by the force of the shell that landed beside him and there was little left to recognise. Antonio, who was fifty or so metres away at the time, identified what remained of the body. A gold ring worn distinctively on the middle finger of his right hand put any doubt aside. It sickened him to do so, but Antonio carefully removed the ring from the incongruously icy severed hand and replaced the hand by the rest of the body. As he drew a blanket over Francisco, he realised that his eyes were dry. Sometimes grief is too great for tears.

It was now late September and within a fortnight, the battle would be over for Antonio too.

It was getting dark and fighting would soon be over for the day.

'It's very quiet out there,' said a fellow militia. 'Maybe they're retreating.'

'Some chance,' replied Antonio, reloading his rifle.

He spotted some movement in a copse above them and raised his weapon. Before he had the chance to fire he felt a sudden, shocking pain in his side. He sank to the ground, slowly, unable to cry out or shout for help, and his comrade thought he had tripped over one of the rocks that littered the hard, treeless terrain they were crossing. Antonio felt light-headed, detached. Was he dead? Why was someone leaning over him, a kindly, muffled voice asking him something he could not understand . . . ?

When he came round, the excruciating agony of it all was more than Antonio could bear. He was delirious with the pain and bit down, hard, on his own arm to suppress the need to scream aloud. Supplies of chloroform were running out in the medical tent and the air was thick with screams. There was little more than brandy to anaesthetise these men, whether it was from shrapnel wounds or amputation that they so desperately needed relief. Days or perhaps weeks later, detached from both time and place, he watched himself being eased on to a stretcher and slotted into a compartment of a train specially adapted for the wounded.

A while later, emerging slowly from this dream state, he found himself in Barcelona which, though under attack, had still not fallen to Franco. The train had trundled north from the Ebro to take the wounded to safety, the red cross on its roof a plea for clemency to the Fascist pilots that prowled the skies.

The process of recovery for Antonio was like the transition from darkness to light. As the weeks went by, the pain gradually decreased, his breathing became deeper, his strength returned; it was like a slow but magnificent dawn. When his eyes remained open for more than a few minutes at a time, he realised that the figures that constantly moved around him were women, not angels.

'So you're real,' he said to the girl who held his wrist to take a pulse. For the first time he could feel the cool pressure of her fingers.

'Yes, I'm real,' she replied, smiling down at him. 'And so are you.'

She had watched the life in this skeletal figure ebb and flow in the past few weeks. It was the same for most of the patients here. It was a matter of luck and the efforts of the nurses, who did their very best as each day more of the dying had arrived to fill the wards to overflowing. The lack of medicine meant that many died unnecessarily. Their malnourished state gave them little resistance to any infection and there were men who had lived through the onslaught of the Ebro, only to be wiped out by gangrene or even typhoid in their hospital beds.

Antonio knew nothing of the previous few months' events but as he emerged once more into the world, he learned of them. The Battle of the Ebro was over. At the end of November, three months after they should have admitted the complete failure of the entire initiative and retreated, the Republican leadership had finally withdrawn what remained of their army. Massively outnumbered and outmanoeuvred at every stage, they had been too stubborn to admit defeat until thirty thousand of their own men lay dead and more than the same number again had been wounded.

It was rarely quiet in the ward. Apart from the sheer volume of patients, the sound of conflict infiltrated almost continually. It was quieter than the battlefield, but the bombardment was continual and the thundering cracks of anti-aircraft fire punctuated the occasional moment of peace. As Antonio became more conscious of these sounds, he pondered what was to come next. He was walking a little each day now and gaining strength by the hour, and it was nearly time to leave the confines of this ward, which had become his home. If only he could go to his real home to see his mother. He yearned for sight of her, and his father too, but of this there was no question. Nor was there any possibility of rejoining what remained of his militia. He did not have the strength yet.

When the Fascists' assault on Barcelona intensified, Antonio moved into a hostel. He was with many others just like himself who had been displaced and weakened but who hoped to take up arms again in the future. They were still soldiers.

The New Year crept in. 1939. There was no cause for celebration. A sense of the inevitable permeated the streets. The shops had been stripped of food, fuel had run out and the last desperate calls for resistance echoed around empty streets. Barcelona was fatally wounded and nothing could save her now. On 26 January Fascist troops marched in and occupied the almost deserted city.

Chapter Thirty-one

WHEN BARCELONA FELL, half a million began their journey into exile, all of them weak from months of undernourishment and many recovering from injury.

Antonio found himself in the company of another member of the militia, Victor Alves, a young Basque, who had been conscripted at the age of seventeen. Untrained in the use of a rifle, he had been wounded on his first day on the Ebro; his family had left a few weeks earlier for France and he hoped to be reunited with them.

There were two possible routes into France and the two men had to weigh them up. The first was over the Pyrenees. For Antonio and Victor, recovering from wounds, the craggy terrain would not be the only problem. Snow would impede them every step of the way. Antonio had heard that children were almost waist deep in it in some places, and the elderly and infirm regularly lost their sticks in the deep drifts. Many slipped and stumbled on the ice and the going was painfully slow.

In addition to this, though Antonio and Victor might have had very little to take with them, there were few who had resisted the urge to take some possessions and their discarded chattels buried in the snow created further invisible hazards for those behind them. In the springtime, when the mountain's white blanket had melted away, there would be a curious trail of bric-a-brac uncovered in the thaw. Useless but sentimental items – a precious perfume bottle or a religious icon – and useful but unsentimental things – a metal cooking pot or a small chair – were scattered along the way.

The alternative to the treacherous mountain route was the coast road, though the danger there was the border control. They agreed that they had no alternative but the latter, and set off, part of a huge column of people making their way north.

Everyone struggled with household items, blankets, bundles of clothes and anything else they had considered essential for their journey to another life. Women on their own with several children had the most difficulties. Antonio often tried to help. He had brought nothing with him but his rifle. He had no other possessions and was used to living in the same clothes for weeks on end. There were many others, though, who had packed as much into a bag as they could fit and now struggled.

'Let me help you,' he insisted to one woman, whose own child carried a baby while she fought tearfully with a bag whose handles had snapped under the strain. A third child tripped along next to them, snugly shrouded in several blankets. Between them, Antonio and Victor carried both baby and baggage and soon they were distracting the little boy with a marching song. Antonio thought back to his journey out of Granada with the band of militia when they had sung to boost morale. It had worked then and it worked now.

Even Antonio, who had seen the most appalling sights on the battlefield, was still occasionally shocked by what he saw on the way. Women gave birth while female relatives gathered round them to shield with their skirts the mystical moment of entry into the world.

'What a dangerous time to be born,' muttered Antonio as he heard the plaintive cry of a new-born.

It was a two-hundred-kilometre trek, and after a week of walking Antonio finally reached the border at Cerbère. He looked across towards the sea and for a moment felt a flicker of optimism pass through him. The Mediterranean caught the shafts of sunlight that penetrated the heavy February clouds, and in the patches of leaden grey water there were expanses of silvery light. There before them was France, another country. Perhaps they would find a fresh beginning there. In this great exodus, the trail of the ragged and forlorn had to believe in a new start, a promised land. There were some who were indifferent now to their own country, a place where they had neither family nor home nor hope.

Though most in this queue had given up their burdens, soldiers clung on to their rifles. There was nothing else they required. Working on the stiff catches through long nights of boredom, they were now confident that these battered Russian weapons would keep them safe.

'What's happening up ahead?' asked Victor.

'I don't know,' answered Antonio, craning to see over the forest of a thousand mostly behatted heads. 'Maybe they've closed it again.'

It had been rumoured that the French had shut the border for a while. They had been overwhelmed by the numbers. The crush of people was now building up behind, but everyone seemed subdued, no one was impatient. They had come this far and just a few metres in front of them was their destination.

After an hour or so they began to move forward. Antonio could see the border control and heard the unfamiliar sound of French voices. The harsh tone was not what they had expected.

'*Mettez-les ici!*'

The words may have meant nothing but the gesticulation and the pile of guns and possessions to one side of the road said everything. The French were making their message clear. Before they left Spain, the weary exiles were expected to leave their arms behind, and many were being forced to dump their possessions too. A few metres ahead of them, Antonio noticed an old man engaged in a furious altercation. That would be a mistake, he thought to himself, to start a fight with the border guard, especially when you were as frail as this old warrior. What ensued was worse.

They made him empty his pockets in front of them and when they noticed his fingers folded into a fist, one of the guards shoved him in the shoulder with his bayonet.

'*Qu'est-ce que vouz faites? Cochon!*'

Another grabbed the old man from behind while a third, realising that the fist contained something other than an intention to lash out, prised the bony fingers open one by one until the palm was exposed. What did they expect to find? A handful of gold, a secreted pistol?

On his outstretched hand lay nothing more than a small mound of dirt, a pathetic sample of Spain's soil that he had brought with him over the mountains.

'*Por favor*,' he pleaded.

Before he uttered even the last syllable of his entreaty, the guard had brushed the grit from his hand, sweeping it away in one stroke. The man looked down at the specks of earth, the remnants of his *patria* that traced the veins of his palm.

'*Hijo de puta!* You bastard!' he cried out, choked, his passion spilling over. 'Why did you . . . ?'

The guards laughed in his face and Antonio stepped forward to hold the man gently by the arm. Tears coursed down his face, but he was still full of fury and poised to lash out. This anger would only provoke these French to further insult and there was nothing to be gained from that now. The precious Spanish soil had already been trampled beneath their boots. The old man was given another shove in the back. If he did not make any further fuss he would soon be in France.

Now the guards turned their attention to Antonio. One of them grabbed the end of his rifle. It was a provocative gesture, and totally gratuitous, given that the pile of abandoned weapons by the side of the road was a clear indication that they had to enter France unarmed. It hardly needed reiteration. Antonio handed his over without a word.

'Why should we give them up?' Victor spat under his breath.

'Because we have no choice,' answered Antonio.

'But why are they making us?'

'Because they're afraid,' said Antonio.

'Of what?' exclaimed Victor incredulously, surveying the emaciated men, women and children around him, some bent double like large snails under the remaining burdens they carried, all of them bowed over with exhaustion.

'How can they be afraid of us?'

'They're worried that they might be letting in a bunch of armed communists who are going to overrun their country.'

'That's mad . . .'

To some extent it was, and yet they both knew that in among the shambolic ranks of broken militia, there were extremists and that in France rumours of *rojo* behaviour had been wildly exaggerated for the duration of this conflict. For those who had expected a welcome, there was to be only disappointment. The presence of the International Brigades in Spain had given them the idea that support and solidarity from other nations was something they could expect anywhere and everywhere, but it was a false one. The cool brutality of the border guards wiped out the remaining hope they might have had.

Once beyond the border post, the road wound down towards the sea. The coast was wild and rocky, the air sharper than in their own country. But the walk was downhill for a while, and that in itself was a relief. The movement of the crowd seemed mechanical now. They were chaperoned by French police who were impatient to move them along.

'I wonder where they're taking us.'

Antonio was thinking aloud. There had been rumours that the French, though unwilling to let them inside their country, had prepared somewhere for them to stay. Anywhere to rest their heads would be a relief after these days of shuffling along in freezing temperatures.

As they came down towards the sea, the dampness penetrated their bones. Victor did not respond to his companion and the two men walked along in silence. They were almost paralysed with cold, and perhaps this numbed their reaction to what they now faced.

Antonio had assumed that they would turn inland, away from the cruel space of the sea, but soon they were approaching the vast expanse of beach whose sands stretched further than the eye could see. They saw huge enclosures marked out with barbed wire and did not immediately realise that these areas were their destination. Surely these were pens for animals, not human beings? In some places the fencing stretched out into the sea itself.

'This can't be where they're going to keep us . . .' Victor allowed himself to say the unsayable. He looked across to the line of black guards who were now guiding people with the blunt ends of their rifles into the enclosures.

'We've swapped the Moors for these bastards? Holy Mary . . .'

Antonio could sense his friend's rage building. He shared his disgust that the French were using their Senegalese troops to keep the Spanish exiles in order. Many of them had experienced the brutality of Franco's Moorish soldiers, the cruellest of all the Fascist forces, and they thought they recognised the same heartless expression on these black faces.

They did not listen to the appeals of families who were keen to stay together, separating them according to the rules of arithmetic rather than kindness. All they cared about was the efficient subdivision of this massive horde of people, and to divide strictly according to numbers was the only way they knew to keep control. The French feared that their small border towns were going to be swamped by refugees and their concern was not without foundation. The town of St Cyprien, which had a population of little over one thousand, would soon find itself home to more than seventy-five thousand strangers, and the only place this town had for them was the huge expanse of unusable land right by the sea: the beach. It was the same for the other towns further along the Côte Vermeille at Argelès, Barcarès and Septfonds too. The only place they could find for the refugees was on the sand.

Living conditions were appalling. To begin with, the refugees were housed in improvised tents made out of wooden stakes and blankets, with no protection from the elements. In the first weeks the beaches were battered by rain and gales. Antonio would volunteer each night to keep watch for an hour, otherwise people would get buried alive in the sand, the loose particles whipped up by the wind to form mounds over the weak and vulnerable. On these desolate wastelands, sand filled eyes, nostrils, mouths and ears. People ate sand, breathed it and were blinded by it, and the relentless exposure drove some men mad.

There was very little food and one small spring to serve the first twenty thousand who arrived. There was no proper treatment for the sick. Thousands of severely wounded had been evacuated from the hospitals of Barcelona, and in many of them gangrene had taken hold. The guards separated out those who showed symptoms of dysentery; the repellent stench was usually enough to identify them and they were left to rot in a makeshift quarantine. Other diseases were rife too. Tuberculosis and pneumonia were both common and each day the dead were entombed deep in the sand.

Perhaps the thing Antonio hated most of all was the way in which they were led en masse to defecate. Certain areas by the sea had been designated for the purpose and he dreaded the moment when his turn came to strain into the sea under the contemptuous glare of the guards. To be taken to this foul area of the beach where the wind sent soiled scraps of paper and sand flying into the air was the most degrading thing of all.

Apart from certain daily routines such as this, there was a sense of utter timelessness on the beaches. The continual washing in and out of the waves and their relentless pounding rhythm echoed nature's disregard for the human tragedy being played out on these sands. The days turned into weeks. For most people time passed unmeasured, but Antonio kept tally by cutting notches on a stick. For him it alleviated the agonisingly slow passage of time. Some, fearing they might go mad with boredom, devised ways of combating it – games of cards, dominoes and wood carving all helped. A few even made sculptures out of the scraps of barbed wire they found sticking out of the sand. Occasionally in the evenings there would be poetry readings and from time to time, at the dead of night, the dark, piercing sound of *cante jondo* could be heard coming from one of the tents. This was the most primitive form of flamenco song and its pathos made Antonio's hairs stand on end.

Then one night, there was a dance performance. The guards looked on, bemused at first and then mesmerised by the spectacle. It was dusk. A small area of solid dance floor had been constructed from old crates that someone had found by a food tent, and a young woman had begun to dance. There was no music to accompany her, just the sound of rhythmic clapping which grew and swelled and became an orchestra of palms, some soft, some sharp, rising in a crescendo and fading away as the strikes of the woman's feet on the boards guided them.

The dancer was scrawny, once more buxom perhaps, but months of near starvation had melted away her curves. The sense of rhythm, which lived in the untouchable part of her, remained and the sinuous movements of her arms and fingers were accentuated by their painful thinness. Strands of her dark hair, matted with salty spray, adhered to her face like snakes and she made no attempt to brush them away.

She may not have had the heavy tiers of a flamenco skirt swirling about her ankles or the accompaniment of a guitar, but in her mind she had both of these and the audience felt and heard them too. Her best fine-fringed silk shawl had been incinerated, along with everything else she owned, when her house had been struck in an air raid. What she twirled around her now were the tattered remains of a headscarf, its fraying hem a distant echo of an expensively tasselled edge. The audience gathered quickly, and men, women and children witnessed an incongruous display of sensuality and passion in these heartless surroundings. The dance made them forget and for its duration drowned out the sound of the waves. She danced on and on in the cool of the night, hardly perspiring. When she seemed to have no more to offer the audience, she would begin again with the gentle tapping of a heel. The spectacle summoned memories in every spectator, of the *ferias* and other happy times that had comprised the now annihilated normality of their lives. In their own minds, every member of the audience was somewhere far away, over the mountains, in a home village or town, with friends or family.

Antonio thought of his sister. Where was Mercedes now? he wondered. There was no means of getting news. He still occasionally sent heavily coded letters to his aunt Rosita in case there was a possibility that she could pass them on to his mother. For all he knew Mercedes could be somewhere on these beaches. He wondered if she had found Javier and if she was still dancing. For a moment Mercedes seemed more real to him than the woman who danced before him. The furrowed brow that scored a deep trench in this woman's face reminded him of how his sister used to concentrate while she danced. There the similarity ended, though, unless the picture of Mercedes that he carried in his mind was out of date. Perhaps she had lost the childlike roundness of her features and now looked as birdlike as this gaunt creature in front of him. He wished he knew.

At the end of a *bulería*, the joyful dance that seemed so out of place here, a small child, his face plastered with dirt and snot, had pushed his way to the front of the crowd.

'*Mamá! Mamá!*' he snivelled, before the *bailaora* swept him up into her arms and disappeared again into one of the far huts, mindful once again of where she was.

After a few weeks went by, the French announced a rebuilding programme. There was a surge of new purpose. Able-bodied men such as Antonio and Victor were instructed to begin dismantling the shanty town of ragged tents and to start constructing wooden huts in ordered rows. Being occupied with manual work engaged both their minds and bodies, but it disturbed them too. Even the burning of the old rugs, some of which had been dragged across the mountains by those who sheltered beneath them, was a painful separation from the past. The new *barracas* might give them better protection, but there was a depressing sense of permanence about them.

'So this is home now, is it?' many of them mumbled.

They had perceived this camp as somewhere temporary, a place to pass through before finding somewhere else more amenable to live. Suddenly it seemed as though it might be for ever.

'We're not exiles, we're prisoners,' Victor said with determination. 'We have to get out.'

'I'm sure they'll work out what to do with us soon,' Antonio reassured him, even though he agreed with him entirely.

'But we can't go on pretending that this is some kind of safe haven!' continued Victor, his youthful fighting spirit refusing to wane. 'Shouldn't we be trying to get back to Spain? We're just sitting here playing cards, listening to people reading Machado's poetry, for God's sake!'

He was right. They were captives in this outdoor prison.

Currently the only way of getting out was to volunteer to become part of a working party. Having been loaded onto a cattle truck and driven to an unknown destination many miles away, men were then inspected for strength like livestock and hired out for heavy-duty manual tasks such as repairing roads and railways, and farming. It hardly constituted liberation. It was more like slavery.

Like many fighting men, Antonio calculated that staying in the camp might put them in a better position to escape back over the mountains and resume the struggle against Franco. He also felt committed to teaching a small group of children who gathered each day to watch him draw letters in the sand. At all costs he wanted to avoid the possibility of finding himself hundreds of kilometres away in an unknown French village, the unpaid labourer of a hostile nation which just about tolerated his presence but no more.

He had enough regrets over being out of Spain as it was. When he had fled Barcelona all those weeks earlier, he had followed the northward-fleeing crowd. Since then he had agonised. Perhaps he should have headed south to Madrid. What had seemed like a safety net had become a noose that had closed in tightly around him.

In many of the militia there was a residual belief that while Madrid still stood everything was not quite lost, and they should be there to protect what remained. For some, survival was about resignation. They began to watch the sunrise and to appreciate the brief but intense moment of beauty when they could look across the landscape and see their own country emerge through the mist. It seemed close enough to touch.

For a few months they retreated into the safety of routine and a pattern of rituals that helped them map out their days. They gave street names to the rows of *barracas*, and even hotel names to the huts themselves. In ways such as this they tried to make their lives worth living.

For some it was about small acts of rebellion and subversion, such as the carving of a sand bust of Franco that was coated in syrup to attract the flies. Victor had been one of the instigators of this and his confrontational attitude had already been noticed.

The guards knew he was one of the troublemakers and they were waiting for him to step out of line again. His slowness to join the queue for dinner one day was all it took. He was buried that night, right up to his neck, in the sand. It filled his eyes, ears and nostrils and almost choked him to death. Even the guard took pity and at three in the morning gracelessly held a cup of water to his lips.

Antonio nursed Victor when he staggered back to the hut that night. The boy was half demented, crazy with thirst and rage. His body could scarcely accommodate the hatred he felt for these guards and his anger was murderous.

'Try to think of something else,' said Antonio calmly, sitting at the end of his bed. 'Don't let them have the satisfaction of your anger. Keep it stored up for later.'

This was easy to say, but an act of such sadism had provoked deep hatred in this fiery youth.

In the spring, the skies became bluer and when the sun emerged fully, the grey sands turned gold and the sea reflected the bright sky. It was only then that they remembered how they used to love beaches. Once places of recreation where the children had splashed in the surf, this coastline now mocked all those happy memories.

But the spring brought with it the worst day of all. News reached them that the Nationalists had entered Madrid. What had been inevitable for many months had become a reality. On 1 April 1939, Franco announced his victory. He received a congratulatory telegram from the Pope.

In Granada there was great celebration and flag waving amongst Franco's supporters. Concha lowered the shutters, locked the door of the café and retired into the apartment above. It would have been insupportable to see the glee and triumphalism on the faces of all the right-wing citizens of Granada who were such an overwhelming majority of its population. She emerged two days later and looked out of her windows at a new and hostile country. It was one she had no wish to see.

Many refugees had to face the reality that returning to Spain would be dangerous. What had been a temporary escape would now be longer term. There was no amnesty for those who had fought against Franco and returning militia were in no doubt that they could be arrested the minute they set foot back in Spain. There were reports of mass executions of Franco's enemies. The safest option was emigration.

'Why don't you apply too?' suggested Victor, who had just discovered his family had already set sail for Mexico.

'I couldn't give up on my country,' said Antonio. 'My family might not even know I'm alive, but if they do they'll be expecting me to find my way back.'

'We probably wouldn't stand a chance of getting a place anyway,' said Victor. 'I've heard the evacuation committee has been swamped with applications.'

He was right, the *Servicio de Evacuación de Republicanos Españoles* received two hundred and fifty thousand requests and only a small number of these could be granted places on the boats that were leaving. Victor was lucky, though. He got a place to go to South America and was soon to embark. His father's name was recognised by the *Servicio* and was influential enough to get him passage.

The French were keen to repatriate all these refugees to whom they had reluctantly given a temporary home and Franco wanted them back too. Loud-hailers sent out messages urging people to cross back over the mountains into a new Spain.

It was a dilemma for them all. France was threatened by invasion from Germany and, for anyone who stayed, there would be new dangers.

'The one thing I won't be is a slave for Hitler,' declared Antonio.

He decided to take his chance and return to Spain. He would make his way back to Granada. Surely the new regime needed teachers as much as the old? Every day since he had been away he had thought of his parents and wondered what their lives were like. Even though he had continued to send them letters, he had received nothing for over a year but he hoped his father might have been released by now, given that he had committed no crime.

Without a photograph of them, their image in his mind had faded. He could recall his mother's black hair and upright bearing, his father's rotund stomach and crinkly grey hair, but if he saw them at this moment he feared he would fail to recognise them.

Many others felt the same urge to go home and, like Antonio, chose to ignore the terrifying reports of executions and arrests. He set out with some other militia who had also fought on the Ebro and who, like him, were eager to leave France, where they had encountered little other than hostility. Their route took them over the Pyrenees and, as they climbed, Antonio took a last look back at the hated beaches. He wondered if he would ever rid himself of the filthy taste of grit or the memories of the gratuitous cruelty he had seen on that sandy wasteland.

Chapter Thirty-two

As he came over the mountains and saw the plains stretching towards Figueres, Antonio had expected to feel a surge of pleasure at the sight of his own beloved *patria*. No such thing happened. It looked different to him now. Spain was his own country and yet it was a foreign place, somewhere now ruled by a Fascist. He hoped his love for it might be rekindled when he got back to his own city.

As he stood on this mountain ridge, watching an eagle soaring high into the sky, Antonio looked south. More than nine hundred kilometres southwest of where he stood was Granada. How he envied the bird his power of flight.

Once they were down the mountain, the men went their separate ways. It was safer that way. Antonio's plan was to take a route through the bigger towns. It would be more anonymous, and it would give him a greater chance of avoiding curious eyes. There were so many people returning to their homes that he was sure he could slip through incognito. He had not allowed for the watchfulness of either the Civil Guard themselves or for the informers who reported their slightest suspicions about any newcomers.

It was around eight in the evening when he approached the outskirts of Girona. Night was falling so this seemed a safe enough time, and he had chosen a quiet street to walk down. Seemingly from nowhere, two uniformed men stepped into his path and demanded his name.

He had no satisfactory papers and his appearance left no room for doubt about which side he had fought on in the recent conflict. It was nothing to do with a uniform or a tell-tale red star badge.

These Civil Guards could simply sniff out a supporter of the Republic and former member of their militia, and this was enough to warrant arrest.

He was incarcerated close to the town of Figueres where conditions were predictably primitive. As he entered prison, Antonio was tossed a rough blanket and cigarettes. He now understood why the latter were considered more important than food. The straw mattress he slept on was infested with lice and the only way of keeping them away from his face at night was to smoke.

A week later Antonio was summarily tried and sentenced to thirty years' imprisonment. For the first time in more than two years he addressed a letter directly to his mother in Granada. The Fascists were happy to guarantee the delivery of missives that further demoralised the families of such subversives as Antonio Ramírez.

The hardship in prison was no revelation to Antonio. He did sometimes wonder how resistant to physical suffering a man could become without losing his humanity. The sheer discomfort of camping out on stony ground in the freezing temperatures of Teruel, the blazing heat of Brunete, the searing agony of his injury, which had made death look like a welcome escape, and the abject squalor of the early days in the sand camps of France: all of these had left their mark. The scar tissue that formed around these wounds, both physical and mental, was tough, and pain had become an ever-diminishing sensation. Antonio was anaesthetised.

The prisoners' food was minimal and monotonous. Breakfast was a bowl of gruel, lunch was beans, and supper the same, sometimes with a fish head or tail. Occasionally there were tinned sardines.

The months passed. Antonio and most of his fellow prisoners were stubbornly resistant to the cruelty of the guards. A few of them literally pined away, as men do when there is nothing to live for, and no hope of this changing.

They kept themselves occupied with talk of escape, but the only attempt that had been made had been so cruelly punished, and in view of them all, that they did not have the stomach to repeat it. The screams of those involved seemed still to echo round the yard.

For a while the most subversive activity they could engage in was a refusal to sing the new regime's patriotic songs, or to talk during the sermons which they were obliged to listen to in the courtyard. Even for that they could be punished. No excuse was too flimsy for the guards to beat them with loaded riding crops.

The most terrifying moment of each day was the reading of the *saca*, when the names were called out of the men who were to be executed the following day. One morning at daybreak, a longer list was called out. This was not the usual dozen or so; this time the names went on and on. There were hundreds. As he stood there in the aching early morning chill, Antonio felt his blood freeze.

Just as the human brain will pick out the one face it recognises in a crowd, Antonio heard his own name in the almost indistinguishable hum of all the others. Among the monotonous list of Juans and Josés, the words 'Antonio Ramírez' jumped out at him.

There was silence as the list finished.

'All those named – in line!' the order was barked.

It took several minutes for the men who had been named to move out and form a queue. Without any further explanation they were herded out of the prison gate. The air reeked of the sour odour of men sweating beneath filthy shirts. It was the smell of fear. Are they really going to kill all of us? Antonio wondered, his legs shaking with such terror that he struggled to control them. There was no time for goodbyes. Instead furtive glances were exchanged between a few of them who had formed a bond during their long period of incarceration together. Those staying looked at those leaving with pity, but all were united in the common determination that the Fascists should not see fear on their faces. It would give them too much satisfaction.

Antonio found himself being marched out of the prison and towards the town. It was not uncommon for prisoners to be moved from one gaol to another, but in these numbers he knew it was unusual. As they approached the railway station, the great crowd of them was ordered to a halt. He realised that they were going on a journey.

For many hours, the train rattled along.

'It's like being in a crate,' Antonio heard one man murmur.

'Nice of them to leave the lid off,' responded another.

'Unlike them really,' said another sarcastically.

Even though they were being taken to a new place, the way they were treated was just the same. More than one hundred of them stood in each cage trundling south. Some clung on to the bars, peering through the slats at the changing landscape, which was gradually flattening out as the day went on. Others, stuck in the middle, could see only the sky.

For a few hours they were lashed by rain but eventually the clouds passed away and Antonio judged from the sun that they were heading roughly south-west. After many hours, the train rattled to a halt and the gates of their cages opened. They tumbled onto the hard, dusty, ground, many of them relieved to rest their exhausted legs.

A group of armed soldiers stood guard over them, weapons cocked, looking for an opportunity to use them. Even if they had wanted to escape, the landscape provided no opportunities. In one direction there were a few outcrops of rock, in the other, nothing at all. There was nowhere to run. A bullet in the back would have been the reward for anyone trying it.

With unconcealed contempt, a few lumps of bread were thrown into the middle of them and the prisoners swarmed around it like a shoal of fish, grabbing, snatching, desperate, all remaining dignity gone.

Antonio watched a dozen men reaching towards the same piece of bread and was sickened by the sight of his own wasted, filthy-nailed hand trying to grab a crust from another man's fingers. They had been reduced to animals, turning on each other in this way.

Then they were loaded back into the train and, for many hours more, they trundled on until the train juddered to a halt. There was a momentary stirring among them.

'Where are we?' shouted someone in the centre.

'What can you see?' called out another. 'What's happening?'

It was not the end of the journey. Antonio fell out of his cattle cage once again and saw a dozen trucks waiting for them. They were ordered to climb aboard.

The men were more tightly crammed in than ever, moving in one united motion as the trucks swayed this way and that over bumpy ground. After an hour or so, there was a crunching of gears and the sudden application of brakes. They were all catapulted forwards in one jolt. Doors opened and then slammed shut, bolts were drawn across, there was the sound of shouting, orders, an altercation somewhere. Once again bowels stirred with fear. They seemed to be in the middle of nowhere, though in the far distance Antonio thought he could see the outskirts of a city.

There was a general murmuring among the men.

'Seems odd to have brought us all this way just to kill us,' pondered the man against whom Antonio had been jammed face-to-face for the past four hours. The foul stench of his breath had almost asphyxiated him. He knew that his own could not be sweet, but this old soldier's toothless mouth and rotting gums had literally made him retch.

Antonio was about to respond when someone cut across him: 'I think they would have done away with us by now if that's what they planned.'

'Don't be so sure,' said another pessimistically.

The debate continued until they were interrupted by an order barked out by one of the soldiers. They were instructed to walk along a track that led from the road and soon they saw their destination. A row of huts now came into view. For many the relief was too much. They wept, certain now that they were going to live another day.

They were marshalled into rows on a piece of ground in front of the huts and addressed by an army captain, his mean mouth and sharp cheekbones all that they could see of his face. It angered Antonio that his eyes were obscured by the peak of his cap. The crowd was silent, expectant, for the first time optimistic, as they watched his thin lips move.

'Owing to the generosity of our great General Franco, you

have undeserved good fortune,' he said. 'On this day, you have been given another chance.'

There was a murmur of relief among the crowd. The tone of this speech disgusted Antonio, but the content of it excited him. The captain continued. He had a message to deliver and he was not going to be deterred.

'You will no doubt have heard that a law has been passed to allow the Redemption of Penalties through labour. For every two days worked, your sentence will be reduced by one day. For scum like some of you, this is more than you deserve, but the Generalissimo has decreed it.'

He sounded like someone swallowing a bitter pill. Clearly he did not approve of this leniency, and would have preferred to see these men suffer the maximum punishment, but Franco's word was supreme and he was obliged to carry out orders.

He continued: 'More importantly, you have been selected for the most glorious of all tasks.'

Antonio began to feel apprehensive. He had heard of prisoners being used as forced labour on building projects, such as the reconstruction of towns like Belchite and Brunete, which had been devastated during the conflict. Perhaps this was his fate.

'This is what El Caudillo said when he announced his plans for this project. I quote . . .'

The captain drew himself up to his full height and adopted an ever more pompous tone. The irony was that his voice was considerably deeper and more masculine than that of Franco, with whose reedy, strangulated tones they were all familiar. '"I want this place to have the grandness of the shrines of old . . . to be a restful place of meditation where future generations can pay homage to those who made Spain a better place . . ."' His singsong delivery of Franco's words was almost worshipful, but his voice soon reverted to a harsher tone.

'The place that you have been chosen to construct is The Valley of the Fallen. This monument will commemorate the thousands who died in this fight to save our country from the filthy Reds – the communists, the anarchists, the trade unionists . . .'

The captain's voice had gradually risen. He had worked himself up into such a fury of revulsion that his cap shook and the veins stood out on his neck. His hysteria was barely repressed. Those closest to him felt the spray of furious spittle that flew from his lips on the utterance of those last words. He was almost screaming now, though there was little need, given the total silence of his audience.

Everyone had heard rumours of this plan. What it confirmed to them was that they were in Cualgamuros, not far from Madrid and close to El Escorial, the burial place of the kings. Franco had one clear purpose in this project. Although this place would commemorate the soldiers who had died for his cause, it would principally be a mausoleum for himself. The fanatical, power-intoxicated captain had finished speaking now. He left it to his inferiors to marshal the prisoners into the huts.

'So now we know why they have brought us all this way . . .' said the old man who had been by Antonio's side all journey. 'I suppose it makes a change from being locked up.'

To some people this old man's resilience had been a tonic, while for others his relentlessly cheerful voice had begun to grate. After all these months, years even, of hardship, it seemed extraordinary that anyone's voice could be so completely free of bitterness.

'Yes, it looks as though we'll see a bit more of the sky,' Antonio responded, trying to sound positive.

The hut that was to be their new home was very different from the last prison they had been in, where for days on end they were shut away in a windowless cell, the only light source an electric bulb, which had illuminated them twenty-four hours a day. It was squalid here, but at least there were windows all down one side and two rows of around twenty beds with a decent space between each one.

'This doesn't look so bad, does it?'

Above the cacophony of a thousand other men gathering on the scrubby ground outside the huts, all waiting to receive their next instructions, the old man's cheerful voice challenged Antonio. He wondered why some people were so richly endowed with a cheerful disposition when all around them the world seemed to be disintegrating.

Laid out on the straw mattresses were brown uniforms and orders were given to put these on.

'You could get two of me in here,' said the septuagenarian, rolling up the sleeves and trouser legs. He looked absurd. 'Lucky there isn't a mirror.'

The old man was right. He did look ridiculous, like a child in his father's clothes. For the first time in perhaps months, Antonio smiled. It was an unfamiliar feeling. His laughter reflex had atrophied many months before.

'How do you manage to be so cheerful all the time,' he asked, struggling to do up his buttons. His fingers were stiff with cold.

'What,' said the old man 'is the point of being any other way?' Arthritic hands were not making it easy for the older man to fasten his jacket either. 'What can we do? Nothing. We're powerless.'

Antonio thought for a moment before responding. 'Resist? Escape?' he suggested.

'You know as well as I do what happens to anyone who does. They are destroyed. *Completely.*' He spoke the last word emphatically. His tone had changed altogether. 'For me it's about protecting the human spirit,' he continued. 'For others it will be about fighting until their dying breath. My resistance to these Fascists is to go along with them, to smile, to show them that they can't crush my soul, the very core of me.'

Antonio was surprised by the answer. He had not expected it. Like everyone who had been in that cattle cage, this man had looked like a destitute labourer. Materially, he had even less. He did not even own the clothes he stood up in. His accent and the way he phrased his words suggested something else, though.

'Has it worked,' enquired Antonio, 'this approach of yours?'

'So far, yes,' the old man said. 'I have no religious faith. You could say that I am an atheist and have been for many years. But a belief in protecting your own essence, believe me, gives you such strength to survive.'

Antonio looked over the man's shoulder at the sea of two hundred other men now reduced to a shapeless blur of humanity by the dung-coloured uniform. It was an amorphous mass, where individuality had finally been annihilated, but in its midst were doctors, lawyers, university professors and writers. Perhaps this man was one of these.

'So what did you do before . . . this?' asked Antonio.

'I am a professor of Philosophy at the University of Madrid,' he answered unhesitatingly, with a deliberate use of the present tense.

He continued now, happy to have Antonio's attention, 'Look at how many people have been driven to suicide. Probably thousands of them. That's the greatest victory for the Fascists, isn't it? One more prisoner condemned to the fires of hell – and one less mouth to feed.'

The man was so pragmatic, so realistic about their situation that Antonio was almost convinced. He had seen several suicides himself. The worst of these had been only a few days ago in Figueres before they were moved here. A man jumped up to grab the light bulb that hung by a wire from the ceiling and in a swift movement, before he could be stopped by either friend or Fascist, he had struck the bulb on the edge of a chair and plunged the jagged shard into his vein.

Guards had eventually arrived to drag away his body. They had seen it all before. It was too much bother to shorten the flex.

'Well,' said the university professor, jamming on the round hat that had sat on top of the uniform. 'I think we're meant to get started.'

His cheerful enthusiasm was, for a moment, infectious.

'You see this?' he said, pointing up at his hat. The 'T' with which it was emblazoned stood for *Trabajos Forzados* – Forced Labour. It marked him out as a slave.

'Yes,' responded Antonio. 'I see it.'

'They can enslave my body,' the professor said, 'but my mind is my own.'

For every individual there had to be a reason to survive and this man seemed to have found his.

By now the rest of the room had cleared. In spite of their empty stomachs, they were expected to work today. There were two hours until darkness and their enslavers were not going to allow them to be wasted.

Marching in single file through an area of dense forest, the new arrivals eventually reached the edge of the site. As they came into the immense clearing, the very scale of what they saw shocked them.

Thousands upon thousands of men worked in gangs. The motion was continuous, streamlined, ordered, and it was clear that they were engaged upon some relentless, gargantuan, never-ending task. As they moved in one direction they bore a load, and then returned empty-handed for another, like ants moving to and from their anthill.

Antonio's group was taken towards the vast exposed face of the hillside. At first glance it looked as though they had been assigned to literally move a mountain. The noise was deafening. Occasionally from within they heard a rumble. It was obvious what they were expected to do. A gigantic hole was being made in this towering rock. Any orders would have been inaudible in the cacophony that greeted them. There were piles of stone in front of them. Some men worked at breaking them down with pick-axes. Shards flew everywhere. The rest picked up the fragments in their bare hands and began to carry them away. Frequently, there was the shout of an order, a castigation, a raised stick. It was a vision of hell.

Antonio's hope that working in the open was going to give them a glimpse of the sky was soon dashed. The air was opaque with dust. Even the illusion of freedom that had been dangled in front of them that afternoon had evaporated. With one hand the Fascists had given, and with the other they had taken away.

Chapter Thirty-three

WHILE ANTONIO WAS building Franco's tomb, Concha Ramírez was still running El Barril, determined to keep the family business going. Like anyone who had been on the wrong side during the conflict, she suffered from the stigma of having a husband and son in prison. Concha was continually harassed by the Civil Guard and her premises often subject to search and scrutiny. These were purely tactics of intimidation but there was nothing she could do to prevent them. Many of those in her position found that their children could get nothing but menial work, and some, whose children tried to return home after fighting for the Republic, were immediately incarcerated. One of Paquita's brothers had been executed that month.

One Thursday afternoon, a few months after Franco declared his victory, Concha was in the kitchen and heard the sound of the café door being pushed open. It had been a busy lunchtime.

A late customer, she thought with irritation. Hope they aren't expecting anything to eat.

She bustled into the bar to tell the latecomer that she had finished serving food, and stopped in her tracks. She tried to speak, to say a name, but nothing came out. Her mouth was dry.

In spite of his hollow eyes and the unfamiliar stoop of his body, she would have immediately recognised this man in a crowd of a hundred thousand others.

'Pablo,' she whispered inaudibly.

He stood there, one hand gripping the back of a chair. He could no more speak than move. Every last shred of energy and willpower had been spent on reaching home. Concha crossed the room and held him in her arms.

'Pablo,' she whispered. 'It's you. I can't believe it's you.'

And that was the truth. Suddenly Concha Ramírez did not trust her own senses. Was this pale shadow her husband? For a moment, she wondered whether this frail, insubstantial being that she held in her arms was even real, or just a figment of her imagination. Perhaps Pablo's death sentence had finally been carried out and this was just a spectre that appeared to her. Nothing was beyond the realms of possibility in her imagination.

His silence did not reassure her.

'Tell me if it's you,' she persisted.

By now, the old man had taken a seat. He was so weak with hunger and exhaustion that his legs could no longer hold him.

Looking into hers with his own watery eyes, he spoke for the first time. 'Yes, Concha, it's me. It's Pablo.'

Now, holding both his hands in hers, she wept. Her head shook from side to side with pure disbelief.

For an hour they sat like this. No one came into the café. It was the dead hour.

Eventually they rose and Concha led her husband up to their bedroom. Pablo lowered himself unsteadily onto the edge of the bed, the left side. It had been empty for so long. His wife helped him undress, removing the ragged clothes that hung off him, and tried to conceal her shock at his emaciated body. His was an unrecognisable torso. She turned back the covers and helped him climb in. The unfamiliar coolness of the sheets chilled him to the bone. Concha followed him into the bed and held him in her arms, transforming the warmth of her body to him until he almost burned. For hours they slept, two slim bodies entwined like stems of a vine. People came and went from the café downstairs, puzzled and mildly concerned by Concha's absence.

It was not until he woke that Pablo asked after Antonio and Mercedes. Concha had dreaded this moment and had to tell him what she knew: that Antonio was now in prison and that she had heard nothing from Mercedes.

That same day they puzzled over the reasons for Pablo's release. It had come out of the blue. One night, following the daily reading of the death list, he had been taken to one side and told that he would be leaving the prison as well. What awful trick was this? he had wondered, his heart beating with sheer terror. He had not been able to ask questions, fearing that any response on his part might jeopardise this reprieve.

With the necessary papers to validate his release, he had worked his way back to Granada, by truck and by foot. It had taken him three days. And all the while he had puzzled, why him?

'Elvira,' said Concha. 'I think it was something to do with her.'

'Elvira?'

'Elvira Delgado. You must remember. The wife of the matador?' Concha hesitated.

Pablo seemed to have forgotten so much, so many details from his life before imprisonment. In the past twenty-four hours she had sometimes noticed a blankness in her husband's expression and it alarmed her. It was as though some part of him had been left behind in his prison cell and had not returned to Granada.

She continued, undeterred. 'She was Ignacio's mistress. I believe she used her influence and got her husband to intervene for you. I can't think of any other explanation.'

Pablo looked thoughtful. He had no recollection of the woman Concha referred to.

'Well,' he reflected finally, 'I suppose it doesn't matter why or how it happened.'

Concha was right. It was Elvira Delgado's doing, but there was no question of finding her to say thank you. Any acknowledgement of her involvement would compromise both parties. Many months later Concha passed Elvira in the Plaza de la Trinidad. Concha recognised her from her regular appearances in *El Ideal*, but even if the familiar face had not caught her eye, the vision of glamour in a red, tailored coat extravagantly trimmed with fur would have made her look twice. Others turned to stare. The woman's full lips were painted to match her crimson outfit and the black hair, piled high on her head, was as glossy as the dark mink that edged her collar.

Concha's pulse quickened as Elvira approached. It was strange for a mother to come face to face with the sensuality that had so seduced her own son, and to acknowledge its power. No wonder he had taken risks to be with her, thought Concha, as she drew close enough to notice the smooth perfection of her skin and to catch a whiff of her scent. It was tempting to speak to her but the younger woman's purposeful stride was so very sure. Elvira's eyes were fixed determinedly ahead of her. She did not look like someone who would take kindly to being accosted in the street. A huge lump had risen in Concha's throat as she thought of her beautiful son.

Pablo told Concha little about his time in prison. He did not need to. She could imagine it all through the lines on his face and the scars on his back. His entire story, with all its physical and mental torture, was etched on him.

It was not only because he wanted to put those four awful years behind him that made him stay as silent as possible about his time in prison. Pablo also believed that the less he described to his wife, the less she would dwell on what Emilio might have suffered before he died. The prison guards were imaginative in their cruelty and he knew they kept their worst for homosexuals. It was better to keep her mind off the whole subject.

What he hated more than anything now was the sound of tolling bells.

'That noise,' he moaned with his head in his hands, 'I wish someone would just take them away.'

'But they're church bells, Pablo. They've been there for years and they're probably going to be there for another few.'

'Yes, but a few other churches have been burned down, haven't they? Why couldn't that one have been?'

The nearby church of Santa Ana was where they had been married and their eldest two children had taken their first communion. It had been a place of such happy and significant memories but was somewhere he could no longer abide. In prison, the collusion of the priest with the torture of its inmates made him as guilty as the guards themselves. His spiteful and cynical offer of last rites to those condemned had made him the most despised individual in the entire institution. Pablo now hated everything to do with the Catholic Church.

In the last prison, where he had spent a whole year, his cell had been in the shadow of a bell tower. Night after night they tolled on the hour, wrecking the precious little sleep he had to remind him of the relentless passage of time.

Each morning when she woke and found Pablo beside her, Concha rejoiced. His presence constantly surprised and thrilled her, and over the coming months she watched him gaining strength and vigour.

A month or so after Pablo's return, a letter was delivered. It was concise and carefully worded.

Dear Mother,

I have moved to another part of Spain, my glorious *patria*. I shall not be able to come to see you for a while as I am working on a special project for El Caudillo to help rebuild our country. I am at Cualgamuros. As soon as I have permission, I shall invite you to visit.

From your loving son,

Antonio

'What does it mean?' asked Concha. 'What does it really mean?'

The terse words and the formality of tone made it obvious that Antonio was hiding something. His reference to Franco as El Caudillo, 'the great leader', had to be ironic. Antonio would never use words that implied such acceptance of the dictator except under duress. The letter bore all the evidence that the writer knew it would be censored.

Pablo read it for himself. It was so strange that his son made no reference to him. He felt he no longer existed.

'He doesn't mention you because he assumes you are still imprisoned,' said Concha. 'It's safer that way. Better not to draw attention to the fact that you have family in prison . . .'

'I know, you're right. They'd just use it as an excuse to victimise him.'

They puzzled a little more over what if anything lay between the lines, and wondered what the special project might be. All they deduced was that their son was in a work camp and that he had become one of the hundreds of thousands of men being forced to labour for Spain's tyrannical new regime.

'If he's working at least they'll want to keep him alive,' said Concha, trying to sound optimistic for her husband's sake.

'Well, I suppose we'll just have to wait and see. Perhaps he'll write again soon and tell us a bit more.'

Neither of them admitted that their stomachs churned with anxiety and they sat down to reply to the letter together.

Antonio was overwhelmed with pleasure when he received the envelope with a Granada postmark. Tears pricked the back of his eyes as he read that his father had been released from prison, and when he reached the sentence where his mother promised to come and visit, he thought his heart would burst. Labourers at Cualgamuros were allowed visitors, and some families even set up home to be close by. It might take Concha a few months to plan but the idea of the visit sustained them all.

Chapter Thirty-four

ANTONIO WROTE BACK. His second letter gave them more detail of what he was actually constructing and he even sent them some money. To give the project legitimacy, labourers were paid a salary, albeit a pittance.

'There's something particularly cruel about having to construct a memorial for your enemies,' said Pablo. 'It's a sick joke, really.'

By now Antonio was almost accustomed to the new routine of his life. He was strong and capable of carrying sizeable loads, but there was little to alleviate the tedium. Death and injury were common inside the mountain, and new workers were continually sent in to replace the killed and maimed.

One day Antonio found that he had a new job. It had been his greatest fear. He had tolerated the worst imaginable conditions and pain that will push a man to breaking point, but the irrational fear of being trapped inside a mountain was greater than all of these. Claustrophobia was something he could not control.

Those assigned to the rock face walked in darkness towards their work. The further they went in, the lower Antonio's temperature dropped. His sweat was cold, all encompassing, dominating his whole body. For the first time in these years of extreme suffering, he had to restrain himself from weeping. It was irrational. It was not the darkness but the oppressive sense of the mountain above him that terrified him witless. So many times before the explosions began, he would have to suppress his desire to scream but occasionally, when they stopped for the stones to fall in front of them, he would allow himself to roar with fear and with the hopelessness of it all, his tears mingling with the filthy sweat that ran down his body and soaked him right down to his boots.

The granite was resistant, but each day they went a little deeper into the darkness. Only a megalomaniac would conceive of such an immense cave of this kind, thought Antonio. It was no less than an underground, man-made cathedral. Sometimes, first thing in the morning, there would be a quiet mystery about it. Before the drilling and the hammering began, he tried to make himself imagine he was going somewhere peaceful, church-like, but soon the terror of claustrophobia overwhelmed him again and he saw himself walking into the centre of the earth, perhaps never again to return.

He endlessly repeated to himself that he would soon be out, but with no light and without a wristwatch, there was no means of knowing when. Eventually he retraced his steps, but each day seemed an eternity.

Weeks turned into months. Progress was slow. In the overall scale they scarcely seemed to have scratched the mountainside. The workers began to learn more about this grand scheme. It was supposed to be finished in one year.

'That's about as likely as Franco sending us home for Christmas,' said Antonio. 'We've already been here for a year, haven't we? And it looks the same as when we arrived!'

He was right. It would be twenty years before The Valley of the Fallen was completed, and it would take twenty thousand men to finish it.

Each week dozens of workers were dying, killed in explosions, crushed by landslides of rocks, or electrocuted. Many of those who laboured at the rock face itself contracted a sinister disease. As they drilled and hacked at the rock face, the air became filled with dust and, though they held sponges to their faces, microscopic particles of silica found their way through and filled their lungs with crystals.

The work was exhausting and the teams of workers were in a constant state of flux. Friendships were hard to form. On rare occasions someone would be granted their freedom but others were less lucky. The professor had been taken away only a few weeks after their arrival at Cualgamuros. It appeared that he had been guilty of committing many, albeit bogus, crimes against the state, the most offensive of them being that he was an intellectual and a Jew. Even as he had been taken from the hut at the crack of dawn one day, he had smiled at Antonio.

'Don't worry,' he had said. 'At least I won't be going to Mauthausen.'

Professor Díaz had spent a year in France under German occupation. Many of his fellow Jews had been rounded up and removed to the notorious concentration camp. Antonio had admired Díaz enormously. He was the only person he could have called a friend in this godforsaken place, and even if the man himself faced his execution with stoicism, Antonio was horrified by the prospect of it.

After this, Antonio made no new friends. At the end of each day, lying exhausted on his straw mattress, he would close his eyes. Only his imagination saved him from insanity. He practised hard to free his mind from this place and they were simple, familiar images he needed. Never of women – such urges had become distant memories now. Usually he was sitting at a table with Francisco and Salvador, there was the alluring fragrance of brandy, the sound of conversation, the sensation of a fresh *polvorón* crumbling to sweet powder on his tongue. No one could reach him here and eventually he slept.

It was the man who slept on the mattress next to him that first noticed there was something wrong with Antonio.

'I don't know whether you cough all day – it's too noisy to notice – but you're doing it all night long. Every night.'

Antonio could detect a note of irritation.

'It's keeping me awake,' his neighbour complained.

'I'm sorry. I'll try to stop, but I must be doing it in my sleep . . .'

The close, smoke-filled atmosphere of the huts encouraged the spread of germs, as did the dampness in the Guadarrama air, and Antonio was not the only worker who tossed and turned throughout the hours of darkness.

Within a few weeks, Antonio himself ceased to sleep. All night he sweated, and now, when he coughed, he saw his palm was stained crimson with blood. He was racked with chest pains.

Antonio was one of many who contracted silicosis. The hated mountain had buried a part of itself within him.

The sick were not kindly treated and many worked until they collapsed. Antonio intended to do the same but one day his body would no longer obey him. For days he could not lift himself off his sweat-soaked bed. He experienced none of the peace that is meant to descend before you meet your maker and through a haze of delirium, all he felt was anger and frustration.

One night there was a passing glimpse of his mother. Antonio had some distant recollection of receiving a letter from her to say that she was planning to visit and he wondered if this was her, standing over him with her dark hair and tender smile. He experienced a fleeting moment of peace, but no other angels came for him and even in a state of semi-consciousness he knew that he was losing hold. The priest that sometimes exploited such men for a last-minute conversion did not bother to visit. Antonio was regarded as beyond spiritual reach by the authorities.

Finally, after some hours of delirium, he was aware of the most terrible, burdensome sadness. He was saturated with tears, sweat and grief, and everything was sliding away from him. Death now rolled in like a high tide and nothing could hold it back.

Throughout the past year, though they had both been entirely unaware of it, Javier Montero had been living only metres away. Along with his father, he had been rounded up in Málaga when the city was overrun in February 1937 and he had spent the entire duration of the war in prison. His only crime was to be a gypsy and by definition, therefore, a subversive. His path and Antonio's had almost crossed a hundred times, but both had become so stooped that they rarely looked up. The intervening years had ravaged them both.

Javier was in a group whose grim task that day was the burial of any dead. Occasionally he caught sight of his once beautiful hands now folded over the handle of a spade, bleeding, calloused, criss-crossed with granite cuts. It had been four years since his slender fingers had wrapped themselves over the fingerboard of his guitar and almost as long since he had heard the sound of music.

'You know, we're probably the lucky ones,' said his fellow gravedigger as they swung their pickaxes at the hard earth. 'I reckon this is softer than that granite.'

'I suppose you might be right,' answered Javier, trying to appreciate the levity in his tone.

They moved the body into position and lowered it into the grave. There was no shroud and the earth from Javier's spade fell directly onto the man's face. These were Antonio's last rites. There were no rituals on this hillside.

Neither gravedigger looked but for a few minutes they kept silent. It was the most and the least they could do.

A few days earlier, Concha had set out from Granada to make the long-promised visit to Cualgamuros. At the entrance she was obliged to register herself and then, having stated her business, was directed to a small building, situated slightly apart from the long rows of dormitory huts, which stretched away into the distance.

She gave Antonio's full name and then the sergeant ran his finger down the lists of workers' names. There were dozens of entries and she stood patiently while he turned page after page. He sighed, apparently bored. Though she could not read any of the names upside down, Concha could see that some of them had lines through them.

Then his finger came to a stop, halfway down a page.

'Dead,' he said dispassionately. 'Last week. Silicosis.'

Concha's heart almost stopped beating. His words came like stab wounds.

'Thank you,' she said politely. She was determined not to show any weakness in front of this man and wandered out blindly, not really knowing where she was going now.

It was five o'clock in the afternoon and some of the workers had returned to their huts after a twelve-hour shift. Javier glanced out of his window. He noticed a woman. Apart from the wives of labourers who had come to live nearby, it was rare to see anyone female, but what made him look twice was that it was a face he thought he recognised. He slipped out of the hut and hastened after her.

The woman was wandering slowly now and it took only a moment for him to catch her up.

'Excuse me,' he said, touching her lightly on the arm.

Concha assumed it was one of the guards about to reprimand her for wandering into a forbidden area. She stopped. She could feel nothing now, certainly not fear.

Javier had not been mistaken. Though her hair was now streaked with grey, she was unchanged.

'Señora Ramírez,' he said.

It took Concha a few moments to realise who this skeletal creature actually was. He had changed considerably but the huge distinctive eyes remained the same.

'It's me. Javier Montero.'

'Yes, yes,' answered Concha, so quietly that birdsong would have drowned out her voice. 'I know . . .'

'But what are you doing here?' he asked her.

The first thing that went through his mind was that Señora Ramírez had learned that he was here and had come with news of Mercedes.

'I came to see Antonio,' she replied.

'Antonio! He's here?'

Concha's head dropped. She could not answer but the tears that ran down her face told him enough.

They stood for a while. Javier felt awkward. He wanted to embrace Señora Ramírez as he would his own mother, but it did not seem appropriate. If only he could comfort her in some way.

It was getting dark now and Concha knew that she would have to leave soon. She must be out of here by nightfall. When her tears had subsided, she finally spoke. There was one thing she must do before she left.

'I don't suppose you would know where he was buried. I would just like to go there before I leave,' she said with all the self-control she could muster.

Javier took her arm. He led her gently towards the burial ground, which was situated a few hundred metres beyond the huts. In the clearing among the trees she could make out the section of ground where the earth had been recently disturbed:

it was ridged like a ploughed field. They approached the spot and Concha stood for a few moments, her eyes shut, her lips moving in prayer. Javier remained silent as the realisation dawned that Antonio's burial must have been on his shift. Even the sound of his breathing seemed intrusive.

Eventually Concha looked up. 'I must go now,' she said decisively.

Javier took her arm again. They passed a number of workers on their way to the gates, who gave him quizzical looks. There was something he was desperate to know and he could not let Señora Ramírez leave without asking her.

'Mercedes . . .'

Concha had almost forgotten about her daughter in the past hour, but she had known that the moment would come when she had to tell Javier that Mercedes had gone to look for him and never came back.

'I can't lie to you,' she said, taking his hand. 'But if we hear from her I'll write to you straight away.'

It was Javier's turn to be lost for words.

As the gate clanged shut behind Concha, she shuddered. Drawing her coat tightly around her, she hastened away. In spite of the fact that her son was buried there, she could not get away fast enough.

One day, an immense cross would soar one hundred and fifty metres into the sky on the mountain top, majestic, arrogant and victorious. With the figures of the holy saints kneeling at its base, it would be positioned above Franco's tomb and on some days its long shadow would touch the wooded place where Antonio's body lay in an unmarked grave.

Part 3

Chapter Thirty-five

Granada, 2001

THE SHADOWS WERE lengthening over the square outside El Barril as Miguel's words died away. Sonia had almost forgotten where she was. She was astonished by what he had told her.

'But how could all this have happened to one family?' she asked.

'It wasn't just the Ramírez family that these things happened to,' replied Miguel. 'They weren't unusual. Not at all. Every Republican family suffered.'

Miguel's energy seemed to be flagging, but he had been tireless in the telling of this story. Sonia viewed the café with different eyes now. The sadness of what had happened to these people seemed to linger there.

The old man had talked for several hours but there was still a part of the story missing. It was the part that she was most curious to know.

'So what did happen to Mercedes?' she asked. The pictures of the dancer on the wall above them were a constant reminder of why she was really here.

'Mercedes?' he sounded vague. And Sonia worried for a moment. Perhaps this obliging old man had forgotten of her existence. 'Mercedes . . . yes. Of course. Mercedes . . . Well, for a long time there was no contact at all because letters could be so incriminating and she felt her mother was probably under enough suspicion without being accused of having a *roja* for a daughter.'

'So she was still alive then?' Sonia's hopes were raised again.

'Oh yes,' said Miguel brightly. 'Eventually, when it was safer, she began to write letters to Concha here at El Barril.'

Miguel was rummaging around in a chest next to the till.

Sonia's heart beat furiously.

'They're here somewhere,' he said.

Sonia was trembling now. She saw in his hand a neatly tied bundle of letters written by the girl whose photograph had come to obsess her.

'Would you like me to read some of them to you? They're in Spanish.' He came to sit down on the chair next to hers.

'Yes, please,' she said quietly, staring at the yellowing dog-eared envelopes he held in his hand.

He carefully removed a dozen fine airmail sheets from the envelope at the top of the chronologically ordered pile and unfolded them. The letter was dated 1941.

The script was unfamiliar. Sonia had never seen her mother write by hand. Her illness had made it difficult and in her memory Mary had always used a typewriter.

The letters from one side of the paper showed through to the other, making the task of reading a challenge. The old man did his best, reciting each sentence in Spanish before translating into rather old-fashioned English.

> Dear Mother,
>
> I know you will understand why I have not written for so long. It was because I was anxious not to incriminate you. I know I am regarded as a traitor for staying out of Spain and I hope you will forgive me for this. It seemed the safest way for all concerned.
>
> I want to tell you what happened after I left for England on the *Habana* four years ago . . .

With every minute that passed, the expanse of water between Mercedes and her homeland widened. The wind got up not long after they set sail and, as they sailed out into the Bay of Biscay, the waves began to roll. The roughness took everyone by surprise. Many of these children had never been on a boat before, and the violence of the rocking motion terrified them. Many had begun to cry as they sensed their disorientation and were gripped by the first gagging moments of nausea.

Even the colour of the sea seemed alien. No longer blue, it was now the colour of churned-up mud. Some of the children were immediately sick and as the journey continued even the adults were retching. Soon the decks were slippery with vomit.

In spite of Mercedes' protest, Enrique was separated from her and put on an upper deck. For many hours she lost sight of him and felt that she had already failed his mother.

'You aren't here only to look after those children,' scolded one of the older assistants.

She was right. Mercedes' role on this journey and beyond it was to take care of a bigger group and her concern for just two of the children was frowned upon by several of the teachers and priests.

That night, the children slept where they could as the boat rolled up and down. Some of them nestled into the bottom of a lifeboat, others curled up on huge coils of rope. Soon Mercedes was incapable of offering them comfort. Queasiness overcame her. When the rough seas became calm again the next day, the relief was immense. The coast of England had been in sight for some time but only when the sea ceased to hurl them around did they notice the thin dark line on the horizon that was Hampshire's coastline. By six thirty on that second day they were docking at Southampton.

The dead flat calm of the harbour was complete sanctuary, and as quickly as it had arrived, the awful seasickness disappeared. On the deck of the ship, small hands held on to the railings and peered over to look at this new country. All they could see were the dark harbour walls that loomed over them.

There was the noisy business of docking the ship to be completed and they heard the alarming clank of the anchor chain, and huge ropes as thick as arms were thrown down on to the quayside. Grizzled men looked up at them with a mixture of pity and curiosity. They meant no harm. There were shouts in a language they did not recognise, gruff aggressive voices and the bellowing holler of the docker who had to make himself heard above the general cacophony.

The sun came out through the clouds but the novelty and excitement of this adventure had worn off. These children wanted to be at home with their mothers. Many had become separated from siblings during the journey and it took time to sort them into groups but the hexagonal badges helped, and each one of them was soon allocated to a helper. Mercedes had hoped for the opportunity to get to know her charges on the journey, but the storm had stolen the moment.

Before disembarkation the children underwent another medical examination and coloured ribbons were tied to their wrists to indicate if treatment was required: a red ribbon meant a journey to the corporation baths for delousing, a blue ribbon meant that infectious disease had been diagnosed and a visit to the isolation hospital was required, and a white ribbon showed a clean bill of health.

All the poor mites looked bedraggled. Hair, so beautifully brushed, ribboned and carefully plaited almost two days earlier, was now matted into hard clumps. Smart knitted jumpers were stained by vomit. The *señoritas* did their best to make them presentable.

Finally, the children had to be reunited with their possessions and given back the very little they had brought with them. Small girls now clutched a favourite doll and boys stood bravely, like little men. By the time they were all assembled and ready to leave the ship they had been docked for some time.

The curiosity was mutual. Everyone stared, wide-eyed. The Spaniards looked at the English and the English gazed at the foreign children edging their way along the deck. Britain had heard so much about the barbaric behaviour of the *rojos* in Spain, how they had burned down churches and tortured innocent nuns, that they expected to see little savages. When these wide-eyed children, some of them still managing to look smartly dressed, came into view, they were amazed.

Among the first English people the Spanish children saw were members of a Salvation Army band. Mercedes did not quite know what to make of them, in their dark uniforms, blasting their bright tunes from gleaming trumpets and trombones. They seemed rather military to her, but she soon learned that they meant well.

Southampton looked like a town in fiesta. Its streets were bedecked with bunting and the Spanish children smiled, imagining this was put up to welcome them. They would discover only later that it was left over from the celebration of the recent coronation.

Those who had been given a clean bill of health were driven in double-decker buses from Southampton for a few miles to North Stoneham, the place that was to be their temporary home. It was a huge encampment spread over three fields, with five hundred white, bell-shaped tents in neat rows. Each tent would accommodate eight to ten children, with boys and girls separated. '*Indios!*' exclaimed some of the children with excitement when they saw them.

'They think it's all a big game of cowboys and Indians,' said Enrique scornfully to his sister, who stood next to him clutching her doll.

For Mercedes it immediately invited comparison with the makeshift tents that people had improvised on the road from Málaga to Almería. Here there was order, safety and, most touching of all, kindness. In these green meadows they had found sanctuary.

The organisation was impressive. As well as the divisions between girls and boys, there were separate areas for the three groups of children, divided according to the politics of their parents. The organisers wanted to minimise the aggression between rival groups.

The camp was its own self-contained world with its own rules and routines. Queues for food were orderly, though it did take four hours to serve the first meal. Much of what they were given tasted strange to the evacuees but they were grateful for it and acquainted themselves with new flavours and tastes like Horlicks and tea. Mercedes found some of the children in her care were hoarding food; for so long they had worried about where the next meal was coming from.

They picnicked in the sunshine but for many days they were

anxious whenever they heard the sound of aeroplanes passing over towards the nearby airfield in Eastleigh. They associated the sound so strongly with the threat of air raids. After a while they began to lie back on the soft English grass and watch the pale puffy clouds, safe in the knowledge that bombers were not going to blot out the sun.

The children were kept busy with lessons, chores and gymnastics, but the discipline was kind, and every effort was made to ensure that this place did not feel like a prison. Each day there was a prize for the tidiest tent and Mercedes made sure that her little charges often won the competition. All of them suffered in some way from aching homesickness, but even the youngest managed to keep their tears until night-time.

The refugees were much greater in number than originally expected, but the pressure was soon lifted when, in the first week, four hundred were taken to a Salvation Army hostel and within a month one thousand more had gone to Catholic homes. There were some food shortages, but not of the same scale that many of them had experienced in Bilbao. One mealtime, Mercedes scrutinised the old and battered knife and fork she was using and remembered that every single item in the camp was from a voluntary donation. Though they were reasonably well protected from the attitudes of the outside world, she knew that the British government had refused to fund their stay in England. Furious efforts were going on to raise money to feed and clothe them and they relied entirely on the kindness of strangers.

Though they were protected from articles in the newspapers that were hostile to their arrival, one piece of news that was not kept from the Spanish refugees was the fall of Bilbao to the Nationalists. Only a month after they had sailed away from it, the city had fallen. It was a very black day at Stoneham. Many of the children ran amok, crying and screaming, panic-stricken at the thought that their parents could now be dead. Enrique, along with some other boys, ran out of the camp, determined to find a boat so that they could return to Spain and fight. They were soon found and brought back to camp. Mercedes spent the night comforting Enrique, assuring him that his mother would be all right. As she sat with him, she thought of Javier too and once again hoped that he had got out of the city long ago.

News of Bilbao's capture created a dilemma for everyone.

'Surely we can't go back now?' said Mercedes to one of the other assistants.

'No, I don't think we can. I think the children would be in even more danger than they were before,' replied Carmen.

'So what's going to happen to us all?' asked Mercedes.

'Your guess is as good as mine, but I don't think we can camp out forever in this climate!'

At some point soon everyone at the camp in North Stoneham would have to be moved somewhere more permanent. The Basque Children's Committee was already working hard to find a solution. Up and down the country, they were establishing 'colonies' in which to house the children, and the destination for each *niño* could be arbitrary. For some it could be another tent, an empty hotel, or a castle. For Mercedes it was a country mansion.

At the end of July she accompanied a group of twenty-five children, including Enrique and Paloma, to Sussex. They took the train to Haywards Heath and at the railway station they were welcomed by the town band and children who had brought gifts of sweets. It was a warm and happy day. From there a bus dropped them in a village fifteen kilometres away and after that it was a short walk from the village until they reached the gateposts of Winton Hall.

The eagle-topped pillars were imposing if dilapidated. Some of the bricks were dislodged and one of the moss-covered eagles had lost a wing. Nevertheless, they created an intimidating impression of what was to come. The children joined hands and marched in pairs along the kilometre of rutted driveway. Mercedes walked with Carmen, the teacher in charge of the group. In the past two months the two women had become close friends.

It was hot. The temperature made them feel as though they were back at home. The as yet unharvested fields around them were pale and parched and the sky was a clear, bright blue. Butterflies basked on the buddleia bushes that grew in profusion along the way, and the younger children squealed with delight at the Red Admirals that fluttered around their heads. They picked buttercups and daisies from the verge and made up a song. Their walk seemed to pass in no time and they even forgot the weight of their bags.

Mercedes was the first to reach a bend in the driveway where the house came into view. She had seen pictures of English stately homes in books, so she had some idea of what they looked like, but she would never have imagined that one would become her home. Winton Hall was built of a sandy coloured stone and had more chimneys and turrets than some of the younger children could count.

'It's a fairy castle!' exclaimed Paloma.

'Are we coming to live with the new King?' asked her friend.

The owners had been watching their progress along the driveway from an upstairs room and were now at the top of the steps to the entrance. Two spaniels sat at their feet.

Sir John and Lady Greenham had all the trappings of the English landed gentry without any of the wealth. Winton Hall had been built by Sir John's grandfather, who had been a wealthy industrialist, but over the years its fabric had begun to disintegrate around the subsequent generations who lived there.

'Welcome to Winton Hall,' said the master of the house, coming down to meet the arrivals.

Carmen was the only one of the group who spoke any English. The children had learned a few words since they arrived, but could not make conversation.

Mercedes knew only 'Hello' and 'Thank you'. Both of these were useful in this situation and she managed to splutter them out.

Lady Greenham remained at the top of the steps, eyeing them all coolly. It had not been her idea to invite the refugees here. It was her husband's whimsical notion. He was a distant relative of the redoubtable Duchess of Atholl, who had established the Basque Children's Committee; now that they had been dispersed from the camp she helped them to find homes around the country. Lady Greenham remembered clearly the first time she had heard of her husband's plan to open up their home. 'Oh, do let's help these poor dears!' he had exhorted. 'It won't be for long.' He had just returned from a meeting in London where the 'Red Duchess', as she was known, had canvassed for support.

Sir John was a kind-hearted man and could think of no reason why they should not invite a group of harmless young Spaniards to fill some of their dusty rooms. They had never had children of their own and it was a long time since the corridors of the house had been filled with any kind of life, apart from the occasional mouse.

'Very well, then,' his wife had reluctantly agreed. 'But I'm not having boys. Only girls. And not too many of them.'

'I'm afraid we can't do that,' he answered firmly. 'If there are siblings, they have to stay together.'

Lady Greenham was full of resentment right from the beginning. Though it was in a state of dusty decay, she retained a strong pride in their home. They had long since dispensed with the servants, who had kept the place immaculate, and now only had a short-sighted housekeeper who occasionally flicked a duster at the cobwebs. Even so, Lady Greenham had a strong awareness of the house's past grandeur and her social standing as its chatelaine.

The children filed up the steps and into the hallway, their eyes as wide as saucers. Dark portraits looked down at them. Paloma giggled.

'Look at him,' she whispered to Enrique, pointing at one of the ancestral paintings. 'He's so fat!'

She won herself a disapproving look from Carmen. Even though she was sure that their hosts did not understand what she had said, it was obvious what had amused her.

Lady Greenham's rather fixed smile faded. 'Now, children,' she said, not the slightest bit perturbed that they did not have any idea what she was saying, but raising her voice in case it helped their comprehension. 'Shall we just establish a few rules?'

They gathered in a circle around her. For the first time Mercedes took a closer look at the Englishwoman. She seemed about the same age as her mother, perhaps forty-five. Her husband, who had strands of reddish hair brushed ineffectually across his bald head, was probably a few years older than she. His complexion was densely freckled and Mercedes tried not to stare.

Carmen translated as Lady Greenham spoke.

'There is to be no running up and down the corridors . . . Shoes will be taken off before you come in from the garden . . . The drawing room and the library are out of bounds to you . . . You must not over-excite the dogs.'

They listened in silence.

'Boys and girls, do you understand all these rules?' said Carmen, to try to break the tension.

'*Sí! Sí! Sí!*' they all agreed.

'Now I shall show you where you're going to sleep,' said Sir John.

The children's feet clattered up the bare broad staircase after their hosts.

Lady Greenham stopped and turned round. The children halted too.

'I think we have already broken a rule, haven't we?'

Carmen flushed. 'Yes, they have. I'm so sorry,' she said apologetically. 'Now, children, go back down the stairs and remove your shoes, please.'

They all did as they were told and their dusty shoes now formed an untidy pile at the foot of the stairs.

'I'll show you where to put them later,' said Lady Greenham. Her own court shoes hammered along the corridor now as the walk to their bedrooms continued.

One thing Mercedes had observed was that, in spite of the temperature they had been enjoying earlier, as soon as they had stepped over the threshold of this house, all the warmth of the day was left outside.

The boys were to be accommodated in a room on the first floor, which had high ceilings, huge sash windows, and a large faded Persian rug, and the girls were to be divided into two separate musty-smelling rooms in the attic, which had once been servants' quarters. There were several beds in each and they were expected to share in whatever way they could. Carmen and Mercedes would sleep top to tail with the girls.

It was suppertime. Initially the housekeeper, Mrs Williams, was as unwelcoming as her mistress. In the kitchen she gave them a series of 'don'ts'.

'Don't leave your plate on the table. Don't bang your cutlery. Don't waste food. Don't let the dogs eat any scraps. Don't let any peelings go down the sink. Don't forget to wash your hands before meals.'

Each one was delivered with a mimed demonstration of what they 'Must Not Do'. Then she smiled – a broad smile that involved every muscle in her face, including her eyes, her mouth and the dimples in her cheeks. The children could see that this woman had warmth in her heart.

In the grand dining room, where grimy crystal chandeliers hung down from the ceiling, the long table was incongruously laid with green china from Woolworths and tin mugs. Lady Greenham was hardly going to use her finest porcelain for these little foreigners.

Their first meal was a dish made from mince followed by tapioca pudding. Most of the children managed to force down the fatty first course but the tapioca was more of a struggle. Several of them gagged violently and Paloma was profusely sick on the floor. Carmen and Mercedes rushed to clear up the vomit. It was imperative that Lady Greenham did not get to hear of it, since this was the sort of calamity that might prove her husband's folly in inviting these children here.

The housekeeper, loyal as she was to her employers, did not want the new arrivals to get into trouble so she helped clear up and promised not to mention what had happened. She would serve something called semolina from now on, rather than tapioca.

The following day, after a breakfast of bread and margarine, the children were allowed to explore outside. They were baffled as to where its limits lay. There was a formal garden with overgrown lawns and brick-edged parterres, where weeds seemed to grow in greater profusion than the roses, against whom they waged an impressive battle. Rather mystifyingly there was a huge sunken space; they deduced from the presence of a now bottomless rowing boat that was stranded in the middle, its oars sticking out of the mud like flagpoles, that it had once been an artificial lake. Some of them walked around it, but found the pathway overgrown and impossible to negotiate. Beyond the lake in one direction was woodland and in the other there were fields, some of them grazed by cows.

There was a little folly in the garden, which had obviously been a retreat for someone who enjoyed painting. It was circular, so that the light could come in from all sides. An easel leaned against the wall, and the old table was covered with daubs of oil paints, tubes of which still lay on the surface. Paintbrushes stood, tips down, in a cup. No one had been in here for years. Two of the older girls, Pilar and Esperanza, were entranced by this secret hide-away and found some paper and scraps of charcoal. The paper was damp but useable and they began to draw. Hours later they were still there, utterly absorbed.

Mercedes was drawn to a wooden summerhouse by the lake and pushed open the door. It was full of old deck chairs.

'Let's put some of them out,' said Paloma, who was exploring the estate with Mercedes. She dragged one of them into the sunshine, only to discover that the canvas had rotted. 'Never mind,' she said cheerfully. 'Perhaps we could mend some of them.'

Later that week, that was exactly what they would begin to do.

Some of the children found the walled area where a few vegetables were still growing. In the past they had been cultivated in industrial quantities, but now only a few onions and potatoes grew. One of the girls went into the greenhouse and found some strawberries growing in a trough. She could not resist eating one and was in a state of anxiety for the rest of the day over whether Lady Greenham had counted them and would notice the missing fruit.

Other children had discovered a disused tennis court and, in a nearby pavilion, the old, rolled-up net. Carmen, with some of the older boys, was now attempting to erect it. The lines were still just about visible, and once they had rooted out some old rackets, all with a string or two broken, a few had begun to pat a ball back and forth across the net. It had been many, many months since they had had fun like this.

At lunchtime Sir John came to find them. He could hear their laughter and found a group of the children trying to keep a ball in play.

'What's this?' asked Carmen, holding out a giant wooden hammer for him to identify. 'There are several of them in a box.'

'Ah,' he said smiling. 'That's a croquet mallet.'

'A croquet mallet . . .' repeated Carmen, none the wiser.

'Shall I show you how to play after lunch?'

'It's a game, then?'

'Yes,' he replied, 'and we used to play it on that lawn.' He pointed to a huge flat sweep of grass that was now covered in patches of moss. 'It's a bit bumpy now, but no reason why we shouldn't have a go.'

After a lunch of potato soup, some bread and a lump of cheese that the children thought rubbery but quite enjoyed, they were back in the garden. There was a croquet lesson. Sir John had set up the hoops and now taught a group of them the strange and quirky rules of the game. Even the boys were dismissive of the option to drive another player off the lawn, and adopted a more gentle strategy. They had witnessed enough aggression in their short lives.

The delightful romance of all the garden's different spaces captivated everyone, and on this perfect English summer's afternoon, they all temporarily forgot about the past and enjoyed the present. There was the freedom to run around and the opportunity to sit quietly too. A few of the younger ones had found a bench in the sunshine and started to draw.

Carmen had kept in touch with some of the other teachers, and conditions in some of their colonies made her appreciate more than ever their good fortune in being at Winton Hall. At one place, the children found themselves being used as free labour in a laundry, and at some of the Catholic-run homes, the nuns did not hesitate to punish misdemeanours with beatings.

Those who were in Salvation Army camps seemed to have

most complaints: 'The stern faces of women in bonnets who make us sing English hymns only remind me of why we had to leave Spain,' wrote Carmen's friend. 'People in uniform forcing us to conform to their religion! Doesn't that sound familiar?'

It seemed to Mercedes that though their actions were often well meant, some of those who ran the colonies failed to appreciate what these children had suffered.

Chapter Thirty-six

One warm summer's day passed after another and the mood at Winton Hall was generally one of content. Many of the children had recently received letters from their families in Bilbao. Enrique and Paloma were among the lucky ones and now knew that their mother and little brother and sister were all safe.

In the mornings, the children had a few hours of lessons but afternoons were for recreation. One day a group of them were trying to recall the words of their favourite songs and the steps of some traditional Basque dances. It mattered so much to them that they should not forget the good things about home. Over the coming days they rehearsed until they were word- and step-perfect. They would perform them to Sir John and Lady Greenham and Mrs Williams, if they were interested.

That night after supper, they put on a performance. Even Lady Greenham managed to applaud. Sir John's enthusiasm bubbled out of him.

'That was marvellous,' he said to Carmen. 'Really marvellous.'

'Thank you,' she said beaming.

'And I've got an idea! I think you should put on a show in the village!'

'Oh, surely not,' Carmen replied. 'I think the children would be much too shy.'

'Shy?' exclaimed Sir John. 'They seem anything but shy!'

'Well, I'll talk to them about it later,' said Carmen, not wanting to dismiss his idea. 'Do you think that people would pay?'

Over the past few weeks she had become aware that money for their keep was in extremely short supply. Although the Basque Children's Committee waged an enthusiastic campaign for donations, the British public were not always prepared to dig deeply into their pockets for children whom they regarded as communists. In every colony the exiles were coming up with ways of earning money.

Sir John was right. That night the children all voted unanimously to perform for the public if it could be arranged.

'But it's only three dances and five songs,' one of the older girls put forward. 'Do you think that's enough if we're charging for tickets?'

There was a general murmur of agreement that this might not be enough. Mercedes did not hesitate to put forward another idea.

'I could dance,' she said. 'They might not have seen flamenco before either.'

'It would certainly make a more varied programme,' agreed Carmen, who knew of Mercedes' past. 'But who is going to accompany you?'

'Well, there isn't a guitarist here,' Mercedes said, trying to make light of it, 'but I could teach you some clapping rhythms.'

Several hands shot up in the half-light. There was certainly no shortage of enthusiasm.

'And I have these,' came a voice from the bed at the far end of the room. It was Pilar. They all turned round when they heard the purring sound of castanets. It was like the sound of a cicada, and on this hot night, they almost imagined they were at home. Pilar had been playing with the castanets since she was three or four, and the fourteen year old now had extraordinary mastery over them.

'Perfect,' said Mercedes. 'We have our performance.'

The dancing troupe grew now to twenty, and everyone rehearsed frantically for three days. The ones who were not dancing made posters and Sir John had them put up in the village.

To Lady Greenham's chagrin, Mercedes practised in the hallway, where the flooring was solid enough to take the force of her steps. The girls sat on the stairs to watch her and peeped through the banister. They had never seen anyone quite like her and were completely mesmerised, clapping and stamping their feet with appreciation whenever she rested.

Pilar sat at the back of the hall. She quietly tapped the beat with her hands first of all, working out the rhythms and then, inaudibly to anyone but herself, she worked out the patterns for the castanets. Only when she was completely sure of them did she move forward and begin to play for Mercedes. She exploited every complex variation of castanet sound, making them trill and sing and snap and clack.

'That's wonderful, Pilar,' said Mercedes. She had never heard castanets played more eloquently.

On the night of the performance, every seat in the village hall was filled. Some had come out of pure curiosity to see these 'small, dark little people' as they were described by the Basque Children's Committee. For them it was rather like going to the zoo. Others came simply out of boredom. There was little other entertainment in an English village.

The Basque dances charmed the audience. Mrs Williams had managed to find them suitable material, and the girls had made their own costumes: red skirts, green waistcoats, black aprons and simple white blouses. They danced with vigour and enthusiasm. Everyone clapped and called for an encore.

The songs enchanted the audience too. Sweet voices in perfect unison sang out '*Anda diciendo tu madre*' and even the most hard-hearted people in the audience melted. Mercedes, standing in the wings, felt a lump rise to her throat as she heard them sing that last word, '*madre*'. They were so far away from their mothers and most of them had been so extraordinarily brave.

Mercedes was the last item on the programme. The contrast between her and the innocent naïvety of the Basque dances could not have been greater. It was nothing like those mechanical performances she had given on the journey towards Bilbao. Here into this hall, with its leaking roof and an audience of stony-faced Englishmen and -women, she brought all of her pain and longing. She was wearing the red polka-dotted dress that she had been given all those months ago by the bar owner. She had put on plenty of weight since then and it was now perfectly moulded around her re-emerging curves.

If the audience had evaporated into the air on this warm night, it would not have mattered to her. Tonight, she danced for herself. Some of them understood it and were drawn in. They eagerly followed every expressive movement with their eyes and appreciated the emotion she was laying bare. When the castanets crackled in the air and matched the rhythm of her feet, they found the hairs on their necks standing on end.

Others found her performance baffling. It was strange, incomprehensible and alien. It made them feel distinctly uncomfortable. At the end of the performance, there was a moment of silence. None of them had ever seen anything like it. Some then clapped politely. Others burst into rapturous applause. Several people rose to their feet. Mercedes had divided them.

The reputation of the Basque singing and dancing, and the flamenco soon spread. It was even reported in the local paper. Letters came from other villages and towns in the south of England asking the refugees to perform, and all invitations were accepted as the payments contributed to their upkeep. Once a week they packed their costumes and travelled to another destination. The contrast between the innocence of the traditional Basque dances and the flamboyant style of flamenco was unique wherever they took it. Not a day passed when Mercedes did not think of Javier, and when she danced it was as though she revived him freshly in her mind and conjured him up again. She needed to keep in practice for when they met again, she told herself.

A few months of relative happiness went by and the only person who did not seem to be enjoying the holiday camp atmosphere of Winton Hall was Lady Greenham.

'Why does she look like she's sucking a lemon?' Mercedes commented to Carmen one evening.

'I don't think she's that keen on having us here,' answered Carmen, stating the obvious.

'So why did she invite us?'

'I don't think she did. It was all Sir John's doing,' replied Carmen. 'But actually I think she's just one of those people. You know – never really happy.'

Lady Greenham's lips were even more pursed than usual when she strode into the dining room at breakfast time. Sir John was sitting having a cup of tea at one end of the table. He enjoyed the formless hum of a language he could not understand.

'Look!' said his wife, slamming down a copy of the *Daily Mail* on the table in front of him. 'Look!'

All the girls had stopped talking. They were alarmed by her apparent anger.

'BASQUE CHILDREN ATTACK POLICE' shouted the headline.

Her husband turned the newspaper over so that no one else could read it. 'That may be the case, which I doubt, but it hasn't happened here, has it? And you should *never* believe what you read in that newspaper.'

'But they're clearly not to be trusted!' Lady Greenham said in a loud whisper.

'I think we should go outside to discuss this,' Sir John hissed angrily.

They both left the room and the sound of raised voices could clearly be heard. Some of the children listened at the door, though they understood almost nothing. Carmen pushed them out of the way to hear.

Sir John admitted that he had heard of minor incidents in the villages close to some of the colonies – scrumping of apples, for example, and the occasional scuffle with local boys, and perhaps a broken window or two – but he was absolutely certain that nothing of the sort could happen at Winton Hall.

Lady Greenham's ambivalence about their presence had always been obvious but now Carmen saw the whole picture. This frosty Englishwoman was happy to do good works for charity as long as it did not intrude too much on her life. Her husband's 'project' had taken it over completely, and she would never feel comfortable with these outsiders. They were foreign and therefore, in her eyes, potentially feral.

Carmen said nothing to the girls, but confided to Mercedes.

'I don't think we should do anything about it,' said Mercedes.

'We must simply prove her wrong,' agreed Carmen. 'The children's behaviour must be exemplary.'

For the next few months, this was how it was. They gave Lady Greenham no cause for complaint.

From November 1937, parents began to write to the Committee. They wanted their children home. Bilbao was no longer being either blockaded or bombarded. In April 1938, Señora Sánchez, whose apartment block had been struck during an air raid, had found new accommodation. She was now ready to reunite her family, and Enrique and Paloma packed their things to return.

Mercedes travelled with the children by train to Dover, from where they were to catch a boat to France before making the onward journey down through Spain. As she sat in the railway carriage with the oranges and golds of the autumnal landscape floating past, she studied her two charges. In the past year, Paloma had remained a little girl. Her doll, Rosa, sat on her lap, just as she had done on the train journey from Santurce to the dock the previous May. By contrast, Enrique had changed substantially. He still had the same worried look, but he had turned into a young man. She allowed herself to imagine the reunion with their mother and felt a stabbing at her heart.

'I'm not sure about going back,' Enrique said to Mercedes when he saw that his little sister had dropped off with the motion of the train. 'Some of the boys are refusing to go. They don't believe it's safe.'

'But your mother has written to you. She wouldn't be suggesting it if she thought it might be dangerous, would she?' Mercedes said to reassure him.

'Supposing it's not her suggesting it, though? Supposing she was forced to write the letter?'

'That's very suspicious of you,' Mercedes said. 'I'm sure the Committee wouldn't be letting you go if they thought there was any chance of that.'

It had not occurred to Mercedes that there was anything untoward about these letters that regularly arrived to summon children home. It seemed the most natural thing that they should be going back to Spain, and it was what had always been planned. Many parents would rather have their children standing beside them raising the fascist salute than thousands of kilometres away in a foreign land. The rumblings of war were now happening across the whole of northern Europe, so 'home' had to be the safest place for anyone.

Mercedes hugged the two children close before handing them over to the person who was chaperoning a whole group back to Spain. Enrique held back his tears, but neither Mercedes nor Paloma could manage to restrain theirs and their farewells were tearful. Promises to meet again were heartfelt.

As she watched the boat leave, Mercedes fought against her desire to return to Spain. With no idea where Javier could be, and real fear of what might happen to her if she returned to Granada, she knew she was better off staying in England. She still had plenty to occupy her here with the children who had not received summonses from their parents. Some of her charges knew these would never come, if both their parents had been killed. Mercedes took the train back to Haywards Heath and returned to Winton Hall, where some new children were due to arrive from another colony, which had been shut down. The initial ninety colonies were gradually reduced in number as more evacuees returned home.

A diminishing group of them continued to put on their dance performances but there was anticipation at every venue now as their reputation grew and the attitudes of local people towards them softened. Occasionally another flamenco dancer would join Mercedes, and two brothers from another colony in Sussex, who were accomplished guitarists, sometimes came too.

When Madrid fell in the spring of 1939, Franco wanted every evacuee and exile still in England to return. Many were warned against it. Destitution, persecution and arrest were all distinct possibilities.

Mercedes realised she now must take a risk. She wrote a short, careful letter to her mother to tell her where she was, hoping for a response that would give her guidance on what she should do.

In Granada, Pablo and Concha wept with joy when they received the letter and knew that their daughter was alive and safe.

'She's been looking after children all this time!' exclaimed her father, studying his daughter's neat handwriting. 'She was only a child herself the last time we saw her!'

'And she's still dancing . . .' said Concha. 'It's so wonderful that she's still dancing.'

They endlessly pored over the letter, and then they discussed how to reply.

'It will be so wonderful to see her again. I wonder when she's coming,' enthused the old man for his only daughter.

Concha came straight to the point. She tended to lead discussions and decisions these days. Pablo had been slow since his time in prison.

'I think she should stay in England,' she said bluntly. 'We can't let her come back here.'

'Why not?' asked Pablo. 'The war is over.'

'It's still not safe, Pablo,' Concha said dogmatically. 'It's not the best thing for Merche. However much we want to see her.'

'I don't understand,' he said, slamming his glass down on the table. 'She's just an innocent young woman!'

'Well, the authorities wouldn't see her that way,' Concha insisted. 'She left the country. That's seen as a hostile act, and she has delayed returning. Believe me, Pablo, she's likely to be arrested. I have to know she's safe.'

'But what about Javier?' appealed Pablo. 'She'll want to come back to visit him.'

This was what Concha feared more than anything. If Mercedes knew that Javier was alive and at Cualgamuros she would almost certainly return. For her daughter's own sake, she chose to keep this information from her.

At Winton Hall, Mercedes eagerly awaited the response. Eventually, with other letters that came from Spain with stamps showing the new dictator, an envelope arrived from Granada. Even her mother's handwriting made Mercedes tremble. Its familiarity made her seem so unbearably close. She tore it open, hoping for news of everyone, only to be disappointed. There was a single sheet and two stark sentences.

'Father and I look forward to having you at home again soon. Your sister sends her love.'

There was so much to read between the lines. Mercedes was thrilled by the news that her father was at home again, but she was puzzled and disappointed by the lack of mention of Antonio. She feared the worst. The second sentence was blatantly clear, though. Her mother's nonsensical reference to a sister gave out a clear message: 'I don't mean what I say.' Even if Concha Ramírez could not say it in so many words, for fear of the censor's eye, Mercedes knew she was being told not to come home. The rebellious child had long since gone. The mature young woman now heeded her mother's advice.

Chapter Thirty-seven

In May 1939, as Winton Hall finally said goodbye to the last of its *niños* from Bilbao, Mercedes knew it was time for her to go too. The house had provided her with security and a roof for two years and she knew she would look back on its grand spaces and romantic gardens with fondness.

Many of the *señoritas* were taking up domestic positions and others trained as secretaries. All of them now began English lessons. In the past two years in England very few of them had learned more than a handful of words. Living and socialising only with fellow Spaniards, their main concern had been to preserve their own language and culture. Staying in the United Kingdom had been the last thing on their minds.

Like Mercedes, Carmen could not return home. Her father and brother had both been arrested during the early months of Franco's regime. They had joined the resistance and when the authorities caught up with them, they had just destroyed a bridge outside Barcelona. Both were now sentenced to death. Carmen's mother had also been imprisoned.

When the time came to say farewell, Lady Greenham was almost warm. They suspected this was because she was happy to see them go, but her thin-lipped smile gave nothing away. By contrast, Sir John's eyes were brimful of tears. He did not shed them, but they could see he was awash with emotion. They promised to come and visit, and he nodded silently before turning away.

Mercedes looked forward with both excitement and trepidation to the next few months. Just as she had done when she got on the boat in Bilbao, she hoped that this time of exile would not continue for ever.

The obvious place to go was London. There was a sizeable Spanish community there now, and job opportunities too once she had learned the language.

'It's strange being back in a city,' said Mercedes to Carmen, as they walked out of Victoria Station into a busy street.

'A bit of a relief really,' replied Carmen. 'I'd had enough of the countryside.'

'I'd had enough of Bilbao by the time we left, though,' commented Mercedes.

'Well, London isn't Bilbao. We're going to enjoy ourselves here! I'm certain of it.'

The London street was packed with people. They all looked smart and purposeful to the two Spanish women.

They had already been offered a room to share in Finsbury Park by a Spanish couple and took a bus to their destination. Sitting on the top deck, in the front row, they enjoyed their journey through the city. They could hardly believe their luck in being here. Hyde Park Corner, Oxford Street, Regent's Park, all these places they had heard of, but the reality of them exceeded expectations. They were full of colour and glamour and vitality. Eventually the conductor called out their stop and they got off. It was only a five-minute walk to their new home: a Victorian terraced house in a pretty street where cherry blossom was in full, glorious bloom.

Their landlords had come to England before the conflict and had eagerly supported the efforts of the Basque Children's Committee. Mercedes and Carmen were made to feel very welcome. Even the pretty painted ceramic tiles they had stuck on the walls and some framed scenes of the Sierra Nevada made them feel at home.

But the threat from fascism grew, just as those who had supported the Republic in Spain had feared, and war broke out across Europe. In September 1940, London was blitzed, and for eight months afterwards was under constant attack.

'So now our own country is at peace and we're being bombed . . .' said Mercedes one night as she and Carmen cowered, terrified, in the Anderson shelter at the bottom of the garden.

'There is something ironic about us sitting here in a foreign country, *still* being targeted by Germans,' Carmen mused. 'But anyway, you're wrong. Our country isn't at peace. How can it be when there are hundreds of thousands of political prisoners?'

This war against Hitler was a terrible one but when it came to the point where children were being evacuated out of London, there was no comparison between the atmosphere there and that in Bilbao when people had decided to leave. In Spain the country had turned against itself. There was nothing so poisonous happening in England. There was fear, but no terror.

The residents of the terrace often spent the whole night in the shelter. It was the safest place. Mercedes and Carmen would talk for hours about their pasts and what might happen in the future. The latter could take almost any course so there were no boundaries or limits to their dreams. The territory was unmapped.

English lessons and domestic work kept Mercedes busy. From autumn 1941, what kept her happy was *El Hogar Español*. The exiled Prime Minister of the Republic, Negrín, had signed a lease on a building in Inverness Terrace, which became the focal point for Spanish exiles who could not return to their own country.

It was the heart of their social and cultural life, and everyone mixed in to socialise and sometimes to sing, from those like Mercedes who were polishing English mantelpieces, to intellectuals and exiled politicians. They even held fiesta weekends. For these events, Mercedes put aside her feather duster and danced. The whirl of her tiered skirt and the sound of her metal-tipped shoes made her feel whole each time. This was who she was and in her mind she was transported home. There were others who could sing, dance, and play the guitar or the castanets, and on a warm night when the windows were open, people would gather in the street below and listen to the gunshot cracks of the stamping feet and the soulful tunes of the flamenco guitar. From time to time a few of them, including Mercedes, would even perform to the public.

She had begun to receive regular letters and some favourite photographs from her mother now and in return finally wrote to tell her story. She deduced from the way Concha described her father that he was not the man he had been. This saddened her, and made her yearn to be at home to help. Subsequent letters told her a little more about what had happened to Antonio, and also relayed general news of Spain. She concluded that Carmen was right. While men were being wrongly imprisoned and treated as slaves, theirs was not a country at peace. Every time she received a letter with a Spanish postmark, she hoped for a moment it might be from Javier. She knew her mother would forward anything he sent. Not even for an hour did Mercedes give up hope.

As the years went by Mercedes' English improved. In 1943 it was good enough for her to train as a secretary. Shortly afterwards she applied for a job in Beckenham, which she was lucky enough to get, and realised that the journey from Finsbury Park would be too long. Carmen was happy to move as well, and they found a flat of their own in south London.

Life was as good as it could be, given their sense of displacement. They did not manage to get to *El Hogar Español* as often now, though Mercedes was invited to dance at least once a month there and her vibrant performances always drew an appreciative crowd.

Mercedes tried not to think too much about the strain her parents were living under. They were running the café reasonably successfully under the new regime, but the continuing grief over the deaths of their three sons never lessened. Concha sometimes thought there were no more tears left to fall, but that was the great deception of a sadness that lasts a lifetime. It is constantly renewed. Each day meant another walk across freshly broken glass. Each step had to be so careful and tentative, simply to allow them to negotiate the pain of getting from morning to night. The quiet ticking of the clock was about as much noise as they could bear once their customers had left for the evening.

Letters got to England, if slowly. Concha always tried to sound cheerful, but she was keen to discourage her daughter from returning. 'You must be having a lovely life there,' she wrote, 'and if you come home you will find it so different.' It was her way of keeping Mercedes away from a country that would be full of memories and empty spaces.

Mercedes' letters to her parents gave the impression that she was settled in her new life. Though their daughter always read between the lines of their correspondence to her, her parents never thought to look beyond the surface of hers, or to question the impression of contentment that she spent so much time creating.

The lack of truth in their correspondence did not mean there was no love between them. It merely meant that they loved each other enough to want to protect the other party.

There was one event that Concha could not conceal. In 1945, Pablo died. It had been one of those severe Granada winters when the raw air reaches into the chest and curls around the lungs, and he had not been strong enough to survive it. It was the hardest moment for Mercedes to bear since she had sailed away from Bilbao.

When the war in Europe ended and men returned from the front, the Spanish girls' social life became focused around the local dance hall, the Locarno. After six years of conflict and anxiety, dancing was the perfect antidote. It was a way of sharing what it was to be alive and it did not require any coupons. Everyone of their age danced the waltz and the quickstep, and as the craze for Latin American dancing swept in, Mercedes and Carmen easily picked it up.

Dance halls were where young men and women conducted their courtships, and most had one clear objective: to find a spouse. Mercedes was an exception. The last thing on her mind was to find a soulmate. She already had one, and when she went out on a Friday and a Saturday night she had no desire for anything beyond the life-enhancing thrill of the dance.

The men danced with different girls each night, some of them that they had known for their whole lives, and others they got to know, but all the while they had in the back of their minds the question of whether they might marry one of them.

The first time Carmen and Mercedes had appeared at the Locarno, they caused a stir. With their dark looks and thick accents, they seemed really foreign and exotic. Although they wore the same kind of dresses as the local girls, that was where the similarity ended. 'They're as dark as gypsies,' people muttered.

They had been going to the Locarno every Friday and Saturday for more than a year when Mercedes was asked to dance by a young Englishman she had not noticed before.

'May I?' he asked simply, holding out his hand.

It was a tango. She must have danced with a hundred men before, but he was a cut above the rest. Later that night, she went over the dance again in her mind and every note of the music came back to her.

For this young man the experience of dancing with Mercedes had held its magic too. The feeling of her light, slight body responding to the merest touch of his palm was very different to the measured clumsiness of most English girls. At the end of the dance, when he was once more sipping a pint with his friends and she was back with her friend, he was not sure that he had really danced with her at all. It was just a memory, something insubstantial.

The following week, Mercedes hoped that the slim, fair Englishman would ask her to dance again. She was not disappointed and smiled her acceptance when he approached. This time it was a quickstep.

He had felt something keen and urgent in the way she danced. Without comparison, she was better than anyone he had ever danced with before, and he realised that her movements were not just a sequence of responses to him. Occasionally he felt her giving him direction. This dark Spanish girl was much more powerful than she looked.

'I've met someone who is a wonderful dancer,' Mercedes wrote to her mother. 'Even when they are trying their best, most of them are so clumsy.'

Mercedes' letters to her mother always talked about dancing. It was a cheerful subject unlike any other, and Concha was delighted when Mercedes wrote one day to say that she had won a competition.

'I'm partnering that very good dancer I told you about. And we have done really well. We have the County finals next weekend, and if we get through we'll be in the Regionals,' she wrote excitedly.

For several years this partnership continued and they never met anywhere but on the dance floor, and occasionally for a cup of tea beforehand. They won every competition they entered and their style and grace as a partnership dazzled everyone. No other dancers had a chance against them. Watching them was sheer exhilaration and the judges always spotted the joy on Mercedes' face as she whirled past them.

It was not until 1955 that he proposed, nearly a decade after their first dance. Mercedes was taken aback. In all that time it had not occurred to her that her partner was in love with her. She was completely devastated by the proposal. As far as she could see it had come out of the blue. She loved Javier and only him, and was full of irrational guilt.

Carmen was tough with her. She had found a husband for herself three years earlier and already had her second child on the way.

'You need to face something, Mercedes,' she said. 'Are you ever going to see Javier again?'

It was a question Mercedes had not dared to ask herself for more than five years now.

'Don't you think that if he was still alive you would have heard from him?'

She knew Carmen was probably right. Javier knew her mother's address, and if he was alive he would have written and Concha would have forwarded the correspondence. All the time, though, there was the nagging doubt that letters could go astray and that somewhere, somehow the man she loved so much was still alive.

'I don't know. But I can't give up on him.'

'Well, you mustn't give up on this one either. He is here *now*, Mercedes. You would be mad to let him go.'

The next time they danced, Mercedes tried to see her partner in a different light. She had always regarded him more like a brother than a lover. Could that ever change?

After the session, they had a cup of tea. Mercedes felt it was appropriate. They needed to talk.

'All I wanted to say was that you can take as long as you like to think about it. I shall wait. Twenty-five years, if necessary,' said her dance partner.

Mercedes studied his face as he spoke. She saw such warmth and kindness that she wondered if she might melt. The pale blue eyes looked into hers and she could see that his words were completely sincere. There was no mistaking his love.

It took her much less than twenty-five years to make her decision. Within a few months she realised that she would be a fool to let this sweet man go.

'You can't be doing the wrong thing by marrying him,' teased Carmen. 'If you're as compatible as that on the dance floor, imagine . . .'

'Carmen!' exclaimed Mercedes, blushing. 'What a thing to say!'

She wrote to her mother to tell her of her engagement. Mercedes was keen for Concha to travel to the wedding but she was an old lady now and had too many anxieties about the journey, not least whether she would be allowed back into Spain afterwards. Mercedes understood completely. A month before the wedding, a package came from Granada. Mercedes was intrigued when she recognised her mother's shaky handwriting on the brown paper, and saw the rows of stamps with Franco's head blackened by the franking machine. Her hands trembled as she struggled to cut through the string with a pair of blunt kitchen scissors.

It was the white lace mantilla that Concha had worn for her own wedding. For forty-five years it had been kept in waxed tissue paper and had survived when so much else had been lost. It was intact, if a shade darker perhaps, and unmarked. Its safe arrival seemed little short of a miracle. Beneath the layers of brown paper, her mother had padded the package out with a copy of the Granada newspaper, *El Ideal*. Mercedes put it to one side to cushion the contents. It was a month or two out of date now but she would look through it later. Even the sight of the masthead made her stomach somersault.

Inside was also a letter from her mother and, in the envelope, a simple, unadorned gold chain.

'I wore this on my wedding day too,' she wrote. 'My mother gave it to me and now I am giving it to you. It had a crucifix once but I took that off some time ago and now I seem to have lost it. I think you know about my feelings for the Church.'

For Mercedes, the only slightly sour note aside from the fact that Concha would not be there on her wedding day, was the disapproval of her fiancé's parents. Mercedes was foreign and some people were afraid of foreigners in those days. As far as they were concerned she had come from another planet. They were not that happy either that she was a few years older than their son, but by the time they walked down the aisle together as man and wife, they had come round a little.

The marriage took place in the registry office in Beckenham. The bride wore a simple knee-length, fitted cotton gown with three-quarter-length sleeves, which she had made herself and her hair was 'up' in the Spanish style, with the extravagant lace mantilla cascading over her shoulders. Carmen was a witness and the guests were mostly Spanish exiles who, like her, had remained in the United Kingdom.

Victor Silvester, the great band leader who had seen them dance many times, sent them a telegram that was read out at their small reception in a local hotel: 'To the happy couple. May your marriage be as perfect as your dancing.'

Chapter Thirty-eight

MIGUEL HAD ALMOST got to the end of the pile of letters. Sonia could see that only one sheet remained in his hand. It was past midnight now and Sonia was worried that he might be getting too tired to go on. Mercedes' story, if it ended here, had a happy ending and perhaps she should be content with that.

'Are you sure you aren't too tired to keep going?' she asked with concern.

'No, no,' he replied. 'I must read you this one. It's the last she wrote, not long after her wedding.'

> England has provided the safe haven I longed for. I still feel an alien in some ways, but there are plenty of kind people here.
>
> Of course, what has kept my spirit alive, and has done ever since I got here, is dancing. It is the one thing that English people seemed to know about Spain: that there are people who dance in big flounced dresses and clack on castanets. Performing reminds me of who I am and yet sometimes it's better not to dwell too much on that.
>
> And, of course, what has made me happiest of all is the wonderful man I have just married. I could tell straight away when we met that he was younger than me, but he has a kind face and he can dance, as the English always say, 'like Fred Astaire'. Even though he is fair-haired and pale-skinned and not at all like a Granadino I am sure you would love . . .

Sonia held her breath. She hardly dared hear the name.

. . . Jack.

Sonia had bitten her lip so hard that it bled. Her neck and chest throbbed with the pain of unshed tears. She was determined not to let Miguel see what impact the letter was having on her. She was not sure it was the right time to explain. He still had a little more to read:

> No one here really knows anything about Spain and I have told my new husband very little about Granada, and certainly nothing of the horrors of our war.
>
> I still wonder what became of Javier, and think of him often.
>
> I know you understand why I haven't returned, given all that's happened to our family and probably the man I loved too.
>
> Mercedes

For the first time, Sonia noticed that she was not alone in fighting back the tears. Miguel's cheeks were damp with them. She was puzzled that he should be so upset when the story was not new to him, and she put her arm around him, handing him one of his own paper serviettes to mop his face.

'I can see you were fond of them, the Ramírez family,' she said gently.

They sat for a few minutes in silence. Sonia needed some time to reflect. There was no doubt now. This was her mother's story and until today she had never known a word of it. She was shaken to the core of her being, and clearly her father would be too if he learned the details of his wife's history. She would have to consider carefully whether such knowledge was really of use to someone in the last years of his life.

Mercedes' tale lay on the table in front of them and Miguel's misshapen old fingers picked up the pages, carefully folded them along their usual creases and returned them to the envelope. Sonia registered that these letters had been read and reread many times. It was strange. Why should these letters from her mother to her grandmother mean so much to Miguel? Her heart quickened and she could not quite tell why. Nor could she bring herself to ask this question.

Miguel was looking at Sonia now. She could see that he wanted to say something.

'Thank you for listening to all of that,' he said.

'You mustn't thank me!' replied Sonia, trying to contain her emotion. 'It's me who should be thanking you. I did ask you to tell me.'

'Yes, but you have been such a good listener.'

Now was her moment. She yearned to show Miguel the photographs she carried with her and now that she knew for certain that Mercedes Ramírez and her mother were one and the same, it did not seem ridiculous any more.

'There is a reason for that, you know,' she said digging into her handbag for her wallet.

She found two photographs, one of her mother as a teenage girl in flamenco costume and the other of the group of children sitting on the barrel.

Miguel had picked up the former.

'That's Mercedes!' he said excitedly. 'Where on earth did you get that?'

She paused. 'From my father,' she answered.

'Your father?' exclaimed Miguel incredulously. 'I don't think I understand . . .'

A moment or two passed before she could actually make herself say the words.

'Mercedes was my mother.'

The old man could not speak. Sonia was worried, but within moments he had recovered. He was shaking his head from side to side in pure disbelief.

'Mercedes was your mother . . .'

He was silent for a moment, and Sonia was almost unnerved by the intensity of his gaze.

'And look,' he said, pointing to the children in the second photograph. 'You realise who these children are, don't you? That's Antonio, Ignacio, Emilio . . . And your mother.'

'It's extraordinary,' responded Sonia quietly. 'It's really them.'

Miguel got up slowly. 'I think you need a drink,' he said.

Sonia watched him cross the room and a wave of affection for him swept over her. He returned with two glasses of brandy, and they sat for a while longer. There seemed so much more to say.

Sonia explained why she had been drawn to Miguel's café rather than any other.

'It's the prettiest one in the square,' she said. 'But perhaps it was something familiar about the barrel. I think that picture of them all as children must have been in my mind.'

'It was almost as though you recognised it,' mused Miguel.

'Well, it is a distinctive feature, isn't it? And I have only just realised what the name of the café means . . . El Barril. I really must improve my Spanish!'

Sonia noticed the clock. It was one thirty. She really had to go. For several minutes, she and Miguel embraced each other in a strong hug. He appeared reluctant to let her go.

'Miguel, thank you so much for everything,' she said.

How inadequate these words sounded, but there were none that would have been enough. There were tears in his eyes as she kissed him firmly on both cheeks.

'Will I see you before you leave?' he asked.

'My plane isn't until the afternoon, so I have a few hours in the morning,' she said. 'I'll come back for breakfast.'

'Come as early as you can. There's somewhere I want to take you before you go.'

'All right,' said Sonia, squeezing his arm. 'I'll see you in the morning. Eight thirty?'

The old man nodded.

Just as Sonia was putting a key in Maggie's lock, her friend came up behind her.

'*Hola!*' she said cheerfully. 'Have you been out for a secret salsa?'

'Not exactly,' Sonia replied. 'I've had a really extraordinary day.'

Maggie was too excited about her own evening to ask any questions. Though she was tired, Sonia sat up with her and heard all about the new man in her life. This one really was going to be special. Maggie could feel it in her bones.

Before they went to bed, Sonia told Maggie that she might need to come and stay again for a few days quite soon.

'You're welcome any time,' said Maggie. 'You know that. Just let me know when and I'll make sure I'm here.'

After a few hours of sleep, Sonia took the now familiar route back to El Barril. Miguel knew she would be punctual and already had a *café con leche* waiting for her on the bar. Soon they were leaving the café and going round the corner to where Miguel's battered Seat car was parked.

'The place I want to take you is just a little way out of the city, so we need to drive,' he said.

They drove for twenty minutes, negotiating Granada's complex one-way system, passing along wide tree-lined boulevards and winding their way through cobbled streets scarcely wide enough for a single car. They skirted the edge of the oldest *barrio* and then the road began to climb.

They did not talk much on the way but even their silences were comfortable. Sonia was busy enjoying the spectacular views of the landscape that surrounded Granada: the flat fertile plains and the dramatic Sierra Nevada. No wonder this place had been such a prize for both Moors and Christians, she thought.

Eventually they reached their destination. Outside a massive ornamental gateway several dozen cars were parked. It looked like the entrance to a French chateau.

'Where are we?' she asked Miguel.

'This is the municipal cemetery.'

'Oh,' she said quietly, remembering that he had encouraged her to visit this place once before.

As he was parking the car, a funeral cortège arrived. In addition to the hearse, there were eight gleaming limousines from which a large party of well-dressed mourners emerged. The women all wore black lace mantillas behind which their faces were hidden. The men's dark suits were well-fitting, made-to-measure, elegant. The whole group walked slowly, sombrely, behind the coffin and disappeared through the gates, leaving the chauffeurs to lean against their polished bonnets and enjoy a smoke.

Miguel looked across at them and Sonia could feel that he had something to say. His voice had an edge. She recalled the hint of bitterness that she had noticed in her very first encounter with him. It had surprised her then and did so again now.

'There were many people killed in the Civil War who were deprived of a burial like that,' he said. 'Thousands of them were just thrown into mass graves.'

'That's awful,' said Sonia in a hushed voice. 'Don't their families want to find out where they are?'

'Some of them do,' he said. 'But not all of them.'

They got out of the car and wandered in. Sonia was astonished by the volume and scale of the tombs. Graveyards in England were very different from this. She thought of the South London cemetery where her mother had been buried, and shuddered. It was a huge acreage of grass with row upon row of small headstones, each space a coffin's width and length. She only stopped to visit once a year, but always drove past it on her way to visit her father, and through the railings it was easy to spot the most recent graves. They still had fresh flowers, wreaths of gaudy yellow and orange, 'DAD' in red carnations or 'MUM' in white chrysanthemums, or the occasional heart-stopping teddy bear. With few exceptions, the older ones had nothing or a few dead blooms in a jam jar. Artificial flora were ubiquitous; those who brought them chose to ignore the notion of *memento mori*.

This Granadino graveyard was a very different place. Some of the departed here had tombs the size of small houses. It was like a village made of white marble, with streets and small gardens.

It was a place that invited contemplation and there were few other people here on this Wednesday morning. Neither Sonia nor Miguel felt obliged to make conversation.

The space was divided into several dozen separate spaces, *patios*, in each of which there were numerous large tombs, crosses and memorial stones recording the names of the dead. What struck Sonia most forcibly, apart from the huge dimensions of this place, was that no grave seemed to have been abandoned.

There were flowers on them all, which made absolute sense when she read the most commonly inscribed words: '*Tu familia no te olvida.*' 'Your family will not forget you.'

Most had been true to their promise.

'Can I wander up there?' asked Sonia, impelled to explore.

Miguel had stopped to buy a small plant at the entrance and she imagined he might not mind being alone for a few moments. She walked purposefully up the pathway that seemed to lead to the boundary of the cemetery, only to find, when she reached it, that there was another area beyond the wall. It almost seemed limitless this place, in both directions. She had no idea how long she walked. She was fascinated by the grandeur of many of these tombs. Some had angels that guarded the entrances to family tombs, fluted pillars and elaborate stone wreaths, there were ornate iron crosses as well as simple marble ones and everywhere – flowers. She saw a few women carrying watering cans and one with a dustpan and brush, doing the housework, lovingly sweeping particles of gravel from her ancestors' threshold. It was one of the most touching things she had ever seen.

She retraced her steps and eventually found Miguel not far from where she had left him sitting on a stone bench.

'Sorry I've been so long,' she apologised.

'Don't worry. Time stands still here.'

'That's true,' smiled Sonia.

She sat down on the bench beside him. It was late morning now. The sun was strong and they were grateful for a shade-giving tree. Opposite them was a huge wall. From top to bottom, there were six tiers of memorial stones. In front of each one was a ledge where people had placed small vases of flowers.

'Do you recognise those names?' asked Miguel.

Directly in front of them, second row from the bottom, she read aloud three names:

Ignacio Tomás Ramírez
28-1-37

Pablo Vicente Ramírez
20-12-45

Concha Pilar Ramírez
14-8-56

She noted the plant that Miguel had bought earlier, its pink blooms just brushing the letters of the last name, and next to it a bouquet of glorious red roses now slightly wilting.

'It looks as though someone else has been to visit them too,' said Sonia.

There was no response from Miguel and she turned to look at him. He was shaking his head.

'Just me,' he said, his old eyes glistening. 'Just me.'

Sonia now had to ask the question that had been on the tip of her tongue since the previous night, when she had recognised the depth of his emotion on telling her the Ramírez family's story.

'Why?' she quizzed him. 'Why were you so attached to this family?'

For a moment it seemed hard for him to speak. He swallowed and it was as though he had to gulp for air before he could say the words.

'I'm Javier. Javier Miguel Montero.'

Sonia gasped in disbelief.

'Javier! But . . .'

There was only one gesture that seemed a natural response to this revelation. She gently took his old hands, and for a while they looked into the watery depths of each other's eyes. Sonia recognised what Mercedes had seen all those years earlier, and Javier gazed at the reflection of Mercedes that he saw in the face of her daughter.

Eventually Sonia spoke.

'Javier,' she said. It seemed strange to use this name now and the old man interrupted her.

'Call me Miguel,' he said. 'I've used the name for so long now. Ever since I first arrived back at El Barril.'

'Of course, if that's what you prefer, Miguel,' said Sonia. There were so many burning questions, but she did not wish to cause him any more pain.

'Can you tell me what happened?' she asked gently. 'When did you come back to Granada?'

'I was released from my duties at El Valle de los Caídos – the Valley of the Fallen – in 1955,' he said. 'I had "redeemed myself through labour", that's what they said. The fact that I hadn't committed a crime in the first place was neither here nor there. I turned up at El Barril one day, completely unannounced. I had no family left in Málaga or in Bilbao, and I was physically destroyed by my time at Cualgamuros. Two of the fingers on my left hand had been broken and were badly deformed, so I knew I couldn't make my living out of being a *guitarra* any more. I didn't really know what to do with myself.'

Miguel paused for a moment.

'Quite simply, I couldn't think of anywhere else to go. Concha made me welcome and invited me to make my home with her. She treated me like her son.'

'But Concha died not long after you came back,' commented Sonia.

'Yes, she did. She became sick quite quickly, but I nursed her as well as I could.'

'Did she ever write to Mercedes to tell her that you were here?'

'No,' Miguel answered bluntly.

'I suppose it would have come out that she had known for years that you might still be alive . . .'

'. . . but she had told me that Mercedes was living in England and that she was settled.'

'But she loved you so much.' Sonia choked as she spoke. 'And you loved her?'

'I did,' he said, 'but I knew she was happy and I was glad for her. It would have been cruel to take that away. She had experienced enough unhappiness . . .'

The pair of them sat in the sunshine for another hour or so. Sonia felt in no position to judge her grandmother's decision to withhold information from her daughter. If she had not done so then Sonia would not be here now.

She sat there admiring this nobility, this fathomless love.

Chapter Thirty-nine

UNLIKE SPAIN, WHICH was moving into summer and not looking back, April in England still seemed caught in the depths of winter. It was icy cold when Sonia's plane landed that night, and there was a thin layer of snow on the ground in the car park. Sonia's hands were blue by the time she had scraped her windscreen.

She arrived home to an empty house and felt like a stranger breaking and entering. It was as though she was examining the clues to someone else's life. She peered into the drawing room. A vase of dead roses sat in the middle of the coffee table and petals were scattered over copies of *Country Life* and *Tatler*. On the mantelpiece, there was a row of invitations to drinks parties and a couple of what James called 'stiffies', invites to formal corporate events, which required the use of card several millimetres thick. One of them was to a buck shoot in Scotland. The invitation was for that day. Perhaps that was where James was now.

On the floor by the kitchen door were a dozen empty bottles of red wine and in the sink, uncharacteristically for James, who loathed anything not to be washed up and put away, was a glass with sediment encrusted in the bottom.

Sonia took her bag upstairs and went to bed, automatically going into the spare room. It had almost slipped her mind, until of course she turned the key in the lock, that her growing estrangement from James had been one of her reasons for going to Granada. London had seemed so remote while Miguel was telling his story.

The week passed frostily. Sonia would not have expected anything different. Her highlight was a salsa class that Friday from which she came home invigorated.

After the deadening few days of being back in the office and the strange domestic atmosphere, the life-enhancing, heart-lightening enchantment of dancing lifted her once again.

That weekend there was a long-standing invitation to visit James's parents. She dreaded it even more than usual but James clearly expected them to go. Appearances needed to be kept up, and cancelling would raise all sorts of questions. For James and Sonia it was much easier to continue in silence and they managed to maintain it for the entire journey. It would have been the perfect opportunity to tell James about her extraordinary discoveries, but she had no desire even to mention them. These were precious things and she could not bear the thought of either his mockery or his lack of interest.

Some old family friends, including James's godfather, were invited for dinner and Sonia observed that she was the only one of the five women not wearing pearls. For her this defined absolutely her sense of not quite fitting. She looked across the tarnished silver and best Wedgwood at James and realised that there was not the slightest possibility that anyone would give the lack of warmth between them a second thought. None of the married couples around the table seemed to address any remarks to each other. Perhaps this *froideur* within marriage was completely normal in the shires.

The big, draughty rectory had last been redecorated in the 1970s, and in the twin room she and James always shared when they were staying, there was an apricot-coloured sink in the corner and shreds of wallpaper hanging from the walls like peeling skin. The curtains must have been grand once, with their swags and drapes and silk trimmings, but now they looked depressing. Diana, James's mother, barely noticed the gradual stages of dilapidation and left her husband to fix the odd broken door handle or dripping tap. This, Sonia told herself, was how the English upper-middle classes liked to live, in a sort of genteel decay, and perhaps it explained why James was so fastidious about the décor of his own home.

After she had renovated the house all those decades ago, Sonia's mother-in-law had turned her attention to the garden and was now a slave to its carefully laid out borders and tyrannical vegetable garden, which supplied them with astonishing gluts of courgettes or lettuces at certain times of year, obliging them to live at times on a very limited diet, and then for months providing nothing at all. As an essentially urban creature, Sonia found this lifestyle baffling.

The single beds had allowed Sonia and James to keep their distance, but that night, when James came upstairs after a late session of port and cigars with his father, he sat clumsily on the edge of her bed and poked her in the back.

'Sonia, Sonia . . .' he drawled, the last word right in her ear.

Already rigid with cold, in spite of the hot-water bottle she clasped to herself for comfort as much as warmth, Sonia stiffened.

'Please – leave – me – alone,' she willed him.

He reached under the blanket and shook her shoulder.

'Sonia . . . come on, wake up, Sonia. Just for me.'

Though she was good at playing dead, he knew full well she was awake. Only the truly dead would have slept through the level of noise he had made and the roughness of that shaking.

'Bugger it, Sonia . . . for Christ's sake.'

She listened to him stamp across the room and the sound effects of his clumsy preparations for bed. Without looking, she could picture the corduroy trousers, shirt and pullover lying in a twisted heap on the floor by the bed and the highly polished brown brogues randomly left, ready to trip them should they have to get up in the night. Then she heard the noisy spitting as he cleaned his teeth and dropped his brush back into the tooth mug, yanking the cord to turn off the light above the sink and her ears, acutely tuned in to these sounds, picked up the sound of the little plastic knob gently banging against the mirror.

He threw back his quilted counterpane and the bed springs creaked as he finally lay down. Only then did he realise that he had left the ceiling light on.

'Bugger, bugger, bugger . . .' It was his mantra. He stomped across to the switch by the door and then stumbled in the darkness back to bed, tripping predictably over his own shoe. There was one further expletive and then silence.

Sonia exhaled with some relief and then rolled over. James's consumption of port would keep him soundly asleep all night.

Early the following morning, Sonia went downstairs to make herself some tea, her breath emerging in clouds of vapour. Her mother-in-law was already sitting at the kitchen table, her gnarled, gardener's hands wrapped around a steaming mug.

'Help yourself,' she said to Sonia, pushing the teapot across the table towards her, scarcely looking up from the newspaper.

Perhaps it was their draughty houses that made these people so cold inside, reflected Sonia, watching the stewed brown liquid splash into the chipped mug that sat on the table.

'Thanks . . . so how's the garden?' she asked, knowing this was one thing that her mother-in-law had feelings for.

'Oh, you know. So-so,' she said still not lifting her eyes from the newspaper.

To an outsider this understatement would have been hard to interpret, but Sonia knew her dismissive attitude conveyed a level of indifference to her daughter-in-law.

As was routine, they all went for a walk with the Labradors that morning. Diana looked imperious in her full-length Barbour, and mocked Sonia for her urban faux fur jacket. She strode ahead with James, determined to keep the pace of the outing going while her husband Richard brought up the rear, a slim figure limping slightly, still dependent on the stick he had used since a hip replacement a year ago.

For some inexplicable reason Sonia felt slightly sorry for her father-in-law today. He looked worn out, faded like a very old shirt. When she tried to make conversation he was monosyllabic, with the coolness of someone who preferred the company of his own sex. On the whole he was a man who was quite happy with silence as long as it was occasionally punctuated with the sound of a barking dog. They continued their walk around the lake. The cold had now penetrated the soles of her boots and Sonia felt chilled to the bone. In his own time, Richard broke the silence.

'So when are you going to give James a son and heir?' he asked. The bluntness of it, though quite typical of the man, took her breath away. What sensible answer could she possibly give? What answer of any kind at all?

Part of her wanted to deconstruct the question, to challenge him on every single word: on the notion of her 'giving' James a son, as though it would be a gift to him, the ludicrous idea of a baby being an 'heir', which she supposed simply reassured them they were landed gentry, and, most important of all, why the emphasis on 'a son'?

She swallowed hard, astonished at the impertinence of the question. A response was expected and the options were limited. She could not tear this man to shreds or use the one simple word she would like to use, to tell him the probable, shocking truth: 'Never'.

A nervous laugh and a noncommittal response would probably do.

'I'm not sure,' she answered.

By the time they arrived back at the house, they were all numb with cold.

For the first time in the past couple of days, the house actually felt warm. James stirred the embers of the fire in the drawing room and soon it came to life.

It was a solid enough scene, observed Sonia, as she set the big kitchen table for lunch. For a moment she questioned her own restlessness. Then James walked into the kitchen and she remembered at least one reason for her dissatisfaction.

'Where will I find the corkscrew?' he demanded, swinging a bottle of claret in each hand.

'In the top drawer, darling,' replied his mother indulgently. 'Lunch is nearly ready.'

'We're just having a pre-prandial,' he told her. 'It can wait half an hour, can't it?'

It was a statement rather than a question, as he proved by leaving the room before his mother had time to protest.

After lunch, James and his father drained a second bottle of wine and the remains of a bottle of port, retiring eventually for a game of snooker in the old derelict stable. By the time they returned, Sonia was ready to go and her bag was packed in the hall.

'What's the hurry?' asked James groggily. 'I need some caffeine!'

'OK. But then I would quite like to get back to London.'

'We'll go when I've finished my coffee.'

Sonia let him have the last word. She was already bored with the exchange and would conserve her energy for when it mattered.

Diana appeared in the hall now. 'So are you leaving soon?' she said, addressing the question to James.

'Sonia seems to think so,' said James facetiously, hamming up the part of the hen-pecked husband.

During the four-hour journey to London, while James listened to an entire Dan Brown novel, Sonia mulled over the proposition Miguel had made before she had left Granada: that she should now inherit the family business.

At five o'clock the following morning, James threw open her bedroom door.

'I'm still waiting,' he said.

'What for?' asked Sonia sleepily.

'An answer.'

Her genuinely quizzical expression irritated him.

'Dancing or our marriage. You *remember*?'

Sonia looked at him blankly now.

'I'm flying to Germany until Friday and it would be nice to have the answer when I get back.'

Sonia picked up the hint of sarcasm in his voice and she could see he had not quite finished.

'I assume you won't be out as usual,' he added.

Sonia literally had nothing to say. Or nothing that she wanted to say now. James picked up his bag and a moment later he was down the stairs and gone.

Chapter Forty

SONIA WENT TO the office and worked furiously that day. At lunchtime she rang her father and asked if she could come and see him in the evening.

'I promise I won't get there too late,' she said. 'And there's no need to worry about supper or anything.'

Jack Haynes liked to have eaten by six and was normally in bed by nine thirty.

'All right, darling, I'll make you a sandwich. I think I've got some ham. Will that do?'

'That will be lovely, Dad. Thank you.'

She had a lot of ends to tie up in the office that afternoon and by the time she left it was already six thirty. The rush-hour traffic out of London was heavy and it was gone eight by the time she rang her father's bell.

'Hello, my sweet. This is a lovely surprise. A Monday evening! How lovely. Come in. Come in.'

Jack's delight in seeing Sonia never diminished. He bustled about as usual, putting on the kettle, finding a napkin for her, getting out the biscuit tin. Her sandwich, on white bread, cut into triangles with a few slices of cucumber arranged on the side, was already on his small dining table set against the wall.

'Thanks, Dad. This is lovely. I hope you didn't mind me coming in the week.'

'Why would I mind? The day of the week doesn't make too much difference to me, does it?'

He went off to make the tea. When he returned, she had not touched her food. She could not eat.

'Sonia! Come on. Eat up. I bet you haven't had anything all day. Do you want me to get you something else?'

'No, Dad, really I'm fine. I'll eat it in a minute.'

'Are you feeling all right, darling?'

Sonia smiled at her father. Nothing seemed to have changed in thirty-five years. He had always fussed over her eating and worried about her looking 'peaky'.

'I'm fine, Dad,' she said gently. Sonia was so nervous she could see her hands shaking, but she had come here to tell him something and she could not leave without doing so.

'I've been in Granada again,' she said quietly. 'I met someone who knew Mum. I never knew her name was really Mercedes.'

'I always called her Mary. No one here could pronounce her Spanish name.'

Jack carefully pulled out the chair opposite Sonia and sat down.

'How wonderful to come across someone from her past! You lucky girl! And did they remember much about her?'

Her father was smiling, eager, curious to know everything Sonia had been told.

His daughter told a carefully edited version of the story. She mentioned Javier once in passing but decided that her father should not be made to feel second-best to anyone. He had given Mercedes Ramírez the happiest years of her life and that bright gem should never be tarnished. She would work out how to introduce Miguel when the time came.

Jack Haynes had known none of this. He had respected his wife's desire to leave her past behind.

'She always told me that she could dance away sadness and bad memories,' he said reflectively. 'And I believe she did. While we were spinning around the dance floor, she became as light as a feather. She couldn't have danced like that with the weight of the world on her shoulders!'

'It must have been such a huge help to her,' said Sonia. 'Perhaps it really was all that dancing, all that exhilaration, that helped her to survive. I know exactly what she meant by dancing away sadness.'

They sat for a while. Jack looked at his watch. It was hours past his bedtime.

Sonia sipped a glass of water.

'And the man who took El Barril has offered the café back to me.'

'What? He's giving you the café?'

'Not exactly, but technically it still belongs to the Ramírez family, and I am the only surviving member of it.'

Jack was more astonished by this than anything.

'What would you say if I went to live in Spain? Would you come and see me?' said Sonia, her voice now full of unconcealed excitement. 'Because I wouldn't go unless you did.'

'But what about James? Does he want to go?'

'James isn't coming with me.'

Her father needed no further explanation. He would not have dreamed of prying into her relationship with James.

'Oh, I see,' was all he said.

It all seemed rather sudden to Jack, whose life had only changed in small increments from one decade to another, but this younger generation saw things differently.

'Yes, of course I would come and see you. As long as you cooked me something nice and plain! And would you still come and see me?'

'Yes, Dad, of course I would,' she said, touching her father's hand. 'We will probably even see more of each other than we have done in the past. The flights are really cheap, too. And there was something I wanted to ask you. Do you mind looking after a few boxes of mine? Just for a while?'

'Of course not – they can go under my bed. I've got a bit of room there.'

'I'll pop back with them tomorrow, if that's OK?'

'It will be lovely to see you twice in one week! Just ring and say when.'

Jack Haynes had not seen his daughter looking so happy for years. They held each other in a long embrace.

'You do understand why I'm going, don't you?' Sonia asked him.

'Yes,' he said. 'I think I do.'

After a small whisky, Jack Haynes slept soundly and had sweet dreams of doing the paso doble with a dark-eyed Spanish girl.

The journey back to Wandsworth took less than twenty minutes at this time of night. When she got in, Sonia collapsed on to her bed. At seven the following morning, she woke up, still fully clothed. There was a busy day ahead of her and she needed to get going.

She began with her clothes. Most of them would be completely inappropriate in her new life. Suits and long dresses she packed into carrier bags, along with winter coats she had hoarded for a decade, and scores of high heels that she would never wear on the Granadino cobbles. There were hats that she had worn to weddings, and handbags in every shade of most colours. She had dozens of scarves, most of which she did not even recognise. By the time she had finished, there were twenty-three bags bursting with contents. She drove them immediately to the Oxfam shop, in case she had a change of heart. There was one garment over which she had demurred. It was the dress she had been wearing at her engagement party in a champagne bar in Mayfair. It was a flimsy piece of lilac chiffon that James had bought and she had been obliged to wear. It had not been quite 'her', but its association with a time of happiness lingered on.

There were other things that went straight into the dustbin: a filthy old Barbour and some wellies that would definitely not be needed in Spain. She had files full of old paperwork, job application letters, CVs and bank statements dating back to university days. All of these could be thrown away.

She made up a box with her favourite CDs. Most of it was music that James did not listen to anyway, so he would not miss them, and on the top of the box she threw in the few stuffed toys from childhood that she would never part with.

Sonia kept herself busy all day, deliberately burying herself in trivia in order to detach herself from the enormity of her actions. Only when she stopped for ten minutes to make a cup of tea did the reality of what she was doing hit her. She was removing herself from James's life. There was terrible sadness but as yet no guilt. As she stirred milk into her tea, she looked around the kitchen and realised that she had left no impression on this room. It had always been James's place and it still was.

There were a few more things to sort out in the bedroom so she climbed the stairs with her tea. One thing she was absolutely resolute about was that she should take nothing that was not hers. The house would remain absolutely intact; she had no desire even to take anything that was jointly theirs. Men are rarely on their own for long, she mused to herself, and she was fairly certain that someone else would soon slot in to take her place. It was as this thought came into her mind that the jewellery box on her dressing table caught her eye. She opened the lid and took out some of the junk jewellery on the top layer. Underneath, there were some small drawers and inside these some family heirloom jewellery that James's mother had given her to wear for formal occasions: emerald earrings, a ruby pendant and some rather hideous if very valuable brooches. Sonia removed them and put them in the safe, which was where James had always told her to keep them. In a little drawer all on its own, she remembered there was a gold chain. Her father had given it to her when her mother had died. She found it now and put it round her neck. Her hands trembled as she did up the clasp.

Then she went back to see her father. He was his usual sweet self, if a little subdued.

'Are you sure you are doing the right thing?' he asked as they stowed two boxes under his bed. 'I'm a little worried about you.'

'I know what I'm doing looks rash, but I have never felt so sure of anything, Dad,' Sonia answered. 'I promise you I've thought about it.'

'Very well, darling. But if you change your mind, you can always come back here, you know that, don't you?'

He said nothing else.

'I've got something here,' said Jack, shuffling across to the other side of the room. 'I thought it would be nice for you to have these now.'

On top of the dresser was a brown paper bag. He handed it to her.

Sonia knew immediately from the shape and weight what was inside.

'Your mother never even considered throwing these away,' he

said. 'She would love to think of them being taken back to Granada.'

The paper rustled as Sonia pulled out the shoes. There they were. The soft leather and the steel toe- and heelcaps worn right down, just as Miguel had described them.

'They even look my size,' said Sonia. 'Perhaps I shall wear them one day . . .'

They were both silent for a moment.

'Why don't you come out soon, Dad?' she said to break the tension, caressing the shoes absent-mindedly as she spoke. 'Come in a few weeks. I'll have sorted out where I'm living by then.'

They embraced warmly, and Jack watched as she disappeared down the stairs.

It was her last day in London; tomorrow she would be flying back to Granada. She rang Miguel and told him she was returning.

'I'm so glad,' he said. 'I hoped you would be back soon.'

Now all that remained was to write a letter to James. She had been dreading this, but she did owe him a response to his ultimatum and perhaps an explanation too.

Dear James,

I think you probably know my answer now. It's as simple as this: for me, dance is an expression of being alive. I can't give it up, any more than I can give up breathing.

I don't expect you to forgive or understand my decision.

I do not want to take anything from you. I have no interest in a share in the house or a proportion of your income. I think what we owe each other now is simply our freedom.

The solicitor has my address, so he will forward correspondence to me there.

I wish you well, James, and I hope in time you will wish me the same.

Sonia

She wrote several drafts of the letter, many of them much longer, but this simple, uncomplicated note seemed to express all that she wanted to say. It was left on the kitchen table. That was the first place James would go to on Friday, when he arrived from the airport and needed a drink.

She had already packed a suitcase, essentially containing favourite clothes that had not gone to the charity shop, and ordered a cab for the following morning.

At five o'clock, the alarm went off. After she had showered and made the bed impeccably, Sonia went downstairs. Taking a final, sad glance around, she dragged her case over the threshold, double-locked the door and posted the key back through the letterbox. She walked towards the waiting car.

Flying north to south later that morning, she watched the changing landscape of Spain through the plane window. She observed the jagged peaks of the Pyrenees melting into gentle foothills and then giving way to the vast open expanses of land now cultivated on an almost industrial scale. Images of Jarama, Guadalajara and Brunete flashed through her mind but the scars of warfare had long since been erased.

When the plane began its descent from a cloudless sky, she thought of how many weeks it had taken her mother to travel the same distance. For Mercedes it had been months, for her less than an hour. There was a glimpse of Granada in the distance as they came in to land and her heart raced with anticipation.

The plane was half full so it was only moments before Sonia was at the top of the steps and feeling the sweet warmth of the Andalucian breeze on her face. Soon she was crossing the tarmac. It was only a short distance to the terminal building and she knew that Miguel was waiting for her.

Her footsteps were light. Her heart was dancing.

Author's Note

The military coup led by General Francisco Franco in July 1936 in Spain was meant to be swift and decisive. Instead, it led to a three-year civil war that devastated the country. Half a million people died and an equal number went into exile, some of them never to return. After 1939, hundreds of thousands of Republicans still languished in prison and many faced the firing squad and burial in unmarked graves. Those who had fought against Franco experienced years of repression and even when the fascist dictator died in 1975, many people in Spain still maintained their silence about their experiences.

Under the Socialist Prime Minister, José Luis Rodríguez Zapatero, whose grandfather was executed by Francoists, a new Law of Historical Memory was passed in October 2007. The law formally condemns Franco's uprising and dictatorship, bans symbols and references to the regime on public buildings and orders the removal of monuments honouring Franco. It also declares the political trials of Franco's opponents during the dictatorship to be illegitimate and obliges town halls to facilitate the exhumation of bodies of those buried in unmarked graves.

The '*pacto de olvido*', the pact of forgetting, is finally being broken.

Victoria Hislop
June 2008

Read on for an exclusive article by Victoria Hislop on the inspiration behind *The Return*

Spain's Civil War:
A story of shame and secrecy

My interest in the Spanish Civil War, the backdrop for *The Return*, was ignited during a trip to the city of Granada in southern Spain and specifically on a visit to the summer home of Federico García Lorca, the poet and playwright. Lorca was a major celebrity in Spain during the early 1930s, charming, handsome, clever and versatile, and was adored by liberal-thinking Spaniards. His visits from Madrid to see his wealthy and well-connected family would even be reported in the local papers. On my walk around his house, which is something of a shrine, I learned that Lorca was one of the Civil War's most famous victims. He was arrested during the first month after it broke out in 1936 and executed a few days later, shot in the back (some say in the backside) near a village outside Granada, and hastily buried in an unmarked grave. The event caused a national outcry.

Lorca may have had left-wing ideas, but he was not an active member of the Socialist party and it was always suspected that his critics were those who despised him for his homosexuality rather than his politics. Being gay made you an easy target under the brutal and deeply conservative regime that was to come into power under Franco.

My curiosity about the Civil War was aroused by what I discovered that afternoon, and I learned soon after that around six thousand other people had been assassinated in Granada alone during the first few months of this three-year conflict. Given that this is a very small city (you can walk from one end to the other in not much more than twenty minutes) I realised that the war must have been a cataclysmic event. It was puzzling to realise that I had visited Spain so many times and not been aware of it.

A Granada street, 2008

When I began researching for *The Return* in 2005, I was told that something in the region of fourteen thousand books had been written about the conflict. It's a daunting figure and makes it even more curious that so many English people, even those who live in Spain, are largely ignorant of it.

Until I began my reading (starting off with histories of the war by Paul Preston, Hugh Thomas and Antony Beevor), the only knowledge I had of this conflict had been sketchy. We learned nothing about it in school history lessons and, as is still the case now, the syllabus was dominated by the two wars of the twentieth century in which Britain was directly engaged. The Spanish Civil War is scarcely a footnote in the textbooks. I had read Ernest Hemingway's *For Whom the Bell Tolls* and in 1995 saw Ken Loach's film, *Land and Freedom*, about an idealistic Englishman who goes to fight with the International Brigades against Franco, and I think my know-ledge was reasonably typical. I am not even sure I realised that, unlike the two other European fascist leaders of the same period, Hitler and Mussolini, General Franco was in power for nearly forty years.

Wandering around in the city of Granada, I began to look for other monuments connected with the Civil War, particularly to the victims. I could not find even one. I did however find a monument to José Antonio Primo de Rivera, who was the founder of the right-wing Falangist movement whose beliefs were adopted by Franco for his fascist regime. Primo de Rivera was sentenced to death by the Spanish Republican Government and executed on 11 November 1936, and his body is now buried next to Franco's. Somehow the existence of his monument in Granada seemed less surprising once I had been told that the Falange party still exists in Granada and that, every 4 January, a group of uniformed members of this right-wing party still hold a ceremony (I am told with goose-stepping) to celebrate the handing over of the keys of the city by the Moors to the fifteenth-century monarchs Isabella and Ferdinand. I realised that there must still be mixed feelings in Spain towards Franco and that there were many people in Spain alive today who must have fought on his side.

An image of Franco in a Granada café

I made a few enquiries with the Spanish friend with whom I was staying, who bluntly told me that he knew of no monuments in Granada to those who had been on the losing side and in fact the Civil War was not something anyone really talked about, himself included. I was rather chastened by his response and realised I was not going to get any more information out of him. I subsequently learned that Spaniards in towns and villages all over Spain, especially people of the generation who were alive at the time of the war, still refuse to talk about it, almost to the point where they pretend nothing much happened. I found all these conflicting attitudes fascinating.

Once I had begun to read up on the war, it became apparent that it had become a source of shame for many people. When Franco died, and democracy and the monarchy were restored, there was to some extent a quiet agreement to carry on, to build a solid future and not to mention the past. A few generations later, people began to question what had happened to their relatives and in which unmarked grave they might lie, and bodies are now being exhumed. It is a delicate but nevertheless very current issue and only recently has an act been passed which actively encourages the putting up of memorials to commemorate the Republicans who lost their lives fighting for the legal government.

Simultaneously with this movement to remember those who were on the losing side, revisionist historians (most famously a man called Pio Moa, whose books are bestsellers) maintain that Franco was not such a bad thing and that the Republic he overturned was corrupt. The two sides are bitterly opposed and hostile to each other, and paint very different pictures of certain events. An illustration of this is the destruction of Guernica. One historian claims only seventy-three people were killed there, and others maintain that thousands were massacred. They can't both be right and both accuse the other of ridiculous claims.

Early on in the course of my research for this novel, I knew that I was not going to be persuaded by the revisionists. Even if there were books that gave both sides of the story, I came across some episodes and places that evoked the extreme cruelty of the Fascist regime and profoundly influenced me. They meant that I could not have adopted anything other than a 'left-wing' approach.

On another trip to Granada I spotted an advertisement in the local paper for an exhibition of photographs taken during the Civil War. It was taking place in a small village outside the city and on a wet Saturday afternoon something compelled me to make the trip. My friends and I were the only visitors in the hall where they were on display. The pictures were taken by a Canadian, Norman Bethune, an idealistic left-wing doctor, who had pioneered a mobile blood transfusion service that he was using to help wounded Republicans in Spain. In February 1937 he encountered the exodus from Málaga by 150,000 people who had fled from the Fascists overrunning their city. He rescued many wounded adults and children and helped them to reach Almería in his vehicle, and his photographs are an extraordinary visual record of the reality of this conflict: ordinary citizens reduced to terrified, destitute, ragged refugees. As well as the pictures, the exhibition displayed written testimonies, by children as young as nine or ten, of their experience on that road, during which they were bombed and strafed from the air. Bethune's images encapsulate the horror of this war and when, a while later, I found myself travelling on that same very exposed road, from Almería to Málaga, the brutality of the way in which these people had been attacked was easy to imagine.

Then there was El Valle de los Caídos, the Valley of the Fallen, Franco's grand burial place where many labourers died during its twenty-year construction. The taxi driver who drove me out there from Madrid was positively hostile when I told him that I was not interested in the nearby burial place of the Spanish monarchs at El Escorial but only in Franco's tomb. It was a startlingly clear April morning and there was a stirring and dramatic beauty about the landscape and the sight of the massive cross that could be seen sitting on a mountain top from many kilometres away. The basilica is said to be bigger than St Peter's in Rome; it is underground, dark and chillingly damp, and has literally been gouged out of the mountainside.

Franco's tomb

The basilica at El Valle de los Caídos

As I walked in and my eyes got used to the gloom, I could see a priest conducting a mass. In a semi-circle around him was a choir and several worshippers on their knees in the pews. And there, on the floor of this huge space, was Francisco Franco's tomb, strewn with flowers. I was really sickened by the sight of it and by the reverential atmosphere. I watched some nuns crossing themselves and wondered to myself how they could have reconciled any of Franco's actions with their religious faith, and realised I would never begin to understand. Outside, against the bright blue sky outside, the huge cross appeared to reach higher than ever into the sky. Marking a dictator's tomb with such a symbol seemed a mockery.

The cross above Franco's tomb

Another thread of the story of this war which took me to a specific location concerned the people who fled over the Spanish border to France when Barcelona fell. They were given refuge on the beaches along the Côte Vermeille at Argelès, Barcarès and St Cyprien. As I describe in the story of my character Antonio Ramírez, thousands of them were herded into pens on these vast, open sandy beaches where they stayed for months. Many of them died there. Nowadays these places are holiday resorts, but I could not help but feel their desolation and think of the lack of humanity with which the Spaniards were treated and the cruel irony of them being housed on beaches which today are places of recreation. However golden these sands may be, they are strangely haunted. At certain places along the sea front, there are monuments to commemorate the camps and those who died in them, and each name represents a life whose story will probably never be told. These plaques look incongruous next to the rows of deckchairs for hire, and ice-cream sellers.

Something else which I had to go and see for myself rather than rely on a reproduction in a book was Picasso's painting of Guernica in the Reina Sofia Museum in Madrid. For many people, this is the quintessential image of the Spanish Civil War and it is a truly iconic work of art. Standing in front of the huge canvas is like being in front of a cinema screen and seeing the whole of the war being re-enacted in front of you – animals, people, buildings, landscape, a whole country being torn apart, turned upside down. It is a powerful and almost raw portrayal of terror. It almost says everything there is to say about those three years. The real thing has an aura that holds your attention and will not let you look away.

Another aspect of the war which I read about and to which I was able to add another dimension was the story of the four thousand or so Basque children who were evacuated to England from Bilbao in May 1937. I was fortunate enough to meet some of them who have lived here ever since, because it was not safe for them to return. They described to me what it was like to leave their parents for an unknown country and to live with total strangers. Those children who were kind enough to share their experiences with me are now in their eighties and are all truly exceptional and brave people. Nothing I might have read could have provided such a vivid insight into the way people suffered during the Spanish Civil War or during the period following it, when the aftershocks continued to be felt.

Victoria Hislop

The Last Dance

AND OTHER STORIES

In ten powerful stories, Victoria Hislop takes us through the streets of Athens and into tree-lined squares of Greek villages. As she brings to life their distinct atmosphere, she creates a host of unforgettable characters, from a lonesome priest to battling brothers, and from an unwanted stranger to a groom troubled by music and memory.

These bittersweet tales of love and loyalty, of separation and reconciliation, captured in Victoria Hislop's unique voice, will stay with you long after you reach the end.

'Beguiling… Her characters are utterly convincing and she has perfected her knack for describing everyday Greek life' *Daily Mail*

'Stunning… Intricate, beautifully observed and with a painter's eye for imagery, in these stories Hislop evokes Greece, its people, its customs and traditions with a sensitivity that reveals her deep knowledge of not just the place but the human condition' *Express*

'Lyrical, twisty short stories' *Evening Standard*